Over the Broad Earth

A NOVEL FROM THE *SAGA OF FALLEN LEAVES*

J.L. FEUERSTACK

ILLUSTRATED BY ALANA TEDMON

Printed in the United States of America

ISBN 978-1-956019-27-8 (paperback)
ISBN 978-1-956019-28-5 (ebook)

**Canoe Tree
Press**

4697 Main Street
Manchester Center, VT 05255
Canoe Tree Press is a division of DartFrog Books

To all the Comrades I ever had...

AUTHOR'S NOTE

As stated above, this is a work of fiction. I have done my utmost to tread lightly regarding subjects that may provoke emotional responses particularly regarding depictions of religion, physical and mental illness, warfare, terrorism, genocide, and abuse. I hope you will take time to explore works of non-fiction pertaining to the various personas and eras that make up the history of our species. Finally, I encourage you to listen to the works of classical and folk music mentioned in this story (notated in italics) particularly when reading the chapters in which the songs are referenced. Although the story is fictional, my intent is to inspire thoughtful reflection while providing entertainment.

DEMONIC LINEAGE

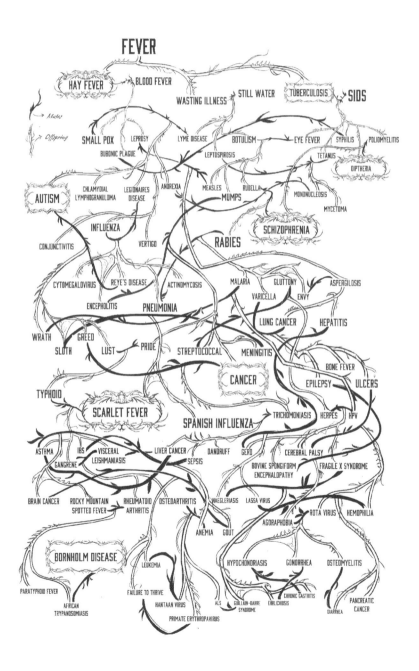

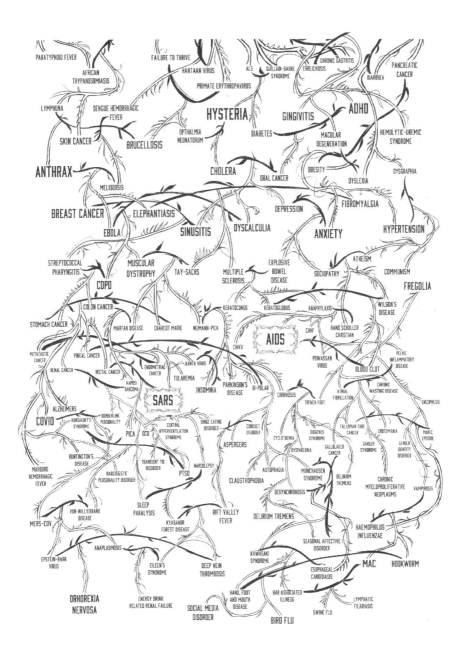

ANGELIC LINEAGE (ASIA)

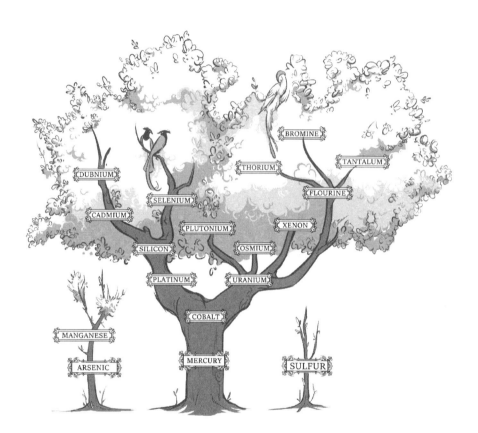

The House of Mercury was founded by the creation of Angels of Asiatic appearance. The descendants of Mercury resemble humans from the Far East. The House of Arsenic (and its descendant Manganese) and the House of Sulfur resemble humans from Europe or the Near East; however, they historically have maintained close ties with the Asian Houses.

ANGELIC LINEAGE
(NORTHERN EUROPE)

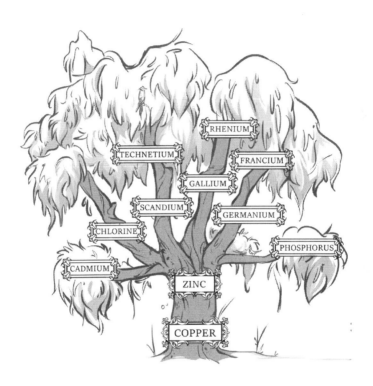

The House of Copper was founded by the creation of Angels of Northern European appearance. The descendants of Copper resemble mortals from Scandinavia and the Baltic.

Angelic Lineage (Africa)

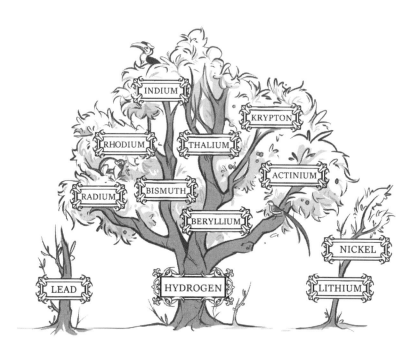

The House of Hydrogen was founded by the creation of Angels of African appearance. The House of Lead, along with the House of Lithium (and its descendant, the House of Nickel), are of Mediterranean origin. Historically they have maintained close ties with the House of Hydrogen and its descendants.

Angelic Lineage (Europe)

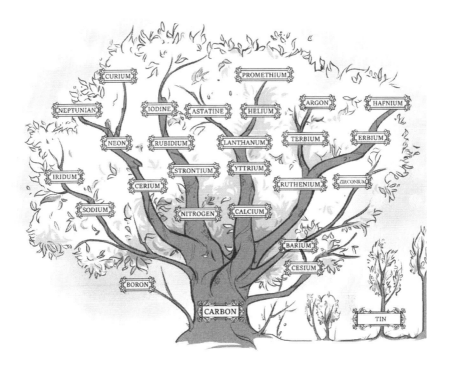

The House of Carbon was founded by the creation of Angels of European appearance. The House of Tin was founded in similar fashion and maintains close ties to the House of Carbon.

ANGELIC LINEAGE
(EUROPE, THE NEAR EAST, & THE NEW WORLD)

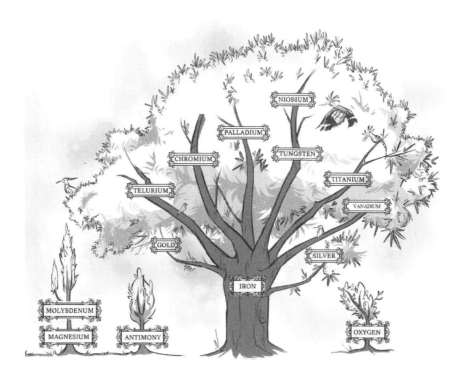

The House of Iron was founded by the creation of Angels of European and Near Eastern appearance. The Houses of Oxygen and Antimony resemble mortals from the Near East and historically maintain close ties with the House of Iron.

The House of Magnesium (and its descendant Molybdenum) was founded by the creation of Angels of Native appearance. Descendants of Magnesium resemble indigenous mortals. These Houses historically maintain close ties with the House of Iron.

OVERVIEW OF THE REALMS

The universe consists of three overlapping realms: The Ethereal Realm (the home of the ancient Elementals, races of Fire, Earth, Air, and Water), the Celestial Realm (the home of God, Satan, and their armies of Angels and Demons), and the Mortal Realm (the home of humans and other earthly flora and fauna).

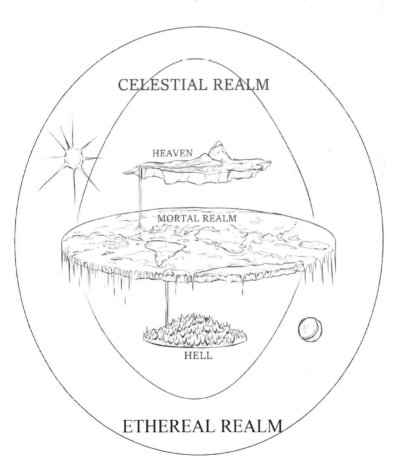

CELESTIAL CREATURES INTERACTING WITH THE MORTAL REALM

Demons/Angels are invisible to mortals when they travel to the part of the Celestial Realm that directly overlaps the Earth. Celestial creatures are inhibited by the Mortal Realm even when they are within the Celestial. They cannot walk through walls or objects. They are subject to natural laws, such as gravity.

POSSESSION

Demons/Angels and other Celestial creatures enter the Mortal Realm through the possession of mortals.

Based upon its skill, a Celestial creature can possess a mortal from varying distance) as long as its mind is stronger than the mortal's mind.

While in possession of a mortal, the Demon/Angel has access to the mortal's memories, language, skills, etc. The Celestial creature controls the mortal entirely. The mortal does not have memory or awareness of the time of possession beyond a hazy recollection.

CELESTIAL TRAVEL

Celestial creatures can travel between locations (in the Celestial Realm or Mortal Realm) by combining any two of the four elements (Air, Fire, Water, and Earth). Combining these elements in the shape of the required symbol, along with the symbols associated with the desired location, creates a portal. This portal can only be opened in the vicinity of mortal or natural structures that form a doorway (such as a door, a cave, or an archway). Celestial creatures can open portals from within the Celestial Realm or while in possession of a mortal host. However, they must vacate a host to pass through the portal.

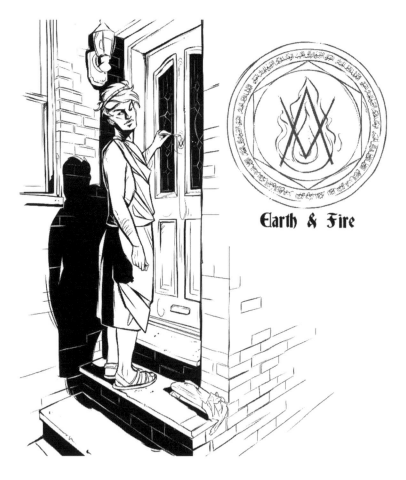

Earth & Fire

WARFARE BETWEEN CELESTIAL OPPONENTS

Angel posessing a mortal

Demon within the Celestial Realm

The conflict between Demons and Angels is restricted to areas in which mortals are engaged in warfare or war-like violence. When Demons or Angels kill each other in the Celestial Realm, the victim is immediately and permanently deceased.

While possessing mortals, Demons and Angels are able to see friends/foes that are currently in the Celestial Realm. Demons and Angels that are in the Celestial Realm are able to tell whether or not a mortal is possessed.

Angels and Demons cannot be injured while they possess a mortal. However, if the mortal they are possessing is killed before they can vacate, the Angel or Demon within the mortal will experience a seizure.

In this scenario (the Angel in the Mortal Realm and the Demon in the Celestial Realm), it is impossible for combat to take place.

Option 1: Combat in the Mortal Realm can occur if the Demon possesses a mortal. In this circumstance, the Angel and Demon would battle with mortal weaponry and would not be vulnerable to injury. Either would be sent into a seizure if his host was killed.

Option 2: Combat in the Celestial Realm can occur if the Angel exits his host. In this circumstance, the Demon and Angel would fight with celestial weaponry and would each be vulnerable to immediate injury and death.

Transitioning Between Realms

All Celestial creatures (Demons/Angels, Wraiths/Familiars, Priests) can bring objects small enough for them to carry from the Mortal Realm into the Celestial Realm. Once the Celestial creature is holding the object, it is no longer visible to mortals. Celestial objects, such as Angelic or Demonic weaponry, clothing, etc., do not transfer to the Mortal Realm when an Angel or Demon possesses a mortal.

AND THE DEVIL MAKES THREE

CIRCADES STOOD IN SILENCE atop the windswept hillside. An overwhelming sense of exhaustion emanated from his temples and coursed through his extremities. He looked out across the barren expanse of land on either side of the Yalu River. The air battering his face was the harbinger of the approaching winter destined to ravage the peninsula, just as the two beings who stood before him had brutalized his understanding of the world. The brothers were alike in appearance – dark hair and dark eyes, the younger one slightly taller. The main contrast between the two entities was attire; one wore a black robe and the other a white robe. Neither spoke.

Circades broke the silence. "And so we meet, for we have much to address. You have killed my father, and my mother, my sisters, and my brothers. You have killed my contemporaries. You have killed the old ones, and you have killed the children. You have left only me." Circades paused and met the gaze of the younger and then the older brother. Neither looked away. *They have no shame, Circades thought.*

He continued. "You have won a great victory through cunning and treachery, and so you have gained the World. Yet, you do not understand the World. That is why you come to this small, rocky isle. I know everything there is to know about the humans. Without me, you will be hopelessly lost, which I imagine is why you have left me alive. When I am gone, my kind will cease to exist. So, what now? What of this earth, of which my kind were the stewards? You must understand and properly administer it, or all life upon it will die."

The white-clad Spirit Walker responded. "Then you shall tell us."

"I will tell you some things," Circades said, "but first you must reveal your given names, for I know you only as Abaddon, the Destroyers."

The entity in white executed an exaggerated bow. "I am God, and this is my brother, Satan."

Circades nodded. "If only such civility were present within you when you arrived upon this world, you might have refrained from slaughtering my people." He sighed, knowing he gave the beings too much credit as it was not just them, but the internal divisions they had exploited that had doomed his race. "Be that as it may, God and Satan, I am Circades, and the conversation we shall have today will be the determinant for your race, the mortals, and all living things upon this earth," he said.

He looked at the beings standing before him and wondered about their origins. They resembled him and the mortals in appearance, but they traversed effortlessly between the Celestial and the Mortal Realm. He could not, and the mortals could not see, much less imagine, the Celestial Universe.

"You know very little of the world you have won," he said, "so allow me to illuminate you. The mortals are the key to life upon this earth. They are different from all other animals; they possess within them a soul, an inner regenerative spark. It frees their behavior from instinct and releases psychic energy into the Cosmos that fuels all the bonds holding the constructs of life together. When their lives conclude, they are fed through the element that consumed them. In such a manner, all souls are reincarnated into new mortals.

God paid attention. Satan kicked at a loose rock, apparently bored.

"This is important, Spirit," Circades said. "The one who understands what I am saying has the key to eternal power."

Satan snapped to attention. Circades continued.

"My race, the Titans, shepherded the mortals. We ensured they passed through either Earth, Water, Fire, or Air in their demise, thus maintaining the balance of energy. Even in all the untold centuries to come, I could not teach, nor would I teach your kind the ancient ways that would enable you to replace my race. You will guide them only through water, and that will be enough. Which of you is to be the ruler of this world? I believe you, God, are the Elder. Within your customs, does the responsibility fall unto you?"

God answered in the affirmative while Satan objected. Circades cringed.

"How will you resolve your differences?" he asked.

God said, "Negotiation," while Satan said, "Combat!"

The wind whipped past them, the only sound while Circades considered the impasse.

"We will draft an accord," he said, "an agreement by which you will be governed, a way through which, in time, perhaps peace will reign over the world."

Thus, the three sat upon the island within the Yalu River for many rotations of the moon, where they argued, learned, and eventually negotiated terms for the Accord. At long last, the agreement was completed.

THE DIVINE DICTUM
(DICTAMEN DIVANAE)

Adopted by the Rulers of the Celestial and Mortal Realm on their First Meeting in the First Year after the War of the Two Realms.

We, the undersigned, acknowledge the need for the stewardship of the psychic energy contained within mortals in so much as it is requisite for the homeostasis and indispensable to the continuance of all life within all realms: Mortal, Celestial, and Ethereal.

Having considered the claims of God and Satan to the rights, privileges, and responsibilities of rule over the Mortal and Celestial Realms, we note the following claims. God's: Primogenitor, the Mandate of Heaven, and Moral Authority. Satan's: Auctoritas, Divine Right, and Charismatic Authority.

We recognize the hopelessness for establishing a peaceful resolution between the claimants, God and Satan.

Established here within are a totality of the confines, restrictions, rules, procedures, processes, and mandates governing the conflict between God and Satan and any subordinates, agents, dependents, or associates, authorized or self-proclaimed, who act on the behalf of either God or Satan.

Bearing in mind that the resolution of the claimants' assertions is the primary prerogative of God and Satan, this accord will be binding over all aspects of existence for God and Satan and any subordinates, agents, dependents, or associates, authorized or self-proclaimed, who act upon either God or Satan's behalf.

Having considered and noted the above, the following terms are immutable and unamendable.

Judicial Authority

1. Declares that the Titan, Circades, is the sole and final arbitrator of any disputes, allegations of misdeeds, requests for clarification, verdicts, determinations, applications, or other administrations of the agreement referred to as the Divine Dictum.

A. All requests for an audience pertaining to the Divine Dictum shall be made in a reasonable, timely manner concerning the discovery of the matter in question.

B. All parties, Circades, God, and Satan, must be present for any litigation pertaining to the Divine Dictum. A failure on the part of either God or Satan to present himself at the time of proceeding will result in an immediate finding in favor of the present party. No effort may be conducted on the part of either party to inhibit, hinder, or interfere with the other's participation, attendance, or access to proceedings pertaining to the Divine Dictum. Either party may request a solitary sidebar meeting with Circades for clarification of an item of the Divine Dictum. If revelations of a breach of the Divine Dictum are identified during such a sidebar, full proceedings will be immediately called to order.

C. God and Satan are entitled to a single representative of their choosing during all proceedings pertaining to the Divine Dictum.

D. Circades will render fair, impartial, and unbiased verdicts after litigation. Once proceedings have begun, all parties are obligated to remain present until the conclusion of litigation and any determinations.

Internal Administration

2. Compels both God and Satan to monitor and ensure the compliance of all subordinates, agents, dependents, or associates, authorized or self-proclaimed, who act upon their behalf.

A. God and Satan must each develop, fund, and support the existence of an internal organization responsible for monitoring the adherence of their affiliated parties to the Divine Dictum.

B. God or Satan will be determined to have adhered to the Divine Dictum when acting upon the assessment of these monitors to punish any violations of the Divine Dictum by any affiliated party. Punishment for infractions of the Divine Dictum must be administered in a reasonable, timely manner from the time at which they are reported. Penalties for violation of the Divine Dictum must be of a lasting and irreversible nature (death or maiming of a substantially impactful manner).

C. Members of the monitoring organization must be of a unique subspecies. They may be the amalgamation of other affiliated subspecies of God and Satan. Members of the monitoring organization may act in concert, in assistance of, or collaboration with other associated forces of God or Satan, so long as such actions are undertaken for brief instances.

Secrecy

3. Strongly affirms that Mortals must never discover the existence of the Celestial or Ethereal Realms or gain knowledge of the inhabitants of the Celestial or Ethereal Realms.

A. Declares accordingly that all forms of hostility between the forces of God and Satan must occur within reasonable proximity to combat involving mortal participants, or within reasonable proximity to warlike violence conducted on the part of mortal participants.

B. Affirms that when in possession of a mortal body, forces of God and Satan must endeavor to conceal their presence from their host(s) as well as any other mortals with whom they may interact.

C. Encourages all efforts toward the immediate disposal (death) of any mortals that gain unintended knowledge of the Celestial or Ethereal Realms or the inhabitants of the Celestial or Ethereal Realms.

D. Approves the elevation of the collective mortal consciousness to a level below the threshold of comprehending the Celestial or Ethereal Realms upon the joint agreement of God and Satan.

Protected Status

4. Solemnly affirms that the species created by, utilized, or indentured to God or Satan for any period of time or for any purpose are afforded protection against excessive maltreatment, unwarranted abuses, or any unduly cruel actions.

A. Declares accordingly that all species created by, utilized, or indentured to God or Satan for any period of time, or any purpose, are entitled to due process regarding any form of lasting or severe punishment.

B. Further proclaims that all the species created by, utilized, or indentured to God or Satan for any period of time or, any purpose, are entitled to own, possess, or otherwise maintain private property. The aforementioned private property of God's and/or Satan's forces is protected against unreasonable search and seizure on the part of God or Satan or any acting upon their behalf.

C. Affirms that all species created by, utilized, or indentured to God or Satan for any period of time or for any purpose are permitted to enter into matrimonial contracts based upon the mutual agreement of both parties. Exception may be taken in instances where marriage will result in the creation of a new species or will significantly enhance the species by pairing two exceptional individuals. Under such circumstances, nuptials may be instigated by decree or familial arrangement without the consent of the parties to be wed.

Governance of Hostilities

5. Proclaims that God and Satan and subordinates, agents, dependents, or associates, authorized or self-proclaimed, who act upon either God's or Satan's behalf are confined by and held to the standards and limitations imposed upon their armaments and defensive capabilities.

A. Proclaims that all Celestial weaponry is limited to handheld arms consisting of blades or blunt edges. Although it is possible to throw such weaponry, armaments whose primary purpose consists of ranged functionality, such as bows, javelins, and all other ranged weapons, are forbidden from Celestial combat. An exception to this exists for the resolution of internal disputes or contests designed to resolve matters of honor.

B. Declares that all forms of armor, protective gear, shields, or like materials are prohibited from use within the Celestial Realm. An exception to this exists for any aesthetic pieces that fail to provide any practical protection. An additional exception to this exists for the resolution of internal disputes or contests designed to resolve matters of honor.

C. Further proclaims that all subordinates, agents, dependents, or associates, authorized or self-proclaimed, who act upon either God's or Satan's behalf, whose primary task shall consist of combat-related functions must be born within the immediate confines, locale, or presence of combat taking place within the Mortal Realm.

Agreement

1. Notes that all parties upon signing have agreed to all aspects, conditions, and details of this accord, in good faith.

Satan   *Circades*   *God*

Thus, the War of the Two Realms concluded with the emergence of a new conflict. God and Satan, having vanquished the Titans, grappled with one another for control of the Mortal and Celestial Realms. Circades, God, and Satan departed the small island. The Devil headed north while God went south. The Ancient (Circades) boarded a small boat and sailed along the Yalu. As each of the three went his separate way, all felt highly confident that the coming war would end swiftly. Yet, as often has been the case in the wars of Gods and men, the conflict took many unexpected turns.

The Meet at the MET

Franz Sauber dropped a token in the turnstile, walked through, and immediately put a handkerchief to his nose. The rank smell of body odor and decay threatened to overwhelm him even as the Demon within him reveled at the stink.

Sauber stood on the spit and blood-riddled platform. He heard a voice.

"Got any change, buddy?"

He looked to find a disheveled man holding out a cup in his leathery hands. Sauber reached for a coin. When the quarter clanked against the metal, the beggar snarled.

"A thousand-dollar, tweed overcoat and all I get is a lousy quarter. Get screwed."

From within Sauber, his undetected but very much controlling Demon smiled. Schizophrenia "Schitz"[1] Incenderos Nervosa had little patience for anyone who was not, or who had not been, a warrior. He could see through the beggar's façade.

There's nothing wrong with this man, Schitz thought. Let's give him a reason to beg.

Schitz touched the man's hand. Suddenly, the man began to twitch and scream obscenities. Losing control of all bodily functions, the man soiled himself and fouled the platform.

Next time, say thank you, Schitz thought.

Franz Sauber backed away in horror. To his relief, he heard the train approaching. Just before it stopped, he looked back at the beggar. A police officer had his nightstick across the man's neck. Sauber hustled into the car; within him, Schitz smiled.

Wish I could help you, officer.

---

[1] Pronounced "Skits"

Sauber waved to the conductor and searched for a seat. The car overflowed with travelers. A happy couple, married according to the rings on their fingers, snuggled closer to one another near the rear of the car.

This might be fun, Schitz thought.

He waved his hand in their direction. The woman's eyes narrowed into a provocative leer, and she launched herself at her husband, her mouth open, her hand guiding his towards her breast. The lights blinked off, throwing the car into darkness. Schitz wiggled his fingers again.

When the light came on, the woman had her hands around her husband's throat. His eyes bulged in bewildered terror. Just when the man's face turned purple, Schitz flashed his hand in a dismissive fashion, and the couple returned to their original positions, though both wore expressions of complete bewilderment.

You're lucky I'm just fooling around, Schitz thought. *Otherwise, one of you would be dead.*

Still in search of a seat, Schitz maneuvered Franz into the next car. Sparks from the rail popped past the windows, a pleasant light show for regular travelers, a terrifying sight for the uninitiated.

Cigarette butts littered the floor. A man selling yo-yos and artificial flowers squeezed by on the left. Franz filched a red, plastic rose – because Schitz wanted one.

A half-dozen young people wearing ill-fitting evening wear and brandishing bottles of alcohol they were too young to possess huddled together in the middle seats. They talked in the loud voices of adolescent insecurity, certain everyone who could hear them would be impressed by their overdressed, drunken bravado.

Schitz raised his hand to unleash havoc, then hesitated. One girl sat by herself. She was the only young lady without a corsage. Heavy chested and plain, she bore the telltale signs of Schitz's ailment. Franz leaned over the seat and presented the stolen rose. The girl's eyes lit up with joy, and the moment his hand touched hers, an aura of wellness spread across her face.

Schitz scowled. "Don't get in the habit of healing people, old boy," he said to himself. "You'll put yourself out of business."

The loudspeaker crackled. A heavily accented voice said, "Lexington and 51st... Lexington and 51st."

They look like they are fleeing Pharaoh's army, Schitz thought. He sneered at the mob. *I've seen Pharaoh's army. You wouldn't stand a chance.*

Franz sauntered towards the door, the last departing passenger.

"Hurry up, mister," the conductor said. "We ain't got all damn day, you know."

Franz apologized. Schitz reached. By the time he passed the uniformed functionary, the conductor's eyes reflected the maniacal gleam of insanity. Schitz hurried his host to the end of the platform where they could watch the departure. The train lurched forward and rolled out of the station but not before Schitz saw the conductor enter the driver's cabin and begin to club the unsuspecting operator with a fire extinguisher.

Schitz turned away from what could only be described as a hellacious circus. He dismissed thoughts of the carnival of delight and looked on to the monolithic aperture of a stairwell ascending to the brighter world above the subway platform. The old beaten brass handrails looked golden.

Franz hesitated. Schitz remembered a time where he ascended a set of stairs much like this one, only at the end of it lay in wait seemingly inevitable demise.

Stairway to heaven," he thought.

At the top of the steps, he avoided a puddle of vomit and made his way to 51st and Lexington. The tingling on his face let him know he was free of the catacombs of New York City's underground. He crossed the avenues and saw a truck driver throwing newspapers at a newsstand whose attendant was absent.

Looking down at the driver, Franz thought, *I'm running late. I don't have to time to think of these trivial things when there are greater matters at hand.*

He walked with brisk steps through the deserted urban environment until he stood in front of his destination. Schitz gazed at signs and posters adorning the Metropolitan Museum of Art and made his way past the loose chains slouched across the entrance. After a few feet, the slight brush of a hand took him by his right shoulder. Franz turned. He saw a silver-haired, blue-eyed man with reddish cheeks and an unnatural, vibrant flush in his face.

The old man's false teeth slipped and caused his words to hiss and slur – an expulsion of mumbled hostility and alcohol-soaked breath. The night watchman stumbled forward and into Franz, who at this point had already realized the man was of no threat to him. Franz took hold of the man's light blue sleeve and held him at arm's length. Bold lettering in a brass nameplate announced "O'Keefe."

Franz grabbed the security officer's hand and squeezed until O'Keefe's eyes registered pain. The grip rendered the aging inebriate incapable of speech.

Walking past O'Keefe and up another set of steps, the sound of the distant wailings of the guard followed by delirious laughter. Beyond the glass doors that made for the entrance of the MET's central atrium, Franz proceeded past an ancient obelisk. The Egyptian exhibit invariably stirred a barrage of memories. He paused for a moment and thought of days long past. A name slipped past his lips.

"Anna."

"It's good to see you're looking well," Zinc said, an absentminded tone within his voice.

"Sorry about that," Schitz replied. "I got caught up in the obelisk. Something about that obelisk haunts me."

"Ah, memories," Zinc said. "Too many."

"Are we anything else other than our memories now?" Schitz asked. "I mean, look at you and me after all these years. That we can stand together in the same place, it's as if now we're more of an idea."

"I can't live on memories," Zinc answered moodily, "I can only live in the now. If I only could sustain myself on memories, I'd kill you where you stand."

"That hasn't worked too well in the past," Schitz said. "But maybe that's just how I remember it." He chuckled. "Enough pleasantries. I have eight new diseases graduating shortly from the Academy. I should be able to send them on missions that will give them over to you. The Ivory Coast is picking up as of late. But I will need a substantial number of Angels to balance the equation. The eight fledglings are being guarded right now by Anorexia herself. Let me reiterate that she is not to be touched."

Zinc sighed and waved his hand, dismissively. "That provides slight complications. But still, manageable."

"Good," Schitz replied. "There is talk amongst our intelligence service that your leadership is undergoing a challenge. Is that something I should worry about destabilizing our agreement?"

"That's not something I would worry about if I was you," Zinc said.

"Fair enough," Schitz said. "Regardless of whether what you say is true, things are getting dangerous for us to keep continuing like this. I don't know about you, but I'm feeling some pressure from these late-night rendezvous."

Zinc nodded. "It seems like both our populations are dropping drastically; hopefully, we can decrease our activity."

"Maybe," Schitz said. "That's not necessarily a bad thing. My bigger concern is if your boss or my boss finds out about what we've been doing."

"I don't want to think about the justice that would be doled out if that were to happen," Zinc said with a shudder. "There's a lot in play right now. Besides, we're two sides of a triangle now."

Schitz thought of AIDS and The Ancient, wondering about which triangle Zinc was referencing. "Well, we need a way to communicate. And face to face is getting too dangerous," Schitz said.

O'Keefe's cackling laughter echoed over their conversation.

"We will have to limit our communication through shattered minds," Zinc said.

"There's nothing shattered about them," Schitz said with a smile as he recollected the orgy of psychosis he had unleashed upon the subway car. "They're a perfect, complexity of systems."

"No matter how you frame it, my side has long since stopped trying to decipher what it was that they were saying or attempting to trace it back to you."

Schitz nodded and thought of his colleague, AIDS. "There are other challenges to using those channels, but I suppose we must use it for now."

"Well, that's one issue down," Zinc said. "What about the third factor, The Ancient."

"The Fossil?" Schitz asked. "I see no danger of him cracking into the mind of anyone, let alone the mind of a lunatic. So, I doubt he'd figure out we're working together."

"I'm more concerned about what his play is," Zinc said. "He hasn't approached either side, but he has been active, accumulating worldly wealth and power. Hardly the vagabond lifestyle he had been leading for millennia."

"It is a concerning mystery," Schitz said. "Hopefully, pertaining to his search for his girl."

"If we have to defend ourselves against him, things might get sloppy," Zinc said. "That's why we need to tighten up now. Have you gotten AIDS under control? It seems like he's everywhere."

"It's a delicate situation," Schitz said defensively.

"That's not a positive development," Zinc said. "You question my control. Are you sure you can hold up your part of the bargain?"

Schitz waved his hand in dismissal of the quip.

"Well, don't let him wipe out humanity," Zinc said. "Remember our balance is not just Celestial beings; the mortals must be in balance as well."

Schitz inhaled fiercely but remained calm, and replied, "There are new Demons from the current academy class crafting their disorders; they're working at the CIA cooking up something much worse than AIDS. I'll keep them in control and AIDS and all the others." He added, "Don't forget about your Co-Commander Uranium II cocking everything up with the damned nukes. Now the defunct Soviet government is so caught up in capitalism it can't keep its own organization straight. Tell me that's not a greater threat than AIDS to the stability of the mortals."

Zinc shrugged. "Just another part of the equation, I suppose. But it is an equation that keeps becoming more and more complex. What's worse, AIDS or Oppenheimer and the Manhattan Project? We've both put things in play that could bring the house down."

"It seems like we're both in need of better housekeeping moving forward," Schitz said with irritation in his voice.

Zinc smirked, cycling back to a statement Schitz had made earlier. "Your boys really do like the CIA."

"And you like the UN," Schitz replied with disgust in his voice.

"Can't hide your distaste for our global empire?" Zinc asked.

"Even working together with you, I could never like the United Nations; I didn't like you when you were the League of Nations," Schitz said. He laughed without humor.

"I don't think we liked *us* when we were the League of Nations," Zinc said.

Both laughed, but neither took their eyes off the other. It was as it had always been, an alliance of untrusting equals.

CIRCADES PAINSTAKING ETCHED THE details of his message into the clay tablet.

"I probably should focus my scattered mind on other endeavors, for I am weary, and I find my thoughts to be chaotic and ineffectual. I ache with the fatigue of a man who has outlived his time and then outlived it again, and again, and again. I am strained and stretched and plagued mercilessly by my memories, as though I was chased by relentless hounds that never tire in the pursuit of their quarry. What else am I to do, but think of you? What else am I to do but try to find you? How can I be whole without you?"

Circades set the tablet in the sand to dry by the sun's unremitting rays. He marveled at how different his writing was from the Sumerians'. When he closed his eyes, he could still picture her face: her flowing black hair, her deep, haunting eyes, her luscious soft lips, her slender neck adorned with beads of bone and copper. For a moment, she was there before him in all her royal beauty.

"Pulwabi," he whispered aloud, "they have begun calling me 'Lalartu' – the ghost, The Ancient, and yet you are the ghost to me.

Still, I see you standing before me. Oh, how I miss you."

Circades strained as though the image in his mind's eye could respond to him if he could only focus intently enough. But she disappeared as swiftly as she had arrived.

Circades opened his eyes, now damp with tears. He winced at the brightness of the Mesopotamian noon. He craned his neck. In the distance, he could hear the clatter and commotion of battle, an all-too-familiar sound. Annoyed by the distraction, Circades closed his eyes again, more intent than ever to avoid the menacing distractions that separated him from his memories – and his love.

He sat by the banks of the Euphrates and felt the warm breeze blowing over the river.

I will find you, Pulwabi, he thought. *I know I will.*

Chapter 1
Birth and Death in Battle

The infant gazelle was still slick and sticky, having fallen from the womb of its mother moments earlier. Bits of dirt and grass clung to its quivering flanks as it rose uneasily to its trembling feet. Within a few moments of birth, a gazelle can stand on its own legs, and within a few hours, it can run. In many ways, the gazelle was similar to the infant born a stone's throw away.

Schitz was born with the knowledge that he was born a Demon – delivered into the world with an eternal debt to serve the Lord of Demons by destroying Angels. He was born with the knowledge of humans, that they are both weak and powerful, that they are both cunning and ignorant, and most of all, that they are the tools with which Demons and Angels did battle. And just like the teary-eyed fawn, Schitz was born weak and vulnerable, for no knowledge can protect an infant, naked and wriggling, birthed in the heat of combat. As decreed in the Divine Dictum, Schitz was born in the Mortal Realm. As ordered by the unforgiving nature of fortune, Schitz was born in the calamity of combat while his mother possessed a doomed mortal woman.

In the moment when his eyes opened and beheld the sun through squinting lids, his mind took in a scene of carnage: blood-soaked sand, the agonized wailing of men, the terrified whinnying of maimed horses, and the putrid, intoxicating smell of death. Schitz looked up to his mother, yearning for protection and guidance. She was a powerful woman, adorned in battle attire with a grim look of determination etched on her face. Her host was not yet ready to succumb to the fatal trauma of possessed birth. Schitz saw a dark aura surrounding the woman who had given him life. Schitz's mother placed him on the ground by her side with her right hand, and with her left, plunged a blade into the midsection of an enemy. Schitz felt cold chills running through his body as fear and exhilaration filled him.

He watched with uninhibited fascination as his mother wrenched the blade from the man's insides, bringing forth from the howling victim a river of blood as strong as the Euphrates. She spared no second thought as she swung her blade towards the next, onrushing foe, severing a tendon in his leg, and then plunging her hungry blade into his throat as he collapsed onto the ground. Schitz looked on, giddy with bloodlust, as he watched the man choking on a torrent of gore that flowed from his mouth and nose onto the battleground.

As metal continued to crash against flesh, Schitz felt the sensation of being lifted into the air. With uncontrollable terror, Schitz turned to behold the figure that had snatched him from the side of his mother. His fears were instantly allayed as he gazed upon the serene, youthful face of Elise, the Demonic midwife. She possessed a quiet calm amid the maelstrom.

"Have no fear young master, while I have strength in my body, no harm shall befall you," she said in a soothing whisper.

Schitz felt a dizzying sensation as the midwife broke into a furious run. He was looking up at the sackcloth silhouette that was now his unholy caretaker as she made a run for an unknown destination. What little hope he had now rested in the arms of an unknown phantom. Elise made a full sprint, tilting toward the camp tents of the warring legions carrying the life she was sworn to protect and seeing dusk rising over the dunes. She hoped their lives would outlast the sunset. The blood-red sky between her and the tents was a seemingly endless dune of crimson; chariots whizzed past in the chaos. No one knew who was on anyone's side. The melee had transformed into a chaotic sea of calamity.

One step to the left and she could be met by death; a similar demise awaited inches to her right as well. No guarantee lay before her; even injury was certain death. Her footing was unsure as the sand, soaked with the entrails of the dead and dying, turned to mud. Before she could reach the apex of the dune, she looked down on a sight worse than any she could have imagined.

Out in the distance before the tents, a blur blotted out the sun, and a deep crimson haze pushed against her – a sandstorm bringing with it every blood-soaked grain from one side of the valley to the other. She removed her headwrap and placed it atop the face of the infant she swore she would die to save.

Her charge looked up at her and saw the fearful grimace. Still, in Elise's dark, almost unseeable eyes, he saw a spark of determination. He felt her rise higher and higher along the dune, and the skies grew oppressively nearer. A shroud fell from her hand onto his face, and everything went black.

Elise knew that her window of opportunity was rapidly fading like the sun. If she could not reach the tents through the battle and the storm, there was no hope for her or her charge. Peering down from the dune, she could see a regiment of horses sweeping across her path and breaking through the flank of the mortal formation; a maneuver meant to sever the rear guard's last stand. Before she could take the next step, the sound of a clattering impact accompanied by a suffocating loss of breath gripped her. With her eardrums ringing and her lungs pleading from pain radiating through her body, Elise dropped the delicate infant on the edge of the dune. She looked over her shoulder, expecting to meet the demise that would end in her failure; all she could see was the sun. As she turned back, she beheld a dismounted rider, the source of the impact, careering down the dune

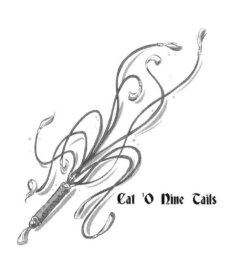

Cat 'O Nine Tails

alongside the baby Schitz. Without hesitation, Elise flung herself in pursuit, rolling through the blood-soaked sand to the base of the hill of carnage. Sinking into the flowing floor, Elise felt the grip of the sinking sand as panic gripped her throat. With an outstretched hand, she grasped the staff of an unfamiliar battle standard. Its flowing flag depicted an Angel slaying a serpent. Hauling herself to her feet, she clutched the helpless babe. Wrapping Schitz in her arms, she was filled with an overwhelming sense of determination.

A vision of shining gold armor holding up a golden sword met Elise's eyes. The backs of her brethren pushed forward in a concerted phalanx; their heels dug deep into the sand. Just above their heads stood a bright white horse, whinnying triumphant and defiant, front legs stomping downward on the foe. Each hoof was laced in gold and drenched in blood. Above the horse's foam-riddled mouth was a helmet from which cascaded blonde hair. Elise saw piercing blue eyes just above the visor. A golden arm stretched up to heaven and raised a golden sword. The other arm brandished a golden handled cat of nine tails. Elise shuddered as she beheld the weapon; the handle was the head of an eagle; the braided cords were its wings and talons. They dripped with blood. To the left of the menacing golden vision, a metallic oxblood apparition of silver reflected the sun's dying rays and smashed in the heads of every poor soul before it. Unlike the white one, this horse spat blood from its mouth and had no eyes, only vacant gaping reservoirs that mirrored its dark coat.

"Brother, let us wipe clean the blood of these instruments with the battle standard of our enemies, for the glory of the one true father," Gold shouted.

Silver replied with maniacal glee. "We will slake our thirst with the rivers of blood flowing from your victory, Brother!"

Together, they said, "Thus, may our favored weapons never know their sheath until we reach uncontested victory. Heaven Prevails."

Several rows away, a recruit clasped his spear and looked down at his shield. He prayed that his leader would never have need to call upon his services. Distinctive shouting broke his train of fear; around him, all the new cadets could hear Gold and Silver's battle cry.

Silver's right hand swooped horizontally, and like a farmer's scythe, eviscerated the wheat that was the foe with a blow from a mighty hammer. As the recruit watched the slaughter, Gold and Silver projected their own essence through their hosts, so that the mortals and Angels within were almost indistinguishable from one another.

Elise witnessed Silver's brutality. She was transfixed by the sight of two hapless mortals as they wilted to the force of the apparition's menacing hammer. She fled in horror. Obstacles confronted her at every turn. She stepped under the belly of a charging warhorse; she narrowly avoided a hail of arrows that impaled the hapless beast. The equine let loose with a terrifying whinny – the horse's protesting shriek against an undeserved death – then crashed to the ground crushing its rider.

Before her in the sand, Elise saw a pair of sandals. She followed up the ankles, calves, legs, hips, waist, torso, chest, shoulders, and neck to a face set with rage. A battle-inflamed warrior banged his sword against his shield.

Magnesium looked down on Elise with the knowledge that his prayers had gone unheeded. He saw the shadow beneath him and was filled with the knowledge that his sole purpose for being was to annihilate this foe and her dastardly charge. His whole life's purpose stood before him, vulnerable and ready for the taking. As he drew in the scenery through eyes blurred by sweat and grime, he felt his hand quiver in anticipation of the kill and the plaudits that would follow his success. His heart raced, and the scene before him turned to a reddish sandy mirage where his prey was no longer visible.

Water & Air

Elise seized the fortuitous moment, leaped to her right, and bolted past him. She passed under his shield even as she felt the whoosh of a blade as it barely missed the nape of her neck. Pressing on, she ducked sword blows, and the whizzing hail of stones hurled from slings. The air burned as specks of windblown sand embedded in her lungs. She hurtled towards her objective. Collapsing to her knees in an exhausted heap at the entrance to the nearest tent, Elise frantically traced the symbols and began the incantations requisite to open the gateway to freedom.

"Air," she cried frantically through gasping breaths. "I have enough to air, but this is too chaotic."

The sandstorm buffeted her. Groaning inwardly, she searched in vain for her satchel of water. With dismay, she realized she had lost in the frenzy of her run. As she scratched the ancient holy symbols at the entrance of the tent, she was met with a searing, debilitating agony in her left arm. The child fell to the floor beside her severed limb. Panicked, she turned and beheld the terrifying face of the silver cavalryman, now dismouted and set upon his butchery. Around him lay a pile of mortal corpses; his gigantic hammer was embedded in what had just been the head of a foe offering a miserable attempt at resistance. Elise looked on in horror as Silver dropped the hammer and raised a sword high above his head. A look of malice etched across his gray eyes. It seemed to her that the Angelic brothers, Gold and Silver, had an uncanny knack for finding mortal hosts that mirrored their Celestial forms.

As though from a fountain, Elise was bathed in the blood of her would-be executioner as a dark shadow passed between her and her foe. Glancing down at the wriggling Schitz, vulnerable and alone, Elise realized that her blood, intertwined with the blood of her enemy, had supplied the much-needed water for the gateway to open. With frantic haste, she used her remaining strength to alter

Earth & Water

the symbols from air and water to water and Earth, as her blood soaked into the sand. She watched on in amazement as the once towering and silvery menace lay writhing in agony, his true form revealed since his mortal host had been slain.

Her savior, a bright-eyed youth, slowly raised an ornate dagger, only to gasp and clutch at his own throat. Elise looked on in disbelief. Her savior's head leapt from his body, severed by an ornate sword wielded by a golden Angel. The new attacker looked over his kill with grim satisfaction, then turned to dispatch Elise who used her final ounce of strength to hurl herself and her precious charge to safety through the entranceway of the tent and the portal she had opened.

Somhetti stood at the top of his island citadel in the Tigris River and looked at the horizon. Across the river to the north, the Acadians had set their battle formations. Far to the south side of the river were his comrades, legions of the Babylonian standard of Ishtar. His pitiful regiment of seven soldiers (if it could be called such) was the only thing standing between the two mighty forces. Somhetti had positioned six men inside the small citadel; the seventh served as reconnaissance on the northern border. Somhetti turned to his second in command, Hamu.

"I need an inventory of our rations."

"Yes, sir."

"And has Vormir returned from his scouting foray?"

Hamu shook his head. "There has been no sign of him in a fortnight."

Somhetti frowned. "Bring me the parchment."

He used a soot-covered finger to outline the battle formations across the river to send them to the friends of Ishtar. With parchment in hand and a soot-laden index finger, Somhetti made the shapes and drew the pictures corresponding to each formation: a horse within a square, a javelin within a square, an arrow within a square, and a chariot within a square. On a clay tablet, Somhetti used different colors to indicate how each square was governed. He sought to convey the magnitude of the forces the foe had arrayed against them. At the head of the formation, he traced an emerald square designating units of composite bowmen. Somhetti traced a red box to representing the foe's javelin units – he'd never seen such long spears. He drew a white square to show cavalry and shuddered as he recalled the ferocious assault of the foe's mounted riders.

Somhetti worked on the schematic until he was satisfied.

Taking a cuneiform tablet, Somhetti folded the parchment paper around it. He slipped a leather thong from around his neck, the one upon which hung an amulet, a gift from his wife. He secured the parchment around the tablet.

He turned to Hamu. "Take this information to the south side of the Tigris. Once you have delivered it, you are free from your oath of allegiance. Do not return but continue to Babylon and deliver this pendant to my wife. I want my son to have it."

Somhetti's scout Vormir broke camp two hundred cubits out from the shoreline of the Euphrates, where the full moon backdrop was pierced solely by the tower of the citadel. Always chastised for his cowardice, Vormir had vowed that he would make everyone in the tower citadel of Annukai recognize his merit. He had planned for his shift to fall on a holy holiday known by all members of the Babylonian elite. He knew he would face the least amount of possible resistance.

Vormir ate the last of his rations, never worrying about the day to come, for in the dawn, he would once again be home within the citadel. And Somhetti would choose another scout, always neglecting to select his brother, Bashir, the real coward who was renowned for his mattress saturating capabilities. Vormir glanced towards the spires of the citadel.

That place could be a sanctuary, he thought, *or it could become my tomb.*

The dunes appeared to move even though there was very little wind. Vormir stood still and squinted. Moments later, when the movement reoccurred, the scout realized, to his horror, that he was not watching shifting sand, but the approach of a massive army – helmets and shields shimmering in the moonlight – moving directly towards the citadel.

"BRING ME THE PRISONER," Silver said with a slight sense of amusement as he peered down at the rune that his men had ignorantly presented to him as an amulet of Babylon, with a perceived value incongruent with its true worth. Hamu collapsed in the sand bound to the oar of a broken rowing vessel, which they had used to cross the Tigress. Hamu's face never looked up to see his captures for fear that any eye contact would result in his immediate physical reprimand. Being brought several paces from where he was kept, he was stopped suddenly and kicked in the back so that he was knocked upon his knees. And now, a palm fully gripped with his hair pushed his face deep into the sand. In that instant, Hamu thought of everything; his childhood back in Babylon, his mother, his first kiss, the first day he was taken for conscription from his peaceful home.

What was it all for? he wondered.

And just as quickly, he saw where it had all led. Above him towered, with its muscles sweaty and veins pulsating, a black steed, an unearthly warhorse. Past the behemoth, he beheld the silver patterned continence of a battle-scarred, grimacing, half-toothed, bald warrior glowing in the moonlight. His armor shone with the aura of a deity, and for the first time ever, Hamu thought he was in the presence of Ishtar and the rising beast of a horse he confused for a chimera.

"What is your name, half-man?" the warrior asked.

"Hamu son of Hamuson of House Hammurabi," the mortal said.

"There are sons of Hammurabi conscripted to the citadel," the apparition replied, "no son of Hammurabi would be assigned to a post so low."

"My family doesn't know I'm here," Hamu said.

"So why are you here?" the deity asked.

"To deliver a message for the commander of the citadel," the mortal answered with a quiver in his voice.

"No, why are you *here*? To escape the trappings of royal privilege? Copper, we've got a meat bag who thinks he's a hero," the Angel said, laughing.

"Is that so, Silver?" Copper VII asked.

"Yeah, well, then show him what happens to heroes," Silver said.

Looking up at Silver, Hamu saw him brush the right side of his horse. He stroked it softly several times, then violently jerked its right ear. Reacting to the signal, the horse lifted its right hoof, and hovered it just above Hamu's collar bone.

"If he is of value to whoever holds the citadel, he may be better used for bargaining in the case of their surrender," Iron II said, replying to Silver's torture of the mortal.

"Your overly sympathetic approach to war is most taxing," Silver said.

"What is he, but another tool in our mission? Furthermore, the siege on the citadel is but a secondary objective in Gold's vision for the conquest of this patch of Earth; spending all these men on this siege will reduce our likelihood of victory," Iron II said.

"Keep him alive? If not for your tutelage when Gold and I were young in the artistry of the sword, I would put an end to you," Silver said.

He spat on the ground.

"Perhaps this mortal will yield some greater reward," Copper VII said. He shifted back and forth restlessly, visibly uncomfortable with the son's disrespect towards his father.

"I've never seen a purpose for these mortals beyond their basest design," Silver said. "For now, I will hold off on skewering him." He turned to Hamu. "Get to your feet. There's still work to do."

Hamu looked up through the froth spewing from the steed's mouth. He saw a shimmering, sand-colored mount laden with intricately crafted armor. The rider held a shield in which the reflection of even the palest moon would shine with the brilliance of a hundred suns. Hamu covered his eyes. The rider spoke in an unknown tongue.

A loud voice sounded from the left – the same odd language. It sounded angry. Hamu shifted his gaze and saw someone astride a black steed. The horse wore battle dress though it was less elaborate. Whatever was said made Silver's horse lower its hoof. Hamu breathed a sigh of relief. The rider threw a round metal object; it fell on Hamu's neck and tightened.

Somhetti's hands shook as he peered from the window. He took dirt from the satchel that lay on the floor beside him. He formed a circle with the sandy soil at the base of the window, a gateway. He recited the incantations then took an ox horn full of sacred water. The room began to shake. Somhetti spilled the water on the ground but missed the circle of earth.

No exit appeared.

Somhetti swore violently and pounded his fist on the circle until his hands bled. When he had regained his equilibrium, Somhetti tried to wipe the earth from the base of the window and attempted the same ritual under the opposite window. He formed a circle inlaid with the traditional letters, wiped the blood from his knuckles, and spat on his palms. Relying once more on the recitation of mantras, he spoke the words, and let the blood and spit drop. Nothing happened.

In disbelief, Somhetti arose and looked out of the window at a bright light that was coming ever closer. The first volley had been fired, and the sound of shouting from beneath his chamber grew louder and louder as the steps pounded heavier and heavier. This would be it. The door shuddered until its hinges gave way. Relief flooded through him when he recognized some of the few familiar faces remaining in the citadel.

Khartoum spoke first. "They've breached the beachheads, and they've cut off our access to the wells, and we've no rations left."

"Go to the base of the citadel," Somhetti ordered.

With his own needs in mind, he knew that each one of these men would only be a tool for his escape. He looked past the armaments room and beyond the mess hallway to the iron gate; all that stood between him and death.

IRON II TURNED TO one of the conscripts of an unknown rank and told him to approach the gate with an offer of parlay. "Give them our terms of surrender."

The conscript turned to another soldier and instructed him to go forth with the decree. The soldier looked up at Iron II with a knowing stare and Iron II returned his acknowledgment by demanding that the first conscript do as he was told, and him alone. Magnesium, clutching his arrow within his mortal host, watched as his superior now had to make the journey up to the gate. The unknown conscript marched his way up to the gate and delivered in hand a parchment which he could not read, even if he wanted to. Trudging toward the gate's mouth, he peered inside at the men that stood on the far side of the barrier, telling them that their commander wished to set them free from the oppressive Hammurabi regime.

"If they would only read, whoever amongst you can, the generous terms of surrender and agree to them in their entirety." Khartoum ordered him to slide the parchment through one of the arrow holes of the gate and then turned and handed it to the only man who could read among them: Somhetti.

Somhetti read the parchment to those within the citadel. "Relinquish your arms and swear fealty to the all-high Zargon the Great, and you will be allowed to return to your lands where you may till them and die of old age."

Beneath the writing inlaid with red wax was a symbol all too familiar to Somhetti. Rolling up the parchment, Somhetti told his men to form a circle. Looking into their desperate eyes, he could see they were eager to acquiesce to any demand that would allow them to see another sunrise.

Somhetti spoke. "They have offered you men a double-sided agreement. You may relinquish your arms, and in return, you and all your families will only know serfdom all the days of your lives. They want you to forfeit every firstborn male child and relinquish all rights to your wives. If you do these things, you may live."

Khartoum looked down in disbelief. He shouted in anger. "They will make dogs of us all."

"Better to be a living dog than a dead man," Salim said with despair.

"You don't even have a wife or sons," Aramish said with disgust.

"Wife and sons, none of you have seen your wives or sons in ten winters; you think your wives and sons haven't already mourned for you?" Urlish asked.

"But we're not dead, and when they see us, we'll be welcome again," Salim said.

Khartoum replied, "Do you not think news of the defeat has not traveled back to Babylon already; we're already dead."

"Then what's to stop us from accepting their terms?" Salim asked.

Somhetti turned to Umon and said, "You've been quiet ever since the siege was raised. Now is the time, if ever, to speak."

"I only know what I know because I am alive. Do you know where we go when we die?" Umon asked.

Somhetti sighed and rolled his eyes.

Khartoum drew his sword and said, "What does that even mean?"

Umon replied, "It means that living under the yoke of one king is no different than that of another, and old age suits me well."

"Coward," Khartoum said.

"Well then, if it's a vote, Salim and Umon have lost."

Salim raised his sword. "Who says it's a vote?"

Umon froze as Khartoum, Aramish, and Urish raised their scimitars.

Aramish then spoke. "Cool your passions, Salim; if all of us are ever to see another sunrise, killing each other will never bring it about."

Salim said, "I only wish to live. I just want to live."

"But wait, Salim," Somhetti said. "They also want us to deliver one amongst you as a sacrifice to Zargon's deity in good faith, only then will we be allowed passage."

Umon, with shaking voice said, "I'd rather die by the side of you good men, than live, knowing that I did so by your death."

Salim nodded, unable to muster words.

Somhetti thought, *Of all the ways this could have ended, this is the least likely.*

He looked past the men, out of the mess hall to the gate where the messenger awaited a response. "You men to the gate, I'll burn this blasphemy from the highest window as our response, then let each of us face our fate with the honor and dignity worth of Hammurabi's finest," he said.

With that, Somhetti took to the stairs, clutching the fuel for his final attempt at escape.

Magnesium watched, alight with the anticipation that sat in the depths of his stomach, as he saw the messenger that stood in his intended place, slump to the sand, an arrow protruding from his hapless body.

"There's but one foe of consequence in the citadel, and we have not only Copper VII and Iron II, but also Silver, what fears could I possibly have?" he asked himself.

A great voice echoed behind him, "Make ready the volleys."

Iron II, looking down at Magnesium from where he sat on his horse, instructed the men around him that their detachment would now take orders from Magnesium. These words brought a return of dread as Magnesium prepared the men for the initial assault. As torches illuminated the battlements above the gate and defiant war cries resounded from the depths of the citadel, its inhabitants clearly prepared for heroic death throes.

Somhetti gasped for breath as he crested the final stair into his chamber past the wooden shards that had once been his door. Beneath him, he beheld with confusion, the all too sudden sound of battle at the gate. Surely, the attack had not commenced before his signal. As he approached the window to make ready the gesture of defiance, he was knocked back by a stone that squarely struck his leather breastplate. As he lay upon the floor, it occurred to him that something had gone drastically awry, and he was gripped by a fear that clasped at his throat. One of his men must have initiated the assault in their heightened state of fervor, and now all too quickly, his odds began to dwindle again.

Thinking back to the halls of knowledge in which he had been imparted with the decrees and incantations requisite to traverse betwixt the realms of Earth and Hell, he desperately tried to recall a domain which he had rarely attempted to invoke – fire instead of water and earth. He tried to mimic from memory the parchments another student beside him used every day.

If only Leprosy was here. He recalled Leprosy's last-minute escape from the field of conflict; she burned a quiver of arrows at the base of a camp tent and so easily stepped out of harm's way. His hands were shaking as he lit the parchment and set it on the ground. Scooping up yet another handful of earth, the Demon within Somhetti frantically traced a thinner circle with greater detail. He hoped that the blood from earlier would not muddle the elements he was attempting to combine. He etched the ancient symbols and began the incantations.

As the window started to shake, he could not tell if it was because of him or because of the volleys, but in a moment, all hope vanished as it became clear that no pathway was forthcoming. He did not see the possibility of finding a host. Somhetti beheld his dim reflection in the moonlight as he peered into the burnt glass on the wall. The dread that possessed him, with the knowledge of his forlorn situation, was unlike the approbation felt before by Stillwater, the Demon that possessed Somhetti. Stillwater was also surrounded by an unremitting foe, the never-ceasing horde of Angels that had broken his lines and scattered his comrades farther up the riverbank. Somhetti ran his tanned hands through his dark hair while in the glass reflection, the pale hands of the Demon within him stroked sandy hair.

The irony that the sole source of water in the citadel had run dry was not lost on Stillwater, the well Demon within Somhetti. Although his signature sickness was a blight that originated from the wells of humans, a dry well would be his undoing. Something as trivial as opening a gateway was now beyond him as his mind had melded with his host. His escape route was blocked. After all, why had he allowed his host to waste time dispatching Hamu with the trinket? He could have done far better things and not risked losing the amulet. Stillwater was a lost cause. His mind had melded with his host's. He would never recover. Desperate, he combed through his mind to find a way to pry away from the earthly being and to escape the approaching foes.

He heard a panicked voice. "Somhetti! They're coming up the stairs."

Somhetti saw the face of another failure in his dark hour. "Hamu, why have you returned to the citadel?" he asked.

"They captured me on the shores before I could reach the Tigris.

They told me to run up the stairs and tell you they were coming – something about an amulet that you had given me," Hamu replied.

"What about that damn amulet?" Stillwater asked. "Why in all of Ba'al's creation would I care about that in a moment like this?"

"You gave it to me. You told me it was of grave importance as it was the birthright of your son," Hamu said.

Stillwater looked at the darkened glass mirror again. He tried to piece together all the momentary lapses of reason he had recently been experiencing. Stillwater vaguely recalled sketching out the enemy's location on a parchment for Hamu. He struggled to discern the difference between his own intentions and those of his mortal host, Somhetti. Stillwater had spent too much time inside the same mortal and was suffering from a melding of minds.

It was then that he noticed a light aura surrounding Hamu that had never been present earlier, and in that moment, he knew the enemy was upon him.

"Somhetti, if you will just tell these things about the amulet, maybe there is still hope for both of us," the Angel said from within Hamu.

"You speak to me of hope when we both know there can be no deals between Demons and Angels," Stillwater replied.

Hamu smiled and let off a nearly inaudible hiss as the rest of the contingent entered the room.

Iron II walked around Hamu to his right, and immediately following him, Copper VII strode to the left, and behind the three of them, Magnesium stood with his arrow at the ready. Looking around the room, Iron II noticed several ritual gateways that never came to fruition.

"In a hurry?" he asked.

"You weren't going to leave us all to ourselves in this citadel?" Copper VII said.

"I think this Demon intended to turn and run guys," Silver said from within Hamu as they all broke out into laughter.

Stillwater knew that aside from killing him, the amulet was a point of interest; his only hope was to delve into the mind of Somhetti for some glint of knowledge that could be parsed for a moment more of time. But he knew, as all Angels and Demons know, trying to delve too deeply into a host's psyche can cause divine insanity – something from which no one had ever recovered.

"The amulet," Somhetti said, "was an acquisition from a Babylonian occupation. There are scores of them that were moved out of the ziggurats, and only a select few know where they have been taken."

Before Silver could speak, Iron II interjected. "You know the sum of those runes could invoke not only the Titans but the powers of the Ethereal as well. If you were to attempt any favor with those beings of doom, you would destroy your own cause as well as ours."

Stillwater replied, "Desperate times call for desperate measures."

"Desperation indeed," Copper VII said.

"Look at all the earth, blood, spit, and tinder all over your chamber. Why would you send a mortal with a rune if it were so valuable?" Iron II asked.

Silver said, "Why would you not just take it through the portal with you, unless," he paused, "your Dark Lord would punish you for such efforts just as much as we are likely to do."

Stillwater scrambled, performing the mental contortions requisite to access Somhetti's memories. As Stillwater filed through the mind of the Babylonian commander, he was beset by disjointed and confusing images, ancient memories that were too old to have been experienced by Somhetti but as clear and lucid as recollections of yesterday.

How is it that this soul remembers his past incarnations, as though he walked the Earth as we do through countless lifetimes of men? This must be The Strain, Stillwater thought.

Fearful of losing his mind, Stillwater broke free from Somhetti's memories. "Indeed, the Dark Lord does not know that some of us in the ranks have reverted to alternate methods; a small coven has been brokered between several of us. If you forfeit the amulet and let me down from the citadel, I can ride east to Babylon, and you can trail me. From there, I can take you the rest of the way to the location of the runes," Stillwater said.

"Treason," Iron II replied. "You can't jump sides; there's no place for you in Heaven."

"Not Heaven," Stillwater said, "but in the Mortal Realm. I want nothing more to do with this struggle. In the end, the filthy meat puppets will do away with us all."

Laughing, Silver reached behind his back and let loose the leather strappings of his whip. "You know nothing," he said, "and I can smell your lies from here, Demon. Whatever disease you bring forth, humans will know its cure, be it upon the sunrise or by and by."

Stillwater looked once more out the window he so longingly thought could also be his freedom. The sky had changed to a deep red. Still, he didn't jump; he looked back at Silver, feeling the shame of his vain attempt to parlay with the foe at the cost of his honor and loyalty to his side of the supernatural conflict. He steeled himself.

"You also lie, Silver, for the sun is upon us, and I am still here, and so I will remain."

Raising his arm, Silver let loose the momentum of the silver-tipped talons of the whip he had recovered from Gold's most recent mortal. Magnesium ducked the whip and let loose an arrow. It missed. Magnesium silently cursed his haphazard weapon. Iron II drew his war hammer and made ready to pounce on Stillwater while Copper VII raised his great shield and spear. Stillwater drew his scimitar.

To his right, Copper VII held an impenetrable shield. Silver stood in the center with his infamous eagle whip. Iron II's hammer stood ready to deliver a killing blow from the left. In the moment, Stillwater decided to bolt forward and engage Iron II; he knew one of the three had already been selected to inflict a mortal injury to the body of Somhetti. Stillwater swatted away Iron II's hammer and engaged him. To his surprise, his exposed right flank remained unchallenged. Cursing loudly, Silver pulled down on his eagle whip only to find that its talons had lodged in the stone ceiling of the chamber. Copper VII hastened to the center of the room. Turning to Magnesium, Silver reached for the leather belt that held his sword and felt a flash of indescribable pain as Stillwater's blade sliced from the left side of his kidney to the right side of his rib cage.

Falling from his host, Silver collapsed onto the stone floor in a writhing heap. He was trapped in the total agony that accompanied the jarring, writhing convulsion of his exit seizure. Immobilized on the floor, he looked about in horror as blurred, watery images of the room flashed before his helpless eyes. He lay stricken and vulnerable, having been cut from his mortal armor. All his mind could focus on was the thought that he had been defeated because his infallible weapon had bitten into the ceiling rather than into a foe. Magnesium looked at Silver in disbelief – he'd never seen the mighty Angel in such a state of weakness. Magnesium stared at the carcass Silver had just departed – the Zargon cavalry commander.

"Magnesium, cover Silver," Iron II said from his own human.

Without hesitation, Magnesium slipped free from his human host with fear deep in his mind. He would be unable to re-enter his own human shield, and there were no additional mortals present. His fears were swiftly banished by the realization that in the airy, Celestial Realm, he was not met by Stillwater, who also had shed his human carriage and was now raising his hellish dagger in preparation for a fatal strike against the helpless Silver. Flinging himself forward, with more haste than skill, Magnesium felt the slicing pain of Stillwater's weapon as it glanced off his short sword and struck his cheek just below the eye. In a flash, Stillwater retreated, and Magnesium stood alone in the Celestial over the recovering Silver.

Stillwater grunted in frustration at having missed a vital strike in his one attempt before entering the soldier that had been vacated. He had lost his opportunity to strike a deathblow to an Angel of the highest order. As he assumed his new body, he swiftly nocked an arrow from the soldier's quiver, and, drawing to full lock, loosed the bolt true and straight into Somhetti's neck nearly a second before the two disembodied Angels, both clamoring to enter the mortal, had reached their target.

An unappreciative Silver bellowed at Magnesium, "You fool, get out of my way," even as Somhetti's lifeless corpse collapsed to the ground. Knowing that skill, but in truth luck and his enemies' overzealousness, had gifted him this opportunity, Stillwater was fully aware that he was within the body of one of Zargon's conscripts and could pass unhindered to the river. He flew towards the battered doorway and took to the stairs.

Realizing the sudden reversal of fortune, Iron II ordered Copper VII to shout from the window not to let Stillwater through.

Copper VII's voice cut the air. "His mortal's name was Hamset, you fool."

Iron II chased after Stillwater; Silver and Magnesium followed close behind. With swift pace, leaping from landing to landing, the four of them made their way to the army waiting outside. Iron II instructed Magnesium to take his human host forthwith and then commanded Silver to tail Stillwater in his Celestial form.

Upon crossing the beaches toward the river, Zargon's army laid down a wall of shields and spears, barricading any possibility of escape. As he ran toward the barrier, Stillwater understood that his only option was a game all Demons played as children called "flesh hop." As a fledgling, he was always the best at leaping nearly fifteen pineal glands before developing a hint of overwhelming fatigue. He would make every jump count. The well was just behind that wall, and just behind that was the bubbling river. If he could only reach the soldiers at the bank, he could flee to freedom.

From behind him, Iron cried, "Spear him."

To his right, Silver ran along his flank with his dagger drawn and a wild hunger in his eyes. Stillwater knew he could not flesh-hop from his current distance. He would have to leave his body and jump before he could close the distance.

Iron II grunted and gasped with his exertions, knowing full well that he was slowed by his human vessel. Ahead of him, he beheld Stillwater's racing body, nearly close enough to jump into any one of the assorted soldiers, with Silver running beside him, a dagger poised to deliver the Celestial deathblow. Should Stillwater make it to the wall of spears, there was a chance he could make it down to the embankment and live to see another day. Overhead a moving shadow cast a blinding light on the sand. A brilliant copper spear, reflecting the rising sun, descended and impaled the mortal Stillwater possessed from his back clean through his chest. He collapsed forward with the spearhead lodging in the sand upholding his wriggling, dying body. Iron II watched as Silver pounced onto the writhing Stillwater like a lion onto its prey, slitting the throat of the Demon and then proceeding to sink his teeth into the gaping wound.

Silver arose from the bloody wreck, still in Celestial form with Demonic blood running down his face and dripping onto the sand. Iron II felt a calming sense of relief as he slowed his run and gasped for air and heard Silver, with both of his bloodied hands to the sky, shout his familiar battle cry, "Heaven Prevails!"

Running forth from the wall of shields, a soldier took off his helmet and tugged the spear out of Hamset. He clutched his fallen comrade in his arms and wiped the dirt from his face.

His grief was genuine. "What have you done, Brother, to deserve such an ending?"

Looking up at General Malto, Hamadu asked the question again, only louder so that all the men could hear, "What has my brother done to deserve such a demise?"

His outcry was followed by the clanging of shields and spears against each other, the shrill voice of mutiny and discord. Raising his hands up and outward to the wall of shields, Iron II spoke. "Be calm, brethren; let me state this tale of most unfortunate outcome. When first we stormed the citadel, we wondered why their gates were already closed and how an unarmed man nearly slipped through our ranks and away to Babylon. And I tell you now, when we stormed the chamber of the commanding officer, he begged us to let him live if he revealed the name of the traitor amongst us. You all remember how he shirked his command to approach the gates. He did so knowing full well the treachery that lay in wait for our emissary and instead sent his commanding officer to his demise. You all saw this to be true, did you not?"

"My brother was no traitor," a man said. "Arraruk, you remember when my brother pulled you out of the way of that chariot, and you, Maltodeer, you were there when my brother held the bridge over the Euphrates by himself against a battalion of javelinists. And Maltok, was it not my brother who jumped in front of the arrow that was destined for your head; the scar which is still fresh on his shoulder tells that tale. I ask all of you now, men, was my brother a traitor?"

Before the men could respond, Iron II lifted the amulet in the morning sun and said, "Such rare riches can sway even the most ardent of soldiers to treachery and betrayal. Your brother was once a good man, but all men may fall to weakness and temptation when offered such wealth."

The men began to make judgments of the two testimonials, and yet again, the spears and shields clamored together repeatedly. Iron II knew the Angels could simply depart their mortals. However, he feared any late-arriving assistance for Stillwater and did not wish to meet any foe without the option of human armor. Thus, he committed himself toward preserving his current possession.

Iron II drew his hammer and slammed it against the sand. Reaching for his horn, he blew the battle note that silenced the wall of spears and shields. Silver, seizing the opportunity, possessed a high-ranking mortal. Both Silver and Magnesium possessed influential mortals. Iron II knew that together they could sway the troops.

Iron II shouted for silence. "You have not heard the fullest extent of this treason. When Hamset held the bridge against the javelinists, was it not curious that an entire battalion allowed him to see another day? Was it not strange that Hamset knew where the chariots were heading before he pulled you aside? Was it not curious that Hamset would know the positions of the enemy archers when he pulled your head from the arrow's flight? I put it to you now, surely a traitor is a conspirator, and thus he must have allies. So now Hamadu, brother of Hamset, son of Hemodon, would it not stand to reason that you would be your brother's aid?"

Before Hamadu could answer, a stone was thrown at his back. Hamadu stumbled and turned back to the wall of spears from which Akmadon had launched the missile. Silver, having thrown the rock, said, "It must be true. Hamadu is a traitor and deserves the same fate, each one the like."

And within the ranks shouted another, "Hamset's death was too good for him; Hamadu should know something far worse."

A faint cry echoed over the rows of troops, "Stone him, stone him."

"I will not waste another spear on this traitor," Iron II said from within the general.

The men put down their shields and tied Hamset with bindings. Akamadon instructed them to dig a hole in the sand where they buried Hamadu neck deep. Magnesium looked on in terror. Since they had achieved their goal, he wondered what good would it do to kill this man, but his thoughts whirled, and all he could do was see himself as another soldier following orders. The men formed a circle and acquired stones, but most of the stones were small, the size of a man's palm. This would not be a quick death. Hamadu cried out to the soldiers who had fought beside him for years. Not long after, Silver took the handle of his scimitar, and knocked Hamadu's jaw out of position with a sickening crack. Hamadu was unable to call out to his former comrades. Soldiers circled him, and hurled stones destined to shred the skin from his head piece by piece.

Upon reconvening, Iron II had begun to lecture Silver about the danger he brought to his clan when he recklessly exposed himself to such harm as the Standard Bearer.

"If you fall in battle, all the Silvers of your House would be rendered impotent in the eyes of men; your namesake would be naught and your linage would be condemned to the lesser tasks of the Creator," he said. "You and your brother were tasked with bringing about the great final victory over the Demons. Getting yourself killed by a cornered foot soldier is hardly the return expected on such a significant investment."

Silver grimaced as his father sermonized. Distracted from his chiding, Silver noted an Angelic Familiar holding a newborn Angel gently in her arms. The midwife was guarded by a stout, hefty Angel. Silver surmised the warrior to be the proud mother of the newborn; she seemed little worse for wear from the ordeal of birthing her progeny. As Silver and Iron II drew closer, they observed the Familiar as she began the incantations required to open a gateway.

"Is this what is to be considered birth in combat, Matron Zinc?" Silver said with a sneer when he was within earshot.

"Oh, I remember your own birth quite well, Silver. It was only after your father had cleared the field of Cain's children that you and your brother were brought forth into this world. Is it any less honorable for my clan to follow in your traditions?"

Silver looked down at the young babe and grinned. "Well, if this is to be the leader of the House of Zinc, I think there is no question which house will be bringing forth the final victory and which will be mopping the Heavenly halls."

Iron II sighed. "My young lord, I think it best to leave the new mother and her retinue to their own matters."

"Ah, indeed, each to his own prescribed role," Silver replied. "I don't suppose you mind us using your gateway," he said, stepping through before he was provided with a response.

The experience of passing through the portal back to Heaven arrived with a euphoric and disembodying sensation that was accompanied by a Heavenly Chorus, to the tune of *Es ist ein Ros' entsprungen.*

> *Let glad tidings reverberate and resound,*
> *Telling all of redemption's greatest story*
> *That which was lost has now been found.*
>
> *Renewed in the light of Heavenly glory,*
> *Delivered from the suffering of Hellish plight,*
> *And all that which is sickly and gory.*
>
> *Now walk onwards towards the light,*
> *You have paid your fare with contrition,*
> *Suffer no longer in the darkness of the night.*
>
> *Your destination is not solely for saints' admission,*
> *Though you will walk on Holy ground,*
> *But for all who will engage in sin's abolition.*
>
> *Bathed in the grace in which all evil is drowned,*
> *Go towards that place where love and light abound.*

Similarly, the descent to Hell was also accompanied by a sense of euphoria for the Demonic forces and an iteration of their own chorus.

Let all passersby hear this our hymn and declaration.
We emerge clad in the trappings of victory.
Purged of all weakness through the test of conflagration.

Rewarded for our devotion and our loyalty.
Let all join in the triumphant battle cry.
In honor of the true and only Royalty.

Our Lord that reigns over all on high
He imbues his subjects the might of lions,
And gives us strength to pull Angels from the sky.

Armed with his wings our environs,
We proudly are free to take our flight,
Over the world that we claim as his proud scions

Victorious in our just and noble fight
To cover all in the peace of darkest night.

The trumpets sounded with each of Gold's heavy, battle-weary steps. The clatter and clamor of combat was replaced by the calm of the Heavenly Halls. Gold felt submerged in water as he received the muted plaudits of those who considered themselves his peers. Slowly, he strode past the cohorts of Angels; youngsters hungry for the first taste of combat, battle-hardened veterans fresh from the rigors of warfare, wise retired Standard Bearers all standing in formation, all at attention. Called upon to acknowledge the recent victory, Gold felt heaviness behind his eyes, an appeal for sleep, or at least rest, for he had sustained numerous Celestial injuries. As he strode past the ranks of Heavenly warriors, he closed his eyes and let the blare of trumpets and the rhythmic pulse of the organ run through his veins. Gold felt chills run through his body as he was filled with renewed energy.

He opened his eyes as he took his place at the head of the Gold Household. He removed his Heavenly weapons, a short sword and three daggers, and placed them gently on the cold marble floor.

Slowly rising to his feet, Gold felt the warmth of light filling the chamber. The music reached a staggering crescendo that brought Gold's pulse to a fevered pace, and then in unison, the Angels broke into song. Gold joining them in the familiar refrain, set to the tune *Loué Soit Dieu le Seigneur.*

> *We stand on guard with not a single hint of trepidation,*
> *We stand on guard, to the foe's ever-present consternation,*
> *Yes, we stand on guard, battle-scarred, weathered, and hard,*
> *Ready for any possible situation.*

> *We fight for God, the primogenitor of all creation,*
> *We fight for His honor, and it brings us the greatest elation,*
> *Yes, we fight with might, for all that is good, noble, and right,*
> *That his temple may never know any desecration.*

> *We wait for the Holy Spirit that Its guidance may always command us,*
> *We wait for Its blessing, which will render us invincible and glorious,*
> *Yes, we wait for that day, patiently, hopeful, we pray,*
> *For when we will be left standing victorious.*

> *We clear the way for Christ, the bringer of all Holy Redemption,*
> *We clear the way with demonic purging, for Earth's reclamation,*
> *Yes, we clear the way, one step further with each serpent we slay,*
> *So that all are free to partake in the Lord's adoration.*

> *If we should fall amidst the battle's havoc, turmoil, and confusion,*
> *We will not beg, nor offer our foes collaboration, parley, or collusion,*
> *Yes, if we should fall, we will fall having given our all,*
> *Let that be our final rest and consolation.*

At the conclusion of the hymn, *Engellied,* the Anthem of the Angels, Gold found a beguiling thought in the back of his mind. Almost like an itch, initially, it only barely registered upon his consciousness, but slowly, as he watched God's stately form emerge from the secret passages where even Angels did not tread, the itch-like thought grew in intensity.

How am I any different from him? Gold asked himself, looking up at God as the Heavenly deity assumed the pulpit. *I may not have created the world, but whispers in dark corners claim that he didn't either; they claim the ancient Ethereal elementals that took no side in the war between Heaven and Hell were the true creators. Regardless, the identity of the Creator is irrelevant; what matters now is the individual with the power to rule the Earthly and the Celestial Realms. God does not fight the battle. God did not scatter the forces of Satan; I did, well, I and my brother.* He glanced to his right, and beheld his younger brother, Silver. His brother was taller and stronger, built for brutality. He had dark gray hair that complemented his pale complexion. Silver nodded curtly, having noticed Gold looking at him.

Oh Brother, do I have plans for us.

THE RIVER'S BANK WAS cool and serene as the night enveloped the dunes. The victorious living had departed the field of battle, leaving the vanquished, quiet dead. The Euphrates flowed peacefully past the citadel, past the thicket where fawn and mother rested, past Lalartu, "The Ghost," yet another nickname the wandering Titan had acquired. Circades had no concern for the lives and deaths of Babylonians and Akkadians any more than he cared for the lives or deaths of Demons and Angels. A singular focus possessed him: Pulwabi. Somewhere, her soul had found its way through the rivers of reincarnation back to the Mortal Realm, and so he longed to find her. The Ghost swore that whether she was young or old, he would hold her close when once again he found her. He gazed down at his tablet, content with the message he had left for her. He raised the hardened clay from the damp Earth and beheld the cuneiform in the moonlight.

Ever since my soul was split,
I've been looking for the other half of it,
I found its reflection in another,
The woman destined to be my lover,
Side by side we would sit,
As the flames danced from the fire pit.

Mankind was new,
And so were you.

I lost you to the flow of time,
Wondering when again, you would be mine.

The Ghost placed the tablet beside the river. He knew she would know it was for her if by some miracle she were to come across it. He shivered slightly in the cold, nighttime air of the desert and slowly collected the remaining tablets, holding them delicately in his arms as a mother would a newborn. Thus, he set out across the desert to scatter his message, wherever the winds of fate saw fit to send him.

Chapter 2

Education

Sitting in the crescent-shaped rows of the amphitheater of Academy Hall in the seat respective of his age, Schitz raised his hand.

"Yes, Schizophrenia," the instructor said.

"The destruction of the Heavenly host and all his unholy offspring."

"Correct, Schizophrenia, that is part of the endeavor, but what is the ultimate goal?" the teacher asked.

"Peace," Schitz said.

The instructor sighed. "Yes, peace, but you lack the second part; if we are to achieve peace, the destruction of the Heavenly bodies is necessary, but what other goal are you lacking?"

Schizophrenia paused for a moment to reflect on his few years of education in the Academy and was prepared to complete his thought. Before he could raise his hand, the Instructor, Hayfever, said, "Yes, in the back."

"The assimilation of all human vessels to the completion of our essence and under our control," a confident voice said.

Fire & Water

"Fantastic, Rubella," Hayfever said, "and what is completion?"

"The subjugation of all earthly inhabitants so that we control the means of psychic energy," she replied.

"Correct, so you see you cannot have peace, Schizophrenia, by simply killing the false God of light alone. We must also wipe clean the slate of the Earthly Realm, placing our authority over all mortals.

Through the completion of both those endeavors, the darkness will creep over all creation, and we will finally know peace through victory and control of the Celestial and Mortal Realms," Hayfever said.

Schitz looked back to where Rubella was sitting. He was highly annoyed he had not been allowed to give the answer to the question. Beside Rubella sat her brothers, Mumps and Measles. They passed parchment to one another. For far too long, this trio of siblings had been a thorn in his side. Hungrily, Schitz awaited the later courses of the day, for this year they would finally be allowed to enter the training compounds and test their mettle against each other. Finally, he could prove to everyone that he was the greatest of his class.

"Hey Schitz, have you been practicing with any of the weaponry back in the caverns," Autism asked.

"No, I haven't had a chance," Schitz said, thinking back to how his Wraith and he had been working furiously day and night with all the weapons she could illicitly procure for him. He was not meant to have contact with anyone outside of his instructors and classmates. Schitz continued. "I haven't had a chance because..."

The soft pat of a crumpled-up piece of parchment halted Schitz before he could finish his lie. He sat still, turning his attention over to Hayfever, looking for any acknowledgment of the recent offense, but Hayfever was busy drafting up the symbols used in the various modes of teleportation. Looking back up, Schitz took a gaze at Rubella, laughing quietly with Measles and Mumps while trying to avoid Hayfever's wrath. Schitz leaned over, picked up the crumbled parchment in his lap, and continued looking straight at Hayfever. He pulled apart the parchment.

He was still looking at Hayfever when Autism fell over from his chair laughing.

"Something you want to share with us, Schitz?" the instructor asked.

"No, Sir Hayfever," Schitz replied, mentally cursing his classmate.

"Are you sure?" Hayfever asked.

"Yes, I'm sure, Headmaster," Schitz replied through a constricted throat.

"Your counterpart would indicate otherwise, I'm sure," Hayfever said. "Autism, what is it you find so funny? These etchings that I've placed for you to look at will save your life someday, perhaps not all of them, but the one that is signature to your abilities is the one that can keep you alive. You must have a clear mind when channeling these forces. If you are distracted or your mind wanders, you will be unable to complete the transition. The combination of some elements, such as fire extinguished by water, requires the utmost concentration and a swift hand. But there is a payoff in that such a difficult combination requires less detail within the periphery destination symbols."

He paused before continuing. "I see something in your hands, Schitz. Why don't you come down here?"

Reluctantly Schitz stood up and let the paper drop from his hands.

"No, no, no Schitz. The parchment that you just dropped, bring that with you. I'm sure it is the source of Autism's hilarity."

Schitz reached down, picked up the parchment, and began to tread toward Sir Hayfever. The level of anxiety gripping Schitz grew; he could no longer speak. He did not know what was on the parchment, but based on Rubella's snickering and Autism's uncontrolled laughter, he guessed this would certainly be a nail in his coffin. The trio of siblings was a source of continuing anguish.

"Now Schitz, stand beside me, look up to the class, and I want you to recite aloud what you thought was so funny that you had to share it with Autism," Hayfever said.

Before Schitz looked at the paper, he took an inventory of every single face, counting them as he had since he first began in the Academy. The number always being the same: thirteen.

"Sir Hayfever doesn't have a seat for you under his desk; maybe you'll have better luck satisfying Sir Tetanus," Schitz read aloud, his eyes widening as he recited each word from the parchment. He felt his innards swirl down to the pit of his stomach with each passing word. He felt nauseated as he stared at a crude stick figure drawing that depicted an unspeakably grotesque act featuring renderings of Sir Hayfever, Sir Tetanus, and a female-looking student, with an identifying label stating simply, "That's you."

Aghast, Hayfever said, "Give that here, Schizophrenia. Have you no shame, no common decency? Clearly, you are insinuating that Rubella is a cheap, low rent contagion to be basely used."

"No, I did not write it; they threw it at me," Schitz said.

"Do you expect me to believe that again?" Hayfever asked. "How many years have you kept up this rivalry with Rubella? Why must you bump heads with her; she is the best student in our class. And with Mumps, who is the most promising warrior we've seen in ages? And Measles who has demonstrated the ability to spread even quicker than disease-carrying fleas could carry him?"

"I swear to you that I did not write this note," Schitz said.

"Truly? With what appears to be a female depiction in a class that only has two females – Rubella with whom you have had problems with for years and Anorexia who is far too feeble to pose a threat to anyone."

Influenza shifted uncomfortably. With her short hair and androgynous features, the instructor had once again forgotten to include her among the females.

"Do you expect me to believe that it is you?" Hayfever asked.

Schitz, his eyes lit with anger, looked up at Autism, hoping he would confirm who'd thrown the note. Autism's face remained blank.

"Tell me, Schitz. You volunteered for every extra credit course, every trip. You can recite every hymn backwards and forwards. You've established your ability to understand our history, and yet you score mediocre classifications across the board. I know you do not have the distinction of being of a terminal affliction, but that of a mild disorder of the mind. For the life of me, I cannot understand why you have such a lackluster scholastic career."

"Go, take your seat," Hayfever said. "No, not next to Autism. I want you to sit beside my desk."

The instruction was met by uproarious laughter from the students. "Quiet down; now let us continue with the portal symbolism," Hayfever said.

But before Sir Hayfever could finish the rest of his lecture, a deep, resonant gong reverberated throughout the Academy; the black bell had rung, and it was time for everyone to enter the second phase of their school day.

The students left Sir Hayfever and walked up the stairs of the amphitheater. Schitz reached the top where Autism had been waiting for him.

"Why didn't you tell him that they threw that parchment at me," Schitz asked in frustration.

"I don't know; it's just like all the other times. Whenever something really shocking happens, it's like I succumb to my essence."

"Why can't you practice the lessons Sir Hayfever told us about controlling our own affliction, so it doesn't compel us to suffer in its nature?" Schitz asked with a groan. "Never mind, let's just get on to the combat sessions. I've been practicing with Elise."

"You told me you haven't been practicing," Autism said.

"I lied Autsy, okay, it's part of what we do. Why are you such a slow learner?"

"I scored better than you on the finals," his friend replied.

"Shut up!"

Walking past the roadwork that made up the Academy, Schitz looked out across the amphitheater before him, a honeycomb cut into the Earth and stretching out until it reached the façade of the great, dark anointed one: a statue of splendor unparalleled throughout Hell – a Minotaur as some of the humans have been known to call it. The beast was muscular and brooding with a saber in hand and the insignia of the Lord of Demons, the five-pointed star upon its regalia. It was carved out of the wall in the volcano that was repurposed as their combat training school. The passageway at the base of the statue's feet glowed with an orange light – the luminescence of flowing magma – a unique and dangerous illumination scheme. The rest of Hell was dimmer, lit by the glow from the River Styx, the Earth's moon, or – when needed – torches. The extra light from the volcano more closely resembled conditions the Demons would encounter in the mortal world. Schitz had been waiting for this day a long time. He wanted to show Rubella and her two minions his worth.

"Hey Schitz, at least he didn't make you sit under his desk," Rubella said.

Measles spoke before Schitz could respond. "That's for later."

Schitz looked towards his fellows for support. Autism stood in silence. Anorexia just rolled her eyes.

She never says anything ever, just once I'd like to hear her say something, Schitz thought.

Assembled in the training arena was every manner of weaponry fashioned by man: longbows and short bows, swords and scimitars, spears and javelins, an array of killing machinery only slightly blunted and dulled to minimize their lethal effects. Once the captured mortal instruments were brought across the boundary, they would have the same impact upon Celestial creatures as they had been designed to have upon humans. Schitz's excitement grew from within the pit of his stomach. It spread throughout his entire frame. He trembled with anticipation at the chance to demonstrate his worth to any possible doubter.

Sir Tetanus's voice filled the arena. "Today is the first where you will learn what you will do every day from now until the final victory or, more likely, until your final, personal sacrifice. You will fight within humans. Therefore, you must be educated to fight superior to all humans."

He paused for effect before continuing. "Additionally, you will learn to slay Angels."

Tetanus gestured to an array of weaponry. Demonic weaponry was like what mortals carried though it was simpler and smaller, designed solely for the closest of encounters. Daggers, short swords, and throwing knives appeared to be the entirety of the weapons designed to combat Angels.

"The techniques will be the same whether felling a man or an Angel; you must first disarm and then dispatch of your foe. These weapons are merely your tools. You must fashion first your heart and then your mind into the instruments that deliver the killer blow. To this end, you will train tirelessly. As you will see, not only new cadets, but all our Lord's contingent return here regularly to hone and maintain their skills. After all, as humanity develops new weaponry, so too will you master all new forms of combat."

At Tetanus's instruction, the cadets formed into two lines facing one another. As always, Schitz found himself the odd student out.

"No, this will not do; I have never known a sibling to possess the depths of cold-heartedness requisite to deliver the killer blow," Tetanus said to Rubella, who had lined up across from Measles. "In time, you will learn to drill with your younger brother as an adversary, but for now, I'll work with him."

Tetanus yanked Measles out of the line by his collar with his massive left hand. At the same time, he pushed Schitz into Measles's place.

His burly voice boomed. "To begin, we will practice simple attack and defense. You may fail every time in which you attack. Expect it. However, if you ever fail to defend, there will be no more reason to worry about ever attacking again. Always protect yourself. You will soon learn; the best defense may actually be a forceful offense."

Catching himself in his own love for oration, Tetanus summarized. "We will review all of this in depth in due time."

Schitz knew Tetanus had delivered this speech many times before. He felt anxious with anticipation as he envisioned smacking Rubella over the head with a wooden sword or poking her in the ribs with a blunted scimitar. Schitz was disappointed as the initial instruction centered solely on choreographed patterns of attack and defense, with no opportunity to strike the opponent. Tetanus moved swiftly from one pair to the next with loud, pointed instructions. "Square your feet. Keep your head up. Swing through your opponent. Remember, you will be trying to strike your adversary, while defending yourself from an opponent who wishes to deliver the fatal blow."

He concluded with heightened emphasis. "Do not aim for their sword. Aim for their body."

Slowly the fledglings began to incorporate his instructions into their practice.

Suddenly, Hayfever entered the training arena with a purposeful stride and gestured for Tetanus to step away from the training. Schitz felt a foreboding shiver run down his spine as he beheld Hayfever clutching a familiar piece of parchment. Schitz hated Rubella to no end. Schitz was agonizing over the parchment when he was clattered over the head with Rubella's wooden sword. Falling to the ground, Schitz could hear a cacophony of humiliating laughter. He gazed upwards through blurry vision to see a concerned look in Rubella's eyes. It quickly melted away as she joined in the laughter. With wobbly legs, Schitz regained his feet only to find the giant hand of the instructor pulling him away from Rubella and supplanting Measles in his place.

"Now see if you can inflict the same on your brother, for regardless of the foe, you must never hesitate when aiming to deliver the fatal blow," Tetanus said.

Schitz regained his composure and, with wincing head pain, resumed a defense position, albeit with greater fragility and trepidation. As Tetanus prepared to swing, Schitz readied to block. A bone-crunching pain shot through Schitz's hand as wood collided with his thin, bony fingers. He opened his mouth to howl in agony. However, the sensation of pain was too intense, and only a minuscule, hissing groan emanated from his gaping aperture. A quick succession of painful blows followed as Schitz continued the exercise. Each time Schitz attacked or defended, Tetanus deftly rapped him across the knuckles. Schitz felt overwhelmed and humiliated as he gritted his teeth.

The day had started with such high hopes, but as Schitz limped back to the barracks, Tetanus's parting words rang in his ears. "Maybe now someone's fingers have learned a lesson regarding disrespectful drawings."

"WHO CAN TELL ME the Demons' standard plan of attack," Iron II asked calmly, gazing upon the sea of hands. He pointed; "Cobalt, the younger."

"Swiftness," the youth answered with certainty in his voice.

Iron II visibly suppressed an eye-rolling response as the class broke into laughter.

"Thank you, Cobalt, the younger," Iron II said. He regained control of the class with a quiet glare. "That is a good place to start. Who can continue with more specificity? Zinc?"

"The flanker assault. They move with a blocker who attacks the edge of our original formation, attempting to pick off whoever is at the flank. When we respond by enveloping the attacker, their reserves, two additional Demons usually hit the exposed portion of the new flank, while the blocker flees. After that, the reserves flee as well. Then they regroup and repeat the same or relocate altogether."

"Draw it!"

Zinc rose to his feet and walked to the front of the white, marble amphitheater that comprised the Heavenly classroom. Zinc enjoyed having the eyes of the class upon him. He felt as though he would burst with happiness. If he could drink in their attention, he would imbibe it all until his cup overflowed. Zinc strode to the large slate stone behind the professor's lectern and dipped a thick stick in the bucket of ash. In a rudimentary yet swift fashion, Zinc sketched a series of Xs and Os symbolizing the movements of Demons and Angels hidden amongst mortal fighting units.

"Good," Iron II said curtly. "Now draw another angle from which they can attack the flank."

Zinc drew another set of three Demons and repeated the same diagram.

"And again."

Zinc repeated the exercise.

"Again."

Once more, Zinc drew another potential angle for attack.

"Good," Iron II said. "Now, what can you tell me about all of these potential angles of attack?"

Zinc glanced at the board and then spoke. "The flanks are extremely vulnerable."

"Correct," Iron II said. "This is why we must rely on our numerical superiority and our discipline. There will be a time when everyone in this room is on the flank of an assault. Once there, you will be vulnerable, and you must remain steadfast. You must count on your comrades. You may sit down, Zinc."

Zinc began to make his way to his seat when the instructor held up a finger. "Unless you think you have it in you to demonstrate our response to the flanker."

Zinc snapped to attention. "Gladly," he replied. He returned to the slate and dipped the stick into the ash.

Zinc marked an array of isolated individual units in the ranks behind the forward phalanx of Angels. Zinc pointed to his figures. "Loosely aligned beyond the first rank, the relay team can respond to envelop the fleeing blocker regardless of whichever rank he takes. Whichever Angel gets to him first slows him down, and the others move in to surround and eliminate him."

"What is the primary challenge for the relay team when pursuing the flanker?" Iron II asked.

Zinc paused for a brief second. "The relay team and the flanker are possessing members of the same army, so bringing him out of his body for the kill requires friendly fire, which must be taken with finesse, so as not to alert suspicion among the mortals."

"Very good; very, very good," Iron II said. "Take your seat, or the class shall forget who the instructor is and who is the pupil."

Iron II chuckled to himself as Zinc headed to his seat. Zinc grinned even though he heard the jeers from the younger members of the Gold and Silver Houses, Peter and Samuel. They whispered, "Teacher's pet" and "Faggot."

"I'd rather be the teacher's pet than a retarded buffoon who still counts on his hands, you inbred morons," Zinc said under his breath, mimicking in exaggerated form the youngest Silver's tendency to count with the aid of his digits.

"Here's how Pyrite and Shiny count...ah one, um two, ah, three, um...seven," Zinc said to the amusement of his peers within earshot. He loved the scowls he saw developing on Peter and Samuel's faces – they hated their nicknames.

"All right, all right, settle down," Iron II said, clearly disinterested in whatever sidebars had broken the silence. "We have reviewed these strategies ad nauseam, and I am certain that each and every one of you grasps the concept even if only a few of you can describe it close to as elegantly as Zinc. The reason I mention them again from scratch now is because we will no longer conduct combat training one-on-one. From this point hence, the classroom will be melded with the field. Carbon III and I will take you through all aspects of what you will do upon graduation, and all of you will complete every action to perfection. You will fight in form with our proven strategies, you will practice developing and inflicting your cures while under duress, and you will practice opening gateways while on the run. This will signify your transition from cadets into full-fledged members of God's army."

"Yeah, we'll see who's retarded and who's getting their ass kicked once we get on the field," the young Silver whispered.

"You for both as usual," Zinc said quickly.

SCHITZ BREATHED HEAVILY, FIGHTING for air as he tried to force his burning muscles to respond. Finally, with great effort, he dragged himself to his feet. He glared over at Tetanus, who had tripped him.

"Why are you angry, young Schizophrenia?" the instructor asked with a grin.

"We hadn't started the drill yet; I didn't expect to be hit," Schitz replied.

"Halt, halt the drill," Tetanus said, his voice bellowing across the broad field that lay adjacent to the glowing blue River Styx. "Schizophrenia here did not think he should have been hit."

With this, he swung his wooden staff and knocked Schitz to the ground with a blow over the head. Schitz grunted as the dust of the field once again assaulted his face. He winced from the pain in his head and wounded pride. The class erupted in laughter. As he rose to his feet, Schitz made eye contact with Rubella, who was flushing red from laughter.

"What?" she asked. "For once it's not me doing it to you. Why didn't you see it coming?"

Schitz wished more than anything that he could be invisible. He imagined himself floating away down the river with the human souls on their way back toward reincarnation.

"The point is one worth absorbing," Tetanus said. "If the enemy kills you while breaking the rules, you will still be dead, even if they themselves are punished with death later. Don't rely on restrictions. Consider this. When will you utilize these combat maneuvers?"

Silence descended over the encircled cadets. Schitz eventually realized the query was asked of him.

"In combat, obviously," he replied.

"Yes, they will occur when embedded in human combat, and why do we fight amongst the humans? And before you answer, by the Devil, you will drop your attitude, or I will have you running between here and the barracks until you are vomiting out your innards."

Schitz snapped to attention. "Operating Clause 3 affirms that mortals must never discover the existence of the Celestial or Ethereal Realms or gain knowledge of the inhabitants of the Celestial or Ethereal Realms. Section A declares accordingly that all forms of hostility between the forces of God and Satan must occur within reasonable proximity to combat involving mortal participants or within reasonable proximity to warlike violence conducted on the part of mortal participants. Section B—"

"That's enough," Tetanus said, "however, what if there is no battle, and no other mortals around."

Schitz was silent for a moment, "Then I suppose we can kill each other."

"Exactly," Tetanus said, "but in the time you took to work out the legalistic merits of action versus inaction, you'd be dead, and even if they were observed by a Familiar, there would be no repercussions from their own internal discipline because they did not reveal knowledge to the mortals. So..."

"So, we must be prepared for the unexpected and not be limited by the traditional guidelines of the Divine Dictum," Schitz said.

"Precisely," Tetanus said. He swung toward the other students. "Resume positions!"

When Tetanus announced for the drill to recommence, he swung his staff at Schitz again. This time, Schitz side-stepped the blow before running to the next position in the simulated assault.

"He can be taught," Tetanus said with a smile as he watched his nephew run along the training course.

THE DAY'S TRAINING EXERCISE concluded with Hayfever's arrival. Hayfever was joined by his sultry, curvaceous mate, Bloodfever. Schitz marveled at her flowing crimson locks and sensual frame. Bloodfever had been the source of many a sweat-drenched dream for a pre-pubescent Schitz before he began the sequestered portion of the Academy. Schitz found himself both wanting to glance at the attractive female superior and to look away. He felt as though his furtive thoughts were etched across his forehead for all to see. Schitz glanced at the remainder of Hayfever's retinue, SIDS and Tuberculosis, who were the grandparents of Rubella, Measles, and Mumps. Schitz observed a striking similarity in appearance between SIDS and Rubella. The pair looked almost akin to distant sisters because Demons only aged to the appearance of a human in their mid-thirties – at most. Schitz felt sickened by the realization that Hayfever, Bloodfever, SIDS, and Tuberculosis were the only surviving members of the grandparent's generation.

The ranks of the Demons were minuscule when compared to the Houses of the Angels. Schitz shuddered as he recalled the hordes of Heavenly foes arrayed against this small contingent. The eldest generation was festooned in black attire from head to toe. Schitz could feel a pulsating chill circulate through the cadet Demons. The Sequester was an arduous time in which the fledglings were isolated from all but their instructors, and yet those assembled before them were not teachers. Bloodfever raised her hand, silencing the muffled whispers that circled the training pit. She spoke with a smoothness that mirrored her frame.

"As our youngest warriors, your presence is required at a state function. However, the Sequester is still in effect; you will not speak to your parents or to us. Now to your barracks and your dress uniforms, from there assemble in the Great Hall. You will come to attention with your company, not your kin."

The youngsters plodded to the long row of beds that composed the training barracks. Schitz gazed at the familiar inscription carved into the wooden frame on the roof of his bunk by a former student.

"Born to die, we are all but passing through; fallen leaves from Yggdrasil, the undying tree."

There were hushed whispers among the cadets as they pulled on their dress uniforms, black grieves, helmets, and breastplates, and fine black robes too delicate for the field. Schitz glanced over at the cluster of siblings that had tormented him so relentlessly. He overheard a soft whisper from Mumps, "It must be a funeral."

"Well obviously, nitwit," Rubella said sharply.

Schitz felt a sense of intrigue as he watched the scourge of his day interact menacingly with another. Rubella was fierce and undeniably beautiful, but whatever attractiveness lived in her lithe frame was overshadowed by her razor-sharp tongue. While dressing, Schitz noticed Autism through the gap between their upper and lower bunk. The lad was grinning uncontrollably. When he caught Schitz's gaze, he gestured with a nod of his head, directing him to look over his shoulder. Schitz turned and felt a smile burst across his face. Mononucleosis was staring furtively at Anorexia's pale wire-thin frame.

"Really? Even today, my man?" Vertigo said as he walked past Mono and slapped him heartily on the back. Mononucleosis jumped and returned to reality.

Schitz laughed along with the others while Anorexia's white complexion metamorphosed into a crimson subcutaneous rose. She quickly pulled her dress robe over her breasts. Schitz admired Vertigo, the star lead of the class whose humor boosted everyone. Moreover, unlike his challenger for the top spot of the class, Vertigo was a friend to all. He never bullied, never truly made others feel bad or embarrassed. Mono shoved Vertigo playfully.

The revelry was short-lived as the cadets exited the barracks and were presented with the cold hard reality that they were going to the funeral of a parent of some of their comrades. Schitz, like the others, had barely known his parents. He had spent his infancy with his Wraith, Elise, and then entered pre-training. His mother and father had been there, but only intermittently. Pre-training was replaced by training, and then the Sequester, years away from any others but his classmates and his instructors.

The cadets entered the Great Hall and snapped to attention. The hall was lit by torches, amplifying the light that drifted in from the Styx. The flickering torches sent eerie shadows across the Hall's many pillars and statues. Schitz realized that his parents' generation was already assembled on the far side of three altars that occupied the center of the cavernous room.

Schitz was shaken to his core; three altars meant three deceased. A solitary loss was monumental in Hell; to have sustained three fatalities was indescribable. Schitz could not bring himself to look. Instead, he scanned their formation for people he knew. His eyes met a familiar stranger, his father. Diphtheria looked severe as always. Only then did Schitz dare to look to the middle of the Great Hall. The scene burned itself into his mind. On the three altars rested Wasting Illness, the grandmother of Rubella, Measles, and Mumps, her daughter, Eye Fever, the trio's mother, and Poliomyelitis, Schitz's mother.

Schitz felt a constriction in his throat and burning in the corners of his eyes. His mind involuntarily trailed back to his birth. He barely knew his mother, and yet the sense of loss was profound; it was the loss of all that was promised after the Sequester. In a moment, he had lost all the hope of a family, somebody on whom to rely.

Well, half of it, Schitz thought as he once again glanced up across the hall and beheld his father. His face was stern. Schitz glanced to his right. The remainder of the grandparents' generation was assembled in a single file. To the left of the altars stood the solitary figure from an age all but lost, an elder even to the grandparents.

Fever cast a stoic figure. His shadow seemed to stretch farther than any others in the flickering display of torchlight.

Schitz glanced around the cavernous, elaborate Great Hall. Painstakingly etched columns rose to an ornate, engraved ceiling decorated with scenes of carnage and war. A circle of Wraiths screeched away on violins, the music at once soothing and scratchy. Schitz would have looked for Elise, but the Wraiths wore long, hooded cloaks that concealed their identities. The stirring melody of the strings grew and grew, rising like a whirlwind, only to die suddenly to an eerie silence.

Emerging from a tiny staircase in the marble floor beside the altars, the Priests appeared. Armed with incense and torches, the holy men and Priestesses spoke in melodic unison. "For the faithful have laid down their lives for the Lord and for us all, therefore let us honor the price of victory."

Schitz reflexively joined in the chorus of "Hallelujah."

The Priests continued, looking up toward the observation gallery. "Lord on high, with your permission, we will proceed."

In that instant, Schitz realized that the Devil, Satan, Beelzebub, the Lord of Darkness, known by many other names whispered in fear in all corners of the world, the great purifier, ordained to bring an end to the ceaseless river of mortal reincarnation and thus provide the world with sleep, was looking down on the proceedings. His presence had gone unobserved among the other youngsters as well, and in unison, all silently craned their necks to see their leader. Physically, he was slender, tall, pale with a crop of short black hair. He wore a simple black robe, no different from their own, and yet the power projected by the silent figure was palpable. He wore a sharp crown with many points, amplifying his horns. Upon his chest he wore more decorations for valor than any Demon could hope to earn. The Lord raised his scepter aloft, and the Priests continued. "Let us pray."

The violins, played by the Wraiths, took up *Lacrimosa*. Schitz remembered the words from his classroom instruction. When he had memorized the hymn, he had not prepared himself for the emotion of the moment. He felt his throat tighten as he forced the words to his lips.

Weep no more, dear,
Feel no fear here,
All that is dust, must return to dust.
All that is Ash, once again becomes Ash,

Weep no more, dear.
Feel no fear here,
All that has been awoken, must be unspoken,
All that has been born, must one day be torn.

Glory fades like the ebbing light,
As we are all overtaken by the creeping night

Rest in the Lord's arms,
Safe from all harms,
Peaceful in the deliverance from all of life's pains
Nothing but the Lord and his attendants remains.

Amen.

Schitz felt numb as he trudged back to the barracks. The air felt heavy, thick with the unpleasant silence. Upon reaching the doorway of the barracks, he came to loggerheads with Rubella.

"Ah, after you," he said cautiously, instinctively dropping his eyes to the ground.

He felt a surprisingly soft hand rest on his shoulder. Schitz looked up and peered into Rubella's piercing blue eyes; it was as though he was seeing them for the first time.

"Your mother was a strong warrior; you should be proud of her."

Schitz felt as though the wind had been knocked out of him. He would have more expected a punch to the solar plexus.

"Thank you," he said. "Your mother and grandmother were fierce warriors. I'm sure you'll live up to their expectations."

Rubella nodded and looked away before walking into the barracks. The dormitory was quiet. Wasting Illness had been the grandmother of Rubella, Measles, and Mumps as well as Anorexia, Autism, Legionnaires' Disease, Chlamydial Lymphogranuloma. She was the mother of their mother, Lyme Disease. The training had lacked a sense of gravity before the funeral. Schitz wondered if he would ever have an answer to the question rattling around in his head. As he collapsed onto his bunk and looked up at Autism's bunk above him, he wondered what it was like, the Mortal Realm. For the first time, he questioned whether he had the makings of a warrior.

THE STONE HALLS OF the palace of Babylon were cool in the night air. Wind swept across the balconies and terraces of the hanging gardens, carrying with it the scent of burnt incense and the dying aromas of the day's final meal. The night was deep and dark and still, but not silent; water flowed through the garden's intricate irrigation system, the catlike call of a peacock sliced through the night air. Schitz felt tension coursing through his body as he crept along the colonnade of massive pillars, edging ever nearer to the Great Hall. He could still hear Tetanus's clearly articulated instructions, ringing in his ears. "This is not a combat foray. Your objective is to practice body-hopping and to get back safely. On the off chance that you encounter an Angel, you are to disengage and return home immediately."

Schitz had not been to the worldly realm since the terrifying ordeal of his birth. He wondered to himself if he was ready to be there in the seemingly unending, expansively broad world of man. For all the time spent training, everything he had studied felt real for the first time. He shivered as he crept farther along the walkway.

They had been sent to the city in pairs. Schitz hesitantly glanced to his right and sighed. He had been paired with Rubella, the top of the class with the bottom of the class, the salutatorian with the second from the anchor, and so on. Rubella had been oddly quiet since leaving the underworld. Schitz noted that she appeared visibly rattled as she crept beside him.

"Are you alright?" Schitz asked in a hushed whisper.

"Of course," she said with determination etched in her voice, disjointed from her expression. "I'll just feel a little better once we find bodies to jump into. I feel exposed here in the Celestial."

Schitz was disarmed by her honesty. Reflexively, he put his hand on her shoulder. "It will be all right," he said, "we'll get through this, and before you know it, you'll be bragging to Tetanus about how you jump from body to body, effortlessly."

"Shut up," she said with a smile.

Schitz saw something in her countenance that he could not place; he banished the thought momentarily. "Look, there are some quarters for the nobility."

With stockinged steps, the duo crept along the cold stones and peered into the room. Schitz saw a young couple asleep, entwined, their naked bodies a bird's nest of limbs. Schitz felt a sense of embarrassment at seeing such a personal, intimate scene. He blushed a little.

"What should we do," Rubella asked.

"I suppose we should do what we came here to do. Relax, it will be easy," he replied.

Schitz took a deep breath, wondering if his reassurance was factual. With great effort, Schitz and Rubella jumped into the two sleeping bodies. Suddenly Schitz was in awe as he possessed the form of the young mortal. It felt odd to him to be in the body of a more mature man, as he was still an adolescent. Schitz's thoughts were interrupted as Rubella sat up in the bed beside him. She had a gleeful smile on her face.

"We did it," she whispered in hushed enthusiasm.

Schitz nodded with delight. It was only then that he felt bashfulness. He realized the human he had possessed was naked; so was the body Rubella had assumed. He glanced down ever so slightly and beheld the figure of the lithe, young Babylonian. He could see through the flesh façade to the Demon he knew so well, and she, too, was so beautiful. How had Schitz never seen it? The enigmatic look had returned to Rubella's face.

"What is it?" Schitz asked.

"I don't know," she replied coyly.

Schitz's heart pounded. He felt more nervous than he ever had during any training or any lesson.

"Why don't you pay attention to me?" Rubella asked suddenly.

The vulnerability in her voice caught Schitz unawares. "What do you mean?" he asked with baffled surprise.

She almost sounded pleading, which was entirely uncharacteristic.

"It's no secret that all of the guys in our class are in love with me," she said. "They're always competing for my attention, but it seems like the attention of the one Demon that I want, the one Demon that I wanted for so long, I can never have."

Schitz reached out and touched the shoulder of the woman across from him. It felt odd to control another entity's body, and yet he was more concerned with what Rubella had to say.

"But you always torment me and insult me," he said with surprise in his voice. "If you wanted my attention, why did you make my life miserable?"

Rubella sighed and placed her hand on Schitz's thigh. "There was a time when you laughed at my jokes and taunts, and it hardly seemed that it tormented you," she said, gently caressing his leg, a small smile forming in the crease of her mouth.

Schitz was whisked back years in the past to a time when he was much younger. In the vibrancy of his youth, he remembered when a young Rubella and he shared jokes and laughter exclusive to themselves. Within his mind's eye, he could see her pushing him to the ground, playfully taunting him.

"I've wanted it to be like those days again for so long," she said with pleading in her voice. "When I felt like I could no longer capture your attention, I tried to do it in the way that I always had, but you no longer seem to think of my jokes as funny or cute."

She sounded as though she was about to cry; the river of tears held back just barely at the brinks of her eyes. Schitz moved his hand down from her shoulder and rubbed the small of her back.

"I never thought of it that way," he said softly.

Silence descended over the room, awkwardly cloaking the couple as they sat in bed. Suddenly, Rubella's lips were pressed against his own. Schitz's mind whirled; he had no idea what to do, but the warmth of her tongue against his own excited him to no end. With ferocity, he caressed every part of her delectable body with ceaseless hunger. It was all new to him and more fascinating and wonderful than he could ever imagine. Suddenly, Rubella broke the embrace and sat back in the bed. Schitz was fearful that he had done something wrong.

Before he could speak, Rubella said, "Let's leave these mortal bodies. I've wanted so long to explore you; I don't want this heavy flesh between the two of us."

All the fear and anxiety of being in the world was replaced by the excitement of feeling Rubella pressed against him after the pair exited the room. The exertions of the mortals who had continued their own expressions of affection could be heard emanating from within, but these were of little interest to Schitz and Rubella.

After a long while, Schitz pulled back from kissing Rubella. He gazed at her deep blue eyes and marveled at her soft yet angular features and her blonde hair that terminated just above her shoulders. Schitz had enjoyed pressing her against the wall of the palace, kissing her with all the strength he possessed. It felt as though years of misunderstanding, tension, and longing had been expressed in those few moments of passion.

Switching back to reality, Schitz whispered, "We'll have more time for this once we get back home."

"I hope so," she replied with a sultry smile.

The two adolescents explored the palace grounds, leaping from one individual to the next. When Schitz grew tired, Rubella motivated him to continue. And when Rubella found herself lagging, exhausted from the exertions of overcoming mortals' minds to gain entry, Schitz encouraged her to press forward. They encountered numerous mortals whose mental strength prevented possession, however, they continued undeterred. The anxiety of being in the Mortal Realm was replaced by the excitement of young love and exploration. It was only when they turned a corner in the cavernous palace and came across a pair of mortals that the frolic once again became a cold reality. Walking towards Schitz and Rubella was a pair of armed mortals locked in a tense, hushed conversation. Immediately, Schitz recognized the shimmering aura.

"They are possessed by Angels," he said.

Schitz and Rubella were paralyzed with fear. The Angels appeared to be unawares. Instinctively, Schitz reached to his waist and drew the sword belonging to his host. In a single smooth movement, he plunged the sword deep into the midsection of the man standing before him. He heard the crack of bones as the sword pierced the sternum of the mortal and knew he had penetrated deep into the soft vital organs. Schitz was taken aback at how easy it was to land a fatal blow. He watched the aura collapse out of the man into a shivering convulsing heap upon the floor. Without waiting for a response from the second Angel, Schitz grabbed Rubella by the wrist and led her on a flight through the palace. Several swift turns later, they approached a doorway. The exercise demanded that each partner carry one of the two elements required for a return to Hell.

Schitz reached for his satchel of earth and said, "I'll carve the symbols, you be prepared to throw the water on them."

He heard a groan of dismay in response and looked at Rubella.

"I must have spilled it," she said. They heard frantic footsteps growing louder.

"It's no matter," Schitz said, "follow me. Whoever's coming is an Angel, probably in Celestial form. He'll try to flank us. He's either looking for a human to jump into or waiting for one of his comrades to cut us down so he can engage us in the Celestial."

Schitz opted for the boldest recourse. He traced the symbols around the doorway, then led Rubella towards the approaching footsteps. Fear smeared its way across Rubella's face.

"You're leading us into the hands of our enemy," she said, but she moved when Schitz tugged her hand. They ran in the direction of the sound. At the last moment, Schitz stepped into a narrow hallway. They crouched against the stone walls. The only sounds were the footfalls and water trickling through the irrigation system.

Only after the steps echoed into nothingness did Schitz realize he'd been holding his breath.

"This way," he said.

Schitz and Rubella passed rooms where the nobility sleep, the armament rooms, and the servants' quarters. They reached the kitchen.

"I'm sorry I spilled the water," Rubella said.

"No, don't be ridiculous," Schitz said. "In all that commotion, not even Tetanus could blame you for dropping your water."

Rubella smiled; Schitz found a jug of water then drew the ancient symbols around the doorway to the kitchen with the remaining earth from his satchel. Rubella sprinkled the water over the dirt, and they recited the incantations in unison. They watched with glee as the doorway opened. They stepped out of the human forms one final time, entered the Celestial, then stepped through the gateway back to home.

Upon arriving back in Hell, Schitz and Rubella were met by the excited faces of the rest of their class. Measles and Mumps bounded over to Rubella. With the intimate knowledge shared among siblings, they perceived a different energy between their sister and Schitz. Measles and Mumps both nodded at Schitz and asked Rubella how the two of them had done.

"He was absolutely amazing," Rubella said with emotion dripping from her voice. She clutched Schitz by the arm. "I was so nervous, but Schitz always knew what to do. We ran into two Angels, and he saved us."

Rubella's announcement drew the attention of the other arriving apprentice Demons. Schitz noted that neither Measles nor Mumps appeared shocked at Rubella's sudden drastic change of affection towards him.

"Is that so?" Measles asked said with fascination in his voice. "Did you really encounter Angels?"

Schitz nodded curtly. Soon they were descended upon by Vertigo, Conjunctivitis, Autism, Anorexia, Influenza, Legionnaires' Disease, Mononucleosis, and all the others.

"We encountered an Angel as well," Vertigo said.

"What did you do?" Schitz asked.

"We ran like hell," Vertigo said. "What did you do?"

"Schitz killed the human that one of the Angels was possessing," Rubella said. She sounded like a proud mother.

An explosion of murmurs and questions descended on Schitz. He'd never felt more alive. He turned to Vertigo and assumed a cavalier tone.

"Well, we turned a corner, and they were right on top of us, so we couldn't run. I ran the closest one through, and then we took off."

Schitz shrugged to indicate that he saw nothing special in the actions he described, while internally he was a tumultuous sea of excitement.

Hayfever's voice pierced the noise. "A word, Schizophrenia Nervosa."

Chills shot through Schitz's body as he gazed at the professor. Rubella squeezed his hand – a reassuring gesture. Steeling himself outwardly, Schitz broke from the group. He caught the glance of Vertigo's supportive nod in his periphery.

I could have never imagined all this, Schitz thought, *a kiss from a beautiful girl who cannot keep her hands off me – the praise and admiration of my peers.*

He was awash in the waters of redemption, as though he had never been the butt of jokes, had never been the dunce of the class. He walked with purpose and confidence and followed Hayfever into the Lecture Hall.

Hayfever placed his hand gently onto Schitz's shoulder. "My, my, my, how the most unlikely of pupils can surprise us," Hayfever said. "Tell me this, why did you kill the Angel's mortal vessel?"

Schitz's throat constricted. He heard himself speak, but it was like someone else's voice. "I had no other choice; I did what I had to do."

"Why not run?" the instructor asked.

"With two Angels a mere foot away, we would have never made it. I needed to capitalize on the moment of surprise and indecision. It was there for the taking," Schitz said.

"And if they had stolen that moment?"

"They didn't," Schitz said.

Hayfever stopped and gazed down at Schitz.

"Then why did you not finish off the Angel?"

Schitz thought for a moment before responding. "Our orders were to avoid combat, so once I had established enough of an advantage to escape, I followed our directive, nothing more, nothing less. I needed to protect my partner and to follow orders."

Hayfever's stoic countenance broke into a broad grin. He removed a hand from Schitz's shoulder and ruffled his hair affectionately. "The Wraiths were out in force tonight, observing your actions."

The searing heat of a blush coursed across Schitz's cheeks when he realized his private moment with Rubella had been observed by a cloaked watcher.

"And may I tell you that your report was the most favorable by far," Hayfever said. "It is one thing to acquire academic knowledge. It is yet another to excel on the training ground. But to excel in the heat of the contested moment when you and your foe hold equal footing, and favor and chance stand between the two of you at an even marker, that... well that is something altogether more impressive, more unteachable, and more telling than any instructor's evaluation."

Schitz felt as though he would burst with delight. "Thank you, sir," he said.

Hayfever continued, "You have charisma, Schitz, and you may well be a leader. Autism and Anorexia have chosen to follow your ideas of cultivating infections of the mind rather than the body. Others will follow you, too, but promise me this: do not dismiss or disregard the lessons I have imparted to you. They have been crafted over countless eons by those who went before us. You must carry forth the essence of the wisdom I have imparted to the final victory, even if you adapt it to your own visions."

Schitz nodded in agreement. "Yes, sir"

"That's my boy, now send in Rubella next, will you?" Hayfever asked.

Schitz nodded. As he climbed out of the amphitheater, he felt a strange anxiety and piqued interest regarding Rubella's upcoming assessment. He felt as though she was something of his and was concerned. He realized that he wanted Rubella to be his. In one moment of affection, she had afflicted him with a virulent, incurable malady with which he had no experience.

MONTHS PASSED, AND THE class continued to advance, making ever deeper penetrations into the human world. An increasing sense of preparedness covered everything the young Demons did. On the parade ground, Conjunctivitis, Autism, and Mononucleosis snapped their heads in perfect unison as Tetanus commanded the squad to "face-right." Rubella worked her way through the crowd of Babylonians, leaping freely from mortal to mortal as she scanned the square for signs of Angels.

Schitz raised his hand in the amphitheater and said, "The most recent elevation of humans' consciousness came at the end of the second age. They developed a knowledge of their species in the form of recorded history and writing. Additionally, The Strain of humans that remember past incarnations developed."

"Very good," Hayfever said.

The youngsters had come into their own and formed a sense of solidarity as they approached the end of their tutelage.

"They still don't respect me," Schitz said wistfully. "I mean, I might not be a laughingstock, but I'm still at the bottom of the class, and everybody knows it."

Rubella shifted as she reclined against Schitz in the open field. It was perpetually lit, as all of Hell, by the light of Earth's moon and the flowing waters of the Styx. She tilted her head backwards towards Schitz.

"But why does it matter?" she asked.

Schitz thought for a moment. He had never considered why it mattered so much to him, what the rest of the class thought of him.

"I guess I don't know, Bella. I just..." He trailed off. "I've always felt different from everyone else. Like, when I hear something in class, I always think, why? Why do things have to be the way that Hayfever says they are? Isn't there another way to look at things? I mean, even with a disease, we were tasked with cultivating specific illnesses; what's so wrong with mine infecting the mind?"

"So, you want your being different to mean you are better rather than worse?" Rubella asked. Her eyes reflected intense interest.

She kissed him on the mouth. He felt flushed with passion and excitement. Schitz fought to breathe. He placed his hands on her waist as she slowly climbed on top of him. Momentarily breaking the embrace of tongues, Schitz whispered, "Have you given any thought to the future? I mean, after graduation."

In the moonlight, her eyes appeared almost silvery as she gazed deeply into his.

"I don't know what the future holds in store," she replied, "but I do know that wherever I am, I want to be with you."

Schitz smiled. His whole world felt dizzyingly unstable. In a few weeks they would graduate, then he would once again meet his father, if he were alive. But what role Schitz would have in shaping the destiny of the cause remained to be seen.

"Have you thought about your father much?" he asked.

"Not really something I'm thinking about right now," she replied playfully. "You think too much; the future will sort itself out. For now, why don't you worry less about asking why, and more about just getting to the front of the class? Can your mind disease kill people?"

Schitz shook his head. "It's not about killing them; I inspire fear, I drain resources. I'm more impactful. A dead human is just a dead human, but an infected mind can send ripple effects of fear throughout countless multitudes."

Rubella smiled. "Whatever you say, handsome."

She ran her hands through his hair, gently stroking his horns.

"I want you," she said.

A strange fear clutched at Schitz's chest.

"Are you sure?" he asked. "You know there is no going back for a Demon. We mate for life."

"Yes, I want you," she said, leaning her face close to his so that their noses were nearly touching. Her small petite mouth spread ever so slightly in a seductive grin. All sense of bluster or bravado abandon Schitz. He knew both he and Rubella were inexperienced. As the male, he felt an extreme sense of responsibility for the outcome. He wanted more than anything to do a good job.

"To be honest, I have no idea what to do," he said. He cringed at his own words.

Rubella smiled. Her giggle put Schitz at ease.

"Start with this," she said in a soft voice while placing both of his hands on her thighs.

Schitz inhaled sharply as she moved his hands under her tunic and began slowly raising them towards her stomach. When she pulled the ruffled folds of her robe over her head, Schitz's pulse pounded in his temples – and elsewhere. He gazed hungrily at her beautiful form, the curvature of ample breasts, her firm taut midsection, and the small patch of hair above her sex. Schitz began running his hands over her body, caressing her back as he moved his tongue over her nipples. He was pleasantly shocked as her delicate yet firm hand searched under his own robe until she held his erect manhood in her hand.

Mimicking her moves, Schitz dared to place his hand between his lover's legs. He was overwhelmed with arousal as his fingers met her wetness. Rubella groaned and began to pump her hand in synchrony with Schitz's stimulating movements. Schitz was sucking at her slender neck when he felt the warmth of her womanhood slide down onto him. He gasped, but he could hardly hear himself over Rubella's moans. Initially, Schitz was overwhelmed with pleasure and sought to impale her with every thrust, but he eventually slowed and enjoyed an intensity he'd never experienced.

Schitz gazed into Rubella's wild, wide eyes. Her mouth was open, but she no longer made any sound.

"I love you," he said in a gasp. His voice was oddly high.

"I love you," she said. "It's always been you."

Without warning, Schitz reached the precipice and lost himself within her. Slowly their exertions came to a halt. Schitz breathed heavily; he felt excited and relieved and curious all at once. Rubella was quiet. She clutched her discarded robe against her body and nestled into him. She whispered from the shelter of his arms.

"I wish we could stay here forever; I wish we never had to go back to the barracks."

Schitz clutched her tightly. A wish is a nice thing, but he knew it would not protect them from reality. Schitz did not wish; he simply clung tightly to her and attempted to savor every second, knowing full well that he was no longer the boy who had snuck out earlier in the evening.

THE CLOSING WEEKS OF the Academy were a blur. Schitz was enthralled with the routine of entering the mortal world by day, followed by nights of passion with Rubella. Schitz had reluctantly taken Rubella's advice and restrained his novel thinking in class. He concentrated on regurgitating the Devine Dictum and the strategy lessons. Schitz had initially seen these efforts met with a rise from the bottom of the class. However, his initial bravado in the Mortal Realm was soon equaled and surpassed by his classmates. He was no longer the butt of vicious ridicule, but there was an intangible missing element. He did not want to be tolerated; he wanted to excel, he wanted to lead, and yet he still heard the criticisms, especially the critiques of his malady.

He had been the first of what they had termed the Psychologicals and had been followed by his friends Autism and Anorexia. Schitz had been heavily criticized for developing a disease that afflicted the mind – one that did not result in a fatality. Schitz had bemoaned the call for "death" or better "painful death" or better still "lingering, painful death," from Hayfever. He had watched with envy as the others – Legionnaires' Disease, Chlamydial Lymphogranuloma, Conjunctivitis, Influenza, Mycetoma – emerged with the symptoms of the afflictions with which they would scourge humanity. They were destined to create fear and to send souls through the river Styx on their way back to reincarnation. If Schitz's envy regarding those developing traditional lethal afflictions was the appetizer, the entrée was Vertigo's development of a virulent psychological condition in which mortals became dizzy, nauseous, and eventually became unable to stand. They devolved into seizures and death. Vertigo had brought the innovation Schitz had sought to create and had elevated himself to the top of the class, ever vying with Rubella for the pinnacle spot.

These thoughts had been aimlessly running through Schitz's mind as he walked alone down the halls leading from the barracks to Hayfever's quarters.

"Come in," Hayfever said.

Schitz pushed the weighty door aside with effort and entered the room. A flood of imagery rushed through Schitz's eyes. Hayfever's room was breathtakingly ornate, with a massive bed covered with leopard and lion furs. The walls were decked with ancient weapons, and his desk was ornamented and impressive. Hayfever sat at his desk while the others in the room stood about awkwardly.

Rubella was present, and her father, Botulism, a short, stocky fellow, Vertigo and his father, Bubonic Plague, a massively tall, muscular monstrosity with long black braided hair, along with Schitz's own father, Diphtheria, a serious, fit man who was dwarfed in the presence of Bubonic Plague.

Schitz snapped to attention. "Schizophrenia Incenderos Nervosa reporting as ordered."

"At ease," Hayfever said. He appeared almost annoyed at the formality.

Schitz stood at ease. Hayfever rose to his feet.

"We are here today because of," he paused, "because of an issue." He continued, irritation heavy in his voice, "Schitz, are you familiar—"

Bubonic Plague erupted. "Just ask him about Rubella!"

The room shook with the anger in his voice. Hayfever glowed red with heat and venom.

"I remember when you were just a pup. You will not interrupt me as your father or as your generational and practical superior. Is that clear?"

Schitz had never seen this side of his generally docile Instructor. Bubonic Plague scowled at the reprimand but nodded.

Hayfever continued, "Schitz, are you familiar with Operative Clause 4, Section C of the Divine Dictum?"

Schitz poured through his memory. "Operative Clause 4, Section C states, 'Demons are generally free to mate with a Demon of their choosing, exceptions may occur when mating is required to create a new species, or in the case of two exceptional Demons that may further the species, then mates may be assigned through decree or familial agreement.'"

Hayfever looked at Schitz with a mournful gaze. "A good recitation, Schitz."

Schitz glanced over at Rubella. Her eyes were wet and glued to the floor. He longed for her to look at him. He was having trouble breathing.

Bubonic Plague's coarse voice brought Schitz back to reality. "We were going through the process of exercising that exception. What is the nature of your relationship with this girl?"

For the first time since his arrival, Rubella glanced up at Schitz with a pleading look in her eyes. She might have moved her head slightly to signal "no." Schitz glanced from Rubella to Vertigo. He felt a seething hatred course through his veins at the thought of this golden, spoiled brat entering his mate.

Ever since the outing into Babylon, Schitz had feared losing Rubella, but to see it unfolding before him...

"Well?" Bubonic Plague towered above him.

"We... we... we love each other," Schitz said. "I intend..." He could not continue.

"We get the idea, young man," Botulism said. He sounded sympathetic. "We're all adults here, or nearly adults, just tell us this, have you and my daughter... have you... ah... progressed?"

Schitz nodded.

Bubonic Plague threw his hands in the air while Botulism looked around the room for guidance.

"It doesn't matter as long as all parties agree, it can be overlooked," Bubonic said.

"I don't agree," Schitz said. "I do not agree at all."

Bubonic Plague's voice was a snarl. "It's of no concern to you, you insolent dog. We are talking about producing a line of Demons that will be exceptional, that will carry us to the final victory. My son is outstanding. This girl stands at the top of her class. There is nothing else to consider."

Botulism nodded in agreement. Schitz tried to focus on Rubella, but the room was spinning. Vertigo looked smug. Schitz wanted to strike him across the face.

"There is that," Botulism said. "But there is another consideration." He turned to Rubella. "What do you want, daughter?"

Rubella never hesitated. "I want Schitz, and he wants me, Father."

Bubonic Plague slapped a huge paw onto the desk. "It isn't up to you – it isn't up to your... your sentimental father." He screwed up his face in a mocking gesture. "'What do *you* want, daughter.'" The anger raged across his eyes. "It does not matter what she wants!"

All eyes locked on Hayfever. He sighed with the weight of the decision.

"In accordance with the letter of the Resolution, when there are two exceptional Demons identified, they can be betrothed to one another by decree."

Bubonic Plague folded his arms across his chest and smiled triumphantly. Vertigo, emboldened by his father's words, glanced at Rubella with thinly concealed lust.

"Then it is resolved," Bubonic Plague said.

Rubella began crying and covered her face with her hands. Hayfever raised his hands in surrender.

"I will present the proposed betrothal for approval," he said.

For the first time, Diphtheria spoke.

"There is another way."

"Go on," Hayfever said.

Schitz's father stood straight. "This is a matter of honor. I suspect what we have here is mere posturing. There are very few females in this current generation. Bubonic seeks only to ensure the continuation of bloodline, so he is trampling on the de facto pairing of Schizophrenia and Rubella. It is a grave insult of Schizophrenia's honor to claim that Vertigo's superior enough to invoke Operative Clause 4, Section C. I propose that they are equals. As such, a resolution of ill-afflicted honor is required without further delay."

The air left the room.

No one dared speak while Hayfever mulled the situation. "Matters of honor are traditionally reserved for accusations of treason or impure blood," he said.

"The current matter is applicable. It is, in all honesty, the only possible solution," Diphtheria said. "You summoned my son. He reported as ordered. He recited the Devine Dictum without error. How can you claim he is inferior to a classmate? It is a grave insult."

"If you are so bent on sending your only pitiful offspring to destruction, my boy will dispatch of him without spilling a droplet of sweat," Bubonic Plague said.

A small smile twitched at the corner of Diphtheria's mouth. "Lead the way," he said.

The group descended the steps to the river Styx. Schitz felt as though he was outside his own body looking in. He had imagined a typical day of drilling and training, a night of slipping away with Rubella. As they approached the riverbank, they were joined by a gaggle of onlookers; apparently, a Wraith had spread the word of the spectacle.

As an array of Demons, Priests, and Wraiths drew near, Hayfever said, "Choose your seconds."

Vertigo spoke first. "Mononucleosis!"

The boys embraced – comrades in arms.

"Autism," Schitz said. His selection nodded. The pair stood apart, reluctant participants in a drama neither completely understood.

Hayfever pointed to a small skiff. "All aboard," he said.

Schitz turned to his father. The older man raised a palm.

"This is the world we live in, son," he said. "I do not want you as my son if you do not stand up for yourself. Now, kill him and be done with it."

Schitz stepped onto the waiting boat. He glanced at Rubella; she placed her hand over her heart then looked away, full of dread and anxiety.

By tradition, the seconds rowed across the broad, peaceful river. Schitz peered into the luminescent water and watched countless souls who had died with fear and hatred in them. Their energy gave strength to Hell as they continued on to reincarnation.

Schitz envied the mortals, although they were unaware of their endless life. They did not understand how death served as a passageway to their next iteration. Schitz knew his death would mean the eternal end of his existence. He shivered slightly.

Today may be my last day; I may never touch Rubella again, or laugh, or feel the wind on my face.

Schitz looked over to Vertigo, who sat in silence. Schitz did not want to kill his popular classmate.

"Why are you doing this?" Schitz asked.

Vertigo replied, "I honor my father as you would yours. What else is there to say? Why are *you* doing this? Could she possibly be worth all this nonsense?"

"Of course," he said. "She is worth anything in the world. If you knew even a little bit about her, you would not ask such a foolish question."

The island of Duellum was a small rocky interruption in the flow of the river. Schitz looked at the patches of dried crimson staining the foliage – gory reminders of fallen combatants. Hayfever opened a large stone cabinet to reveal a cache of weapons. In all his training, Schitz had only encountered Celestial weapons or dulled mortal weapons in the form of close range, small implements. Now he beheld long swords, spears, bows, all manner of human weaponry, effective and sharp.

As though he had read Schitz's mind, Hayfever spoke. "The Divine Dictum holds that all available weaponry must be at the disposal of the participants when there are internal disputes. Vertigo, as the challenged party, you select the implements of battle."

Vertigo selected a pair of long menacing spears and two short swords. Schitz wrapped a leather scabbard belt around his waist and slid the sword into place. He picked up the spear and stretched a little.

Hayfever led the group to the middle of the island. Schitz and Autism stood face-to-face with Vertigo and Mononucleosis. Hayfever spoke.

"Your seconds will bear witness that the fight was fair and that honor was upheld."

Autism and Mononucleosis nodded sternly. Hayfever continued, "The duel is over when one combatant either concedes or can no longer carry on the fight. At my command, you will turn and walk ten paces. From there, the contest will commence. Let honor be upheld."

"Turn," Hayfever said.

Schitz's hands trembled; bile churned in his stomach. He had been trained to kill Angels – his mortal enemies. He never imagined a fight to the death with a classmate – even one he did not like.

He saw Rubella in his mind... his mother, Elise... his father.

"March!"

Schitz began to walk in slow, measured steps.

He remembered passion in the grass...

"Eight... nine..."

He thought about adventures he might never experience.

"Ten! Commence!"

Vertigo rushed forward.

He thinks he will dominate. He will tire.

Schitz never moved. He readied his spear, then threw it.

He missed.

Vertigo smiled, a crooked expression of smug satisfaction. Without any reaction at all, Schitz drew his sword. He was pleased to have jettisoned the spear's weight.

Vertigo jabbed with his spear. Schitz sidestepped and parried. Vertigo continued to thrust, vicious, driving stabs at first but growing weaker as the heavy spear drained his muscles of strength.

When Vertigo pushed the spear forward with an uncommitted shove, Schitz grabbed the shaft and pushed just as Vertigo recoiled to launch another attack. The combined motion – one pulling, the other pushing – threw Vertigo off balance and he sprawled to the rocky ground.

Schitz stepped forward and lowered his sword until it touched Vertigo's throat.

"The fight is concluded," Schitz said.

"Yes," Vertigo said.

Schitz thrust his arms to the sky and turned to face his second. He'd won – and Rubella was his. He sheathed his sword, then looked at Autism, whose face was pale with dread.

Schitz turned back toward Vertigo. Halfway through the turn, he felt the slick, burning sensation of a razor flaying his cheek just below his left eye. He howled in pain and rage.

"I never yielded, you fool," Vertigo said.

Schitz saw blood on the top of Vertigo's sword – his blood. He brought his hand to his face and winced. He could smell the cloying coppery aroma and knew instinctively that the wound, though serious, was not fatal.

He watched Vertigo's chest heave as his opponent resumed the attack. Although he had drawn his sword, Schitz contented himself to dodge and duck. Sweat poured from his face and stung his wound. Fatigue began to weaken his legs – his vision grew blurry. He was suddenly thirsty beyond all reason.

Schitz blocked another tired swing. Metal clashed against metal.

Vertigo drew back and swung his blade horizontally, neck-high – a killing blow. Schitz made no attempt to parry the blow. When he ducked, Vertigo lost his balance and stumbled. Schitz slashed his sword across Vertigo's exposed back. The boy collapsed onto his stomach. His sword skipped away across the stones.

This time, Schitz placed his knee in the small of his opponent's back. He grabbed Vertigo's hair, pulled it back, and lay his sword across the boy's exposed throat.

"The pain means you can feel. You are not paralyzed... yet," Schitz said. "Do you concede?"

Vertigo rasped his answer through clenched teeth. "Fuck you."

Schitz pulled back on the hair, then slammed Vertigo's face into the rocks countless times. He heard a sickening crunch of teeth and bones.

This time he shouted. "Do you concede?"

"I, con—" Vertigo said.

"Too fucking late," Schitz said. He dragged his right hand up and back, opening Vertigo's throat with the edge of the sword. A torrent of hot blood spurted onto the ground, gushing in pulses until the heart quit beating. Schitz rose to his feet and walked to the far bank of the island as far away as he could get from the onlookers on the opposite bank. He submerged his head in the cool waters of the Styx. When he withdrew it, his face was healed.

He ran his hand over his face. *Nice scar*, he thought. Schitz splashed water on his face again and hoped it would conceal his tears.

Schitz stood at attention. He felt a pervasive numbness. The time spent in Sequester had changed him. He'd lost his mother and killed Vertigo. He'd ventured into the mortal world. Still, he felt like uncertainty incarnate.

He was unsure if he was prepared to fight and die – was not certain about moving forward with Rubella. All the youthful exuberance, the anticipation of being a glorious warrior, the innocence of first love, his belief in the victory that he would help usher in, it had all been ripped from him. He felt an aching in his temples, a dull coursing fatigue running through the length of his body.

To Schitz's right and left stood the remainder of the graduating class. Not yet battle-hardened, but no longer untested, it was their time to take their place amongst the ranks of Hell. Schitz could feel a maturity in the phalanx that had not been there before, but somewhere along the way, insidiously, it had crept into all of them. Graduation was a formality; they were already soldiers.

The band of Wraiths took up the anthem of Hell, The Hunter's Song, and despite his numbness, Schitz felt a chill run down his spine, a sensation only the patriot will ever know. As the tune of *Loué Soit Dieu le Seigneur* began, Schitz cleared his throat and joined in the chorus of familiar voices.

> *We stand firm, though the foes volleys fall upon us like showers,*
> *We stand firm through the passing of many countless hours,*
> *Firmly we stand, awaiting the Lord's command,*
> *Ready to unleash our company's many powers.*

ZINC FLUSHED WITH PRIDE and accomplishment as he stood at the lectern. The weight of the valedictorian's medal around his neck felt glorious. As the band of Familiars struck up the Heavenly anthem, *Engellied*, to the tune of *Loué Soit Dieu le Seigneur*, he felt a sense of complete accomplishment. Zinc cleared his throat as he began leading his class in song.

> *We stand on guard with not a single hint of trepidation,*
> *We stand on guard, to the foe's ever-present consternation,*
> *Yes, we stand on guard, battle-scarred, weathered, and hard,*
> *Ready for any possible situation.*

SCHITZ GLANCED FROM SIDE to side as he beheld all of those in attendance. His father stood at the front of the senior demons. As always, he wore his unreadable, scowling glare. Schitz continued singing.

> *Forward we bound, when unleashed upon the dastardly foe,*
> *Forward we leap, like hunting hounds upon the beleaguered doe,*
> *Eagerly we spring, letting the battle cry ring,*
> *Swifter than any arrow loosed from a bow.*

Schitz thought of his handful of Angelic encounters. *Am I fierce to the enemy?* he wondered.

ZINC GLANCED ACROSS THE rows of his graduating class. He felt immensely lucky. For countless centuries, his kind had battled the Demons that sought to destroy God's fragile worldly kingdom. He counted himself fortunate that he was born in a time when he and his comrades would smash them into oblivion. He sang the next verse even louder.

> *We fight for God, the primogenitor of all creation,*
> *We fight for His honor, and it brings us the greatest elation,*
> *Yes, we fight with might, for all that is good, noble, and right,*
> *That his temple may never know any desecration.*

SCHITZ CONTINUED TO SING.

> *Proudly we take our place amongst the Lord's trusted appointed,*
> *Bathed in the blood of the foe and in the oil of victory anointed,*
> *Proudly we feast on the flesh of the vanquished deceased,*
> *Our enemies dismembered and disjointed.*

Schitz thought of the Angel whose throat he had cut. He could relive the scene in his mind's eye, the blood, the writhing, the comingled sense of accomplishment and relief.

Zinc continued to lead the class through the glorious hymn.

> *We wait for the Holy Spirit that Its guidance may always command*
> *us,*
> *We wait for Its blessing, which will render us invincible and glorious,*
> *Yes, we wait for that day, patiently, hopeful, we pray,*
> *For when we will be left standing victorious.*

He felt his pulse pounding in his chest as he envisioned himself standing victorious on the field of battle. He imagined a pile of dead Demons and his classmates triumphant.

Schitz glanced over at Rubella. He felt a sense of attraction and pride as he took in her lithe, elegant figure. He imagined the body of Hell's Valedictorian that he had come to know so well. As though feeling the weight of his eyes, Rubella glanced over her shoulder and met Schitz's glance, crinkling her nose in a tiny smile. Schitz winked at her as he continued to the next verse.

> *We bring forth the peace of the everlasting and the tranquil night,*
> *We bring forth all that is needed and what's more all that is right,*
> *Justly we come, to undo all that must be undone,*
> *We will never tarry or weary in our fight.*

ZINC'S ATTENTION WAS DRAWN to the youngest of the Carbon sisters, Cecilia Carbon. He mused at how her dark hair stood in stark contrast to her brilliant white robe. Seeing her future husband gaze upon her, the young Angel glanced down bashfully. Zinc continued singing.

We clear the way for Christ, the bringer of all Holy Redemption,
We clear the way with demonic purging, for Earth's reclamation,
Yes, we clear the way, one step further with each serpent we slay,
So that all are free to partake in the Lord's adoration.

SCHITZ THOUGHT OF THE future. He wondered what it would entail, victory or death?

If victory calls for us to offer ourselves a sacrifice on the altar,
We will not hesitate, nor will we cower or will we falter,
Preparedly, we go forward, no loss is too untoward,
Merrily we go forth to the slaughter.

ZINC THOUGHT OF THE future. He had topped the class, but he had yet to see action. The only three Angels in his class to encounter Demons during training had not returned to tell the tale. Zinc was confident it would be different for him. With confidence, he led the class through the final verse.

If we should fall amidst the battle's havoc, turmoil, and confusion,
We will not beg, nor offer our foes collaboration, parley, or collusion,
Yes, if we should fall, we will fall having given our all,
Let that be our final rest and consolation.

SCHITZ SNAPPED BACK TO attention in full unison with the others of his class. The Devil rose to his feet from the reviewing stand of the Great Hall. Schitz saluted, bringing his right arm, open-palmed across his midsection so that it lay across his left elbow, parallel to the ground. Schitz felt ready, no matter what his fate held in store.

ZINC RAISED HIS RIGHT hand to his right eyebrow in salute to the Lord God Almighty as the graduation ceremony concluded. He was ready for the future, whatever it entailed.

CHAPTER 3

GOLDEN SANDS

THE WARM WINDS SWEPT with effortless ease across the dunes of the Sahara, shaping the sand to their will. The sun sank steadily towards the horizon, casting its brilliant dying rays over the city that would later be known as Thebes. As the shadows grew over the city, Pharaoh Amenhotep gazed across at the many wonders of his city: the necropolis, the temples of Luxor and Karnak, and many other-worldly beauties such as his stately palace. The scent of the evening meal was pleasing to the mortal part of the God-King, warming his smell the same way the spectacular sunset warmed his eyes and his soul. Amenhotep considered the vastness of greater Egypt and all the wonders contained within his mighty kingdom. He had reunified upper and lower Egypt upon his arrival in this, the city of Waset.

Gold was immensely pleased with himself as he gazed upon the city and the dunes through the eyes of the possessed Pharaoh. "This will be my land; its people my people, and I will be their God."

He extended both of his arms upwards, clenching his fists with tenacity, trembling with excitement.

"Aren't there some challenges to that?" his brother Silver asked from inside the Royal Chamber. He had possessed the body of General Ahmose. The general was a staunch friend of the Pharaoh and named after the Pharaoh's late father. He was revered by the royal family, a fitting choice for Silver. Gold, despite his love for Silver, was vexed by the interruption.

"Such as?" he asked.

"The atrophy," Silver said bluntly.

"Walk with me, young brother," Gold said in a stately tone.

The pair descended the steps from the royal chamber past the well-armed contingent of Royal Guards, holding long spears (used for much more than ceremony) and sporting razor-sharp short swords at their waists. Gold and Silver continued to the entryway of the palace, where artisans were busy completing a statue of Horus that incorporated the body of Gold while still retaining the traditional head.

The Captain of the Guard saluted and then bowed to the Pharaoh. "I shall take my constitutional, Captain," Gold said without interest.

"Yes, Sire." The captain opened the gate. The pair had barely trod a handful of paces when commoners began lining the path on either side of them. The peasants prostrated themselves on the dusty ground. They were frantic in their approach but took care not to obstruct the monarch's path. The feeble and sick held their hands upward. Gold reached into a massive camel-leather satchel that adorned his waist, and removing a golden coin; he placed it gently into the hand of a man afflicted with smallpox.

Gold said, "Arise, my servant, for you have been freed from the torments that so unjustly afflicted you."

The man, now visibly radiant, rose to his feet, free of sores or any sign of illness. Though he did not look at Gold, the man began to shout. "Praise be to the God-King, his mercy and kindness, his power and knowledge, his greatness astounds and humbles us his faithful devotees."

Gold continued his way, beaming as he dispensed the healing mineral, the effects of which were substantially enhanced by his being near it. A king might surround himself in a room of gold and have years added to his life; a sickly pauper could be raised from a coma should Gold press a coin into his grubby hand.

"So, you see, my brother," Gold said upon returning to the palace, "we need not worry about the atrophy because we will heal the sick as we always have."

"Then, aren't we still just tools of Heaven," Silver asked as the pair returned to the royal chamber.

"Oh!" The voice belonged to Mehytenweskhet. "I did not realize you had brought company..."

"I will be with you in a minute, my beloved," Gold said. He ignored her seductive tone and turned to his brother. "We will not go back to Heaven," he said, "so, we will not be a part of Heaven."

Silver raised an eyebrow.

Gold continued, "Let them fight it out with the Demons over and over and over again. I, for one, have a greater plan. I will build my own worldly kingdom, and I will reign free from the perpetual war, free from any master. And I... uh... we will be Gods among these people."

Silver smiled and nodded. Then his expression dropped. "But what about the time limits of staying in these bodies? I'm already feeling the itch to flesh-hop. It's been a few weeks; you can't have a coup every month."

Gold smiled. "When I was in the desert to the north, I saw a strange man. He was not Angel or Demon or Elemental. I was mesmerized that the legends were true; the survivor of the Titans, the arbitrator of the Divine Dictum, still lives. I followed him as he searched from town to town, always questioning, always looking. I was amazed that he stayed within the same body, apparently his own, as I jumped from host to host. I observed him as he conducted many a strange prayer, and I concluded that one of them must be the mechanism by which his clearly mortal flesh never aged, and his immortal mind stayed young."

Gold paused and appreciated that he had Silver's wide-eyed attention. He continued, "I tried to mimic the incantations I overheard and to retrace the symbols I saw him draw. Then, one day, I felt my thoughts melding with that of the host; I felt a critical need to jump. Still, I held on. I tried my best, while his strange language was still fresh in my mind."

"And?"

"And," Gold looked a little annoyed, "I instantly felt free of the melding as though I had just freshly accessed the host's pituitary. I tried it a few days later to the same effect. I've been doing so with the Pharaoh here, and the result is astounding. I will teach it to you, and we will bring our wives here, and whoever else is honestly drawn to us by the beam of our light."

Silver nodded eagerly, exhausted of all counter-arguments.

"I learned much from tracking the Titan," Gold said. "And I believe that I gained an understanding of the amulet you snatched from the Demon. But that is a matter for another day. We will build our Kingdom, it will be glorious and ever-lasting, and no force from

Heaven or Hell will dare attack us because to do so would weaken them to their ideological enemy."

Gold smiled and grabbed his brother by the shoulder, shaking him soundly. "We were too good for them, too bright. This, my brother, this is the final victory."

"Yes," Silver replied, "and in my life or, need-be-it, my death, I will defend you and our new home."

I<small>T FELT LIKE CENTURIES</small> since Schitz had been within the walls of Babylon. It held a fond place in the depths of his heart – the site where he had first experienced Rubella's love. Those days before the duel with Vertigo and before graduation from the Academy now seemed quite innocent. With the Sequester complete, he had been assigned to a unit where he would no longer enter the mortal world solely for acclimation. No, now he would participate in combat sorties.

The Babylonians, embroiled in a conflict with their Assyrian overlords, were led by Shamash-shum-ukin; Babylon had amassed a considerable following of allies to resist the rule of Ashurbanipal, Shamash-shum-ukin's brother. Schitz stood outside the Assyrian encampment looking at the mighty walls of Babylon. He wondered how many Angels had assembled within its walls awaiting the upcoming battle. Schitz remembered bungling upon the Angels with Rubella when they had been cadets. He felt deep loneliness, wondering where Rubella was and what she was doing. He wondered if she would be part of the assault the following day.

After graduating from the Academy, Schitz and the members of his cohort had been separated and placed into Hell's battle formations. However, since they were still not considered full-fledged warriors, they were not entirely free to move about independently. Schitz and the others were considered trainees. Only upon the completion of ten missions in which their unit recorded a fatality would they be deemed to be initiated. Hell's battle formations consisted of eight squads:

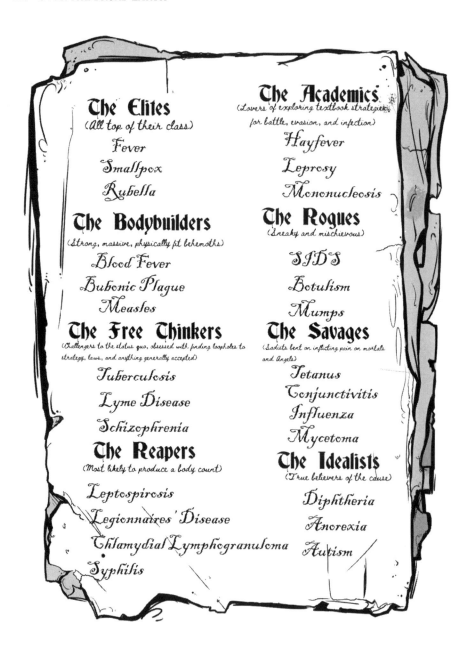

The Elites
(All top of their class)

Fever

Smallpox

Rubella

The Bodybuilders
(Strong, massive, physically fit behemoths)

Blood Fever

Bubonic Plague

Measles

The Free Thinkers
(Challengers to the status quo, obsessed with finding loopholes to strategy, laws, and anything generally accepted)

Tuberculosis

Lyme Disease

Schizophrenia

The Reapers
(Most likely to produce a body count)

Leptospirosis

Legionnaires' Disease

Chlamydial Lymphogranuloma

Syphilis

The Academics
(Lovers of exploring textbook strategies for battle, evasion, and infection)

Hayfever

Leprosy

Mononucleosis

The Rogues
(Sneaky and mischievous)

SIDS

Botulism

Mumps

The Savages
(Sadists bent on inflicting pain on mortals and angels)

Tetanus

Conjunctivitis

Influenza

Mycetoma

The Idealists
(True believers of the cause)

Diphtheria

Anorexia

Autism

Twenty-six fighters, half of them fresh graduates still completing their training, were all that stood between the Devil and defeat. Twenty-six soldiers to cover the broad Earth, from Mesopotamia to the Great Rift Valley, from Europa to the lands across the Western Ocean. The responsibility was humbling.

Schitz looked down at his true form through his mortal clothing. He wore a long gray robe split in the midsection by a broad, brown leather belt and covered by a long cloak that bore a resemblance to the wings of a bat. He wore a scabbard for a Celestial short sword on his left and five Celestial throwing knives on a bandolier. Schitz appreciated the sense of belonging he found in the unit in which he was a trainee. The blades of his weapons were all inscribed with the phrase Cogitationes Posteriores Sunt Saniores: "Second thoughts are even wiser."

The ground shifted behind Schitz, and he turned to see that he was joined by his Demonic colleagues.

"Everything is in place for tomorrow," Tuberculosis said.

Schitz nodded. He tried to look calm; he was anything but tranquil. He worried about the coming day's action; he was worried about Rubella.

"You're nervous," Lyme Disease said. Her voice was soothing. She was Autism's mother. Schitz found it somewhat odd to be working with her while Autism was off with Anorexia, and Schitz's father, Diphtheria.

"I just want to do the right thing tomorrow," Schitz said.

"That's all you have to think about," Tuberculosis said. "Forget about that little mate of yours, forget about your fear of dying, forget about us. Focus on what you need to do. If you do that, you'll have plenty of time to think about everything else afterwards, believe me."

Schitz nodded curtly. His mind was reeling. The more he attempted to suppress his concerns and worries, the stronger they resisted.

"Let's review," Tuberculosis said as he traced the layout of the city walls and the interior structures with a sagacity born of countless incursions within the ancient city. They had been among the Assyrians for several days, but as their numbers were low, unnecessary risks were considered treason. With so few Demons, each life was precious and not to be thrown away in a cavalier fashion. Constant intelligence reports from the Wraiths outlined the position of Angels within a given city.

"They are expecting a fight," Tuberculosis said. "They will position the majority of their troops here at the entrance in anticipation of the Assyrians' attempt to breach the walls." He traced arrows in the sand corresponding to the troop movements that would follow. "We will scale the walls here," he said, marking a position along the wall perpendicular to the main gate.

The plan echoed within Schitz's mind. He'd been over it so often; he could see it happening. They would scale the wall with grappling hooks and enter the city. Then they could either assist the main force or continue to the royal chambers, an area likely to contain Angels tasked with coordinating the defense.

"Committing four squads to the same battle is quite the considerable risk. Avoiding casualties must be of the utmost concern," Tuberculosis said.

"All right," Lyme Disease said, "let us check our gear and hold an audience with the Wraiths."

THE HEAVENLY HALLS WERE abuzz with activity. Angels were rushing to and fro. Familiars were frantic to impart intelligence. Priests were busy performing the return ritual. Portals were opening and closing. Yet to Zinc, it was muted and of little interest.

"I still do not understand why I cannot take part in the battle," he said as he watched recent graduates from his Academy class prepare to enter the Mortal World.

His father, the Standard Bearer of the Zinc House, sighed heavily. "Your time will come, my son, and when it does, there will be no reprieve in sight until hard-earned retirement, victory, or death. Enjoy your youth; do not heedlessly long for the hazard wherein a single unfortunate step may undo all skill and preparation."

"But I am ready," Zinc said with frustration in his voice. He felt doubt creeping into the edges of his mind as he began to question his readiness.

"I thought I was prepared when I was a bright youth as well," his father said, assuming a softer tone. "Then I saw how distressing, cold, and dangerous combat is."

"I just want to know, already," Zinc said, feeling frustration build. "I want to know that I can do what is required of me."

Zinc looked up at his father. Though Angels did not age like humans or even Familiars, somehow despite his youthful appearance, the Standard Bearer's countenance conveyed a rugged, hardened effect of age, an effect matched by his untamed, dark flowing hair and his coarse beard. Zinc met his father's piercing blue eyes, which for the moment seemed to soften in care for his son.

"I have great plans for you, my son," the Standard Bearer said. "You will elevate our House above all others. You will earn us a spot alongside the Lord's right hand."

Zinc felt a creeping sense of elation slowly overtaking the recesses of his soul.

"Therefore, I will not have you wasted with menial tasks such as the current impending battle," his father said.

He rustled his son's hair affectionately, then strode towards the portal doorways. He turned back towards his son. "I will represent us today; tomorrow is yours," he said with a broad grin brimming with paternal pride.

Zinc raised his right hand to his forehead in a crisp salute. As his father disappeared into the crowd of departing Angels, Zinc was shoved from behind. He stumbled but regained his footing. His robes fluttered as he whirled around to find the source of his imbalance. He beheld his former classmates Peter and Samuel, youngsters of the Gold and Silver Houses, snickering and cocky as ever.

"Oh, teacher's pet has to stay home again," the Gold youngster said with a mocking tone of false pity.

"Sir Iron II probably has some pots for him to polish," the young Silver said while making a crude gesture with his hand.

Zinc, steeled by his father's aspirations, dismissed the mockery of his peers. "Well, if it isn't Pyrite and Shiny. Try not to die today," he said. "It would be a pity if you were already cut down before I got the chance to show you up."

"Oh, we're not going to the battle," Peter said as he began walking toward the portals.

"Yeah, we're going somewhere way more important," Samuel said.

Peter hissed under his breath. "Shut up."

"What?" Samuel said, now on the defensive. "He doesn't know anything."

Zinc briefly wondered about the idiots' designs but quickly turned his thoughts to more productive matters. If he could not fight, at least he could train. Zinc resolved to make the most of the time until he was prepared for combat.

THE WALLS OF BABYLON were a towering, steep face of stone. Schitz swore under his breath as the mortal's hands burned against the ropes. The agonized thoughts of his host bombarded his own, as he willed himself up yet another length of rope toward the ramparts. The clatter and commotion of a pitched battle rose in the distance. Schitz felt a rush of frenzied excitement, fear, and confusion. His mind whirled with thoughts of the larger scope of the battle, the war between Hell and Heaven, Rubella, his father, and countless other random images. He pushed them down and out of his consciousness as his elders had instructed him; he focused on the job at hand, and at long last, reached the summit of the great wall. The hand of the host possessed by Tuberculosis extended and assisted in pulling Schitz over the edge of the wall.

Breathing raggedly, Schitz gazed upon the scene. As predicted, the Babylonians and Angels had moved all their forces to the main gate to counter the primary assault. Thus, Schitz and his contingent had infiltrated unbeknownst to the foe. They descended the wall down a set of steep stone stairs where Tuberculosis ordered them to hold. The streets were eerily abandoned. Schitz felt the unnerving sense of being watched as he looked at the rows of quiet stone houses that comprised this quarter of the city. They waited for word on the battle, which was expected via Wraith messenger.

Tuberculosis fumed visibly from within his host as the minutes stretched onwards without the arrival of a Hellish emissary.

"We can't wait forever," Lyme Disease said from within the body of a lithe, female Assyrian archer.

"By the sound of it, the battle appears to be progressing further into the city," Tuberculosis said calmly. "However, that bodes little either way with regards to our compatriots."

Schitz shifted anxiously from side to side as he awaited the elder's determination.

"We will go at once to the Royal Chambers," Tuberculosis said. "We will trust that our comrades have the situation in hand and will not squander our undetected arrival."

Briefly, Schitz thought of Rubella and the others and desperately hoped that his squad leader had not abandoned them to a grisly fate. Once more, he forced the thoughts aside and, with stocking steps, followed his compatriots through a maze of narrow corridors, which would lead them to the palace. The archer led the way, her bow drawn with an arrow nocked, followed closely by her swordsmen companions.

THE ANGELS HAD FIELDED a sizeable contingent in response to reports from the Familiars that indicated Demonic plans for a massed movement of forces on Babylon. The Standard Bearer of the Zinc clan glanced over a map of the city painted on the worn, tanned hide of an old horse. The layout of the city was awash with triangles, squares, and circles corresponding to the various mortal, Heavenly, and Hellish units. Zinc the Elder, looked up from the map and beheld the Royal bed chamber of Shamash-shum-ukin, now converted into the Angelic Headquarters. Zinc mused at the coordination, for there had been a time when the Heavenly notion had simply been to amass all the Angelic hosts and march with numerical superiority to crush any Demon whosoever dared show his face. These tactics had left God's army awash in blood. The Demons were far nimbler and more tactically proficient.

No, he thought, *this coordination is better, for we must not throw lives away with reckless abandon.*

A Familiar appeared. "The trio of the Strong Ones has moved up the right flank." He was gasping for air. The messenger pointed to the edge of the Babylonian formation. Zinc the Elder, looked at the Familiar. She was a handmaiden of his own house, the one who had looked after his eldest surviving son. This Familiar had not yet reached full age and still possessed some physical beauty to her, which was heightened by her quivering lips and all too apparent panic. "They are a leviathan," she said. "They have cut down a score of the forces we sent against them."

"Plague and his retinue," Zinc said. He and the other senior figures arrayed around the map and looked toward Iron II, the most storied among them.

"Shall we leave this planning and take charge of the field?" Lord Carbon III asked. He was clearly anxious for the old ways. Iron II pulled the map from Zinc's hand. A pang of emasculation shot through the Standard Bearer's body as he was forced to defer to his superior.

He had his say in the initial movements, now he offers his criticism when we encounter setbacks, he thought, but he knew better than to overtly mock the Commander.

"No, I feel as though they have not yet shown their full hand," Iron II replied coolly.

Carbon III spoke. "Now we have seen three groups of three. However, our intelligence predicted more. We shall not join the battle until we are fully aware of the situation."

Babylonian Swords

His face heavy with frustration, Copper VII spoke. "It would be useful if Gold and Silver were here."

Iron II looked at Copper VII with a steely glare but uttered no reply. Iron II's sons, Gold and Silver, had been granted charters for their own Houses, and Iron II feared in the depths of his soul that their elevation had corrupted their characters. He kept his doubts to himself. They were not a topic for idle consternation or a convenient excuse for the current situation.

Iron II addressed his men. "Copper VII, Antimony I, Sulfur II, Tin I, Lead III, Carbon III, Oxygen I, and Zinc I, you have all brought to the fray nearly a dozen warriors from each of your Houses." He glanced from Standard Bearer to Standard Bearer. "When accounting for my own allotment, we have fielded a force ten times the expected Demonic force. Yet you plead for Gold and Silver?"

A drab silence fell across the absent King's chamber.

Iron II's voice rang with the force of irritation. "Familiars!"

From the shadows, an assembly of fragile, robed males and females emerged from the corners of the chamber.

"I charge you with this decree," Iron II said through gritted teeth. "Find the remaining Demons your division predicted would be here or confirm beyond a doubt their absence."

In an instant, the Familiars vanished.

"Make ready to join your commanders already in the field," Iron II said. "When word returns, we will clear all Demonic presence from the battle."

A SOLITARY ARROW TORE through the hot afternoon air of the seemingly empty palace garden. It struck a fleeting shadow just below the jaw. Slicing through flesh, veins, and the windpipe, the missile felled the Angelic Familiar.

"Another one," Lyme Disease said in delight as the Familiar crumpled to the ground.

The Familiar and the Wraith were such weak creatures; they could not possess humans and dwelt neither entirely in the realm of the Celestial nor in the mortal world. They were susceptible to both supernatural and worldly weapons. While Angelic and Demonic corpses never rotted and lay where they fell, Familiars and Wraiths almost instantly dissolved into a putrid lump of flesh a mortal would likely mistake for the remains of a cat or dog, or the limb of a human.

"You do have an eye for spotting those pesky things," Tuberculosis said.

Schitz thought of Elise. With his mother gone, she was the closest maternal entity he had left. He silently hoped that she was safe from harm, wherever she might be.

"We can go no farther in these meat sacks," Tuberculosis said, gesturing across the garden to the entrance of the royal chambers, which was protected by a handful of alert guards. He continued. "Even if we kill them silently, it would be a waste of time. To the Celestial." He turned to Lyme Disease. "Cover us, then follow as swiftly as you can,"

Schitz held his breath as they slinked past the guards. In the Celestial, they were invisible to the humans, but an attuned mortal might feel their presence. It was always best not to flirt with the laws of the Divine Dictum and to expose oneself to mortals. While possession, especially possession in wartime, was nearly never detected, walking too close to a non-possessed mortal could give away some notion of a spiritual being.

The halls of the palace were cool compared to the gardens, which were bathed in the afternoon heat. Schitz and Tuberculosis trod with quiet purpose through the palace. With each step, Schitz felt his muscles tense under his black and gray robes. In the Celestial, he felt naked. He was armed with only a few knives, a short sword, and a dagger. He would have felt more protection from a mortal body.

I wish we had Celestial armor, he thought. *All these cursed rules agreed upon when the Devil and God entered this wager.*

They reached an intersection of corridors. Tuberculosis held up his hand, and Schitz held still. He crouched with his back pressed against the wall and felt the tingle of a single bead of sweat meandering down his temple. He held his breath as though exhaling would blow a veritable trumpet of noise throughout the quiet hallway. The pitter-patter of approaching feet within the Celestial announced the arrival of Lyme Disease behind them. Tuberculosis seemed disinterested. He raised his sword slowly, with menacing purpose.

A voice in the Angelic tongue echoed from around the corner. "Do you hear that?"

Schitz was shocked as two petite, Heavenly Familiars, one male and one female, came around the corner. Tuberculosis brought his sword crashing down on their heads. The blade sawed its way through skull and brain alike, spilling a pile of gore onto the mortal and Celestial floor. The victims had been denied even the moment requisite to utter a scream. Each half-decapitated, heads severed at the top jaw. They collapsed onto the ground. Although he knew the business that he and his kind dealt in, Schitz was still shocked to witness such sudden violence. He had killed before–Vertigo and the Angel when he had snuck away from the Academy–but seeing the two unarmed Familiars hewn down in such a manner turned his stomach.

Lyme Disease whispered from behind. "More of them. I thought I'd have gotten them all by now."

"Well, tread quieter from here on out," Tuberculosis said. "I believe our presence has still gone unnoticed."

The trio pressed on in the Celestial, keeping to the shadows, moving through the dancing illuminations cast upon the walls by the numerous burning lamps lining the palace corridors. The flicking lights appeared ever more ominous when commingled with the Hellish intruders.

THE PITCHED BATTLE THAT spelled the fall of mighty Shamash-shum-ukin and his Babylonian rebellion was cataclysmic in scale, both for the mortal and supernatural elements involved. The Demons had pushed forward aggressively and dispersed, as they usually did; however, instead of fleeing back to Hell, the Demons countered a second time with renewed reinforcements. Falling back a second time, they then countered with still more reinforcements. The Angelic ranks had been caught in disarray by each counterattack and were rendered into a whirling, leaderless mess, uncertain of whether to attack, hold their ground, or retreat. As the battle wore on in favor of the attacking Assyrians, it also turned in favor of the Demons. Slowly, with each felled soldier, each bloody step forward, the outcome became more and more evident. The desperate Babylonians rushed forward, trying in vain to stop the foe from pouring into their city, whilst the Angels were killed and scattered each time they attempted to assemble and press their numerical advantage.

THE STONY GROUND ALONG the route to the Ishtar gate had been dusty and brown when dawn had broken. Day had transformed it into a crimson and stained surface covered in fallen soldiers and discarded weapons and armor. Still, the Assyrians pushed forward in an unremitting effort to smash what resolve remained in the Babylonian defenders. The heir to the Iron Household gazed out upon the scene.

"Curse my elder brothers," he said. He thought about Gold and Silver, then spat. "While they have been given their own Houses and lauded with praise, I have been left to assume the House of Iron. But what will I inherit?"

He watched more of his kin fall under Demonic blades. His thoughts mirrored the reeling, exasperated conjectures of the Babylonian commander he possessed.

What will happen to the city and my holdings? the mortal thought.

With a slight mental exertion, Iron the Younger, suppressed the mortal's thoughts. He grabbed a nearby Familiar by the scruff of her robe and lifted her off the ground.

His voice was the growl of a wolf. "Tell me now. Why are we receiving no word from our high commanders?"

"I do not know, Master," the terrified Familiar replied as she wriggled, visibly uncomfortable within his grasp. Her fear heightened as Assyrian archers began firing bolts in the direction of the Babylonian commander and, by extension, his invisible captive. The arrows wisped past Iron and the Familiar like angry wasps.

"When I fall, they will bury me in the halls of my fathers, with honor and fanfare. You..." he spat again, "... you wench... you will rot on the ground like a flea-ridden dog. But maybe you can find some honor before that by finding out what our leaders would have us do. The day is not yet lost. Bring me word!"

With his final instructions issued, Iron flung the Familiar in the direction of the royal chambers. A moment later, an arrow struck his host in the stomach, piercing through his armor and plunging into his innards.

So much for your lands and holding, Iron thought, regarding his human as he looked about for an alternate vessel, *and so much for mine.*

RUBELLA FOUND HERSELF IN awe of Smallpox and Fever as they dealt out death and destruction in an almost elegant dance. They shifted between the Celestial and mortal possession with a free-flowing effortlessness that lacked any sign of exhaustion. An observer would be hard-pressed to tell whether they were more lethal in their own form or when they were cloaked in their fleshy vessels. Rubella, for her part, did her best to keep up. Hayfever, Leprosy, and Mononucleosis had initiated the first wave and had scattered following some initial success. When the Angels had pressed forward in their customary attempt to envelop the Demons, her cohort had sprung forth and eviscerated the foe.

Her first kill had been effortless. Fever had stepped from within the body of an Assyrian and parried an overhead blow from the onrushing Angel, one of three charging toward him within the Celestial. After blocking the strike, he had tripped the foe and quickly dispatched the remaining adversaries. Rubella, trailing Fever, came face-to-face with the fallen Angel. He had dropped his sword looked up at her frantically. He glanced down to his waist for a dagger, then in bewilderment looked for a passing mortal to possess. In the end, he did neither effectively.

As he reached for an onrushing Assyrian, Rubella plunged her short sword into his chest. The young Angel's white robe instantly turned a dark red around her blade. Their eyes met for the briefest of seconds.

Rubella thought, *He could have been handsome if we weren't trying to kill each other*, as she beheld his short black hair and thin, angular features, his light gray eyes. She was pulled from her thoughts as she withdrew the blade from his chest cavity and stabbed him a second time. The enemy slumped over her blade—all life extinguished. Rubella kicked the lump that had seconds before been a living thing and wrenched her sword free once more. She felt exhilarated.

"I got one," she shouted aloud. Still, nausea churned in the pit of her stomach as she considered the ghastly act she had just committed.

Moments later, she found herself separated from her comrades. She felt vulnerable and gripped by terror, naked within the sea of swirling combatants. She looked about for a mortal to possess. As a female Demon, she could only possess female mortals, a supreme inconvenience on the battlefield. At last, she spied a female warrior among the Babylonian ranks and stepped forward to assume the added layer of protection.

She had nearly reached her destination when an overwhelming pain emanated from her left shoulder blade. Rubella collapsed to the ground and felt additional pain as her knees struck the stone. Instinctively, her hand touched her back; it was wet and sticky. She touched a foreign object protruding from the source of her pain, halfway between her armpit and her spine. She pulled the knife from her back by the handle, crying aloud as it cut on the way out as well. She glanced about for her attacker and beheld a handful of Angels rushing toward her, three in the Celestial and two protected by human shields.

Rubella thought of Schitz and her father. She longed to see them again. The realization that she would not made her sadder than she had suspected, more than the fear of death. She readied her sword in her remaining effective arm, an awkward feat as she was naturally left-handed.

As the Angels closed on her, neither the attackers nor Rubella saw the arrival of Bubonic Plague. Within the Celestial, the hulking figure raised his axe, a gigantic curved and razor-sharp blade affixed to a pole the height of most men or Demons. The weapon had required a thorough review to verify that it complied with the Divine Dictum. The Devil himself has been surprised that a Demon could wield such an instrument of war.

Now the blade, forged by the most diabolical of Hell's blacksmiths and fashioned in the shape of a rat, crashed into the three Angels within the Celestial, harvesting the trio in a singular sweep. It severed a head, sliced a torso, opened an abdomen in a single downward arc. Without hesitation, Bubonic stepped into a mortal known by his fellows as Gilgamesh, namesake to the Mesopotamian king of lore.

The Assyrian mortal, suddenly imbued with supernatural strength and determination, readied his sword, and brought it crashing down on the helmet of one of the remaining Angels. The force of the blow was so paranormally strong that it split the mortal vessel's head down to his throat. Bubonic stepped back into the Celestial, leaving his mortal host to be memorialized by the hammer and chisel of history, and planted a heavy foot atop the chest of the writhing, seizing Angel.

Plague spat on the Angel's face before crushing it with the handle of his axe. The monstrous warrior turned to the remaining Angel to find that he had begun flesh-hopping away with the rapidity born of otherworldly fright.

"Pathetic coward," Bubonic Plague shouted over the ceaseless clatter of combat.

"You saved me," Rubella said as she collapsed to the floor under the weight of her injury. "Not yet," he replied with grim determination. Bubonic heaved her over his shoulder and rushed away from the point of contact between the two armies. Each jostling step sent pain through Rubella's back, and white flashes through her field of vision.

"I'm going to die," she moaned as Bubonic Plague came to a halt.

"Hardly. A wound like that is probably closer in pain to childbirth than death, and you'll have to do that in combat as well," he said with a crooked grin.

"You saved me," Rubella repeated.

Bubonic Plague looked down at her quizzically. "Of course I saved you. Why are you surprised?"

"Ver... Ver... Vertigo," Rubella said.

Gilgamesh

Bubonic Plague sighed. "You would have made a good daughter-in-law, but I am a soldier of Hell. I am not going to hold a grudge against you, your father, even the boy's father." He looked towards the western wall of the city. "No, my grudge is with your wimpy, feeble mate, who deprived me of a son and Hell of a fine fighter. My vengeance is for him and him alone. But that is a conversation for another day."

Bubonic Plague reached around Rubella and patted her on the back, firmly striking her wound. She winced and howled in response.

"Look, it's not that bad," he said with a chuckle. "If it were, you would have fainted."

"It hurts like a motherfucker," she replied bitterly.

"Well, it's nothing that a bath in the Styx won't cure," Bubonic said. "I still remember the first blade I pulled out of myself. I still have it back home."

Rubella had not realized that she was still clutching the Angelic throwing knife in her deadened left hand until Bubonic plague took it and placed it in her belt.

"Now you're still in the fight," he said, "and we need you. So, buck the fuck up and do your job."

Rubella nodded sternly and looked back toward the point of contact between the two armies.

"That a girl," Bubonic said and then charged off into the battle.

SCHITZ AND HIS COMPANIONS reached the edge of the royal chamber. They took up positions at the doorframe—Schitz and Lyme Disease on one side and Tuberculosis on the other. They could hear the Angels within.

"We cannot wait any longer for a Familiar to return." The Angel's voice was gruff and menacing.

Schitz peeked into the room and saw a tall Angel with long dark hair and a scruffy beard addressing an Angel of similar appearance with a shock of long gray, braided hair. All the Angels in the room possessed a mortal.

"Agreed," the gray-haired Angel said. "Wherever the Demons are, whatever their numbers, our units surely need us. Curse these useless Familiars."

Tuberculosis held up nine fingers. Schitz and Lyme Disease nodded in unison. Tuberculosis moved his hand in a circle. Schitz and Lyme Disease understood the signal—all nine were possessing humans. Tuberculosis shrugged and visibly suppressed a laugh.

They had arrived secretly only to be rendered impotent by a lack of mortals available for possession. Celestial beings could not attack anyone in the Mortal Realm. The same rule applied in reverse. A Demon or an Angel that was occupying a mortal could only attack an enemy in the Celestial Realm by leaving his or her host. With no humans to occupy, the Demons could only watch the Angels in frustration. Even if the Angels saw them, there would not be a battle unless the Angels decided to abandon their hosts and step into the Celestial for a brawl.

The King, Shamash-shum-ukin, came around the corner of the corridor. The monarch ran at full tilt in search of his advisors and generals. Tuberculosis pointed toward the approaching king and then towards himself, indicating he intended to possess the mortal. Schitz shook his head.

He focused and aimed his malady at the mortal king. Shamash-shum-ukin slowed his run. When he reached the royal chamber, he unleashed a violent, frothing tirade of utter nonsense, incoherent wailing, and unrelated phrases.

With a wild look in his eyes, the king whirled and shouted. "It must burn. You all must burn."

He heaved over a pair of giant oil lamps that stood at the entrance of the royal chamber. Fiery oil poured over the carpets and climbed the tapestries lining the walls. The room was engulfed in billowing smoke and intense heat, an instant conflagration.

Tuberculosis grinned wildly and gestured for the others to follow him. Within the Celestial, the element of fire could not hurt them. They entered the inferno and found the mortal hosts withering and succumbing to smoke and flames. A couple of Angels had managed to step into the Celestial. They saw the Demons and readied for battle.

Tuberculosis and the leader of the Angels began to swing at each other in a fierce succession of strikes and parries. Schitz found himself immediately on the defensive as two other Angels attacked him deftly from either side. He could do little else to avoid their blows except to duck and parry. He made no attempt to strike. In the chaos and commotion, Schitz was vaguely aware of Lyme Disease moving from one foe to another. In a matter of moments, she had dispatched the Angels who had been caught out by their hosts' mortal death throes. They'd been thrown into the shock of uncoupling.

Earth & Fire

The two Angels attacking Schitz saw the horror poured out upon the floor of the royal chamber—they gawked as their comrades were massacred. The two fled past Schitz and out of the room, soon followed by the Angel that had been engaging Tuberculosis.

The trio of Demons pursued their quarry. The fleeing Angels led their tormenters down a palace hallway. Schitz wondered whether they would regroup and reengage in the battle. Farther ahead along the corridor, a portal opened. Schitz noticed a solitary Familiar who had utilized earth and fire to open a Celestial doorway for her beleaguered superiors. The slinking, shadowy creature did not wait until the Angels reached the doorway to jump through herself. A moment later, the three Angels piled through the portal and vanished to safety.

Tuberculosis let out a mighty whooping yell, and slapped Schitz across the back. Lyme Disease shouted in turn and raised Schitz off the ground, spinning him around with strength that surprised him.

"What an amazing idea, young lad," Tuberculosis said as he ruffled the youngster's hair and once more patted him on the back.

"But they got away," Schitz said, slightly confused.

"A minor matter," Tuberculosis replied. He turned to Lyme. "How many did you slay?"

"Six by my count," she replied giddily.

"Six," he echoed. "Six Standard Bearers. That will be crossed swords to your Knight's Pentagram for certain."

Schitz's mind recalled the senior Demons at his mother's funeral—how they were festooned in their medals. Hell offered a series of decorations for valor in battle. The Pentagram Second Class was a circular badge with the symbol of the Devil and a pentagram star. The Pentagram First Class consisted of the same circle-enclosed star attached to a ribbon. The Knight's Pentagram was worn around the neck; the crossed swords mentioned by Tuberculosis was one of the highest possible additions that could be awarded to a holder of the Knight's Pentagram.

Tuberculosis grinned. "We caught them completely unawares and decapitated their leadership. Surely our comrades will have taken the field."

Schitz thought of Rubella and the others as Tuberculosis led them through the palace towards the sounds of combat. For all the day's tension, Schitz had only momentarily been locked in battle with the enemy, yet still, he felt exhausted and longed for the contest to be settled.

Upon reaching a bulwark of the palace, the trio discerned scenes of devastation. The Babylonian army was well in its death throes. The Assyrians were massacring the remaining males, children, and the elderly, whilst eagerly grabbing maidens and matrons. Some even set upon the conquered women of Babylon in the blood-drenched city streets. Fires had broken out across the sacked city.

Schitz turned his gaze back to the palace. The fires started by Shamash-shum-ukin had spread into an all-consuming, relentless blaze.

"Babylon is bathed in fire and put to the sword," Tuberculosis said. "Pity."

The most notable facet to Schitz within the imagery of conquest and annihilation laid bare before him was the lack of Heavenly or Hellish involvement. The scene appeared bereft of either supernatural element.

A Wraith emerged from the combat, approached the trio, and saluted crisply—his open palm parallel to the ground across his body.

"Lord Bubonic Plague sends his regards and reports, 'The day is ours entirely, not a single Demon lost to the foe.'"

The words brought relief to Schitz. Rubella had survived.

Tuberculosis returned the Wraith's salute and replied, "Then away with us, let us make for more pleasant pastures, now that our work here is done."

Lyme Disease completed a portal at the entryway to the palace as flames approached from within, and the ceaseless cacophony of earthly slaughter continued to ring over the dying city.

"THIS WAS AN UNMITIGATED disaster," Iron II said stoically.

He reclined in the leathery chair that accompanied the desk within his dwelling space. Iron II slowly lifted an elegant, golden chalice to his lips with an air of ambivalence and imbibed the Elixir of the Angels. Although the waters of the Enuoe, the Heavenly River through which peaceful souls passed on to reincarnation, caused madness in Angels, distilled variants provided medicinal tonics or, as in the current case, intoxicants.

"There is no sense in dwelling on that which is lost, especially when so many perilous circumstances lay before us," Iron II said before he sipped again from the chalice.

Zinc glanced about in envious awe. He had only ever seen the rooms and corridors assigned to his father's people. The House of Zinc had been founded by his father, a descendant of Copper V, a gifted charter following successful service against the forces of Hell during campaigns in the Indus Valley. Still, as one of the newer houses, the dwellings of Zinc were extremely humble by comparison. Lord Iron II's abode was much larger and more luxurious than anything Zinc could have imagined: ornate wooden armoires, a liquor cabinet, an elaborate series of bookcases, chaise lounges, and small tables. The walls were lined with trophies from countless battles, both Hellish and mortal weaponry, armor, trinkets, and all sorts of preserved animal skins. Zinc's attention settled on the head of a massive bear. He gazed open-mouthed at the enormous, malicious teeth and colossal snout. After further inspection, he realized the lower jaw had been removed to allow the enormous beast to be worn as a headdress. Its body would hang like a cape.

"The battle claimed the lives of scores of Angels. Not one confirmed death among the Demons," Lord Iron II said between swigs. "It has been many a year since my House assumed the honor and responsibility of leading the forces of the Lord Almighty. And now, clad in the vestments of shame and humiliating defeat, I must turn the burden of command over to another." The alcohol was thickening his tongue. Words came with some effort and arrived at the listeners' ears in a mangled state.

Iron II paused and glanced across the room, his gaze moving from one to the next, surveying all assembled: Lord Mercury, Lord Arsenic, Lord Lithium, Lord Nitrogen, Lord Magnesium, and Lord Zinc. Each of the surviving Standard Bearers was present along with his eldest son.

"We are in the middle of a cataclysmic crisis," Iron II said. "We lost six Standard Bearers and innumerable soldiers in a battle that we sought out, a battle we planned for, an operation assessed and choreographed for every possibility and eventuality." Iron II sighed and shook his head before pouring more Elixir into his vessel. "We are so greatly diminished that we can no longer mount any large-scale operations. We are compromised with regards to intelligence gathering due to the loss of seasoned Familiars." Iron II grunted with frustration. "We lost the leaders of more than a third of our houses. If our situation were not bad enough, Gold and Silver have undoubtedly gone rogue with the entirety of their households. They used the preparations for the battle as cover to move out the remainder of their families and Familiars."

An image of Zinc's schoolmates and their passing conversation by the portals flashed across his memory. *They have gone. They have gone to treachery and deceit,* he thought. Zinc's mind was a whirl with questions, for, in all his instruction on the history of Heaven and Hell, he had never heard of an Angel or Demon defecting.

"The law is unbending and perfect, and thus it is to be enforced to the letter," Iron II said. "Therefore, the houses of Sulfur, Lead, Antimony, Copper, Tin, and Oxygen will be unincorporated and committed as vassals to the surviving Houses."

Zinc thought of his fiancée, the youngest Carbon sister. He had been promised her hand in a mostly ceremonial strategy, for though she was from an ancient house, her position within the birth order made her far from prestigious. Her House was old, but the Standard Bearer had resigned himself to the role of chief educator and elder statesman. The merger between a lower daughter from a less active House and the firstborn son of an emerging House was a good combination. However, the dynamic of power was about to change substantially; the Houses of Carbon and Iron were going to inherit a substantial number of the surviving fighters.

"The House of Carbon will take two," Iron II said, gesturing to Lord Carbon III. Heaven's classroom instructor appeared to have aged far beyond the thirty-odd year maturation limit. The battle and its repercussions had drained away all vitality—and youth.

Carbon III patted his eldest son on the shoulder. "It is time for me to reserve myself solely to the classroom and to the company of other retired Standard Bearers, such as my father and Lord Iron I. Thus, I leave this decision in the capable hands of my eldest living son. Gentlemen, I give you Lord Carbon the Fourth."

There was a moment of solemn applause that echoed the despair within the room. Lord Iron II raised his chalice. "Come; all of you join me in a drink."

Iron's eldest son handed out less ornate goblets. The chalice felt heavy in Zinc's hand. He had never imbibed the intoxicating drink. As he peered into its murky depths, he wondered if there could be a less celebratory occasion. The drink tasted like pure fire and made Zinc wince.

"Thank you all," Carbon IV said.

Zinc beheld the newly appointed Standard Bearer. He was tall and lanky with red hair cut short and a neatly cropped beard. He had wild eyes and appeared much less reserved than Carbon III, the school instructor. The younger looked like a hunting hound first unbounded from his restraints and freed for the hunt.

"We will receive fealty from the former houses of Sulfur and Antimony," Carbon IV said. Iron II grinned broadly. Carbon IV had only taken control of one powerful House (Sulfur), leaving the other (Copper) for Iron.

The completeness of the political situation emerged. Carbon IV was married to a daughter of the house of Iron. The bonds between these houses would be further intensified now that they controlled such a large portion of the Heavenly contingent. Iron II rose to his feet, somewhat unevenly, as the Elixir coursed through his system.

"We shall receive fealty from the former Houses of Copper and Tin. The remaining former Houses of Lead and Oxygen will go to whoever can bring Gold and Silver to heel."

Following the pronouncement, Iron II collapsed into his seat in a rather unceremonious fashion. Zinc glanced back down at his own chalice and realized he had yet to attempt a second sip of the potent drink.

"Heaven can barely afford this fracture at such a time," Iron II said in a voice steeped with frustration. "Bring their Houses back, and to our new leaders will go the survivors of the Gold and Silver Houses as well. I will present this to God, and I am sure he will accept."

The assembly concluded. Zinc took another swig from his chalice and grimaced before setting the cup down on the nearest table.

As they left the room and began walking the corridors that led to their own humble abodes, Zinc's father spoke. "See, my son, you longed for combat, and now it is upon you. You will bathe in the blood of your foes and drink the bitter taste of the lethal contest."

"I think I've had enough bitter tastes for one evening," Zinc replied.

The Standard Bearer laughed heartily from deep within his chest. "It is an acquired taste, made easier by trying days."

"So now I am ready?" the son asked.

"Carbon IV and Iron II have divided much of our remaining force between them, although the blood of this colossal fuck up is still wet upon the sand. The only way they can justify it is to pass on power to the next generation. Four defunct houses are barely a squad compared to the number of the fallen who already pledged fealty to Carbon and Iron. Sulfur and Copper alone had subsumed several fallen houses that fell during bygone times."

"I'm ready," Zinc said.

"I believe you are, my boy, I believe you are," Lord Zinc said as he patted his son on the back.

"To the final victory," shouted a chorus of triumphant voices as all manner of goblets, chalices, and glasses were raised aloft. A powerful drink known throughout Hell simply as "Brew" spilled out from the overflowing cups.

"And to our heroic comrades!"

A chorus of hurrahs echoed across those assembled on the banks of the Styx. There had been the presentation of medals for those who had played an integral part in the battle. Tuberculosis, Lyme Disease, and Diphtheria received swords to their Knight's Pentagrams, Measles received a Pentagram First Class, and Rubella had received a wounded in action Pentagram. Additionally, it was announced that a statue would be erected in the Great Hall depicting Bubonic Plague and Lyme Disease's contributions to the battle in the slaying of Angels and Familiars, respectively. Following the formal ceremony, overlooked by the Devil, the happy combatants had filed out to the banks of the Styx for merriment and revelry.

Schitz wandered gleefully among the drunken escapades, overcome jointly by Brew and joy at the outcome of the battle. It seemed undeniable that they had broken the back of Heavenly resistance and that the long dreamt of victory was at last in sight. It was said that Brew was bitter to counter the sweet taste of victory; however, at the moment, Schitz found the harsh taste quite enjoyable.

As Schitz meandered through the crowd of celebrating Demons, his attention was drawn to Rubella. She sat by the edge of the water; her robe was opened, exposing her lithe, muscular back. Schitz watched as a Wraith painstakingly etched an ink pattern under her skin with a stiletto. After a few moments of stabbing in the ink, the Wraith dipped a cup into the waters of the Styx and poured the water over her back to heal any injury committed by the blade. Rubella smiled broadly when she noticed her mate.

Schitz beheld her smooth wet skin and how she held the front of her robe up to cover her breasts. Her hair was pulled forward over her shoulders.

"My back was injured, so I figured this was the best way to cover it," she said with a smile.

"I'm glad you're all right," Schitz replied, fully realizing how devastating it would have been for her to be more severely injured or killed.

He shuddered, then took further inventory of the work being conducted by the Wraith. The servant was nearly finished decorating her skin with an elaborately detailed set of wings that ran from the tops of her shoulders down to the small of her back. A large pentagram occupied the space between the wings.

"That's lovely work," Schitz said, longing to touch her.

The Wraith nodded without taking his attention from the task at hand. "Humans always think us and the Angels have wings," Rubella said, "so why not?"

"It's a great idea," Schitz replied.

The Wraith finished his painstaking task, and Rubella raised her robes back over her body. When the Wraith took his leave, Schitz reached to touch Rubella's arm. She recoiled ever so slightly.

"What's wrong, Bella?" Schitz asked, panic coursing through his body.

"It's nothing," she replied dismissively.

"No, it is something," Schitz said. Frustration and disappointment tore at his soul. "For so long now, you've kept me at the edge of your affection one day, and then at the heart of it the next." He sighed. "I do not understand why this has to continue on forever."

"It hasn't been forever," she said. Her irritation was visible. "Vertigo—"

Schitz cut her off. "Vertigo; did you care so much for Vertigo that you now find me detestable?"

"No," she replied, now flushed red with heightened temper, "but you denied us a worthy fighter for our cause. What if he had been here today?"

"And that would be worth having him as your mate?" Schitz asked. He shook with rage at the thought of Vertigo being inside Rubella.

"Well, how many Angels did you kill out there?"

"I," Schitz paused, "I helped in other ways." He cringed. The words were feeble—he wished he could take them back.

"Sometimes, I think it was all a mistake."

Schitz's mind was awash in competing thoughts: his perceived uselessness in battle, the Angel he had secretly killed, Vertigo, Rubella. He longed with every fiber in his being to hold her, to kiss her, to reassure her, and to be reassured by her. Schitz longed for sobriety and clearness of thought.

Still, when he glanced down at his cup of Brew, he paradoxically took another swig.

"Look, it is not the mountain of emotion we are making it here," Rubella said as the redness in her cheeks slowly began to evaporate.

She gently touched his forearm. "I love you. I am sorry for what I said. I am glad I chose you, but this is hard. Look at them," she said, gesturing toward the merrymakers a few strides away.

No one was paying attention. Schitz was relieved.

"They hate you over the slaying of Vertigo," Rubella said, "and at times, I find it hard to blame them, let alone to shoulder the hatred I may experience by association."

"Association! You mean your betrothal to me?" he replied indignantly. "Do you want to go through with the wedding?"

"I do," she said, but her response was tepid. "I really feel trapped, though. Having already laid together, it would be scandalous to refuse marriage, and with you having slain Vertigo to protect your claim."

"I didn't do it to protect a claim," Schitz said. He felt a constriction in the pit of his

Chalice of Brew

throat and burning within his eyes. "I love you, and I want you for myself."

"Just forget it," she said. "It's just, Bubonic saved my life today and—"

"Plague?" Schitz's voice shook with anger and uncertainty.

He glanced across the sea of celebrating Demons and quickly spotted the hulking, bearded giant. "I hate him," Schitz said.

"The feeling is mutual," she replied curtly.

Schitz sighed. "I need to rest."

"Aren't you going to continue celebrating?" she asked. "Why don't you stay?"

"No, it would appear that the commonly held perception is that I didn't earn it."

With that, he flung his cup to the floor and strode off defiantly toward the junior bed chambers.

"HAVE YOU HEARD THE news?" Elise asked.

"How could I have not?" Schitz was sullen, his response clipped. "All of Hell is abuzz with the talk of the miracle birth."

Elise was matter-of-fact. "Influenza and Legionnaires' Disease will be the preeminent force in Hell now," she said. "Twins are quite common, but triplets, and non-fraternal, two girls and boy."

Schitz nodded. "Encephalitis, Reyes Disease, and Pneumonia; good names."

"The boy, Pneumonia, is quite cute," Elise said, "however, they are the offspring of Bubonic Plague's linage. He will tout his own contribution."

"I heard him claiming that Vertigo would have sired a superior breed of Demons in vast numbers as well," Schitz said.

"You must patch up whatever rift has begun to grow between you and Rubella," Elise said. She placed her hand on Schitz's shoulder. "You must produce exemplary offspring, or you will never be safe; the Devil only cares for those Demons he sees as warriors and producers. You must ensure that if you are not deemed worthy in battle, then you are at least a worthy sire of offspring."

Schitz gritted his teeth in frustration but nodded in agreement with Elise's synopsis. "You're always looking out for me," he said with a half-grin.

Chapter 4

Echad Mi Yodea

"We must be patient," Zinc the Elder said to his son as they sat upon the rocky outcropping overlooking a barren stretch of the Nile. Zinc beheld his father's strong jaw and his cold blue eyes from within the Celestial Realm and felt pride to be alongside the Angel with whom he shared so much in common. Zinc, though not yet matured, resembled his father in many ways, though not in temperament. His father always advised caution and patience. Still, the younger man yearned for the fruition of their purpose. The elder Zinc ran his fingers across the sand.

"The situation is finely poised," he said as he traced a map in the earth. "The forces of Gold and Silver are arrayed here in Egypt proper. The Hyksos hold the North, and the Nubians hold the Kush to the South."

Zinc knew much of the Hyksos, as the Demons were fond of possessing them due to their extreme mobility in utilizing war horses. Until Gold and Silver assumed control of them, Egypt had been the Angels' army of choice in the region, although each side switched when circumstances dictated. Nubia was a mystery to Zinc. As a fringe civilization, it had received less attention from either side of the supernatural struggle.

"Additionally, the captive Israelites comprise another large population within the area," the elder Zinc continued. "We must choose wisely in our approach, for as Silver and Gold have taken Egypt, we, too, must take and hold a population, so that we may have mortal vessels with which to wage the struggle."

Zinc alternated his attention between his father's rudimentary drawing and the world outstretched before him. He felt chills throughout his body at the thought of defeating Gold and Silver and elevating his House.

"We must choose wisely, and then we will no longer be patient, but swift," his father said. "As soon as the Hellish scouts get wind of this defection and the current schism born of it, all of Heaven might fall to the hands of the foe. We must conclude this matter with haste once it begins."

"And what of the other Houses?" Zinc asked.

"There will be no collaboration in this endeavor, my son, for the reward for victory is too great. As you will come to see in time, there are as many casualties to the hordes of the abominable host as there are to political jockeying and incessant scheming."

Schitz cursed aloud as he walked along the gently flowing depths of the Nile. He felt frustrated beyond words. He was still considered

to be an unskilled warrior and a poor cultivator of disease. The rift with Rubella seemed ever-widening.

He looked up at the clear blue sky and the ever-present sun, which radiated on the barren, dusty land. He felt isolated, alone, and miserable. A deep, aching sadness weighed him down. He felt detached from his Wraith Elise, who, despite efforts to compensate for his lost mother, could not relate to his problems. He was isolated from his peers, even Autism and Anorexia, who continually made efforts to lighten his mood. He felt lost with regards to Rubella. They were due to wed, but she was oscillating between loving affection and vapid neglect, usually as the result of the treatment she experienced from the other Demons because of her choice of a mate.

Schitz allowed his sulking, self-pitying mood to be temporarily interrupted as he beheld the small slave encampment that stretched out before him. It consisted of miserably small, deplorable dwellings. The captive Israelites existed in conditions worthy of pity. Schitz saw small groups of women tending to their young children and their abodes. He saw sickly, emaciated men in various stages of decay, gaunt from overwork. Schitz sighed as he walked through the slave encampment within the Celestial.

He glanced from mortal to mortal. Their clothing was ragged, and their bodies worn, yet he perceived a certain admirable mental fortitude. Schitz had forayed into the Mortal Realm as he did on most days, not to engage the Angels in battle but to propagate illness amongst the humans. They were fresh souls for the Styx and thus more power for Hell. The energy from the departed filled the water of the Styx with regenerative properties and enabled Demons to open portals to and from the Mortal Realm.

Schitz reflected on the development of his disease. He felt proud of his affliction of the mind. He was certain he had innovated a new idea. He still remembered the day he had raised his hand during the lecture and suggested afflicting the mortals' minds in lieu of their flesh.

There had been skepticism until Vertigo devised his illness, a paroxysm that led humans to fall to their death. Hayfever had called it the perfect refinement of an "undeveloped idea." Schitz felt his temper flare at the thought of Vertigo. Within his mind's eye, he could still see him winking in response as though he had somehow assisted Schitz. He turned his attention back to the task at hand. Slowly he focused on the mind of a woman tending to a cooking fire. After a few moments, she began to rock repetitively. A shudder passed through her body.

Ima, the woman, started to repeat things under her breath. She kept calling for her mother over and over. Schitz turned to his next victims, a pair of slight boys, mock fencing with a pair of small sticks. Schitz crouched upon his haunches and watched the innocent swordsmanship of the scrawny youngsters. Slowly he infused their minds with the dizzying madness of his design. The sticks began to swing more and more violently until they snapped on impact. The children, with fierce, ravenous eyes and barred teeth, began to claw and bite at one another. A mother rushed to intervene.

Schitz stepped closer to her and began to work upon her mind.

The woman began to howl. "They must bleed, they must bleed!" She raised a fist-sized stone, rough and jagged in texture. She hesitated for a moment before crashing it down on the boys, first one then the other in unremitting savagery. She did not stop even when their twitching, shattered remains gave out the final spasms of life, and their bowels evacuated their minor contents on the dusty sands. And still, Ima continued to wail and rock in place.

"That was chilling." It was a smooth feminine voice a few steps over his shoulder.

Being in the Celestial, Schitz knew the only being who could see him were either of Heavenly or Hellish disposition. He whirled around and drew his short sword. His eyes met a young Egyptian woman. She bore the trappings of noble birth, a white robe of the highest quality, ornate bangles, and a large golden headdress.

Schitz perceived the Angelic aura around the woman and beheld the Angel possessing her. The Angel mirrored the mortal in many ways: shoulder-length black hair, petite features, round eyes, olive complexion. Schitz felt assured enough to face a single Angel in combat. However, he did not expect to encounter an unaccompanied foe. His eyes darted frantically from side to side, seeking the woman's confederates.

"Oh, please relax," she said as though she were an audience to his thoughts. "I am alone, and I have no intention of fighting you."

Schitz gazed in stupefaction as she strode past him with silken steps. Her small feet in her diminutive sandals barely made an imprint on the sands. She reached into an ornate satchel and retrieved a handful of golden coins. Nonchalantly, the young Angel tossed the golden coins to Ima. Like snow melting with the encroachment of spring, the woman's lunacy faded upon contact with the metal.

She prostrated herself before the Egyptian. Next, the elegant noblewoman walked toward the butcher of the children. She placed a golden coin into the slave's quivering hand.

"I release you from this Hellish burden," the Angel said softly.

She drew a golden dagger from her waist and plunged it into the woman's throat. "And I release you from the guilt of deeds you unwittingly committed. Go peacefully."

The noblewoman addressed a crowd of cowering, kneeling slaves. "I will not tolerate violence amongst you lot," she said, "not against each other, not against us your benefactors. If a jackal strolls into your camp, I expect you to show it hospitality and let it on its way. I expect you not even to raise your foot in violence toward a scorpion should you encounter one upon your path. You will be soft and malleable and will thus receive our continued grace."

The Egyptian woman retrieved a fistful of golden coins and tossed them to the cowering subordinates. "Come now," she said under her breath to Schitz, "let us to the gratuitous luxury of conversation."

The two walked along the Nile. With each step, Schitz felt an uneasy yet exhilarating sensation. The back of his throat tingled.

"I am a maiden of the House of Gold," the woman said. "They call me Anna."

"My name is Schizophrenia Incenderos Nervosa," he replied, "but most people call me Schitz."

"Those are weird names," Anna replied with a laugh.

Her laughter filled him like water refreshing a man in the desert. Still, there was a deep sense of foreboding. Though beautiful, the

Angel was his enemy. Schitz thought of what Rubella would say if she saw them standing there laughing by the Nile.

"You say so much without saying anything at all," Anna said. "It is written all across your handsome face."

Schitz blushed.

"Meet me here at this spot again tomorrow," she said. Without waiting for a reply, she walked away.

Schitz stood still as a statue and watched her figure fade into the distance.

"THEIR WEAKNESS IS THE Atrophy," Zinc the Elder said as he addressed the cohorts of his House. Zinc looked toward his father and felt a swell of pride and love for the Angel that had given him life. His father added, "They have taken unto them the captive nation of Israel. Gold and Silver use this population to avoid the atrophy that comes from lack of service. They keep the Israelites in a state of constant degradation from overwork and privation, only to heal them and thus fulfill their biological mandate to aid humanity."

Zinc looked across those assembled, his father's younger brothers and their offspring, his cousins. His aunts had been married off to other houses; his uncles' wives had arrived from other clans. He wondered if his cousins would accept his ascension to the throne of the House when the time came. Under the laws of Heaven, they had no choice, but it was not uncommon for coups to erupt over succession. Zinc did not enjoy the closest relationship with his cousins or uncles. He knew they perceived him as soft and spoiled, ever kept under his father's watchful eye.

Zinc looked at his mother. He sighed and wondered why she seemed so singularly focused on the elevation of the House. For as long as he could remember, every conversation he had with the husky Angel was tied back to the same theme.

"Be top of your class so you may elevate this House."

"Learn from your father so you may elevate this House."

Even in his younger years: "You must be brave and bold so you may elevate this House."

Zinc was the eldest of eight children and often wondered if his parents had agreed to split their family. It seemed that he received the entirety of his father's attention while his siblings received his mother's. Zinc thought of his brothers and sisters standing behind him. They were much younger than he. The next in line had had just entered the senior portion of the Academy. Zinc knew several would-be siblings had not survived the ordeal of birth amongst mortal combat.

Zinc's father kept droning. "We will act today to assume control of a large portion of these mortals and begin steps to lead them from bondage and thus deny this resource to Gold and Silver."

Zinc hoped that when the House was elevated, his father would lead them for many years before safely retiring. Zinc wondered what motivated the older generation: the final victory or the successful conclusion of one's career; so few survived to reach the requisite number of decorations required to leave active service.

"Once we depart, we will not return until the matter is resolved," his father said.

An uproar of whispering swept through the assembled. Zinc the Elder raised his hand for silence. "I know this is not our way. You fear Demons will nip at our flanks even when we are massed. This is a valid concern. However, all intelligence indicates that the Demons have been probing into Asia Minor and the Mediterranean and Arabia following their recent successes. They either appear uninterested in Egypt or see it as too fortified."

After this assessment, the most senior Familiar, a shadowy, short man with wrinkled features and a swift yet hobbled gait, nodded in agreement. Zinc's father concluded, "Make ready yourselves, arm your persons heavily, steel your nerves, and secure your courage to your very hearts, for we hunt our own and we will only return once draped in the vestments of victory."

The crowd cheered. As Zinc raised his voice in the chorus, chills ran down his spine. Regardless of their differences, this was a united House. They were blood and relations. He felt proud; he felt at home. He knew they could trust him, and he could trust them. Zinc was hungry for battle. In his very soul, he felt a deep thirst to bring the separatists to justice.

A SCORPION CLICKED ACROSS the uneven, rocky, sandy stretch along the Nile River. Schitz watched its progress as he waited for yet another rendezvous with Anna. He had met her several times since their initial encounter. They had shared about their respective families and cultures. He found Anna to be highly intelligent, uproariously humorous, and overwhelmingly seductive.

He heard a familiar voice. "I've given a thought to your problem."

Schitz looked up from the scorpion and was met by the dark black eyes of the Egyptian noblewoman and Angel within her.

"My problem?" he asked. "I'm more interested in how you keep yourself within that body without melding minds."

"Oh, so you fancy this body," she replied with a playfully arched eyebrow.

"Just tell me your secret," he said.

"Maybe," she replied, as she drew a golden axe from her waist, "if you can disarm me."

Schitz smirked and drew a short sword from the scabbard of the Egyptian guard he had possessed. "I promise I won't hurt you," he said, brimming with confidence. He was certain he possessed the prowess to beat any Angel in single combat.

"Don't go too easy on me," she said with a grin.

She swung the axe with unbridled fury. Schitz managed to ward off the initial blows. He was caught off guard by the skill with which the lithe woman wielded the axe. When he finally attempted a counter, she deftly ducked, dropped her body to the ground, and swung her extended right leg. She caught him across the ankle, knocking him to the ground.

She leapt to her feet and held the axe to the soldier's throat. Schitz abandoned his host and rolled into the Celestial.

"I wouldn't have sent you into a fit by killing your mortal vessel," she said.

She slipped into the Celestial herself. Schitz stared at her cascading black hair, much longer than he'd surmised. Her white robe opened low enough to expose a small amount of cleavage.

"You... you are gorgeous," he said.

She grinned. "Everyone else in my clan is blonde and of fair complexion. Therefore, my father makes the likely correct assumption that I am the product of a dalliance. I stand out from the others. I am not held in high regard."

"Your hair is beautiful," Schitz said.

He stepped closer to her. His heart pounded in his chest. A thought of Rubella flicked through his mind but was replaced by the memory of her most recent coolness when a Demon had mentioned Vertigo in passing.

"We're all just lonely beings, aren't we? Well, you and I, at least," she said. "Your problem is your arrogance."

Schitz stepped away. "I beg your pardon?"

"You assumed that you would disarm me effortlessly. Why? Because I am an Angel? Because I am a female? That noblewoman over there is strong because I am strong," she said, gesturing to the woman, who stood flirting with the guard Schitz had possessed. "We lend our strength, our skill, all of ourselves to our hosts, just as we draw their language and experiences from them," she said.

Schitz nodded though he was not certain he fully understood.

"Let me guess," she said. "Like us, you have an Academy where you learn fighting skills and strategy, and afterwards you continue to train sporadically."

Schitz nodded.

"You train little beyond what is organized for you. Like my people, most of your kind are content to spend their time gambling, drinking, and procreating."

Schitz nodded again.

"Well, my darling Demon, good looks and wanting to be good won't make you good, and simply doing what your instructors schedule for you will always leave you mediocre. Are there those among your ranks who train on their own?"

Schitz considered the ranks of Hell's fighters. He knew that a few jogged together along the banks of the Styx, and others sometimes practiced exotic fighting methods on their own. Obviously, the followers of Bubonic Plague's Body Builders clan did all they could to grow their brute strength and sheer muscularity.

Schitz nodded, and a sudden feeling of shame crept into his mind.

"What's wrong?" Anna asked.

"I feel lazy," Schitz replied.

"But you see, don't you? There is nothing to stop you from doing all those things and more; nothing stopping you except yourself. Feed your hunger to be great—not just in battle—feed it in preparation and honing."

Schitz could sense a rising tide of purpose.

Anna kept talking. "The Angel I believe to be my actual father, imparted to me an ancient and overlooked doctrine. It is called the Thirteen Steps. If you can truly become a master of all thirteen modalities, you will be undefeated in battle."

"Why did it fall out of practice?" Schitz asked, intrigued.

"The legend is that imparting too much knowledge can lead Angels to feel they no longer need God. They want to break away," she replied. "I don't know where they got that ludicrous idea from."

Schitz laughed as she referenced the current situation of the Gold and Silver Houses. He leaned his face close to Anna's. "Do you wish to teach me?"

She rested her forehead against his and closed her eyes. Schitz's heart raced.

"I will teach you so much," she replied.

In the days that followed, Schitz went through a rebirth. He was baptized into a training regimen.

"One is standing," Anna said.

Schitz mimicked Anna's pose. She stood with one leg extended in front of her, parallel to the ground. He groaned as he followed her in yet another single-leg squat.

"Again!"

"Two, running."

Schitz had run, and run, and run some more along the banks of the Nile and through the expanses of the desert before Anna gave her blessing. His feet protested each step; his lungs burned, but there came an overwhelming sense of achievement when he passed Smallpox and Hayfever as they jogged along the banks of the Styx. He could sense their confusion as he whipped past them.

"Three is wakefulness."

"Do you Angels sleep?" Schitz asked with a laugh.

"Don't be a fool," she replied with a smile, "all supernatural beings must rest to recover from injury or after an extended battle, even if they don't fully sleep."

Schitz shrugged. "I was pretty certain I'd outgrown outright sleeping, and I've never been critically injured."

A sinister expression spread across Anna's beautiful face. "Thus, I present to you the Angel-be-good stick, well, Demon-be-good in your case."

Schitz looked on in horror as Anna pulled a menacing-looking club from behind her back. Without taking her eyes from his, she wrapped it in a thin cloth.

"This should dull the blows, slightly," she said.

Following the savage beating, Schitz lay on the desert sand. The worldly ground felt like the softest of mattresses.

"Please let me sleep," he said.

"No," Anna replied. She laughed and smacked him across her face. "Stay awake, feel the pain of the healing, master it."

"Four is reflexes."

She approached him with her blunted club.

"This time you get to dodge it," she said with a maniacal grin, "otherwise, we repeat lesson three."

Schitz bent his knees and readied himself.

"One more thing," Anna said.

"What's that?"

"Eyes closed."

THE RECENT GRADUATES FROM the Academy were afforded shared rooms within the corridors of Hell until they were married. Anorexia moved the heavy wooden door aside with notable difficulty, as she entered the room. The skinny Demon collapsed onto her own bunk and sighed heavily.

"Is everything all right?" Rubella asked.

"They're just all so demanding," Anorexia replied with exasperation heavy in her voice.

"Oh, the boys?"

"Yes," Anorexia replied. "They are tireless in their pursuit."

"Well, there are more males than females within our ranks right now," Rubella said.

Why are we having this conversation?, she thought.

"Even my own brother, though," Anorexia said. Frustration was evident. "Just today, he was complaining about a lack of women, and he told me that sibling marriage is not prohibited."

Rubella raised an eyebrow. "That is pretty gross."

"Tell me about it."

"Well, is there anybody you fancy?" Rubella asked.

If we must talk about this, I ought to act interested.

A cloud passed across Anorexia's pale face. "No... not really. I mean... I know Mononucleosis has always been obsessed with me. I might just have to give in and marry him."

"How romantic."

"Well," Anorexia said, "we're not all as lucky as you and Schitz."

"I'm sorry, babe," Rubella said. "I didn't mean to sound harsh. I just would hate to see you settle for creepy Mono. Besides, I'm not that lucky."

"How so?"

"Well, all of Hell blames Schitz and me for Vertigo's death," Rubella said.

"I think it's romantic that Schitz killed him for your hand," Anorexia said. She clasped her bony hands to her chest. "So very romantic."

Rubella felt a pang of defensiveness. "Would you have preferred he killed him for you?" Her voice was flat and hard.

"No, no," Anorexia said. Somehow, she grew paler. "That's not what I meant."

Rubella sighed. "It's just so tough being hated."

Anorexia patted Rubella on the head. "I can't imagine, but if it helps, I don't hate you at all."

"Thank you, love," Rubella said.

"Hey, us girls have to stick together, with all these sex-crazed Demons around here," Anorexia said.

Rubella's thoughts drifted to Schitz. "Can I tell you something?" she asked.

Anorexia nodded.

"I have been utterly terrible to Schitz. I have taken out my disappointment with Hell's response to the Vertigo fiasco on him, and I feel terrible about it. I have driven a wedge between us, and I have no idea what recourse I have to fix it." Rubella fought back tears. "I have loved him for so long. I don't know why I always give him such a hard time."

Anorexia embraced her with sisterly affection. "None of it is easy; they teach us how to fight, not how to love."

"You know," Rubella said, "even when I teased him when we were younger, I only did it because I wanted his attention so badly."

Rubella did not doubt that her roommate was in love with her fiancée, but she decided not to speak of it.

Anorexia's voice carried a lot of unspoken pain. "I think he will be very happy if you quit blaming him; if you are kind to him—if you show him some of your feminine grace."

Rubella's mind swirled. She had always thought of Schitz as belonging to her, even when they were children. The realization that another female could love him was overwhelming.

"I will," she said.

ANNA'S DEMANDING VOICE NEVER stopped. "Five is defense." She pounced like a crazed animal and swung her axe in an unrelenting attack. Schitz blocked every swing with his sword.

"Very good," she said. "You've been practicing."

"I have to," Schitz said. "I don't want you to kill me." He cocked his head. "I have a question."

"Okay."

"How do you continue to find Egyptian women who all look alike."

Anna's smile was wicked. "Do you fancy the mortal host or me?" she asked. "There's no secret. I step out of the mortal, and then back in."

Egyptian Khopesh

"You are astounding," Schitz said, "utterly astounding. You break all the rules."

This time there was no smile. "Six is attack."

Schitz swung his sword at the Egyptian noblewoman from within the body of a soldier. She grinned broadly with each attack, encouraging him.

"Yes, good, attack… again."

Schitz was not about to tell her that he was exhausted.

"Seven is disengagement."

"Do you ever take a break?" he asked.

"Are there nap times during a battle?" She waited. He had no answer. "I didn't think so," she said. "All of us will encounter a time when we must break off from combat."

Schitz swung his sword at Anna. Instead of blocking his assault, she stepped to the side, tripped him, and broke into a run.

"Eight is balance within," she said after they had jogged for a while.

They sat beside the banks of the Nile, legs crossed, eyes closed.

"Feel the breeze upon your face," she said. "Feel the ground beneath you. You must be aware of all that is around you."

"How much longer?" Schitz asked.

"Until you learn everything." She stood. "Nine is control of distance."

Schitz watched as she drew an Egyptian bow. He drew his own.

"Kill the scorpion," she said.

"Where?" Schitz asked.

"The far side of the river," she replied.

Schitz squinted. "Is that a scorpion or a shadow? You must have supernatural eyesight."

"Shoot the scorpion."

It was not a request.

Schitz loosed the arrow and watched as it landed a few feet away from the creature. Anna released her bolt and hit the target dead center.

"How did you do that?" Schitz asked.

"Practice," Anna said. "You must control the distance between you and all things."

Anna punctuated her sentence by nocking another arrow and firing it into the scorpion again.

"Well, that doesn't count," Schitz said. "It was a stationary target."

Anna laughed and rubbed Schitz across the back. For the next few days, Schitz was a Demon possessed. He threw knives at targets along the banks of the Styx, and he shot a bow at every imaginable target along the Nile.

Schitz's Notebook *Egyptian Archer*

I can remember this possession so clearly. I recall the weight of the bow and the strength of the mortal, as I tried to hit an impossible target upon the far side of the Nile. How fondly I recall those days with Anna.

Anna shouted from the back of a galloping horse as they rode side by side.

"Ten is control of animals."

When the ride was done, they sat in the Celestial and watched the river. Anna drew an Angelic dagger and sliced Schitz's forearm. When he yelped, she shook her head.

"Eleven is control of pain," she said. "Own it, make it yours; master it."

Schitz gritted his teeth until the pain subsided. Anna handed him the weapon.

"Now, do it to me," she said.

Schitz winced as he drove the blade home. Anna closed her eyes and hummed as the blade cut through her soft, smooth skin. Schitz

ECHAD MI YODEA • 153

watched as her face reflected a near-sexual satisfaction.

When he returned to Hell, Schitz dipped his arm in the Styx for healing and then contemplated the lesson. He drew his dagger and repeated the process until he had mastered the lesson.

The lessons recommenced in the morning.

"Twelve is humility."

Her hand brushed his; Schitz's pulse spiked. Anna looked at him with steely intensity.

"You must never underestimate any entity, friend or foe. You must see all as the potential bringer of your destruction. You must kill all hubris. Meditate on the meaning of this."

They continued their walk within the Celestial until they had reached a small cluster of trees.

"This has been quite the education," Schitz said. "I'm excited to complete the training."

"You have no idea," Anna replied.

Schitz did not want the lessons to end. "Wh... what is the final teaching?" he asked with some hesitation.

This time her voice caressed his ear. "Thirteen," she said, "thirteen is surrender." She pushed Schitz against a tree. "You must surrender to the inevitability of whatever is going to be."

She put her hands on his shoulders and forced him to the ground. She never took her eyes from his as she straddled him and raised her robe. He saw her long muscular legs and her smooth, delicate, feminine sex. Anna slid herself forward and pressed her womanhood against his mouth.

She groaned. "Give in."

Schitz lapped at her body like a thirsty man who'd found a running spring. Anna's moans grew louder. Then, without warning, she pulled herself away, crouched over him, and opened his robe. She sat and pushed him inside her. He was astounded by her ferocity. Anna gyrated her hips and dug her nails into his back.

"Take me," she said. "Take all of me."

Schitz rolled over and pinned her into the earth.

"Yes!" She was shouting now.

He felt an animalistic impulse rising within him. The pain of her nails in his back and her teeth on his chest drove him into a frenzy. He placed his forearm across her throat and drove himself inside her.

"Take me," she said, croaking through her constricted windpipe. "Break me. Don't stop. Ruin me for any other man."

Her eyes rolled back into her head. Her frame shook violently with spasmodic convulsions. Schitz, overwhelmed with an animalistic passion he did not understand and could not control, lost himself in spasms of pleasure.

When they were both spent, they lay at the base of a palm, intertwined. And for a while at least, the rest of the world did not matter.

"WHERE IS SCHITZ?"

Frustration reverberated in Tuberculosis's voice.

"I'm here," Schitz said, turning the corner. He was in a hurry; he knew he was late.

He did not know Tuberculosis had posed his question to Rubella.

A pang of guilt shot through Schitz when he saw his mate.

"I've been training," Schitz said in a voice he knew sounded too casual. He forced a smile. When Rubella turned, he saw a deep sadness in her eyes.

"You have been doing an inordinate amount of that recently," Tuberculosis said. "Remember, this is a grueling campaign, not a sprint. You must not burn yourself out."

Lyme Disease jumped into the discussion. "Besides, you need to allot time for starting a family and building our ranks."

She patted Rubella on the back.

This conversation needs to end, Schitz thought.

He nodded acceptance and hoped it would be a sufficient response.

"Well, thank you, Rubella," Tuberculosis said with a huff. "You may return to your own squad."

She saluted before turning to Schitz. She kissed him upon the lips briefly but with abundant affection.

"I love you," Schitz said.

"And I, you," she replied. She leaned in and whispered, "Whatever stresses we have been going through have been by my cause. I promise you things will be better. I love you so much, and I am so sorry. I don't care what anybody else says. I am happily yours."

Schitz's gut twisted, but he recovered sufficiently to kiss her on the forehead and reply, "Thank you, everything will be fine, just stay safe."

Rubella went to join her squad, and Tuberculosis began to talk.

"We have confirmation of a rupture among the Heavenly contingent," he said.

Schitz tried his best to feign shock upon receipt of the intelligence of which he was already aware.

"The Angels have taken up positions within the Hyksos, the Egyptians, and the Israelites. We will be traveling to Kush, where we will attack from the South once their civil war has commenced."

Competing emotions set Schitz's stomach at war with itself. He was concerned for Rubella and fearful for Anna's safety. He was also worried about how he would fare in combat.

The briefing continued. "Wraiths report a multitude of apocalyptical events in Egypt, the likes of which we do not fully understand. They must be related to the Angelic civil war; regardless, we must be prepared for anything. This is definitely our greatest ever opportunity to crush them beyond recovery," Tuberculosis said. "Now, let us away."

ISSACHAR WAS A STRONG, tall Hebrew; he had not buckled under the yoke of bondage but had built up immense fortitude. He scanned the desolate streets of the area surrounding the palace with a keen eye. The Egyptians were hidden away within their homes, within their palaces, within their massive tombs, anywhere save out of doors. Zinc admired Issachar's strength and skill in battle; he had been a good selection.

Zinc searched his thoughts, ever aware of the draining sands of the hourglass that would force his departure. He feared that his mind would meld too much with the host. He turned and silently motioned to his companions to move forward. He was shocked when both held their places, staring at him defiantly. Rachael and Benjamin had possessed cousins of Issachar's, just as they were cousins to Zinc. Once again, Zinc felt his concerns regarding the willingness of the House to follow his commands rise within him.

"Your father has gone too far," Rachael said in a hiss, "this is insanity."

"Aye, is this now the time that rank insubordination rears its ugly head, so as to undo our progress?" Zinc asked.

Benjamin tried to counter with a conciliatory tone. "Cousin, surely you see that frogs and locusts are one thing. But wholesale genocide is quite another. We cannot murder children and expect to stay within the good graces of the Lord. We are acting like Demons."

"God has abandoned this place," Zinc said with a seething wrath in his voice. "The Lord wishes only for a swift end to this matter. So, let it be us who bring about its conclusion, and thus reap the reward."

Satisfied he had squashed the mutiny, Zinc gestured toward the nearest doorway. "There, no mark of blood upon the door. Thus, there shall be blood spilt within."

"I will not be party to the killing of children," Rachael said indignantly.

"Cousin," Zinc said, "if I have to start this slaughter with you, I shall, for we will commit this deed tonight. Can you not see it? We have strangled the defectors with this Hebrew insurrection; they cannot leave their fortress to heal the sick and will soon succumb to the atrophy, whereas we heal the Israelites from our maladies and grow stronger. The shudder we send through this empire tonight will collapse Gold and Silver with all certainty."

"You speak so calmly of dealing out death," Benjamin said. "Have you ever actually taken a life?"

"Cousins," Zinc said as he raised his hand to his face in frustration,

"I am my father's successor. I bear the weight of leading this House someday. I will reward loyalty with favor and punish dissension with great malice. Do not force my hand over the lives of these inconsequential objects. When they die, they will be reincarnated."

"But they will pass through the Styx, giving power to Hell and branding you a traitor!" Rachael lunged at Zinc. Benjamin grabbed her.

"How dare you," Zinc said. He had raised his dagger without thinking.

"Look," Benjamin said, "we will get nowhere with this incessant debate. We will cover you, and you shall commit the killing."

Benjamin looked at Rachel, who shrugged. Zinc nodded. "A most agreeable solution. Thank you, Cousin."

Zinc slunk into the Egyptian dwelling place. He worried that his cousins were right; would he be able to take life so callously? His shoes muffled with rags, he slipped across the dirt floor without a sound. The family was of modest means and slept together, curled in a bundle in peaceful rest. The couple was young; a single child lay between them.

With paternal-like care, Zinc lifted the child from the sleeping couple. A part of his mind yearned for the child to be a girl. He sighed as he undid the swaddling clothes: a boy. He drew his dagger and readied himself.

He heard Rachel's whisper. "Wait."

Zinc knew he could not hesitate. He plunged the knife into the child's soft belly, then ripped sideways through the midsection, eviscerating the hapless infant. Zinc watched as a flood of gore showered down on the sleeping couple. The Egyptians woke and began to scream.

Zinc dropped the lifeless husk onto the couple.

"By this, you will know that I am the Lord," he shouted. Then he raced past his confederates and out of the house.

When Rachel joined him, he grabbed the collar of her robe and slammed her against the wall. "I will do as my father commands, and I will do whatever it takes to achieve victory. Never, ever, stand in my way," he said with his face less than an inch from hers.

Rachel's ashen face nodded. He turned to Benjamin, who bowed his head and said, "All fealty to the Standard Bearer and his Heir Apparent."

Thus began a night of uninhibited mayhem and slaughter. Before the sun rose in the eastern sky, the trio had indulged in a banquet of blood—a slaughter destined to change the face of history. They returned to the Hebrew settlement saturated in crimson and covered in gore.

Rachel and Benjamin never took their eyes from the dirt. But Zinc strode into the camp with his head erect, triumphant in the knowledge he had established his place as the next leader of his House.

THE KINGDOM OF NUBIA fascinated Schitz. The inhabitants were darker than Egyptians and held differing language and customs. Schitz spent time familiarizing himself with the army and its weapons, axes, spears, and bows like the Egyptian arsenal. He felt ready to test his newly cultivated skills. His thoughts invariably drifted back to Anna. Schitz sighed and gazed across the desert toward the North.

"Where are you, my beloved?"

Schitz had no idea how he wished to proceed with regards to Anna and Rubella. However, he knew that Anna was sorely out of reach, a reality that brought a deep sadness to his heart. He turned his attention to the detachment of Nubian infantry armed with curved short swords and thin, iron-tipped spears. The warriors wore a skirt-like lower garment made of leather or leopard skin depending on rank and a strap that crossed the chest. They were rugged and physically fit troops.

Suddenly, from within the cluster of soldiers, a cloaked apparition emerged and grabbed Schitz forcibly by the hand. Having been in the Celestial, Schitz was alarmed to feel the contact on his body. He looked down to perceive Elise.

Of course, he thought. *A Wraith can touch both the Celestial and the Mortal Realm simultaneously, as they exist somewhere between the two, a small benefit in comparison to their vulnerabilities.*

Elise pulled Schitz away from the assembled infantry to the edge of a cattle pasture. Schitz gazed at the boney cattle, emaciated in the unrelenting sun.

"What are you doing?" she asked. Her quiet voice did not mask her fury.

"What is it, Mama?" Schitz replied. But he knew; oh, how he knew.

"My dagger is still wet with the blood of two Wraiths that witnessed you copulating with that Angel," she said.

Schitz inhaled a ragged breath as the seriousness of the situation fell upon his shoulders. He looked at Elise and then sat down.

"I love her," he said. His voice was more whimper than a whisper. "She has been good for me."

"All your new training?" she asked.

Schitz nodded, fighting back tears.

"That has been noticed by many. You overwork yourself, like a man possessed, rather unlike a Demon."

"I feel better, though," Schitz said.

"Maybe you are," she said, "but you know how dangerous this affair is for the both of you. And what of Rubella?"

Schitz shuddered. "I love Rubella so much, but things have been difficult. She flies into a rage at any thought or mention of Vertigo."

Elise nodded. "This is a difficult situation and one that will take time to heal, but your love is strong enough to overcome this indiscretion, no matter how passionate it was."

"I feel lost, Mama," Schitz said.

Elise embraced her charge. "You have grown so much and so fast since I lifted you from your mother's arms and carried you from the field. I promise you, as long as I have strength in my body, I am here for you."

Elise turned her attention to the Nubian troops. "Put everything into today's work; all of your new training, all of your Academy training, all of your feelings. Use them to drive your effort. There will be time afterwards to sort out everything else."

Schitz rose to his feet and embraced his Wraith. "Thank you," he said softly.

"You don't have to thank me," she replied. "Just do well."

Schitz nodded and walked back towards the troops. He stepped into one of the commanders and shouted to those assembled, "It is time; let us to the battle; Egypt is ours."

A cheer echoed from the ranks of those assembled as they marched toward the contingents that were being corralled by Tuberculosis and Lyme Disease.

REBEKAH EXITED HER HUMBLE dwelling as the sun broke over the horizon to the east, bathing the slave camp in orange rays of searing light. The young Israelite shouldered her heavy reed basket laden with the household's clothes and rags. She struggled her way down to the river. Rebekah preferred to leave early before the morning heat was too intense. The bank was deserted, and she took a moment to appreciate the gently flowing river.

Rebekah had never informed another soul of her condition— it terrified her. She had no idea why she had memories of past lives every bit as fresh as things she'd experienced yesterday. She did not understand how she should interpret the images she saw of events yet to transpire, but they were as clear to her as the morning sky.

She soaked the soiled garments in the river and hummed a tune of her own creation. She had crafted it while watching a beautiful Egyptian noblewoman train in combat with a companion. The song was a way to interweave her past memories and future visions.

She started softly. In her mind, she could hear the steady beat of animal-skin drums and the sounds of accompanying voices. "Echad mi yodea? Echad ani yodea. Echad Eloheinu, Eloheinu, Eloheinu, Eloheinu, Eloheinu Shebashamayim uva'aretz."[2]

---

[2] Who knows one? I know one. One is our God, in heaven and on earth.

Gold addressed his army. "Today, we fight them," he said to the assembled inside the barricaded palace.

"The Israelites or the Hyksos," Silver asked. His lips were pursed in thinly veiled frustration.

Israelite Khopesh

"All of them," Gold said. "Today, we will show them that we are gods in our own right."

Gold grabbed his reluctant brother by the hand and raised it above his head. He shouted across the room. "Assemble our forces!"

The members of both Houses raised their voices in a cheer of hope and defiance. "Hail Gold and Silver.

Shnayim mi yodea? Shnayim ani yodea. Shnei luchot habrit,
Echad Eloheinu, Eloheinu, Eloheinu, Eloheinu,
Eloheinu Shebashamayim uva'aretz.[3]

Lord Zinc looked at his brothers. "Rally our forces and assemble them on the banks of the Red Sea; send word to Gold and Silver we will meet their forces there," he said.

A spark of intense sensation jetted through young Zinc's body when he heard his father's command.

One of Zinc's uncles rushed to the Head of the House. "Reports indicate that Iron II and Carbon IV are on the move with a massed force of Hyksos to the North, my Lord; they have the rest of Heaven in tow with them undoubtedly."

"It is of no consequence," the Standard Bearer said. "If we are to claim authority for our House, we must be able to stand on our own and outmaneuver the older Houses. Make ready all preparations."

---

[3] Who knows two? I know two. Two are the tablets of the covenant. One is our God, in heaven and on earth.

Shlosha mi yodea? Shlosha ani yodea. Shlosha avot, Shnei luchot habrit.
Echad Eloheinu, Eloheinu, Eloheinu, Eloheinu,
Eloheinu, Shebashamayim uva'aretz. [4]

The Nubian infantry moved swiftly across the barren, rocky earth. Dust clouds churned up by chariots and marchers clogged the air like a scirocco. Schitz coughed as the mouth of his mortal tasted grit, but he moved forward at an exhausting pace. Ahead were the chariots with Lyme Disease and the cavalry commander possessed by Tuberculosis. The assembled force was an impressive array of bronze and animal skins. The soldiers bristled with spears and quivers that clattered as the force advanced. In his mind's eye, Schitz envisioned the other prongs of the Nubian attack led by other squads of Hell.

Arbah mi yodea? Arbah ani yodea. Arbah imahot, Shlosha avot,
Shnei luchot habrit. Echad Eloheinu, Eloheinu, Eloheinu,
Eloheinu, Eloheinu, Shebashamayim uva'aretz.[5]

The Israelites stood with their backs to the Red Sea, shoulder to shoulder in organized ranks; a slave army, but an army nevertheless. They lacked armor or chariots, they were clad only in humble robes, and they were armed solely with rustic swords and a handful of bows, but Zinc was confident that the anger bred from oppression and hardened with labor would prevail. He stood to the left of his father, who had assumed the body of the leader Moses.

To the Standard Bearer's right stood his oldest sibling. Arrayed behind them, the Household of Zinc was posed to claim its place at the seat of power. A pillar of dust announced the arrival of the Egyptian forces.

---

[4] Who knows three? I know three. Three are the Forefathers. Two are the tablets of the covenant. One is our God, in heaven and on earth.

[5] Who knows four? I know four. Four are our Matriarchs. Three are the Forefathers. Two are the tablets of the covenant. One is our God, in heaven and on earth.

Chamisha mi yodea? Chamisha ani yodea. Chamisha chumshei Torah,
Arbah imahot, Shlosha avot, Shnei luchot habrit.
Echad Eloheinu, Eloheinu, Eloheinu,
Eloheinu, Eloheinu, Shebashamayim uva'aretz.[6]

Gold held his hand above his head, then lowered it in a chopping motion. "Attack!"

His chariot barreled forward over the broken terrain.

Gold shouted encouragement to his forces. "Spare no one. We will wipe these usurpers from the face of Heaven and Earth."

Not far away, Silver echoed the sentiments. "For our Victory!" He led a contingent of cavalry toward the assembled Hebrews.

Silver could feel the anger coursing through the mind of the mortal he possessed. The man had awakened to find his son brutally slaughtered; he yearned to drink the blood of the Israelite young who were cowering behind the fighting force. Silver smiled with maniacal glee as his horse plowed onward.

Shisha mi yodea? Shisha ani yodea. Shisha sidrei mishnah,
Chamisha chumshei Torah, Arbah imahot,
Shlosha avot, Shnei luchot habrit.
Echad Eloheinu, Eloheinu, Eloheinu, Eloheinu,
Eloheinu, Shebashamayim uva'aretz.[7]

Moments before the leading elements of the Egyptian charge reached the Hebrews' front line, Zinc (within Moses) and his confederates reached into the dusty earth and removed stakes as long as palm tree trunks. They'd been hardened in cooking fires and filed to menacing points.

---

[6] Who knows five? I know five. Five are the books of the Torah. Four are our Matriarchs. Three are the Forefathers. Two are the tablets of the covenant. One is our God, in heaven and on earth.

[7] Who knows six? I know Six. Six are the books of the Mishnah. Five are the books of the Torah. Four are our Matriarchs. Three are the Forefathers. Two are the tablets of the covenant. One is our God, in heaven and on earth.

"Steady," the Standard Bearer said.

Charging horses impaled themselves on the stakes. Riders flew through the air and were set upon with savage glee as soon as they hit the ground. Chariots buckled and overturned. The Hebrews pushed forward into the enemy in a storm of hacking and stabbing. The sand greeted the resulting blood with an eager thirst.

> *Shivah mi yodea? Shivah ani yodea Shivah y'mei shabta,*
> *Shisha sidrei mishnah,*
> *Chamisha chumshei Torah, Arbah imahot,*
> *Shlosha avot, Shnei luchot habrit.*
> *Echad Eloheinu, Eloheinu, Eloheinu, Eloheinu,*
> *Eloheinu, Shebashamayim uva'aretz.*[8]

A panicked Gold observed the chaotic fray from within the Celestial. The melee was a maelstrom of confusion. He was unaccustomed to fighting at even odds; the Demons usually hit and ran, while these Angels stood their ground, inviting pitched battles. Gold and his forces were unable to envelop the foe; each separate encounter occurred at even odds. Gold's troops began to tire from the atrophy. He had been forced into the battle to prevent his army withering since his foes had cut off his supply of mortals to heal and through which to gain energy. Gold swore as he watched another of his forces felled by the Hebrews. The helpless Angel (trapped in the throes of a departure seizure) was quickly dispatched within the Celestial by one of Zinc's Angels.

Gold's attention was drawn to his bastard daughter, Anna; she moved so fluidly and clearly, unfazed by her circumstances. He watched in amazement as she slipped between the Celestial and Mortal Realms, hacking off limbs, cutting throats, blocking and dodging attacks. She defended against two possessed Hebrews from within an Egyptian, stepped in the Celestial, killed a stricken

---

[8] Who knows Seven? I know Seven. Seven are the days of the week until Shabbat. Six are the books of the Mishnah. Five are the books of the Torah. Four are the Matriarchs. Three are the Forefathers. Two are the tablets of the covenant. One is our God, in heaven and on earth

Angel, stepped into a different mortal female, lifted a fallen spear to her hand with her foot, and ran both Hebrews through. This Angel of death then returned to the Celestial and threw a knife with each hand. She struck the wriggling Angels (who'd transitioned back into the Celestial) in their throats.

Gold fought his way through friend and foe and slapped her upon the shoulder.

"We must turn one of their flanks and make a break for the sea. I can open the waters," he said.

She nodded curtly and said, "Their right. More are coming from the left."

"Pass the word to all you can; we must flee."

*Shmonah mi yodea? Shmonah ani yodea Shmonah y'mei milah
Shivah y'mei shabta,
Shisha sidrei mishnah, Chamisha chumshei Torah, Arbah imahot,
Shlosha avot, Shnei luchot habrit.
Echad Eloheinu, Eloheinu, Eloheinu, Eloheinu,
Eloheinu, Shebashamayim uva'aretz.*[9]

"There, yonder," shouted Zinc the Elder, "Iron II and Carbon IV. We will not let them take this field."

Zinc drove his sword through a mortal Egyptian's throat while looking for enemy Angels.

"Brother," he shouted over the clatter of weapons and screams of dying men, "you must maneuver to the right to put ourselves between our late-arriving comrades and the foe. My son will cover the gap left by your exit."

Zinc felt a rush of energy. He was eager to fulfill his father's important command. The Hebrews maneuvered between the onrushing Hyksos and the Egyptians, a suicide mission for their

---

[9] Who knows Eight? Eight are the days until the brit milah. Seven are the days of the week until Shabbat. Six are the books of the Mishnah. Five are the books of the Torah. Four are the Matriarchs. Three are the Forefathers. Two are the tablets of the covenant. One is our God, in heaven and on earth.

mortals. Zinc rushed into the gap left by the departing forces. He was the sole Angel in the area and soon found himself faced by Egyptians possessed by familiar faces, his old classmates, Peter and Samuel, and another of their kind he did not recognize. Zinc was surprised by the look of fear in their eyes.

Zinc blocked two quick attacks head-on before ducking under a third. He dragged his blade across the midsection of the foe he did not recognize. He watched as the blonde maiden fell to the sand seizing violently. He nearly decapitated her with his dagger after he stepped into the Celestial. From there, he turned on his old classmates, who arrived too late to assist their accomplice.

"Now, I put an end to your undeserved sense of superiority," he said.

Three strokes later, Zinc ran Samuel through. Peter fled into a mortal Hebrew. Zinc stepped into an Egyptian and fired an arrow into the target's throat.

He returned to the Celestial and found Peter seizing after he was ejected from the dying Hebrew.

"You always were fool's gold," Zinc said.

He sliced his classmate's throat. Zinc's chest rose and fell in ragged, heaving breaths. He had held the line.

Tishah mi yodea? Tishah ani yodea Tishah yarchei leidah
Shmonah y'mei milah
Shivah y'mei shabta, Shisha sidrei mishnah,
Chamisha chumshei Torah,
Arbah imahot, Shlosha avot, Shnei luchot habrit. Echad Eloheinu,
Eloheinu, Eloheinu, Eloheinu, Eloheinu, Shebashamayim uva'aretz.[10]

Schitz watched the swirling carnage in amazement. Tuberculosis spoke solemnly from the chariot. "For the time being, we will let

---

[10] Who knows Nine? I know Nine. Nine are the months until birth. Eight are the days until the brit milah. Seven are the days of the week until Shabbat. Six are the books of the Mishnah. Five are the books of the Torah. Four are the Matriarchs. Three are the Forefathers. Two are the tablets of the covenant. One is our God, in heaven and on earth.

them do our work for us. However, be ready to charge upon my signal."

He inscribed a message upon a sheet of papyrus in Nubian characters. The mortal orders carried a secret, encoded message.

"Boy, carry these orders to the other commanders," he said to a young messenger.

Asarah mi yodea? Asarah ani yodea Asarah dibrayah,
Tishah yarchei leidah Shmonah y'mei milah Shivah y'mei shabta,
Shisha sidrei mishnah, Chamisha chumshei Torah, Arbah imahot,
Shlosha avot, Shnei luchot habrit. Echad Eloheinu, Eloheinu,
Eloheinu,
Eloheinu, Eloheinu, Shebashamayim uva'aretz.[11]

The Hyksos arrived and crushed the mortal Hebrews between themselves and the Egyptians with swift ferocity. Within the Celestial, progress was significantly slower as the Angelic forces of Carbon IV and Iron II, along with their adherents from other Houses, were careful to avoid harming forces from the House of Zinc. As a result, they were unable to gain access to the remaining soldiers of Gold and Silver. Carbon IV and the others watched as the forces of Zinc finished off Angel after Angel.

"They flee," Carbon IV said in frustration to his comrade Lord Iron II. He gestured to a mass of Gold and Silver Angels retreating the field within the Celestial.

"We cannot reach them," Iron II said. "All that is to be claimed from this field will belong to the upstart. Still, let us gain our fill of mortal slaughter so that none of these meat sacks who have known Gold and Silver shall live to see the morrow."

They set upon the slaughter of the opposition.

---

[11] Who knows Ten? I know Ten. Ten are the Commandments. Nine are the months until birth. Eight are the days until the brit milah. Seven are the days of the week until Shabbat. Six are the books of the Mishnah. Five are the books of the Torah. Four are the Matriarchs. Three are the Forefathers. Two are the tablets of the covenant. One is our God, in heaven and on earth.

*Achad asar mi yodea? Achad asar ani yodea Achad asar kochvayah,
Asarah dibrayah, Tishah yarchei leidah Shmonah y'mei milah
Shivah y'mei shabta,
Shisha sidrei mishnah, Chamisha chumshei Torah, Arbah imahot,
Shlosha avot, Shnei luchot habrit. Echad Eloheinu, Eloheinu,
Eloheinu, Eloheinu, Eloheinu, Shebashamayim uva'aretz.*[12]

Gold collapsed to his knees and retrieved an elaborate jeweled amulet from around his neck. He placed it upon the ground and traced ancient symbols around the talisman. He prayed his observations of the mysterious Ancient had been accurate. He uttered the incantations he had learned from spying on the Titan.

Then Gold shattered the Amulet against the ground. He watched as his blood dripped down on the shattered charm. He felt an unfamiliar power traveling through his body. He turned and faced the sea, fully aware of his enemies bearing down upon him and howled at the sea.

"I command you, element, to heed my instruction: part!"

*Shneim asar mi yodea? Shneim asar ani yodea
Shneim asar shivtayah,
Achad asar kochvayah, Asarah dibrayah, Tishah yarchei leidah
Shmonah y'mei milah Shivah y'mei shabta, Shisha sidrei mishnah,
Chamisha chumshei Torah, Arbah imahot, Shlosha avot,
Shnei luchot habrit. Echad Eloheinu, Eloheinu, Eloheinu,
Eloheinu, Eloheinu, Shebashamayim uva'aretz.*[13]

---

[12] Who knows Eleven? I know Eleven. Eleven are the stars of Joseph's dream. Ten are the Commandments. Nine are the months until birth. Eight are the days until the brit milah. Seven are the days of the week until Shabbat. Six are the books of the Mishnah. Five are the books of the Torah. Four are the Matriarchs. Three are the Forefathers. Two are the tablets of the covenant. One is our God, in heaven and on earth.

[13] Who knows Twelve? I know Twelve. Twelve are the tribes of Israel. Eleven are the stars of Joseph's dream. Ten are the Commandments. Nine are the months until birth. Eight are the days until the brit milah. Seven are the days of the week until Shabbat. Six are the books of the Mishnah. Five are the books of the Torah. Four are the Matriarchs. Three are the Forefathers. Two are the tablets of the covenant. One is our God, in heaven and on earth.

As the Red Sea split to reveal dry ground, every individual soul, mortal and supernatural, stood in silent, terrified awe at what they were witnessing. Schitz quivered. He fought the thoughts of his mortal vessel, who longed to run from such a powerful scene. He looked toward Tuberculosis, who wore a knowing smirk.

"The legends were true," Tuberculosis said as a broad grin spread across his face. Tuberculosis lowered his hand. "Attack!"

The Nubians charged into the raging battle. Schitz breathed easily as he ran toward the mêlée. He propelled his host forward. The enemy drew closer with each stride. Axe in hand, his arms pumped like pistons. He saw the mortals and Angels with crystal clear acuity.

Shlosha asar mi yodea? Shloshah asar ani yodea Shlosha asar midayah.[14]

Gold led his surviving faithful at full tilt through the exposed seabed within the Celestial.

Shneim asar shivtayah.[15]

Zinc the Elder, still within Moses, and his fellows within the Hebrews chased their quarry with savage intensity as they followed across the parted sea.

Achad asar kochvayah.[16]

Schitz cut his way through the Angels that had not entered the sea. He slipped between the Mortal Realm and the Celestial even ahead of Tuberculosis and Lyme Disease. He plunged his sword into a mortal's chest, moved into the Celestial and sliced the seizing Angel's throat, his fourth kill in quick succession.

---

[14] Who knows Thirteen? I Know Thirteen. Thirteen are the attributes of God.

[15] Twelve are the tribes of Israel.

[16] Eleven are the stars of Joseph's dream.

Asarah dibrayah.[17]

Anna heard Gold's shout "Shut" from a few strides ahead of her. She looked over her shoulder as the walls of water began collapsing inwards. She ran forward with survival-driven vigor.

Tishah yarchei leidah.[18]

Zinc looked down at his feet as the ground violently shook around him. He ran with all his might, longing to reach the far bank of the sea.

Shmonah y'mei milah.[19]

The Nubians shouted in victory as they walked across the field littered with dead enemies of Egyptian, Hyksos, and Hebrew origin. Schitz watched the waters close on those who had ventured into the sea. The mortal Egyptians abandoned by Gold and Silver, being the last to enter, were caught in the raging waters.

Tuberculosis patted him on the shoulder. "You were frighteningly fierce today."

Schitz smiled broadly. "I know."

Shivah y'mei shabta.[20]

The Hebrews emerged soaked and waterlogged from the Red Sea. Zinc could taste the bitter, salty water through the thoughts of his mortal. His father swore loudly as he gazed across the barren landscape, searching in vain for the survivors of the houses of Gold and Silver.

---

[17] Ten are the Commandments.

[18] Nine are the months until birth.

[19] Eight are the days until the brit milah.

[20] Seven are the days of the week until Shabbat.

Shisha sidrei Mishna. Chamisha chumshei Torah. Arbah imahot. Shlosha avot.[21]

Gold stood back from the portal he had opened within the cave opening in the hills of the Sinai.

Shnei luchot habrit.[22]

Rebekah concluded the final verse of her song.

Echad Eloheinu, Eloheinu, Eloheinu, Eloheinu, Eloheinu, Shebashamayim uva'aretz.[23]

Rebekah fell to the floor, emerging from her trance. She wondered at the mysteries of her song, for many of the verses pertained to things yet to come to fruition. She looked about the banks of the river and realized it was night. With the knowledge that her people were no longer in Egypt, Rebekah left the washing and strode off into the desert.

SCHITZ RECLINED ALONG THE banks of the Styx in quiet contemplation. The battle had been a success, yet his return to Hell had been bereft of much joy. He knew that even if Anna had survived the battle, the odds of which were low, he would still never see her again. He sighed and gazed across the river. The pain that followed the end of the affair was all-encompassing. He had unburdened his heart to Elise, and she had recommended that he put his thoughts elsewhere.

---

[21] Six are the books of the Mishnah. Five are the books of the Torah. Four are the Matriarchs. Three are the Forefathers.

[22] Two are the tablets of the covenant.

[23] One is our God, in heaven and on earth.

Schitz's Notebook

The chariot is the perfect weapon of modern war. It enables swifter movement than traveling by foot and greater control of ranged weapons as opposed to riding a mount. The chariot allows armies to travel greater distances without falling prey to exhaustion and strikes fear into the hearts of the enemy. The only drawback is the skilled workmanship required to construct/repair.

9/10

He suppressed an involuntary smile as he heard his wraith saying, "Anything but more exercise."

He looked at the bound volume of papyrus in his hands. From a young age, Schitz had cultivated a fondness for writing. When Elise had presented him with the notebook upon his graduation from the Academy, he had been filled with enthusiasm to fill its pages. Now more than ever, the need for distraction felt paramount. He mulled over a subject upon which to begin and immediately thought of Anna. Schitz quickly banished the idea of producing further evidence of his dalliance. His mind turned to the battle; he thought of the chariots employed by the Egyptians. These machines of war were a marvel to him. Suddenly, Schitz found himself tracing the likeness of the weapon on the page. In that moment, it dawned upon him. "I will use this notebook to catalogue the various mortal instruments that pique my interest."

He set down to work, and, as Elise had predicted, somewhere along the route of his efforts, he felt slightly less pained.

THE TRAPS AND FALSE hallways of the pyramid would not deter the hordes of grave robbers in the centuries that followed, nor would the fear of divine retribution from beyond the grave. Yet, the first of many visitors to the tomb had not come to take, but to add his own contribution to Pharaoh's final resting place. The walking shadow, known to the locals as Nebusemekh, had carefully installed the anchors and wooden riggings for his rope, which allowed him to descend into the depths of the structure in the dead of night. The climb to the vent that had granted him access had been exhausting. Still, he was motivated by his soul-consuming task, and his desire pulled him past the staggering climb and beyond the pitfalls and traps in the grand gallery to his destination, the Queen's chamber. Nebusemekh had used his keen vision to navigate through the dark of the pyramid's massive innards; however, upon arrival

Horus

at his destination, he lit the various torches that lined the walls of the Queen's resting place. The chamber was marvelous. Golden statues lined the walls, elaborate papyrus scrolls hung throughout the chamber, ornate hieroglyphs adorned the four walls, ornaments and coins lay strewn across the floor. They glittered in the flickering lights of the flames.

"Oh, my beloved," he said aloud, "how unworthy would even these riches be if you were resting here." He sighed deeply as he imagined her smile, the smoothness of her skin, her long black hair.

"How ironic," he continued, "wherever I go, I am known as the ghost, but it is you who dies, and yet returns."

The Ancient One felt a deep well of sorrow in his heart. He longed to speak his words to his beloved instead of to the open silence surrounding him. Slowly, Circades selected a portion of the wall and set upon it meticulously with his chisel and file. He hummed and thought of Pulwabi's smile as he inserted his own hieroglyphs into the running narrative.

I found you once more in an age of gold,
And in hieroglyphs, our story was told,
By the river's winding bend,
I found a princess whose beauty knew no end.
In the shadow of the pyramids bold,
We watched our story of love unfold.
The sands of gold and waters blue.
Could not match the beauty that was you.
I lost you to life's spinning wheel,
All but for the blink of time we could steal.

Upon completion of the final details of paint upon the stone, Nebusemekh stepped back and admired his work. His own writing fit perfectly within the contribution of the artisans. The Ancient smiled. The Queen had been a beautiful woman: long flowing hair, deep piercing eyes, petite features, and curvaceous femininity. Men found her enthralling, and while Nebusemekh appreciated her beauty, his oath of love to another would never be broken or replaced. He knew that were Pulwabi to read the words; she would know they were composed for her. Then with the silence of a ghost, he killed the fires and left the Queen's final resting place.

CHAPTER 5
SUCCESSION

"Your victory, if you can call it that, was far from complete," Lord Iron II said.

Zinc quivered with irritation. He glanced about the Standard Bearer's luxurious chamber and shook his head vehemently. He might have done something foolish, but he felt his father's staying hand on his back.

"Do not heed the words of this drunken fool. Wait, and watch what happens."

Iron II continued his slurred speech. "Do you not agree, Lord Carbon IV?"

The neophyte Standard Bearer, Carbon IV, hesitated. Iron II slurped Elixir from a chalice. While Carbon IV was clearly under Iron II's influence, the younger leader seemed to desire some level of amenableness with the Zinc House. He stuttered and cleared his throat and looked anxiously from side to side, as though searching the room for his absent father. Iron II glared at Carbon IV and awaited a response.

A knock at the door broke the awkwardness and interrupted the frozen tableau of discomfort.

"Come," Iron II said.

He raised his chalice, signaling to his son that his cup was empty.

A frail, elderly Familiar, clad in an elegant dark robe, strode confidently into the room.

"Ah, Artorius," Iron II said. His appreciation for his House's oldest surviving Familiar was evident. "What news do you have for us?"

The Familiar walked to the front of the room with purpose and placed his wrinkled hand upon his master's shoulder. Iron II looked disheartened; he searched the Familiar's face for answers.

"Shall you adjourn this gathering?" Artorius asked. "You might prefer for me to present the decree to you in a more private setting."

"Nonsense," Iron II said. "Let us hear the news."

Artorius filled the silent chamber with a gravelly voice. "It is the will of our Lord God that all shall pay great thanks to Lord Zinc for his industry, his bravery, and his fighting prowess in driving Gold and Silver from their stronghold in Egypt." Artorius stepped in front of the elder Zinc. "Thus, our Lord, the one true God, presents to his humble servant Sir Zinc admittance to the Order of Highest Merit."

The Familiar reached into his pocket and extracted an ornate cross, the highest award any Heavenly soldier could receive.

Artorius cleared his throat and continued in obvious discomfort. "And to his eldest son, the Lord our God, the most revered, bestows admittance to the First Order."

Zinc could barely believe he had been recognized for his efforts. The First Order was a simple, blue cross with a gilded edge. It was worn on the left side of the recipient's robe. Artorius pinned the medal upon Zinc's chest. Zinc flushed with pride—he'd been recognized by God himself. An uncontrolled smile burst across his face. The Familiar tapped him on the side of the arm and nodded.

Artorius turned to those assembled. "Additionally, the Lord God decrees that the disbanded former Houses of Lead and Oxygen will pledge fealty to Lord Zinc and his House as will all the returning members of the former houses of Gold and Silver."

Artorius raised his voice to be heard over the buzzing whispers. "Yes, several members of both houses have abandoned their dissent and returned to seek the Lord's forgiveness. They will be interrogated to the fullest and then fall under the dominion of the Zinc house, for the Lord has tired of so much Angelic bloodshed."

Zinc could not believe the words he'd just heard. Lead, Oxygen, Gold, and Silver, albeit remnants of the final two, were his family's servile forces. In a single action, his father had elevated the House of Zinc to the highest reaches of Angelic power.

"Lastly," Artorius said, "evoking the Divine Dictum and his power as our Lord, God hath decreed that it is time for the eldest son of the Iron House to assume the duties of Standard Bearer."

The son of Lord Iron II had been in the process of bringing more

Elixir to his father. Now he stood frozen in the middle of the room. He fumbled the pitcher he was carrying and nearly dropped it.

The deposed Iron II rose to his feet. "Come here, my boy."

He shook his son's hand, then began passing out chalices to everyone in the room. Zinc was filled with further validation of his elevation when Iron II handed both him and his father particularly elaborate goblets. Having completed his humble task, Iron raised his own cup and spoke.

"I am humbled and honored that the Lord has so chosen to deem me worthy of retirement. I am filled with paternal pride in the knowledge that my eldest will carry forth the traditions and grandeur of this noble House. To Lord Iron the Third."

A unison of hearty voices cheered, "To Lord Iron the Third." The new Lord Iron appeared more like a frightened hart than a triumphant ascendant.

Zinc winced when he sipped the bitter liquor. His father (Lord Zinc) stepped toward the new Lord Iron and said, "In the spirit of tonight's gathering, I, too, announce the ascendancy of my own eldest son."

Chalice of Elixir

Zinc felt a shock akin to being struck by a weapon. Suddenly, his legs wobbled, and the room spun. His father's voice echoed as if it were at the end of a long tunnel. The room rang with a new shout, "To Lord Zinc the Second," and everyone raised their glasses. Zinc recovered enough to snap a salute to his father. The former Lord returned the gesture with a glint of satisfaction in his eye. Zinc stepped close to his father and summoned all the strength he could put into his voice.

"I will not rest until glorious death or the final victory," he said. He struck his chest with his fist.

His father grabbed him by either shoulder and rested his son's forehead against his own.

"I know that you speak the truth."

The assembled Angels gave another shout and continued to drain their Elixir.

"I PROMISE YOU, I tried everything I possibly could," Tuberculosis said. He shook his head.

Schitz sighed and looked about the elder's room in frustration.

"I just don't understand," he said. "How are they ever going to take me seriously or move past this undying obsession with Vertigo if they never acknowledge my good work? I did well."

Tuberculosis's voice was calm. "You will find that receiving praise and distinction is more the exception rather than the rule."

Schitz scowled.

"You did very well," Lyme Disease said. "Your deeds are worthy of a Pentagram Second Class at least. To have dispatched seven Angels single-handedly and so quickly, amazing work."

Schitz looked at the medals around his squad mates' necks and grimaced.

How many more do I have to kill, he thought. *If I can get one of those, no one will ever mention Vertigo again.*

Tuberculosis reached into the pocket of his robe and withdrew the remains of the Amulet Gold had shattered. He looked at Lyme Disease.

"Your father, Stillwater, was obsessed with the Elemental Tools," he said. "Artifacts long believed to be mere legend."

"He told me of them often," Lyme Disease said. "They are rumored to be the garments and possessions of the Titans, the tools with which the Titans interacted with the Ethereal Realm."

"Indeed," Tuberculosis said, "and it is said that whoever controls one of these items possesses the power to command the elements themselves."

Schitz was stunned by the conversation. Most Demons were loath to discuss the Titans, the race that had dominated the Mortal Realm before Satan and God. The Titans had been defeated by a unified army led by the Devil, or God, depending on which side was telling the story. Following the colossal battle, the Titans were eradicated. Their offspring had been rendered weak and impotent through crossbreeding with mortals and were allowed to survive. They were enslaved as Wraiths and Familiars. Thus, Hell and Heaven acquired their servant classes.

"My concern," Tuberculosis said, "is that The Ancient has transgressed his neutrality and thrown his lot in with the forces of Heaven."

Schitz had heard whispered rumors of the mysterious entity known only as "The Ancient." Tales of him circulated through the dormitory of the Academy. He was described as a dark, menacing force, the father of many a nightmare.

"I did not know he was real," Schitz said.

"Oh, he is real," Tuberculosis said. "Worse yet, he is even more powerful than the legends. He is the last of his kind, the last surviving Titan. He possesses primordial knowledge that imbues him with destructive capacities beyond our wildest dreams. Until this moment, he was largely ignored because he remained neutral and disinterested in both the war that eradicated his race and our war with Heaven. However, it would be devastating were he to be our foe."

"We are not entirely certain that he is in league with our enemies. He was not present at the battle, only the Amulet," Lyme Disease said.

"True," Tuberculosis said, "however, I do not understand how an Angel could have used it, for it required lost ancient rites and incantations."

"It would be impertinent to make him a foe if he were still neutral," Lyme Disease said.

"Indeed, that is why we are going to seek him out," Tuberculosis said.

Schitz's mind reeled. His squad leader's intentions were surprising and dangerous.

"It will be perilous," Lyme Disease said.

"It will also be unsanctioned," Tuberculosis said with a touch of mischief. "We will not be informing the Devil or any of our colleagues of this endeavor. The Free Thinkers alone possess the cunning mindset needed to engage with such a wily character as The Ancient. Besides, nobody is aware of the details surrounding the parting of the sea. It is best for us that it remains so."

Tuberculosis swept the shattered Amulet back into his pocket.

Lyme Disease asked, "When do we leave?"

"Tout suite," Tuberculosis replied.

"THEY SAY HE IS a member of the race that came before," Zinc's father said in a stoic voice. "He is a Titan. They once ruled all realms, mortal and Celestial."

Zinc nodded. "In the Academy, they told stories of him in hushed whispers. They say he is immortal, possessing the powers from whence the universe was fashioned. They say he cannot lie, but if he does not wish to answer, he will kill you on the spot. He is reportedly the one who set down the Divine Dictum to establish order between Heaven and Hell. And they say he is the one who maintains it."

His father waved a dismissive hand. "They say a lot of things, but I will find him,"

"I am uncertain what I will do in your absence," Zinc said.

His father stepped closer and interlocked his fingers behind Zinc's head. He focused his cold, blue eyes. "I have kept you to myself, my son, held you closer than your brothers or sisters. I have kept you close so that even your mother might seem less than kin to you. I did this to impart all that was good in me to you. You are strong and wise and will be more than capable in my absence."

The father patted the new Lord of the Zinc House on his cheek. "Had I held onto my title, I would have done you a grave disservice," he said. "The new Standard Bearers of Iron and Carbon are still wet behind the ears and have not yet assumed the mantle of leadership.

Should they gain such a footing while you were still under me, you would never surpass them."

Zinc shrugged. "I still wish you weren't leaving, all the same."

"We must find out how Gold and Silver were able to remain so long within mortal hosts without the melding of the minds. We must know how Gold parted the waters as though he had command over the elementals. To this end, it is not a choice but a requirement that I go, but I will be with you through your training, your intellect, and your strength."

He saluted. "Lord Zinc."

The son awkwardly returned the salute. "Good fortune to you, Sir Zinc," he said.

THE WORLD IS BECOMING *so inextricably interconnected,* The Ancient thought as he stalked through the woods that lined the edge of the Jōmon settlement. *Look how these travelers from Korea bring their pottery and iron working here to Honshu.*

The Ancient had been given the name Fuyūrei by the local inhabitants, who saw him as a wandering ghost of no particular malevolence. Still, he was to be respected.

An apt assessment, Circades thought. He took care in his movements. He didn't want to expose his presence to the mortals. They could see him, clearer than they could see Wraiths and Familiars. Demons and Angels within the Celestial were, at most, passing shadows, an apparition in the corner of a mortal's eye.

The Ancient gazed at the bamboo structures of the Jōmon village. It was midday, and despite a heavy rain, the inhabitants were going to and fro as they completed the various tasks of life. Fuyūrei longed to engage in fellowship with the mortals, to feel the bonds of shared experience with others. He suppressed his urge for connection. He knew all too well that knowledge of the supernatural contaminated a mortal's soul. It was the mystery of the unknown beyond death that kept the soul pure, and fueled the energy that bound the Mortal, Celestial, and Ethereal Realms through the cycle of death and rebirth.

The Ancient recalled the emergence of their cursed races with a shudder. Neither Titan nor mortal, the Celestial walkers had slaughtered his kin in their bid to conquer the realms. With their victory, the beasts had inherited the burden of maintaining order. He had allowed them the ability to raise the mortals' awareness, a dangerous yet sometimes necessary action. When the forces of Heaven and Hell agreed to such an action, then the mortals' understanding of the world increased. This agreement had been executed before, and mortals had gained knowledge that they were different from the animals. They learned about their collective intergenerational history and grew in an understanding of how to manipulate their world. The Ancient recalled the first enhancement of mortal knowledge in what was known as the Garden of Eden, when the Demon, Slithering Sickness, delivered the agreed-upon elevation of human consciousness.

The Ancient thought of these developments as he watched the effects of the cultural exchange between the peoples of the islands and the mainland. He cared far less for the impact on the mortals and more for his own personal vested interest. As the population grew and the mortals multiplied, the difficulty of his quest to locate the reincarnated soul of his beloved increased.

The Ancient strode away from the encampment and toward a nearby stream. He watched from the edge of the wood as the Jōmon women bathed in the flowing waters. He searched the souls of maidens back through their various incarnations for the one soul he longed to find. A darkness settled over him as his task did not provide the desired return. Once more, he had failed to find his beloved.

A taunting voice banished the silence. "Is this the way the last mighty Titan fills his time, as a voyeur of unsuspecting mortals?"

The Ancient turned and saw a solitary Angel in the body of a Yayoi warrior. The Ancient observed the features of the Angel within the man: long, dark hair hung down to his shoulders in a chaotic unkempt mess that matched his rugged beard. He had strong angular features and piercing blue eyes. Despite his perpetual hunt for his beloved,

Fuyūrei was unable to avoid the dramas and personalities of Heaven and Hell.

"How I pass my time is entirely up to me and should be of little concern to any other, Lord Zinc," he replied. He was clearly irritated by the interruption.

"My son is now Lord Zinc," the Angel replied, beaming with paternal pride. "'Sir Zinc,' is more than fine."

"A pleasure," The Ancient said. He returned his attention to the women near the river.

"I mean no offense," Sir Zinc said, "but I am concerned about how freely you are sharing your considerable wisdom."

Fuyūrei looked at the former Standard Bearer. "I will take no offense until after you explain what you mean."

"I simply wish to know how a group of usurping Angels could so mimic your powers."

"Such as?" The Ancient asked.

"Such as elongated possession of a human without the melding of minds, or utilizing relics to control the elements," Zinc said.

"These are things I learned about only after they took place," The Ancient said. "I make no effort to hide my behaviors. You found me easily enough, and you see what I am doing." He pointed to the women. "If anyone has gleaned anything from me, they did so by watching more and talking less."

LYME DISEASE COULD NOT hide the excitement in her voice. "They are in league together."

Schitz stood next to her and watched the Angel cloaked in mortal flesh as he talked with a man by the river who appeared to be in the Celestial and the Mortal Realms simultaneously.

"We can't be sure," Tuberculosis said. "The conversation alone is not enough to confirm collaboration. Besides, there is no court to which we could bring a grievance even with solid evidence. After all, we would be accusing the only judge. We need to be cagier."

Schitz took in every aspect of the mysterious entity they had tracked across the globe through three cycles of the moon. He was tall and tanned; he had strikingly pronounced, clean-shaven features complemented by dark eyes and wild, dark hair. Although he had purportedly lived millennia, he looked no older than a mortal of thirty.

"We will capture the Angel," Tuberculosis said.

Schitz and Lyme Disease spoke at the same time. "Capture him?"

Schitz had never heard of any Angel or Demon surrendering to a foe. Both could slip into the Celestial at will.

"Sure," Tuberculosis said. "We will ascertain all the information we need without risking an exchange with The Ancient."

"I understand the objective," Lyme Disease said. "I fail to understand how we are going to achieve something no one else has ever done."

Tuberculosis smiled. "Schitz, go and possess the leader of the Yayoi scouts and lead them in an attack on the women. Lyme Disease, I see a maiden standing guard down there. Her bow is ready. Make her use it. I will remain in the Celestial to prevent the Angel's flight. We must be careful. We want to capture the Angel alive; an unprecedented achievement."

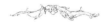

Sɪʀ Zɪɴᴄ's ᴠᴏɪᴄᴇ ᴇᴄʜᴏᴇᴅ with skeptical relief. "So, the balance of power remains intact?"

"Indeed," The Ancient said. "Now, if you would excuse me, it seems there is some pressing business at hand."

Sir Zinc whirled and saw members of the Yayoi rushing through the woods toward the stream. He also saw a duo of Demons, one in the Mortal Realm, the other in the Celestial.

He drew his bronze sword and ran toward the river, confident he could outrun the pursuing Demons. The veteran Angel broke through the trees. The Jōmon women fled in disarray. The Yayoi fell on the slower females, ripped their garments, and hoisted them over their shoulders in lustful glee. Most of the Yayoi scouts ignored the archer who was shooting as fast as she could.

The bow-woman had been possessed by a tall, curvaceous Demon with a bounty of long crimson hair though her human was a short, dark-haired mortal. Sir Zinc stepped into the Celestial a moment before an arrow struck down his host. He continued running through the stream.

Over his shoulder, he saw his pursuers, one in each Realm.

Time to fight, he thought.

He drew his short sword and readied himself.

TUBERCULOSIS AND SCHITZ RUSHED toward the waiting Angel.

"Remember to hold within your mortal," Tuberculosis said.

Schitz's pulse throbbed in his neck; he closed the distance between himself and the foe. The Angel, though in a defensive position, was clearly vulnerable. Schitz jumped onto the body of a panic-stricken Jōmon woman who had been too frozen in terror to flee from the marauders.

At the same time, Lyme Disease took possession of the woman's body. As Schitz feigned manhandling her, Lyme Disease whispered a warning.

"The dagger in his belt, the dagger in his belt, the dagger in his belt."

Schitz looked at Tuberculosis, who had engaged the Angel. They were matched with exquisite parity so that the clash of Celestial blades and the movement of bodies was more of a dance than a depiction of violence. The Angel blocked Tuberculosis with a high guard and immediately attempted to strike him with a roundhouse kick. The Demon dropped his sword arm and blocked the kick before spinning to generate momentum for another attack.

The Angel ducked under the blade and attempted to bring his own down upon Tuberculosis, who rolled out of the way. He jumped to his feet and renewed his assault on the Angel with a lunge toward his midsection. The Angel parried and continued to maneuver. He was careful never to turn his back toward Schitz and Lyme Disease.

When their swords locked, Tuberculosis drew a throwing knife with his free hand and sliced at the Angel's midsection. The Angel caught the Demon by the forearm and pushed him backwards away from him.

"Throw me over your shoulder," Lyme Disease said as she slipped out of the woman. Schitz hoisted the vacant mortal while Lyme Disease charged toward the Angel. Tuberculosis backed off and threw his small knife at the Angel. Schitz marveled at the Angel's dexterity. He harkened back to Anna's training; he could hear her sultry, feminine voice from within the Egyptian noblewoman, "You must never underestimate any entity friend or foe. You must see everyone as the potential bringer of your destruction."

The Angel dragged his blade across Tuberculosis's thigh. The senior Demon howled in frustration and fell into the shallow, rocky stream.

He called to Schitz, "Don't just stand there, help us, you young idiot."

Schitz leapt from the body of his host. He was grateful for his training, as, upon his exit, the Angel deftly disengaged from Lyme Disease and swiftly swung his blade toward Schitz's throat. Schitz managed to parry the blow but was knocked aside by the strength of the Angel. He watched haplessly as the Angel bounded into his former host.

Sir Zinc felt the familiar rush of exhilaration that accompanied success upon the battlefield. He had handled a markedly adept foe and escaped. He would have preferred to kill his assailant, but he'd been outnumbered, so he contented himself with being alive and free.

The Yayoi raiders had already fled the stream, and he would join them soon from within the sole mortal available for possession. Sir Zinc smiled. There were no mortals left for the Demons to possess; the female Demon could not re-enter the woman his raider was carrying. It was indeed a grievous error for the senior to call for aid from the junior, forcing them all into the Celestial and allowing him access to the sole remaining mortal.

Zinc looked back for a last triumphant glance. When he turned, however, he saw something unexpected. Both the female and the junior Demon were huddled next to their stricken leader. Written across the face of each were smirking, sardonic expressions that Zinc could not quite understand. Then the exquisite redhead raised her right hand, pressing her long, delicate thumb and middle finger together, and produced a snap that rang out across the Celestial.

A bolt of terror inched its way through Sir Zinc's body.

Shit!

As soon as she snapped her fingers, the message Lyme Disease had worked so hard to imbed within the mortal's mind took effect. Schitz watched as the Jōmon grabbed a dagger from the belt of the Yayoi and plunged it viciously into his back. The fatally wounded man collapsed to the ground. The affected mortal continued stabbing the body until she emerged from her trance. She looked down on her bloodied hands and the wet, shredded clothes demolished by her would-be abductor. Naked and distraught, she ran back to the village along the banks of the stream.

Tuberculosis rose to his feet and removed the drawstring around his celestial robe. "Leave the lady to hers," he said to Schitz.

Schitz marveled at the perfect execution of Tuberculosis's scheme to make Zinc think that the Demons had abandoned their hosts prematurely. The overconfidence of their foe had allowed them to guide him toward possessing the Yayoi. A fatal mistake.

Zinc wriggled and flopped like a landlocked fish while Tuberculosis issued orders.

"Steady him."

Lyme Disease and Schitz held the writhing Angel still, and Tuberculosis bound his hands and feet with their drawstrings. Once the Angel recovered, they raised him to his feet and marched him to the edge of the clearing. Lyme Disease snapped a shoot of bamboo to serve as the crossbar for a rudimentary door. Schitz drew the requisite symbols for a return to Hell, then looked past the opening portal to the far bank of the stream where he beheld a solitary figure who was watching their exploits.

Simply gazing on The Ancient filled Schitz with a sense of dread. He did not quit looking at the old Titan until the portal closed.

THE NEW LORD ZINC paced the length and breadth of his dwelling place. He had found precious little time to relax in his new abode since he had assumed control. Thoughts of his missing father overwhelmed his strained mind, and he wondered if he would ever enjoy the benefits of his elevated position. There was so much to do, and each item seemed of pressing importance: locating Gold and Silver, the consolidation of his recent acquisitions, his upcoming wedding. The subjects all clamored for his attention.

Zinc turned his attention to the maiden of the Gold House, who patiently sat upon a chair alongside his desk. With quiet comportment, she had allowed him to rant and rave about his situation. He beheld her now as though for the first time. Her long black hair, vibrant olive complexion, and piercing dark eyes all rendered her quite stunning. Zinc felt a particularly intense sense of arousal with the knowledge that such a fine specimen was entirely at his disposal.

I can order her to submit to me whenever I choose, Zinc thought.

With great resolve, he suppressed his lusty thoughts and addressed his Angelic chattel. "They tell me you are the most adept of all your House in the arts of combat."

"I'm surprised you don't remember yourself," she replied smoothly.

"You were a little bit ahead of me at the Academy, but I do recall a few joint exercises," Zinc said.

The Angel, known as Anna of the Gold House, nodded in reply.

"I want you to assemble a team of your choosing," Zinc said. "Pick only the best warriors from among the House proper and the vassals. Take as many as you need and find my father. Take Familiars as well if you so need."

"I understand that circumstance has contrived to make me your underling," she said, "however, I feel obliged to point out that failing to lead such an expedition on your own may make you appear weak to your colleagues."

Zinc ground his teeth in frustration.

She continued, "To entrust such a mission to a conquered servant may lead to the impression that you are unwise, to say the least."

Zinc's skin crawled at being chastised by the scum that had so recently defected. He smacked her across her face. His hand stung from the impact, but he noted his victim neither flinched nor uttered a note of distress; she simply absorbed the blow and returned her gaze to his eye.

"Do not presume to lecture me, deserter," he said. "I send you so that I might remain and attend to the tasks of the state. I will not prioritize my personal search for my father over my obligations here in Heaven. Such my father taught me, and in doing such, I honor him. Besides, I send you to show my respect for technical prowess over lineage or standing."

Anna nodded.

"Return my father to me safely, and you will have a position of luxury and contentment," he said. "That is all."

The lithe Angel rose to her feet and exited the room. Zinc collapsed in a heap upon his bed.

"Father," he said, "I am not certain how long I can do this without you."

THE GREAT HALL WAS eerily quiet. "I never knew surrender was an option," Schitz said. He smirked at Tuberculosis.

"Too often in the heat of battle, we concern ourselves with what we wish to do," Tuberculosis said. "But if you can surmise the course your enemy desires to take, then you gain a step—a significant advantage."

"I wish you had been an instructor at the Academy," Schitz said to the sagacious elder.

"Hayfever and Tetanus did fine by you, young lad," Tuberculosis said. "Besides, my ideas are too radical ever to be considered worthy of academic instruction." His smile looked a little sad.

Schitz nodded and turned his attention to the assembled. His contingent of his father, Diphtheria, his aunt Syphilis, and his academy mates Autism, Anorexia, and their brother Legionnaire's Disease stood next to Rubella's group. He saw her father Botulism and her brothers, Measles and Mumps. It was a small gathering due to the unrelenting efforts of Bubonic Plague to brand Schitz as an outcast. All of Hell had been invited. Those who came had chosen Schitz over Bubonic Plague, at least for that day.

Schitz turned his attention back to his grandfather, Tuberculosis. Unlike the mortals who would only ever know a grandparent as an old relic of their youth, Schitz had matured into the physical peer of his father's father. Tuberculosis could still best Schitz on the training ground and academically. Schitz had great respect for the Demon, but there was a level of distance that he never fully understood.

Tuberculosis had insisted on a strictly professional relationship when Schitz had entered the squad. His grandfather had refused to answer any questions pertaining to their bloodline, his father, or his personal life. He expressed affection as a comrade rather than a relative, which was more than Schitz could say of his father. Other than his involvement in the duel with Vertigo, his father had remained distant.

Schitz was pulled from his familial thoughts as a quartet of Wraiths began to work the strings of their violins. The notes of the old hymn hung in the air and added warmth to the cold stones.

"Ah," Tuberculosis said, "*Not for me, but for Thee.* I love the old hymns. What a fantastic choice."

Schitz nodded. He watched as the bridal procession approached the altar. "I wish circumstances would have allowed for a more festive occasion."

Tuberculosis patted him on the back. "It would be foolish of you to think that anybody other than those who are here should matter. It would also be foolish to imagine that you are the first of our lot to kill a colleague over a mate rivalry. These politics and inclinations are old within our kind. As the season changes, so will the pall Bubonic Plague casts over you and your bride."

Schitz nodded, and said, "Though he is powerful. I heard that the Devil tasked him with the interrogation of your prisoner."

Schitz stole a glance over his shoulder to the doorway that led to Satan's dwelling place. He had hoped that the Dark Lord would attend and bless the wedding.

"The glory was in the capture," Tuberculosis said with glee. "Who cares who is afforded the honor of carving that wretched beast into food for dogs? Enjoy today. It is one of the few days that has nothing to do with our constant struggle. Savor each moment, and they will sustain you all your life."

Schitz heard a nostalgic note and wondered if Tuberculosis recalled his own marriage to SIDS. Schitz's grandmother had not come to the wedding, although it was reported that it was less due to her siding with Bubonic Plague and more to do with a summons to Satan's company. The Rogues were known for their interrogation skills. Schitz was certain that SIDS was prying forth many a Heavenly secret from the lips of the Angel they had captured.

Schitz eagerly drank in the scene as Rubella slowly neared him with regal steps. For most of their lives, Demons wore functional attire, simple robes, sandals, maybe a cloak. The only adornments anyone chose were decorations awarded for valor in battle. However, on the day of a wedding, the attire was much more overstated. Schitz was clad in a robe made of too fine a material to wear within the Mortal Realm. His shoes were more elaborate than his usual sandals, both in the intricacy of their interwoven design and the patterns burned into the leather. Over his shoulders was draped the skin of a lion. Schitz had felled the beast in the Mortal Realm, a ceremonial prerequisite to matrimony. Rubella approached and stole the entirety of Schitz's thoughts.

She was dressed in a bright crimson robe. On the day of matrimony, practicality was discarded. Rubella's robes were elaborate and tight, revealing her feminine frame. Her footwear, also crimson, was thin and gave the impression that she was nearly barefoot. She was adorned from head to toe in jewelry cut from obsidian.

The procession was led by a Priest who continued past Schitz and assumed his position closest to the altar. Rubella stopped next to Schitz and took his hands in hers as she faced him. Behind Rubella, now standing between the contingents of Demons, stood an array of Wraiths. Tradition held that the Wraiths stood guard to prevent any violence between families during the ceremony. Schitz could feel a slight tremble, but he could not tell whether the source was Rubella or himself.

The ceremony was brief and to the point. The Priest began, "Let us give thanks to our Lord that he sees fit to bind together these two souls."

The officiant then unrolled a scroll that bore the signature of the Devil. "Our Lord decrees that by this bond you join into one flesh and one blood, only to be separated whence one's blood hath run out. Do you each accept this decree?"

Schitz felt a constriction in the back of his throat. He fought to fill the hall with a confident, assured voice as he said, "I do."

"Present your hands," the Priest said.

Schitz and Rubella held their palms upwards. The Priest drew an opulent ceremonial dagger from its scabbard. In a swift, merciless motion, he dragged the blade across their respective palms. Schitz winced slightly. For the briefest of moments, he could hear Anna saying, "Eleven is control of pain."

Schitz rapidly fought to banish thoughts of the Angel with whom he had shared such intense intimacy. But the harder he tried to put her from his mind, the more vivid the images became.

Schitz returned the present as he heard the Priest say, "In the name of the Lord, I proclaim thee wed."

With the conclusion of the ceremony, the Priest retrieved a lavish chalice from atop the altar and poured water from the Styx over the couple's hands. Schitz smiled and whispered into Rubella's ear. "No matter what challenges we have faced before, I pledge to you all of myself from this day forth. I promise we will know happiness and joy together. I love you so much."

Tears leaked from the corners of her eyes as Rubella echoed her affection for Schitz. "I love you, too."

Schitz pulled Rubella close to him and kissed her. He drank in every sensation of her soft tongue against his own, only remembering the crowd of those assembled when a cheer of jubilee echoed throughout the hall.

"Nervous" was an understatement. Zinc lowered his arm from the salute and glanced around the room. Marble walls adorned with paintings merged seamlessly into ornate tile floors. Statues stood guard in every corner. The high, canopied ceiling rested on gorgeous, carved columns. Bookcases as tall as four men lined one complete wall and displayed every imaginable volume. A bar, behind which stood every concoction known in civilization, stood on the opposite side of the room in a perfect juxtaposition of "education" and "enjoyment."

On a luxurious leather couch in the middle of the room, sat the source of Zinc's trepidation, The Lord of Heaven himself: Almighty God.

"Relax," he said. "Have a seat."

Though his tone was friendly, every word from His mouth carried the substance of a Divine command. He had a fair complexion and jet-black hair, which was cut short and neat. Lean and toned, his soft amber eyes were both disarming and penetrating.

Zinc attempted to steel himself for the encounter.

"Would you like something to drink?" God asked.

"No, thank you, my Lord," Zinc said. He sank into an inviting chair.

"Let me begin by saying how pleased I am to meet such a promising Angel," God said. "I'm told that even though yours is a newer House, you are making astounding progress. Congratulations. Heaven needs such leadership."

God paused, and Zinc used the opportunity to find his voice, "Thank you, my Lord."

God nodded. "Second, I am saddened to tell you that I have dispatched Familiars to recall the detachment you sent in search of your father."

Zinc felt a pang of confusion and sadness. He was glad to be sitting. He might otherwise have collapsed.

"I'm so very sorry," God said, "but he is lost."

Zinc fought to remain calm. He said, "I will miss him greatly and will strive to honor his legacy."

God nodded sternly. "Your father had sought answers from a perilous source, though in the end, it was Demons who took him."

"Not The Ancient?"

"No," God replied. "The Titan did not kill your father. Lord Zinc, we reside in a world that is held together by many mysteries just as it is held together by the elements. How Gold and Silver fell into the dangerous knowledge surrounding the Amulet that parted the Red Sea is a mystery to me. But I know Gold and Silver remain at large, and the forces of Hell have decimated our numbers. We must refocus on gaining the initiative. I have received word from the Familiars that there is a young Macedonian King by the name of Alexander III. I have it on good authority that he holds within him much potential and that he will bring the sword to all who stand in his way. It is imperative that we formulate a strategy in which we are always either possessing him or those immediately around him. In such a manner, we will use his superior troops to crush the Demons. Only then will we turn our attention to Gold and Silver. This is my task for you."

Zinc nodded.

"Also," God said, "until the traitors are brought to heel, we must not permit the descendants who have returned to leave Heaven. We cannot risk their feeding information back to their old Standard Bearers."

Zinc cringed as he recalled Anna's rebuke.

"Yes, my Lord," he replied.

"WHAT DO YOU THINK about Greece," Rubella asked as she and Schitz reclined by the banks of the Styx.

"For a honeymoon?" he asked.

"No," she laughed. "All the talk about the next big campaign."

"The Greeks are crazy," Schitz said. His tone grew somber. "Thermopylae was unpleasant, to say the least."

Schitz's mind drifted back to a barren plain that stretched along the Malian Gulf. His squad had attacked a corps of Angels during the outset of the battle and pursued them; however, once entrenched within the Spartan phalanx, they were impossible to dislodge.

"They are talented at war," Rubella said, "and should they unite, they will be able to march across the entire world."

"I supposed that is why there are many reports of the Angels congregating around Macedonia," Schitz said.

He rolled over from his back and placed his hands behind Rubella's head. "Whatever the future has in store, all I want is to share it with you."

He kissed her and enjoyed her enthusiastic reciprocation. As their passion peaked, she gazed into his eyes with longing.

"Give me your progeny," she said.

CHAPTER 6

THE ARSONIST

Alexander of Macedonia looked out over his court. "We will carry forth our superior language, culture, and ideas across all manner of savage lands and peoples," he said. "Thus, we will bring light to a darkened world. "Prosperity, health, commerce, and progress will follow in the wake of our army, and the untold future generations will thank us for lifting humanity out of the mire and morass of the arcane thinking and practices."

Zinc felt his spine tingle as he heard Alexander espouse the very virtues of the Angels, the very religion of Heaven, to his followers. When Zinc and his compatriots defeated the Demons that dwelled in the darkened corners of existence, they too would bring light and peace unto the world. As the vigorous young king so eloquently put it, peace would follow in the wake of their army, both mortal and Angelic.

Zinc took in the assembled Angels within the court within both the Celestial and Mortal Realms. Zinc had instructed his younger brother Ervin to possess the Macedonian. Zinc wished to save his own possession for a more critical time. God had forbidden the use of any of the knowledge Gold had acquired to prolong possession times. In a decree, God had referenced "the dangers of invoking knowledge that was better lost to bygone ages."

In the time since his father's death, Zinc had attempted to foster a better relationship with his mother and his siblings along with his extended family. His pride swelled when he gazed across the court and saw his brothers, sisters, and cousins ready to lead the forces of Heaven. His attention shifted to his cousin Rachael with whom he had conducted the Passover slaughter. Oddly enough, she has become one of his most staunch supporters since their time in Egypt. Zinc felt as close to her as any of his siblings.

Zinc's attention shifted back to the matter at hand, the unification

THE ARSONIST • 199

of the Angels and the Greeks. Just as Alexander was in the process of purging dissenters and ascertaining loyalty, so too Zinc required the subordination of several Angelic Houses that failed to defer to his authority, mainly those of Carbon and Iron. The loss of his father had provided those elements with a renewed desire to resist his ascent to power.

The conversation unfolded in tandem. Alexander and the mortals debated the merits and the particulars of an invasion of Asia Minor, while Zinc and Angels argued about the authority and strategic control of the Heavenly squadrons.

"You will not direct the sons and daughters of the esteemed House of Iron even if the broader strategy comes from God himself," Lord Iron III said. "On the battlefield, we will be in command of our own."

Zinc was sure that control over individual fighters was an inane argument. His thoughts were mirrored by the Lord of the Carbon House, who attempted to interject.

Zinc cut him off. "I will provide you no argument there. However, control of Alexander and his generals will remain in the hands of the Zinc House if you are to make such demands."

Lord Iron III was flabbergasted. "How does one relate to the other?"

"It is simple," Zinc said with insincere amicability. "That is the exchange for autonomy over your Houses."

Carbon IV shook his head and turned to Iron III. "Alexander should have been the only negotiating point. You've won control of your House, which you already had, but lost any hope of control of the army."

"Quite," Zinc said, "but it was never yours to lose anyhow. This meeting is adjourned. Let us reconvene when we reach Granicus."

"ARE THE REPORTS THAT bad?" Schitz asked.

"Indeed," Elise replied. "This army is going to be the focal point of all future actions. They are motivated, advanced, and led by a technical genius. It was a coup for the Angels to get their hooks into them first."

"Well, we'll just have to nip at their flanks like we always do," Schitz said. "We're always outnumbered."

"Indeed, but this will be dangerous. If you are outside of the Greek formations, you will be severely outclassed. You must be extra careful," Elise said. She patted him on the shoulder. "How are you?"

"I'm fine, Mama," Schitz said, not entirely certain he believed it.

"I know it must be a lot. Those that blame you for Vertigo's demise; your affair with the Angel; your new marriage. All of the normal strains and stresses of combat," she said.

"I compartmentalize my thoughts," Schitz said, "and I surrender to the inevitable."

"Oh?"

"Indeed, try as I might; there is much beyond my control. I accept that," he said.

"Oh, my boy," she said. She embraced him with her sole remaining arm. "You have grown into such a fine Demon."

Schitz embraced his surrogate, shocked to feel the effects of age upon her frail frame.

"The Devil be with you," Elise said as she broke the embrace.

"I'm not sure the Devil likes me very much," Schitz said.

He reflected upon his own mental schism. He was angry at his leader for failing to acknowledge him and for being so easily influenced by Bubonic Plague, yet he was also motivated to succeed and win his leader's approval.

"In time, you will see the magnitude it requires to win his lasting affections," Elise said. "Bubonic will not be your undoing."

Schitz nodded. "Well, I have to be off to rendezvous with the rest of my squad. They anticipate action in Asia Minor."

Schitz hesitated for a moment—an awkward pause. He glanced about the room. Wraiths were not permitted within Demonic quarters when the resident Demon was not present.

"Ah, yes, of course. I will be on my way," Elise said.

Schitz smiled. *She would do anything for me, but she must not become too comfortable, or someday she may cross a line.*

PARMENION SURVEYED THE FORMATIONS of his master's army.

"Oh, how the tides do change," he said. "The Persians have tried to batter down the doors of mighty Greece many a time. Yet here we stand, ready to march over Persia."

A rush of satisfaction rushed through the Macedonian commander's mind. Zinc had taken possession several days before.

"Indeed," Alexander said.

Zinc could discern Ervin inside Alexander. The young general spoke. "The cavalry and infantry are assembled. We must attack at once before the Persians have time to prepare themselves."

Zinc stepped closer and whispered in his brother's ear. "They will hit and run. Our Familiars already report that the Demons are arrayed in their traditional three-party hunting groups. Send word. We will not attempt to envelop them at the outset. We must only defend ourselves until we have reached the Greek mercenaries fighting with the Persians. Then we will surround the Demons."

"Ah, the trap is set, my brother," Ervin said.

"We will take the field today in a glorious manner," Alexander said with a glint in his eye.

Parmenion raised his arm in salute. "Indeed."

SCHITZ RESTED COMFORTABLY WITHIN the body of a Persian nobleman as they both sat in the saddle. He surveyed the scene. The Persian forces were hastily preparing for battle with the Greeks. The air was hot and dry, a typical pleasant day in May in western Asia Minor. The morning sun beamed through a crystal blue sky. The foliage, the dusty barren rocks, and the meandering flow of the Biga River all conspired to render a scenic, placid tableau. The whinnies of warhorses, the clatter of armor, the clanking of soldiers' steps, the rattle of arrows within quivers rebelled against the landscape and delivered an unnatural element of foreboding. Schitz could feel anxiety and conflict amongst the thoughts of the Persian, along with a strong desire to defend his homeland and his people.

The Persian was watching three cohorts of Memnon when Tuberculosis came up alongside within the body of a Persian commander.

"You always find the most ornate armor," Schitz said with a grin.

"What is a man if not his attire? If I must wear these mortals, I prefer the ones with elaborate taste," Tuberculosis replied.

Schitz marveled at the armor. The breastplate was made of many rows of individual bronze sections. Each piece portrayed a painstakingly etched, carving of an eagle.

"They do not trust the Greek mercenaries," Tuberculosis said.

"And why should they?" It was Lyme Disease; Schitz marveled at the fierce Persian woman his compatriot had possessed.

"I feel there is something more to it," Tuberculosis said. "I sense some skullduggery among them. It merits further investigation."

A Wraith appeared from out of a small bush. "My Lord, Bubonic Plague sends word that the battle has begun. There is a great multitude of Angels within the ranks of the Greeks. He spurs you forth to your purpose, my Lord."

Tuberculosis drew his sword and glanced down menacingly toward the Wraith, a servant to Plague. "Tell my son-in-law that I need no instruction as to my purpose. We join the battle forthwith, as was previously discussed and planned. Away with you."

The commander waved his cavalry forward. "Onwards Persians!"

THE GROUND HEAVED AND swelled as though he was on raging seas as Zinc clattered through the Persian lines. The Companions had cut through their mortal adversaries well, but his quarry had yet to present itself. As Zinc brought his sword down upon the head of yet another adversary, the blade deflected off the helmet but crashed down with enough force that the Persian's vertebrae snapped, leaving the man's head at a disjointed angle. His body slumped to the ground.

Suddenly, moving through the lines to the point of their attack, Zinc beheld the Persian cavalry and amongst them a contingent of three Demons. The basic strategy of the forces of Hell was always to attack the numerically superior Angels briefly, score a kill or two with the aid of their undeniably superior fighting style, then flee.

Heaven's general strategy was referred to as "the relay" or "the double envelopment." This tactic called for the initial squad or, if need be, a secondary squad from within the supporting ranks, to surround and strike down the Demon. Zinc had found that in the wheeling tumult of combat, such strategies rarely played out as they did on the training ground. However, under the current circumstances, Zinc was aching with the hope that the Demons would expect the Angels to follow their usual plan.

THE PERSIAN COUNTERCHARGE BROUGHT Schitz and his comrades reeling towards the foe and their Persian hosts into direct combat with the leader of the enemy contingent. Schitz felt overwhelmed with the possibilities. He knew the instructions were to hit and withdraw without being surrounded. However, he could see the value of denying the promising Macedonian general to the Angels.

If I can kill him, Schitz thought, nearing the point of contact on his steed, *I can claim the day's glory.*

The predetermined plan was for Lyme Disease to make the first attack and flee through the Greeks, flesh-hopping back to the Persian lines while Tuberculosis and Schitz hit the Angels that tried to engage or encircle her. Schitz hoped with all his heart that Alexander would be available to him. He forced his mind to be steady as the horse's hooves pounded upon the rocky earth.

Schitz watched as Lyme Disease set upon her target, an Angel amongst the cortege of Alexander, but not the king himself. She managed to land a fatal blow upon the mortal and leapt from her horse into the Celestial. A pair of Angels dismounted into the

204 • OVER THE BROAD EARTH

Celestial to protect their fallen comrade as she shook violently. The others were too slow, and Lyme Disease successfully ran her victim through.

Experience had taught Schitz to expect the Angels within the Celestial to attempt to surround Lyme Disease. This time though, circumstances deviated significantly from the expected. The Angels turned toward Tuberculosis and Schitz and were joined by their brethren, who arrived within the Celestial.

The Angels' maneuver exposed five of them to Lyme Disease. Had she remained in place she could have easily attacked the Angels from behind. However, the red-haired vixen had already begun flesh-hopping through the Greek contingent, entirely unaware of the Angels' gambit. By opting not to surround Lyme Disease, the Angels were in a strong position to face Tuberculosis and Schitz.

"We've become too damned predictable," Schitz said. He stood with his back to Tuberculosis – a classic two-man defensive position.

"It would seem so," Tuberculosis replied. He swung his sword at the nearest Angel with panic in his eyes.

Each of them took on two or three Angels at a time. Schitz dodged one attack, parried a second, then stepped into the body of a Persian nobleman, Rhoisakes. He seized the momentary reprieve to launch an assault on Alexander.

He shouted over his shoulder to Tuberculosis. "Withdraw, I've got this one!"

Schitz knew he had presented the Angels with a conundrum. They would either protect their cherished general or pursue Tuberculosis. Schitz swung Rhoisakes's axe. A sickening sound emanated from a hapless Greek's face as it collapsed under the weight of the blow. Schitz neared his target, the unpossessed Alexander. The general was unguarded.

Schitz swung his weapon. The commander surprised Schitz with his adroit fighting skills. A tingle of warning shot through Schitz.

I have been exposed too long.

He stepped into the Celestial a moment before his mortal host was run through with Alexander's spear. The general mistakenly assumed Rhoisakes would die instantly; his innards were flowing out of a great hole in his gut. The young Macedonian's eyes bulged as his opponent lifted a massive axe above his head and, tapping into some last second of life reserve of power and rage, crashed it into Alexander's head. The helmet split in half. Somehow, Alexander's head remained unscathed.

Within the Celestial, Schitz sidestepped the swipe of an Angel's sword, wheeled, and leapt into the body of yet another Persian, Spithridates. Schitz raised the mortal's sword and readied himself to dispatch the Macedonian general. An unearthly pain, hot and slicing, cut through the host's arm. Schitz watched helplessly as the limb fell to the ground. It settled on the earth, still clutching at the sword. The wound to Spithridates left Schitz feeling woozy but did not pitch him into a full fit.

Schitz fell from the body into the Celestial Realm and began faking a departure fit. A clean-shaven Angel with long, flowing brown hair stood over Schitz with a readied sword. The foe was prepared for an easy kill. Meanwhile, other Angels began possessing mortals from the general's retinue. They had bought Schitz's ruse and saw no need to remain in the Celestial Realm.

Schitz ceased his charade and drew both his daggers. He dug each blade deep into the Angel's thighs, midway between his knees and his hips. The Angel's robes were inundated with a deep crimson that flowed outwards like an overturned wine decanter. Schitz sprang to his feet and fled towards the main body of the Persian army.

RACHAEL'S FRUSTRATION BUBBLED LIKE an angry boil. "They still managed to get two of us," she said. She was riding with Zinc in pursuit of the Demons.

"I'm sorry about Benjamin, Cousin," Zinc said. "Is the wound mortal?"

"I gave him some Manna," she replied, "but I fear it will not stop the exsanguination; it has been a long time since the bread was in Heaven."

"He is strong," Zinc said. "Let us focus on the task that is at hand, and you shall avenge your brother, dear cousin. Then we shall attend to him whatever his state may be."

Rachael bobbed her head and focused on the horizon.

A SURGE OF RELIEF flooded Schitz when he spotted Tuberculosis and Lyme Disease at the predetermined rendezvous point.

Lyme Disease, winded from her flesh-hopping and Celestial running, threw her arms over her head in triumph. "I got one! I didn't see what happened after that."

"Some sort of change in strategy," Tuberculosis said, "tried to spring a trap, but we got away."

"They're still hot on our tails," Schitz said.

The trio looked at the approaching contingent of Greeks headed by the possessed general.

"Quick to these mortals," he commanded, gesturing to a phalanx of Greek mercenaries in the service of Persia. "I will lead this charge; you two will only attack if they attempt to surround me. If they don't, I'll kill the exposed ones, and you can fall back yet again."

"So, YOU WILL FIGHT with the Persians against your own blood," Lydia said. She alternated her gaze between her husband and the outstretched waters that lapped peaceably along their coast.

"Not against my blood," Selsuceus said. "I will fight with Memnon and my fellow Rhodians."

His wife stepped closer. "Madness," she said. "Look upon the lush foliage, the calm, peaceful waters, the hills. This is your home, and it is Greece. Why would you make a widow of me to serve Persian overlords?"

Selsuceus looked at the shoreline of his holdings and turned his attention to the rolling hills and his many gardens. "The Gods have seen fit to bestow us with many of the pleasantries this life has to offer. Still, we are indebted to men like Memnon, who keep our isle pristine and safe. I will fight with him, but I will not make you a widow, my beloved."

Lydia rested her hand on his smooth beard and stroked his chin. "My dear, your visions are not of things yet to pass but of those events already written."

He nodded and attempted in vain to suppress the thoughts that intruded into his mind of faraway places and other lives, thoughts he could neither explain nor understand.

"I just know that I love you too much to leave you," he replied, placing his hand over her own. Despite all the acuity placed within his mind by The Strain of knowledge, Selsuceus was blinded by love.

He could only see his wife, not the Angel within her, the Angel who spoke to him. "Keep your promise when the time comes; ensure that you return to me."

Tuberculosis stepped toward the closest mortal in the front row of Memnon's forces. When he could not take possession, he stepped back, perplexed.

"This mortal is of a very strong mind," he said. He shook his head like he had tasted something bitter.

Schitz watched as Tuberculosis was rejected twice more in quick succession. Anxiety gave way to terror; their plan rested heavily upon occupying mortal armor. Lyme Disease attempted a possession and was similarly rejected.

"This is not a good time to have a problem," Schitz said.

Schitz turned his attention away from the uncooperative Greek mercenaries and back toward the charging Greek regulars who had drawn remarkably close. He heard a grunt and turned to see a horrific sight.

The edge of an Angelic throwing star protruded from his grandfather's sternum.

208 • OVER THE BROAD EARTH

The enemy is within throwing range, Schitz thought.

He wheeled just in time to dodge a whirring blade. Schitz drew his short sword and stole a glance at Tuberculosis. Blood from his grandfather's mouth painted the older Demon's robe a slithering crimson.

It's bad... not necessarily fatal, Schitz thought.

He shouted to Lyme Disease. "We must hold here! We can't move him under duress."

Tuberculosis coughed through a spew of blood. "Go, you two. I'm done."

Pain rushed through Schitz's body. It clawed at the back of his throat and in the corners of his eyes; it ran down his extremities. He

Japanese Shuriken & Celestial Throwing Stars

had lost his mother in his youth and barely knew his father or his grandmother. He had no siblings. Tuberculosis represented his only close family. He looked up to the older man. As he beheld his stricken grandfather on the ground, he remembered a reconnaissance during which they were infecting indiscriminate humans with their respective illnesses. They'd joked about Tetanus, Schitz's uncle, Tuberculosis's son.

"The killer blow," Schitz said, mimicking the academy instructor.

Tuberculosis brushed away tears of merriment. "I don't know why he is so fond of saying that."

Schitz glanced toward Lyme Disease as the foe closed upon them. She launched herself toward the Angels.

"We will not give up on you so easily, old man," Schitz said. He lunged toward the nearest Angel with an overhead swing of his sword. The battle commenced. The Demons' plight grew ever more desperate as a second contingent of Angels arrived.

Schitz was split between defending the listless Tuberculosis and engaging with the enemy. An Angel stepped around Schitz to deliver the coup de grâce to Tuberculosis. Schitz thrust his sword into the midsection of the would-be assassin.

With his sword impaled, Schitz drew a dagger from his belt with his left hand and swept it towards the region where he expected the next blow. The Angel's sword was a much more powerful weapon than Schitz's dagger, but the Demonic blade managed to deflect the enemy's strike. The lack of resistance threw the Angel off balance. Schitz withdrew his sword from the first and drove it through the second. Schitz kicked the Angel squarely in the midsection to clear his scarlet-stained blade. The Angel flopped to the ground, her eyes open in a vacant stare.

He turned his attention back to Tuberculosis on the ground, a trickle of bloody drool at the edge of his mouth.

"He's dead," Schitz said.

The last stand over their comrade had been futile. Schitz sighed and turned his attention to Lyme Disease. She was fighting off a trio of Angels. One caught her sword in a block, then the next swung at her. She parried deftly. The third Angel stepped back and drew a pair of throwing knives. With chilling skill, the Angel threw both blades from her right hand. Lyme Disease, having perceived the threat, blocked the knife screaming towards her head. The second blade caught her in her lower stomach. The wound itself would not have been fatal. However, the injury allowed the other two Angels the opportunity to set upon her.

Each stabbed her through the chest with their sword. As she dropped to her knees, Lyme Disease's eyes locked with Schitz's gaze.

I am responsible for this, he thought. *She stayed here because of me.*

Schitz stared at Lyme Disease from across the battlefield. She was grievously wounded, but he wanted to save her.

She looked at him and mouthed, "Go."

Schitz memorized the features of the Angel who had thrown the knife: long dark hair, small round eyes, angular nose.

I will kill you, he thought. He broke into a run.

Three... four... five... in his mind. Then... *break left.* Again... *three... four... five... break right.*

Each time, a throwing knife sailed past without harm.

"You fought well and bravely, Cousin," Zinc said as he gazed about the battlefield. The encounter has devolved into a rout. "Go attend to your brother. His wounds were grievous, but I have hope he will survive."

Rachael's voice was tinged with bitterness. "One of them got away," she said, "the one who cut him so savagely."

"Two Demons in a single battle is an exemplary feat," Zinc said. "God himself will decorate you. Now go to your brother's aid. I will continue this battle, and one way or another, he will be fully avenged."

Schitz ran through the Celestial. All about him was a maze of impenetrable mortal flesh. He had cursed, he had wondered, he had pled for a solution as he ran. Exhausted, he came upon the remnants of savagery. A trail of Angelic corpses lay strewn in a path like rocks in a shallow stream, one every few strides. Farther along, he came upon a fierce pitched battle between still more Angels and the remnants of the Reaper Squad.

Schitz saw Vertigo's older brother, Conjunctivitis, writhing upon the ground. He appeared to have suffered numerous injuries. Beside him lay the still body of Mycetoma. His throat had been cut so violently that his head hung only by the smallest amount of stubborn tissue. Mycetoma's father, Tetanus, and Conjunctivitis's sister, Influenza, battled a horde of Angels. The enemy, thoroughly bled, was unable to deliver the final strikes that would clear the Demons from the battle and existence.

Schitz assessed the situation and settled upon a bold, idiotically risky plan. As Greek mercenaries loyal to Persia were fleeing or being cut down by the Greek forces within the Mortal Realm, Schitz approached the melee. He shouted a battle cry, then turned as though addressing compatriots behind him.

"Over yonder, fresh meat for the slaughter, onwards Demons."

The potential of additional Demons was more than the remaining Angels wanted to face. Schitz watched in glee as they withdrew from the fray. He rushed to his comrades.

Tetanus slumped to knees. Influenza, the sole member of the Reapers still standing, greeted Schitz. "Where are the reinforcements?"

"That was a bluff," Schitz said.

"Damnation," Influenza said. "We must get out of here before the Angels realize they were duped and recommence their assault."

Schitz nodded. "You take Tetanus. I'll take your brother."

Schitz saw Influenza glance down at Mycetoma's lifeless corpse.

"I am truly sorry," Schitz said. "It has been a bad day for all of us; we will have to come back for him."

The pair dragged their comrades away in search of anything they could use as a door.

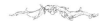

"Today was a hard-fought victory," Zinc said quietly as he stood next to Rachael. He looked down at the stone altar where Benjamin lay in state.

"I find it hard to see victory in today; only disaster," she replied with a hoarse voice.

"He looks peaceful," Zinc said. Benjamin's robes had been replaced to hide the grisly effects of his injuries.

"He looks like he will never tell me another joke, or embrace me close, or listen to my complaining," Rachael said. "He looks dead."

"I am sorry," Zinc said.

She continued, "You know, sometimes I wish we rotted like the humans, then at least it would be over. But when all this is done, all the fanfare, and the eulogizing, and commemorating of valiant sacrifice and hard-won honor, when it's all over, they will put him in the stone floor, and he won't rot. He'll sit there like some broken, discarded thing. All that was him will just sit there. Forever."

Zinc placed his hand affectionately across her back and shoulder. He felt a pang of guilt as he involuntarily appreciated her firm frame. Whereas his fiancée felt soft to the touch, he could not help but notice the muscle tone through Rachael's robe. She spoke through her tears.

"Thank you, Cousin. I know there are many to honor today. I heard you lost a younger brother. I appreciate you taking the time to stand here with me."

Zinc sighed. "Of all my relatives, there are none like you and Benjamin; you didn't change when I took over the House. You grew with me rather than trying to exploit me, I trusted him, and I trust you. I loved him, and I love you. There is no other memorial altar I would stand before, no other I would honor more than your brother, my cousin, and my friend."

"Your words are kind, and I know they come from an honest place," she replied. "They give me strength and resolve towards my purpose."

"The one who killed him?" Zinc asked.

"I will find him, and I will kill him," Rachael replied.

"He is not fully unknown to us," Zinc said.

"No, they call him 'the Scarface.' We do not know his proper Demonic name or even the illness he purveys," she said.

"I wonder which one of our lot gave him that mark across his left cheek," Zinc said.

"Whoever did probably didn't live to tell about it," she replied, "but I'll live to tell the tale of killing him."

After reiterating her vow, Rachael removed her Noble Order, the third-highest award bestowed upon angels. The Noble Order was a cross worn around the neck. She slipped the ribbon around her brother's lifeless wrist and settled the cross into his hand.

Zinc was taken aback. He, too, had been award the Noble Order and could not imagine a circumstance in which it would leave his neck.

"Your medal," he said.

"It's better for Benjamin to have it," she said. "I'd rather not remember today anyway."

Schitz sat alone beside the banks of the Styx, holding his knees close to his chest. He gazed out on the souls of the mortals as they flowed through the river onwards toward reincarnation.

All of them died fearful, sickly, and hateful, he thought. *Now they fuel our effort to gain control over their realm once and for all.*

"Mind if I interrupt your solitude," a familiar voice said from over his shoulder. Schitz turned to see Conjunctivitis approach him, a bottle of Brew in hand. His fellow Academy-mate handed him an empty cup and poured the Demonic drink into it, then filled his own before slumping down next to Schitz.

"Cheers," Schitz said cynically as he clinked his chalice against his comrade's.

"To my continued good health," Conjunctivitis said, "and to the Demon that ensures its continuance."

Schitz could not help but break into a slight grin.

"I never thought I'd be sharing a drink with one of Bubonic Plague's children." He glanced down at the contents of the cup. "Poisonous?"

Conjunctivitis patted him on the back. "We drink from the same cup, figuratively and literally, so any poison you imbibe will sicken us both."

Schitz sighed. "Say more."

"The ire of my father, the loss of a beloved grandparent, take your pick."

"I heard about Blood Fever," Schitz said. "I'm sorry for your loss."

Conjunctivitis shook his head. "And I for yours. For all that has been lost."

Schitz shook his head and drank another sip. "We lost four today."

"Indeed,"

"Four is too many," Schitz said.

"Four is just a number," Conjunctivitis said as he refilled Schitz's cup and then his own. "The number is meaningless. What matters is who we lost: Blood Fever, Tuberculosis, Lyme Disease, and Mycetoma. We lost grandparents, fathers, sons, daughters, worthy fighters all."

Schitz nodded silently in agreement.

"What also matters," Conjunctivitis said, "is that we didn't lose Tetanus, Influenza, and Conjunctivitis."

"Or Schitz," Schitz said.

"If you insist."

Schitz grinned slightly. "Well, don't take it the wrong way, but I'd have traded Conjunctivitis for any of the lot we lost today."

"Absolutely, the only one more useless than him is that Schitz character."

Both Demons laughed until the tears started to flow down Schitz's cheeks.

"Ah, drink, drink," Conjunctivitis said, tilting the bottom of Schitz's cup upwards.

"I'm sorry," Schitz said, lowering his empty cup and wiping his eyes. "I don't know where that came from."

"Look, I'm just a few months older than you. I don't have answers to any of the questions you're asking, but I can sit here with you, because I owe you my life, and I am eternally grateful."

Schitz sighed and said, "I appreciate your company, but you owe me nothing. I'm sure you would have done the same for me. Even if it would have annoyed your father."

Conjunctivitis laughed heartily. "You have no idea the discord between my father and me. He is probably disappointed that you saved me."

Schitz was shocked to hear such a brutal and candid assessment of his colleague's familial circumstances.

"I'm sorry to hear that," he replied. "Dare I ask why?"

"Well, I suppose I can't deny you after saving my life and all," Conjunctivitis said before he took a deep sip from his cup.

Schitz turned his gaze from the Styx back to his Academy-mate. "No, no, you don't have to answer, really. All you owe me is the same when our fortunes are reversed."

Conjunctivitis smiled sheepishly, his pale complexion taking on a red tinge. "Let's just say that unlike my brother, I would have never had any interest in Rubella, or Anorexia, or any eligible maiden."

"Oh," Schitz said. He was slightly confused for a moment. Then, "Oooh."

He looked down at the river awkwardly, then back over at his comrade. Conjunctivitis shifted nervously and brushed his dark bangs off his forehead, only for them to settle back into place.

Schitz shrugged. "Well, I don't see that as such a big deal. It's certainly no reason for your father to hate you."

Conjunctivitis exhaled relief and imbibed once again. "You show your good nature, but you know as well as I do that such," he paused, "penchants as mine put me and my liaison in mortal danger."

"So, you have a mate then?"

"In a matter of speaking," Conjunctivitis said wistfully, "but it is far more complicated than the type of situation to which you are accustomed."

Schitz suppressed his curiosity about the identity of Conjunctivitis's lover.

"It was terrible." Conjunctivitis let out a mirthless laugh. "My father was incessant in pairing me with Leprosy. She waited a long time for a mate. Imagine her disappointment if my father had succeeded."

Schitz joined in the laughter and thought of Leprosy. She had married a generation beneath her when she had taken Measles as her mate.

"She's just given birth," Conjunctivitis said.

"I didn't even know she was with child," Schitz said.

"Well, it is quick, you know," Conjunctivitis said, "not like the human gestation."

"Still."

"Yes, they named the boy Aspergillosis. He looks like a brute already. Must take after his father."

Schitz nodded as thoughts of Rubella passed through his mind— blatant reminders of their failure to conceive.

"My sister is pregnant again as well," Conjunctivitis said.

Schitz bit his lip. "She seems cursed by the fertility goddess," Schitz replied. "No offense."

"None taken. I know you and Rubella must be a little frustrated. Everything... uh... work okay down there?"

Schitz whirled, ready to defend his masculinity. But Conjunctivitis was grinning from ear to ear.

"Just fine, thank you," Schitz said.

Conjunctivitis staggered to his feet and executed a sloppy salute. "Oh, I think this Brew has done me in," he said.

Schitz rose to one knee. "Me, too," he said.

"In all seriousness," Conjunctivitis said—they steadied one another, "I can never thank you enough for what you did today. My sister and I are eternally grateful. She won't show it as much because of family politics, but we are both in your debt."

Schitz shook the extended hand. "You are welcome, my friend. Now let us away from the river before we are as soaked with drink as those souls with Hellish water."

RACHAEL SPOKE FROM WITHIN the mortal Roxana.

"How long do you plan to stay with the Macedonian?" she asked.

"As long as it takes to crush the forces of Hell," Zinc said. He had taken possession of one of Roxana's brothers.

"Your brother Phillip, who currently occupies Alexander, and all others who have held the post claim that his designs are lunacy. The Commander sends far too many mortal souls to the Styx. He has the mercy and fair judgment better suited for Demonic possession," Rachael said.

"But don't you see, fair cousin?" Zinc said, "We deny this monster to the Demons, and we will ensure he is disposed of after they are. We cannot concern ourselves with how much fuel is sent to Hell; we heal enough to ensure that a vast supply of mortals die peacefully. They fuel our Heavenly devices. We must destroy the forces of Hell first, and then we can bring peace to the mortals as we saddle them under our perpetual yoke."

"I understand, and I have been in support of these methods but mark my words, there is a darkness in Alexander that chills my very soul." Rachael scratched her chin, a habit when she was vexed. "It resonates even in the thoughts of his mortal bride, who I currently hold in possession."

"I understand your concerns," Zinc said. "Based on what this man has done in Tyre and Gaza, he looks like an arsonist. He means to burn the very fabric of humanity. But that is of no matter. He is our harnessed beast, and we will use his invincible army to crush the Demons. We must stay this course."

Rachael's head bobbed. "I see your logic, though I wonder if it was not imprudent to destroy the Gordian Knot. They claim it held even more power than the Amulet that parted the Red Sea."

Zinc shook his head. "I wonder this often as well. Oh, I recall the rage of Iron III and Carbon IV as though it were yesterday," he replied.

He watched as Alexander and his closest cohorts walked through the streets of his latest conquest, Memphis. Zinc drank in the scenery. He gazed at the columns of the exquisite palace and temple complex, powerful and ornate, strong enough to outlast men and their supernatural overlords.

"I miss my father," Zinc said. "I miss him dearly. I honor him by attempting to make the very best decisions for our House and for Heaven. I do not now believe, nor will I ever, that knowing how he died will ever be of benefit to us. I think it best to destroy the relics of the Titans wherever we encounter them. The last of their kind will not fight with or against us regarding these artifacts."

"So, we will stick with Alexander, although the Demons have not been presenting themselves for battle so readily. What do you plan to say to those assembled?" Rachael asked.

"We will drive into Mesopotamia and on into the heart of Persia," Zinc said. "We will continue with our original plan to build this strong and unified empire. If we sow enough health and peace in the wake of this army, the Demons will just be forced to attack. They cannot afford to allow what we are building. We have already constructed a city like Alexandria in Thrace, Dalyan, Alinda, Iskenderun, and now on the Nile Delta. We have built up Tyre and Gaza. These will be beacons of light and health even if they were first plowed by the swords of war. When the Demons eventually attack, we will destroy them."

Rachael pointed to Alexander. "The plan is working. I just really despise that man. But even arsonist tendencies will serve our purposes. The world will be reborn through fire."

Chapter 7

STRANGERS

S chitz ambled into his humble quarters, distracted by the day's events. He had sown his disease amongst the mortals with varying levels of effectiveness and had shadowed Alexander's army as it cut its way through the Persian heartland. It had been one of the many pedestrian days that seemed to comprise most of his efforts. He could still count on one hand the number of full-scale engagements in which he had taken part: the sack of Babylon, the battle of the four armies in Egypt, and Granicus stood out in his memory. He had partaken in countless smaller engagements; however, it was difficult to tell when and where the Angels would commit a large number of their forces.

Schitz's focus was drawn back to the present. He was startled to find Rubella in their chambers. She was often away on campaigns with her own squad or preparing for her debut of academy instruction, the honor of finishing top of her class.

Rubella was reclining on the lion skin Schitz had worn on their wedding, which now lay atop their bed. She bounded over to Schitz, throwing her arms around him.

"I'm pregnant!"

Schitz experienced the sensation of being doused with cold water, an overwhelming shock crisscrossing his nervous system.

"R... r... really?"

Rubella pulled back slightly. "Are you not pleased?"

"I'm, I'm overwhelmed."

"I am relieved, overjoyed, worried, happy all at once." Rubella exhaled a combination of a sigh and a squeal and wrapped her arms tighter around Schitz. "We did it, my love," she said.

Schitz picked her up off her feet; her muscular legs wrapped around his waist. He kissed her and placed her down upon the bed.

"How do you know," he asked. The process was a mystery to him.

"I can feel the heartbeats inside of me," she replied, flush with emotion.

"Heartbeats?"

"The best part," she said. "There are two."

Schitz was uncertain whether he was more taken aback by the news or by this effervescent side of Rubella. When she was younger, she had a garrulous personality. However, the events surrounding Vertigo and her introduction to war had dampened much of her vivaciousness. Schitz loved seeing the girl from the Academy, his childish tormentor, and the maiden with whom he had fallen hopelessly in love.

"The process is much more difficult than that of mortal women," Rubella said.

Schitz nodded, recalling his own birth.

"The babies will be born through the mortal woman I possess. The instant birth will kill her, thus preventing knowledge of our existence. The tricky part will be protecting me when I seize following her death and taking care of the Wraiths who will bring our children home safely."

Schitz felt warmed and concerned when he heard her utter the words, "our children." A sensation of responsibility overwhelmed him.

"It is decreed that they be born into battle," Schitz said. "Alexander and the Persians are set to engage in the vicinity of the Persian Gates. Alexander is bent on reaching Persepolis."

"This will be a far greater challenge than a normal Demonic birth," Rubella said, a serious nature returning to her voice.

"What makes you say that?"

"Your squad was annihilated, and mine consists of Smallpox and Fever, neither of whom are particularly fond of you."

Schitz sighed. "Even Fever?"

"Well, he's more ambivalent, but Smallpox and Bubonic are the closest of siblings, and Fever desperately seeks to maintain unity within our squad. He will side with his grandsons, Smallpox and Bubonic Plague, on this matter."

"We're all his descendants," Schitz said with irritation.

Rubella shrugged.

"The Reapers owe me a favor," Schitz said, thinking aloud.

"Yes, I heard about how you rescued them singlehandedly, my brave husband," Rubella said. "If not for your persona non grata status, they would give you the Knight's Pentagram."

"I'd settle for a Second Class," Schitz said.

"Oh, I assure you they think you are second class." Rubella laughed.

"Oh, ha, ha, Miss Academy Instructor," he said. "I don't know if it is wise to burn that favor, though. There may be another way."

Rubella cocked her head. "Your father?"

"Yes," Schitz said. "Yours has been distraught since the death of your mother; they say he is volatile in the field."

"And you are not close with SIDS."

Schitz's throat constricted. "I was much closer with Tuberculosis. If only he were here..."

"So, speak to Diphtheria," she said. "Do you have any idea why he is so distant?"

Schitz shook his head. "I have no clue, but now I have reason enough to find out."

"THE DEMONS WILL SHOW themselves, and we shall crush them," Zinc said to the assembled in the Macedonian's chambers.

"I give you this," Lord Iron III said begrudgingly, "the broad strategy is working, and you gave them a bit of a shock at Granicus with those brainwashed mercenaries. However, you need something to knock them out—to outmaneuver and crush them. What is your idea this time?"

The words were less of a challenge and more a plea for victory. Zinc could see it in his comrades' eyes; they were so close to triumph. The battle of Granicus had gone a long way toward balancing the scales. The mobilized Heavenly forces knew that another success of such magnitude could pave the way to the final victory.

"I will be honest with you, my fellows, I do not know." Zinc let the weight of his uncertainty hang in the air. "But I will soon enough, and when we agree on a plan, we will crush the Demons once and for all."

Zinc had learned from his father the value of candor and the means by which it could be wielded to compensate for any shortcomings.

Zinc briefed the Angels while Alexander instructed the mortals. Zinc racked his brain to think of any clever strategy. Rachael remained after the others had departed. Both angels stepped into the Celestial.

"Is it wise to admit that you have not yet thought of a plan?" she asked sternly.

"My father once told me that a soldier can smell doubt within his commander better than any hunting hound his quarry," Zinc said. He could hear his father's voice. He could still see his face and feel his hand on his shoulder. Zinc shook himself from the depths of self-pity.

"Your father was a wise Angel," Rachael said, comfort in her voice.

"He would know how to entice and trap the Demons," Zinc said.

"We need them to overcommit," Rachael said. "As always, they are content to nip at our flanks, to outfight us and flee. In turn, we try to surround them."

"But they always either escape or die hard," Zinc said, as he remembered some of the Angelic casualties from Granicus.

The Familiars who had collected the bodies for interment in the Heavenly halls had noted a brutality in the slaughter, atypical of even the normally ferocious combat between Heaven and Hell.

"A cornered animal is most dangerous," he said.

"Alexander will win this battle by encircling Ariobarzanes when he makes his stand at the Persian Gates, just as Xerxes did at Thermopylae," Rachael said, "but how will we win our Celestial struggle?"

"I'm amazed by your first statement," Zinc said.

"Well, I was speaking to Cousin Jacob. He is occupying the mind of Alexander, and he told me that the Macedonian is obsessed with crushing the Persians. He believes they will best be surrounded if they believe they cannot be. Therefore, he will commit his forces head-on in the appearance that he is unaware of the route by which he can surround their camp."

Zinc nodded. "An extra encirclement they do not see is always ideal, but where?"

"Persepolis," they said in unison.

Rachael shook with excitement. "It is difficult to open a portal in the field. Angels and the Demons typically use the apertures of tents from an army's encampment, but in this case the Persian camp will be sacked, and we can feint that this is our supposed trap."

"In reality, we will anticipate their arrival at Persepolis and ambush them there."

Zinc grabbed Rachael by both of her hands and stared into her gleeful eyes. "I love the way your mind works," he said. "You are brilliant!"

Rachael held his amorous gaze for a moment before she moved forward and passionately pressed her lips against his own. Zinc flushed with arousal as he moved his hand across her robes, feeling her strong yet feminine body beneath. Rachael broke the embrace.

"We can't keep doing this," she said, biting her lower lip. She gazed at him through her round, dark eyes.

Zinc sighed. "They keep asking when I plan to marry the Carbon girl, Cecilia."

"It will cement your position at the top of the hierarchy; bonding you to the Carbon House will weaken Lord Carbon IV's link with Iron III," she said.

"I don't care about politics." Zinc said. "I am enthralled with you. You are everything she is not—brave and ferocious in battle, and meticulous and astute in strategy. I rely on you, and I love you. It's not fair."

Rachael placed her hand on his chest and peered deeply into his eyes. "I feel the same way about you. When you first ascended, I thought you were a blowhard trying to live up to his daddy."

Zinc chuckled.

"I thought you were a savage during Passover," she said, "but to see the Angel you have become, the leader you have become... You elevate our House and bring us closer to the peace of the Final Victory. I am in love with all that you are, both to me and to our cause."

"I want to marry you," Zinc said stoically. "It is not frowned upon to marry within a House. There are those who claim that it maintains purer bloodlines."

"You sound like a Demon," Rachael said.

Zinc smirked. He knew she was correct. There had been a time when Angels and Demons both reflected the various breeds of mortals, some with dark skin and others with light. Some with round eyes, others with almond-shaped eyes. Yet while the Angels had varying Houses that bore resemblances to the plethora of humans from the varying continents, the Hellish bloodlines had converged and created a singular race of Demons, all of which mirrored mortals from Europa or the Mediterranean. There was conjecture among the Angels that the Demons had intentionally weeded out their own kind to acquire a unified resemblance. Thoughts like this made Zinc uncomfortable as his House resembled mortals from Europa. He cringed at the thought of exterminating his own kind simply because of their appearance. His mind briefly cut to the house of Hydrogen, whose members resembled the mortals endemic to Africa.

His mind churned. *Did the Demons really cull their own kind so that their features were all similar?*

He looked at Rachael. "Be that as it may, there is precedent that would support our union."

Rachael sighed. "My love, I want nothing more than to hold you close as my mate. I desire it even more than my revenge, but our love would weaken your standing. It breaks my heart."

Zinc quivered. "What shall we do?"

"The same as we always have," she replied. She leaned her ample chest against him. She glanced about Alexander's vacant tent furtively, ensuring there were no Familiars present to witness the act of their love.

"She is anything but a fighter," Rachael said. "When the time comes for her to give birth in battle, I'm certain she may not survive the ordeal."

A shock ran down his spine. For a moment, he felt a pang of guilt as he imagined his fiancée, petite and gentle. Her freckles and round blue eyes conveyed innocence, and her diminutive frame gave her a perpetually girlish appearance. In the field, she generally performed armed reconnaissance supporting the Familiars and defending them against Wraiths—far from difficult or dangerous work. The thought of killing her seemed unduly harsh. Zinc's thoughts were interrupted when Rachael pulled him onto Alexander's luxurious bed.

Later, as they pulled their robes back on, Zinc stared at Rachael and thought, *I was raised to be apart from my family, to prepare me for greatness, and I have always felt alone in the company of Angels and mortals. Yet with her, I feel a kind of peace I never knew was possible, a peace born from the death of loneliness.*

"What are you thinking?" Rachael asked.

"Just that I love you so much," Zinc replied.

THE HILLS SURROUNDING THE Persian encampment were steep, naturally defensive, and rugged. The Greek advance had stalled upon them for a month of wreckage against the taut Persian lines. While Ariobarzanes held the high ground and the wall stood firm, he could deny entrance to the Persian heartlands.

From within the Persian commander, Diphtheria spoke to his son. "I'm glad that you called upon me with your conundrum."

"Really?" Schitz asked, "because you generally seem very disinterested in me."

"If I were to be honest," his father said, "I would say that I am generally disinterested in you."

Schitz felt perturbed and intrigued by his father's bluntness.

"Why?" Schitz asked. "Even now as we speak, I feel this mortal's thoughts. They are filled with a love of homeland that is surpassed by a love he holds for his father, his mother, his wife, his sons, and his daughters. What is so wrong with me that I am not worthy of such a love?"

"First of all, you are aware you sound like a bitch?" Diphtheria asked.

The words stung but not as much as his father's visible amusement.

"Lighten up," Diphtheria said. "Secondly, try to understand. Our existence is constant pain, fighting, death, loss. To survive, I have steeled myself as best I could. You have had but a taste of what this life entails. The name of my grandfather's grandfather is lost to history, yet he was known by Fever, who I know, and through all that brief history there has been a banquet of blood. You must find your own way to survive through this unending slaughter. I have survived by being a stranger to everyone. Connections to others are distracting."

"Is it easy?" Schitz asked, intrigued to have a window into the Demon that had made him.

"No," Diphtheria answered. "I mourned my own father's recent passing, and my sister's before that, and those of my aunts and uncles. I mourned, never fully knowing them. Yet, I would not want to know them better if it meant putting my life in jeopardy."

"Is that the way it has to be?" Schitz asked.

Diphtheria nodded. "Look at my cousin, your wife's father, Botulism. He has been a wreck since Eye Fever's passing. I often remind him that he must inflict his malady upon the mortals. One day he will fall victim to the Atrophy."

Diphtheria shook his head and continued, "I loved Poliomyelitis deeply. I mean, she was my sister, and it was frowned upon for us to wed. Your grandparents never forgave us. This is Hell, and all Demons are closely related, but our choice was not an accepted one. Yet, we did it for love. When I lost her, I nearly lost myself. I do not want to go through that. I can't go through that. So, you must be a stranger."

Schitz felt a deep sense of pity as he heard his father's words, for he knew them to be full of wisdom and worthy caution.

"The mortals have it so easy," Schitz said.

"Yes," his father said. "Ironically, their ignorance of reincarnation means that they fear death unnecessarily, while we fear it justly."

"When I hear you speak like this," Schitz said, "I feel as though I cannot ask you for the favor that is on my mind."

"You can ask anything. It is up to me as to how I respond. But there is very little I would not do for you. I do love you; I just require distance."

Schitz gulped and began his plea. "Rubella and I need help for her birth."

A conflicted look passed across Diphtheria's face. He then spoke decisively. "I'll do it."

"If it's too much—"

"Don't be ridiculous, even if you weren't my son and these weren't my grandchildren, Hell needs fighters. It is my duty to do what I can."

Schitz sighed in relief.

"I tell you this," Diphtheria said, scanning the Persian positions, "the camp beyond the wall is still part of the battle. Rubella can have your twins there and still adhere to the Devine Dictum. You and I will provide her protection, and it will be the easiest and the first of many births."

Schitz was surprised and confused by his father's expression, and then he realized why; the older man was smiling.

ALEXANDER'S ARMY HAD BEEN stalled for a month by the Persian Gates. Zinc could feel an uncontainable urge in the Macedonian to advance and crush his enemies. The Angel within him also felt this desire to annihilate his foes. Zinc carefully reviewed his order of battle. He had deployed Lord Iron III and his forces to possess Craterus and his troops. They were positioned within the Macedonian main force with orders to proceed with the same frontal assault toward the wall. Lord Carbon IV had been sent to take his contingent beyond the battle to the capital of the Persian Empire, Persepolis, where he would possess a nobleman by the name of Tiridates. This Persian had been entrusted by Darius III to control the treasury and the city. If anybody could shut the gates, it would be him. Zinc, having possessed Alexander, would lead his forces through the secret path, utilized only by a few shepherds, and encircle the Persians.

Zinc's mind meandered back into his own history. After the debacle in Babylon and his rapid ascension, Zinc was still untested concerning the burden of command and the complexities of crafting either mortal or Angelic strategies. The loss of his father had left him mentally bedraggled and unable to focus on anything other than locating his sire. Rumors had abounded that the elder Zinc was in the Far East. Following God's instruction that he cease his search for his father, Zinc had remained in the East, not directly violating his sovereign's decree, yet not fully adhering to it. He came across the state of Wu beside the mouth of the Yangtze River.

Zinc found the city Gusu and its pastoral surrounding to be soothing in nature. He spent time amongst the people; he drank himself into a stupor and lay with mortal women from within unsuspecting hosts. Through these travels, he found himself in the court of King Xiong Zhen. It was there that he witnessed a young man brought before the king. The subject had gained widespread recognition for his philosophies on warfare and soldiering.

"My advisors and courtiers tell me much about your philosophies, Sun Tzu," the king said.

"Yes, my Liege," the young man replied.

"They say you would make a great general," the king said, "that you will lead our forces against Chu and return cloaked in glory."

"Yes, my Liege," the young man replied quietly.

"If you were such a man, I trust you could train any army?"

"Yes, my Liege."

"Then I command you to train my concubines," the king said with a laugh.

Zinc watched from within the body of a royal advisor as the members of the king's harem were brought into the throne room. The girls, all young and beautiful and dressed in the finest silks, giggled when presented with the enterprise. The only individual not laughing was Sun Tzu.

"With your permission, my Liege," the young man said.

Xiong Zhen gestured for Sun Tzu to commence with the exercise.

The aspiring general divided the concubines into two squadrons and instructed each squad to align itself in rows and columns. Next, he inquired amongst the court as to the king's favorite two concubines. There was jovial murmuring amongst the concubines and the court, after which two names were produced. Sun Tzu placed the favored concubines at the heads of each squadron.

"You are the officers," he instructed to each of the favored concubines. "When I give an order, you will deliver it to your squadron."

The concubines giggled in response. Zinc wondered how the young philosopher remained calm while conducting such a humiliating and pointless enterprise.

Sun Tzu stepped forward and stood between the throne and the assembled formation.

"Face Left," Sun Tzu said with a ferocious tenacity his quiet demeanor had yet to reveal. As his command echoed across the throne room, it was met with varying responses; some concubines turned to the left, others looked to the left, still others laughed in place.

"This is my error, my Liege," Sun Tzu said, returning to his docile tone, barely audible over the courtiers' hysterics. He raised his voice slightly as he continued, "In war, it is the general's responsibility to ensure that the soldiers understand their orders."

Sun Tzu demonstrated for the concubines how they were intended to step, pivot, and step so that they were now standing facing a new direction. He then returned to his spot at the head of the formation.

"Face Left," he said. This time a few more concubines turned to the left. However, the majority remained in place and laughed at the spectacle.

"This, my Liege," Sun Tzu said in an authoritative tone, "is the fault of your officers. In war, when soldiers understand their orders and do not follow their commands, the guilt lies with the officers."

Following this summary, Sun Tzu swiftly drew his sword from its scabbard and advanced toward the nearest concubine officer.

Xiong Zhen sprang to his feet and began to shout; all hilarity wiped from his face. "What are you doing?"

"In war, there must be discipline," Sun Tzu said. "There must be the severest of consequences for disobedience."

"Lower your sword," the king said.

"It is the general's responsibility to ensure victory," Sun Tzu replied in a tone as authoritative Xiong Zheng's. "Without discipline, there can be no victory; without consequences, there can be no discipline."

Zinc gasped as Sun Tzu turned from addressing the king and

violently slashed his sword across the concubine's throat. A fountain of arterial spray spewed onto the floor. Gasps of shock resounded within the chamber as the concubine collapsed onto the wooden floor of the throne room, convulsing and choking upon the rapidly expanding pool. Xiong Zheng fell back onto his throne in shocked silence. The second concubine officer, perceiving her fate, began to run towards the exit of the room, only to trip and stumble in her terror. With swift, confident steps, Sun Tzu strode towards her. He grabbed her by her lengthy, black hair, pulling it back as she howled a sickening scream. The general plunged the sword between her collar bone and her shoulder. The scream abruptly silenced; the concubine slumped to the floor.

Silently, Sun Tzu wiped the blade on the dispatched concubine's robes. As he sheathed his sword, Sun Tzu spoke aloud. "Such a beautiful face, even more so the waste that the mind behind it was so consumed with frivolity and childish disobedience."

Zinc could feel a combination of terror, hostility, and disbelief swirling within the thoughts of his host. Yet, as Sun Tzu appointed new officers and resumed the drill with silent, heightened attention from the remaining concubines, the host's thoughts shifted to those of respect and admiration. Zinc realized he was impressed by the warrior-philosopher.

The entire spectacle took on a surreal aspect. Servants removed the bodies of the butchered concubines. They then returned and scrubbed the floor clean, removing any evidence of the violence that had ended the lives of the young girls. Sun Tzu continued to instruct the concubines until they were able to perform all sorts of close-order drills, turning in all directions, standing at attention and at ease, and marching about the throne room, all in unison. Slowly, the pigment returned to the king's face. He watched a gaggle of disorganization and frivolity transformed into staunch, mature beings.

"You will lead my army," Xiong Zheng said with hushed reverence in his voice.

"Yes, Sire," Sun Tzu replied with a curt bow.

In the days and months that followed, Zinc possessed numerous individuals in proximity to Sun Tzu. He could have possessed the general himself. However, he wished to leave him unmarked. The general was a wealth of knowledge, and both Angels and Demons had a way of seeing mortals that had experienced prior possession.

Slowly, the memories of the Far East faded, and Zinc returned to the Macedonian camp. He recalled the matter in which Sun Tzu discussed with several junior officers the merits of a full as opposed to partial encirclement.

"In war, when an army is completely surrounded, its soldiers will band together as brothers and will fight with unequaled ferocity," Sun Tzu said. "Whereas, when an army perceives a route of escape, no matter how minuscule, all will flee to that point. The soldier will see his fellows more as an enemy impeding his escape than as a brother he is willing to die for."

Zinc ruminated on this teaching, the bulwark of his current strategy.

"We will allow the Persian army to escape the gates and return to Persepolis," he said to Rachael.

For a moment, he was taken aback by her beauty, for she had possessed the body of Penthesilea, a gorgeous warrior of Alexander's Companions who was named for the mythic Amazonian Queen. Perceiving Rachael's own beauty mirrored within the mortal's momentarily distracted Zinc.

Rachael smiled. "I see you approve of my host," she said with a smirk.

Penthesilea leaned forward and kissed Alexander heartily, brushing her tongue against his.

Upon breaking from the kiss, she said, "It will be a great victory that is won today."

"THERE, THEY HAVE PRESSED toward the wall again," Diphtheria said as he led Schitz and Rubella through the Persian camp.

"That will more than meet the criteria for the children to be born in battle."

Schitz felt elated and frightened as the moment approached. Hell had been spurred to battle despite the risks due to their depletion in numbers. The threat posed by Alexander's expanding empire was deemed to be too high. The Demonic forces had once again been fielded in a concentrated effort. Schitz took comfort in knowing that the Persian army would be filled with Demons. He desperately hoped they would provide adequate cover for the birth of his children.

Rubella had possessed Youtab, the warrior noblewoman, sister to the Persian commander. Schitz marveled at the beautiful combination created by Rubella and the Persian woman.

"You look gorgeous," he said to his wife from within the body of Ariobarzanes.

"The process will be quick once it begins," Diphtheria said. "We must be ready to protect her once she becomes vulnerable in the unlikely circumstance that the situation on the battlefield deteriorates somehow."

THE SHEPHERDS' PATH WAS narrow; however, the Macedonian and his forces were spurred forward both by their own motivation and their Angelic puppeteers. Their armor and weapons clattered along the rocky path. Bathed in the morning sun, Zinc felt prepared for the trials ahead. He glanced to his right and beheld Rachael within Penthesilea. She bore a face of grim determination; he would not wish to be her enemy. Rachael noticed Zinc's attention.

"The Persian camp draws near; we will surely break their hold on the gates."

I hope, Zinc thought.

He craned his neck to see the path ahead.

Any moment now, he thought as they drew close to the outskirts of the Persian encampment. Adrenaline pumped through him, a sensation heightened by the anticipation of the Macedonian commander.

THE PERSIAN FORCES WITHIN the camp had erupted into a chaotic uproar as news reached the commanders that Alexander's forces had out-maneuvered them and were approaching. Schitz looked at Diphtheria and Rubella.

We are doomed, he thought.

His father turned to Schitz. "Steel yourselves, you lovers. We are undone but not yet defeated."

Schitz drew his sword as the Macedonians began to charge upon the camp. Within Ariobarzanes, he shouted to his Persian troops. "My countrymen, whatever happens here today upon this field, it has been my honor to defend our homeland with you—to defend all which is dear to us."

He turned toward his father, who stood beside him within the general's advisor. "Thank you," Schitz said.

The Greek attack was forceful and swift.

"There and there," Diphtheria said as he pointed out Alexander and his Companions. "I count at least six Angels among their forces."

Schitz agreed with the assessment. He felt his sinews tense. The Angels cut their way through the Persian ranks, closing the distance to them with each moment.

"I expected more," Schitz said.

"It may be a trap," Diphtheria said. "They will expect us to hit their formation and flee. There is a gap in their forces on the left flank, likely intentional. We will hit their line, and I will flee there, trig-gering whatever snare they have employed. This will give you and Rubella a better awareness of the circumstances."

"I thought you couldn't allow yourself to care," Schitz said with a broad grin.

Diphtheria shoved him on the shoulder and winked.

"Better late than never," he said.

FROM ATOP THE HILLSIDE adjacent to the wall of the Persian Gate, Hayfever had a fantastic vantage point of the battle. It did not require the eyes of a seasoned commander to realize the Persians were hopelessly forsaken. Hayfever and his comrades, his daughter Leprosy and Mononucleosis, had engaged and killed several Angels in the initial exchanges along the hillside. He marveled at how predictable the Angelic strategy of encirclement unfolded over and over. For the old instructor, some encounters really were academic.

However, as the situation progressed, the Persians' situation became clearly untenable. Hayfever signaled to the adjacent hilltop where his son Bubonic Plague and his young son-in-law Measles were stationed. The Persian army within the camp appeared to have escaped complete encirclement either through a brave stand or a Macedonian error. Hayfever perceived a gap along the Persian left flank through which a large portion of the army was fleeing, pre-sumably toward Persepolis. Hayfever gestured to Bubonic Plague to maneuver in the same direction as the retreating Persians.

SCHITZ HAD FOLLOWED DIPHTHERIA into close combat with the Angels. He watched as his Father hit their lines and engaged in a quick exchange with the foe. He had deftly engaged Alexander, knocked him to his feet, killed a Companion that rushed to his aid, and then dispatched the Angel in the Celestial. As the Angel stepped into the Celestial to engage his father, Schitz rushed forward within his mortal host and knocked Alexander to the ground again. The Angels faced a conun-drum: pursue the Demon or protect the prized Macedonian. The foe opted to split their forces, half pursuing Diphtheria in the Celestial, half staying to protect Alexander in the Mortal Realm. Schitz found himself engaged in close combat with several possessed Greeks. As he blocked an overhead swipe from one, he sidestepped a thrust from another. Suddenly, an arrow struck one of the Greeks in the throat. Schitz stole the briefest of glances over his shoulder and saw a grinning Rubella within Youtab. Schitz cursed to himself as he watched an Angel writhing upon the ground, for he could not abandon his host. He needed Ariobarzanes to protect Rubella. Since there were no viable hosts nearby, if Schitz stepped into the Celestial to complete the kill, he would be stuck there.

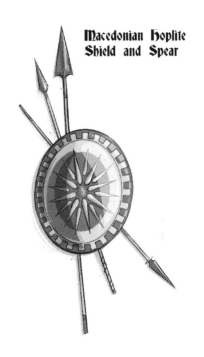

Macedonian Hoplite Shield and Spear

Under the cover of Rubella's well-placed archery, Schitz fell back to her position.

"How are you holding up?" he asked.

"I think it's starting," she said with pain in her voice and her eyes.

Schitz looked down. Youtab's midsection suddenly began to grow. Rubella fell to the ground as a puddle formed on the dusty earth. Schitz turned toward the Angelic possessed Greeks and readied himself as he stood between them and Rubella.

"They'll have to kill me to get to you," he said.

He turned briefly and met Rubella's gaze.

"I love you," she said. "No matter what happens."

DIPHTHERIA HAD FLESH-HOPPED AND fled through the Celestial in the direction of the Persian retreated. With each step, he was aware of the three Angels pursuing him and the potential to encounter more Angels attempting to complete the encirclement. He passed a rise in the hillside and came across a large contingent of Greeks possessed by numerous Angels. The Greeks were holding their position and allowing the Persians to flee unhindered.

"So, this is their subterfuge," Diphtheria said.

For the briefest of moments, he assessed his environs with the powers of observation and intuition built over countless mortal lifetimes. Schitz was defending the birthing Rubella to his rear off the right. To his left was the ambuscade of Angels. Rapidly arriving behind him to the left was a host of disengaging Demons. Diphtheria spotted Hayfever, Leprosy, Mononucleosis, Bubonic Plague, Measles, SIDS, Botulism, and Mumps among them.

If they run through this kill zone, it will be one Hell of a fight, he thought, *but if I stop to warn them, I probably won't make it out myself.*

Diphtheria had little love or concern for the Demons rushing toward the ambush zone, but he knew he could not allow the ambush to play out as the Angels intended. He raised his hands above his head, signaling to the onrushing Demons.

THOUGH HE WAS OCCUPIED defending himself and Rubella against Alexander and two of the possessed Companions, Schitz noticed a solitary, stationary Demon in the distance: Diphtheria. Schitz parried a blow from Alexander and shoved him away. He sidestepped an overhead blow from one of the Companions, grabbed him by the breastplate and shoved him into another.

He looked again at his father. Diphtheria was locked in combat with the three Angels. Initially, he held his own, but a swarm of Angels engulfed him. Schitz swore aloud as he saw his father cut down without mercy. He could not fathom why his father had stopped running, why he was waving to the retreating troops.

Having seen the intended ambush, the large group of Demons broke into countless different directions. Alexander and his Companions fell back toward the larger contingent of Angels. For a moment, Schitz held the gaze of the Angel possessing the Macedonian general. There was a mysterious meaning behind the stare that he could not quite place.

Hatred, fear, irritation?

Schitz focused and tried his best to afflict the mortal with his illness. By the time the Angel withdrew, Schitz was unsure if he'd been successful.

Without fanfare, two young Wraiths arrived beside Rubella. Both were fair in complexion with long black hair reaching to their ankles; they looked like sisters. Schitz watched the first Wraith remove a wriggling infant babe from within Rubella, a girl. The Wraith wrapped the baby within her own robe and fled the battlefield. Schitz watched the Wraith's progress with bated breath.

"Have no fear, master," the second Wraith said in a delicate voice. "We will do everything within our power to keep your little ones safe."

Schitz smiled. "My Wraith said the same thing to me on my own birthday."

The Wraith bowed demurely. Schitz watched, beaming with pride, as the Wraith wrapped an infant boy within her robes. She glanced furtively around and then ran toward one of the half-wrecked Persian tents. She carved the transportation symbols upon the ground before removing a water canister from around her waist.

Schitz looked at Rubella, who was standing beside him within the Celestial. Youtab lay on the ground, dead. He pitied the loss of the beautiful, fierce Persian. He saw the portal open. As the Wraith was preparing to step through the portal, an Angel within the body of a female Greek warrior stepped from behind the tent and stabbed the Wraith through her midsection. The Hellish midwife died whilst uttering a bloodcurdling scream.

Schitz froze in horror. The Greek warrior snatched up the boy by the scruff of the neck. Having just been born, the infant existed somewhere between the Mortal and Celestial Realms and was therefore vulnerable to both.

Schitz recognized the Angel within the Greek warrior—she was the villain who had killed Lyme Disease and Tuberculosis. She ripped her sword across the infant's neck. The tiny body dropped to the ground with a sickening thud. The Angel hurled the severed head at Schitz, a hideous, infantile discus.

Schitz bellowed a colossal war cry that shook the vacant Persian camp. Imbued with an unfamiliar rage, Schitz crashed into the embodiment of the mythic Amazon. Her sword fell from her hand. The two wrestled to the ground.

Schitz was too apoplectic to fear the Angel's ferocity. He drew a dagger from the waist of Ariobarzanes. The Angel broke the mortal's wrist.

Schitz had the thought to flee his mortal host but responded too slowly. Less than a second later, the blade pierced the Persian Commander's heart.

TRAPPED IN THE CELESTIAL, Rubella witnessed the duel. She watched Schitz seizing upon the ground, then watched over her mate with her sword drawn, ready to defend him should the Angel emerge from her host.

The Angel stepped into the Celestial and kicked Rubella squarely in the midsection, knocking the breath from her body. Sprawled across the dusty, rocky earth, Rubella watched helplessly as the Angel raised her blade above Schitz. Rubella drew a dagger from her waist, having dropped her sword, and flung herself towards her stricken husband. The blade struck the Angel in the forearm and diverted her thrust. Instead of hitting Schitz's throat, the blade plowed into his chest just below the collarbone. He howled an unearthly, ghoulish scream.

The Angel grabbed Rubella with her uninjured arm and threw her to the ground. Both women scrambled to pick up Rubella's discarded sword.

RACHAEL WAS ENRAGED WITH the amateurish nature with which the fight had progressed. She had been granted multiple opportunities to end it. However, the Demons were scrappy and had each fought tooth and nail, both in the Mortal and Celestial Realm. After being denied the opportunity to avenge her brother's death, she had turned her attention upon the female Demon, whose offspring she had beheaded. The woman had stabbed Rachael's right arm, rendering it virtually useless. Now, with her less-favored hand, she punched the Demon repeatedly. She had the sense that had she been using her preferred right she would have inflicted fractures and brain damage with her punches.

Rachael groaned in frustration as yet another blow landed less than forcefully, though it was still met with a sickening crunch of facial bones splintering. Satisfied with her efforts, she grabbed the Demon's sword, which had been dropped in the fray and raised it to dispatch its former owner.

When Schitz's vision returned, it was cloudy. His entire body burned with pain. Despite the foggy sight and debilitating agony, he saw the Angel poised to run Rubella through with a sword.

Schitz pulled a throwing knife from his belt and slung it more with hope than skill. The blade struck the Angel in her hip. It inflicted a grievous enough injury for her to crumple upon the ground. Schitz could not stand. He looked and saw the Angel crawling away. He longed to end the Angel who had taken so much from him, but Rubella was severely injured. He screamed at the retreating Angel.

"Tell me your name, cursed beast, that I might know you the next time our armies meet," Schitz shouted.

Without turning or pausing in her task of slow retreat, the Angel replied, "I am a lady of the house of Zinc, and I will kill you and all you hold dear for what you have taken from me, you scar-faced bastard."

Schitz reflexively brought his one useable arm to his face and touched the rough scar Vertigo had given him.

Ah, he thought, so this is how the Angels identify me.

Using all his remaining strength, Schitz dragged Rubella to the portal that had been intended for their son. He reopened the doorway by tracing the ancient symbols in the earth and covering them with blood flowing from his chest wound. He glanced down at the rotting pile of meat that was the corpse of the Wraith. The unidentifiable remains lay next to the headless body of his son.

"I'm sorry," he said. "I'm sorry for the both of you."

THE ANGELS RECLINED WITHIN the Palace of Persepolis. Elixir from Heaven had been brought down in large quantities. It was consumed copiously along with Manna, which was eaten to heal the wounds incurred in battle even if it was significantly less useful outside of Heaven. Zinc felt a kind of reckless abandon brought on by combat and the intoxicant. In a lack of concern for protocol or appearance, he had pulled Rachael close and kissed her in the presence of members of the other Houses. They were neither bothered by nor interested in their leader's predilections.

He raised his half-empty chalice in a salute. "We are on top of the world!"

The tepid response indicated both exhaustion and inebriation. Perched on a luxurious chaise, he looked down at Rachael's head resting in his lap. She slept deeply as she healed from the severe injuries she had sustained. Zinc felt at peace. He turned to his fiancée, Cecilia Carbon, who reclined next to him.

"How are you, fair maiden?" he asked.

"I am well," she replied with a forced smile.

She glanced at Rachael and said, "I just hope that someday I will have a greater share of your time and affection."

Zinc was fully aware of the ridiculous nature of his situation. He lay with both his illicit lover and his intended wife; the former fully intended to kill the latter.

"My Lord brother."

It was his sister.

"What is it, Catherine?" he asked, endeavoring little to conceal the irritation in his voice.

"Ah, it's Katelynn, actually my Lord, but that's no matter," she replied. "Ah... well... it's... it's... Joseph, he's having a fit. He said that the Macedonian's mind is chaotic and painful to inhabit."

"I'm sure he's overreacting," Zinc replied. He sounded calm, but inwardly he was concerned.

The Demon Rachael hated so much had done something to Alexander when they were fighting. Zinc grimaced as he recalled being knocked to his feet twice before he was forced to withdraw.

"Not my finest hour," he said aloud.

"I'm sorry?" Katelynn asked.

"There might be something to it actually," Zinc said, "but it can wait until we have recovered our faculties. Tell Joseph he may quit the possession but remain vigilant in our surveillance of Alexander. He is too valuable for us to allow him to become compromised."

Zinc's younger sister nodded and departed. He felt delicate fingers rubbing his shoulders. Maiden Carbon whispered in his ear. "Just relax. You've earned a moment's reprieve."

Conflict raged inside Zinc. He knew her kindness was precisely what he needed.

THINGS WERE FINE FOR Philea as the sun rose over the Aegean. She enjoyed the peaceful solitude of her estate while her husband and sons were campaigning in Asia. The crisp January air meant she spent most of her day in the comfort of her home. In the early afternoon, when she was contemplating whether to enjoy the carnal pleasures of one of her young slave girls, she began to feel poorly. She experienced a painful, throbbing ache throughout her body, and large painful nodules in her groin and underarms. A deep sense of fear and foreboding settled over the household, and slaves engaged in panicked whispered and frantic discussions. Slowly, the unremitting pain replaced their whispers, and soon even the light faded.

Philea was filled with an overwhelming series of conflicting sensations, all horrible, all painful. She perceived herself to be drowning in a thick, putrid liquid. Helpless and muted, she longed for the nauseating experience to end. Yet it continued and continued and continued. At one point, her head briefly broke the surface of the water. At that moment, to her dismay, she beheld two ghoulish figures sitting on the bank of the river.

CONJUNCTIVITIS RAISED HIS HAND and waved with sardonic enthusiasm as he spotted a soul breaking the surface of the Styx. A moment later, it was pulled back into the translucent depths.

Schitz's drinking companion giggled. "They always have such funny expressions on their faces when they break the surface. So much terror and confusion."

Schitz grimaced and drank another sip of his Brew.

"Oh, lighten up," Conjunctivitis said. "If you get any more morose, I think we will both fall into a stupor."

Schitz sighed. "I guess; I saw my son's terrified face in that wretched soul's expression."

"I'm sorry, mate," Conjunctivitis said. "I can't imagine what that was like."

"It's driving me crazy that I couldn't protect them," Schitz said.

"You can't think of it that way," Conjunctivitis said. "You saved your wife and your daughter. You must be grateful. How's the wound?" He touched Schitz's collarbone. Schitz winced.

"I'm lucky to be alive; she was aiming for my heart. Though she had already butchered it."

"Wow," Conjunctivitis said, "now that is poetic."

"Must be the Brew."

"Well, now you've got another battle scar to talk about when we rule the world, and all we have to do is sit around drinking and reminiscing."

Schitz instinctively raised his hand to his face.

"You know that bitch we fought, she called me 'Scarface.' I guess that's how they can tell me apart."

"That's no good," replied Conjunctivitis. "I'd rather be known as 'handsome' or 'intelligent' or 'dangerous.'"

He laughed heartily at his own joke, which elicited laughter from Schitz as well.

"I just feel a little vulnerable, being known and all that," Schitz said after a moment's pause.

"Yeah, I can see that. But does it really change anything? To have a name among the enemy," Conjunctivitis said.

"I guess if they know my fighting style, they can anticipate me."

"Don't take this as an insult," Conjunctivitis said as he poured himself more Brew from the decanter, "but do you have a fighting style?"

"Well, I've gotten better since the Academy, I think."

"What are your concerns?"

"Well," Schitz said, "I am learning to mix my methods instead of going through a predictable series of moves. I have tried to add a dimension of complexity."

Anna would be proud, he thought before he continued.

"I knocked Alexander and the Angel within him on his ass today, twice. And I would have easily killed him if I had not fought so conservatively, but protecting Rubella was my priority."

"You and your father were very brave," Conjunctivitis said, raising his glass.

Schitz clinked his cup against his companion's. "I wonder, could I have been so brave?"

"You more than held your own, my friend."

Schitz felt a knot growing in his throat. "I heard there was another ambush outside the city."

"It was brutality incarnate," Conjunctivitis said.

"There was a detachment of Angels already in the city. A small group but it contained an important Persian. They held the gate shut. Then the pursuing Angels trapped the Demons within the Persian forces outside the city."

Pressure rose in Schitz's chest; the subtle feeling of claustrophobia.

"But Bubonic Plague was instrumental in breaking them out, correct?" Schitz asked.

Conjunctivitis nodded again.

"My squad was not committed to the battle. I was told he killed numerous Angels and facilitated the escape but at a dreadful cost."

"Who?" Schitz asked.

"Hayfever, our old teacher from the Academy days, and Botulism," Conjunctivitis said.

Schitz winced. He liked his often-comical father-in-law, who, though depressed after the death of his own mate, was always attentive to Rubella.

"He never saw his grandchild," Schitz said.

Conjunctivitis shook his head.

"And I heard Leptospirosis fell," Schitz said drearily.

"Along with our classmate, Mononucleosis," Conjunctivitis said.

"Poor Anorexia. She and Mono just got married."

Conjunctivitis drained his cup and wiped his mouth. "Counting your father that makes five fallen."

A numbing sadness hung in the air.

"I hate to give him any credit, but without Plague, we would have lost the war," Schitz said.

Conjunctivitis shrugged and grinned mischievously. "I owe him even if I wasn't there; after all, he saved Chlamydial Lymphogranuloma."

Schitz said, "Oh, so that's your guy then, is it?"

"Come on," said Conjunctivitis laughing, as he rose to his feet shakily, "this Brew has already got me saying too much. Besides, we can't be late for the funeral."

Conjunctivitis attempted to stand. He put a hand on Schitz's shoulder to remain upright.

"A little too much Brew, my friend," he said. He reached down and helped Schitz.

"You know, my friend," Schitz said, "we are in danger of making these sessions a habit."

"I guess we'll just have to start winning battles again," Conjunctivitis replied.

Chapter 8
The Exorcist

The amphitheater brought a heightened sense of nostalgia for Rubella as she stared out across the rows of empty seats. A cohort typically consisted of multiple subdivisions based on age. However, the upcoming group was unusually small and would all sit on a single row. Rubella reminisced about her own time in the Academy. She could see herself and her brothers seated next to each other. She had so enjoyed the sense of comradery with her siblings and classmates. She remembered trying to get Schitz's attention, teasing him relentlessly. Her grin widened when she recalled the note she had thrown at him.

So childish, she thought, and giggled as she remembered Schitz taking the blame for the drawing.

An authoritarian voice boomed from over her shoulder. "Brings back memories, doesn't it?"

Rubella turned to meet Fever. He was a short and slender Demon with dark black hair and a large, prominent nose that seemed out of place when compared to his other features. "I'm very proud and very relieved with the path you have chosen," he said. "As valedictorian of your cohort, you are the first Demon presented with the honor of an academic position and admission into the Elites. In my time, there have been those like Hayfever who chose to teach but did not join the Elites, and those like Smallpox who joined the Elites but did not accept a position in the faculty. But like me, you have done both, and I could not be happier."

Rubella smiled. Her squad leader had been instrumental in shaping her development. In many ways, his tutelage had made her feel incredibly important, for although Fever was father, grandfather, great-grandfather, and now great-great-grandfather to virtually all the living Demons, he was reclusive and interacted little with others.

Fever set down a stack of scrolls on the lectern. "Summaries of each student within the upcoming class," he said, "compiled by the Wraiths that have been caring for them."

Rubella nodded. It was difficult for her to be separated from her child. It seemed that as soon as she had been reunited with her daughter in Hell, she was once again ripped away from her. Fever spoke as though he had a window into her thoughts.

"I will tell you the same thing I told Hayfever, the same thing my father told me. You have a unique position instructing your children. It means that you see them during the Sequester, which is quite different than the experience of all other parents. You must respect this privilege, and you must treat your children no differently than any other pupils."

A sharp pain cut through Rubella's mind each time she heard Fever use the word "children."

Ever perceptive, he said, "Do not give way to sadness and despair, my young protégé, there is time for you to have many children yet. Think not on what you have lost but on the wonderful Demon you have brought forth into this world."

Fever rummaged through the scrolls and handed one to Rubella.

"But remember," he said, "no different than any other student."

Rubella unfurled the scroll as Fever departed. A smile returned to her face as she read about the stranger that was her daughter.

THE GREEN, ROLLING HILLS and the warm climate of Sicily were an inviting change of scenery for Schitz. He was more than happy to leave the dusty, barren expanses of the Levant[24] and Near East behind for the time being. From his position on one of the many hills, Schitz beheld an endless progression of olive groves, imported by the Phoenicians, centuries earlier.

Everybody is trying to bend the world in their image, he thought.

---

[24] The Eastern portion of the Mediterranean consisting of Egypt, Greater Syria, and the Euphrates.

His thoughts wandered to the dismantling of Alexander's empire. The Angels had tried so hard to establish a kingdom on Earth, and they had nearly succeeded. Had they accomplished their goal, the flood of souls into the Eunoe, the Heavenly river of reincarnation, would vastly exceed the deluge flowing into the Styx. Yet, for all the Angels' work, it had all but collapsed within a few years following Alexander's demise. Schitz wondered if the competition between Hell and Heaven was evenly balanced, for mortals appeared in the most part to be bent upon inflicting the most grievous, frightful horrors on one another, the types of atrocities that sent a soul to the Styx and fueled the Demon's ability to open portals. Yet, despite what they did to one another, all mortals wished the opposite for themselves and the select few others for whom they felt love.

"So, who has the advantage?" Schitz asked himself.

His philosophizing was interrupted by the arrival of the remainder of his detachment. The recent spate of casualties had forced the creation of an ad hoc squad comprised of Leprosy, Schitz, SIDS, and Mumps. Schitz thought of the order of battle as he took stock of his current squad: The Elites (Fever, Smallpox, and Rubella) had not sustained any casualties in the time since his class's graduation. The Savages had lost Leptospirosis, but still had Legionnaires' Disease, Chlamydial Lymphogranuloma, and Syphilis. The Reapers had lost Mycetoma, but still had Tetanus, Conjunctivitis, and Influenza. Each of these squads had the traditional allotment of three Demons, due to the Savages and Reapers having an overload at the time of graduation. The Idealists had lost Diphtheria, leaving them with Anorexia and Autism. The Rogues had lost Botulism, leaving them with SIDS and Mumps. The Bodybuilders had lost Blood Fever, leaving them with Bubonic Plague and Measles. The hardest-hit squads had been the Academics and the Free Thinkers. Leprosy was the sole survivor of the former following the losses of Hayfever and Mononucleosis, and Schitz was the last man standing of the latter, following the deaths of Tuberculosis and Lyme Disease. They had lost just over a third of their population of fighters in the time since his class had left the Academy. However, Hell was not in a crisis because of the loss in terms of numeric proportions. Hell was in a state of emergency because of the type of casualties that had been sustained; the senior leadership had been gutted.

Fever had long held a solitary position, and there had never been a discussion of his contemporaries due to ideological reasons. However, SIDS, now like Fever, was the sole survivor of her generation. Schitz wondered if in years to come names such as Blood Fever and Stillwater would vanish from Hell's lexicon and, therefore, from the mortal world as well. Schitz felt deeply troubled by his own memory, for though it was sharp enough to remember his own birth and the events of his childhood, it was far duller regarding others. Over the passage of the centuries, he slowly forgot the details of his mother's face and the sound of her voice. He feared that the same would be true for Tuberculosis and Diphtheria.

I suppose I have to live if I am to forget them, he thought. *That comes first.*

"The Romans are making their final preparations for the assault upon Agrigentum," Leprosy said

"Very good," SIDS said. "Any sign of Angels."

"We failed to spot any." Mumps was always eager to show his involvement.

Such was even the case in youth, but Mumps was fairly average compared to his burly brother and his genius sister. Perhaps, that is what forced him to be cunning, Schitz thought.

"We will fight within the Roman army, as planned," SIDS said. "Let us hope some Angels arrive. It would be such a waste of time otherwise."

"It's always good to practice," Schitz said.

His mind drifted to his training with Anna. It had served to imbue his personality with a permanent revulsion for hedonism and leisure. No matter whatever else occupied his time, Schitz set aside time to run along the banks of the Styx, to practice with his mortal bow and his Celestial blades, and to strengthen his body and mind.

"Yes, we know how dedicated you are to labor," SIDS replied sharply.

Schitz felt the sting of her ridicule. He did not know why his grandmother, his last surviving immediate relative, had always been so callous towards him. While Tuberculosis had expressed genuine love and care, and Diphtheria had exuded a kind of disinterested support, SIDS seemed to express a genuine antipathy towards Schitz. The reason for this hostility eluded him.

"As long the Wraiths determine that the Romans have not come under interest from the Angels, we will proceed as planned," SIDS said.

Schitz thought of Elise for a moment, the last truly familial relationship he maintained outside of Rubella. Elise was a constant support both emotionally and practically. He thought about her kind in general; descendants of crossbreeding between Titans and humans, they were effectively slaves to Hell. Wraiths were generally considered expendable due to their fragility. However, the scouting and supportive services they provided were essential for the functioning of Hell and its army. Schitz set in his mind to seek out Elise when they returned to Hell; it had been far too long since they had a conversation.

RUBELLA LOOKED OUT ACROSS the young faces eagerly gazing up at her. They comprised the entirety of Hell's hopes for victory. In her lifetime, they had lost fourteen Demons, thirteen in action against the Angels and Vertigo in the dual with Schitz. The seven youths who sat before her would only replenish half that number. In qualitative terms, however, it would take centuries for them to reach the level of skill possessed by the departed, both in fighting prowess and disease cultivation.

Rubella looked first at Influenza's children: Cytomegalovirus, Encephalitis, Reyes Disease, Actinomycetoma, and Pneumonia. Rubella thought it might have been more of a scandal that only two of the children resembled her mate, Legionnaire's Disease. Encephalitis and Reyes Disease, twin girls, both had Legionnaires' gray eyes that matched their silver hair and small angular noses. However, the boys, Cytomegalovirus, Actinomycetoma, and Pneumonia all had dark hair, a trait not found in either parent. Additionally, Actinomycetoma bore a striking resemblance to his namesake, the late Mycetoma.

How salacious, Rubella thought smugly. *Of course, the naming was purported to be in honor of their fallen classmate. Yet, he had grown remarkably to his likeness as the years had passed.*

Rubella shifted her attention to Leprosy's child, Aspergillosis. He resembled his father's build. Even at this young age, he was much taller and broader than his peers. Leprosy, the odd woman in her own cohort, had picked the most physically fit member of the next class. Rubella often cringed at the thought of her sister-in-law being from a prior generation. She recalled the amusement of her peers, claiming that Leprosy had "found a young stud."

Of course, since Demons did not age beyond their prime, it was soon impossible to tell the difference in age between Leprosy and her brother. However, his simple nature would always render him the subordinate of the two. Rubella hoped that her nephew would be good-natured and kind to his fellows like his father and not dark and conniving like his mother, who seemed aligned with Bubonic Plague and his hatred of Schitz.

Thoughts of Schitz brought Rubella's attention to her final student, her own daughter, Rabies. She had dark hair like her father and their fair complexion. She was slightly built yet tall. Rubella imagined she would develop into a strong adult, despite her slender frame, just as her mother had. She swelled with pride, then recalled her squad leader's admonition: "You must treat her as you would any other student."

Rubella began. "Today, you start your formal education though you have already seen battle."

Her thoughts returned to the Persian camp, where she beheld an Angel decapitating her newly born son. She cringed as she watched his body fall like a sack of grain on the hard, unforgiving ground. Rubella collected herself. "And you have already received instruction from your Wraiths and perhaps your parents."

Rubella felt a pang of loss cut through her mind. She had given herself over to her missions and to planning for her position at the Academy. She could not remember a single instance in which she had taken time to attend to Rabies. She had left this task to her Wraith, Constantina.

"Now you enter the Academy," she said. "Now you will hone your intellect and your fighting skills with which you will battle Angels. You will cultivate a disease that will ravage humanity. And most importantly of all, you will learn why we are here."

A sense of calm washed over her, and she realized that all of Hell was counting on her to educate the next generation of warriors.

"Our Lord was present for the moment of creation. For it was his existence that created all things. For he is immortal and wise. In the beginning, our Lord saw to the birth and destruction of all mortal things, keeping existence in a balance. He did this through control of the elements that hold the realms together: water, earth, air, and fire. As his children, you will also learn to manipulate these elements. The world lost balance when the species known as the Titans gained consciousness and rebelled against our sovereign. Thus, our Lord was compelled to craft us, his loyal adherents, to battle these usurpers. The Lord crafted us in his image: immortal, powerful, perfect," Rubella said.

Pneumonia raised his hand.

"Yes, Pneumonia," Rubella said.

The child rose to his feet, his hands by his side. "How are we immortal if we can die?"

Rubella smiled. "Our Lord has blessed us with ageless youth, but it is true that we can fall in combat. He did this so that only the worthiest of Demons would live to see eternity."

Pneumonia returned to his seat. Rubella continued, "It was after our defeat of the Titans that an upstart Demon broke from our Lord's grace and rebelled against him. This deceiver stole our Lord's knowledge and fashioned his own Celestial Realm and his own army: Heaven and the Angels, respectively. Thus, it falls to us to defeat these heretics and usher in the final victory."

Rubella carried a strong sense of satisfaction as she imparted knowledge to the youngsters. She beamed with joy. "There is so much for you to learn," she said, outlining the topics to come, "the customs of our Church, the Divine Dictum, utilizing the elements for travel, strategy, the crafting of disease, and the list goes on and on and on. I hope you are all as excited as I am."

Rubella surveyed the crowd and observed a variety of expressions ranging from disinterest to fascination. She noted that Pneumonia was the most attentive of all. She glanced between him and Rabies, and she began to formulate a plan.

Roman Pilum

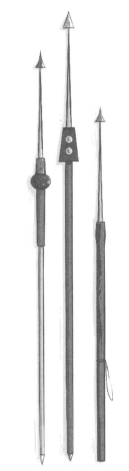

THE ROMAN SQUADRONS ADVANCED with a combination of precision and uniformity that conveyed a forcefulness Schitz had not seen in the ranks of Zargon, Nebuchadnezzar, Ramses, Leonidas, or Alexander. It was improbable that history would elevate the name of Lucius Postumius Megellus to the pantheon of great tacticians. Yet, under his command outside of Agrigentum, he led the perfect accumulation of military knowledge melded into the absolute fighting force. The ranks advanced in lockstep toward the foe. Schitz stood with Mumps and the Velites, lightly armored skirmishers each carrying a spear known as a "pilum." As they approached the Carthaginians, Schitz could sense his host's trepidation. Schitz understood the young Roman's apprehension as he beheld the massed

African forces, a horde of barbarian troops comprised of mammoth war elephants, cavalry, and fierce warriors. Attending to his own concerns, Schitz scanned for Angels inside Hannibal Gisco's troops. He had yet to observe any when he heaved his pilum towards the front lines of the enemy. Schitz stepped into the Celestial as the Velites withdrew through the gaps purposely left in the lines of the heavy infantry.

THERE HAD BEEN A time when Schitz felt naked within the Celestial surrounded by mortal combat, vulnerable to the Angels, bereft of a mortal shield. However, upon the field at Agrigentum, he felt control and calm as he surveyed the destruction wrought by the two warring armies. He was about to speak to Mumps, who had joined him in the Celestial, when he perceived a handful of Carthaginian troops with the light aurora that proclaimed Angelic possession.

"Do you see them?" he calmly asked Mumps.

"Who?" Mumps replied. Anxiety filled his voice, his eyes darted side to side.

"There, amongst the reserves," Schitz said. "Odd that they would arrive so late."

"Maybe it's a trap," Mumps said. He looked over his shoulder towards the ranks containing SIDS and Leprosy.

"They're probably novices," said Schitz, "or more scouting than properly committed to battle."

Schitz assessed the situation. Hell was on the defensive and could not risk casualties on speculative ventures such as Sicily. Schitz had brushed off the possibility of a trap but recognized the possibility of subterfuge. Judging Mumps's skittishness, the second-guessing nature of SIDS, and the hostility of Leprosy, Schitz determined he would have the most freedom of action if he led the way. Additionally, if there were a trap, he preferred to spring it without the hindrance of his compatriots. As he ran forward within the Celestial, his attention shifted to the war elephants in the Carthaginian reserve, and an idea took shape.

"This empire will be even grander than that of Alexander's," Zinc said. He and Rachael strode the broad, cobbled street leading up to the temples of Saturn and Concord and the numerous other houses of worship that comprised the Roman Forum.

She sighed and gazed across the city scene of men and women meandering across the many avenues and walkways. "Their robes are so similar to ours," she said.

"Are you serious?" he replied, taken aback by her disinterest.

"It just feels so pointless," she said. "Your idea was good, but it seems too grand to materialize."

Her words flayed his pride. He was, after all, Heaven's leader. Following the fall of Alexander's Empire, Heaven had issued a vote of confidence, but Zinc constantly sensed his vulnerability to being unseated.

"I've worked so hard to build up my standing," he said.

"I know," Rachael replied. She turned her attention away from the crowd and nestled her head into his chest. "It's all just mundane to me. I long for things beyond this moment's grasp."

"The Demon with the scar?" he asked.

"The Demon with the scar, you, take your pick," she replied bluntly.

Zinc felt another prick to his ego.

"I am sorry it is taking so long to... to mend the situation."

"Cecilia has given you four sons and four daughters, more than enough to carry on your House and to expand new Houses should the need arise. I fear all this breeding has led to true feelings between you two."

Schitz's Notebook

Roman Velite

These troops are just one of countless examples of the Roman mastery of strategy: the spear cannot be thrown back by the enemy, the armour is light but effective allowing for maneuverability. I was unafraid in the face of the enemy when possessing these mortals.

Zinc moaned. "If you can fancy a way to dispose of her quietly, I have already sanctioned it."

"But how can I do it quietly when she is surrounded by Familiars on her pathetic reconnaissance endeavors?" Rachael asked.

Zinc groaned in frustration. "What do you want me to do? They would put me to death for treason if I orchestrated the death of another Angel, and our customs don't allow for divorce."

Rachael looked about the busy scene from within the Celestial and shouted, burying her face in her hands.

"What is pressing the issue so much at this juncture?" Zinc asked.

"My father, your uncle," she said with obvious cynicism, "has insisted that I am not to remain as your concubine. He feels shameful for allowing it and powerless to stop it."

Zinc flushed with embarrassment. What he'd always imagined as private was now very public in nature.

"We all know that a restructuring is coming soon; there will be new Houses incorporated, and new Standard Bearers will need wives to begin their progeny. My father is insistent that I be one of those wives. I will no longer be 'Rachael' but a 'Lady' of a House," she said with a regal air to her words.

"Is that what you want?" Zinc asked. He fought back tears.

"What I want has mattered very little in my life, my love," she replied. "Now come, this is a rare holiday. Where to next? The Colosseum? The chariot races? An orgy? The choice is yours."

Zinc forced a smile. "You always know how to cheer me up."

THE ANGELS THAT HAD arrived at Agrigentum were indeed novices. Schitz managed to bypass them entirely, putting at ease any concerns pertaining to a trap. From within the Carthaginian ranks, he had launched confusion and discord that had resulted in a stampede of the war elephants and a complete collapse of the fighting forces. The remainder of his squad had mopped up the Angels and taken the field much like the conquering Romans. Upon linking up with the rest of the squad, Schitz and the others had departed the field as victors.

They happened upon a small, nondescript town that would be too tiny to have made it onto any map or any history of the isle of Sicily. The inhabitants of the hamlet, the Sicani, had traveled from Iberia centuries earlier. Though they were the constructors and occupants of the village, there was not a mortal soul in sight.

"Any of these doorways will suit our purpose," SIDS said bluntly.

Schitz looked around the apparently abandoned village from within the body of a Roman legionnaire. The hair on the back of his neck bristled.

"Where are the villagers?"

"They probably fled into the woods to avoid any marauding soldiers," SIDS said.

Ever eager, Mumps bent down and began to trace the symbols requisite to open a portal for their escape.

The villagers emerged from the dwellings. The ambush was well coordinated and quickly overwhelmed the mortal legionnaires and the Demons within. Since the Sicani were primitives, fighting mostly with blunt weapons and stones, none of the Romans were killed before the Demons had the opportunity to step into the Celestial.

Schitz surveyed his surroundings. Mumps was thrashing about upon the ground. The mortal he was within had been restrained by several of the Sicani and was pinned to the ground, a fate shared by the other Romans as well. Although the legionnaires had struck down numerous villagers, soaking their gladii in primitive blood, ultimately, they had been subdued.

"Just leave the body," Leprosy shouted.

"I can't," Mumps said. Panic etched his face. "Help me!"

Schitz was astonished to see the senior Demons frozen in fearful indecision. He looked over to Mumps and was met with a terrifying image. The man who was inflicting the suffering on Mumps was clad in a long, brown cloak decorated with the pelts and bones of many animals. His head was crowned with deer antlers. The man's muscular forearms bore numerous lacerations in various stages of healing. The cuts appeared self-inflicted and formed the shapes of many ancient symbols.

As Mumps screamed for assistance from within the Roman, the mortal host's eyes rolled back in his head, pure white pools. The Celestial echoed with Mumps's pleas for aid. The mortal host shouted in a Demonic tongue.

Schitz moved to help. He tried to possess the human, a creature he assessed as a Shaman. Schitz was repelled by strong mental forces. Schitz moved into one of the Sicani. He raised his host's crude iron sword. Suddenly, he had trouble breathing. Though he saw no one, it felt as if someone's hands were around his throat.

Schitz looked at the Shaman, whose eyes burned with a reddish fury. Using the Demonic tongue, the crazed holy man addressed Schitz.

"You as well will serve as a fine sacrifice to Dana and a warning to your fellows. You will pay the price for desecrating mortal flesh by your presence within."

The Shaman returned to his assault on Mumps. Schitz watched on, gripped by a terror he'd never known. He trembled, helpless. The Shaman uttered a series of mantras. When he completed his incantation, Mumps was ripped from the body of the Roman.

Mumps appeared within the Celestial; a gelatinous puddle without a single defining characteristic of his previous incarnation.

Leprosy had begun opening a portal near one of the doorways further away from the Romans and their Sicani captors. Schitz was filled with an unfathomable hatred for the erstwhile comrades who were so quick to abandon him. He saw no path to victory over the Shaman and resigned himself to his fate.

Thoughts of Rubella and Rabies passed through his mind along with an overbearing sadness. Then, to his surprise, thoughts of Anna occupied his attention—her sharp smile, her piercing eyes, their passionate embrace by the oasis. He missed her so and would never see her again.

Oh, what I would give for one more moment along the Nile, he thought.

He was readied for his demise, only to be shocked when he experienced not the slightest amount of pain. He looked at the Shaman, who spoke.

"This one is not like the others; there is light in him."

Can he read my thoughts, my memories of Anna, an Angel? Or is it something about my own composition he sees?

His airway cleared and breath returned. He took the opportunity to exit the mortal's body. He raced towards his comrades with a bewildered sense of relief.

"What happened?" Leprosy asked.

"I don't know," Schitz said. He was still angry about their lack of assistance. "Let's just go home."

"I'M NOT SURE I understand," Aspergillosis said. "Why can't we just wait for our Lord's son to arrive. If he is so essential for the final victory, why hasn't our Lord provided him? And for that matter, why hasn't the pretender, the false God, produced his supposed messiah if all of this is foretold in our canon and theirs?"

Rubella did her best to suppress a smile. She loved to watch her students contemplate the mysteries of the Demonic Church.

"Well, would any of you like to answer your colleague?" she asked, pushing them to seek the answer from within the knowledge she had already imparted. "Pneumonia?"

The young Demon rose to his feet and said, "Matters regarding the fulfillment of prophecy are known to the Lord and the Lord alone. We must fight here and now because that is the task for which we were created."

"Very well put," Rubella said. "Now for the ladies, since we are on the subject of the Devil's son, why is it important that you remain pure until you have chosen a mate?"

Rubella felt a swell of pride as Rabies raised her hand.

"Yes, Rabies," she said.

"The Lord and the Falsifier are the sole survivors of their House. Therefore, for the Lord to sire his progeny, he will choose a Demonic maiden whose virtue is pure, a maiden unknown to Demon or mortal."

Rubella found it impossible to suppress a maternal grin. "Very well put."

Fever entered the room. Rubella called the class to attention.

"All rise and salute!"

In unison, the young Demons rose and brought their right hands across their midsections in Hell's salute. For a moment, Rubella wondered if Fever had arrived to tell her off for showing nepotism toward Rabies. However, when she met the senior's gaze, she saw a softness in his eyes.

"At ease," he said to the class.

The students returned to their seats. Fever spoke softly to Rubella.

"I am sorry to be the bearer of bad news, but you must ready the class for a funeral—your brother Mumps. Also, I've been told that there is some bad business pertaining to your husband."

THE RETURN TO HELL had been a blur. The Priests chanted a hymn and lit incense within their thurible.[25] Leprosy and SIDS acknowledged the Priests before rushing off. Schitz remained until the hymn was completed. He was filled with vivid memories of what had happened to Mumps and wondered why he had been spared.

On the way to his room, Schitz was intercepted by the High Priest, who was accompanied by Leprosy and Bubonic Plague. Plague was radiant with apparent delight, sporting a broad grin.

"You are summoned to appear before our Lord Satan for trial," the High Priest said. He avoided eye contact.

"Trial? What is the charge?"

"Treason," Bubonic Plague said. His glee was unrestrained. "And when they find you guilty, they'll do to you what they should have done when you killed Vertigo."

"I killed Vertigo in a sanctioned duel that you instigated, you buffoon!"

The High Priest snapped a command. "Enough! There will be a fair trial, and then our Lord's justice will be administered. Until then, there is no reason for further discussion."

Schitz was led through the Great Hall. He was filled with a humiliating sense of vulnerability. There were Priests performing the return ritual, and Wraiths decorating an altar for Mumps's funeral. Random Demons passed, all staring with peaked interest in Schitz's direction. He felt naked and terrified and enraged all at the same time. For a moment, he was distracted from his own self-pity by a simple black urn atop the solitary altar in the middle of the Great Hall.

---

[25] A metal Censer.

I escaped the Shaman's destruction only to face this horrible new fortune, he thought.

The procession of embarrassment continued past the Great Hall and through a corridor— one Schitz had only seen the Devil use. Despite his circumstances, Schitz was curious. He walked into a room containing a throne and several chairs, an ornate rug, and numerous elaborate trophies from the mortal world. The walls were decorated with captured weapons, animal hides, and armor of all kinds. Behind the throne, a solid, wooden door led to further mysteries. Schitz was led down a different corridor, which was lined by small wooden doors, each containing a tiny peephole. They stopped at a door. The High Priest reached into his robes and retrieved a set of iron keys. The door creaked open with an agonizing groan.

Satanic Incense Thurible

Schitz stepped into the small barren chamber. The door closed behind him. The black stone walls looked like everything else on Hell's grounds. There were no furnishings.

This place is designed to inspire madness, Schitz thought. *What have I gotten myself into?*

SATAN RECLINED UNCOMFORTABLY ON his ornate, black throne. He sighed audibly, restlessly moving his scepter back and forth before speaking with heavily labored words indicative of his indignation.

"I will reiterate. Without this exorcist and his explanation for why he spared Schizophrenia Incenderos Nervosa and killed..."

He looked up, flustered.

"Mumps Paraoyxmos Salivare," the High Priest said.

"Yes, why he spared Schizophrenia and killed Mumps," the Devil said with little apparent interest, "... without this mortal, this exorcist's explanation, there is basically nothing we can say about his supposed treason."

"Supposed treason, my Lord?" Bubonic Plague could scarcely contain his indignation. "You have word from my sister Leprosy, and the little rat's own grandmother, SIDS. The mortal Shaman spared him. Why, if not due to his treasonous nature?"

Satan rose and held up his hand. Everyone fell to their knees.

"Treason indeed," the Devil said. "However, if I condemn a Demon to death based upon suspicion alone, you lot will come clamoring to me every time you have a petty grievance. I cannot have this. Nor will I put down a solider as effective as Schizophrenia over supercilious jealousy."

"Effective, Lord?" Bubonic's sarcasm was undisguised.

"Yes, effective," the Devil said. "I know you and your retinue are responsible for the highest body count on any given day, but there is an efficacy to Schizophrenia. Despite what some people say," he stared at Bubonic Plague, Smallpox, and Leprosy, "and their attempt to diminish his reputation, I have heard whisperings of his success in the field."

Bubonic Plague sucked in a breath to issue a retort, but the Devil continued over him.

"Find the Shaman, or I will release Schizophrenia and unburden my pent-up rage upon you for wasting my time."

"Yes, my Lord," the trio replied in unison.

Satan collapsed onto his throne. "So, at long last, we arrive at the true matter at hand," he said.

He glanced about the room, gazing across the faces of those assembled. They represented the world he had created, Priests, Wraiths, and Demons. The Devil reflected on the ongoing struggle with his brother. Their kind had all but been annihilated in war with the Titans, and yet they could not see fit to rule their hard-fought prize together. Thus, he had created his army to do battle with his brother. He had enslaved the descendants of mixed Titan and human origin, the Wraiths, breeding them with mortals until they had been sufficiently weakened to a permanent servile state. He had created his Demons by mixing with mortal women, a painstaking pleasure through which he created a powerful race he could control. Then, he had fashioned his Priests by breeding Demons with Wraiths. This class, though ageless like the Demons, was not created to fight but to uphold the religion through which he commanded the obedience of his forces. He did not want anyone to fight as his family, but as his devotees.

If I ever defeat my brother, he thought, *I will reveal myself to the mortals, and they will make up the base level of the power structure and worship me. I will feed them disillusionment. That way, the Styx freely flows. But they will bow to me for all eternity only if I am victorious.*

Satan turned his attention back to his underlings. "I have assembled you today because I have decided to disband the Warring Clans."

There was a collective gasp.

Fever replied first. "My Lord, we have always had our fraternities of battle. They solidify our camaraderie and aid the transition of the youngsters from the Academy to active service."

"I know, I know," Satan replied. "You have always had your cliques, the Brains, or the Brawn, or whatever you call yourselves. But it is not working. You do not share enough information among your squads, and you do not work well enough together."

"I most humbly disagree, Sire," Fever said. "Schizophrenia saved the Reapers at Granicus, even after his own squad was cut down."

Satan raised an eyebrow, visibly intrigued. "And we rewarded him with The Knight's Pentagram, I presume?" he asked, turning his attention toward Bubonic Plague.

"There were conflicting reports of the event, my Lord," Mephistopheles, the oldest of the Wraiths, said.

"Conflicting from whom? Let me guess, Bubonic Plague?"

"He did speak on behalf of his children," the Wraith replied awkwardly.

"It doesn't matter," Satan answered. "I have made up my mind, and the clans are disbanded. Current members can still carry any customized weapons or gear, but no new materials are to be made. In place of the clans, we will institute a Triumvirate Council on which will sit elders of the Demons, Priesthood, and Wraiths. This council will strategize all operations and will be responsible for reporting all outcomes directly to me."

The sense of anticipation and intrigue was palpable as the assembled awaited further details of the overhaul.

"I have selected Fever, Bubonic Plague, and SIDS to represent the Demons. Mephistopheles, Elise, and Anubis will represent the Wraiths on the Council. The High Priest Titus and the Priestesses Erin and Desdemona will represent the Church."

Satan glanced across the room. He furrowed his brow. His voice sounded like broken glass. "The High Priest will have final say amongst any disputes as he is my voice in my absence."

Due to his different breeding, Titus appeared slightly older than the Demons, who maintained perpetual youth, though not as elderly as the senior Wraiths. The creases around his eyes grew as he suppressed a grin.

"I expect you all to work together in bringing about an end to this wretched, prolonged conflict," Satan said. "You are dismissed."

ELISE WAS THE FIRST to visit Schitz in his cell. He had heard her soft yet authoritarian voice from the far side of the wooden door.

"What on Earth have you gotten yourself into now, my son?" she asked.

"Oh, Mama, I haven't the slightest idea," he replied.

"Do not do that," she replied.

"What?"

"Do not give up or feel sorry for yourself. Whatever this is, whatever brought it about, there is a solution to it."

Tears streamed down his face. "I won't," he replied, vainly attempting to stiffen his voice.

"I've just come from a meeting," Elise said. Her excitement was obvious. "Our Lord is highly speculative about the allegations against you. It seems that without the mortal exorcist's explanation, you will be exonerated."

Schitz's heart raced with the positive news, but he tempered his exuberance. He knew he still faced the possibility of execution.

"Be patient," she said. "Do not allow the isolation to get to you. Train your body and mind to cope with the deprivation. I will return to you soon, my son."

"I CANNOT EXPRESS TO you enough how little interest any Demon has in going anywhere near the Shaman," Leprosy said.

She and Bubonic Plague walked through the city of Syracuse.

Bubonic Plague ignored his sister's comment. "How do the Angels always manage to build such empires? First Alexander, now the Roman Eagle?" he asked.

"They fought with Carthage here in Sicily," she said, "brief as it was."

"Yes, while they were consolidating their hold over Rome itself," he replied. He looked at the Phoenicians from the Celestial. "What was he like?"

"The Exorcist? He was an older mortal. He dressed in the old way, primitive, furs, and skins."

Bubonic Plague shook his head. "I thought the knowledge of exorcism had been lost to the mortals, but I lifted the lid of the urn, and there was no doubt as to how Mumps met his demise."

Leprosy shuddered. "I never want to see anything like that again." She placed her hands on a young couple as they passed her, inflicting her disease upon them. "It was disconcerting," she said.

"I have no wish to die that way," Plague said. He reached for a mortal and transmitted his affliction. "Therefore, I have sent Smallpox to find *a* Shaman, to take the place of *the* Shaman."

"You are unrelenting," Leprosy said.

"I will avenge my son."

"Is that all this is about?" Leprosy asked. "We all lose our children, parents, spouses."

"That's interesting coming from you," Bubonic Plague said, "since you still have your spouse and child."

"And you still have your spouse and children, Brother," she said.

Bubonic laughed and placed his large hand on his sister's demure shoulder. "Ah, life changes, sister. I swear we were just back at the Academy, arguing whose disease was better."

Leprosy smiled. "What is it then?"

Bubonic Plague looked away across the bustling Sicilian streets. "I was always proud of Vertigo. I thought he was going to inherit the world of Hell on Earth. I thought he would make me proud. Also, when we do win this war and establish our perpetual reign, the Demons of the highest order will be royalty. That's why Fever is hanging around, to be the highest Demon in the afterworld."

"Ah," Leprosy said. "And you thought that your son could help deliver that for you."

"It sounds selfish," Bubonic said, "but it was all I've looked forward to, for us and our family."

Leprosy nodded. "All right, I'll ensure that SIDS and I identify whoever you drag before Satan as the exorcist."

Bubonic pointed and shouted. "Look at that!"

A pair of Angels within the Celestial emerged from around a street corner.

"Not now," Leprosy said. She extended a restraining hand. "There is no battle here; we cannot have you on trial as well."

After Elise, Schitz was visited by Rubella. He longed to touch her body through the cold, lifeless door.

"I miss you so much," she said. "I don't understand why you're here."

Guilt carved at Schitz's heart. He remembered his frequent remembrances of Anna.

"I miss you, too," he replied. "I'm dying to kiss you just one more time."

"Don't talk like that," she said, emotion dripping from her voice. "They'll free you, and you'll kiss me every day, forever and ever."

Schitz blinked back tears. He looked around the bare room for anything to take his attention away from his situation. "How is Rabies?" he asked.

Rubella's voice lightened slightly. "Rabies is with child."

"How long have I been in here?"

He heard a sob through the door. "A long time."

Schitz looked up toward the black ceiling. He tried to work through the competing emotions: sadness, joy, regret, hope.

"I have so many questions," he said. "Who is the father? Have they wed?"

Rubella's answer was a little lighter. "Oh, he is such a bright lad. You would really like him. His name's Pneumonia. I practically forced them together."

Schitz's head snapped back. "Influenza's son?"

"Well, yes," Rubella replied.

"The grandson of Bubonic Plague."

"Well, yes, but—"

"My persecutor!"

Rubella whimpered.

Schitz recoiled at his own personal rage. He realized his feud with Bubonic's lineage had caused his love nothing but grief.

"Don't fret," he said with feigned joviality. "Don't you see the genius of your matchmaking?"

"Genius?"

"Their union is the perfect opportunity to unite our warring factions, maybe not Plague but surely the others."

Rubella's voice lightened instantly. "Do you think, love?"

"Of course," he replied, "but tell me more, does she have a name planned?"

"Maleficorum Incarnatia, but Malaria for short," Rubella said.

Schitz could tell his wife was smiling by the tone of her voice. He was glad he had suppressed his rage.

I'd have preferred for her to marry Autism, he thought, but he chose not to voice his opinion. *I don't know how many more times I may talk to Rubella.*

"My love," he said, "I do not know what course these events will take. If the Devil's decision does not run in my favor, please do not be there when they carry out the sentence. I do not wish for you to remember me that way."

He could hear Rubella sobbing from the other side of the door.

"Also, please don't bring Rabies here. She'll remember me from her birth, and that is best."

Rubella nodded through her tears, then said, "Of course."

Schitz rested his cheek against the door. "No matter what happens, despite all that has happened, I love you so dearly."

ONE DAY WITHOUT WARNING, a small slat opened in the door.

Schitz heard the High Priest. "Hands!"

Schitz slid his hands through the opening.

The High Priest groaned. "No, you dolt. Put them behind your back. Are you daft?"

Schitz winked. "Just don't have your experience with restraints, I guess."

The iron manacles were cold and heavy. The door protested when it swung open.

Schitz was met with a large portion of the Priestly contingent. Titus, the High Priest with his long slender nose, small round eyes, and generously silvered black hair, wore the part of an Infernal Pontiff well. Behind him, the various Priests and Priestesses of the Church stood in elaborate, embroidered robes.

The Priests led him to the throne room. He stood in a makeshift dock. Everyone he knew was present and standing behind him, facing the throne. The Priests stood on his right, and his left, and a trio of Demons huddled around a small table at the base of the steps leading to the throne.

Perched upon the throne sat the Lord of Hell. His demeanor was as haughty and aloof as always, and he appeared irritated by the necessity of his presence. Seeing him in person, Schitz was amazed by his likeness to other Demons. The Devil was not overly muscular; he was of average height and build, a little on the thin side. His dark hair stood in stark contrast to his pale complexion.

But his eyes set him apart, deep and melancholy—two orbs of an endless abyss—a look of vast emptiness imbued with the power to extinguish all life.

Schitz looked away, then was drawn back. He had an intense longing to serve this powerful entity. Since birth, he had accepted his role in the overarching plot of Hell versus Heaven, and the proximity to his Master served as a potent reminder.

I wish this were under different circumstances, Schitz thought.

Satan opened the proceeding. "My loyal subjects, we are gathered here to address a grave matter. A member of my forces stands accused of treason. Schizophrenia Incenderos Nervosa, how do you plead to this charge?"

Schitz's dry tongue clung like a bat to the roof of his mouth. His tongue lost all moisture. His lips quivered. Trying his best not to squeak, he said, "Not Guilty, your Highness."

The Devil continued. "Bubonic Plague, how is it that you level this accusation?"

Schitz watched his nemesis step forward and begin to address both the throne and the assembled throng.

"My Lord, I learned from two reliable Demons that a mortal exorcist spared Schizophrenia's life. The only explanations for such an event are that he is either an Angel or in league with Angels."

A Priest Schitz had never seen before leapt to his feet. "Hold your slanderous tongue, you oversized whelp," he said. "The Purists were ferreting out half-breeds and interlopers before your grandfather's father was a thought in his father's mind. It is not possible that this man is of Angelic breeding. You will not utter such words either here in this public forum or in private."

Bubonic Plague stepped back and raised both his hands in the gesture of surrender. "All right, your Grace, then he is so in league with Angels that the mortal could smell his change in aura."

"You're getting ahead of yourself," the Devil said. He waved his hand in a dismissive fashion. "Are your two witnesses here today."

"Yes, my Lord."

"Then identify them."

"They are Leprosy and SIDS."

The Devil continued to slouch. "Lady Leprosy and Lady SIDS, are the statements made by Bubonic Plague true and accurate?"

Leprosy glared at Schitz as she answered the Devil. "Yes, my Lord. The Shaman exorcised Mumps, brutally killing him; he then turned his attention to Schitz, who was aiding Mumps. However, the Shaman spared Schitz. He said he was not like the others."

"The others being Mumps and yourselves?" For the first time, the Devil appeared intrigued.

"That is what I presume," she replied. "I didn't have time to ask him to clarify."

Her final response brought a small chuckle from the crowd.

"He said something else after that," she said. "But I did not hear it."

The Devil swung a finger across the hall. "And you, Lady SIDS."

SIDS stepped forward, looking mostly to the ground.

"My experience was identical. I can neither add nor amend any detail."

His grandmother's betrayal landed like a punch to the groin. Schitz longed for Tuberculosis.

He would have never stood for such a mockery.

Still, Schitz detected a flicker of relief. As Elise had told him, this testimony was not enough to damn him.

"Is there anything else," the Devil asked.

"Yes, my Lord," Bubonic Plague said. As if introducing a celebrity, he waved his arms. "I give you the exorcist."

Schitz whirled his head in the direction of Bubonic's gesticulation, as did everyone else. The door opened, and the High Priest entered behind a shackled mortal. A collective gasp and frenetic whispering resounded through the chamber. Schitz could not believe his eyes.

This can't be happening, he thought.

The mortal being paraded into the room was dressed in the vestments of a Shaman, antlers and pelts included, but he was not the man who had exorcised Mumps.

"I'm told you exorcised one of my Demons," Satan said.

The imposter recoiled, then regained his composure.

"I did, and I would do it again, Balor," the man replied.

The man addressed Satan as the Celtic Demon King, Schitz thought.

"Why did you spare that one?" Satan asked.

"He is not a Demon," the Celt replied after a nervous glance at Schitz.

"He looks like a Demon to me," Satan said, "and I think I would know."

The Celt gulped. "Th... there is a li... lightness in his aura. I would not kill one of Arixus's servants. You cannot see this because you are too close to him; darkness sees only darkness."

Schitz wanted to shout. The Shaman who had performed the exorcism was a Sicani. The Sicani had originated in the Pyrenees before migrating to Sicily. The imposter was a Celt, a mortal of entirely different heritage, visibly from Gaul. Schitz hoped that the ruse was obvious to the Devil. However, the Dark Lord seemed unfazed.

"All right," the Devil said. "Does the accused have any explanation?"

Schitz gathered himself. *Not the time to stammer,* he thought.

"My Lord," he said. "To begin, this is not the individual who killed Mumps; this is a Celt, and we were in Sicily."

The Devil shrugged. "Is that so? I can't tell the difference with mortals."

The crowd behind Schitz erupted into a violent storm of Demons and Wraiths, simultaneously shouting both that the Shaman was and was not a Celt. The division of opinion existed along the lines of loyalty to Bubonic Plague and Schitz.

Satan raised his hand for quiet. "I suppose I should have seen that coming. They say he is; you say he isn't. It doesn't really matter. As Salvatore, the leader of the Purists, has already established, their work is beyond repudiation. It is not possible that Schizophrenia is a mixed breed, so I really do not care who this mortal is or what he has to say. The main point is that the enemy spared you." He looked at the witness like there was something vile on his shoe. "Oh, you can take him away. Dispose of him in the usual manner."

The Priests removed the witness while Schitz struggled to breathe.

The Devil leveled his gaze on Schitz. "As I was saying, you were spared by the enemy. Do you deny this?"

"No."

"Can you explain why?"

"No, but it's not because I'm a traitor. All my life I have served you faithfully. I am willing to lay down my life for you and for Hell's victory. The reason the real exorcist caught me was because I tried to save Mumps. These deserters did nothing to intervene on his or my behalf. They should be on trial for cowardice."

"All right, all right," Satan said. "The agreed-upon facts are as such: there was an exorcism in the field, and Mumps died while you did not. Everything else is contested, so it comes to me to decide the verdict. We are adjourned while I will weigh the evidence. I will deliver my determination in turn."

He looked at the crowd. "These proceedings have satisfied the rights afforded to the accused by the Divine Dictum."

SCHITZ RETURNED TO HIS cell and fell into a paroxysm of rage. He screamed and swore at the top of his lungs. He punched the stone walls until his knuckles were too bruised to strike anymore. He smacked his forehead against the wooden door until the blood left his face sticky and gritty. He grabbed his hair and howled in animalistic anger.

When he paused for a moment, he heard a voice from the other side of the cell wall. "I take it that your day in court did not go as well as your friend had anticipated."

Schitz rushed to the wall. "Who's there?"

"That may seem like a simple question," the voice replied, "however, after my time here, it is not so easy to say who I am anymore."

"Well, from your speech, I do not believe you to be a Demon," Schitz said.

"No, I am, or better to say I was, an Angel. I was Lord Zinc, and before that, I was Henry Zinc. Now I am a ghost."

"Astounding," Schitz said. "I brought you in, well, my squad and I."

"Oh, I'm certainly happy things are working out for you in that case," the voice said.

Schitz laughed. "I cannot believe they have kept you alive."

"Barely," the elder Zinc said. "They nearly killed me with their interrogation."

"I'm sorry," Schitz said.

"You don't have to say that."

"No, I am," Schitz said. "Death in battle is one thing, but to rot away here tortured and isolated, deprived, that is not fair."

"The one thought that beguiles my mind is my son," Zinc said. "I don't suppose you have any detailed knowledge of Heaven."

Schitz chuckled. "I won't be seeing an Angel anytime soon, and no, I won't be able to tell you much about your side."

"Fair enough," the elder Zinc replied. "For what it's worth, you have my sympathies."

The conversation was interrupted by a harsh bang and the irritating, familiar voice of Bubonic Plague.

"Do you hear me, Schitz?" he asked. The tone was not solicitous. "I have come from a meeting of the Triumvirate Council, and Satan has informed us that you will be put to death. Do you hear that? I wanted to be the first one to tell you. Tomorrow they will lead you out to the duelists' island where you robbed us of Vertigo. They will tie you to a stake, and I..." he chuckled loudly, "... I of all Demons will have the honor of chopping off your weaselly head."

Schitz said nothing. Heavy footsteps receded. Schitz sunk to the floor.

"A word of advice," the elder Zinc said after a moment's silence, "Don't give them the satisfaction of seeing you weak, or sniveling. Face them with a stern, calm demeanor, and you will feel better as you meet your end."

"I've steeled myself for death on the battlefield countless times," Schitz said, "but this, this death feels like a waste."

"That is because it is," his fellow prisoner replied.

The conversation was interrupted again, this time by SIDS. She spoke through the door.

"I know you probably don't want to hear from me right now, Schitz."

His reply was a hiss. "You're correct."

Undeterred, she continued, "I've come to tell you two things. The first, you likely care little for, and that is the reason for my betrayal. I loved Tuberculosis with all my soul, and I swore that I would never lay with another when I lost him. But I am pressed to wed Fever. I bought my chastity with my complacency in your demise."

"So, I suppose I am meant to feel bad for you?" Schitz asked.

"You were never a grandson to me," she said. "That is the second thing I have come to tell you. Your father, Diphtheria, loved Poliomyelitis, your mother, very much. Had she lived, they might have lived as husband and a wife, but while they were siblings, he did not make her with child."

Schitz convulsed as though he had already been struck by the executioner's axe.

"My father was not my father?" he asked.

"Did he treat you like much of a father?" she replied.

Schitz recalled Diphtheria's dying moments at the Persian Gates. He could see it so vividly in his mind's eye. He remembered how Diphtheria stepped in to assist when Bubonic Plague wanted to snatch Rubella away for Vertigo.

"He was a good father and a good Demon," Schitz replied.

"Ah, you wouldn't know the difference, only having one to judge by," she said, "but the truth is, my sweet Polio was taken by another."

"An Angel?" Schitz asked.

Perhaps the Shaman was right, he thought. He clutched his jaw and winced in anticipation of SIDS's answer.

The laugher from the hall was shrill and caustic. "The opposite, entirely," SIDS continued. "She was taken by the Dark Lord himself."

Schitz's head exploded in a spasm of pain. "That would make me, the Son of Satan, the Antichrist, the one foretold to bring about the final victory."

"Oh, calm yourself," SIDS said. "That is our mythology, our religion. We all know the Devil has dipped his bucket in many a maiden's well, and sometimes he leaves a splinter in the water."

Schitz cringed both at the metaphor and the harsh criticism of the Church he had dedicated his life to serving.

Schitz snarled through the door. "So, do you have any suggestions or are you simply here to gloat."

"Well... you could tell the High Priest. Then, one of two things could happen. He might have you released..."

Schitz waited for the other shoe to drop.

"... or, out of fear you will tell someone, he could have you executed before the sun shines tomorrow."

Schitz took a moment to catch his breath. "There's only one thing to do," he said.

"Yes, my grandson?"

"Go fetch the High Priest, you old witch."

THE LORD SATAN'S FINGERNAILS scratched against his throne. Small sparks flicked into the air. The High Priest smelled ozone.

"The prisoner told you this?" the Devil asked.

"Yes, my Lord."

"As far as you know, has he told anyone else?"

"He was abundantly clear that he had told no other living soul, my Lord."

"How does his story affect the Church?" Satan asked.

Titus, High Priest of Hell, did not like to discuss theology with his Master. The Devil was not a creature of great intellectual depth. He much preferred action, violent, fiendish, painful action. But there was no dodging the inquiry.

"Not well at all, my Lord," Titus said. "You did not take the Maiden Poliomyelitis as your Queen. Schizophrenia began his career with ineptitude. He was not an accomplished academic, and he promotes a non-lethal disease. None of those things squares with the prophecies. Your progeny is anticipated to be from the womb of Hell's female consort and to achieve things heretofore unimagined. This Schitz character is, by all reports, rather ordinary."

The sparks increased in size and frequency. "I have two options," Satan said. "I can either strike a bargain with him or kill him in his cell."

"I am not opposed to the second option, my Lord."

"Nor am I," Satan said, "but a convenient jailhouse death will raise questions with which we do not wish to deal. If I kill him and he has told someone else about this theory of his origin, say Rubella, his demise will launch a crisis of doubt, the sort of thing destined to destroy a kingdom."

"So..." Titus awaited.

"So, we find a middle ground," Satan said. "I must say, for a dimwit, this character has positioned himself very well, but he may not like the outcome."

"How is that, my Lord?"

"The Demon Schizophrenia will be exonerated," Satan said. He smiled, all sharp teeth and fetid breath. "But I do not believe the young man will live long enough to enjoy his newfound freedom."

CHAPTER 9

EXILE

The clatter of fire-hardened wooden swords striking against one another resonated along the banks of the Eunoe. Zinc gazed at the mock combatants as they whirled in the dance of imitation battle. They were well-matched, and each thrust was met by an equal parry. Each kick found its equivalent in the corresponding block or dodge. The wooden swords found each other instead of their target each time, over and over.

The young Angels each resembled Zinc so much a casual observer would have been hard-pressed to note a defining characteristic. Yet to Zinc, his sons were as different as night and day. Patrick was hot-headed, ambitious, and impatient. He reminded Zinc of himself. Aaron was calm, analytical, and quiet in large groups. Despite their differences, the pair was inseparable both in proximity and ability. Zinc could not have been prouder.

"That is enough, my boys," Zinc said. He clapped his hands. "Well done, well done indeed."

Both sons breathed heavily. They turned toward Zinc and smiled. "Surely, we are ready for combat," Patrick said with a savage glint in his eye.

"Oh, I'm certain you are," Zinc replied, "but as my father told me, your time will come, my son, and when it does, there will be no reprieve in sight until hard-earned retirement, victory, or death. Enjoy your youth; do not heedlessly long for the hazard, wherein a single unfortunate step may undo all skill and preparation."

Zinc looked at his children and was relieved that he had not deprived them of their mother. Lady Zinc had not so much as won Zinc over, as she had exhibited dogged determination in carving out a substantial part of his life for herself. She had not experienced the full battle hardening that Angels of the line experienced from confrontations with Demons. But her years overseeing Familiars in the Intelligence Service had imbued her with self-assuredness and guile that she had been missing in her younger years. She had been relentless in her demand for his physical attention and had provided him numerous children, for which he was abundantly grateful.

Zinc enjoyed Lady Zinc's intimacy; her girlish, demure frame was petite in comparison to Rachael's strong, muscular body, but he could not deny that he enjoyed ravishing her regularly. His guilt now centered on Rachael. Zinc felt her grow more and more frustrated and distant with each child he fathered by Cecilia, and each year that passed without resolution. He feared deeply that he would lose her. As accustomed and favorable as he found his wife, Zinc felt a unique pull toward Rachael. He knew he would never replicate the feeling with another.

He suspected that had Lady Zinc not continuously been surrounded by crafty Familiars whenever she was in the field, Rachael would have long found a way to murder her. Some days he thought such a resolution would have been for the better. But when he looked at his dueling sons, he knew their development had benefited from having both parents.

"Come," he said, "we must prepare ourselves for the Grand Gathering. I believe there will be a surprise in it that will give heart to you both."

He grabbed his eldest by the neck and rustled his long brown hair. "Especially, you, my fiery Patrick."

TIME HAD DRAGGED FOLLOWING Schitz's gambit. He had remained confined to his cell, though his blooming friendship with the former Standard Bearer of the House of Zinc had provided his mind with much reprieve from tearing itself to shreds with anxiety. They engaged in debates and traded riddles and stories. They spoke of the Mortal World, of food, and women, and drink, and music.

"I tell you this true," Schitz said one day, "if I leave this cell to my death, you will have been one of the best friends I have ever known, whereas if I leave this cell to return to my duty, you will once again be a mortal foe."

"Such is our world," the elder Zinc replied, "however, respect is the common element of which you speak, for whether I am your friend or foe, you hold respect for me, and I for you."

THE GRAND GATHERING WAS a spectacle to behold. The notes of the organ and harpsichord filled the air of the Great Hall as heavily as the incense. The Heavenly choir added their voices to the music. It was a rare event for all of Heaven to be assembled.

Numerous accolades had been heaped upon Zinc in his early years. He now wore them on the luxurious robes of his dress uniform: The First Order, The Most Excellent Order, The Noble Order, and The Glorious Order. All variously ornate crosses were either pinned to his chest or worn around his neck. At his waist was The Spodium, the Celestial long sword of the House of Zinc. He typically left the Spodium in his chambers for safekeeping. Zinc was uncertain whether he deserved these plaudits. However, he could see why they kept arriving despite his failure to deliver a crushing blow to Hell, despite the collapse of Alexander's empire.

Since assuming the role of leader of his House and the unofficial title of Commander of Heaven, the Angels had failed to suffer a single defeat. Scores of Angels had been killed in action, as was the unfortunate reality. However, the particularly high numbers of casualties they had experienced in Babylon and Egypt were no longer occurring regularly. Zinc felt uneasy in the pit of his stomach. He knew Rome was probably his final chance. Heaven had been repopulating, outfitting, and learning the mortals' warfare to a greater level than ever before. He could sense that a climactic confrontation was coming.

Additionally, the incorporation of new Houses, as occurred at the Grand Gathering, would further complicate the politicking required to ensure his hegemony over the forces of Heaven. Still, as he stood with his House, he felt pride and a sense of accomplishment. He looked across the various Houses of Heaven, and he felt a grim sadness as he noted the various retired Standard Bearers.

If only my father were still here, he thought.

The melodious strains of orchestra and choir came to a halt as the High Priest ascended to the altar and turned his attention toward the musicians. The High Priest began to conduct the orchestra. The organ took up the tune of *Loué Soit Dieu le Seigneur*. Zinc joined the rest of Heaven in the familiar refrain.

We stand on guard with not a single hint of trepidation,
We stand on guard, to the foe's ever-present consternation,
Yes, we stand on guard, battle-scarred, weathered, and hard,
Ready for any possible situation.

We fight for God, the primogenitor of all creation,
We fight for His honor, and it brings us the greatest elation,
Yes, we fight with might, for all that is good, noble, and right,
That his temple may never know any desecration.

We wait for the Holy Spirit, that Its guidance may always command us,
We wait for Its blessing, which will render us invincible and glorious,
Yes, we wait for that day, patiently, hopeful, we pray,
For when we will be left standing victorious.

We clear the way for Christ, the bringer of all Holy Redemption,
We clear the way with Demonic purging, for Earth's reclamation,
Yes, we clear the way, one step further with each serpent we slay,
So that all are free to partake in the Lord's adoration.

If we should fall amidst the battle's havoc, turmoil, and confusion,
We will not beg, nor offer our foes collaboration, parley, or collusion,
Yes, if we should fall, we will fall having given our all,
Let that be our final rest and consolation.

The meaning of the words had taken on a graver meaning to Zinc than when he had committed them to memory in the Academy. He had seen death in all its horrific forms; it had been close to him many times. It had been made manifest in the form of the Demon with the scar on his face, the one Rachael obsessed over constantly with thoughts of revenge for killing Benjamin. Thoughts of Rachael pained to Zinc. He wondered if he should still somehow dispose of his wife.

God ascended to the lectern that overlooked the Great Hall as silence returned to the muster.

"Assembly of Heaven," he began, "there is nothing that brings me greater joy than the Grand Gathering. This hallowed tradition of incorporating Houses means that we are strong, we are growing, and we are going to win."

A cheer went up through the ranks. God raised his hand to his eyebrow in salute; a gesture returned smartly by all assembled.

As God descended the steps from the balcony, the High Priest by the altar resumed the service. "The House of Zinc has been selected for two incorporations."

Zinc still felt a nervous tingling whenever he spoke to such a large assembly. Still, he was excited. He turned to his eldest sons. "Come, Patrick and Aaron," he said.

It was not uncommon for a leading House to save its best sons to ensure strong succession and to trade the right to incorporation, referred to as a dispensation, to negotiate for other rights and privileges, or to institute policy changes. Zinc, however, saw the advantage in christening two Houses aligned with his interests.

He and the boys arrived at the altar, and the High Priest instructed all three to kneel. Zinc lowered himself to his knees, facing his sons.

The High Priest began, "Ave Maria, gratia plena, Dominus tecum, Virgo serena." The High Priest commanded, "Rise, Lord Zinc."

Zinc stood. Both sons continued recitation of the prayer dedicated to the woman who was prophesized to give birth to the son of God one day. The High Priest handed Zinc a Celestial long sword that had been resting upon the altar.

"For Patrick," the High Priest whispered with a slight smile.

Zinc received the sword with the blade laid flat across both of his palms. Next, the Priest instructed Patrick to stand. The boy ceased reciting the Ave Maria and rose, placing his palms under the sword as well.

"Recite after me, young Lord," the Priest said. "I, Lord Chlorine, hereby accept The Chlorum, the sword of my House, the protector of my people, and the eviscerator of my enemies."

Patrick echoed the words of the High Priest. Next, the holy man removed a small, white dove from an iron cage resting atop the altar. He sliced the neck of the hapless creature with the razor-sharp edge of the blade and tossed the corpse into a basket beside the altar.

"I swear," he continued with Patrick echoing, "that this shall be the last innocent blood spilled by this sword or any sword of my House."

The blood of the slaughtered dove dripped from the blade onto the white marble of the Great Hall. "Kneel once more as a son of Zinc," the High Priest said. He turned to Zinc. "Lord Zinc, repeat after me. I dub thee Lord Chlorine."

Zinc held the weapon by its handle and gently tapped each of Patrick's shoulders and then the top of his head. "I dub thee Lord Chlorine," he said.

"Arise a Lord," the High Priest said.

Zinc grinned broadly as he presented the sword to his newly invested son.

The process repeated. Aaron received The Phosphoro and was dubbed Lord Phosphorous. Zinc felt extremely pleased with himself as he returned to his Household's formation without either of his eldest sons, for they had taken up solitary positions representing their own Houses. He would secure wives for them forthwith, and they would expand their Houses immediately. He would also send some other members of the Zinc household to support them in the interim.

He took assessment of his holdings. He controlled the former Houses of Lead, Oxygen, Gold, and Silver directly. He received support for his leadership from the oldest Houses, Iron and Carbon. Neither of them desired to go against him; they did not want to be alienated from the seat of power.

The House of Mercury was an interesting offshoot as one of the three houses that physically resembled mortals farther from Europa and the Middle East. They generally focused upon the Far East and the mortals that looked like them, a theater largely ignored by Heaven and Hell, although Zinc did have plans to expand to their region.

The House of Magnesium largely resembled mortals of the uncharted regions across the sea, red in complexion. Like their Asian counterparts, they brought healing to the part of the world that interested them most and only joined large-scale operations in the Near East and Mediterranean.

The last of the ethnic houses consisted of the House of Hydrogen. These Angels resembled Africans and primarily took part in the affairs of the Dark Continent. Zinc did not see any of these Houses as a threat to his centralized power; they were mainly on the periphery and focused on maintaining the independence of their Houses.

The remaining Houses of Arsenic, Lithium, and Nitrogen generally acted together but had little interest in going against the consensus. Zinc surmised they would remain docile if he continued to deliver acceptable strategy and results. He had received two Houses for his sons, who would remain loyal to him. The remaining Houses would receive one incorporation option, either to raise a house or haggle for privileges.

To Zinc's surprise, the people following him chose to incorporate Houses. Iron III selected a younger son to begin the House of Tellurium. Carbon IV tagged his eldest son to start the House of Barium. Arsenic gave rise to the House of Manganese. Lithium birthed the House of Nickel. Nitrogen begot the House of Strontium. Mercury IV fathered the House of Cobalt. The last House to go was the House of Hydrogen.

Zinc watched with half interest as Lord Hydrogen approached the altar. He was a muscular, stocky Angel. He wore his robe cut short. Most other Angels sported a longer style to the ankles. His short robe displayed his strong legs. Zinc was aware of Hydrogen's tactical prowess.

The High Priest spoke. "It has been arranged between Lord Hydrogen and the Maiden's father, Henrik Zinc, that the aforementioned Lord will trade his right to incorporate a House for the hand of Rachael Zinc in holy matrimony."

Zinc felt faint. The world swirled in utter chaos and disruption. He was well aware the entirety of Heaven was looking at him for a reaction. Zinc locked his face in a stoic expression and walked to the altar with his uncle Henrik. They joined a smug Lord Hydrogen.

"I have both procured you a valuable asset and overlooked your wanton disregard for my daughter's honor," Henrik whispered to Zinc.

"For my part," Lord Hydrogen said, "I will be happy never to touch your woman, maybe even to overlook her whereabouts, if you follow my instructions in the field and in the strategy room."

The blood pulsed in Zinc's carotid. "Are you mad? You vastly underestimate me."

There might have been a time when Zinc would have considered the offer and surrendered his influence for a permanent solution to the issue of his cousin-mistress. But now, he saw clearly that he would not squander his father's gift of Heavenly power over his infatuation for Rachael.

"I am the leader of the Houses," Zinc said. "I understand your wife fell to the Demons at a battle along the Sénégal. I wish you and your new wife much better luck."

"If you say so," Lord Hydrogen said.

Zinc stepped forward and spewed his disdain in a violent whisper toward his brawny colleague. "You have made your play, and I give you credit. It was a well-conceived ambush, but you ensnared little at the cost of your exposure. Now, I see your game, and I will be wary to your movements, Lord."

Zinc turned to the awkward face of the High Priest. "All are in accord, Your Eminence."

Then, to Lord Hydrogen, "Best get on with the wedding, with all these new Houses and all the repopulating that has been taking place, I have the mother of all battles to plan, and all Houses will be participating."

He returned to his place at the head of the Zinc household, passing Rachael on her way to the altar. He allowed himself one final gaze. Then, she walked away from him forever.

THE IDYLLIC, SLOPING HILLS and the dense forests of the expanses along the Rhine soothed Elise. The scenery stood in a direct contradiction to the cold, murderous intent of the region's inhabitants. Elise moved deftly over the wooded terrain, and she was not handicapped by age or the loss of her left arm. Although Wraiths aged over the course of several human lifetimes and appeared elderly, they remained nimble and agile.

Mephistopheles had been elated at the inclusion of the Wraiths on the Triumvirate Council, even if they were the lowest of the three entities. As slaves, any measure of authority or self-determination was extremely valuable. Mephistopheles would be the first to point out that the Demons and Priest were slaves, too; all Hellish creatures fell victim to the Atrophy, a wasting away resulting from failure to perform one's prescribed task. Elise's thoughts drifted to her old lover as she weaved her way through the forest. The lives of Wraiths were fragile; existing both within the Celestial and the Mortal Realm made them vulnerable to both. It was only natural that she and Mephistopheles, as the oldest of their kind, would have inevitably fallen into a romantic attachment. Each had been wed to others who had long since died. She loved the companionship of her vivacious and extroverted partner.

They had gone to the Rhineland on Mephistopheles's insistence. As soon as he assumed his position on the Council, he was possessed with the notion that he would contribute a major intelligence coup. They played the game Wraiths had played for centuries when dealing with their Heavenly counterparts. The vastly superior numbers of both Angels and Familiars meant that Heaven could conduct armed reconnaissance. One or two Angels accompanied the Familiars on their missions, which prevented Wraiths from attacking their roguish adversaries. There had been questions as to whether such practices violated the sections of the Divine Dictum pertaining to the intelligence services. However, Hell had generally been disinterested in lodging a formal complaint. Heaven possessed a distinct advantage, as Wraiths were vulnerable to attack from Angels, Familiars, and even skilled mortals.

The game developed by the Wraiths consisted of one Wraith leading a curious pack of mortals toward the Heavenly units. Elise allowed only a small shadow of herself to be seen by the band of Cherusci warriors. The Germanic tribesmen were on alert for Roman legions in the area and had easily taken the bait. They pursued the intruder intently as she weaved through the woods.

Meanwhile, Mephistopheles stalked the Familiars and their protective Angel. As the tribesmen broke through the woods and clattered into the Roman scouting detachment, both sets of mortals naturally fell into a hasty combat. Mephistopheles hurled a throwing knife from his concealed position, striking down a Familiar. The Angel, perceiving an attack from within the Celestial, instantly understood her vulnerability. Since she did not know the act had originated from a harmless Wraith, she stepped into the body of a mortal female warrior, a move that proved to be her undoing. The moment she assumed her mortal shield, one of the Cherusci cut her down with a javelin.

Elise pounced on the seizing Angel. She drew a small dagger and plunged it into either side of her foe's delicate throat. The Angel twitched as her life faded from her. Elise was set upon by a Familiar, but she dropped to the ground and barrel-rolled, knocking her attacker from her feet. Elise scrambled over and raised her bloodied dagger with her sole arm while resting her body weight upon the foe. Elise readied herself to claim the second victim.

Mephistopheles shouted from over her shoulder. "Wait!"

In an instant, Elise became aware of her greater surroundings. The surviving Familiars, like the Romans and the Cherusci, had all dispersed. Mephistopheles rushed over to Elise. He held the Familiar tightly by her neck and spoke.

"You are already dead, young one. All you can do now is decide how you meet that end."

A sense of pity flooded Elise. The young Familiar was pretty, with small, cherubic features, short blonde hair, and large eyes that darted frantically from side to side. Her freckled skin showed little effect of aging. In a certain way, she reminded Elise of her own sister, long since departed.

Mephistopheles continued, "I want to know all of the details of your mission and what you are doing in Germania."

The Familiar began to cry. "I... I... I don't know many details. Th... they want this campaign to go well for the Romans."

"For the Romans? You weren't out here looking for Demons?"

"That t... t... too." She choked on her sobs. "But I was told primarily to assess concerns for the mortal army."

"Why?"

"I don't know. Something to do with the Silk Road."

"The Silk Road is countless leagues from here."

Mephistopheles rubbed his chin as recognition dawned.

"Close your eyes," he said.

She screamed in panic. Mephistopheles turned the Familiar around and pressed her face against the bark of a nearby tree. With a smooth, deft motion, he knocked the Familiar over the head with the handle of his dagger. Elise gazed on in perplexed amazement as the Familiar, unconscious, yet very much alive, slumped to the ground.

"Come on, let's go," said Mephistopheles, a hint of shame in his voice.

"You mean, you're not going to..."

"I couldn't do it," he said. "She is just a child; she reminded me of Erika."

"Me, too," Elise said softly. "Are we getting too old for this?"

Mephistopheles glanced down at the body of the butchered Angel and shrugged. "Hardly, but you know there has to be some limit. That Familiar will probably never harm another soul in her entire life. I mean directly. She won't kill anything. She'll amble along until something picks her off or she retires. I hear they have retirement in Heaven. Either way, they show no mercy to our kind, Wraiths, or Familiars. Both sides mistreat us. I thought I could give her a break."

Elise nodded. She kissed him passionately before saying, "You truly are noble."

As the two headed away from the site of the skirmish, Elise remembered the information they had gathered. "My love, what secret did you discern?"

Mephistopheles grinned. "The Silk Road is the only connection between East and West. Right now, Parthia and Sogdia stand between Rome and the Han. Imagine if Rome were to sweep through Europa and across the Steppes. The Empire would double in size; it would reach the East."

Elise swore in an ancient tongue and then said, "If they absorb the Germans and the Scythians into their empire, they could stretch from the Atlanticus to the Eastern Sea."

"Alexander's dream brought to fruition," Mephistopheles said. "The Angels have always sought to create a worldly empire that mirrored Heaven to deny us access to as many mortal souls as possible."

Elise nodded. "That means they will commit everything towards making this expansion possible when they cross the Rhine."

Mephistopheles picked up his pace. "Come, my love, we must report to the Triumvirate at once."

ZINC SAT WITHIN THE Heavenly chamber designed for strategy and studied a map of the known world. He felt overwhelmed as he looked at the various kingdoms and empires. He wondered if his strategy was even plausible—to cover the earth in an empire aligned with Heavenly interests, a place where healing fed souls to the Eunoe and deprived Hell of energy.

A familiar feminine voice rose over his shoulder. "Always scheming."

For a moment, Zinc was excited when he saw Rachael, but the memory of recent events soon brought him back to reality.

"I heard about Lady Zinc," Rachael said, "that she fell on a scouting mission over the Rhine."

"Yes. Ironic that it finally happened after it was too late for us."

"For what it's worth, I am so incredibly sorry," she said with tears in her eyes. "If I had to choose between my father and you, I would choose you, but I didn't know if I would ever have you, and the shame he felt was killing us both."

Zinc tried to speak but was caught off guard when Rachael pressed her lips passionately against his.

"I will always love you," she said, "and I will always hate that I could never be Lady Zinc."

She turned and left the planning room. Zinc sighed and returned to his strategizing. It was all he could do to try to put thoughts of Lord Hydrogen touching his beloved out of his mind.

THE DOOR PROTESTED, AND the High Priest opened Schitz's cell.

"You have been free of the Atrophy while within these walls," Titus said, "but now it is time for you to resume your work."

Schitz, baffled at this proclamation, stood.

"My sentence?"

"Your sentence will be discussed after this upcoming battle, but for now, we need you and every able-bodied Demon," said the Priest.

Just before Schitz walked out of the cell, he heard a faint whisper. "Fare thee well."

Schitz was not surprised by the wobbly nature of his run. He'd been confined a long time. He threw open the door to his room and saw Rubella readying herself for battle.

Her shout shook the walls. "Schitz!"

Schitz took her in his arms and kissed her. They were naked in seconds and made love with a passion they had not experienced in years.

"We're going to be late," Rubella said between gasps.

Schitz gathered an assortment of throwing knives. "What is going on?"

"I don't know for certain," Rubella said. "Intelligence indicates a movement of Angels en masse. The Triumvirate is throwing everybody at them."

"The what?"

"Oh, you've missed so much," she replied. "The Devil disbanded the clans; we now answer to a council of senior Priests, Demons, and Wraiths."

"Who's on the council, Bubonic Plague?"

"Yes."

"Of course, he is, the overrated buffoon."

Rubella laughed. "A lot has changed. We're grandparents." Rubella beamed. "Two beautiful girls. Gluttony and Envy."

"Interesting names," Schitz said.

"It's the style now," Rubella said. "Your friend Autism married one of my former students, Reyes Disease. She had twins, Lust and Sloth, and has two more on the way. She plans on naming them Greed and Wrath."

"Wow," Schitz said, "it's a lot to take in. When I left, Rome was a fledgling kingdom. On my way, I heard the Romans are now set to conquer the known world."

"Speaking of, let's go," she said. "I hate being the last one in the room."

The briefing took place in the Great Hall. Schitz could hardly remember an occasion other than a funeral for which all of Hell was in attendance. As was customary, the Demons stood with their respective cohorts. Schitz took his place in formation; he was surprised by the warm reception he received.

Conjunctivitis threw his arms around him briefly and thumped him on the shoulders. "Welcome back, old boy."

"Glad you're still with us," Autism said.

"Glad to be here," Schitz said with a broad grin. "I hear you've been busy, you old dog."

Anorexia embraced Schitz and sobbed into his chest. "I was so worried for you."

"Thank you," Schitz said, taken aback by her affection.

Even Influenza, who seemed to adhere to her father's hatred, gave him a half embrace. "It's good to see you well."

The cohort settled into formation. Schitz glanced over toward the parents' generation and felt his own age as he saw Bubonic Plague, Smallpox, Leprosy, Tetanus, and Syphilis. Bubonic Plague stared at him with undisguised loathing. Schitz was taken aback when he surveyed the younger generation and beheld the woman his daughter had become. He regretted his absence during her Sequester and graduation—and when she had brought home her children. Rabies noticed his gaze and offered an awkward half-smile, which Schitz returned.

"I'll be there from now on," he vowed to himself.

The High Priest called for order. "We are gathered here today because we have been presented with a momentous opportunity. Our brave Wraiths have uncovered a massive movement of Heavenly forces across the Rhine. They mean to cross Europa and to reach the Steppes, through which they will gain access to the vast tracts of Asia. We can surprise them at the outset and deal them the most destructive of blows."

Tension seized the room. Everyone recognized the severity of the moment. Heaven was making a move to capture more territory than it had ever held before. Schitz had missed much of the rise of Rome, but if the Caesars were anything like Alexander, the opportunity to halt their expansion was critical. It was rare indeed to possess such specific strategic and tactical intelligence. Schitz's muscles tensed at the thought of the glory to be had in a few hours' time.

Lucius Flavius hated the northern climes of Germania. He longed for his village in the Calabrian countryside. When he closed his eyes, he could feel the warm, sea-swept breeze of the coast. He saw the rolling hills, the olive groves. He could hear his wife's sweet, warm laughter. Lucius longed for the comfort of home; the September Germanic air was cold and hostile. The rain pelted him mercilessly; it clung to his armor and weighed down his red tunic. The soaked wool was heavy and uncomfortable. Mud squelched with each step and clung to his sandals, freezing his feet. His sizeable wooden shield felt slippery in his hand.

"Three Legions are on the move," he said to Quintis Aquilani, a fellow centurion and close personal friend, "in this weather and this disorganized a fashion."

Quintis shook his head. "No scouting units; the column is spread out and mixed with camp followers, but Varus wants to move quickly. He said that if we smash Arminius, there's only one remaining Germanic chieftain between us and domination of the region."

Lucius looked skeptical. "Poor planning wastes the lives of good Romans."

"And good Angels," Lord Magnesium replied from within Quintis.

Lord Molybdenum looked at his father and once more shook his head. "Zinc convinced God that it was wise to throw our whole force into this endeavor, but I would rather be across the great water in the land untouched by this unending war. I can relate to this homesick mortal."

"You will find the balance in time," Lord Magnesium said, "between fulfilling the expectations here in Europa, fighting with the main body of the Heavenly army, and taking time for our side projects across the sea."

"It just feels rushed," Molybdenum said. "Besides, I heard we lost several Angelic scouting units in this region before the primary mission."

"One of which included Lady Zinc," Magnesium said, "so be careful how you voice your concerns."

"I understand," the younger Lord said. "It just feels like an impending disaster."

"It may well be," the elder Lord replied, "but one cannot shirk his duty. All we can do is try to weather the storm, just like these centurions."

VILI GRABBED ANOTHER BUNDLE of sticks in his brawny arms and held the mass of rough wood tightly as his wife, Angrboda, lashed the bunch together with a thin strip of animal hide. Urgency sparked in the air. Across the river, there had once been people like them, who lived freely and worshiped the old Gods. Now, the people of Gaul were oppressed and subservient to their Latin overlords, heathen men who worshiped false Gods and shaved their faces. Though they appeared feminine, Vili knew the invaders were masters of war and required the utmost respect for their capacity for destruction. He breathed deeply as the cool breeze washed over his bare arms.

"We must build this wall high and strong," he said. "This will be where we break their spine when we force them along the narrow road."

Angrboda sighed as she bound yet another set of branches. "This rain is a gift from Odin; it will slacken their bows and bog them down in their heavy armor."

Schitz looked at Rubella within her host's lightweight, leather armor and animal-skin dress. The mortal was a fierce warrior with strong musculature and long braided hair. Her host wore a tattoo of the Valknut on her broad shoulder, a symbol associated with the God Odin and with death. She was an excellent host for his tough, warrior bride.

"Everything is coming into place, although I will say I feel a little put out to pasture, heading up the second ambush site's preparation," Schitz said.

"Ah, cheer up, my love," she replied. "It's good to have you back with me. Now we can all be a family. Well, as much as a family is in Hell."

Schitz smiled broadly and closed his eyes. He relished the cold wind and rain pelting his host's face.

THRONGS OF STUDENTS STROLLED down the narrow, cobblestone streets of Heidelberg in the twilight hours of the cold winter's day. The scene was a flurry of young men in heavy overcoats with top hats and walking sticks and young women in full-length gowns and shawls with many petticoats beneath, the height of fashion for 1850 AD. A light snow fell on the merrymakers as they made their way from Heidelberg University to local establishments.

Within a beerhall, Maximillian Feuerstein took his seat at a well-worn piano. Many beers had been spilled on it, and many carousers had sat upon it, but the old instrument came to life under his boney fingers.

He had to shout over the squawk of the accordion. "Come on, gentlemen, you all know Als die Rumer Frech Geworden."[26]

With great enthusiasm, the young men hoisted their beer steins and raised their voices in happy unison.

> Als die Römer frech geworden, Simserim sim sim sim
> zogen sie nach Deutschlands Norden.[27]

Hands and flasks struck tables:

> ...simserim sim sim sim...

---

[26] When the Romans got cheeky.

[27] When the Romans got cheeky, Simserim sim sim sim sim, they moved to the North of Germany.

Voices rose to the rafters...

Vorne mit Trompetenschall...[28]

The revelers mimicked the sound of Roman trumpets, täterätätätä, before continuing...

...ritt Herr Generalfeldmarschall, täterätätätä.
Herr Quintilius Varus, wau, wau wau. Herr Quintilius Varus...[29]

The verse ended with boisterous mimicking of the sounds of trumpets and battle...

...schnätterängtäng, schnätterängtäng, schnätterängtäng,
schnätterängtäng.[30]

Max plowed into the second verse, and the merrymaking grew in volume.

Nineteen centuries before the raucous student gathering, two armies clashed in a calamitous battle.

In dem Teutoburger Walde, Huh! Wie piff der Wind so kalte.[31]

The battle commenced in ferocious fashion. Bubonic Plague led a score of Demons in possession of fearsome Germanic warriors through the dense fog and rain of the September morning. The situation immediately favored the local inhabitants. The rain had rendered the Roman bow strings unusable. In contrast, the javelins of Germanic tribesmen split the air with deadly precision. Romans and Angels collapsed under the storm of projectiles. Plague led the Demons out of the mortals and into the Celestial.

The cohort of senior Demons was the combination of centuries of

---

[28] Front with trumpet sound.

[29] Rode General Field Marshal

[30] (Mimicking the sound of trumpets)

[31] In Teutoburg Forest Huh! How the wind blows so cold.

training and refined practice. It inflicted brutality upon mortal and Angel alike. Bubonic wielded his gargantuan axe, cracking an Angel's head like an eggshell. While his axe was still stuck in the twitching body, two Angels attacked. Tetanus was quick to cover his peer and stepped between Bubonic and the foes. Tetanus blocked a thrust from one, then dispatched him with the flick of his sword. He kicked the second Angel in the midsection. The Angel scampered into a mortal German; however, the host was immediately brought down by a javelin hurled from nearly a hundred steps away, by Leprosy from within the body of a Germanic tribeswoman. The Angel fell to the ground in a heap, and Plague, who had retrieved his axe, severed his head. He looked at Tetanus.

The Valknut

"You're getting slow, Cousin."

Tetanus smirked. "There's more yet to come, Cousin; let us see who drowns first in Angels' blood."

> *Raben flogen durch die Luft, Und*
> *es war ein Moderduft, Wie von*
> *Blut und Leichen...*[32]

The number of Angels in the field that day was massive, and though the Heavenly forces were initially overwhelmed, they began to regroup.

> *Plötzlich aus des Waldes Düster*

---

[32] Ravens flew through the air, and it was a musty scent like blood and corpses.

Brachen kampfhaft die Cherusker. [33]

Upon hearing reports of heavy casualties, Zinc fled the body of Varus and led a detachment into the thick of the fray. After crossing a small knoll along the windy forest road, Zinc beheld the massive Demon that Angels knew as "the Leviathan" or "the Behemoth." This gargantuan foe was in the process of dispatching several Angels that had surrounded him but were clearly unable to cope with his fighting skills. Zinc plotted his course and flesh-hopped through several Romans. His target was not the Behemoth. At the last moment, he stepped into the Celestial and swung his sword as a feint toward the large Demon, only to drop into a head-over-heels roll that carried him between the Demon's legs. As Zinc emerged on the far side of the Behemoth, he spotted his target, the Demon supporting the Behemoth. Zinc caught the foe off guard and plunged his sword through his heart.

Mit Gott für Fürst und Vaterland Stürzten sie sich wutentbrannt
Auf die Legionen.[34]

Bubonic shouted as he turned over his shoulder to see the wily Angel kill Tetanus. In his moment of distraction, Bubonic felt the searing pain of a Heavenly blade slicing across his midsection. He dropped to his knees and found himself face to face with a snarling, female Angel. She raised her sword, and Bubonic attempted to force his body to overcome his injury to offer up some sort of defense.

"Look out, Lady Hydrogen," an Angel shouted over the fracas.

In an instant, Syphilis arrived at the side of her husband, blocking the swipe that had been intended for him. Deftly she battled the Angels surrounding Bubonic and the corpse of Tetanus. The fearsome female disengaged when her foes were either slain or had withdrawn.

"Come, we must fall back," Syphilis said. "You are grievously injured."

---

[33] Suddenly from the gloomy forest the Cherusci broke in battle.

[34] With God for Prince and Fatherland they rushed furiously to the legions.

"No, they have not run me through," Bubonic said through clenched teeth. "We all must press onwards. The day is not yet ours."

*Weh, das ward ein großes Morden, Sie schlugen die Kohorten, Nur die röm'sche Reiterei, Rettete sich noch ins Frei',
Denn sie war zu Pferde.*[35]

The battle raged along the winding forest road. Many an Angel and Demon fell as the contest wore on. SIDS had been providing ranged support, hurling javelins down upon the Romans from within the Mortal Realm, while Smallpox and Fever brought down their victims once they had fallen into the Celestial. Unbeknownst to the Demon or her host, a pair of Romans had escaped the entanglement upon the road through the aid of the particularly crafty Angels possessing them. Lord Magnesium closed on her from behind and slit the Germanic tribeswoman's throat, while his comrade set upon SIDS within the Celestial, hacking her to pieces with a Heavenly hatchet.

Fever swore and bellowed at the top of his lungs, helpless to avenge her from the roadside as the Angels slipped away.

*O Quintili, armer Feldherr, Dachtest du, daß so die Welt wär'?
Er geriet in einen Stumpf, Verlor zwei Stiefel und einen
Strumpf Und blieb elend stecken.*[36]

The greatest slaughter of the day took place in the swamps north of the main road. Disorientated from the ambush, a considerable portion of the legionnaires fled to the North, mistaking it for the direction of the main route. The Germans had disguised the direction of the road the day before.

"It's not the route!" Aaron was desperate.

"But my Lord has already led a contingent of our House in that

[35] Alas, that was a great murder, they beat the cohorts only the Roman cavalry saved himself in the open, because they were on horseback.

[36] O Quintili, poor general, did you think that was the way the world was? He got into a swamp lost two boots and a stocking and got stuck miserably.

direction, Lord Phosphorus." It was an Angel of the House of Mercury. "What would you have us do? Abandon them? Will you abandon them? If what you say is true, they are there stranded. What then?"

Aaron sighed and swore. "Fine, lead the way."

Da sprach er voll Ärgernussen. Zum Centurio Titiussen:
Kam'rad, zeuch dein Schwert hervor,
Und von hinten mich durchbor, Da doch alles futsch ist.[37]

Fever could sense the impending kill like a veteran hunting hound. They had pushed the heavy Roman infantry into the swamp. The Angels had been dragged along with their hosts. Now Fever led a contingent of siblings into the marsh in pursuit. He grinned broadly and released a menacing Germanic war cry as he led Autism, Chlamydial Lymphogranuloma, Legionnaires' Disease, and Anorexia into the battle.

They raced through the surface fog. Alternating between the Mortal and the Celestial, swapping possession effortlessly, they hewed down scores of Romans and Angels alike. Fever surged forward and fell upon an Angel of Asiatic appearance. She was cowering in a clump of swamp foliage, wailing. The desire for blood filled Fever like a palpable hunger. He looked at the frail Angel. She had been injured in the chaos; blood and muck stained her white robe. Fever raised his Celestial mallet, ready to claim the easy kill.

Suddenly, the water beside the Angel exploded in violent upheaval as a concealed Angel broke the surface and plunged a short sword into Fever's midsection. Fever groaned as the blade cut mercilessly through his innards.

In dem armen röm'schen Heere diente auch als
Volontäre Scaevola, ein Rechtskandidat,
Den man schnöd gefangen hat, Wie die andern alle.[38]

---

[37] Then he spoke with annoyance to the Centurion Titiussen: Comrade, take out your sword and run me through from behind since everything is gone.

[38] In the poor Roman army there was a volunteer, a legal candidate, and he was captured like all the others.

Lord Mercury IV wrenched the blade free from the midsection of the elder Demon and then hacked his neck. As the heap that had been a deadly nemesis only moments earlier slumped into the murky waters, Mercury IV turned to his eldest daughter. Her wound was fatal, and she was already slipping into perpetual sleep.

He whispered in his grief, "You have honored me and our House." He ran his hand along her cheek. "Your final act showed all the bravery I always knew you had."

She shuddered and expired in his arms.

Legionnaires' Disease screamed as he peered through the fog and saw the Angel slaughter Fever. His body quivered with rage and fear. Fever was the sole sire to all living Demons. Legionnaires' Disease could not imagine an Angel who could best the ancient Demon.

When others rallied to his side, Legionnaires' led them in an assault. The Angel was skilled. Legionnaires' Disease was unable to find a weakness. The others joined in the fray. Without surviving mortals in the area, the Angel defended valiantly but fell to the retribution of the Demons. Legionnaires' Disease landed the final, fatal blow, dragging his blade across the Angel's neck.

> Diesem ist es schlimm ergangen,
> Eh daß man ihn aufgehangen,
> Stach man ihm durch Zung und Herz,
> Nagelte ihn hinterwärts, Auf sein corpus iuris.[39]

Conjunctivitis found himself alone, separated from the others along a deserted stretch of the road. Not a living mortal was in sight, only corpses of Roman infantry and camp followers. Suddenly, he was set upon on all sides by a pack of Angels within the Celestial. He side-stepped the first attacker and ran him through. Before the foe's blade fell to the ground, Conjunctivitis grabbed it.

---

[39] It fared badly for him. Before he was hung up, he was stabbed through the tongue and heart and nailed backwards to his body of laws.

In a matter of moments, he had dispatched all the Angels, hacking off limbs and heads until there was nothing left but four piles of dismembered parts on the barren road.

Lord Phosphorous immediately regretted following the sentimental nature that had led him into the swamp. The murky ground had been transformed into a killing field, the likes of which he could have never imagined. The Germanic tribesmen had fallen upon the dispersed Romans, and Demons on the Angels. He fought with desperation and fear.

When he emerged from the swamp, his robes sliced by Demonic blades, his face covered with mud and blood, he appeared more a wild beast than an Angel. He had lost the entirety of the contingent allotted to his House. He fled up the road in the direction he perceived the Romans' flight to have taken.

> Als das Morden war zu Ende, rieb Fürst Hermann
> sich die Hände, und um seinen Sieg zu weih'n, lud er
> die Cherusker ein zu 'nem großen Frühstück.[40]

Roman Gladius

Anorexia looked about the swamp with terror gripping at her throat. She had possessed a Germanic warrior maid for protection. She glanced left and right for Romans and Angels. They were all dead. As far as she could see in the murky waters were dismembered and butchered corpses. They had slain countless Angels and mortals, and now the swamp was a watery graveyard awash in crimson, matching the Roman colors.

---

[40] When the killing was over Prince Hermann rubbed his hands and to dedicate his victory, he invited the Cherusci for a big breakfast.

Her brother Autism arrived through the mist, within a chieftain. He was carrying a golden Roman standard.

"Look at what I found," he said, still out of breath.

"Impressive," she replied through a shaking voice. "Have you seen the others?"

"We're all that's left."

"The Angel's died hard and took down Legionnaires' Disease and Chlamydial Lymphogranuloma."

Anorexia collapsed. "What are we going to do? I don't want to die."

Autism looked about the swamp again. "Calm yourself, sister. This, this is victory. Hard fought, yes, but a victory, nevertheless. The cost of triumph is blood; you know this to be true."

Anorexia tried to compose herself. "What are we to do?" she asked again.

Autism sighed. "Well, there's no shame in regrouping after such an encounter. Let us make our way to the woods where we can construct a portal."

> *Wild gab's und westfäl'schen Schinken Bier, soviel sie wollten trinken Auch im Zechen blieb er Held Doch auch seine Frau Thusneld soff walküremäßig.*[41]

The surviving Romans that had avoided the swamp, and the Angels within their ranks, managed to establish a fortified camp constructed with wagons from the supply train.

"This venture is blown," Iron III said with frustration from within General Varus. "We must collect ourselves and leave this field."

Zinc responded from within one of the General's officers. "We must wait until we have an accurate assessment of the casualty figures. We have killed many Demons today."

Carbon IV stepped forward within the Celestial, clutching his left arm, which was oozing blood from a deep, Celestial wound. Zinc

---

[41] There was game and Westphalian ham beer as much as they wanted to drink. He also remained a hero in carousing. But also, his wife, Thusnelda, drank like a Valkyrie.

cringed. If both the honorable Houses of Carbon and Iron challenged him, he would lose his authority.

To Zinc's surprise, Carbon IV said, "We must carry on. Rome must not be like Alexander's empire."

Next to speak was Lord Hydrogen. Zinc felt his body tighten with hatred as he saw the Angel he loathed more than any other. Zinc desperately tried to banish thoughts of this detestable Angel touching Rachael. Hydrogen pushed a young Familiar towards Zinc with an infuriating grin across his face.

"Tell them of the casualties," Hydrogen said.

The Familiar began. "Artorius is present, so perhaps you would like to hear from a more senior—"

"Report to us!"

The Familiar straightened. "We have confirmation of six Demons that were killed. Likely one to two more have perished as well."

"And our losses?" Hydrogen asked.

"We believe the number to be around one hundred, my Lord."

"How many Standard Bearers?" Zinc asked.

"Five my Lord: Mercury IV, Nickel, Tellurium, Manganese, and Arsenic."

Zinc bowed his head. "Three of those are brand new, just created. Such a loss is tragic but can be expected. This was indeed a hard-fought battle, but not so tipped against us in number. If we rally, we just might deal Hell a hammer's blow yet."

Hydrogen spoke next. "The Familiar says that nearly one-third of Heaven has fallen today, and you seek more blood? Who are the Standard Bearers that will lead when all have fallen?"

"You are of the Intelligence Service, Familiar," Zinc said. "What is your estimate of how many Demons compose Hell's order of battle."

"We estimate it to be in the thirties," the Familiar replied.

"So, if we kill two to three more, this affair is even. I know, Lord Hydrogen, that such a tense affair might be beyond your stomach, but I assure you, those of us who take on the responsibility of leadership know when to attack and when to withdraw," he said. He draped his arm around Lord Carbon IV.

"We need one, bold action," Zinc said. "We break out and seek to inflict a precise blow on a single portion of their contingent. Then we withdraw and assess."

The assembled Lords agreed. Zinc recognized the Familiar as Lilly, the sole survivor from the day his wife fell. He longed to speak to her about the details of that day but saw no opportunity under the current circumstances.

Nur in Rom war man nicht heiter, Sondern kaufte
Trauerkleider;
G'rade als beim
Mittagsmahl Augustus saß im
Kaisersaal, kam die Trauerbotschaft.[42]

"All this action, and nobody came this way," Schitz said from behind the fabricated wall of sticks and earth.

"We're in a good position," Rubella said. "Patience."

"I'm just anxious to be back in the fight," Schitz said.

The next day, the Romans and their Angelic counterparts broke their encampment and continued along the narrow road through the forest. They encountered battlements constructed by the Germanic forces. Once again, javelins fell on the Romans like the heavy September rains. Schitz watched in horror as the Angelic contingent trapped within the ambush exceeded the expected numbers. The horde of enemies was so large it threatened to break the encirclement.

He manned the earthen ramparts with Rubella and Syphilis. Rabies, Cytomegalovirus, Actinomycetoma, and Reyes Disease sallied forth to dispatch the fallen in the Celestial. As they departed, it became clear that the Angelic contingent was massive. Many had seized when their hosts were killed, but there were many more in the Celestial.

"Hold the battlements at all costs." Syphilis dropped a satchel filled with Celestial throwing knives on the earthen wall as she shouted. "And for Satan's sake, cover me."

---

[42] Only in Rome was it not cheerful, mourning clothes were sought after. At midday meal Augustus sat in the imperial hall and came the sad news.

Syphilis leapt into the Celestial and charged toward the others who had already ventured forth.

> Erst blieb ihm vor jähem Schrecken
> ein Stück Pfau im Halse stecken,
> Dann geriet er außer sich und schrie:
> "Vare, schäme dich Redde legiones!"[43]

Rabies had anticipated combat from her earliest days. Yet, as the Romans and Angels moved toward her, she felt a dizzying panic.

"There are too many!" she yelled at the top of her lungs to be heard.

Her brother-in-law, Cytomegalovirus, showed no fear. "It seems we are caught out," he said. "Brace for contact."

Though the javelins cut down scores of mortal Romans and exposed vulnerable Angels, the Celestial was filled with too many Angels to exploit the advantage. Rabies fought for her life. To her delight, she slew one Angel, then another, then another. Her small band of Demons was holding its own.

Still, something told her they would be overwhelmed in a matter of minutes. She watched in horror as Reye's Disease stepped into a Roman to avoid an onslaught from four Angels only for her host to be struck by a javelin. She fell to the ground, shaking. Rabies flung a throwing knife into the back of one Angel and charged a second.

She heard a voice in the distance. "Look out, Lord Chlorine!"

The Angel turned and raised his sword to block Rabies. Her momentum bowled them both onto the ground. Rabies and the Angel scrambled upright and traded ferocious blows.

Shouts of warning filled the air. "Rabies, you must get out of there."

She saw Syphilis running towards her. Dozens of Angels were chasing her in the Celestial. Syphilis blocked, dodged, tumbled,

---

[43] At first, he was left with shock, a piece of peacock stuck in the throat. Then he was beside himself and shouted, "Varus, be ashamed, give me back my legions!

evaded. She jumped briefly into one mortal, then another; at times, she cut down an Angel.

Rabies saw Cytomegalovirus lying dead on the muddy earth. Two Angels shoved swords through Actinomycetoma.

Momentarily distracted, Rabies lost her footing. Her attacker swiped a sword across her thigh, slicing her robe and leg to ribbons. Rabies howled at the searing agony and looked up to face execution.

I will not show fear, she thought.

A shadowy blur passed over her as Syphilis flew through the air and landed a kick into the Angel's chest. Before Rabies could speak, the senior Demon had slung her over her shoulder and started running. Syphilis scooped up a delirious Reye's Disease by the waist and lumbered towards the battlements.

> *Sein deutscher Sklave, Schmidt geheißen Dacht':*
> *Euch soll das Mäusle beißen Wenn er sie je wieder kriegt*
> *denn wer einmal tot daliegt wird nicht mehr lebendig.*[44]

Schitz had never seen such a feat of strength. He stared, slack-jawed, as Syphilis toted the injured Demons toward him. Schitz recovered his faculties and began to hurl Celestial throwing knives at the pursuing Angels. Rubella joined in the effort to cover their comrades.

Angel after Angel fell. Blood spurted from severed throats and punctured lungs. The foes stopped their pursuit and began to throw weapons of their own.

> *Wem ist dieses Lied gelungen?*
> *Ein Studente hat's gesungen in Westfalen trank er viel drum aus*
> *Nationalgefühl hat er's angefertigt.*[45]

---

[44] His German slave, called Schmidt thought: the mouse will bite you, if he ever gets her back because whoever lies dead once will never live again.

[45] Who succeeded in this song? A student sang it, he drank a lot in Westphalia, therefore out of national feelings he made it.

Syphilis heaved her charges over the edge of the battlements and collapsed to the floor. Schitz and Rubella ran to their side. Syphilis had been struck in the back by a throwing star and was spitting blood.

Her words came in gasps. "I brought back the young ones—your young one."

"Shush, don't speak," Rubella said. She cradled Syphilis. "We can never repay your bravery. Save your strength."

"I am done in," Syphilis replied. She coughed out a river of blood. "Look after the young ones. They've been hurt badly. And... losing a host... the first departure seizure can be dangerous."

"We shall attend to them, I promise," Rubella said. "Be at peace. You have saved two fine young women. They will have more children because of you, and their children will have children; until the final victory."

"Until the final victory!" Syphilis repeated. She grimaced and went limp in Rubella's arms.

> Und zu Ehren der Geschichten tat ein Denkmal man errichten,
> Deutschlands Kraft und Einigkeit kündet es jetzt weit und breit:
> "Mögen sie nur kommen!"[46]

Schitz watched his wife holding his departed aunt.

Syphilis was married to Bubonic Plague, but she was a brave warrior, he thought.

He owed her a debt.

Night descended on the woods and the fields along the twisting road that wound through Teutoburg Forest. The Germanic warriors returned to their villages, leaving only the corpses of the three annihilated legions. The bodies remained, food for ravens, as the unrelenting rain continued to fall.

---

[46] And in honor of the stories, they erected a monument to Germany's strength and unity. It announces far and wide: May they only come!

THE FORCES OF HELL traipsed back through various portals and queued for the Priests as they performed the Return Ceremony. They barely had time to slink off to their respective abodes before the High Priest summoned the majority of the battle's survivors to a meeting in the Throne Room. All knelt when Satan entered.

"I will keep this brief," the Devil began. "Our losses have been extensive, and there is much sifting to be done through our remaining ranks. Regarding the accusations brought about against Schizophrenia Incenderos Nervosa, I have concluded that he was the victim of a false-flag endeavor on the part of the Shaman to sow discord within our ranks."

Schitz could not believe the absurd explanation. He glanced around the room, but the attendees were too battle-worn to offer an observable response. Even Bubonic Plague seemed disinterested and self-absorbed between an apparent injury and the loss of his wife.

Satan continued, "Therefore, I find that Schizophrenia is not guilty of treason and is, of course, of pure Demonic Blood. However, I have determined that Bubonic Plague and Schizophrenia's feud has proven incredibly detrimental to the functioning of our forces. Therefore, Schizophrenia is hereby banished to the land beyond the waters to the West, where he will be tasked with locating and dispatching of the Angel Gold. This time-consuming mission will surely give Bubonic Plague and Schizophrenia time to reflect upon how they can best work together. This exile will take effect upon the morrow. You have the remainder of the day to get your affairs in order, Schizophrenia. That is all."

CHAPTER 10

GODS AMONG US

"Lift those stones, you worthless maggots!" The overseer in the stone fields of Nawahocte cracked his whip. "The Gods' monument will not be built with ideas alone."

Nitathl lifted the stone satchel and hoisted it across his back, his scarred and bloody posterior bearing yet another heavy load, ignorant to the dangers of his wounds.

He prayed silently. "Great God Inti, great Sun God, my wounds will be healed in the glow of your light that shines upon even the lowest of our society, for we are the children of your making."

Walking toward the embankment of canoes that would bring the stones up to the monument in the name of the holiest of holies, Nitathl considered himself blessed. In the afterlife, he and his children and his children's children would be credited with building the monument of the creator. Mikhush took the stones and washed his hands in the river to remove the dirt and debris accumulated throughout the endless workday. He cursed the summer of their world because every hour of sun equated to an hour of labor.

"Why do you sulk so much, Mikhush?" Nitathl asked.

"Because I haven't seen my wife since I left to work these dreadful pits," Mikhush replied bitterly.

"Count yourself lucky," Nitathl said. "The overseers will only be credited in the afterlife with holding a lash. You can say your hands helped build the house of God."

"You can keep the afterlife, Nitathl. We're not there yet; we're only here dying."

Nitathl turned away from Mikhush and wandered to the rock pits amid the myriad of laborers, an endless sea of humanity. Mikhush pushed the canoe from the bank and began paddling toward the heavenly Gods' estate. Mikhush was plagued by a haunting memory, a recollection of playing with his fellow youths while his mother called from a hut. When he arrived, to his dismay, a heavily feathered and decorated Shaman stood at the bedside of his father. The holy man sang the familiar hymns and shook a bone rattle over his father's body. Rivulets of sweat made his father appear as if encased in obsidian.

His mother leaned down and whispered, "Your father has the sweating sickness."

Mikhush had heard of this malady in other villages and knew the Shamans could not cure the ghastly disease.

How different life was now that the Gods had graced his people with their presence. Sickness and disease had vanished from the land, and death only arrived as a peaceful transition for the elderly. In an instant, Mikhush felt guilty about his petty, mortal concerns. He looked up toward the sky, high above the Andes. "All praise be to thee our saviors."

Elise pleaded with Schitz. "This is a victory for you, my son."

The Demon stood, legs spread in a defiant pose, arms crossed. His scowl looked like a thundercloud. "They've essentially executed me," he said. "I can't come back until Gold is dead. He took on Heaven and Hell and escaped with his life."

Elise did not reply. She was watching the various comings and goings of the Great Hall.

"Oh, I'm sorry, am I distracting you?" Schitz asked.

Elise wrapped her sole arm around his waist. "I'm sorry, my boy," she said. "I am distracted. Aside from Germania, we received reports of a deeply troubling nature from Judea. There are reports of sightings of the Messiah, the Son of God, The Christ. Leprosy was the only senior Demon fit to investigate. I have just heard from Mephistopheles that they have recovered the soup that was once her body. The mortal purported to be the Heavenly Messiah exorcised her."

She shook as with a fever.

"Well, supposedly, I'm the Antichrist," Schitz said. Sarcasm dripped like syrup from his words. "Maybe I should just go fight him instead of Gold."

"Oh, shut up, child," Elise said. "Your lot thinks Wraiths are simpleminded and ignorant."

Stung by her retort, Schitz pulled away.

"I'm sorry, Son," she said. "We just see so much that Demons do not or chose not to see. The Devil has utilized his privilege with many a young maiden. It would be foolish to think he has not sired a few who call others 'father.' The Church would have you believe his one and only son will be powerful, as if he has not bred with his own creation multiple times, not to mention his pairing with mortals. Still, it is more likely than not that many of you are related to him. In your case, I cannot say. I knew your parents well. They loved each other from early on, as much as SIDS refused to admit it."

Schitz's mind reeled.

So, *was it my blood or my thoughts that the exorcist sensed—or something else*? he thought.

"None of it really matters," Elise said. "Have you brought enough provisions?"

Schitz broke into a small grin. "I am laden like a pack mule."

In addition to everything else, he had countless throwing knives, a multitude of daggers, several short swords, and a pair of long swords.

"Remember, place those in differing caches; familiarize yourself with your surroundings and move slowly. Don't rush or force things."

Schitz held his Wraith tightly. "I know, Mama. It will be okay."

"The Wraiths will check in on you from time to time," she said.

"Thank you," Schitz said. He focused on sounding steady. "I must go now."

Schitz stepped further into the Great Hall, where he was met by Rubella and Rabies.

"How is the leg?" he asked as he pulled Rabies into a reserved embrace.

"Nothing that the waters of the Styx could not repair," she replied.

"You fought very bravely. I am looking forward to fighting by your side when I return."

"I would like that very much," she said.

"Now, my wonderful daughter, I wonder if you might give me a private moment with your mother?"

Rabies stepped away.

"Don't stray too far; it will be but a moment," he said. He turned to his wife. "My life... my love."

The words came with difficulty. Rubella clutched him so tightly, he had trouble breathing. They had made love more times than either could count since his sentence was pronounced, but his desire for her was still boundless. Schitz broke the embrace and placed his hands on either side of her face.

"There is so much to say and so little time," he said. "I know it will not stay quiet for long—the means of my escape from judgment."

Rubella laughed through tears.

"Oh, yes," she said. "You are the infamous descendant of Satan himself? Yes, I have heard the discussion."

Schitz shrugged. "I don't know if that's true, but even if it is, Elise just told me I would not be unique. Before I follow the despot's edict, I need to know if anything ever happened to you."

Rubella placed her hands over Schitz's and gazed deeply into his eyes. "And you would defy the Lord himself for my honor? I know you would, my love, but thankfully I have only known you."

Schitz felt a pang of guilt as he thought of his own infidelity, but pushed it from his mind, flush with relief that Rubella had not been taken against her will.

"Although," she said, glancing down, "within our generation, I know that Influenza's innocence was... ah... compromised by Satan."

Schitz stepped back in revulsion. His voice was a croak. "So, her children?"

Rubella snickered. "Well, I don't know who fathered her children. Surely not all of them came from Legionnaires' Disease, rest his soul. But I do know that Satan presented himself to her and took her for himself as a potential bride. Afterwards, he discarded her. She always felt his interest was a charade to steal her maidenhood; that he never intended to marry her."

"And this is common knowledge?"

"Amongst us girls," Rubella said. "She unburdened herself during the Academy, but what power do any of us have to stop such things?"

"I'm glad Rabies wed quickly," Schitz said, overwhelmed by disillusionment in his leader.

"Luckily, through my place in the Academy, I always had her right under my watchful eye," Rubella said. She spat in disgust. "Ah, the Academy. I am overwhelmed with the loss of Fever and Tetanus. Now I am all that's left to pick up the pieces and carry on our traditions; it is a burden I never imagined I would shoulder."

"You will do amazing work," Schitz said. "You have always been the smart one."

She forced a smile. "The one positive is that I have Rabies to help me; she was top of her class and has accepted a position."

"I am so proud of my brilliant, talented women," Schitz said.

He signaled to his daughter. She returned, and he pulled her into an embrace with her mother.

"We have to be realistic. It is the nature of our lot in life that we may very well not see each other ever again. I want you both to know that I love you so very deeply. You are the best parts of my life."

He kissed Rabies on the forehead, then enjoyed one, last, passionate kiss with Rubella. Without further comment, he made his way to the departure gateways lining the far side of the Hall. The columns featured countless ancient symbols carved into them. With a small amount of dirt, water, breath, or fire from caldrons that stood beside them, a Demon could select anywhere in the world for their arrival. Schitz hesitated. He had never traveled across the waters, but from instruction and the reports of Wraiths, he had a generalized knowledge of where he was going. He dipped his finger into the flammable oil

Fire & Air

pot and traced it along the symbols for fire. He placed a torch into one of the ever-burning flames and ignited the symbol. Finally, he exhaled on the conflagration, while beginning the incantations requisite for travel. His arrival would not be narrowed down to a specific area, so he closed his eyes and hoped for the safest landing. With that, he stepped through the portal and into the unknown.

"I'M NOT CALLING YOU a coward," Lord Hydrogen said as he and Lady Hydrogen walked through the crowded, narrow streets of Volubilis. "I just don't understand how you went through the whole battle without participating in a single meaningful engagement. Your debriefing was a topic of consternation during the inquest into Teutoburg Forest."

"I gave an honest assessment," she replied bluntly before averting her gaze to the many comings and goings of the local inhabitants of the North African city.

"I extol you for your honesty. I just don't understand the rationale," he replied.

"From the beginning, it was clear to me that all of Hell's forces were present, so I sought out the one with whom I have a score to settle," she said.

Lord Hydrogen raised an eyebrow. "The one with the scar on his face?"

Rachael nodded. "That's the one."

"I hear he is of tremendous quality," Hydrogen said, "but next time, maybe you could trouble yourself with some of the others."

"It's not that I sought him out for the challenge," Lady Hydrogen replied. "I have a personal vendetta against him. He killed my brother Benjamin."

"Ah, you two were close?"

"We were twins, but more than just that. My whole life, he was my best friend, my confidant, the one reliable, consistent thing. Then in an instant, that animal took him away from me."

Lord Hydrogen reached for her hand; the touch was awkward for both of them.

"I am sorry," he said. "We have much to learn about one another."

"You mean I'm not just a bargaining chip?" she asked.

Hydrogen sighed. "It is true that I saw a way to influence Zinc through his... his relationship with you, but I did not endeavor to exploit this angle for personal gain or love of power. Look at my House; we are on the periphery of Heaven's forces. We are called upon for the deadliest, most speculative endeavors, but do we have a voice in the setting of strategy or policy? Never."

"That's why you scheme so clumsily." Rachael laughed, harsh and mirthless. "You do it from the good of your heart."

"Excuse me?" Lord Hydrogen feigned offense.

"I heard about how Zinc handled your maneuvering at Teutoburg," she said. "You wanted to stop the slaughter once it was obvious that it was a stalemate."

"Correct."

"You're a kind-hearted Angel," she said while shaking her head. "Zinc cares very much about being in control, more so than he does about anything else..." She paused for a moment. "...even me."

"I need to tell you," Lord Hydrogen said, "I don't need to know about your feelings for him, I will not interfere, but—"

"Stop it!" Lady Hydrogen halted in the middle of the street. Her fists were clenched, her jaw set. "All of Heaven knows I was his concubine, or whatever you want to call it. I presume you can live with it. Otherwise, why would you have married me? Especially when you say your political concern with Zinc comes from an honest place."

Lord Hydrogen made a waggling motion with his palm—maybe yes/maybe no. "When your father came to me, he expressed that he wanted a fresh start for you, and I thought the idea had appeal." He smirked. "And you are so beautiful, that helps."

Rachael laughed. "I agree, a fresh start sounds good, but we will need to fine-tune your politicking." She turned and met his deep, dark eyes with her own. "For example, if you want something," she lowered her voice, and bit her lower lip, "if you want something very badly, the best way to go about it is to make your target believe they want it as well."

"I see," Lord Hydrogen said. "So, my desire at the moment, it is really yours?"

"Now you're getting it," she replied.

She slid closer and pressed her open mouth against his.

ZINC SAT ABOUT HIS lavish room feeling extremely isolated. He had accomplished much in his time stamping his authority over the forces of Heaven. Yet, he was certain he had lost his way. Certain that he could not deliver the final victory. The moment's question was how to proceed with this knowledge. He had given his eldest sons their own Houses, and they had performed admirably at Teutoburg and at several actions in the Levant following that. However, he did not feel anywhere near ready to retire and turn his own House over to another. The only option he could see was to throw his support behind another and work on rebuilding his authority. It dawned upon him that he could shift the paradigm entirely. He could free the Houses, each to their own accord, no more Leading House-Subordinate House relationships. Then with those loyal to him, his sons, and whomever else, he could reassert his authority over Heaven without the burden to provide definitive success. The more he ruminated upon the idea, the more Zinc was in favor of the action.

As he looked around the empty room, he realized that for the first time, he lacked a confidant with whom to share his ideas. He had lost his father, his wife, and Rachael. His room and his world felt very small and very lonely.

THE NOISE OF THE jungle was the first element that Schitz beheld as he stepped forth into the Mortal World, a melodious hum of insects, birds, and animals. Next, he perceived the heat and humidity, an oppressive, overwhelming force that seemed to envelop and subjugate him. Schitz sat upon the exposed root of a massive tree, larger than any he had ever seen in Europe, Africa, or Asia. He clasped his head within his hands and rocked back and forth. The punishment seemed massive; banishment to the New World, exiled with the only hope of return resting in his assignment to singlehandedly kill a Demi-God and his brother.

He cursed aloud and considered how he had structured his efforts for survival weighed against his need to contribute to the cause. He already knew that reports of the Messiah that had exorcized Leprosy would pull Angels and Demons to the Holy Land. He would miss these crusades. All his life, he had striven to avoid conflicts and yet attempted to avoid the label of cowardice. However, despite these efforts, he found himself barred entry to Hell and sent on a veritable suicide mission. He was cut off from Rubella, Rabies, and Elise, and all that was safe and comforting.

A wave of self-pity threatened to swallow him whole. He felt as though life never had a way of working out for him, as it did for others. He looked up into the branches above him and saw a toucan perched upon a bough, peering down upon him.

Schitz observed the bird and thought, *This animal does not know his fate any more than I know my own, and like him, I know that the world is full of food and predators. I, like this winged fellow, will strive to eat whilst avoiding those who would eat me, and like this colorful bird, I will not concern myself with my fate or more substantial problems.*

Schitz rose to his feet. "Gold and Silver fancy themselves gods," he said aloud. "Well, then, I will have to become the destroyer of deities."

With his courage and resolve renewed, Schitz strode out into the jungle. The toucan squawked and fluttered away in a huff.

"I will find my way back to my home," Schitz said. "I will chart a course, and I will not waver."

"Do you really think it's true?" Aaron whispered to his older brother.

Patrick shrugged. "It's possible. I mean, it is what our Church says will happen, and I'm certain God would leave it as much a mystery to us Angels as he would to the mortals. Maybe more of a mystery to us, since he's the mortal's Messiah, and our new leader."

"Wow," Aaron said. "The son of God, the Christ."

Patrick was not paying attention. He had more pressing thoughts on his mind than the fulfillment of the prophecy. He begrudgingly had to admit that his father had been correct about his assessment of combat. The fight, chilling and brutal, had left a mark on his psyche. He no longer wished for his next visit to the Mortal Realm.

Though he had partaken in several uneventful missions since Teutoburg Forest, he no longer yearned for the rigors of combat. Ironically, he had been heavily rewarded, as his detachment had been credited with three kills and he with one personally. However, he had taken little joy in the experience. The Demon he had felled with a last-ditch heave of a throwing star had kicked him with sufficient force to shatter four of his ribs and punctured both of his lungs. He had barely survived the return to Heaven, where Manna had been administered and saved his life.

The Angels responsible for two Demonic deaths died as they charged the earthen battlements erected by the Germanic tribesmen. Lord Chlorine's brother, Lord Phosphorus, was the sole survivor of the portion of the battle referred to as 'The Swamp'—a campaign now discussed in hushed whispers and swirling rumor.

"The Houses recently formed will return to the House of their origin, Nickel to Lithium and Tellurium to Iron. Since Arsenic and Manganese both fell, their Houses will go to the brave Lord Carbon IV," his father said to the Heavenly assembly.

Lord Carbon IV stepped forward; he raised his right arm and spoke.

"This will be a fitting gift for my eldest living son, for Manna can do but so much." He punctuated his sentence by raising his severed left hand. The wound proved too deep and he had lost the limb. "But I tell you this: though my career is cut short, I have never been prouder to fight alongside such Angels as I did on that harrowing day."

A considerable cheer rose from the crowd. Lord Chlorine wondered how the Angels truly felt about the outcome of the day. His father had led nearly three hundred and fifty Angels into battle, and over one hundred and twenty had returned as lifeless corpses. That was the reason Heaven abandoned merely trying to crush Hell with their superior numbers; more troops often resulted in large casualty figures.

"Cobalt, who bravely represented his House, will receive the members of the House of Mercury," Lord Zinc said.

A flurry of whispering passed through those assembled. Phosphorus knew there had been a lot of conjecture whether the survivors of the formidable House of Mercury would stay with their kind or would be parsed out to an older house. In a magnanimous gesture, Zinc allowed them to continue their cultural integrity as the House of Asiatic Angels.

Lord Zinc continued, "It is now with a heavy heart that I must speak candidly with you." An ominous silence fell over the Heavenly assembly. Lord Phosphorous felt the hairs upon the back of his neck stand up as he awaited his father's next pronouncement.

"I believe we are on the cusp of a challenge to my role as the leader of the Heavenly Houses." He paused until the murmuring died. "Come, come. I know you are hurting. You are doubting. We have lost a great multitude of our family and friends. So, when I tell you there is no need for any further strife among us, I pray that you truly hear my words. Moving forward, I will not issue an order to any member of any House other than my own. I strongly encourage all other Standard Bearers to take the same approach. Let us follow up on the costly blow we have delivered to Hell with camaraderie and solidarity rather than politicking and jockeying for authority."

There was stunned silence that was slowly followed by eruptive applause. Soon a chant of "Zinc, Zinc, Zinc" shook the hall. Zinc raised his hands to quiet the crowd, though Phosphorous knew his father well enough to know he was enjoying the moment.

"All hail Zinc, the conqueror of Granicus, Persepolis, and Teutoburg," shouted the new Lord Carbon V.

In stunning unison, the Heavenly Hall was filled with the stamping of feet. Everyone snapped to attention and saluted Lord Zinc. Phosphorous did not doubt that his father would once again gain hegemony over the other Houses, even if he saw reason for granting them a level footing for the time being.

"I AM NOW THE eldest," Bubonic Plague said, "and the burden falls upon me not just to bring victory in the field but to lead us forward strategically."

"And the Council?" Smallpox asked.

Bubonic looked upon his brother with disdain in his eyes. "We are the Council."

"You mean you are," Smallpox replied, bemused, "for I am certain you see no threat from Rubella or me."

"The little bookworm?" Bubonic scoffed. "I still remember rescuing her during the siege of Babylon. She is of little consequence either way, and I know you stand with me."

Smallpox smiled. "Foregone conclusions. And I trust you expect the Wraiths and Priests to bend to your will."

"But, of course, Brother," Bubonic replied with a maniacal grin. "I will not go out in a burst of glory like my beloved Syphilis."

"They built her a statue in the Great Hall," Smallpox said with the slightest hint of jest in his eyes.

"And what good is a statute when your cold body lies under it?" Bubonic asked.

"None at all," Smallpox replied, "but it is nice, a truly epic depiction of her carrying the two young Demons to safety."

Bubonic Plague grunted.

"I only mention it to say, what more is there than lasting glory?

We all fall eventually," Smallpox said philosophically. He sipped Brew from an ornate chalice.

"Do you know how many Angelic trophies line these walls?" Bubonic asked, gesturing with a swipe of his hand that sent sprinkles of Brew flying from his own chalice.

"I haven't the faintest idea," Smallpox replied.

He glanced about his brother's luxurious dwelling space. Plague had recently moved into his grandfather's old abode and had replaced Fever's adornments with his own. Smallpox took inventory of the mortal and Angelic weapons that lined the walls, an impressive array of swords, knives, armor, animal skins. The mortal weaponry and armor covered Sumerian, Babylonian, Egyptian, Greek, Roman, and various other eras. The Angelic weaponry was vast in style and quantity.

"I could not count," Smallpox said.

"Two hundred and fifty-two," Bubonic Plague said.

"Wow," Smallpox replied. His admiration was evident. "That has to be the largest collection of Angelic trophies ever acquired."

"I have two statues in the Great Hall, from Uruk and the Fall of Babylon. Two statues while I still live. I have slaughtered Angels in multitudes, the likes of which Hell has never seen. I will not fall like the others, as you say."

"I meant no offense, Brother," Smallpox said.

"Brother, ah, there's the rub, isn't it? You resemble our studious father. The same can be said for Leprosy, rest her soul. But where does my breeding come from?" Bubonic Plague asked.

Smallpox nodded. "You weary me with the same diatribe," he said. "You're just upset about Schizophrenia."

"I am the destroyer of Heaven," Bubonic said. He drained his chalice. "I am the Antichrist Satan never claimed. But when I deliver the final victory, I will sit at the right hand of our Lord as the true Prince of Hell foretold in our legends."

Smallpox raised his glass. "I'll drink to that."

Bubonic Plague seemed to relax slightly. "I have been working on a strategy," he said with pride evident in his voice. "Now that I am the most senior Demon, I plan to take on a greater educational role at the Academy. I shall begin a special project."

Smallpox choked on his Brew a little. "Have they asked you to instruct at the academy?"

"They will undoubtedly," Bubonic said. "However, it is my own project about which I am most excited. I am going to recruit a select group of the youngsters to form an elite society, a coven of sorts."

Smallpox leaned closer; his interest heightened. "To what end?"

"By myself, I can inflict devastating outbreaks of illness upon the mortals. However, if I train a cadre of followers to inflict my disease upon the world, we can kill all of the mortals."

"That's an interesting endeavor," Smallpox said.

Bubonic's face glowed with excitement. "Think about it," he said. "The entirety of humanity would begin to perish, and as they did, all would die gripped by fear, hatred, anger, all that sends souls to the Styx. Our power would overflow while Heaven starved. Angels would be unable to travel between Heaven and Earth. They would either die in the Mortal Realm, as our powerful army wore them down, or they would wither from the Atrophy."

"I can see that if human deaths rapidly and drastically outpaced human births, then they would go extinct. If they all died in fear, their souls would be trapped in the Styx waiting on mortal bodies that were not being created," Smallpox said. "But how would we then rule over the mortal world? Presumably, we would want to reinvigorate the human race, so that we could rule over them and ensure that we had continual access to the Mortal and Celestial Realm."

An awkward stillness settled over the room.

"I have it," Smallpox said. His voice bubbled with exuberance. He gulped at his chalice before explaining. "There is very little difference between the body of a Demon and the body of a mortal, yes?"

"Yes, of course," Bubonic Plague said. "Satan fashioned Demons through breeding with mortals."

"Exactly," Smallpox replied, "think about it. We die from injuries that would easily be mended by the waters of the Styx simply because the waters lose their potency when taken out of Hell, and we bleed out before we return. I've watched the Priests heal a slit throat post-mortem just so the poor sap would look better upon the funerary altar."

"So, you think the mortal souls could be inserted into the repaired corpses of Demons?" Bubonic Plague asked.

"The very ones that rest under the floor the Great Hall," Smallpox replied. "Ask Satan if it is a possible end game for your plan. If so, I am certain he will support it, and I will do everything within my power to assist you as well."

While Bubonic ran through the facets of the newly completed plan, Smallpox refilled both of their cups.

"It is perfection," Bubonic Plague said. "I applaud you for seeing it through to a fitting conclusion."

"All the pieces were already there," Smallpox said. He raised his glass. "To you and your coven."

"And to the final victory," Bubonic Plague said.

The brothers toasted and drank.

SCHITZ HAD DECIDED TO take Elise's advice to heart, even if the prospect of a protracted exile grieved him. He knew it was lunacy to assume he could simply walk into Gold's empire and murder him.

"I have to study the rain forest, the mountains, the people," he said aloud as he walked through the dense brush. "I have to learn how the entire system has been established and then probe for weak points."

Schitz embarked on an extensive, meticulous endeavor to learn all he could about the Amazon. He studied the geography, the rise and fall of the hills and mountains, the paths of the many rivers, the locations of dense foliage, and clearings. He studied the mortals, the Cacataibo, and the Isconahua nomadic tribes within the jungle, the Tiwanaku and the Wari, city-dwelling inhabitants, the Incas who occupied the highlands. He learned about the foliage and the animals.

As mortal years passed, he slowly became aware of the environment at a level he had never imagined possible. He began to observe Familiars slinking through the jungle and the villages. Schitz resisted the urge to follow them or to engage them. In his initial observations, he deduced that they had seen him as well, and they were much quicker and stealthier.

That will never do, he thought. *I must become faster and stealthier.*

Schitz ran incessantly. He trained himself to fly through the dense foliage and winding forest paths at a full tilt. He wanted to reach the point where he could glide past spying Familiars without their ever seeing him.

Schitz began to stalk the Familiars, remaining undetected as he went. His progress was slow, but he eventually began to track the Familiars higher and higher into the Andes. Within the Highlands, he observed Angels, both within mortal bodies and within the Celestial Realm. It was easy to deduce that the Angels were of the Houses of Gold and Silver, their complexions were pale, and their hair was mostly blonde or silvery-gray. Schitz saw an Angel with dark black hair and felt his pulse quicken.

"Anna?" he whispered to himself.

However, as the possessed mortal stepped out of the shade of a Cerezo tree, he realized the resident Angel was blonde; her hair color had been momentarily concealed within her host.

Schitz cursed softly. *I cannot let thoughts of Anna distract me from my purpose.*

Though he had given himself over to Rubella, he knew his vow was easier to make than to keep. Proximity to the House of Gold evoked strong, confusing feelings.

Prompted by his agitated mental state, Schitz opted to disengage from scouting the Angels. He knew he'd been spotted early in his stay, so he relocated all his Celestial weapon caches, then ceased his activity. He knew he could not operate if reports of his presence reached the Angels. He needed Gold to believe that a Demon had been skulking around the fringes of his empire but had withdrawn.

ZINC WALKED WITHIN THE Celestial across the plains of Ravenna. The breeze from the Adriatic was warm and refreshing. It had been many

Septembers since the contest in Teutoburg, yet Zinc felt as though the season of autumn and that cursed month, in particular, would always bring nostalgic memories of sorrow. Zinc glanced about at the aftereffects of battle—eviscerated corpses, some still twitching or groaning, discarded weapons and armor, flags and standards, and all manner of materials and personal items littered the field.

The Roman Empire had well and truly disintegrated. Though it had taken longer to fall apart than Alexander's kingdom, Rome, the Eternal City, was no longer the ruler of the world. Zinc was relieved that he had abdicated his position as leader of the Angels before the demise of yet another of his mortal empires. Had he stayed with Rome and his position until the bitter end, his career would have been indelibly blotted. His assessment of his current situation was far less bleak than that of Romulus Augustulus, the last Caesar.

As Zinc had predicted, none of the Standard Bearers possessed the ability or cunning to unite the Houses of Heaven. They carried on their own speculative endeavors with little central coordination or leadership. Zinc, for his part, had accepted an invitation to teach at the Angelic Academy. He utilized the opportunity to focus on his own development; he knew his future lay in continually evolving.

Participation in the battle of Ravenna had been a final stage exercise for the current senior class. Zinc had introduced this level of training upon his appointment to the faculty and often wished such training had been available during his formative years. He had taken the young Angels to a field likely to be devoid of Demonic involvement.

Years earlier, the Demons were satisfied to bludgeon the light of Rome into darkness. Besides, the emergence of the mortal heralded as the Messiah drew a great deal of Demonic and Angelic attention to the Levant. Zinc felt safe utilizing the action in Northern Italy for training purposes.

He divided the class between the final Roman Legions and the Germanic Foederati. Within the Mortal Realm, the Angels had engaged in actual battle, maneuvering from host to host, slaying humans, and coordinating with their comrades. Within the Celestial, they fought mock battles with one another using blunted weapons. Zinc could tell that conducting the drill within actual mortal warfare was a useful tool. Many young Angels who had shown promise in the classroom or on the training ground were far less skillful when faced with the grim realities of combat.

"Remember," Zinc said to the assembled students, "we are here to bring death to Demons and humans alike."

To punctuate his point, he stepped into the body of one of Odoacer's men. Zinc forced the host to pause from looting the dead. He pulled a spear from the earth and strode over to an injured Roman. For a moment, he knelt over the Roman and whispered a short series of Latin utterances. Zinc rose to his feet and plunged the spear into the legionnaire's chest. He wrenched the weapon free and tossed it to the ground.

Stepping back into the Celestial, Zinc asked the assembled Angels, "Who can tell me what I did before I killed the Roman?"

A few hands went up. Zinc felt a sense of pride as he beheld one of his own descendants prepared to answer the question.

"Yes, young Zinc," he said.

"You spoke to him about the love of his homeland and glorious death in the service of his people," the young member of his House replied.

"Yes, indeed, quite right. And why did I do that?" he asked.

Zinc's attention was next drawn to a young maiden of the former House of Silver. Although members of defunct Houses were virtual slaves to him through their pledged fealty, their children were mandated to receive academic instruction.

"Young Silver of the House of Zinc," he said.

"So that his soul might travel to the Eunoe instead of the Styx," she said muted, yet confident in her reply.

"Yes," Zinc said, "that is correct. Remember, while you are in possession of a mortal, regardless of whatever else you are doing, you must endeavor to imbue them with such thoughts. Someday you will be able to spread such thoughts to all those in your proximity. The nature of battle inspires fear and hatred. Therefore, it is an aid to the foe. We must strive to counter that by offering the opposite version of the sacrifice."

The students nodded in acknowledgment. Zinc felt very positive when he assessed his new role. He enjoyed shaping young minds and being solely responsible for his own House. Following the departure of Patrick and Aaron to become Standard Bearers of their own, Zinc began building his relationship with Adolphus, his next oldest son, preparing him either to assume command of the House of Zinc, or to receive his own House at the next Grand Gathering.

Zinc was jarred back to the present as his thoughts were interrupted by a hand, held aloft by one of the students, a sandy-complected young member of the House of Hydrogen.

She resembles her mother in her features, though not in complexion, he thought.

Rachael's daughter was quite attractive, particularly her striking, hazel eyes. Zinc pushed the thoughts away. He assumed his typical contemptuous demeanor toward pupils that were not associated with his own House.

"Yes, young Hydrogen," he said as though exhausted by the question that had not yet been posed.

"Is Rome done with?" she asked.

Her voice was ever inquisitive but guarded. She knew her instructor despised her.

"Yes," Zinc replied. "Mortal domains rise and fall like mortal kings. We use them as best we can, as conduits for our purposes: healing practices, knowledge, philosophy. But in the end, they fall, and new ones arise in their place."

The young maiden bobbed her head.

Zinc returned to Heaven and passed through the chambers utilized for making Manna. Irrigation troughs diverted a small amount of the Eunoe. The pipes were narrow; they needed to be small so as not to capture a passing mortal's soul. The water was collected in large vats then mixed with flour made from heavenly wheat grown along the banks of the Eunoe. The mixture was cooked over a large open flame.

As the water evaporated from the dough, it was trapped in linen cloths and sprinkled back over the bread, a process that was repeated many times until all moisture had dissipated. The final product was a white, flaky bread cut into small round wafers. Drinking the waters of the Eunoe caused madness in Angels. However, Manna retained the therapeutic properties of the Heavenly water without the side effect of mania.

Angels ingested Manna to treat wounds sustained in battle. Since the wafers lost potency when they were taken out of Heaven, injured Angels returned to their realm if they were to survive injuries sustained in combat.

The process of baking Manna was assigned to a select group of Familiars. As Zinc passed through the Heavenly bakery, he checked the effect the work had on its inhabitants. It was rumored, with much evidence, that the bakery's workers employed the leftover Manna for other uses. Zinc heard that Familiars crushed the remnants and snorted the powder. The practice allegedly provided Familiars with euphoric sensations. Many of the Familiars in the bakery had distant, vacant stares, a perpetual stupor.

Zinc made his way through the Manna bakery and came across a descendant of the House of Gold.

"Ah, Anna of the Manna," he said, a horrible joke he uttered every time he encountered his subservient.

"My Lord," she said. She was not amused.

"Do you know where Beatrice Silver is by any chance?" he asked.

"She's tending to the vats," Anna replied with disinterest.

What an odd case that one is, Zinc thought. *She has never married and keeps almost exclusively to herself.*

Although certain members of the Gold and Silver Houses had returned, chastened, after the battle in Egypt and been accepted back into Heaven, Zinc remained wary. He knew Anna's reputation as a stellar fighter but made it clear he would not trust her in battle—at least not for a long time. He felt the same way about Beatrice.

Manna

Lost in thought, Zinc almost bumped into Beatrice. She could not be more different from Anna. Beatrice was garrulous and evocative. Though Beatrice had never married, she regularly took lovers—and she had numerous children. The only luxury of being a social pariah was the ability to behave in whatever manner she saw fit.

"Beatrice."

"Yes, my Lord," she replied. Her eyes sparkled, her tone echoed exuberance. "How can I be of assistance?"

"I've come regarding your daughter, Constance Silver."

"Ah, has she gotten herself into some kind of trouble?" Beatrice asked.

"The opposite," Zinc said, imagining that trouble was more the domain of the mother than the daughter. "In fact, she is such a promising student I am considering lifting the ban placed upon her as a descendant of the House of Silver. She might fight in the Heavenly cause."

"That seems like a punishment," Beatrice said with disappointment in her voice.

"I beg your pardon?"

"Our life is fine," Beatrice said. "It's not good, but it's not bad. If she were to fight, she'd likely die. Here, she can be like me; she can serve to avoid the Atrophy and remain free from all the dangers of the war with the Demons."

"That is not honor, or purpose," Zinc replied, taken aback. He felt like he'd been slapped across the face.

"My Lord," Beatrice said, "I was in Egypt. I bought into all the beliefs my Uncle Gold, and my Father Silver fed us. It all was folly, and suffering followed. Please forgive me for the effect it has had on my outlook. I just don't feel belief when I search my soul. I know that I benefit from the work of others, but after all I've endured, this is how I feel."

Zinc pursed his lips and waited.

"But why ask me anyways?" Beatrice asked, her normal jovial tone returning. "You're our all-powerful Standard Bearer; you can command her in any manner you see fit."

Zinc shrugged. "I thought you'd be proud and could shed more light on if I am right to trust her."

Beatrice smiled. "She's a serious girl. Most of my kids try to avoid the Academy and occupy their time with mischief and the sorts, but Constance is a good one. She would do you and your House proud."

Zinc touched his finger to his brow in a small salute. "Thank you for that, Beatrice, and thank you for all you do. The Manna is an important job. We rely on you a lot. Don't let the past weigh so heavily upon you. It is okay to believe in more than simple survival."

THE RAINY SEASON BROUGHT a deluge to Manchuria. For countless days and nights, the heavens pelted the earth with an unremitting torrent. The waterlogged countryside had been a curse for Yang Liang's army. Provisions could not be transported, troops could not move freely, and disease ran rampant. The forces of Goguryeo were fighting on their own terrain and were significantly less impacted by the rains. Thus, they had been able to pick their battles before withdrawing and regrouping.

Similarly, Bubonic Plague had picked the location of the small village outside of Liucheng to suit his purposes. As the rain fell through the night, he stood confidently within the Celestial. He looked across the coven he had created. It had been more difficult than he had initially imagined. Rubella had insisted that only a Demon at the top of his or her class could be appointed to the Academy. In the end, intervention by Satan in the dispute had resulted in a compromise; Bubonic could break the Sequester to recruit Demons to his project, but he would not instruct the cohort, only those who joined his coven.

Thus, Bubonic had acquired his followers. Seven Demons had heeded his call: Pride, Lust, Sloth, Greed, Wrath, Gluttony, and Envy. They called themselves, "The Seven Deadly Sins." Instead of cultivating their own diseases, Bubonic's coven began mastering the application of his illness.

It had been slow going initially; it was not easy for even a young, malleable Demon to copy another's trademark. Yet, with time and patience, Bubonic had instructed his followers in the creation of his malady. He christened the disease brought forth by the coven "Pneumonic Plague." It was slightly different from the original he had created.

Bubonic was giddy when he looked at the fully-grown members of the Black Death Coven.

Pride and his wife, Lust, stepped in front of the group. "To commemorate the occasion," he said.

They each held up a large cloak. Bubonic Plague realized the hood of the garment resembled the head of a giant rat, the animal he had long ago selected as the disseminator of his disease. The robes were made of rat skin and fur.

Bubonic Plague smiled. "My children," he said, "what an honor."

While the assembled Demons applauded with raucous exuberance, he pulled the vestment over his body.

"Thank you," he said, beaming. "The time has come for us to test the application of our illness. Remember, this is not a simple presentation of our disease into the world to send souls to the Styx. We must have a full understanding of how long it takes for them to notice that they are ill, the response of the healthy to the sick, and how long it takes for the victims to die. We need detailed information. You must possess the mortals of this village and read their thoughts as they are falling victim to our designs."

Following his instructions, the Demons set through the small village with savagery and swiftness. By the morning of the next day, not a single mortal soul remained alive. The village sat still as the gray light of dawn flickered through the mist of falling rain. Corpses lay strewn about the township. In fear, the dead had abandoned their own homes and sought refuge from the pestilence. They lay where they had fallen, arms and legs violently contorted. Blackened lesions peppered their bodies; puss and blood erupted from their cavities. The dead told a story of those who they had abandoned: a wife left by her husband, children abandoned by their mother, an old man deserted by his daughter—all dying alone as their brethren vainly attempted to avoid their own predetermined fate.

The silence of the village greeted the eight Demons that walked through assessing their work. Bubonic surveyed the handiwork of his coven and felt as though he had become a deity, a God of death.

He spoke from under the rat head of his hood. "We have successfully obtained one hundred percent casualties in a matter of mere hours. This is what we will do to all of mankind."

He turned to Greed and said, "Go with your sister Wrath and possess the bodies of any nearby Goguryeo soldiers. We will assess if the infection moves from the corpses to the living, and we will utilize them to burn this village. We must keep our potency a secret until the perfect time to unleash it upon the world."

THE SHEEP GRAZED ALONG the grassy slopes, meandering around the haphazard stones that lay at various angles throughout the pasture. Thus was the fallen grandeur that had once been the Roman Forum. Passing lightly through the dispersed flock, the man known as Exspiravit walked past the few remaining columns of what had once been the temple of Saturn. The early afternoon sun was bright, yet this Ancient One felt a chill.

This used to be the heart of the world, he thought.

"Look what they have done to our beautiful city, Pulwabi," he said into the breeze.

He closed his eyes and envisioned the city in its grandeur; the broken pillars rising from the ground, stone floors covering the grass, and the vast emptiness teeming with people of all types.

Exspiravit sighed. "I've longed to hear your view of the modern world," he said. "Has your soul changed?"

He wondered if his beloved one had been a plebian, a patrician, or a slave of Rome.

"Or was she thousands of miles from this place?" he asked aloud.

He removed a worn hammer and chisel from under his humble garments and began to cut into the marble.

I found you next amongst a marble hall,
Behind the eternal city's towering wall,
Like the colosseum's staggering height,
Our love grew taller by day and night,
And though the empire would eventually fall,
It seemed, but for a moment, time would stall.

Antiquity provided many wonders true,
They pale in grandeur when compared to you.
But the wheel of lives once again turned,
And the city we loved to ashes it burned.

The gentle bleats of the sheep floated over the vacant forum. No shepherd was needed, for though the city would forever be associated with wolves, all manner of hunters, wolf and fox, emperor and senator, Angel and Demon, all had departed by the time Circades carved his message in the stone. He looked at his work and closed his eyes while the warm summer sun washed over his body. He sat for a while alongside the stone and conducted an imaginary conversation with Pulwabi, wondering how she would respond to his queries and laugh at his stories, all while holding him close.

SILVER

GOLD

Chapter 11
VENI, VENI EMMANUEL

THE CONCEPT OF NEUTRAL ground was not foreign to the forces of Heaven and Hell. After all, an Angel that killed a Demon outside the proximity of warfare conducted by the mortals was meant to be put to death according to the Divine Dictum. According to the letter of the law, everywhere combat did not occur was neutral ground. In practice, this was not always the case. Many Angels and Demons were willing to risk killing an adversary without the cloak of mortal combat, even though such instances led mortals to claim they had seen Angels and Demons.

Although such an occurrence threatened to hand permanent victory to the non-offending side, Demons and Angels felt vulnerable even when amongst peaceable mortals. Truly neutral ground existed in places consecrated by agreement from both sides. Neutral ground could only be utilized within the Celestial. Since no mortals could set foot upon neutral ground, the premises required proper defenses against intrusion, accidental or otherwise.

Zinc swam from the mainland to the neutral ground of a tiny Grecian Isle. Within the Celestial, it was impossible for him to drown; he navigated the treacherous currents with ease. As he waded ashore, his robe clinging to his body, he was filled with a sense of uncertainty. He made his way forward to the only structure on the island.

The house was old. It was initially a garrison for a contingent of soldiers, placed strategically to defend the approach to Lárissa at a time when the city was its own city-state and had concerns for security. Changing political boundaries had rendered the city far from the edge of Greece and dispelled the need for a barracks. The Angels and Demons each claimed it. Zinc knocked on an elaborate door. The Angels who visited the neutral ground were generally frowned upon for engaging in the hedonistic behaviors that took place therein.

Zinc, however, no longer cared about rumors or whispers. Although he presented himself as unaffected, in truth, he missed Rachael. It pained him to see her happy in her life as Lady Hydrogen. He missed his deceased wife, Cecilia. He regretted that he had seen her as an obstacle for so long and not as a confidant, a spouse, a source of affection in her own right. She had been kind to him. She had been patient, supportive, and had borne him so many sons and daughters.

The heavy, olive wood doors swung open silently, interrupting Zinc's reminiscence. As it opened, Zinc appreciated the intricate carving in the wood of a pentagram and a cross interlaced together, surrounded by wings. He was greeted by a woman. At first, he thought she was a Familiar. But her features were different: pointy ears, sharp teeth, and cat-like eyes. Zinc had never seen a Wraith in person. In battle or while conducting their activities, they were a mere shadow, ever fleeting. The closest he had come to seeing one had been in the books of the Angelic Academy.

Zinc assessed the creature; she was beautiful. She appeared as a mortal woman of two decades in age. She had short, dark hair and amber eyes, the irises of which were oval like a feline. The Wraith was slight and stood about four feet in height.

"Welcome, traveler," she said with a smile. "Please follow me, and I will show you where you can leave your wet clothes."

When the Wraith turned, Zinc looked through her sheer, black robe and admired her taut, lithe frame.

"You'll find replacement robes in here," she said pleasantly, gesturing toward a small doorway. "Just leave your wet clothes there, and they will be dried for you by the time you depart."

Zinc thanked her as he stepped into the room.

He changed and emerged from the room to find the hostess waiting for him. She smiled broadly, fully aware of Zinc's scrutiny.

"You'll find many pleasures beyond your wildest dreams here at the Isle of Neutrality," she said. "However, the rule of neutrality must be followed at all times: no violence of any kind. No threatening or menacing of any form. Other than that, you are free to indulge all of your wildest fantasies."

Zinc was amazed by the lavish artistry of the castle. The hallway was paved with some of the most elegant marble he had ever seen. It was laid in a checkerboard pattern of white and black and intended to appease members of either side of the Celestial divide. Numerous paintings of mastery yet to be attained by mortal artists lined the corridors. They depicted various scenes of Heavenly and Infernal lore.

The Wraith led him into a large atrium. The room was dimly lit by burning torches and littered with an array of lounges and chairs. When his eyes adjusted to the darkness, he saw a handful of occupants.

A Wraith caressed his arm, and with a purr, said, "My name is Helga. Ooo, so strong. Feel free to ask any of the attendants for anything. And if you should need my services for anything at all," she bit her lower lip, "don't hesitate to ask."

The hostess melted into the shadows. He stood for a moment,

awkward in his solitude, then noticed a raised hand beckoning to him. When he got closer, Zinc realized the person was dressed in a black robe, a young Demon. Zinc had seen his kind before, but always in the chaos of combat, always briefly, furtively.

Here sat the enemy, calm and composed, holding a massive, ornate, silver chalice in one hand and a wooden pipe in the other.

"Welcome traveler," the Demon said with a jovial voice. "Take a seat; there is more than enough room."

"Thank you," Zinc said as he settled on a lounge beside the Demon.

The stranger set down his goblet and met Zinc with an extended hand. "Spanish Influenza," he said.

The Demon was young, appearing to have just reached maturity. He had short dark hair, and deep coal-black eyes. These features stood in stark contrast to the Demon's pale skin. He was unusually thin, almost emaciated, with high cheekbones and clavicles that were highly visible through the opening at the top of his robe.

They shook hands. "Lord Zinc."

"Oh, I'm in the presence of royalty," Spanish Influenza said. While he did not laugh, his voice betrayed his bemusement.

"It just means I'm the head of my household," Zinc said.

"I know what it means." The Demon laughed. "You have got to lighten up."

Zinc's laugh was forced and awkward. "Yeah, I think so."

Spanish Influenza snapped his fingers and shouted to an attendant. "Some more Angel's Blood over here for my new pal."

Zinc looked on as a scantily clad Wraith fetched a goblet and filled it with liquid from a cauldron.

"Don't worry," the Demon said. "That's just the name. It's actually a tonic made from Brew and distilled spirits."

"Brew?"

"It's similar to the Elixir you guys drink."

"And that there?" Zinc asked, gesturing to the pipe.

"Ah, this is a weed that grows along the banks of the Styx called Devil's Grass. Dried and aged to perfection," the Demon said. He held the bowl over a candle and drew a deep pull from the pipe. "Now, if you'll excuse me for a moment."

Zinc, confused by the request, glanced down at the pipe and then back at the Demon, who had arched his head backwards and audibly exhaled with his eyes pressed tightly closed. A moment later, Zinc noticed a rhythmic rising and falling from the crotch of the Demon's robe. It was only when a petite Wraith emerged from under Spanish Influenza's vestments that Zinc realized what had been occurring throughout their conversation. The Wraith winked at Zinc as she wiped her mouth and rose to her feet.

"Try some." The Demon held out the pipe once he reopened his eyes.

Zinc gingerly held the bowl of the pipe over the flame and drew a pull. He coughed as the metallic taste of the smoke flooded his senses.

"That-a-boy." Spanish Influenza cackled. "But try to inhale more smoke next time."

Zinc nodded as he felt a tingly sensation running through his body. The second time he inhaled from the pipe, his throat burned less, and he had a greater sensation of swallowing the smoke. He was vaguely aware of the Demon to his right, laughing and clapping his hands.

"This is going to be such a fun day." Zinc heard the words, but they seemed far away and near all at once.

The room alternated between vibrant colors and gray tones as Zinc looked about his surroundings between gulps from his chalice. The drink had initially been strong; however, as time and the effects of the smoke took hold, it became more and more palatable.

"How do you feel?" the Demon asked with an oscillating voice.

Zinc smiled, which brought cacophonous laughter from the Demon.

"But you feel good?" he said. "Don't you?" Spanish Influenza continued.

"I feel better than I have ever felt," Zinc said. He assessed the tingly, nervy sensation that made him aware of his entire body all at once.

"Good," the Demon replied. "Our lives are so often not like this; it's only fitting that you take the time to feel good."

Zinc felt as though he was watching himself from somewhere else. The two clinked chalices. Zinc watched the drink slush from side to side within the cup, then brought the goblet to his mouth. When he lowered the chalice, Helga's face was inches away from his.

Her voice sounded like clothes dropping to the floor. "Having a good time, are we?" she asked.

Zinc stared into her amber eyes. He was shocked by the intense sensation that ran through his body as Helga slithered atop him. With deft dexterity, she snatched the goblet from his hand.

"Finish your drink," she said, a light-hearted command.

As Zinc reached for the chalice, she yanked it backwards and moved her index finger back and forth, chiding, "No, no, no... not with your hands."

The Wraith then opened her robe with her left hand and poured the contents of the cup over her bared body with her right. The drink ran over her breasts and down her stomach before settling into his lap. His entire nervous system overloaded as the cold liquid seeped into his robes while he tasted the sweet drink and Helga's warm skin. While he lapped the Angel's Blood, she opened his robe and straddled him. Zinc gasped with pleasure when Helga put him inside of her.

Zinc surrendered to the competing sensations of pain and pleasure. The room spun throughout the disembodying experience. Sights, smells, tastes, sounds, and sensations bombarded him.

When he had nothing left to give, he was distantly aware of Helga dismounting and fading away into the darkness. He watched her depart, then slipped into a powerful, restful sleep.

He awakened many hours later to a violent jostling and opened his eyes. For a moment, he was confused and frantic. Then he heard Spanish Influenza's jovial voice intoning a mock incantation.

"Return to me, Your Majesty."

Zinc shook his head and tried to clear it.

"Here, drink this," the Demon said as he handed him a small glass.

"I don't think I can drink anymore," Zinc said. He clutched his throbbing skull. "My head is going to split. I fear I am done in."

He groaned and rolled to his side, fearful he would retch.

"I am most certain that you are far beyond that," Spanish Influenza said, "but this tincture is made from the bark of Heavenly Oak and salt from the Dead Sea. It will restore you. Trust me."

Zinc grimaced and swallowed the bitter drink but was immediately grateful.

"Better?" the Demon asked. "Hell of a grand first visit, huh?"

Zinc groaned at the pun but conceded. "Indeed, it was."

"A ride with Helga is a sort of rite of passage here," Spanish Influenza said.

Zinc blushed. "I can't believe I did all of that. Were you here the whole time?"

The Demon swept his hand around the room. "We all were," he said. "You should be ashamed."

Zinc glanced around the room saw other white and black robes dispersed about the chamber.

"Oh my," Zinc said.

The Demon exploded in laughter. "Stop it," he said. "Everything is fine. While you were dreaming, I enjoyed a particularly feisty ménage a trois with a pair of Angels, right here."

"It has been quite a day," Zinc said.

"Why did you come here?" the Demon asked.

Zinc paused for a second, then said, "Despair, I lost my wife and my mistress a while back, and I haven't really recovered."

"That's heavy stuff," Spanish Influenza said. "You didn't ask, but I come here for balance. Like I said before, not much of our life is like it is here. Here there is no judgment, no rules, and no boundaries. I come here to escape the other times when I am a professional, a killer, and a good soldier."

Zinc realized he was in the presence of a formidable foe, even though he was still young.

"I do not doubt that you are those things in totality," Zinc said. "How good that we met here, instead of in the field where I would have to test your mettle."

Spanish Influenza laughed. "It has been a good day. When you return, I would like very much to engage you in scholarly debate. That is also an enjoyable pastime here at the neutral ground."

"What a varied array of activities," Zinc said with a smile.

"Indeed," replied his Demonic counterpart. "Drugs, sex, and philosophy, a potent combination for the stimulation of the mind."

"I will look forward to seeing you again, Spanish Influenza," Zinc said.

"Well met, Lord Zinc," the Demon replied, clasping his hand. "I'm sure one way or another, I will see you soon."

THE STYX MEANDERED THROUGH Hell, carrying mortal souls that had died with fear, hatred, or despair in their essence. Along the bank, bathed in the radiance of the river that illuminated Hell's perpetual twilight, sat the Black Death coven. Bubonic Plague's followers sat cross-legged along the various lengths of a pentagram he had painstakingly depressed into the grass along the river's edge.

"We are gathered together today once more on the eve of combat," he said with a booming voice. "Therefore, as we prepare for the impending spectacle of the deadly contest, let us draw upon the river that heals us."

He filled a large goblet with water from the Styx.

"We thank the Lord for purifying the river with many souls," the disciples said in unison.

"I offer you my comradery, my guidance, and if necessary, my life." Bubonic Plague said. "To symbolize this devotion to you and all of Hell's cause, I offer my blood."

Bubonic drew a Celestial dagger from his waist and opened his wrist. He winced as the blade tore a ribbon of his flesh. He watched as his artery spurted copious amounts of Demonic blood into the vessel. He stopped once the water was strained a dark crimson, then dipped his wound into the Styx.

Plague exhaled slightly as the waters healed the injury.

"We thank the Son for his noble sacrifice," the devotees said in unison.

Bubonic reflected on the way he had injected himself into the Antichrist narrative. He had not been shameless enough to stake his claim outright. Instead, he had alluded to his ancient, noble blood-line, an easily accomplished task for the eldest living Demon. His followers drew their own conclusions regarding the identity of his father. They were confident he was the Son of Satan and the true Crown Prince of Hell.

Anger filled Bubonic Plague as he thought of the coward, Schizophrenia, and his claim to ancestry linked to the Devil.

Be calm. He is gone, and he is never coming back, he thought.

He issued a command. "Drink!"

As the chalice was passed from member to member, Bubonic considered how similar the consumption of blood was to the communion sacrament of the Roman Catholic Church. Once the vessel had been returned to him, Bubonic Plague drained the remainder and placed it into the center of the pentagram. He stepped back to the apex of the symbol and instructed his followers to rise to their feet and to clasp hands. They formed a circle around the pentagram.

"We give thanks for the Infernal Spirit that binds us and all of Hell together as one," they said in unison.

Having concluded the ceremony, Bubonic Plague led his followers toward the Great Hall. He appreciated his sway over the Triumvirate Council; it meant he could always ensure that the members of the coven were all assigned to the same mission.

"Remember," he said as they marched, "we have many great plans ahead. As important as this battle is, you must not be reckless. Your lives now serve a greater purpose as each day brings us closer to the unleashing of the Pneumonic Plague."

He swelled with pride as he watched his coven head forth, ready for battle.

Titus, the High Priest, looked across the meeting table, the gathering of the Triumvirate Council. His eyes darted from side to side, and he drummed his boney fingers on the table. He glanced down at his hand. It was odd that the spaces between his knuckles should seem so hollow and drawn. Priests, unlike their Demonic sires, outwardly aged past the appearance of young adults, though not as old as Wraiths. As the product of breeding Demons with Wraiths, Priests possessed a variable biology. They were the only species containing the blood of Titans, Mortals, Wraiths, Satan, and Demons. The competing blood sometimes led to odd outcomes.

Older in appearance than the Demons, younger in appearance than the Wraiths, and yet I alone, out of all the occupants of Hell, have the need for eyeglasses, he thought to himself.

The High Priest wondered if nature or nurture had produced his gaunt hands and the deep creases around his eyes. He found his title to be a perpetual curse as well as a reward.

If only we could attain the final victory, then I would have my reward: Eternal Pope of the Infernal Church of Satan, he thought.

The Priestess Erin leaned over to whisper, "Titus!"

The High Priest looked up and realized that the Wraith portion of the Triumvirate had arrived and was waiting.

"Please have a seat," he said.

Mephistopheles, Elise, and Anubis took their seats. They all had reached their peak age, all three appearing as haggard, elderly wisps. Their once catlike eyes had dulled and were no longer distinguishable from those of a mortal. Their angular ears had dulled with age as well. Yet, their looks were incredibly deceiving, for the High Priest knew they were wily and cunning, and most adept in the field—even Elise with her amputation.

"You are summoned here today as you have been for over ten centuries, on a basis equal to the passage of the Earth's Moon, to report upon our most pressing concern from an intelligence point of view," he said.

"The Nazarene," Mephistopheles said, unwilling to sit patiently through the High Priest's introduction.

Titus suppressed his irritation.

"Yes," he said. "A thousand years is neither an inconsequential nor a significant passage of time for our kind. You have been allowed time because we have been extremely cautious since Teutoburg. We have focused on replenishing our numbers by limiting ourselves to extremely brief engagements. Even regarding replenishment, we have been cautious of when to authorize procreation, so that steps could be taken to secure the young. In fact, other than Leprosy, Aspergillosis, and Varicella, all exorcized by the Nazarene, we have not experienced a casualty since Teutoburg Forest."

Mephistopheles nodded. "I am aware of the history you have mentioned at every meeting for the last hundred centuries," he said, rubbing his temple.

Titus stared at the impudent Wraith. "I mention it because the Lord of Hell does not wish to pursue any major strategic initiatives until we have a definitive report on the Nazarene. Imagine if he is what they say he is, and we send our entire force afield, and he purges all of them," Titus said. "Bubonic Plague just took his entire coven into the field. It would be helpful if they had information."

"The Crusade has been incredibly helpful," Elise said with a conciliatory tone. "For the first time since the rise of Rome, we have been able to conduct operations in the Levant. The Wraiths have been scouting in Tyre, Nazareth, Galilee, Jericho, and Bethlehem. Once Bubonic aids the crusaders in the capture of Jerusalem, we will investigate there, too."

The High Priest sat up. "This is hopeful news," he said. "We are getting close." He had been staring at Mephistopheles. He turned to Elise. "I believe in you. I trust you and your Wraiths will be able to prove whether this mortal is the Messiah of Heaven or an imitator."

"He is in no way an imitator, regardless of whether or not he corresponds to the mortal dogma that has sprung up around his life," Anubis said.

Everyone quivered as the gravelly voice of Anubis filled the room, for he rarely spoke.

"We know he was mortal. We know he was never possessed by either Angel or Demon. We know his reputation for exorcism comes from his killing of three Demons and over twenty Wraiths. We are talking about a mortal. Other than Lords Iron, Carbon, Gold, Zinc, and Lady Hydrogen, I cannot think of any living Angels with a higher body count. I know not whether he is the manifestation of the lore, but his feats were legendary. The Devil is wise to proceed with caution."

An awkward silence settled on the assembled delegates.

"Well," Titus said following an involuntary gulp, "I am certain you will find us the answers we need."

As a sense of muted satisfaction settled upon his troubled mind, Titus raised his hand. "Hail Lord Satan."

The Wraiths rose to their feet and snapped a crisp salute. "Hail Lord Satan," they echoed in unison.

Titus felt his right eye twitch. He noted that Anubis had saluted but failed to voice the oath. The High Priest decided not to press the issue and allowed the Wraiths to exit.

"We have given audience to Bubonic Plague, Smallpox, and Rubella and to Mephistopheles, Elise, and Anubis," the High Priest said, turning to Erin and Desdemona. "Now, we must confer amongst ourselves."

The weight of his responsibilities made his shoulders heavy. "We already know that Bubonic Plague fancies himself the Antichrist. He is doing everything he can to establish his legitimacy."

"And what is Lord Satan's opinion on the matter?" Erin asked.

"He is conflicted," Titus said. "The Devil knows that the liberties he indulges in with Demonic maidens is an open secret; knows most fear to discuss the subject. Many, like Bubonic Plague and Schizophrenia, can probably claim that he is their sire, which is unfortunate," he paused in frustration, "since the purity of his bloodline and the arrival of the foretold son are such central tenets to our faith."

"Why not embrace Bubonic?" Desdemona asked. "Such a boon would be invaluable to the morale of our forces."

"The Lord is hesitant," Titus said, "because he worries whether Bubonic Plague can live up to the expectations of the Messiah."

"But we cannot risk alienating him because he is essentially the commander of our forces," Erin said.

"Exactly."

"So, what is the plan?"

Titus rubbed his temple. "Satan has entrusted the decision to us."

Erin responded with characteristic bluntness. "Coward."

Titus heard Desdemona inhale in response to Erin's blasphemy.

"I agree," Titus said, "nevertheless, we must decide what to do. I urge you to vote with your conscience. The fate of Hell may well rest upon this decision."

He took a deep breath. "All in favor of supporting Bubonic Plague in his bid to be Antichrist raise your hand."

Not a single hand went up.

"Then it is decided," Titus said. "We will not forsake our honor or our religion for convenience. We will not fashion a Messiah of our own making but will wait for the true Antichrist."

"I would rather die with dignity than sacrifice all we have asked so many to give their lives for," Erin said.

Desdemona nodded. "Even if Lord Satan is not perfect, we should remain true to our beliefs."

Thus, the Church reached its conclusion, a far-reaching decision that would reverberate throughout the halls of Hell and Heaven alike.

SCHITZ WAS INTRIGUED. Two figures lumbered through the dense brush of the rain forest. They bore the dark outline of Demons. He watched and tried to identify them or to ascertain their purpose at least. He readied a Celestial dagger. He knew he had many enemies in Hell, especially after the allegation he had used in his defense. He relaxed when he recognized Autism and Conjunctivitis.

Bounding from cover, Schitz caught both of his comrades by surprise. Autism shrieked and jumped backwards, while Conjunctivitis reached for his weapon. Schitz threw his arms around Conjunctivitis and embraced him.

"You startled me," Autism said.

"Because I am so fierce," Schitz said.

The comrades laughed.

"It has been an eternity since I saw a friendly face," Schitz said. He was smiling uncontrollably.

"Speaking of that," Conjunctivitis said, "what part of your mission has kept you here so long?"

"Gold is no easy foe to take down," Schitz replied. He glanced about the jungle in frustration. Schitz was aware of how impotent his answer sounded. "It's a suicide mission to take on that bastion singlehandedly. Even with you two, it would be impossible."

Doubt creased Autism's face. He opened his mouth, but nothing came out. Conjunctivitis jumped into the void.

"After you left, Satan issued a decree. Any Demon or Wraith aiding you will be put to death."

"That clarifies why Elise never came," Schitz said with disappointment in his voice. "She had promised to visit me."

"It's also been very chaotic for us," Conjunctivitis said. "After Teutoburg, there was a series of shocking developments in the Levant."

"Oh?"

"Yes, and we will tell you all about it," Conjunctivitis said, "but such news will go down best with Brew."

Schitz smiled as his friend retrieved a large carafe and three wooden cups from his satchel.

"I was wondering what you were lugging around," Schitz said.

He rubbed his palms together in expectation.

"Yeah," Autism said. He jerked a thumb at Conjunctivitis. "It was his idea, and somehow I ended up hauling the stuff."

After the drinks had been poured, the conversation resumed.

"I've heard of this Nazarene," Schitz said after a brief prologue by Conjunctivitis. "At the outset of my exile, Elise told me that he had killed Leprosy."

"Indeed," Conjunctivitis said, "as well as Aspergillosis and your grandson, Varicella."

Schitz shook his head. "I never got the chance to know him. If what you say is true, it is disconcerting, to say the least. There is no precedent for such a powerful exorcist other than the one who killed Mumps."

"He also is believed to have killed scores of Wraiths as well," Autism said.

Schitz realized how much he had missed.

"But he was mortal," Schitz said. "His life must have ended centuries ago."

"Indeed," Conjunctivitis said. "He was executed by his fellow mortals at a young age. But after his death, he was widely reported to have completed resurrection."

"Resurrection?" Schitz asked.

"Reincarnation of the same soul into its original body," Autism said between sips of Brew.

"I've never heard of such a thing."

"Hell has been extremely cautious in dealing with this subject. There is much concern that the Nazarene is, in fact, the Messiah foretold in the mortal and Angelic literature."

Schitz's frustration grew. He could not stand being away from the goings-on of Hell.

"Things are progressing, though," Autism said. "We are paired with a mortal army of Europeans and will soon control the Near East. Bubonic Plague has raised a cult with which he plans to make massive gains for our side."

Conjunctivitis rolled his eyes and made a gagging motion. Schitz laughed and spewed a little brew on his robe.

"Make sure you're very careful, you two," he said.

Conjunctivitis reached out and gave Schitz a reassuring thump. "Don't you worry about us."

"How is Rubella and my family?" Schitz asked.

I'm almost afraid to hear the answer.

Conjunctivitis beamed. "She is well and sends her love. She is excelling at the Demonic Academy. Rabies as well. They are both phenomenal instructors."

Autism drained his cup. "I hate to say it, but we should probably go."

Schitz nodded. "You must ensure your safety. Thank you so much for coming."

The friends embraced.

"You have spurred me to my purpose," Schitz said. "No longer will I plan, and stalk, and wait. I must act. I will act. I want to return to Rubella and my child."

"Just get the Brew out of your system first, all right?" Conjunctivitis said.

Nasir Al-Hasan had carried a blade for the Fatimid Caliphate for so long that he could hardly remember the time before his warring duties. A marauding, callous life had imbued Al-Hasan with an extra sense of anticipating battle. That morning the sensation coursed through his body as he walked along the eastern wall of Jerusalem. He felt it in the air as he watched the sun climb over the Mount of Olives. He heard it in the wind as his footsteps gently carried him along the battlements.

Al-Hasan had partaken in the battle a year earlier when the Fatimids captured Jerusalem from the Seljuqs. He had bathed his sword in the blood of the Sunnis. Now the infidels prepared similar treatment for his kind. Al-Hasan looked at the Christian army that had laid siege to the holy city. It was a sea of iron, armor and weaponry, horses, and machinery. He knew the battle would unfold before the sun rose the following day. He closed his eyes and basked in the orange and red rays for a moment.

This could be my last day on Earth, he thought.

Soon, the city would be overtaken by the beast of combat, a ferocious, bloodthirsty monster that consumed indiscriminately.

Zinc felt sympathy for his battle-scarred host as he, too, surveyed the positions of the Crusader army. He suspected the inhabitants of the city were doomed. Zinc had been present during the battle for Antioch where, following their victory, the Crusaders had put the inhabitants to the sword in an orgy of destruction. The irony of a holy war as the source of murder, rape, and even cannibalism was not lost on Zinc. However, he could not force himself to raise his nose in righteous indignation, for he was aware of the hypocrisies of Angelic existence.

He stepped into the Celestial to retrieve his pipe and smoke some of the Devil's Grass he had brought with him from the Isle of

Neutrality. He judged that this brief interaction with the Mortal Realm would not give him away to any of the soldiers defending the wall. Their focus, like Al-Hasan's, was on the enemy surrounding them.

The acrid smoke, already familiar to Zinc, and euphoria overwhelmed Zinc's senses momentarily.

This is a poisoned existence, he thought.

He was sad, lonely, and confused. His confusion centered on what he wanted for the rest of his life and how to go about getting it. He looked at the ancient city of Jerusalem, the holy city of three mortal religions, and detected the slightest glimmer of hope. Battle always offered the opportunity to serve Heaven and to advance his own agenda.

Zinc walked along the wall as the day fully dawned upon the besieged city. He reached the Al-Aqsa Mosque on the Temple Mount.

Mortals continue to fight over this "sacred" ground. First the Temple of Solomon, then the Second Jewish temple, then a Roman place of worship, and now a mosque.

The mosque's cedar beams pre-dated the founding of Islam. Angelic legend held that the city of Jerusalem was the location upon which God and the Devil, along with the deceased members of their race, watered the Earth with the blood of Titans, thereby consecrating it forever.

Zinc passed by the Dome of the Rock. The gold dome offered restorative benefits to those mortals who worshipped under it, a belief that fascinated and frustrated him. Zinc thought about Gold. Following their flight from Egypt, the brothers and their remaining adherents had disappeared from Heaven's attention when the fight with Hell occupied both the Deity and his army of Angels. But the devious duo remained like a neglected tumor—silent, growing, and malignant. Centuries passed, and the whispers grew. Tales of Gold and Silver in the savage lands across the sea began to arrive in Heaven from Familiars scouting the globe. God had forbidden any missions against the rebellious Angels and had given strict instructions for any Angels not of Native origin to avoid the New World. Consequently, Zinc and the others focused on eradicating the Demons.

Still, he heard tales of Gold and saw the deserter's mineral healing the sick across the length and breadth of the world, and Zinc longed for resolution. He knew he could bring closure to his father's final endeavor. Thoughts of his father inevitably brought on a sense of shame.

What have I become? he thought. *I want to fix this.*

Zinc had been part of the contingent assigned to the Fatimid Caliphate to ensure that the Angels held Jerusalem and the Celestial powers offered by the site of the Titans' massacre. The gold of the Dome of the Rock healed mortals. Likewise, teleporting through the doorway of any of the buildings on the Temple Mount issued vast, temporary powers of strength and speed to Angels or Demons.

Several skirmishes with the Demons and their army of European Crusaders had convinced Heaven that holding Jerusalem was an unobtainable task. Most of the Angels had abandoned the city in the face of the siege. Zinc had volunteered his House for a very particular mission, one fraught with danger. However, if they were successful, this mission, like his work at the Academy, would be another step towards rebuilding his image.

Upon reaching the Jewish Quarter of the city, a cramped maze of narrow corridors and rugged winding streets, Zinc was greeted within the Celestial by his three eldest sons, Patrick, Aaron, and Adolphus. Zinc knew he could rely on assistance from his sons' Houses even if he no longer commanded the forces of multiple domains.

Standing next to Adolphus, as was typically the case, Zinc observed Constance Silver. In the time since Zinc had granted her an exception to the Mortal Realm travel ban and combat operations, she had grown into a formidable fighter. Zinc was unhappy that a member of a subordinate House performed noticeably better than any warrior within his own House, but he was happy to have spotted her talent and intellect.

"As-salaam-Alaykum,"[47] he said to his assembled captains. "Surely, the battle will commence forthwith. The crusaders are much less equipped to mount a siege than the Muslims are to withstand it. Therefore, the attack is imminent."

[47] "Peace be with you."

"Likely under cover of darkness to protect their few siege towers," Patrick said.

Zinc loved when his sons showed such promise as field commanders.

"Indeed," he said, "so we have the remainder of the day to prepare." He began using a charred piece of kindling to sketch a diagram of the city on the rough exterior of a stone building. "Remember, they will likely attack from the south and from the north."

He continued with the diagram. Zinc glanced about to make sure no mortals were nearby. His activity would take the form of the story from the *Torah*, the book of *Daniel*, in which an invisible hand wrote prophecy on a wall. Zinc did not need to invite attention, so he was pleased to see that the narrow street remained empty.

Schitz's Notebook

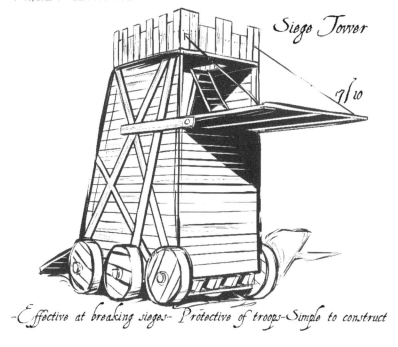

Siege Tower

7/10

-*Effective at breaking sieges- Protective of troops-Simple to construct*

-*Slow to move -Vulnerable to fire -Difficult to construct in desert*

"This action is an armed reconnaissance mission," he said. "We are only resisting the Demons to assist our true aim, which is the acquisition of knowledge. In the time since the life of Jesus Christ, the Demons have withdrawn considerably. They limit themselves to the briefest of tactical engagements and the infliction of disease upon mortals."

The Angels made the sign of the cross when he mentioned the name of the mortal believed by many in Heaven and Earth to be the Messiah. Zinc desperately hoped that the Nazarene was the son of God. However, if he was, God continued to keep him as a strategic reserve. There had been no unveiling or debriefing in Heaven.

"The Demons that have remerged of late are behaving in a novel manner," Zinc said. "Their squad is massive compared to the small trios we are accustomed to encountering, and they avoid hit and run tactics. Instead, they hold a strategic position and then either defend against our attack or advance on us in a coordinated effort."

"Like a Roman Testudo," Constance said.

"Yes, indeed," Zinc said. "In addition, they are led by the Behemoth, the large, abnormally strong Demon. We still know little about his followers and the diseases with which they deal. Additionally, there have been reports of extensive activity regarding Hellish Wraiths in the Holy Land following the progress of the Catholic armies. We need to know what they are planning. Observing the Wraiths has been impossible; they have become quite adept at killing our Familiars and even the Angels that oversee them."

"Indeed, they are deadly."

The voice came from the back. Out of nowhere, Lilly, the Commander of Familiars, stepped forward. Zinc had mixed feelings for the old woman who led the Intelligence Service. Elderly only in outward appearance, Lilly was phenomenally adept in the field. However, she was infuriatingly cautious and often seemed to place the safety of her Familiars above the outcome of the mission.

"Welcome to the briefing," Zinc said.

"Oh, I've been here all along," she replied.

Lilly had been present on the mission on which Lady Zinc had been killed. The Intelligence Officer had never provided a straight answer regarding the details of the engagement.

Zinc returned to the matter at hand. "Our faux resistance must be believable. Therefore, in the South, we will make all efforts to repulse the attack as normal. Any forces you deploy here will be significantly safer; they will not be expected to fall back. In the North, we will only offer token resistance, which should allow the Behemoth and his men to break through the city for our observation. Those you place along the Northern wall will have a very low probability of survival. I would not recommend that any Standard Bearers be there."

Zinc turned his attention to Lilly. "We need to know specifics, names, identifying characteristics, fighting styles, and most of all, any potential weaknesses."

"I concur," she said. "My Familiars will be in place. And where will you be?"

"On the North Wall."

He saw one of his sons begin to stand in objection. Zinc raised his hand, and the boy sat.

"I'll be fine. I just have to ensure things go according to plan." Zinc concluded the meeting. "None of us likes a mission like this. I would prefer that we were here to kill as many Demons as we could. However, if we are going to be successful against this enemy, we need to understand him fully. I trust all of you will do what has been asked."

Rubella looked at the assembled faculty as she prepared to address her colleagues. Pride filled her; she saw the three females around the conference table. Before she had topped her class, it had been unheard of for a woman to hold an academic position. She had been instructed by Tetanus and Hayfever.

Before their time, the scholarly tomes spoke only of male instructors, but Rubella changed everything. She had been followed by Rabies, then Rubella's niece, Cancer, sired by her late brother

Mumps and Encephalitis. Cancer led to Scarlet Fever, daughter of Sloth and Meningitis. Where once it had been debated whether a female should hold a position, the faculty was entirely composed of intellectual, fierce, exceptional daughters of Hell.

Rubella was confident she had reached the time to have a conversation she had been dreading for centuries. The subject had once seemed hopeless, but when Schitz broached it upon the eve of his departure, Rubella reconsidered her reluctance. If someone as innocently ignorant to the situation as her husband could be so appalled by the Dark Lord's behavior, perhaps change was possible.

Rubella addressed the assembly. "I've called you here today to discuss a grave matter of the utmost importance to all of us. Before I begin, we are on the cusp of graduating another cohort, and I could not be prouder of all of you. Fourteen graduates; that is amazing. Our numbers have proliferated since the last great battle, and your skillful teaching has ensured that there has not been any decrease in the abilities of our graduates. If anything, our recent classes containing the likes of the various Cancers, Spanish Influenza, Typhoid, and Hepatitis are the most potent we have seen. I cannot thank you enough for the efforts you have made in shaping these Demons as we once again prepare for broader combat."

"Yes," Cancer said. "What news have you from the Triumvirate?"

"As you know, there is great concern surrounding the Nazarene, which has led to our calculated approach to the Mortal Realm," Rubella replied. "As we speak, the Black Death Coven has begun the final assault on Jerusalem. Their success in the Levant has and will continue to enable the Wraiths to explore the validity of the claims surrounding the Nazarene. Soon we will resume unrestricted operations within the Mortal Realm."

Rubella noticed a visible reaction among the Demons when she mentioned the Black Death Coven. It was clear they were reviled. However, Bubonic's group was the most powerful entity in Hell, second only to Satan himself.

"However, I have not called you here today to update you on the Council or matters of strategy or academics, but another issue entirely," she said before taking a deep breath. "I want to address the role we have unwittingly played in victimizing the Demonic maidens of Hell. We teach them how our Messiah, the son of Satan, will be born of a pure Demonic maid that the Lord will take as his queen. We teach these young, innocent girls that the savior of our people will be brought to us by their lying with the Devil. He rewards this piety by having his way with whichever maidens he sees fit. All the while, he never intended to take any of them as his queen, thus depriving us of his foretold heir."

Rubella's blasphemy ignited an uncharacteristic explosion from the faculty, all speaking over each other.

"We cannot talk on such a subject," Scarlet Fever said.

Rabies was on her feet. "What can be done?"

"This is too dangerous," Cancer said. "He can put you to death solely on the statement you just made."

"Ladies!" Rubella raised her hand. "Yes, this is dangerous, but search your hearts and ask if you are content risking your life for a kingdom that allows such abusive frivolity from its Overlord."

Again, Rabies asked, "What can we do?"

"We must teach our pupils that they have domain over themselves; they can decline his advances," Rubella said.

"Would that not constitute treason?" Scarlet Fever asked.

"The prophecy focuses on the Messiah. Therefore, the ascendance of the Queen is mentioned second. But as with all our doctrines pertaining to mating, a permanent bond, whether sanctified by the Priests or simply agreed upon and sincere between the mates, is a prerequisite to breeding. It would be unreasonable to assume that such would not be the case for the Devil and his bride as well." Rubella's face flushed with the passion of her argument.

"So, we will not have to contravene or modify the teaching," Rabies said. "We simply emphasize the correct order of mate selection. Then a young Demonic maid would not lie with Satan unless she was truly to be Queen of Hell."

"Or at the very least in agreement to his advances," Scarlet Fever said. "Of course, wouldn't they be anyway. I mean, he is the Devil."

"I wasn't," Cancer said. Her voice barely registered but the words reverberated in the ears of the hearers like an explosion.

"I... I'm so sorry," Scarlet Fever said. "I spoke without knowing."

"I was naïve," Cancer said. She was standing, but her eyes locked on the floor. "There were so many girls in my cohort: Meningitis, Lust, Wrath, Gluttony, and Envy. I couldn't believe he had chosen me. But I wasn't ready. When I told him I wasn't... it didn't matter."

A lump in her throat constricted Rubella's breathing.

"I never," Cancer's voice cracked as she began to sob, "I never told Greed, my husband. How could I?"

Rubella rushed from her side of the table but still got there after Rabies and Scarlet Fever, who embraced their shaken comrade.

Rabies spoke first. "You were the strongest student of the first class I taught, and it was an honor to receive you into the faculty. I would have gladly accepted you as Hell's Queen, as my Queen. You were not naïve in thinking you were worthy. Satan was naïve in overlooking your worth."

"Salve Regina," Rubella said. She stepped back from the embrace to kneel before Cancer.

Rabies and Scarlet Fever genuflected. "Salve Regina, Hail the Queen!"

Cancer laughed through her tears. "Arise, subjects. Your love is all I require. Now get up, you look ridiculous."

Once again, all embraced.

"All right," Cancer said, "let's make sure it never happens again."

FATIMA GAZED OUT OF the small rectangular opening in the wall of her humble dwelling. She contemplated the meaning of her continuous memories, instances from past lives, births, deaths, lovers, children. She thought about the rivers of reincarnation: one smooth and calm, the other chaotic and violent.

The earliest memories she had were of a man named Circades, though not really a man but one of the ancient species that had once inhabited the Earth before mortals gained self-awareness. She longed for him with all of her being. A great sadness settled upon her as she looked at the night sky. She knew Circades was likely somewhere in the world. His kind were notoriously difficult to kill—but the Earth was wide and broad, and the odds he would find her were low.

Fatima's sadness was compounded by the news that her parents had selected a bridegroom for her. In their small Christian community of Alexandria, securing a marriage was no small feat. Fatima's family had been ecstatic while she suffered in silence.

"Where are you, Circades?" she said as she stared at the stars, a sparkling blanket of countless gems. She knew mortals were longing for various things across the world. So many of them longed for a savior, whether it was The Savior or their own personal deliverer from hardship and suffering. Fatima considered herself to be a loyal follower of Jesus of Nazareth, yet as she looked across the still night, she knew her deepest longing was for Circades.

She sang a quiet tune to ease her nerves,

Veni, Veni Emmanuel! Captivum solve Israel![48]

Schitz ran through the Amazon tracking the Angels. Each time he grew more confident, maneuvering unbeknownst to his foe.

Qui gemit in exilio, Privatus Dei Filio,
Gaude, gaude, Emmanuel nascetur pro te, Israel.[49]

Zinc watched intently as the Demons advanced in unison within their tight formation, then sallied forth unexpectedly, only to fall back to the strength of their original Testudo. He had directed his contingent as best he could, but the last stand was hopeless, and the Demons and crusaders broke through the Flower's Gate along the city's northern wall.

---

[48] "O come, O come Emmanuel and ransom captive Israel!"

[49] "That mourns in lonely exile here, until the Son of God appear. Rejoice, rejoice Emmanuel, shall come to thee, O Israel."

Veni o Jesse virgula! Ex hostis tuos ungula.[50]

Bubonic Plague brought his rat-shaped axe down on the head of another Angel with crunching satisfaction as the heavy weapon shattered the foe's skull. All manner of blood and brain material escaped from the various original and newly formed openings.

De specu tuos tartari
Educ, et antro barathri.[51]

He shouted to his Coven over the clamor of battle. "Do not tarry."

Plague was a veritable whirlwind, slaying Angels within the Celestial, all while briefly touching mortals and transmitting his malady to them.

Gaude, gaude, Emmanuel, nascetur pro te, Israel.[52]

"Why have you disturbed me?" Satan asked. "I cannot recall the last instance in which my presence was needed at the Academy."

Rubella braced for all that she knew would follow, then spoke. "We have called you here to put an end to something that has gone on for far too long."

Veni, veni o oriens! Solare nos adveniens. Noctis depelle nebulas,
Dirasque noctis tenebras.[53]

Lilly watched as the Demons set fire to the Jewish Temple from within the bodies of the crusaders.

---

[50] "O come, Thou Rod of Jesse, free thine own from Satan's tyranny."

[51] "From depths of hell Thy people save and give them victory o'er the grave."

[52] "Rejoice, rejoice Emmanuel, shall come to thee, O Israel."

[53] "O come, Thou Dayspring, from on high, and cheer us by Thy drawing nigh; Disperse the gloomy clouds of night, and death's dark shadows put to flight."

Gaude, gaude, Emmanuel
nascetur pro te, Israel.[54]

Sacratissimum Cor Iesu

She had followed them intently and closely. As the howling of those in the temple rose over the clamor of battle and slaughter, she took note of what she observed. She was now aware of the names and appearances of most of what was called "The Black Death." With any luck, the other Familiars would be able to fill in the few remaining gaps of knowledge.

Elise slowly climbed down the steps of one of the many tunnels that ran under the ruins of what had been the Church of the Holy Sepulcher.

Veni clavis Davidica! Regna reclude coeliac.[55]

Though centuries had passed, she could clearly see the evidence of something unusual within the tomb. "So, the rumors are true," she said aloud.

Fac iter Tutum superum, Et claude vias Inferum. Gaude, gaude,
Emmanuel nascetur pro te, Israel.[56]

---

[54] "Rejoice, rejoice Emmanuel, shall come to thee, O Israel."

[55] "O come, Thou Key of David, come, and open wide our heavenly home."

[56] "Make safe the way that leads on high and close the path to misery. Rejoice, rejoice, Emmanuel, shall come to thee, O Israel."

Gold and Silver reclined on the luxurious lounges on one of the balconies of their palace.

> *Veni, Veni Adonai! Qui populo in Sinai.*
> *Legem dedisti vertice, In maiestate gloriae.*[57]

The sun descended over the western slopes; Gold sipped more Chicha Morada, a drink the mortals brewed from the local purple corn.

"It is good to be a king, but much better to be a God, eh Brother?" Silver smiled broadly.

Fatima concluded her song, looked again at the starry night, and felt at peace.

> *Gaude, gaude, Emmanuel nascetur pro te, Israel.*[58]

At least I have an immortal love to remember, she thought.

---

[57] "O come, Adonai, Lord of might, who to Thy tribes, on Sinai's height, in ancient times didst give the law in cloud and majesty and awe."

[58] "Rejoice, rejoice, Emmanuel, shall come to thee, O Israel."

Chapter 12

All that Glitters is Not Gold

The sun rose over the summit of the Andes Mountains and bathed the citadel of Machu Picchu in radiant light. Gold smiled as he watched in smug satisfaction.

"Before my arrival, these simple folks worshipped the sun. Now I am all they need to live happy, healthy, prosperous lives," he said to his brother.

They stood on the terrace.

"Indeed, Brother," Silver said. "The fruits of your efforts are magnificent. What was merely the Incan Empire has become your own realm of divinity on Earth."

He made a mocking bow.

"And so, we shall spread forth the empire through Amazonia north, until this entire ignored world is united in our image," Gold said.

Silver was quick to agree. "And with the humans of your dominion impervious to possession by Demons or any Angels other than us, we are free to step from mortal to mortal without vulnerability in the Celestial, and they can never force us out."

Gold's smile resembled the face of a viper. "You err, Brother. Call us not Angels; now, we are well and truly Gods."

This time Silver's genuflection was without sarcasm. "I was wrong to doubt you after Egypt," he said. "This will be a stunning success."

Gold watched the inhabitants of the citadel going about their various daily tasks amid the solid gold walls of the buildings and the golden pathways that ran across the mountaintops.

"We are invincible," he said aloud. "The centuries testify to our permanency. But don't grovel unto me too much; it doesn't suit you."

Gold laughed and playfully punched Silver in the arm.

SCHITZ RAN INTO A group of hunters after several days of wandering the jungle in the Celestial and working up the courage to begin his campaign. The mortals were immensely interesting to Schitz. They were clad in the simple leather trappings of the New World. Their humble primitive attire was interwoven with beads and chains of gold. They walked through the jungle carrying spears and bows but carried the wealth of an Old World king around their necks.

"Gold truly has made an impression here," Schitz said.

He watched the men stalk a wild boar. They felled the pig with savagery. They whooped and shouted as they set upon the squealing beast. Schitz was satisfied that the hunting band would provide him with safe cover from within which he could move closer to the epicenter of the Empire. There, he was sure to find his targets.

Schitz closed the distance to the hunters and was shocked to find himself forcefully repelled as he attempted to possess the leader. Stepping back with wobbly steps, Schitz shook his head. It had been several centuries since he had run into a human with a mind capable of resisting possession.

Shocking.

He aimed for the closest hunter and was once again repulsed.

"What is going on?" he asked, this time aloud. He went from one hunter to the next, all with the same result. Dizzy from his failed attempts, he decided to follow the group.

This is an unexpected challenge.

"THE LATEST HOLY WAR is going well enough," Carbon V said to Zinc. They were standing to receive the sacrament of return within the Great Hall. Both Angels were awash in the dust of the Holy Land.

Zinc appreciated the advice, but it did little to soften the sting of his incompleteness. "I simply want to end him," Zinc said. His voice was loud enough to make Carbon V wince.

"Shh," Carbon V said, a finger to his lips. "It is not God's will; he is much more concerned with the annihilation of Hell. He will attempt to rehabilitate Gold and Silver."

Zinc knew there was nothing he could do; he was a passenger in time—an observer to the events and circumstances around him.

"True," Zinc said.

"What's troubling you, my friend," asked Carbon V. "You seem distracted."

"I hear talk about Gold and Silver everywhere I turn," Zinc said. He looked like he smelled something vile.

"And you feel as though it was an opportunity squandered?" Carbon V asked.

"I just wish I could be permitted to finish what I started. I want to rectify my failure. Since stepping down from my position of leadership, I have had time to consider my other shortcomings."

"You must not think of it as a failure," Carbon V said. "And you must not rush to remedy the situation. Let the legend of Gold and Silver continue to linger. Many of their Houses have fled to the New World; their absence is felt every day on the battlefields of Europa and the Holy Land, so there is talk. Rumors circulate about what is going on in the New World, so there is talk. And inevitably, there is talk of how Gold was expelled from Egypt. As his legend grows, so does the magnitude of your role in 'driving him out' instead of his 'escaping.' You need to do nothing but wait."

"Perk up," Carbon V said, "the siege ladder training should be fun."

"Yes, it will," Zinc said. "If we ever get out of this ridiculous ceremony."

Schitz had exercised caution through the jungle paths and trails on the way to the massive citadel in the Andes. He felt more like a Wraith than a Demon as he slinked through the shadows concealing his aura from the various Angels he observed within the golden city. Thankfully, most of the Angels appeared lax and off their guard, far more concerned with healing humans by handing out gold and silver coins than assessing their environment. The city was astounding. Every building was constructed of solid gold. The sun's reflection was blinding. Even the walkways were gilded.

Schitz watched as injured hunters and gatherers were healed, the sick were made well, and old people were made young. All the while, the mortals proselytized their devotion to the Sun Gods. Schitz's intrigue with the odd society receded when he considered the perplexing situation of his inability to possess any of the mortals he encountered. With every rebuff, his anger grew. He hated the vulnerability of the Celestial. Slowly, the monumental nature of his task dawned on him. If he could not possess a human, he could not kill the humans housing Gold and Silver or their clan.

Schitz realized he could be set upon by these Angels in the Celestial, and in the ensuing combat, they would have the safety of cloaking themselves in mortal flesh. He would not. Schitz felt like a man who had wandered into a den of lions.

He surveyed his surroundings and struggled to suppress this rising sense of doom. He closed his eyes and pictured Rubella; he imagined her soft skin.

"I will get back to her," he whispered under his breath.

Schitz broke into a run and did not stop until he had hidden himself in the dense, dark jungle. He walked through the thick foliage and breathed in the humid oppressing air while he considered his conundrum. He wondered if the Devil and Bubonic Plague were aware of this information but decided that laying blame and suspicion of those who wished him ill offered no solution.

He cursed aloud. The answer was simple; he would have to travel beyond the realm of the empire and return with a war party full of enough humans for his possession. Schitz's knowledge of the New World was hazy, but he knew there were civilizations to the north of Amazonia.

He began a slow journey through the jungle. Progress was monotonous. He continually assessed the possibility of Angelic possessed humans along the various pathways of the empire. He vowed he would not allow the intoxicating desire for his redemption to move him toward recklessness.

The pathways through the jungle were tedious and tiresome for Schitz, even in the Celestial. He groaned as he passed through the seemingly endless entanglement of vines and trees. He passed through numerous settlements of the hunter-gatherers and found that mortal after mortal he was unable to possess. The days began to melt into weeks, then into months.

Finally, he came to an established city. Emerging from the jungle into a clearing, he saw large stone buildings in a grand clearing, box-shaped pyramids that rose high above the jungle floor. He drew closer to the Mayan settlement; each step increased his sense of defeat. The homes and pyramids had initially been built with stone, but the sun glistened off newly added gold decorations. Once more, he was met with dizzying resistance when he attempted to indwell the inhabitants.

What if the entire New World is like this? he thought.

He bypassed the village. He saw a few Angels and was careful not to engage them. They were clearly proselytizing to the villagers, sharing the salvific news of Gold's Kingdom.

They are spreading faster than Bubonic's dread disease, he thought.

"These fools," he said as he tripped and hacked his way through the dense foliage. "They are all focused on these wars for the Holy Land and the Old World. By the time they capture it, the rest of the world will have fallen to The Glitter Brothers."

THE PILGRIMS LAY PROSTRATE on the golden ground as the most recent form of the God walked from person to person bestowing curative coins of gold and silver. The believers had no reason to question why the Holy One chose to reveal himself in differing forms. He always wore his massive golden crown adorned with three feathers and carried a long golden sword. He was never without a razor-sharp golden spear strapped to his back.

The crowd pleaded with the God. "Take us with you; take us unto the holiest of holies."

Gold tested the elasticity of his mind within his current vessel. The man in whom Gold resided had once been a humble shepherd. Gold sensed their thoughts beginning to merge.

This is an excellent time to perform the switch; the ancient ritual I stole from the Titan to counteract mind-melding is wearisome.

Gold pointed to a young man who had recently been healed of a lame leg. "You, rise!"

The genuflecting man hopped to his feet with his eyes locked to the ground. "Quite an honor, my Lord," he said.

"Yes, it is," Gold said. While the others tried to hide their disappointment (they did not want to be banned), the man's family exalted Gold with even greater ferocity, jubilation in their voices, and tears of elation on their faces. The man followed Gold up the steps into the golden temple.

The Priest began shooing out the parishioners. When they reached the altar, the High Priest removed Gold's weapons and handed them to the young man.

Gold handed his crown to Silver for safekeeping. The young man knelt before the altar. Having cleared the temple, the contingent of Priests, all hosts to members of the Gold and Silver Houses, formed a circle around the altar and the trio of Gold, Silver, and Gold's selectee.

Gold climbed onto the altar and lay on his back. He slipped out of his original host and into the body of the young man. The shepherd on the altar, now free of his possession, stared in stupefaction. Gold plunged his sword into the man's chest. The sickening crunch of the blade breaking through the man's sternum was followed by a gush of blood. Gold pulled the blade free and licked the blood from its crimson edge. The Priests carried the exsanguinated body to an ever-burning fire pit at the rear of the Temple.

Gold turned to his sibling, beaming with satisfaction. He addressed the throng of Priests. "Brothers and Sisters, we are invincible and immortal; the world will be ours. Heaven on Earth has arrived."

THE CITY OF TENOCHTITLAN lay beside the expansive Lake Texcoco in the midlands of a narrow patch of land connecting the continents of the New World. The giant, squared pyramids were like those Schitz had encountered farther to the south. The town bustled with the comings and goings of primitive life.

For the first time in a long while, Schitz managed to step into the body of a mortal. His first host was a simple tradesman who scratched out his existence, carving and shaping obsidian arrowheads, spearheads, and other instruments of hunting and war. Schitz delved into the man's mind as he set upon his task within the small stone building that served as both domicile and workplace. Schitz swiftly accessed the native language from within the man's mind as well as the local power structure, a monarch who was both a religious and tribal figurehead. Schitz formulated a plan, one he had to implement before the emissaries of Gold and Silver made inroads into this civilization.

Schitz made his way toward the loftiest of pyramids, typically the best way to locate a society's leader. He jumped from mortal to mortal with excessive frequency with the dual intentions of reinvigorating his sense of flesh-hopping and assessing if there were any mortals that could repulse him.

The grand pyramid was an impressive spectacle rising high above the stone city. As Schitz ascended the many steps of the structure, apprehension crawled along his spine like a snake. Long ago, he had learned not to ignore his sixth sense. At the summit, Schitz saw the source of his concern. Within the internal chamber at the top, the local ruler sat surrounded by Priests clad in leather and feathers and warriors adorned with the skins of jaguars. Standing before the leader were two emissaries, Angels of the House of Gold within mortal Incas. The ambassadors knelt behind two large sacks, each brimming with golden coins and trinkets.

They are lazy and complacent, Schitz thought. *They should have already possessed the local leader. They probably haven't seen a rival Angel or a Demon in ages.*

Schitz did not hesitate. Capitalizing on his foes' lack of aware-ness, he slipped into the Celestial and then possessed the body of the ruler.

"Execute these heathens," he said.

Schitz appreciated the speed at which the warriors fell upon the stunned emissaries, plunging obsidian daggers into their throats and midsections in an unrelenting series of savage blows. The blood spewed on the stone floor of the room in a deluge. Schitz stepped from the ruler and set upon the seizing Angels. He cut open the Angels' throats. When he looked at the mortal leader, Schitz felt a cold pang of fear.

The Divine Dictum, he thought.

The carnage had not taken place on a battlefield, a likely violation of numerous clauses of the contract. It was unlikely that there were any Wraiths or Familiars in the crowd gathered along the steps of the pyramid.

Then, he had a revelation.

Are not the actions of Gold's order a violation of the Divine Dictum? After all, we are forbidden from revealing our existence to the humans.

His mind reeled as he weighed his own actions against those of his Angelic quarry. Schitz realized that Gold had revealed nothing to the mortals; the Angel hid himself within the mythology of the natives.

He is not Gold; he is the Sun God. He does not do battle with Demons or other Angels because he is the supreme and undisputed leader, Schitz thought.

Schitz realized he could employ the same strategy to cover the prohibited killing he had just committed. Since he could not repos-sess the baffled ruler, Schitz looked about for a suitable host.

He stepped into the most senior priest and pulled the king to one side. In hushed tones, he said, "My Lord, you seem confused by both your own actions and what you have seen."

The king's eyes were the size of dinner plates. "I know I ordered the slaughter, but I did not do it consciously—at least, I don't think I did. I don't know what happened."

"My Lord," Schitz said, "these godless heathens were false prophets. They claimed to represent the Sun God, when it is well known that the Sun God speaks through you alone. They were arrogant enough to attempt to sway your opinion with gold. They wanted you to deny your station as the Sun God's only mortal conduit. The great Huitzilopochtli[59] acted through you to blot out these vile cretins. The massacre felt grander because the God himself devoured their blasphemous souls as we destroyed their bodies."

The king absorbed Schitz's words and, in so doing, eradicated any violation of the Divine Dictum. The king turned and addressed the shocked audience. "Forgive me for a moment. I am still shaken by the presence of our God whose vengeance was poured out upon these savage heathens. They came to corrupt us, to rob us of our purity, and to remove us from the light of the Sun God, who shines down upon us perpetually."

The ruler paused and turned toward the priests. "What is to be done with this menace?"

Schitz, thankful for the opportunity to drive the discussion despite being outside of the autocratic ruler, replied, "Surely their influence has spread like a dark shadow across the world. You all heard them boast that they already control the vast jungles and mountains to the south. Their evil is perverse. We must assemble our best warriors and cut off the head of this snake."

Schitz commanded the priests to carry the bodies to the massive altar at the summit of the pyramid. When they completed the task, they lit the fire in an enormous brazier next to the altar.

The king shouted from the pinnacle of the pyramid. "These fiends came to us disguised as friends with the goal of deceiving us and removing us from the favor of the Sun God."

The crowd erupted in a storm of jeering and protestations. The king continued, "Have no fear. Your king and your high priest easily saw through their ruse and invoked the vengeance of the Sun God."

The crowd responded with a cheer that reverberated against the

[59] Aztec war and sun god. Also spelled Uitzilopochtli.

pyramid stones. "The work of the Sun God is not finished," the king said. "We are called to destroy this heathen empire. The Sun God will direct us through the high priest."

Schitz held an obsidian blade aloft; the crowd below looked like a feeding frenzy of sharks. They bumped and slapped one another. They screamed themselves hoarse as Schitz drove the blade into the first body, carved, then held up a human heart.

Blood from the squishy cardiac muscle ran down Schitz's arm. His voice echoed across the plaza below.

"We offer their hearts to our God that he might delight in feasting upon them and instruct us with the desires of his own." He tossed the heart into the flames, then repeated the action with the second body.

"We will send Jaguar Claw," he said.

A senior warrior standing near the spectacle raised his dagger toward the sky. He knelt. The priests painted his face and body with the blood of the butchered messengers.

Aztec Daggers

Schitz assessed how many "vessels' he would need. Every human was someone he could possess. Of course, each one was yet another who might alert the enemy.

Once again, he plunged the dagger into the corpses. This time, two pairs of lungs crackled in the flames.

"We will send Arrowhead and Running Water!"

The brothers rose, one holding a bow, the other a spear. They shook their weapons for the crowd. The priests anointed the pair with the blood.

Schitz continued his gory autopsy—kidneys, intestines, livers—all while estimating how long it would take to reach the mountaintop citadel. He cursed how long he'd gone without a possession. Going forward, he would have to exercise extreme caution lest he meld his mind with the host's.

I've survived this long for a reason, he thought. *I'll be fine.*

He eventually settled on twenty warriors, a holy number for the Mexica. Each month of their twenty-month calendar corresponded to one of the gods. Once the selection was complete, he heaved the husks of what remained of the emissaries down the steps of the pyramid.

Their bodies bounced down the steep stairs and people scattered to avoid contamination. Schitz decided to whip the crowd up a little more. He wanted to cover his own actions within the established mythology.

"Bring forth a living sacrifice," he said, "so that the gods might bless our endeavors."

The crowd cheered with the appearance of bound prisoners. One by one, the captives were placed across the altar. Schitz plunged the obsidian blade deep into the sternum of each sacrifice, cracking open the chest bone to remove the still-beating heart. The hapless sacrifices were then discarded down the steps and torn apart by those who waited below.

Schitz looked up toward the sun as he raised the last heart high aloft.

There is no god up there for these savages, he thought, *but below, I'm sure my Lord will rejoice with the news of such a bloodthirsty people.*

Schitz tossed the fourth heart into the fire and exited the priest, moving into the body of the senior warrior. The war party descended the stairs of the pyramid in a solemn procession. Hands slapped Schitz in encouragement and support.

He did not relax until he and his men were out of the city.

"Have we received word yet from the River Valley civilization?" Gold asked Silver.

"Not yet, Brother," Silver replied.

Gold continued to walk through the streets handing out coins and other small trinkets to the many pilgrims that lined his path.

"We must not tarry in our expansion," Gold said. "We must completely consume this savage New World whilst Heaven and Hell are distracted; only then can we cross the waters and spread across the entirety of Earth."

Silver nodded. "When Heaven and Hell lose the ability to possess all humans," he paused and formulated his thoughts as Gold handed a coin to yet another clamoring mortal, "will they continue to fight over the Earth strictly in the Celestial?"

Gold ruminated on the question while he healed a man with a contorted leg.

"It will not matter what they do, for we will use gold and silver to render humans immortal, curing all ailments, and the Eunoe and the Styx will run dry. Their energy will be completely depleted."

Gold grinned at the ingenuity of his strategy. He continued, "I believe Heaven will come begging for parlay. At that time, we will be installed as the true rulers of the Angels."

A broad grin spread across Silver's face. "And what of Hell?"

"We will extinguish Hell," Gold replied. "I have no need for Demons in my kingdom."

"It is a brilliant plan, Brother," Silver said. "What a concept—harvesting the mortals' energy for ourselves instead of acquiring it from the Heavenly river."

Gold smiled and patted Silver on the shoulder. "Soon there will be no need for death or reincarnation; we will control the energy and the mortals and be crowned the supreme entities of Earth." He squinted, obviously thinking of something. "Find out what happened to the runners we sent to the north; we must not tarry in our efforts."

THE JAGUARS WERE MIGHTY warriors, as fierce as the beasts whose skin adorned their backs. Their weapons were as sharp as the teeth of the dead cats they wore around their necks. Schitz appreciated the swiftness with which they cut through the jungle. They passed along like shadows melding with the trees and vines, silently traversing the rugged terrain with ease. They traveled light and foraged from the countryside and the jungle. Though barefoot, they moved with ease over rocks and roots. They ran and did not tire. They engaged isolated Angels and mortals, dispatching them without mercy or pause.

Schitz made sure to ingrain his orders deep in the mind of each warrior he possessed, one at a time. He did not want the plan altered. When they arrived at the foothills of the Andes, Jaguar Claw instructed five of the warriors Schitz had not already possessed to ascend the summit to the citadel. The leader of the war party informed the five that he and the remaining Jaguars would commence a rampage through the lowlands surrounding the citadel. They would draw out the enemy, then wipe them out, bit by bit, while the five ascending the summit decapitated the leadership of the empire.

The men embraced each other heartily before separating. Schitz stepped into one of the five preparing to climb to the summit. He had left five mortals on purpose. He predicted he would need three just to reach the citadel, meaning he would have two fresh ones with which to battle Gold and Silver. He hoped he had calculated correctly. Running out of mortals or having his mind meld with a host would both be fatal errors.

"I AM THE SENIOR Demon, and you will obey me," Bubonic Plague said. His voice reverberated across the Great Hall. Rubella cringed as she felt the weight of the curious gazes of the many passersby.

"There is no reason to presume that he is dead, or that he won't come back," she said through gritted teeth.

"We need all of the children that can be produced for this cause," he said, exasperation heavy in his voice. "It is time to end this lunacy. You should have wed Vertigo, not that impotent, spineless coward. He is surely dead, and if he is not, there is no way he will succeed at his task. Satan has blessed a union between you and me."

"I will wait for Schitz, my lawful husband in the eyes of our Church," Rubella replied.

"Where are you going?" Bubonic Plague asked when Rubella opened a portal to the mortal world.

"Damascus," she replied bluntly. "Why don't you try doing something useful for a change?"

Before the infuriated Demon could reply, she had gone. Bubonic Plague cursed and stamped upon the ground. Unbeknownst to anyone other than Satan, he had been keeping track of the weasel, Schitz, and his adventures in the new world. The Devil had been intrigued about the savagery of the mortals that engaged in human sacrifice and cannibalism, and he had been concerned regarding Bubonic Plague's account of Schitz's inability to possess humans.

As he opened a portal to the Mortal Realm, Plague hoped he would be blessed to observe Schitz's death. He knew every day brought the exile nearer to a confrontation with Gold. Bubonic was forced to admit that the bastard was persistent; he was shocked by how far Schitz had been willing to travel to find humans he could possess and equally stunned by the breakneck pace with which he had returned to the Andes. Nevertheless, Bubonic thirsted for the death of the impudent parasite, and longed to see his wife wed to a proper Demon, either himself or, at least, Smallpox. Bubonic Plague stepped through the portal, hoping against hope that he would witness the final demise of the Demon he hated with every fiber of his being.

THE ORCHARDS OUTSIDE OF Damascus had been selected by the Crusaders as the route by which to approach the city because of the dual benefit of offering sustenance and cover. A half-century of campaigning in the rugged, barren Holy Land had taught the Christians the value of food and water. Yet, as Rubella arrived from Hell to rejoin the army, fresh with new instructions from the Triumvirate Council, she felt something was terribly wrong. The Muslims appeared well prepared and were utilizing the maze-like nature of the orchards to ambush and hamper the Christian advance.

Rubella sighed with exasperation as she assessed the scene. The knights had dismounted from their steeds due to the heavy fire of arrows and stones coming from the Muslims. The riders and infantry alike took cover behind their shields, a serious hindrance to the advance.

Typhoid, the son of Pride and Lust, exited a Knights Templar to meet Rubella within the Celestial.

"My Lady, do you bring word from the Council?"

Rubella felt a pang of pity as she searched the face of the young Demon. Although Typhoid had already sired an Academy graduate in his daughter Asthma through his marriage to Scarlet Fever, he was untested in terms of brutal, pitched battle. Rubella knew her subordinate longed for the order to withdraw.

"We must press on," she said, trying to rally his spirits. "Damascus is of incredible importance. We will win a great victory for Hell and our Crusader Kingdoms."

To his credit, Typhoid appeared to steel himself for further contact with the enemy.

"We've been trying to push on through the orchards," he said. "We encountered a staunch group of Angels directly before us and a variety of others along our flanks. We've gotten some pretty decent kills along the flanks, but that rock wedged before us is immovable."

Rubella considered the strategic situation. The Demons had captured Jerusalem and immediately begun utilizing the power provided by the ancient ground. To secure their claim, they had also established themselves within the crusader states. Hell had set up a rotating assignment, so that Demons always held the crusader armies of Edessa, Antioch, Cilicia, Tripoli, and Jerusalem. The Wraiths had scoured the Holy Land and determined that the Nazarene, once immensely powerful, had departed for Heaven.

Therefore, the Triumvirate decided to resume normal operations.

The Angels countered and crushed the kingdom of Edessa. As a member of the Triumvirate, Rubella was in command of the mission. She found herself leading a mixed force of veterans and neophytes. Autism, Conjunctivitis, and Pneumonia composed the experienced troops while Typhoid, Streptococcal, Dandruff, and Ulcers were still untried. She divided her contingent into smaller teams and sent them to probe the Angelic positions.

"Autism and Pneumonia are still pushing forward on the flanks?" she asked Typhoid.

"The last I was informed, yes, with decent success," he replied.

They had the neophytes split between them to complete their squads. Rubella had taken Typhoid to form a dyad to bolster the collapsing flanks. Typhoid had been on his own when she went to brief the council.

Is the resistance significant, or has Typhoid simply had enough? she wondered.

She opted to press forward before reestablishing contact with the rest of her detachment. She and Typhoid each jumped into a Templar Knight. He leapt into a baron from Normandy; she took a woman of noble birth in Burgundy.

With the heat of the day and the battle raging around them, they came upon a force of Muslim Cavaliers, dismounted and possessed by Angels. Rubella tapped Typhoid on his arm. The metal of the mailed glove clanked against his shoulder plate. She raised her long sword and asked, "Are those the Angels you spoke of, ones that gave a strict reckoning?"

"Aye, my Lady," he replied.

"Then let us pay them back twice in turn. I will dispatch them in the mortal flesh, you deal the fatal blow in the Celestial. I will cover you."

"Aye, my Lady," he said, though clearly frozen with fear.

"Come," she said with a maniacal laugh. "Deus vult."[60]

---

[60] God wills it. (The motto of the Crusaders)

Rubella and her comrade attacked with savage efficiency. Rubella knocked aside a possessed enemy's sword and struck him between a gap in his armor at the base of his breastplate. After running the mortal through, she blocked an attack from another possessed mortal, stepped into him with her shoulder and plunged her sword into his exposed throat. Having killed two possessed humans, she anticipated Typhoid's arrival within the Celestial and joined him there.

As he plunged his Celestial dagger into one Angel and then the next, she defended him from an onslaught of Angels attempting to protect their own. Rubella cut down the Angels attacking Typhoid and left a trail of their entrails and blood on the soft floor of the orchard.

A scattered remnant of the Angelic force fell back, and a familiar face stepped from behind one of the orchard's many trees. Rubella returned to an earlier time. She recalled the pain of childbirth, anxious concern for her babies, and the sense of vulnerability. She remembered how the female Angel before her had decapitated her infant son and stabbed Schitz in the chest.

Rubella was vaguely aware of Typhoid preparing himself to attack.

She shouted a warning. "No, Typhoid, run to the flank and bring Autism and his retinue immediately."

The novice hesitated to leave his commander, a sentiment she much appreciated. But she knew the specter in front of them was far too lethal for a neophyte. Typhoid would only be a liability.

"I have given you an order," she said.

"My Lady," he said with a nod.

Before he departed, Rubella caught his gaze, and for the briefest of moments, remembered his early days in the Academy. She recalled how he passed a note to Scarlet Fever during one of her lectures. He had looked so panic-stricken when he realized he was discovered that she had felt compelled to direct her attention elsewhere.

Such innocence in youth, she thought.

"You have fought bravely, Typhoid," she said, "and you have made me very proud."

Typhoid departed to carry out her order.

Rubella turned to her adversary. "Lady of the Zinc House," Rubella said.

She sheathed her Celestial dagger and drew the long sword from her waist.

"Lady of the Hydrogen House now, yet well remembered," Rachael replied. "Is that your son? Did you bear another?"

Rubella felt the hairs upon her neck stand on edge. The Angel strolled forward, dragging the tip of her sword upon the ground.

"As a matter of fact, yes," Rubella said. "All of my pupils are my children, and after today you will never hurt any of them again."

The Angel laughed, a falsely feminine titter. "Oh, I will drink that one's blood this very hour."

Rubella noticed the slightest distraction pass through the Angel's eyes and was aware of a Demonic Celestial body arriving behind her.

"Be careful; this one's dangerous," Rubella said before a slicing pain cut through her midsection.

She gazed down in shock and horror and fought in vain for breath. She traced the path of the Celestial dagger buried in her liver up the arm of the Demon until she came to the face of Spanish Influenza. He wrenched the blade free and stood calmly alongside her. Rubella wobbled and buckled. He stepped towards her with the body language of concern, least his treachery be observed.

Rubella struggled to breathe. "I taught you," she said. Biting cold gripped at the core of her body. She felt wetness spreading from her wound, running down her leg, and filling her robe.

"My brother was your grandfather," she said.

"Satan said to tell you that you should have stayed out of his bedroom business," Spanish Influenza said.

Before she could reply, Rubella collapsed to the ground. In the dizzying grip of agony, she was vaguely aware of her assassin's departure. She fell onto her back and gazed up at the clear, cloudless sky.

Rubella assessed her situation. She was in dire circumstances, but if support arrived to drive away the Angel, she might not bleed out before they returned her to Hell and the healing waters of the Styx. She had been undone by the sudden arrival of a Demon; now, that was all that could save her.

The Angel's face blocked Rubella's view of the sky.

"I spent some time in Assyria," Rachael said. She rolled Rubella over on her stomach. "I was there during the reign of Ashurnasirpal II. Do you know his preferred method of execution?"

Rubella groaned as she felt the Angel cutting at her robes with a Celestial blade. Naked and helpless, Rubella's body began to tremble.

Rachael's voice was the low growl of a jungle cat. "They took the skin from the condemned while they still breathed. It's quite phenomenal. If done correctly, a human can survive a complete flaying, so that they live for hours or even days after the deed."

Rubella's scream pierced the sky. "Help me! Somebody, help!"

"Is your husband alive?" the Angel asked. "Are you calling for him?"

Rubella sobbed as her pleas went unanswered.

"You know, he is the one I want," Rachael said, "but I am so happy to do this to you. I do hope he is still alive. He has eluded me for so long."

"He lives, and he will kill you for this," Rubella said.

"Oh, I doubt it," Rachael replied. "But I hope he tries. I might do to him what I'm about to do to you—unless I can think of something more painful."

"I will neither beg for my life, nor will I give you the satisfaction by voicing my suffering, so just get on with it."

"As you wish." Lady Hydrogen let out a long, harsh laugh, then drew a dagger. "Ashurnasirpal II liked to start with the thighs."

She dragged her Celestial dagger along the inside of Rubella's buttock until it was resting on her tailbone. "However, I prefer the base of the spine."

Rubella fought with all her remaining strength not to scream as she felt the blade sliding beneath her skin, cutting through layers of tissue and muscle. The Angel moved the blade with agonizing deliberateness, a snail-like pace of pain upwards along the spine.

Rubella forced herself to recall the day Schitz had been banished from Hell, in particular the moment when he had embraced both her and Rabies. In that brief instant, all three of them had been together. Rubella wished deeply in her heart that the moment could have been longer, but she was grateful to have enjoyed it at all.

I love you both, she thought.

The blade reached the top of her head and began removing her scalp.

Rubella focused for a moment longer upon the memory of Schitz and Rabies and then yielded to the coming night, and finally, the cessation of her torture.

THE JAGUAR WARRIOR'S WIFE was vivacious and possessed an unquenchable libido. On many a night, he awakened to find her straddled atop him, or working vigorously to rouse him from slumber, at least the part of him she needed. The warrior appreciated the memories of the pleasure he took from her, but the thoughts were a double-edged sword, for he wondered how she occupied herself while he was away. The idea of her hunger pulling her to another bed sent pangs of blood-boiling jealousy through his body.

Schitz grunted with frustration; neither the erotic memories nor the jealous thoughts of the warrior mattered to him, but they were an indication that he was overstaying his time of possession. Schitz gazed toward the summit of the mountain. He wondered about Rubella and what she was doing in his absence. The sun crept toward the western slopes. They would reach the citadel by the break of dawn if he pushed the Jaguars to their limit.

I have no choice, he thought.

And he jumped into the penultimate mortal.

THE CONTINGENT OF DEMONS stood in a single file as the Priests continued with the Return Ceremony. Autism stared at the black marble floor of the Great Hall.

A familiar, feminine voice arose from over his shoulder. "First, Schitz is banished. Now we lose Rubella." It was Anorexia. "The numbers from our class have dwindled so."

Autism turned and beheld his sister's thin face. "I don't know which is worse, dear sister, having lost an old friend or knowing the pain Schitz will encounter when he gets back."

"If he gets back at all," she replied with a heavy voice.

"Indeed," Autism said, "if he comes back."

DAY BROKE OVER THE Andes. Schitz led the five Jaguars into the outskirts of the citadel. In hushed tones, he spoke to the warriors, reporting the observations he had made in the dark.

"The temple is home to the leaders," he said, tracing a box in the dirt with his index finger. "It has an entrance towards the front that leads to the main street and one in the rear leading to the houses of the more opulent families."

He turned to the one mortal he had yet to possess.

"Cipactli, you will go to the rear entrance and wait. When the fighting starts, enter the temple through the rear entrance."

He looked at the others. "Mazātl and Itzcuīntli, you will guard the front entrance. Do not be reckless with your lives; you will only hold off any reinforcements while we are within the temple."

The men nodded.

"Cuāuhtli, you will enter the temple with me," Schitz said.

The only acknowledgement was a slight flicker of the eyelids. Schitz did not wish to enter the temple with the last mortal he could possess. He intended to use Cuāuhtli, Mazātl, and Itzcuīntli as bait, and he wanted to save the last viable vessel as a last resort, just in case.

The Jaguars made their way toward the temple. They crouched low to the ground and moved silently along the exteriors of the buildings. Whenever they came upon a guard or a citizen, they fired their obsidian-tipped arrows with brutal accuracy, silently cutting them down. Schitz watched a pair of lesser Angels writhing on the ground, seizing.

He was forced to bypass them; he could not step into the Celestial.

I hate to miss an opportunity to dispatch the enemy.

He watched Cipactli break away from the crowd and head to the rear of the temple.

There goes my last hope.

Even in the early morning hours, a cluster of pilgrims was arrayed across the steps of the holy site. Schitz raised his bow and fired an arrow into the chest of one of the pilgrims. His fellows followed suit. Pandemonium erupted. Schitz glanced over his shoulder and saw several warriors with the auras of Angelic possession rushing down the street toward the temple. The early morning sun reflected off their golden armor. The pilgrims scattered from the steps and called to their god for rescue. Mazātl and Itzcuīntli took their positions on the stairs and fired arrows toward the onrushing foe. Schitz led Cuāuhtli into the temple.

Rafael Della Cruz rested his musket against the wall of the ancient building and removed his heavy helmet before he marveled at the treasure trove. His eyes beamed at the glittering storehouse.

"Dios mio!"[61]

The other men cheered and jumped with joy. "Oro, oro, esta oro aqui!"[62]

"We are richer than our wildest dreams," the Spaniard said. "And the king will be ever so pleased."

Gold and other ornamentation lined the walls of the holy place. A tall man wearing a large crown of golden feathers stood at the altar.

Schitz froze.

"Gold," he said aloud.

---

[61] Oh my God.

[62] Gold, gold, it's gold here.

"None other," the Angel said from within the priest. Without warning, he picked up a spear and hurled it at Schitz.

Cuāuhtli shoved Schitz out of the way. The spear bore through the native with a sickening squish. He collapsed, a torrent of blood pouring from his heaving mouth.

Schitz raised his bow. Gold sprinted toward him. Unable to get off a shot in time, Schitz dropped the bow and drew an obsidian dagger in each of his hands. Schitz ducked and dodged as his foe hacked at him with a sword.

Schitz heard the clash of battle from outside; his comrades were holding off reinforcements. But his focus was on Gold's maniacal attack. The Angel was a whirlwind of savage ability. Schitz narrowly avoided a thrust to his gut by rolling. He popped to his feet and wrenched the spear from Cuāuhtli. Schitz blocked a downward swipe with the shaft and countered by swinging the blade at Gold's throat. The Angel swayed backward, barely avoiding the edge.

"You're not bad," Gold said with a smile.

"You're a little bit rusty," Schitz said.

Gold parried a thrust and stepped closer. Anticipating the move, Schitz swung the shaft at Gold's head. When the Angel ducked, his crown clattered to the floor.

Schitz flipped the spear over, snagged the crown with the butt end, and flung it at Gold. The heavy ornament cracked into the human's knee, and Gold buckled with a groan.

Schitz raised his spear to deliver a death blow. Before he could strike, a knife bounced off the spear's tip only a hand's width from Schitz's ear.

Gold smiled. "Just in time, Brother," he said.

Silver, short sword in hand, shrieked and launched himself at Schitz. The Demon planted the blunt end of the spear on the floor, lifted, and kicked Silver with both feet.

With ferocity born of desperation, Schitz used the spear to keep the brothers at bay. They menaced him with swipes and swings but were wary of the glistening spear tip. The stalemate was broken when Cipactli entered through the rear entrance, unobserved by the combatants. He raised his bow and fired an obsidian-tipped arrow through the throat of Silver's host.

Schitz reveled for a moment in the execution of his plan. *His timing was perfect*, he thought.

He stepped into the Celestial and swung his sword at Silver. Another blade came from the side and blocked the attack. Gold had stepped into the Celestial in his brother's defense. Schitz's sword slid across Gold's, and instead of slicing Silver's throat, it smashed broadside into his jaw, shattering bone and teeth.

Schitz rolled across the ground and possessed Cipactli, for he could not risk being stuck without a mortal shield.

In a moment, Schitz's former host, Quiyahuitl, ran Gold's former host through with the golden spear. Schitz fired an arrow into Quiyahuitl's back, piercing his heart thus denying Gold a mortal he could possess. The Demon rushed across the room and quickly reacquired the spear.

Gold stood in the Celestial. His eyes darted from side to side like a trapped animal. Schitz possessed the only remaining mortal in the room. If Gold fled within the Celestial, Schitz would dispatch his brother. Silver twitched in agony on the floor. Gold's gaze went from his brother to the rear entrance of the temple and back.

"Surrender to me, and I'll spare your brother," Schitz said.

Gold spat. "You've hardly won, besides there are no accords between your kind and mine."

Schitz glanced over his shoulder toward the main entrance of the temple.

"How long do you think your men can hold out?" Gold asked. "The entire city will be crashing in here soon."

Schitz wondered how many arrows his confederates had remaining in their quivers.

Schitz had anticipated the possibility of a stalemate but not the upper hand that the injured Silver gave him.

"You know he'll die if you take much longer," Schitz said, pointing a taunting finger at the writhing Angel.

Schitz dropped to a knee and drew an obsidian dagger. He kept a keen eye on Gold, who hovered over Silver like a bedraggled lioness protecting a wounded cub. Schitz began sawing at the neck of the fallen king. Upon severing the head, Schitz grabbed the golden crown from the floor and strode toward the sunlight, which bathed the main entrance of the temple.

"I'll be with you two momentarily," he said to Gold.

THE GARDENS BEHIND WALTER Ackell's estate were a welcomed sanctuary from the festivities for Lieutenant Scott Mitchell and Ackell's eldest daughter, Evelyn. The cocktail party in honor of the men who would soon be departing for France was not on either one's mind.

"This war's been going on for years," the young lieutenant said. "It won't last much longer. We always knew I might get called over."

"I know," Evelyn replied in her Southern drawl. "I just know that I'll miss you ever so much."

"Well, I got you something to remind you of me," the young soldier said.

He dropped to one knee. Evelyn raised her hands over her mouth.

"Oh, my good Lord," she said.

"Now, don't get too excited," Scott said. He blushed and removed a humble gold band from his pocket. "It's tough to afford anything fancy on a lieutenant's salary, but I hope you'll have me anyway."

"Oh, of course, I will, and oh, I really do love it!"

Evelyn smiled through a veil of happy tears.

A RIVER OF FALLEN bodies meandered up the street and continued up the stairs of the temple, arrows protruding from their stricken bodies. Mazātl and Itzcuīntli were not fairing much better; both men bore the wounds of several arrows about their bodies. Yet the Jaguars held the top stair, their chests heaving from exertion.

Schitz climbed up above them on the smooth sloping stone,

which ran along the staircase, and raised his voice above the fray. Luckily for Schitz, his Aztec comrades had killed the Incan hosts of many Angels. Those that had not fallen victim to departure seizures were too frightened to storm the temple in the Celestial.

All action stopped when Schitz made his pronouncement.

"Your false God is dead," he said.

He punctuated the sentence by flinging the severed head of the Gold's mortal into the crowd. The surviving Jaguars hooted and howled with delight over the deafening silence that fell over the assembled mass. Schitz raised the golden crown upwards toward the sky and smiled at his massive luck when a solitary cloud drifted in front of the sun.

"We are the representatives of the true Sun God," Schitz shouted, "your false idolatry has angered him."

The cloud blocked the blinding sunlight. Schitz lowered the crown onto his head.

"The Sun God has abandoned your people in his anger, and soon, his vengeance shall be fully poured out upon you. Go from this place at once."

The writhing sea of humanity that followed Schitz's instruction could only be born from a genuine fear of divine retribution. No sooner had his voice echoed into nothingness that the streets became virtually empty. Schitz anticipated the arrival of a supporting contingent of Angels; however, with all their potential hosts rushing homeward, the Army of Heaven seemed unable to step out into the Celestial.

Schitz suppressed a smile. "This just might work," he said.

The flight away from the battleground shook the ground like an earthquake or cattle stampede. The exhausted surviving Jaguars collapsed on the steps. Only time would tell whether they would see the sunlight of the next day or succumb to their many wounds. Schitz mounted the smooth stones that served as the banister to the staircase and continued to the roof of the temple.

If I were Gold, I wouldn't be waiting around for my hapless reinforcements, Schitz thought. He ran as fast as he could. Upon reaching the edge of the roof, he flung his mortal over the edge while jumping into the Celestial and catching the edge of the roof with his hands, he dropped to the rear entrance of the temple. Gold was in the process of opening a portal in the doorway, his injured brother prone across the floor beside him. The last mortal crumpled on the rear staircase.

Schitz's feet caught Gold squarely in the chest and sent him reeling away from the doorway. Schitz drew his Celestial sword and lunged at the beleaguered Angel. Gold managed to block the blow with his own sword, but he could not ward off another kick to the ribs. Gold grimaced, and his sword clinked across the floor.

"I give you good price," Steven Wu said from behind the counter of his Canal Street jewelry store.

"Naw, man, how you want me to drop a grip on that weak-ass chain?" replied his less than interested customer.

"I give you good price; is twenty-four-carat." Mr. Wu remained insistent.

"Naw, G, not for that thin-ass chain; you must be buggin'."

The customer turned to leave; the storeowner reluctantly attempted to retain his attention.

"You wait, you wait, I make better deal. I give you special deal."

The cacophony of car horns and loud voices muted as the customer shut the front door and stepped back into the jewelry shop.

Lying in Schitz's intimidating shadow, Gold shouted at Silver. "Go, save yourself!"

Schitz did not bother to turn away from his quarry.

"Is he able to move?" Schitz asked with smug satisfaction painted on his blood-creased face.

Gold cowered. "I was building something great. Wh... wh... wh... why did you have to come here?"

Schitz shrugged. "I'm just following orders, but if I had to guess, if Hell and Heaven can't work out an accord, two's company and three is definitely a fucking crowd. There's just no room for you."

Schitz raised his sword above his head.

"Wait," the Angel said, his voice pleading and pathetic. "I can give you—"

"Let me guess," Schitz said. But he didn't. Instead, he buried his sword into the Angel's skull.

Then he finished the thought. "You can give me gold."

Schitz pulled his sword free and brought it down a second and third time until he was satisfied that no life remained within the shattered Angel.

To his surprise, the maimed Silver had managed to open the portal and depart.

Schitz's Notebook

Aztec Jaguar

Itzcuintli

I will forever owe a great debt to these remarkable warriors. For I doubt that I would have triumphed over Gold and Silver without them. The Jaguars are versatile, fierce, intelligent, and relentless. I will always hold them in my memory with the warmest of recollections and admiration.

"Well, it's no matter," Schitz said aloud, flush with his victory. He had killed Gold, shattered his empire, and maimed Silver; surely, he had fulfilled his obligation. He stooped over his fallen foe.

Rising to open his own portal, he spoke into the void. "Strange, I don't feel nearly as vulnerable in the Celestial now."

He gazed down to his left hand in which he clasped Gold's severed head. "Why do you think that is?"

THEY GAVE GOLD A funeral in Heaven with full honors; Silver received a Divine pardon.

How quick they are to claim the fallen as their own, Silver thought with disgust. *They see the world as they would like it. Then again, Gold was a hero, the slayer of Demons, the prolonger of the lives of human kings, no longer now.*

Silver shook his head and mumbled to no one. "Be he their hero, or their villain by his actions, he will always be my brother by his blood, and I will honor him ten-thousand times more than the most ardent mourner here. I will remember the Angel, not the myth."

Silver noted the way they cut their eyes at him, uncertain if they were afraid, in awe, or just merely curious. Reflexively, he touched his silver false teeth. He knew he had always been slightly more emotional than others, but now Silver was sure that he looked haggard, weathered, akin to those mortals whose minds had been sheared and shredded by the Demon that had killed his brother and maimed his face.

Silver thought less of himself and more of his fallen kin as he took his place closest to the altar. His throat closed as he beheld the painting of his mentor and closest friend. The golden arrow that rested below the solemn portrait was an all-too-present reminder of all that Gold would now be to the world.

"We flew too close to the sun, Brother," Silver said aloud as he knelt by the altar. Then glaring at the High Priest, he snarled. "Well, what are we waiting for?"

Then from the secret chamber that led to the only gallery box in the cavernous Great Hall, a bright light emerged from behind the doors that held the holiest of all secrets, and He stood in observance.

The violins took up *Sarabande*, the funeral hymn of the Angels, and the Priests took their place at their proscribed stations. Silver's voice was hoarse as he began the drearily familiar lyrics in unison with those in attendance.

Hear how, the bells tolled,
When Requiem, was told,
With darkness, descending,
And sadness, unending,

The Priest stood before Silver, decked in his finest most ornamental robes. He shook the thurible, which clanged from its chain as the incense wafted over the assembled. The Priest reached out and fanned the heavy smoke towards himself before covering his ears in solemn accordance with the ritual.

See how, widows cry,
Nary an eye is now dry,
Of all those assembled,
Fraught and quaking; how they trembled,

The Priest shook more incense from the thurible in Silver's direction. He wafted the incense upwards past him toward the ceiling before covering his eyes with open palms. They were moist and clammy with beads of sweat.

Feel now, the dead corpse,
Cut down, without remorse,
Note how, the veins chilled,
For all blood has been spilled,

Rising to his feet, Silver's knees ached from having knelt on the cold stones. Slowly, he regained his footing and placed his hand on his brother's arm. It was still and rigid. He felt a deep emptiness in the pit of his stomach as he gazed upon the corpse, a black cloth covering Gold's neck and the place where his head should have been. Silver imagined his brother's face where the fabric was. He chose to remember Gold's face as peaceful, serene in death as it never was in life.

Taste now, the acridness,
There is no cure for this sickness,
Of eternal silence,
Brought upon by unholy violence.

While the congregation continued the hymn, Silver stepped back from his brother and knelt. He opened his mouth as the Priest placed the sacramental bread within. Silver gagged slightly as he quickly swallowed the dry wafer before accepting an elaborate chalice that was, of all things, golden. Silver drank a deep draught of the sacramental wine. After draining the goblet, he placed the cup next to his brother.

Smell now, the foulness,
As death now, surrounds us,
Wrapped in the putrid wings,
That envelop all mortal things.

The Priest returned to wafting incense toward Silver, who was now feeling light-headed from draining the entire chalice of wine. Purposefully, the Priest focused as he wafted the smoke towards his nose and then down to the ground, before placing his hands over his nose.

Angelic Incense Churible

Weep now, with full remorse,
There is no other recourse,
The living; for the dead cry,
Knowing that one day they too will die,

Silver moved his hands up to his temples and gripped them in accordance with the ritual. The rite had seemed odd when Silver had done it for his uncles and his cousins, but he felt the true purpose as he completed the gestures in honor of his brother. He rose to his feet and snapped to attention, his chest out as he joined in the dark chorus.

> *Honor now, the sacrifice,*
> *No other price, will suffice,*
> *For it is the lot of those who serve,*
> *To give all, and never lose nerve.*

Silver raised his hand in salute.

> *Offer yourself, to God,*
> *Who all on Earth and Heaven laud,*
> *And your own death will have meaning,*
> *Long after you are no longer breathing.*

Silver's voice rose above the others as he sounded the last verse. He locked eyes with the sovereign figure as the hymn concluded, but he could find no answer to what thoughts were marauding behind his king's solemn, unshaken demeanor. However, God seemed pleasantly relieved.

SCHITZ SAT ALONE IN his room, reclining on the lion's skin spread across his bed. He clutched the rugged fur tightly between his fingers. He wanted to cry but had already emptied all that was within him into the cat's pelt. His body trembled and heaved as he drew in ragged breaths and reeled under a foreboding sense akin to claustrophobia. The torture of knowing he would never again get to hear her voice, feel her skin, see her smile, ever, left him with the sensation that the universe was requiring him to hold his breath forever.

His homecoming had been painfully anticlimactic; he had arrived with Gold's head and completed the Return Ceremony. The Priests had taken the Angel's head, while Schitz retained the crown and golden sword for himself. Schitz had then sought out his mate only to encounter Elise. The Wraith had already heard word of his return and was waiting for him outside of his quarters.

Schitz could tell from the look in her eyes that she bore ill tidings. He felt hollow as she clutched him close to her.

"There, there, my boy," she whispered.

It stung with heightened poignancy that Rubella had been taken from him while he had been banished. All he could do was lock himself away in his quarters and weep as he drank deeply from the well of inconsolable sadness.

Chapter 13

Single Combat

A huge map teetered on an undersized easel in the Great Hall. Lilly pointed to a sketch of the Behemoth tacked to the margin. "Let us review," she said. "Bubonic Plague leads the Black Death Coven, but this one is the problem."

Zinc had seen the hulking warrior a few times from a distance, and although trepidation pricked at his spine, he relished the opportunity to take on such a storied enemy.

Lilly continued her debrief. "He is strong, quick, and comfortable fighting multiple opponents. Overwhelming him is not an option. However, isolating him by killing the rest of the Coven would be a good place to start."

Zinc glanced about the room. His son Patrick, Lord of the Chlorine House, and his son Aaron, Lord of the Phosphorous House, were part of any operation he undertook. Zinc was proud of the Standard Bearers he had sired. They had married well and built their houses into influential Heavenly entities. They had sired long lineages of their own, and their loyalty to him was paramount in his plan to ascend to the summit of Heavenly power once more. His son, Adolphus, and daughter-in-law, Constance Silver, sat against one wall.

After the Siege of Jerusalem, their centuries-long liaison had come to light. Zinc wished he had enjoyed the benefit of his experiences when he had been in his son's position. Despite the taboo, he had encouraged the union. The couple was probably the most powerful in Heaven because of their adroit field abilities and an all-encompassing knowledge of tactics and strategy. Zinc was confident in all four of his commanders.

"Our first point of vulnerability, identified by scouting, is the duo Pride and Lust," Lilly said. "They are married and almost always fight side by side."

Lilly pointed to sketches of Pride and Lust.

"We know their partnership has led them to develop skills allowing them to work in tandem. Lust is an expert archer. She can hit targets accurately from distances well in excess of three hundred yards, if we are using the English system. She typically strikes opponents in the vulnerable places between armored plates such as the neck or in the armpit under the pauldron. Lust is incredibly strong. The mortals she possesses fire arrows at an unheard-of velocity and can easily puncture chainmail with their bolts. Pride is an expert at close combat, both in the Mortal and Celestial Realms. He typically operates ahead of Lust and cuts down the Angels she has dispatched with her arrows."

Zinc thanked Lilly for her information and assumed the lead. He addressed the broad components first. "All reports indicate that the Demons would like to open a second front for the spread of their plague. They are making progress from Genoa and Venice over land. However, they would vastly accelerate their expansion if they were to break out from another port, especially in the North. Hence

Calais. The conditions of siege and the location of the port city are perfect for maximizing the spread of their disease. Lilly's reports predict that the Demons may already be there."

He moved into the strategic portion of the plan. "Lord Phosphorus and his House will lead an assault on the gate to draw attention. If the Demons sally forth to engage our force, their effort will include Pride. In turn, Lust will provide cover from atop the walls. Lord Chlorine and his contingent will man an English trebuchet, which will fire on Lust's section of the wall. When Lust is killed by our siege engine, I will dispatch her since I will have infiltrated Calais within the Celestial. Then we will withdraw."

English Longbow

Zinc liked both the plan and his commanders' reaction to it.

He added a warning. "There is a high likelihood for casualties among the force that acts as bait," he said. He locked eyes with Aaron. "The probability of killing Pride outright is low. However, he will be most distracted when the trebuchet takes out his wife. If you have the opportunity to strike, try to take him out and withdraw immediately."

THE SKY OVER THE fortress of Calais was cloudy. Sophie Deschamps nocked another arrow to her bowstring. The light spring rain would do little to affect her arrow's path. From within the French woman, Lust calculated the various parameters of wind, distance, elevation, and movement before letting the shaft fly. Unlike its predecessor that had harmlessly clattered off an English soldier's helmet, this arrow found its way to the target, striking the English man-at-arms in the throat.

Schitz's Notebook

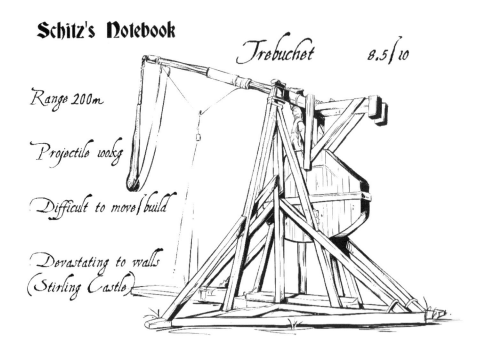

Trebuchet   8.5/10

Range 200m

Projectile 100kg

Difficult to move/build

Devastating to walls (Stirling Castle)

Lust watched as an Angel fell on the damp, muddy Earth in agony. She reached into her quiver and drew another arrow while the rest of her Coven departed the fortress within a contingent of French infantry who were ready to engage the attackers and the Angels within.

SCALING WALLS HAD NEVER come easily to Zinc. Hampered by the rain, he led his men into the castle at Calais as the clatter of armor and jostling of metal issued the universally distinguishable sound of an army at the alarm. With great pains to maintain their covert arrival, Zinc, Adolphus, and Constance had spread out and taken up positions around the courtyard below the wall. Zinc peered up through the rain plinking against his head and watched the possessed archer above him atop the wall. He readied a Celestial dagger and waited.

Henry Cooper, or Harry Coop as his fellows referred to him, had developed a distinct reputation among the operators of the siege engines. Within all of Edward III's army, none was better at finding his mark, whether with stone or incendiary. When Patrick Chlorine possessed him, Harry was preparing his mighty trebuchet. The combination of ballistic knowledge represented the highest level of expertise the world had yet witnessed. He held his thumb and index finger aloft, squinting through the space between his digits, as the rain pelted his steel helmet and ran down his hand.

He judged the distance to his target, the height of his target, and the weight of the stone projective. The sling-release mechanism was in the correct place. He was sure because he had checked it multiple times. With one last look towards his comrades engaged in fierce combat at the wall of the castle, he turned toward the possessed crew manning the trebuchet.

"Loose!" The wooden beams groaned as the counterweight released. The massive, moving parts heaved into action and launched the stone toward its target.

ALTHOUGH HE WAS TYPICALLY more than happy to engage the Angels in combat, Bubonic Plague was irritated by the day's events at Calais. He had assembled the Coven to orchestrate a massive outbreak of the Black Death. His plans had been for the plague to break the siege and then to infect the English as well. He hoped he could then spread the infection both to the British Isles and south through the continent.

Conjuring Pneumatic Plague, the combination of the Coven's efforts, required time and focus. The interruption of the Angels leading a localized attack on the gate frustrated Bubonic to the utmost.

From within a French soldier, Bubonic brought down his mortal mace on yet another English infantryman, crushing through his mail, fracturing bones and puncturing organs. The man collapsed to the ground, and an Angel fell onto the muddy ground within the Celestial. Bubonic's follower Pride had already dashed ahead of the others within the Celestial. He drilled a throwing star into the Angel that was seizing at Bubonic's feet, thus allowing his commander to remain within his mortal host.

Bubonic smiled. His force had cleared the English and Angels who had so ambitiously attacked the main entrance with ladders. The wooden apparatus and many of the men lay haplessly on the wet earth following his Coven's resistance. He had sent Lust to the wall for top cover with her bow, while he led the others into the fray.

Bubonic Plague watched as the Angels stood before him in the Celestial several paces beyond Pride. Their number had been decisively

French Mace

halved, and without surviving mortal hosts, they appeared to have lost the will to continue the skirmish. Upon initial assessment, Bubonic believed they had killed five to seven Angels, not a bad endeavor. He shouted to his adversaries as they began to fall back. "Done so soon? Well, come back any time you like."

As soon as he had uttered his taunts, a solitary projectile sailing over the combatants' heads caught his attention. He tracked its swift course and watched it cut through the air before slamming into the section of the wall manned by Lust. Bubonic grimaced. Particles of stone and dust erupt in a cloud of debris, masking the area where the Demon had been a moment earlier.

"Subterfuge!" He cursed. "Perfidious wretches!"

Bubonic Plague knew that the well-placed stone had been coordinated with the attack. He looked at Pride. The Demon was staring at the place where, only moments before, his wife had stood. Pride was too lost in thought to notice the blade hurtling through the air.

"Look ou—"

The warning was cut short by the thud of a throwing knife burrowing into Pride's chest. Bubonic howled, but not even his screaming protest could resurrect his colleague.

THE STONE FROM THE trebuchet blistered into the wall. Zinc watched the body of the French archer tumble through the air. The mortal woman's frame crumpled and broke on the ground. The Demon within began to writhe in agony. Zinc rushed to her while she was immobilized, only to arrive at the same time as Constance.

"Ladies first," he laughed as he deferred to his daughter-in-law. He watched her lift Lust's chin and open the Demon's arteries with two precise cuts. The edges of Constance's mouth curled in a tight smile. She watched the Demon exsanguinate.

Adolphus had already opened a portal utilizing the mud at the base of an archway.

"One down," the young Angel said.

Zinc slapped him on the back. "I love when things go according to plan," he said.

CHALICES OF ELIXIR CLINKED against each other in the Great Hall and voices of jubilation rose and fell among the Angels and Familiars. Though they had just attended the funeral and internment of six Angels of the House of Phosphorous, there was little effort among the survivors to render a somber or subdued affair. All told, the intricately complex operation had been executed with minimal losses. By comparison, two Demons had been killed and the Angels had prevented an outbreak of the Pneumatic Plague.

"All right, all right!" Zinc shouted to be heard. "We have another mission to begin planning."

"We have identified the next area likely to be hit," Lilly said. "It fits within Bubonic Plague's personality to be enraged by setbacks and to redouble his efforts somewhere else in the North of France. Based upon this and the movement of the French Army, we have identified Brittany as his next target to expand the plague."

Zinc laid out the plan. "With the removal of Lust, we now possess a distinct advantage with regards to ranged combat within the Mortal Realm. For our next endeavor, we will exploit this change in the dynamic."

Bubonic Plague surveyed the camp of Duke Charles of Blois. The French commander had assembled a massive fighting force in hopes of expelling the English from Northwestern France. Bubonic was less concerned with the objectives of the hapless French military and much more anxious about the duke's decision to utilize large numbers of Genoese mercenaries. The hired fighters were already carrying the seeds of the infection. Plague knew this would assist in conjuring another massive outbreak in the yet-to-be-affected coastal region.

Plague felt conflicted. He was thrilled with the spread of the disease. He watched the knights of nobility attended by their squires, professional men-at-arms, lower-class mercenaries and for-hire troops, camp attendants, and numerous support elements. The outbreak of the Black Death had torn through Asia and the Middle East and was rampaging through Southern Europe. In some locales, there were not enough left living to bury the dead. Fright and panic ran rampant. Bubonic felt the unremitting urge to accelerate the spread of the disease.

On the other hand, the embarrassing loss of Pride and Lust infuriated Plague. He'd spent eons building the Coven only to lose two of his best in a moment of bumbling idiocy.

Plague began to run through the population of Hell in his head. He decided that the last two classes were already too developed to shape in his image. Plague would have to wait until the next cohort. Then he would claim the grandchildren of his current flock.

Bubonic's musings were interrupted by an alarm. An English relief force had been spotted clearly attempting to break their siege upon La Roche-Derrien. Plague groaned aloud and thought, *How have they become so good at finding us?*

He decided he would fight within the French and resume the propagation of Pneumatic Plague afterwards.

He issued commands in his characteristic bellow. "To the mortals!"

He immediately possessed a French knight. Through his visor, Plague beheld the battlefield in its entirety. He spotted the Angels within the English ranks. The force sent to relieve Dagworth was composed of lightly armored pikemen and archers. As the French knights dismounted from their steeds, the ground shook under the weight of the heavily armored men.

Plague called to his contingent. "Whilst they remain hidden in their mortal hosts, we will break the English line. You know the order for progressing within the Celestial."

It was predetermined prior to battle that sorties into the Celestial would be conducted first by Greed, then Wrath, followed by Sloth, Gluttony, Envy, and lastly, Plague himself. Everyone had a backup.

The battle unfolded for both the French and Demons in a manner that could have been transcribed in a strategic tome. The French knights broke the line of pikemen and began to slaughter the lightly armored and outnumbered troops. Unseen by the mortals, the Black Death Coven broke through the English lines within their French hosts and began to cut down their Angelic counterparts.

When the first Angel fell in a departure seizure, Greed rushed to dispatch of the foe and was met by a fierce contingent of Angels. They were no match for the Demon, who dispatched several Angels before falling back into a different French knight. The process repeated itself. Angels were engaged within the Mortal and Celestial Realm with equal effectiveness. The Coven advanced with mechanical efficiency, shifting between realms with precision and ruthlessness.

The Angels, though superior in number, could not break the phalanx of mortal hosts or the Celestial testudo of Demons. The survivors eventually broke ranks and fled amongst the retreating English. Shortly thereafter, the Anglo commander Dagworth surrendered to the French.

"At last, we can resume our endeavor," Bubonic Plague said. He surveyed the battlefield strewn with the dead and dying.

The victorious French and their Genoese mercenaries were loosely arrayed, picking amongst the fallen and corralling the captured. Greed, in his typical manner, was rifling through the personal possessions of the butchered Angels. Familiars would soon arrive to ferret away the bodies for internment, but not before Greed claimed his trophies: jewelry, weapons, hair, teeth, ears, whatsoever caught his attention. Bubonic watched his adherent claim the grisly rewards of victory.

As he turned to his other devotees who were standing in closer proximity, he said, "That was more like it!"

He had no sooner spoken than a force of the English that had been besieged within the town sallied forth and caught the dispersed French troops in a state of disarray.

Plague whirled to Greed. "They have regrouped! They have unleashed a strategic reserve."

He groaned with the realization that the Angels had always planned for two phases of battle. Against the first group, Greed would have been able to hold his own, but the fresh arrivals overwhelmed him within the Celestial before he could acquire a mortal host. Bubonic watched helplessly as one Angel, and then another, landed a successful stab until Greed collapsed. Then, without explanation or reason, the Angels fled the field.

Alone with his thoughts, Bubonic fumed. The French duke was the captive; Dagworth was free.

It is with great swiftness that defeat can be snatched from the jaws of victory by blundering overconfidence, he thought as he watched the English restraining the enemy commander. He took some small consolation in completing the outbreak of Pneumatic Plague with the surviving members of the Coven following the Angelic withdrawal.

However, the victory was muted. The Coven was essentially cut in half, and the outbreak was much less dramatic than he had intended.

The Black Death coven was left to lick its wounds and contemplate its next action for the elimination of humanity.

"WE HAVE IDENTIFIED THE next member of the Black Death Coven for execution," Lilly said. She addressed the assembled members of the Houses of Zinc, Chlorine, and Prosperous. "But we are uncertain how to exploit the identified weakness."

"Just brief us on the intelligence, and we will formulate the plan," Zinc said with excitement in his voice.

Lilly appeared annoyed. She glared, then continued, "Wrath has a bad habit of remaining within hosts longer than she should. Females on both sides face the challenge of having fewer mortals available. Most mortal armies hold no more than thirty-five to forty or so female soldiers per one hundred. However, we have noticed that even when an alternate host is available, Wrath likes to remain in her current dwelling. This behavior exposes her to the melding of minds. Additionally, her temperament is volatile, which in a state of melding would expose her further."

Zinc stroked his chin. "I already know how we can do it, distasteful as it might be."

Upon leaving the briefing, Zinc was in high spirits, elated to be leading his House and comrades in a series of victories. His focus on the task of defeating the Black Death had been an effective medicine against his personal loneliness. Yet, as he walked through the Great Hall, all his joie de vivre was extinguished by Lord Hydrogen's approach. Zinc's blood boiled; he hated Hydrogen more than all the Demons of Hell combined. Hydrogen unleashed a toothy smile made all the brighter by his dark complexion.

"I heard you were back," Hydrogen said. "You are the Leader of the Heavenly Armies, now rebranded as The Demonic Assassin."

"Is that so?"

"I do not know whether to be overjoyed or despondent with your change in strategy," Hydrogen said.

"Meaning?"

"For the longest, my House has restricted itself primarily to Africa. After all, we are tied to the region from whence God visited himself upon their mortals and created our ancestors."

"Is this going somewhere?" Zinc asked. "I'm well aware that you and those like you generally prefer to remain to your own enclaves."

"Unless called upon for wider battle," Hydrogen said. "In the past, it's always felt like being led to slaughter, after which we are cast again to the fringes. However, now you seem uninterested in our services, and it is an odd feeling, with you fighting for the survival of humanity and Heaven."

"So, you are never satisfied?"

"I am frequently satisfied," Hydrogen said. The corner of his mouth twitched in a mocking grin.

Zinc flushed at the innuendo and raised his fist. His foe backed away, both palms extended.

"That was misspoken," Hydrogen said. "I meant no disrespect, and we have no need of juvenile bravado. The truth is this: I am concerned. The Demons began this plague in the Far East, and the Asian Houses of Cobalt and Uranium were helpless to stop it. If the Demons focus on my continent, I feel concern for the houses of Hydrogen and Bismuth."

"There is no racism in Heaven," Zinc said, "and the continent is not yours. I travel all over the world fighting the Demons and healing the mortals. If you choose to remain in your preferred abode, that is up to you. If the Demons go to Mauritania or Aksum or Mapungubwe, I will fight them there."

"I do not know if that is the best strategy," Hydrogen said. "I propose that we make the various claims that exist over different regions official. You will be sovereign of Europa and the Levant. I will rule over Africa. Lord Cobalt will have dominion over Asia and Magnesium over the New World. That is already how it is. So, if we respect these boundaries and do not interfere in one another's operations, we will be free to administer as we see fit and to request aid from one another rather than to demand it. We would be able to determine how and to what level we assist one another without the fear of being branded a coward."

This plan reeks of Rachael's influence, Zinc thought. *And I cannot rightly refuse at this time. I am completely inundated with fighting the Black Death.*

He'd sought out the responsibility of stamping out the plague as a means of achieving dominion over all of Heaven. Now, he was on the verge of losing authority over most of it.

"Fine," Zinc said. "I presume you have already spoken with the others?"

"I have," Hydrogen replied. "Also, there is something else, a peace treaty of sorts."

"Oh?"

"I have a daughter who is ready to marry," Hydrogen said. "I would consider it an honor were you to take her as your wife, so that you might continue to expand your noble line."

Anger burned through Zinc. He could not treat the offer as the insult it was intended to be, a jab at his miserable loneliness. Nor could be stomach the idea of marrying Rachael's daughter.

"I am still mourning my late wife," he replied, "but I thank you for your offer."

Hydrogen retreated the way he came, and Zinc slumped in the realization he'd been outmaneuvered.

LORD PHOSPHOROUS SAT IN the cramped confines of the baggage wagon. He breathed evenly and slowly. He knew that he could suppress his aura if he focused. He faced an arduous task. He had spent much of the day waiting for the French Army (led by his father Zinc and brother Chlorine) to attack the English supply camp. Before taking up his concealed position, Phosphorus had filled the minds of several mortals with a specific, morbid task. Then, within the Celestial, he had slinked into the wagon to conceal himself.

The Demons were close by and appeared uneasy as they fell back. Phosphorus could hear their gigantic leader barking orders and shouting commands. Soon after, arrows began to fall amongst the tents and supply wagons, intermittently at first but in ever-increasing rapidity. The storm and clatter of combat grew ever nearer. His pulse quickened as the trap he had set took effect.

When the French Army reached the camp, a trio of Englishmen grabbed the archer within whom Wrath resided because Phosphorus had commanded them to assault the mortal the minute the camp fell into disarray.

Phosphorous leapt from the supply cart. Underneath the wagon, he found the mortals raping the mortal Wrath was within. The Demon should have fled for the Celestial at the outset, but as discussed in the briefing, she was prone to remaining within hosts longer than was advantageous.

May God have mercy on my soul, he thought. *What evil have I instigated?*

Phosphorous was aware of the extent to which possessors experienced the sensations of their hosts. Like many Angels, he had experienced intercourse while possessing a mortal long before he had ever bedded a fellow Angel. He watched the violation, both revolted and aroused by the spectacle. He made sure that Wrath saw him standing over her within the Celestial, ready to strike her down should she abandon her host.

Phosphorous heard the Behemoth calling for Wrath to join the testudo as he was certain the other Angels had arrived among the French in the frenzied attack. Wrath screamed for assistance, though her Celestial pleas were muffled because her host's face was being pressed into the mud.

Wrath gargled out a threat. "I'll kill you for this. Stand back so that I can depart and fight you on even terms, you coward."

Wrath appeared to attempt to exit the mortal even though she risked being stuck down upon departure. Phosphorus readied his dagger, immediately frightened at the prospect of fighting the enraged Demon in single combat. To his relief, bafflement painted Wrath's face, and she remained within the battered mortal. Panic spread to the Demon's eyes. She tried to escape her mortal bindings again, in vain.

Phosphorous bent over the mass of bruises and whispered, "I'm sorry we stooped so low."

He sprinted to a tent and began making the ancient symbols on the ground with shaking hands. To his astonishment, the portal opened without the addition of a second element. Only then did he realize that he had begun to cry.

WRATH HOBBLED THROUGH THE remains of the looted camp. When she came on Bubonic and the others, she was sure they were within the Celestial, but she could barely see them through the mortal's eyes. She knew the pain pummeling her belonged to her host, but the two had become indistinguishable. She knew she had been ravaged.

She fell into Bubonic's arms. "What do I do? I am melded."

He stepped into a passing mortal, an English infantryman who had returned to the camp after the French withdrawal and drew his sword from its scabbard.

"No!" Her voice was a shriek. "The departure seizure will kill me."

"It's your only hope," Plague said.

The blow removed the mortal's head from her shoulders. A violent seizure gripped Wrath. She could hear the mortal Plague had possessed addressing other non-possessed soldiers that had witnessed the execution.

"She's a witch," he said calmly. The passersby shrugged in reply.

Then the encroaching darkness came to claim her.

BUBONIC PLAGUE STRODE THROUGH the Great Hall with frenzied steps and the eyes of a madman. He paced and fretted as he waited. Finally, his target emerged from the gate of return. Plague unceremoniously brushed his way past the Priests performing the Return Ritual, grabbed Spanish Influenza by the scruff of the neck, and walked him out of earshot.

"Have you attended the debauched comingling of Demons and Angels on the neutral ground?" he asked.

Though posed as a question, Bubonic already knew the answer. The younger Demon went pale with fright.

"Yes... I... uh... I frequent such places from time to time."

"Someone has taken a disturbing interest in me and the Coven. I need to know who it is. Go wherever it is you go—I do *not* want to know—and send a message to the other side. Whoever is after me needs to come out into the open. I challenge him, or her, to meet me in Guillac, where I will meet them in single combat."

Spanish Influenza saluted and replied, "I will deliver your message. But it may take some time; there is no set schedule of attendance."

Bubonic's stare could have melted a glacier. "Just ensure that it is delivered."

AT HIS DESK, AGNOLO di Tura, a chronicler from Siena, penned his summary of the pestilence.

"They dig ditches now, instead of graves, and yet still the ditches overflow. The old bury the young. I myself have laid five children within the earth. Nevertheless, it is not enough to slake the hunger of God's retribution. Surely, this is the end of times long foretold. Who among us can hope to escape this most violent, most black death?"

POPE CLEMENT VI STOOD on the edge of the Rhone River and watched its gently flowing progress as it meandered through his home region of Avignon. He often wondered why such trying times had descended on his papacy. Yet, as always, he humbled himself before the will of God.

Having completed the ceremony consecrating the river, he turned to Cardinal Aubert and said, "The river is now holy ground and acceptable for the proper burial of the faithfully departed."

"Soon, the need for burial will be a thing of the past, Holy Father," Aubert said.

"For this is the End of Days?" Clement asked.

"There is little doubt," the cardinal replied.

"I disagree," the pope said. "It is undoubtedly the will of God, as are all things. It is undoubtedly a test, as are many things. It remains to be seen if it is the End of Days. If it is, it makes little difference to us, for we will continue to serve God Almighty as best we can while we await the mysteries of his Revelation. Anything else would be presumptuous."

"Indeed, Holy Father," Aubert said.

Pope Clement looked at the river he had just ordained as a mass burial site and sighed. "Although not a soul in Heaven or Earth could fault you for rushing to such a conclusion."

"AND WHY ARE WE here?" Conjunctivitis asked as the forces of Jean de Beaumanoir and Robert Bemborough took to the field in Guillac, Brittany.

"You are my children," Bubonic Plague said. He looked at Conjunctivitis and Influenza. "Your place is by my side when such times as these present themselves."

In truth, Bubonic was frustrated to have been forced to call upon his son and daughter to fill out the ranks of the Black Death. He had also called up Measles from his old clan, the Bodybuilders. He completed his contingent by bullying a few Demons into compliance: Spanish Influenza, Dandruff, and Bone Fever.

He looked at the Demons he had summoned to replenish the Coven and was overburdened with a sense of failure.

"And why are they here?" his irritated son asked. He gestured towards the assembled mortals. Bubonic looked at a group of knights, squires, men-at-arms, and nobility.

"Jean de Beaumanoir has called out Sir Robert Bemborough for single combat. They have enhanced the confrontation to consist of ten knights and twenty attendants on each side, more or less," he said.

"This is all incredibly stupid," Conjunctivitis said. "I am amazed that the Angels responded to your challenge. I am amazed at the mortals' behavior. I am shocked and amazed and—"

"Please do shut up." Bubonic's face flared in rage. "For once in your life close your mouth and try to make me proud."

When Zinc took to the field, his feet dragged as if stuck in the mud. His arms had no life, his legs no spring. He had been surprised to hear of the challenge when he had last traveled to the Island of Neutrality. He did not feel positive about this development in his campaign to defeat the Black Death Coven. Despite his misgivings, he steeled himself for the encounter at hand.

As the combatants drew near, Plague stood within Jean de Beaumanoir. Zinc, occupying Robert Bemborough, began to doubt the assortment of Angels in his entourage. He had initially refused to bring his sons as he feared the odds of survival in facing the Demons in open combat were far too low, and he did not wish for their Houses to be dissolved. However, news of the duel had spread like wildfire throughout Heaven.

Iron III and Carbon V had insisted they join. To his surprise, Zinc was approached by Lord Hydrogen and Rachael.

"Do you plan to take all the credit?" Lord Hydrogen had asked with a broad smile.

"I thought you had what you wanted," Zinc replied.

Hydrogen took the bait. "All that you wanted, perhaps," he said. He touched his wife on the thigh.

"Don't act like children," Lady Hydrogen said. "This is bigger than any of us."

"Indeed," Hydrogen said. "This is too grand a stage for one House or one region. We come to aid you freely on our own accord, fully understanding the risks. We ask nothing in return."

They all agreed. The Standard Bearers and a relative of their choosing would represent the Houses in combat. The final roster consisted of Zinc and Adolphus, Chlorine and his son Antonius, Phosphorus and his daughter Electra, Carbon V and his younger brother Phillipe, and Hydrogen and his wife Rachael. Additionally, they had agreed that the rules of succession would be suspended. The Houses of any fallen Standard Bearer would remain autonomous. Lord Iron III and his son Jens had been selected to act as witnesses.

Bubonic Plague stood within his host and met with Zinc.

"Terms?"

"I believe we must cease our endeavors once the mortals do," Zinc said. "In such environs, our presence in the Celestial would be observable once their combat concludes."

"Agreed," Plague said.

Zinc's flagging confidence was not bolstered in the least by looking at Bubonic's dark features and menacing scowl.

"I propose that once these sacks of meat return to their lines, we abandon them," Bubonic said with a snarl, "and complete our business in the olden manner."

"Strictly, the Celestial?" Zinc asked. He struggled to make his voice sound as stern as possible.

"You have gutted my force with trickery and knavishness that should fill you with shame and self-loathing," Bubonic Plague said. "You have a chance to reclaim your honor on this field by facing your foe eye to eye."

"I agree to your terms," Zinc said, "but not to your sermonizing and hypocritical condescension."

The grin of a ravenous tiger spread across Bubonic Plague's face.

"I will kill you at last, and when I do, I will sink my teeth into your abdomen while you are still breathing, you impudent sap," he said.

Zinc returned to his lines, fuming.

Am I a joke to the world? he thought. *Hydrogen steals my woman, and then they both have the nerve to impose themselves upon the final battle I contrived. This Plague offers threats and insults as though we were young children.*

He shook his head. *It is no matter.*

Zinc relayed the terms to his confederates.

"Well, any last advice? Words of inspiration?" Lord Hydrogen asked. He laughed. No one else did. He held up his hands in apology.

"I fear the weight of the day got the better of me. Now, as I look upon them, I have misgivings."

Zinc squared his shoulders. "Those Demons are not the Black Death Coven," he said. "We have gutted their ranks so thoroughly that they have filled their cadre with imposters and cheap imitations. Look at their leader; he wears the guise and vestments of a rat. You would have him ruling over this world?"

"No!"

"You would have him rule over Heaven?"

"No!"

Zinc looked at his sons. "Today, I fight by your side again, but not as your father." He looked at Iron III and Hydrogen. "Not as your fellow Standard Bearer." He looked at Rachael. "Not as your confidant."

He swept his hand across the line to include them all. "Today, I fight by your side as your brother, for we are all kinfolk most dear. Should I fall today, I count myself lucky to die in such esteemed company as this, on such a historic day, for today we fight to eradicate the plague these Demons have brought upon the world. Today we fight to eliminate this age-old threat from existence. For today we fight for Heaven!"

The speech was met by a rousing cheer. Hydrogen stepped forward and punched him playfully in the arm before shaking his fist in the air.

"You restored me, Lord Zinc," he said with his ever-present smile.

Zinc turned to face the foe.

"On my command," he shouted, "send them back to Hell."

On the other side, Conjunctivitis said, "It looks like they are raring for a fight."

"As well they should be," Bubonic Plague said.

Feeling the need to motivate the troops he had harangued and pressed into service, Bubonic Plague stepped forward.

"I know that most of you are not adherents to my Coven. Today is bigger than me or the Black Death. Today is bigger than the ten Angels that stand across the field from us. Today is about the final victory. My adherents and I have plotted a course through which we intend to bring about the long sought-after prize. And who has felled them in their efforts? Those treacherous, conniving fiends through devious trickery and duplicitous, underhanded dealings. When they do such, they are not just denying me, or the Coven, but all of Hell of the prize of the final victory—the victory that your grandparents, and parents, and brothers, and sisters, your sons, and grandsons have died wanting to see. Today, do not fight for me; fight for that. If you fight not for this brotherhood, fight for the dream of victory. Today make that victory our reality."

"All right, old man," Conjunctivitis said. He stood next to his father.

"I am not an original member of this Coven." He drew his Celestial dagger and began cutting a swath of rat pelt from his father's cloak. "But today, I am the Black Death." He draped the fur over his shoulders and tied it in a knot so that it rested over his robes like a scarf. He removed another section and tossed it to Influenza.

"And so are you," he said. She tied the gnarly shawl around her shoulders.

Sloth, Gluttony, and Envy quickly provided bands of rat fur from their own cloaks to the other members of the contingent.

They began chanting in unison, "We are the Black Death, we are the Black Death, we are the Black Death."

"Your speech was good," Conjunctivitis said. He pointed to the gray fur draped on the Demon's shoulders and flicked his bangs. "But that's how it's done."

Plague smiled and rested his forehead against his son's. "No father has ever been prouder," he said.

The ensuing battle was fought with such frenetic violence and savagery that it was long remembered within the annals of medieval and supernatural lore. As the mortals set upon each other with lance and spear, the Celestial combatants attacked with daggers and swords. The mortal battle progressed to swords and maces; the Celestial contest devolved into a battle of knives and even fisticuffs. Zinc found himself strangling the Demon known as Dandruff with his bare hands as the battle reached its climax.

No one died easily. Demon and Angel hacked one another, inflicting the most grievous of wounds. Plague looked on helplessly as two Angels forced his son to the ground and stabbed at his midsection.

In his last moments, Conjunctivitis tore out an Angel's throat with his teeth.

In a grief-fueled rage, Plague hacked an Angel to bits with a dagger. Had the Demons been organized and more accustomed to working together, the traditional testudo of the Black Death Coven might have succeeded. However, under the chaotic circumstances, the Hellish forces experienced a disaster. Soon Bubonic Plague and Spanish Influenza were the sole remaining Demons facing Zinc, Lord Hydrogen, and Lady Hydrogen.

All the survivors were bloodied and exhausted. Spanish Influenza had picked up Bubonic Plague's axe but was using it more as a crutch than a weapon. He was visibly dizzy, having sustained a blow to the head that had removed one of his horns. With five remaining combatants in place, the mortal contest ended.

"It is over; the mortals have stopped," Spanish Influenza said. He dropped the axe and fell upon the muddy ground.

Plague looked about the bloodied field and beheld the shattered remains of the Black Death. Sloth, Gluttony, and Envy all lay dead. He glared across the pitch at the Angel he had spoken to at the outset, and with heavy, labored strides, made his way toward him.

Plague walked past Spanish Influenza and scooped up his axe. The Angel had fallen to the ground and appeared defenseless under the weight of his accumulated injuries. As Plague raised his axe, preparing to end the irritating foe, he heard one of the other surviving Angels speak.

"You will cost your side the war. Look around you. If you land that blow, all manner of witnesses will report you being observed by the mortals. You will be finished."

Bubonic turned and saw an Angel of dark complexion lying upon his back, a Demonic dagger protruding from his ribs. Bubonic grunted and turned away, stopping to scoop up Spanish Influenza, who he slung over his shoulder before departing.

"THE FIELDS OF FRANCE are so regularly watered with English blood, one could reason that next spring we will see Edwards, Richards, and Henrys sprouting forth from the earth," Schitz said. His voice danced with amusement. He gazed across the countryside surrounding the monastery of Les Augustins.

"If only replacing destroyed life were that easy." The sweet voice came from the young French woman standing in front of him.

"What do you know about the difficulty of replacing life, Joan?"

The Angel possessing the maiden now addressed Schitz. "This vessel may be ignorant of the pains of childbirth, but I am no stranger."

Schitz grinned. "Ah, so you are well versed in the means of rec-reating life."

"This is not a suitable conversation for a fair maiden," she said without rebuke.

"'Fair' is an apt way to describe both of you," Schitz said.

"Flattery will not save you," Lady Calcium said.

"If you were going to engage me in combat, you would have done so at our first meeting," he said. He feigned a wide yawn.

Schitz thought back to his encounter with the Angel during the siege of Orléans. He had slain a handful of Angels before he encoun-tered a single hold out, the very leader of the French contingent. There was something intriguing about her; she was astoundingly confident, self-assured, attractive.

Finding no pressing need to force the encounter, Schitz had jumped into a French officer. Schitz later learned the Angel inhabit-ing the French leader was Lady Calcium, wife of the Standard Bearer Lord Calcium. She had been intrigued by a Demon who was willing to converse with her.

As the English surrendered, she had instructed him to meet her outside the monastery.

He snapped back to the present.

"True, enough," she said, "but I might turn on you at a moment's notice."

Schitz beheld the woman and the Angel within; there were striking similarities. Both wore their dark hair long, flowing down their shoulders; both were slender in build with delicate features and striking eyes. When he first met Joan in battle, she had been clothed in armor. Now she stood before him in a simple tunic and riding boots. His gaze settled on the Angel's thin neck around which he saw a pair of ornate chains.

Schitz's Notebook

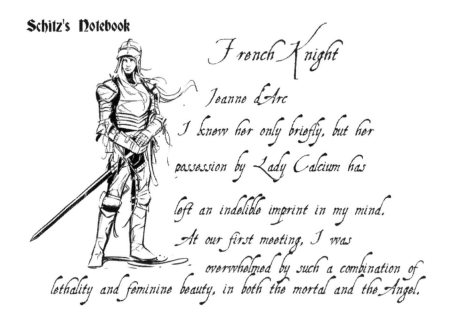

French Knight

Jeanne d'Arc

I knew her only briefly, but her possession by Lady Calcium has left an indelible imprint in my mind. At our first meeting, I was overwhelmed by such a combination of lethality and feminine beauty, in both the mortal and the Angel.

"Can I help you?" she asked.

"Those are beautiful, from what I can see from here," Schitz said.

"That's a little forward," Calcium replied.

"Your jewelry," he said. He blushed.

She pulled a silver rosary and a silver chain from which hung a cross.

"One cross isn't enough?"

"Oh, I'm sorry," she replied with a feigned apology, "will they make you burst into flames?"

She menaced him with the chains. Schitz laughed and leapt back in mock horror.

"They belonged to my parents," Lady Calcium said.

"Ah, mine are gone as well," Schitz said.

Calcium's face was solemn. "I suppose that is our lot. I'll pass these on to my children or grandchildren someday."

"How many children do you have?"

"Quite a few," the Angel replied. Her gaze shifted from Schitz to some faraway place for a moment. The soft breeze of the May evening blew over the hillside.

"Do you?" she asked, breaking the silence.

"Yes," Schitz replied, "although I am but a stranger to her. Perhaps it is better that way."

Suddenly he could see Rubella reclining along the bank in the glowing light of the Styx.

"I had a wife once, but..." he swallowed, "she is gone now."

Calcium rested her soft hand on his shoulder.

"I wonder what she would think if she saw me standing here talking to you like this," he said.

He wiped his eyes.

Calcium smiled. "I don't know what she would say, or what my husband would say, but as you said, loss is our lot in life. We must be entitled to a few liberties."

Schitz gazed into her striking eyes—then began to feel lost in them.

"Do you make a habit of befriending the enemy?" he asked. He remembered Anna.

I wonder what happened to her.

"Never, but for you, I'll make an exception," Lady Calcium replied.

Skepticism tickled Schitz's brain.

"Why?" he asked.

"Because I felt something when I saw you, a commonality perhaps. I thought, 'Yes, he is like me.'" The comment was sincere and disarmed Schitz's concern.

"So now what do we do?" Schitz asked. "I don't know how to befriend a female, other than to sleep with her."

Lady Calcium laughed. "That is most certainly not how you should speak to a maiden or a Lady of an Angelic house," she paused with a devilish grin, "but I'll let you slide."

She hesitated a moment.

"I can't promise that circumstance will not render us enemies," she said, "but I will do my best to avoid killing you, Sir Schitz."

She kissed him lightly on the cheek before she turned.

"Fare thee well, Lady Calcium," he said as she walked away.

"I T'S A SHAME WHAT they did to that human you were within," Schitz said as he strolled through the countryside of Hertfordshire.

"Barbaric," Lady Calcium said. "Humans, I doubt they'll ever change."

"Will we?" Schitz asked.

"What's troubling you," she asked.

She was uncertain why she maintained this friendship with the Demon. Yet, every time her hand grazed against his, or their eyes interlocked, she felt a warm shiver run down her spine.

What is this magnetism that draws me back to him again and again? she asked herself.

"I just feel heavy, lately," Schitz said.

Lady Calcium thought that her companion looked rather dashing within a mortal who was in the armor and trappings of the House of York.

"Why?" she asked. She rubbed a sore shoulder, lingering fatigue from the Battle of St Albans. Schitz stopped and stared at her with his patented soul-piercing gaze.

"I'd rather not sully our time together with my concerns and worries," he replied. "I enjoy your company far too much for that."

"Always the flatterer," she said.

Why am I giddy? I feel like a schoolgirl; like he passed me a note in class. Her next thought brought her to a stop. *Shall I tell him I love him?*

Schitz's Notebook *Onager (Siege of Orléans)*
6/10

—*Light weight projectile —150m -275m Range*
—*Easily maneuvered - Not effective against walls*
Best against infantry —Simple to construct

Feelings of guilt and memories of her husband and her children and grandchildren crossed her mind. Lady Calcium's dilemma was interrupted when Schitz changed the topic.

"I think they'll call this the War of the Roses," he said. "A lovely caption for a deadly conflict."

"Why do you say that?" she asked. She was still wrestling with her last question.

"Well, as you know, York and Lancaster both represent their house with a rose, and my title sure rolls off the tongue better than the York and Lancaster Wars."

Lord Calcium would not have approved of the loving look Lady Calcium directed at "her Demon." Nor would he have liked the purring quality of her voice.

"Maybe they'll call it The War of Mad King Henry the VI," she said.

Will he notice my tone? My Lord Calcium says it's my "bedroom voice."

Her heart melted when Schitz smiled. "Anything is smooth when it rolls off your tongue," he said.

She felt warm and wet.

I must tell him.

"Still," Schitz said, "I really like your proposal. After all, driving Henry insane was some of my better work. It is a habit of mine to afflict defeated leaders."

"I shouldn't compliment your devilry," she said, "but you make it very hard not to compliment you."

"I appreciate your commendations, milady," he said.

He bowed.

Her knees went weak.

"I'd like to see you again soon, Lady Cal," Schitz said.

"Must we part so soon?"

Don't sound so pathetic!

"I fear the eyes of Wraiths and Familiars," he replied. "But it won't be long. Meet me in Paris in a week's time. I'll wait by the main gate at noon; we'll slip off somewhere."

Her heart fluttered. Her breath came in short bursts.

"Fare thee well then, my white rose," she said.

Schitz waved. "And you as well, my red rose."

THE CITY OF PARIS enjoyed as much peace as one could expect in June of 1455. Yet, for Schitz, danger was ever-present.

In such a hazardous world, why am I carrying on this liaison with Lady Calcium? he thought. *This would be simpler if my attraction to Lady Calcium was only physical. I could either have her and be done with it or steel myself and exercise some discipline.*

He knew he preferred the former and had no doubt a coupling would be well worth his time. He had enjoyed a brief dalliance or two within a mortal host since he lost his darling Rubella.

Ah, Rubella... I thought I would be yours forever.

He could still see her face. He could still hear her voice. But he felt a strong attraction for this Angel, this Lady Calcium. He was more concerned with losing her than with rejection. He could sense how she longed for him.

"I'll do it," he said. "I'll tell her today."

He waited with nervous energy. Romance was so different from lust. He had lain with many women, Celestial and mortal, but he had only experienced romantic affection for Rubella and Anna. He desperately hoped this romance would enjoy longevity. He waited and watched. The midday crowd came and went; new arrivals passed through the gates from the countryside; merchants peddled their wares; children and dogs ran to and fro.

He saw her. Schitz stepped into the Celestial so it would be easier for Lady Calcium to spot him. She was elegant and regal.

Yes, today I tell her, Schitz thought.

She waved and quickened her step. Then... from behind the beautiful, beloved face, three additional Angels emerged.

Schitz stepped into a passing mortal. A shriek Schitz would remember until his dying day pierced the moment.

"Betrayal!"

Schitz watched a tall, blonde Angel plunge a dagger into Lady Calcium's back. The assassin's two stocky male attendants joined in a quick, terrible slaughter.

Rage thrummed through Schitz. He rushed into the Celestial and charged the Angels, wholly disregarding that no mortal combat was taking place in the vicinity. The portal through which Lady Calcium had arrived was still open and the Angels had turned to depart.

He drew his sword and lunged toward the Angel at the rear of the murderous procession, obviously a grizzled and battle-worn veteran of many arduous encounters. For reasons Schitz never understood, the Angel paused and made a half-turn toward the slaughtered Lady Calcium—perhaps to admire his handiwork. The hesitation gave Schitz an opportunity and he drove his sword up to the hilt into the Angel's chest. They tumbled into the portal.

Schitz's eyes burned from a bright light emanating from all sides. He raised his free hand to cover his eyes. When his sight adjusted, he was filled with abject terror.

"Fuck, I have killed myself," Schitz said.

He had no doubt that he was standing in the Great Hall of Heaven.

Slack-jawed Priests stared at the Demon who was sprawled across the white marble, a pristine surface displaying an ever-growing crimson stain. Schitz withdrew his sword and wiped the bloody blade on his robe.

I may be a dead man, but I will not go alone.

Still burning with anger born of anguish. Schitz slashed his sword through the air and cut the throat of the other male assassin. Before the foe collapsed to the ground in a bloody heap, Schitz swung at the neck of the blonde Angel.

He watched in grim satisfaction as her head jumped from her shoulders. The nearby Priests huddled together in their white robes like a gaggle of frightened geese. He set upon them with a violent fervor, hacking and swinging.

The hands they raised in useless defense only fed his hungry blade with severed fingers and amputated arms. Too afraid to move, the Priests caterwauled as he cut them to pieces.

Standing in a growing pool of blood, Schitz bellowed a war cry and blasted an assortment of chalices to the ground from the top of the altar.

A horde of Angels descended on Schitz from all sides. He moved through them like a fish swimming through the reeds. Nothing could touch him. He avoided countless blows from swords and spears and mauls and maces. He was the perfect embodiment of fear and zeal.

Schitz abandoned precision in favor of mayhem; he slashed tendons and severed limbs. His mission was to inflict as much pain as possible before someone felled him. With no mortals to occupy, he knew it was fight, then die.

Pain from the bee stings of throwing knives and stars began to register, and exhaustion pulled at his arms and legs. But the fury of his wrath propelled him to yet another blow—still another strike.

Another column of fresh Angels closed in on him. Having fallen onto his back, Schitz recognized his defensive liability. He inhaled what he knew to be his last breath.

I made a good accounting of myself, he thought. *This will be a good death.*

His sword clattered against the stones, dropped by exhaustion and surrender to the inevitable. Schitz wondered if there was really nothing waiting for him on the other side of the curtain, no parents, no lovers, no friends, no enemies, nothing. So he'd been taught from his earliest days. He hoped he was wrong.

He rose to his knees and awaited the end.

"Halt!"

The voice rolled like thunder across the hall. Schitz opened his eyes and peered up at the Angels that stood over him, weapons raised.

"Take him prisoner," the voice said.

Rough hands dragged him to his feet. A sharp pain erupted at the base of his neck, and the room went black.

Schitz awoke in a bare room devoid of windows or furniture. The floor and walls were the same white marble as the hall in which Schitz had arrived.

He remembered his cell in Hell. *Same room, different color,* he thought.

Nausea struck him at the same time he was aware of the throbbing pain in his head. He looked at the door, sturdy and immovable. He tried to stand but lacked the strength.

Schitz crawled about the small cell on his hands and knees. He found initials carved into one wall—MM. Underneath were a series of hash marks. He counted well over a hundred.

What type of soul could spend that much time here and not succumb to the Atrophy.

He wondered if he had been sentenced to a slow, wasting death locked in this bare room or if the walls had the same effect as the Demonic cells, warding off the Atrophy. He knew he would succumb to the Atrophy much quicker than the immortalized MM without supernatural aid. He wondered if he possessed Lord Zinc's strength; the old boy had endured his imprisonment without impairment.

Questions swirled.

Will I be interrogated—tortured?

Will they execute me?
If so, in what manner?
Will I burn like Joan?
Will they simply watch me waste away?

He resolved to accept whatever fate lay before him. He thought about Rubella.

What would she say if I had to tell her I got myself killed over a woman, and an Angel at that?

Schitz thought of his life and felt unsatisfied. He had not fulfilled his full potential. He had hoped to bring humanity to its knees but only afflicted a small segment of the population.

Though he hated the Devil, Schitz believed in the cause of Hell and the just reward of rest for its fighters. He knew he would die without seeing the immortality that would accompany Hell's final victory.

Self-pity settled into his heart when his thoughts circled back to Lady Calcium. He could not believe how unlucky he was; as soon as he had opened his heart to love once again, the object of his affection was cut down before his eyes. He wondered if the Familiars had collected her body and whether they would hold a funeral mass for her. Schitz deeply wondered more than anything whether Lady Calcium returned his feelings. He hated that he would never find out.

Schitz staggered to his feet and punched the hard marble wall. He looked over towards the door and noticed the tiniest sliver of an observation window.

"I won't let them see me crack," he said. In defiance, he began Hell's anthem.

We stand firm, though the foes volleys fall upon us like showers,
We stand firm through the passing of many countless hours,
Firmly we stand, awaiting the Lord's command,
Ready to unleash our company's many powers.

Forward we bound, when unleashed upon the dastardly foe,
Forward we leap, like hunting hounds upon the beleaguered doe,
Eagerly we spring, letting the battle cry ring,
Swifter than any arrow loosed from a bow.

Proudly we take our place amongst the Lord's trusted appointed,
Bathed in the blood of the foe and in the oil of victory anointed,
Proudly we feast on the flesh of the vanquished deceased,
Our enemies dismembered and disjointed.

We bring forth the peace of the everlasting and the tranquil night,
We bring forth all that is needed and what's more all that is right,
Justly we come, to undo all that must be undone,
We will never tarry or weary in our fight.

If victory calls for us to offer ourselves a sacrifice on the altar,
We will not hesitate, nor will we cower or will we falter,
Preparedly, we go forward, no loss is too untoward,
Merrily we go forth to the slaughter.

When he finished his rendition of defiant protest against his jailors and against the world itself, Schitz was greeted by the pitter-patter of a solitary set of hands clapping on the other side of the door.

"Bravissimo!" It was the same authoritarian voice that had called off Schitz's execution in the Great Hall.

The door opened without a sound. A tall man strode into the cell, with strong, angular features and broad shoulders. He was adorned in the garb of a mortal king. He wore a golden crown and carried a scepter. What struck Schitz most was how similar his appearance was to Satan's, though there were observable differences.

"God, I presume," Schitz said. His tone was neither submissive nor hostile.

"The one and only."

Schitz eyed the sizeable sword at God's waist. "I am honored you have come to kill me yourself."

"I thought we might at least have a conversation first. Your incursion is all anyone has been talking about."

Schitz nodded. "It was not intentional. I completely intended to kill the Angels, but I did not mean to... uh... enter your house. To be honest, I didn't even know it was possible for me."

God laughed and shook his head. "Neither did I. It's never

happened before. We've taken a few prisoners, but there's never been an unannounced visit."

Schitz was impressed. The Devil would never confess to being unaware or wrong.

"Was it worth it?" God asked.

"Not really," Schitz said.

"No?"

"She was worth all of Heaven and Hell," Schitz said. "For her, I'd gladly throw my life away, but if I could go back, I'd act differently."

"Spoken like a true lover," God said.

"I wasn't though," Schitz said.

"Really?"

"We were respectful adversaries who enjoyed conversation, but I never touched her, not once," Schitz said.

Why am I so defensive? Why is this so awkward?

God stared at Schitz. "Be that as it may, you did love her, as lovers do."

"Yes," Schitz said, "but I kept my feelings to myself." His voice cracked. "I do not know if she had any deeper feelings for me."

"Oh, she did," God said.

He reached into the pocket of his robe. Pain pierced Schitz's heart as God's hand reappeared. He was holding Lady Calcium's rosary beads and crucifix chain.

"Look at the back of either one," God said.

Schitz flipped to the obverse side of the cross and squinted to read the engraving—masterfully rendered.

S.I.N.

Tears formed in the corners of his eyes. His lip quivered.

He swiped at his cheek, then reddened at being so moved before a stranger, no less the grandest of his enemies. God spoke.

"Liaisons between humans and Angels are dangerous; liaisons between Angels and Demons are beyond hazardous. That is why my army and your army have special units, whose tasks are to ferret out and eliminate half-breeds."

"Was that who murdered Lady Calcium?" Schitz asked.

God raised an eyebrow at the word "murder."

"No. You murdered her sister, her father, and her brother-in-law just before you eviscerated my unarmed Priests and a multitude of my soldiers, but you did not encounter any of my half-breed hunters. She was killed over a family matter."

An uneasy silence descended on the room.

"She was good," Schitz said. "She did nothing wrong; she did not betray her marriage or her cause. There are neutral grounds where Demons and Angels are permitted to meet, and it is not seen as perfidy."

God swept his hands back, a bow of agreement.

"Our relationship was a form of that, just less official and mobile in location," Schitz said.

God chuckled. "An engaging legal argument, but let's be honest. You were probably going to assist in the violation of her wedding vows on the day she died."

Schitz opened his mouth to protest, but God waved his hand and continued.

"It doesn't really matter. Your side will deal with the issue as they see fit if they know. If not, the matter is closed. I see no need to file a protest regarding the Divine Dictum; your incursion was an unfortunate accident. I think it is fair to say it balances out the over-zealousness of my Angels killing Lady Calcium outside the confines of mortal warfare."

Schitz's eyes narrowed.

"I'll be going back to my side?"

God's face was blank. "That depends. We have a variety of reasons to kill you: your trespass in Heaven, your relationship with Lady Calcium, your killing of unarmed Priests, or simply because you are our enemy. I, however, detest executions. They represent humanity in its basest form. I have rarely condoned them within my ranks."

"So, what then?"

"You will face an opponent of my choosing in combat. If you win, you will be free to go. If you lose, there will be no mercy. I know beyond a doubt that is a far more generous offer than any of my Angels would receive in Hell."

Schitz recalled the elder Zinc, captured by the Free Thinkers, who still languished in a cell.

"You make a point."

"Let us to it," God said. He stepped out of the doorway and gestured for Schitz to follow. "Time waits for no man, be he mortal or God."

God laughed when Schitz slipped Lady Calcium's rosary and crucifix chain over his head.

"A question," Schitz said.

God inclined his head.

"What is the truth about the Nazarene?" Schitz asked. "Was he really your son? Is he here?"

God tried without success to suppress a smile. "I think you have other things to worry about right now."

James Butler, the Fifth Earl of Ormond and the First Earl of Wiltshire, was the staunchest Irish supporter of the Lancastrian cause. As a result, he had been forced to abandon his armor and don a monk's habit at the conclusion of what would later be known as the First Battle of Saint Albans. The York victory would have repercussions far beyond the halls of London.

The Earl dressed in civilian clothes and made a swift return to Erin's Isle. The Earl's rivals, James FitzGerald, Sixth Earl of Desmond (south) and Thomas FitzGerald, Seventh Earl of Kildare (north), had backed the house of York and would likely feel emboldened to move against him domestically. Butler landed his remaining forces on the coast along the border of the native Irish lands of Mac-Murrough and the Anglo-Irish Wexford lordship from whence he planned to cross the countryside until he had returned to his lands and Ormonde Castle.

Zinc had escaped from the battlefield and possessed the Earl. He had begun the day with the soldiers of York. However, in the melee, most of the Angels had swapped into the bodies of the defeated men of Lancaster. Zinc fought desperately to suppress his host's varied, anxious thoughts.

It's getting time to vacate this body, he thought. *I've spent enough time here; I do not want to be rendered ineffective.*

Isolated and separated from any other Angels, Zinc saw the benefits of remaining in the commander's position for as long as possible. But he was always required to weigh the ever-increasing melding of his mind with the human's psyche. This time, both he and his host had the same thought.

How shall I proceed?

For the moment, Zinc forced himself and his human to relax. He took in the spectacular Irish countryside. The men seemed happy to be home and marched with just a slight spring in their step despite debilitating exhaustion.

The men began to sing a folk marching song.

> *Some say the Deel[63] is dead, the Deel is dead, the Deel is dead.*
> *Some say the Deel is dead and buried in Kirka'dy.*
> *And some say he rose agen, rose agen, rose agen, rose agen.*
> *And some say he rose agen Awa wi the English army.*

Bagpipes and drums joined in the tune.

Schitz and God walked past a horde of curious and jeering onlookers. Their march concluded at the River Eunoe. Schitz noted the similarity of the illuminating, blue water to that of his native Styx, though the Eunoe appeared lighter in the perpetual daylight of Heaven than the Styx did in Hell's never-ending twilight. A small footbridge led to an island in the middle of the river.

Schitz recalled Vertigo, and the first time he had taken a Celestial life. Once again, he was surrounded by enemies. One-on-one, any Angel is at a disadvantage against a Demon, but Schitz warned

---

[63] The Devil

himself against the alluring fallacies of hubris. He vowed to be cautious, as Anna had taught him. He had searched the crowd in vain for his ancient lover.

Surely, she is no longer living, he thought.

He forced himself to focus.

"Your weapons," God said. He gestured to a table next to the entrance to the bridge.

Schitz approached the table and immediately recognized his own Celestial equipment, a short sword and a pair of throwing knives. He retrieved the familiar weapons and began across the bridge. On the barren island, Schitz saw a towering Angel. He had long flowing black hair and wore a tight-fitting robe that displayed his muscular physique. The Angel brandished an oversized battle axe.

Schitz reached a deep, thin mark cut into the ground. The Angel sneered at Schitz and turned to face the riverbank. Schitz nonchalantly followed suit. God had ascended upon a small platform. The Angel raised his axe high aloft in his left hand and brought his right over his heart in a closed fist. Schitz suppressed a giggle as he brought his right hand across his chest to the crook of his left elbow and snapped his heels together in Hell's salute. God raised his right arm, scepter in hand, and the jeering and murmuring of the crowd fell silent.

In the voice he must have used at Mount Sinai, God said, "May Providence shine upon the more deserving!"

God lowered his hand, and the roar of the crowd rose like a storm. Schitz drowned out the violent epitaphs; he heard the tattoo of drums and the nasal wail of bagpipes. He hummed to himself as the Angel stepped into a readied stance.

Some say the Deel is dead, the Deel is dead, the Deel is dead.
Some say the Deel is dead and buried in Kirka'dy.

The Angel advanced towards Schitz. Schitz tossed his sword. It clanged across the rocks and drew a perplexed look from the Angel. Schitz breathed deeply and withdrew a throwing knife in each hand. He felt the heft of the blades and judged the distance. As he anticipated, discarding his primary weapon confused his opponent. The pause was all Schitz needed. He tossed the first knife aloft in a high arching motion. Barely a moment later, he hurled the second knife directly toward the Angel's throat. The Angel deflected the incoming knife with the handle of his axe. Schitz was in a headlong rush. The Angel raised his axe in anticipation at the precise moment Schitz's first blade found its target. The knife sliced into the Angel's right shoulder just behind his collar bone. Although it was a non-lethal injury, the timing was perfect. Schitz scooped the sword from the ground. The Angel's right arm buckled from his injury.

Schitz raked the sword across his foe's abdomen. The great axe crashed to the stone floor. Schitz's slashing run carried him past the Angel's grasp. When Schitz wheeled, the Angel was on one knee, watching his intestines slip to the ground like so many sausages.

Schitz kicked his enemy in the back, then drove his sword between the Angel's first vertebrae and the base of his skull. Schitz thrust his arms aloft in triumph and absorbed the jeering crowd's protests as if they were thunderous applause.

He wrenched his sword free, wiped the blade, and slid it into the scabbard with a flourish and a bow. He strode to the entrance of the footbridge with all the confidence of a victorious gladiator.

She stood in the crowd on the other side—the Angel he hated more than any other—the one who murdered his son, his grandfather, his father, his wife. Schitz pushed back a momentary thought to kill her, a move tantamount to suicide. He passed by her and winked. He walked down the Heavenly River and traced the sacred symbols on a rock.

He decided to use an ancient doorway; not anything direct to Hell in case he was followed.

He blew on the symbols to provide air, then began the requisite incantations.

THE EARL'S SOLDIERS CONTINUED their folksong as they marched past a cluster of ancient ruins.

And some say he rose agen, rose agen, rose agen, rose agen.
And some say he rose agen Awa wi the English army.

Without warning, a portal opened between the stones of the henge, and the shadowy aura of a Demon emerged into the Celestial. Zinc readied himself for combat. In a series of lightning-fast moves, the Demon jumped into a nearby soldier, then jumped back into the Celestial and began to make marks on the Earth. Before Zinc could react, the mysterious foe altered the portal and disappeared.

"So be it," Zinc said.

THE THRONE ROOM APPEARED much larger when not crowded with onlookers. Schitz was not happy.

My repudiation and banishment were very public, he thought. *Where are all the people when I am redeemed and reestablished?* The only ones in attendance were the Devil, the most senior Priests and Wraiths, and Bubonic Plague.

The Devil began slowly. "It would seem that Schizophrenia has neutralized a grave threat. He comported himself respectfully during the prescribed probationary period."

Damning with faint praise, indeed.

The Devil glanced from side to side and mirrored the sullen faces of Titus and Bubonic Plague. But their displeasure made the moment all the more glorious for Schitz.

The Devil continued, "We could not allow a strong third party to establish a foothold on Earth. Had we permitted Gold and Silver to secure a worldly kingdom, we might have won our battle with Heaven only to discover the prize we sought was already occupied by another. We owe Schizophrenia our thanks for dislodging them from their positions."

Schitz was torn between appreciation for the thank you and his disdain for Satan's ineptitude and abuses. The Devil rose from his throne and walked to Schitz. The High Priest followed. Schitz was surprised to see the High Priest place a Pentagram Second Class in the Devil's hand.

The Devil pinned the medal on Schitz's robe. "Your contributions have been many and oft-overlooked. Should you continue your trajectory, I believe you will receive greater accolades moving forward. Such is the case for those who stay within the light of my favor."

The Devil returned to his throne and raised his voice. "Your trial period of return from exile is now complete. You are free to pursue any endeavors that will contribute to our cause and correspond to the rank and station fitting your order of graduation from the Academy."

Schitz recalled Tuberculosis's admonition that medals and statues often came when they were least sought after or desired.

"Now, let us turn our attention to our primary objective, the destruction of Heaven and the final victory," the Devil said.

Schitz was amused to observe that while the High Priest's face brightened at the change of subject, Bubonic Plague's posture visibly wilted.

Bubonic's voice did not carry its usual bluster. "The numbers of the Black Death Coven have dropped dramatically. The Angels have been very resourceful in targeting our members. The plan to drain the Eunoe by eliminating the human supply chain via the plague is no longer a feasible strategy."

Silence settled like a foul-smelling blanket. Schitz discerned there had been considerable resources poured into Bubonic's scheme. Although Schitz was heavily invested in the outcome of the greater conflict, he was simultaneously gleeful to see his sworn nemesis suffering such humiliation.

"So, we will train more members for the Coven," Satan said. His voice fell like a hammer; each word measured, each syllable aimed at Bubonic.

"I don't know if that will work," Titus said. "I mean, if the Angels have prioritized the elimination of members of the Coven, won't they just continue to do so? My Lord, the only original member is Bubonic Plague."

"Then... we... will... train... more," the Devil said, "unless you have some other workable solution."

Schitz snickered but stopped when Satan glared at him.

"You can leave now," the Devil said. "The remainder of this gathering is for senior leadership only."

Schitz saluted crisply and departed. He smiled so hard he thought his face would split.

IN THE TYPICAL BUREAUCRATIC fashion of Heaven, many years passed between the actions of the twenty-sixth day of March in the year of Thirteen Hundred and Fifty-One and the rewards attached to them. Yet, the emotional wounds of the day were still fresh among those affected by the slaughter. Zinc felt nothing as he received the highest possible commendation, The Golden Halo. The golden circle suspended from a ribbon around his neck. A wreath of gilded olive leaves sat on his head.

Each of the surviving Angels received the same recognition. Zinc glanced at Lord and Lady Hydrogen beside him. The trio received Heaven's raucous applause. He saw his own mood reflected in their hollow, vacant expressions. Zinc's favorite sons were gone, Patrick, Aaron, and Adolphus. He looked to the crowd and saw Adolphus's widow, Constance, weeping. Since the battle, he seldom saw her anywhere other than in the Manna bakeries.

What hollow glory there is in defeating the Black Death when its progenitor, Bubonic Plague, still lives.

THE TRIUMVIRATE CONDUCTED ITS inquest into the duel at Guillac. Many Demons had died, some from recklessness. Still, the Devil remained supportive of Bubonic Plague. Satan was insistent that new members be added to the Black Death Coven.

Bubonic was irate and would not listen to reason. Though Titus implored him to listen, after a lengthy debate, Bubonic Plague abandoned the halls of Hell. He was last seen walking into one of the rocky caves along the banks of the Styx. In subsequent years, most claimed that he died of the Atrophy; but despite regular searches in the caverns, no one ever found his wasted remains. Others regularly talked about his survival, how he haunted the area—a specter that wandered in and out of the grottos and fissures along the Styx.

The holdouts girded their arguments by pointing to the continuation of the dread disease bearing Bubonic's name. They could not, however, explain why he was never seen. His defeat in the duel represented the last time he took to the field in the service of Hell.

He remained only in legend...

...the only Demon impervious to the Angels...

...and, perhaps, the fabled Antichrist.

THE MARRIAGE OF COUNT d'Ostrevant to the daughter of Duke Philip of Burgundy had sent the town of Cambray into a bubbling fever of activity. Forty knights were to participate in a joust as part of the nuptial celebrations. Through the marketplace, the site of the tournament, a hooded and cloaked figure passed the merchants and carpenters and men-at-arms. He rose no alarm or interest from either the peasants or the nobility.

The man known as Le Fantôme trudged through the mud brought on by the light rain. He entered the blacksmith's shop in a huff.

"The work has been completed," the blacksmith said. He was a jovial, heavyset man whose face glowed red from his exertions.

Le Fantôme stooped and inspected one shield from the hay-strewn floor.

"And with plenty of time to spare," he said.

The smith missed the sarcasm. "Well, not really, my Lord. The joust is today, begging your pardon."

Le Fantôme decided to temper his cynicism.

"My good man, I am not your Lord. I am simply a messenger," he said.

He withdrew a large coin purse from his pocket.

The blacksmith weighed the small bag in his palm. "Well, nobility is as much about having gold and about having God on your side. My fortune in receiving this order is indicative of the latter; this bag certainly brings me closer to the former."

Le Fantôme smiled. "A clear conscience is the highest form of nobility."

He turned the shield he held in hand. The blacksmith's effort was solid. More importantly, he saw the lettering ordered by his employer meticulously etched into the design.

"Nice work," Le Fantôme said. "You like the verse?"

"Begging your pardon, but I am merely an illiterate laborer, my... I mean, sir. But I did have a priest read it to me. Quite interesting."

Le Fantôme checked every word.

I found you in the time of ladies and lords,
At the joust amidst the clatter of swords,
There you stood my princess fair,
Who gave me a ribbon from her flowing hair,
Chivalrous I strove to win your accords,
As I plucked at my loot and sung to its chords.

You were my lady, and I was your knight,
In that dark age, we found a glimmer of light.
But as the moon must wax and wane,
So, life must end to begin again.

Le Fantôme, Circades in disguise, smiled and raised his hood over his head. "It's an old verse. The author of which has been lost to time. Please make sure that the shields are disseminated before the joust."

"My sons are ready to deliver them at the very moment," the blacksmith said with pride.

"Sons, plural," Le Fantôme said. "You didn't need that bag of coins to be rich."

Circades stepped out of the shop and walked towards the center of the town.

He mumbled to himself. "Oh, Pulwabi, will I ever find you?"

Chapter 14

POWDER

The room was dark. Despite the inhibited vision, the groans and gasps painted a graphic picture of what was happening in the pleasure den on the Isle of Neutrality.

"Want to talk about the last time we saw each other?" Zinc asked.

"What is there to say?" The Demon snapped his fingers at a passing Familiar, then motioned for her to serve Zinc. She brought a goblet of Angel Blood.

"You didn't fight me during the duel," Zinc said.

He was overwhelmed for a moment with memories of his dead sons; he could see Aaron's vacant eyes, Patrick's opened throat, and Adolphus's white robe, stained deep red.

"That was not my fight," Spanish Influenza said. "I have no appetite for barbarism; better to fight under natural circumstances than contrived ones."

Zinc tilted the cup and gulped the bitterness inside in hopes of quieting the images of his butchered sons. He wiped his lips with his sleeve.

"I just needed to know where we stand," he said.

Spanish Influenza let out a small snigger. "First, you need a refresher class in manners. More importantly, although I enjoy your company, there is no 'we.' My heart was not in the fight, but that's no reason for us not to drink together."

Zinc's mood refused to lighten. "I meant to kill you that day," he said, "but I am thankful it did not come to that." He drained his drink before asking, "If your heart was not in the fight, why were you there?"

Spanish Influenza took an exaggerated breath. "I guess we are going to talk about this. You are a killjoy, my friend. The big, ugly one, Bubonic Plague, he knew something about me—something very bad that I did under the instruction of my Lord. If the rest of Hell knew, I'd be an outcast. That gave him power over me."

"Why do you speak of him in the past tense?" Zinc asked.

"Oh, you haven't heard." Spanish Influenza dragged an index finger across his throat. "He's dead; killed himself, he did."

Zinc shot to his feet; his goblet clanked on the floor. "He's dead?"

The Demon nearly laughed himself off the chaise. "Invested in that idea much, my friend?"

Zinc picked up his cup, which was immediately refilled, downed it in several gulps, then shook his head. "I just... uh... I never really knew if he could be killed. He seemed invincible. How did he die?"

A sheepish grin painted Spanish's face. "Well, I haven't actually seen the body, but the old warrior spirited himself away in a cave some time ago. Surely the Atrophy has claimed him."

"Problem, gentlemen?"

A pale, rail-thin Demon with cropped, dark hair stood next to them, hands on her hips.

"Ah, sorry if we disturbed you, dear daughter," Spanish Influenza said.

Zinc spewed Angel's Blood from his nose. "Daughter?"

"Do I not strike you as a family Demon?"

Zinc looked around and considered the libidinous displays underway in every inch of the room. "At this point, who am I to judge?"

Spanish Influenza did the introductions. "Sepsis, this is Zinc; Zinc, Sepsis."

"Charmed, I'm sure," she said.

She stared daggers into Zinc; not necessarily weapons of destruction but certainly ones with serious perfidy attached. Zinc clasped her small, thin fingers in a dainty handshake only to be surprised when she yanked him to his feet.

"Excuse us for a moment, Father," she said.

"Oh yes, please, at least get out of my vision, you heathen," he said with a deep laugh.

"The apple doesn't fall far from the tree," she replied as she led Zinc into a different corner of the room.

Zinc had become familiar with the way interested parties typically grabbed the attention of somebody, or bodies, in which they were fascinated. However, with Sepsis, the encounter took a novel turn.

Once she pushed Zinc onto a chaise longue, she yanked opened his robe and then began to choke him. She was not the least bit playful.

He reached to break the hold and free his throat from her surprisingly firm grasp. Sepsis let go, then struck him about the face and chest with a series of violent blows. Zinc could not catch his breath because she had straddled him.

He heard muffled giggling and turned to see a trio of young, female Demons eagerly looking on from a nearby lounge. Zinc flushed. He had grown accustomed to the exhibitionist nature of the neutral ground, but Sepsis was clothed and beating him for the viewing pleasure of the observers. Zinc felt a unique sense of vulnerability that was new to him. Sepsis recommenced the choking.

"This is for me," she whispered in his ear. "You are nothing but a means to an end."

She punctuated her sentence by slapping him viciously across his face. For a moment, he considered disengaging from the tryst as he winced at the pain in his cheek. However, when he turned his face back, Sepsis hiked up her robe and slid forward to sit on his face. Zinc gasped for air; she grabbed him by his hair and pulled his face into her. Her thin fingers grasped his hair savagely and yanked at his scalp with unimaginable pressure. Slowly, her legs began to quiver.

Zinc was drowning in the cascade of her feminine satisfaction. At the precise moment he started to faint, she deftly dismounted and pivoted. Zinc gasped for air. In his state of confusing pain and arousal, he lost track of her momentarily, then climaxed almost instantly when she took him in her mouth.

The sexual gymnastics brought an uproarious giggle from the audience.

"What a schoolboy," Sepsis said. "I wasn't too hard on you, was I?"

She dragged her nails across his bare chest.

Zinc considered himself well versed in carnal knowledge prior to the encounter. When he returned to Spanish Influenza, he was beginning to grasp how much more there was for him to learn.

Spanish Influenza spoke. "Whatever you are about to say, I would prefer it not be about anything that transpired since you left here."

"Oh... oh... yes... I mean... no... I mean, never... obviously." Zinc hated to stammer.

Makes me sound weak.

He recovered. "It's weird to think of you as a father."

"A little hedonistic for parenthood?" Spanish Influenza asked.

"Precisely."

"Oh, I am," Spanish said. He snorted a line of red powder from a golden plate. He wiped his face. "Then it's probably even weirder for you to see me as a grandfather and her as a mother."

"It is."

"But you must have children and a wife back home," Spanish Influenza said. He offered the plate of powder to Zinc.

Zinc accepted the plate. "My wife is dead," he said. "I have some living children, fewer after recent events. To be honest, as time passes and my children have children, and their children have children, I lose track. Now, it's just the House of Zinc and those who married into it. The rest of the relationships, who is my grandson, great-granddaughter—all that is irrelevant. Angels come and ask me for permission to marry or for other dispensations, and they are strangers to me."

"It is better that way," Spanish Influenza said. "Lessens the attachment. I mean, I watched you throttle my son Dandruff to death, and yet I can sit here talking to you after you defiled my daughter. So, detachment is a good thing. It may be the only thing keeping you alive at this moment."

Zinc stared into the distance. "Now that I think about it, you have killed at least two of my sons."

The Demon's laugh carried the cold wind of sorrow and pain. "And yet, here we sit. We are... thoroughly terrible parents!"

"Perhaps it is the nature of our existence."

"Cheers to that," Spanish Influenza said.

They clinked goblets and drank. Zinc reflected briefly on the irony of losing sons and then cavorting with their killer.

"What is our debate topic tonight?" Zinc asked.

"We have a rousing topic. Is there the possibility of peace without total victory for one side?"

Zinc swirled the dregs of his drink. "Interesting."

"We will call the meeting to order." He wobbled to his feet. When he quit swaying, he unleashed a loud, though slurred, call for attention.

"Demons and Angels of the Neutral Ground, if you will be so kind as to cease from your pleasure seeking for a moment, the time has come for this evening's discussion. I pose the question first to Lord Zinc: Can there be peace without total victory?"

Though his mind was addled from sex and drugs, Zinc stood. He knew the easy answer was no. But he liked a good intellectual challenge.

He started to speak, then caught a glimpse of Sepsis. She peered at him with her dark eyes and spread her legs ever so slightly. She was flanked by the Demons that had watched their coital encounter.

"Ah... yes," he said. "Yes, I believe there was a time when the founders of Heaven and Hell faced a mutual enemy. Should an existential threat arise that nullifies the significance of our current struggle, it is possible we could find an accord absent a definitive victor."

He heard whispers of protest from around the darkened room. He sat to an unfamiliar sensation, not happiness, but at least the absence of overwhelming sorrow. He raised his chalice to his lips and listened as the next speaker launched into a drunken, but passionate, rebuttal.

Zinc and Spanish Influenza smirked at each other. They shared the same thought.

His argument would carry more weight if he were wearing clothes.

THE RUINS OF THE Karnak Temple refused to wilt to the sun's unremitting assault. Ancient hieroglyphics squinted into the blazing rays as if to say, "We've faced fiercer adversaries."

God stalked through the rubble with his hands clasped behind his back. He kicked aside a small rock and watched it plink its way from side to side down a crumbling corridor. He looked at Smallpox.

"So, after all this time, he refuses to meet me face-to-face?"

There was no answer.

"So many things pass into antiquity; why should my relationship with my brother be any different?"

"Due respect, Your Almightiness," Smallpox said. "I have come with a singular purpose and stand under the strictest instructions to discuss nothing else. What... ah... how do you feel... uh... what is your reaction to the proposed elevation?"

"I remember when we elevated humans the first time," God said. "They evolved from simple animals with virtually no knowledge of their species' past, no sense of language, and no culture, into what we have now."

He gestured to the ruins.

"So, you are in agreement?" Smallpox asked.

God held his palms up either in supplication or surrender. "Why not? Let us roll the dice and see where they carry us. I, too, have grown tired of the current limitations. The mortals have hacked at each other with sword and spear for millennia. Let us see what they do with the next elevation of consciousness."

Eager to conclude, Smallpox nodded.

"We will begin by making the ancient symbols," God said. He wished his brother had come. Working with a proxy was always so tedious.

"After you, sir," Smallpox said.

"WE NEED YOU, FATHER." Rabies's voice carried a note of pleading. "Won't you at least consider?"

Schitz shook his head. "They elevated Anorexia and Autism to the Council. Surely either of them is more qualified to teach at the Academy. They both finished ahead of me in my graduating class."

"It's not about academics," Rabies replied. "We have instructors to teach theory and strategy: Cancer, Scarlet Fever, Sepsis, Anemia, and me."

"An impressive roster and all-female. Your mother would be so proud of you all. More to the point, she would strictly adhere to the tradition that only the top of the class teaches at the Academy."

"It is true," Rabies said, "she was a strong believer in that tradition. However, the trend that I have observed is terrifying and requires correction."

"And what is that?"

He looked at his daughter with pride and love. And pain—she looked so like her mother.

"Our advantage against the Angels in combat is fading," she said. "There have always been unexpected variables that influence the outcome of battle, but with each passing generation, the skill gap between our side and the Angels is shrinking. With their superior numbers, we cannot afford to lose our advantage in fieldcraft."

"What would you have me do, my love?"

When he dropped his feigned irritation, Rabies smiled.

"Teach combat training," she said with a broad smile. "Your friends on the Council have already approved a waiver for you to join the faculty."

"My friends?" Schitz's head snapped back.

"Anorexia and Autism," Rabies said. "They have always supported you."

Schitz realized he'd outlived a great many of his Triumvirate Council enemies.

"I guess I do have friends on the Council now," he said. "Good."

"The next cohort is ready. And there is something new; something called 'firearms.'"

"I've heard. Disgusting concept. Combat without contact. Death by distance."

"Don't start talking about the old days, Father," Rabies said. "There are bigger issues."

"Like?"

"They raised the level of humanity's consciousness," Rabies said. "It presents a significant challenge to all of us. It's up to you to ensure that it doesn't translate into our losing any ground to the Angels."

"So, joining the faculty. Does that make you my superior?"

Rabies let out an uncharacteristically girlish giggle. "Only during times of academic instruction."

COBALT STOOD BESIDE HYDROGEN in the Great Hall of Heaven. The heads of Asia and Africa once again convened.

"I believe that your efforts towards self-determination have been a pyrrhic victory," Cobalt said. The Asiatic Standard Bearer added, "Dominion of your region of the world also comes with the responsibility of maintaining it."

"Rather stating the obvious, no?" Hydrogen asked.

"Yet something too often ignored by the Houses on the far corners of the globe," Cobalt said. "Just Look at the Black Death. It started in my region, but its impact in Europe people remember. If we could have snuffed it out in Asia, perhaps millions could have been saved."

Lord Hydrogen nodded. "I agree, however, the right to abstain from foolhardy endeavors, dreamed up by a self-appointed leader of Heaven, is invaluable. It is a matter of life and death to those of us on the fringes of power."

"I am not on the fringe of power," Cobalt said. "I have built up the Houses of my sons, Platinum and Uranium, into an invincible contingent. We answer to nobody and control the largest landmass on the globe. I gladly postulate that I should be considered as the next leader of Heaven."

Lord Hydrogen shook his head. *Every Standard Bearer thinks he is the next great thing*, he thought.

He looked at Cobalt and said, "Well, the agreement stands, at least for now."

Cobalt shifted uneasily. He chose his words with great care. "I'm certain you have noticed that Magnesium and Molybdenum failed to create any new houses. They have built up their negotiating power by hoarding dispensations and now possess the ability to shape your arrangement quite substantially."

"Do you know how they might intend to alter it?" Hydrogen asked.

Cobalt shook his head. "I wouldn't worry," he paused for effect, "unless you want to gain more authority for yourself."

"I don't foresee engaging in a power struggle with the natives," Hydrogen said. "I have little interest in their region of the world."

Cobalt chuckled. "It might be harder to convince the natives of that. They were traumatized when Gold and Silver set up an enclave within their domain. I think they see potential enemies wherever they look."

Lord Hydrogen mentally cursed his colleagues. They were always scheming and plotting, ever seeking out the routes to power and influence over Heaven. "Stay safe," Hydrogen said. He was more than ready to end the conversation. He shook Cobalt's hand.

"And you," Cobalt said.

Though his grip was firm, insincerity glinted in his eyes.

Lord Hydrogen watched the Asiatic Standard Bearer depart, cutting a forceful path through the masses of Angels milling about the Great Hall. Hydrogen moaned in frustration. He had cajoled Zinc into accepting the division of authority. The arrangement had shielded the House of Hydrogen and his son's House from being called to participate in haphazard, poorly planned missions. However, the division of authority seemed to have generated an intense thirst for power among other factions.

Hydrogen pursed his lips. *The duel with the Black Death has brought me closer to Zinc*, he thought. *Still, I doubt true friendship can blossom between us if Zinc feels spurned by Rachael. We look like we are all at peace—one with the other—but I have a sense of impending disaster.*

Nostalgia flooded through Schitz. It had been a long time since he'd walked across the black, marble floor leading to the lecture hall of the Demonic Academy. The mortal implements he carried with him felt heavy, but not as heavy as his memories.

With every step, he missed Rubella more. The abortive liaison with Lady Calcium had done little to reduce his loneliness. Each time he opened himself up to the possibility of a connection, Demon or Angel, he was rewarded with disappointment and heartache.

He set up for his instruction and reminisced about another painful loss, Anna. In many ways, hers was the purist relationship of his experience, brief though as it was. He had never concealed his involvement with a fellow Demon from her, and still, she had loved him and claimed a part of him for herself, a part that would always belong to her.

Schitz looked up and realized the room had filled. The current cohort was joined by some post-graduate students. There were thirty-one in all, the largest assemblage he'd ever seen in the Amphitheater.

This is over 70% of all living Demons, he thought.

In addition, there were Wraiths, Priests, and Priestesses. Elise waved from the back corner. It seemed all Hell wanted special weapons instruction from the legend that was Schizophrenia.

The room fell silent when he looked from his notes and stepped into the well at the front. Rabies winked at him, flush with familial pride. She stood and addressed the assembled.

"We are facing a dire time in the history of our people. The Angels are numerous and have become adept at targeting our strongest warriors."

The energy in the room dropped and Schitz suddenly understood the weight he'd volunteered to carry.

Rabies kept going. "That being said, we have a wealth of experience here; Hell's second-oldest Demon and one of its most adept warriors. This morning, I give you the legendary killer of the Angel Gold, Schizophrenia Incenderos Nervosa."

The one who'd been considered a dunce, a dullard, and a coward, held up his hands to silence the thunderous applause. Almost all his critics were dead. The generations in front of him saw only the snake who'd shed his skin of failure and disrepute and emerged as a cunning and calculated viper.

"Thank you, Rabies," he said. He held up a clumsy wooden contraption. "This is the Harquebus. It is not the first firearm. However, it represents the first major advancement in gun powder weaponry, something destined to define both mortal and Celestial combat henceforth. Understand this: the sword is disappearing as an instrument of war. How we battle in the Celestial will change dramatically as well. For now, that is the totality of your lesson on firearms."

The assembled began to murmur among themselves in shocked disbelief.

Schitz spoke over the babbling. "Of those assembled here for training within the eldest cohort, who was first in their class?" he asked.

Scarlet Fever rose to her feet and saluted. "I am."

"Ah, you are already an instructor here at the academy," Schitz said. "Why are you still training?"

Scarlet Fever's confidence wilted a bit. She flinched when she said, "Because the senior faculty instructed me to."

Schitz's iron gaze stifled a ripple of snickers.

"Show some respect," he said. "Let me ask you this, Scarlet Fever; how much do you wish to contribute to the final victory?"

"With all that I am," she replied, still blushing.

Schitz heard himself quoting Anna. "If your hunger to be great is as large as you say, feed it, but not just in battle; feed it in preparation and honing."

For a moment, Schitz was back in the desert—running, fighting, and loving. He continued to quote his long-lost lover. "Wanting to be good won't make you good, and simply doing what your instructors schedule for you will always leave you mediocre."

He motioned to Scarlet Fever. "Step forward."

Schitz placed the lug, the iron rod stabilizer for the Harquebus, on the ground, then rested the long body of the musket on the loop at the top.

"Hold the firearm like this," he said.

He whispered to her under his breath. "Don't feel bad. When they see you as honest and flawed, they will see your authenticity and follow you with more loyalty for it."

Schitz corrected her posture. "Hold this weapon until you can no longer maintain the optimal firing position, then pass it to the next member of your cohort," he said. "The rest of you, fall into formation."

The students left their seats and assembled in the open area at the front in three lines.

After the three ranks assembled, Schitz said, "Sound off!"

Scarlet Fever, still maintaining her hold on the Harquebus, said, "Scarlet Fever; daughter of Sloth and Meningitis."

Down the line, the troops proudly asserted their lineage.

"Spanish Influenza, son of Sloth and Meningitis."

"Typhoid, son of Pride and Lust."

"Trichomoniasis, daughter of Greed and Cancer."

"Herpes, son of Streptococcal and Gluttony."

"HPV, daughter of Malaria and Wrath."

"Lung Cancer, daughter of Aspergillosis and Envy."

"Hepatitis, son of Aspergillosis and Envy."

A thought tickled Schitz's brain. *They are all descendants of members of the Black Death Coven.*

The next generation began to shout.

"Sepsis, daughter of Spanish Influenza and Trichomoniasis."

"Liver Cancer, son of Spanish Influenza and Trichomoniasis."

"Asthma, daughter of Typhoid and Scarlet Fever."

"Gangrene, daughter of Typhoid and Scarlet Fever."

Almost immediately, in an obvious attempt to stand out, the next two soldiers stepped forward. "And her brothers IBS and Visceral Leishmaniosis."

The new approach started a trend. Herpes and HPV's children saluted as a group, Bovine Spongiform Encephalopathy, Cerebral Palsy, and Fragile X Syndrome.

The daughter and son of Varicella and Lung Cancer, Epilepsy and Ulcers, were followed closely by Brain Cancer (daughter) and Rocky Mountain Spotted Fever (son) from the loins of Liver Cancer and Asthma.

IBS and Sepsis had produced Anemia and Gout, a girl and a boy; Visceral Leishmaniosis and Gangrene were well represented by their twins, Osteoarthritis and his sister, Arthritis. Not to be outdone, Hepatitis and GERD had produced a beautiful daughter in Naegleriasis and an equally striking son in Lassa Virus.

Ulcers and Cerebral Palsy's children, Rota Virus and Hemophilia, were so androgynous that Schitz only knew their genders because he checked the roster, and Agoraphobia, daughter of Bovine Spongiform Encephalopathy and Epilepsy, bore an uncanny resemblance to the cattle that her father routinely infected.

Still, Schitz's confidence soared. He recognized a room full of talented, well-trained fighters.

The Final Victory is closer than ever, he thought.

His voice rolled across the troops. "The steps I will teach you are designed to purify mind and body. The first is standing."

He noticed an eye roll.

"Is there a problem, Spanish Influenza?" he asked. He identified the miscreant by name to show the class who was in control.

"No, Schizophrenia," Spanish Influenza said, but the sarcasm in his voice was unmistakable. "It just seems this lesson might be better suited for the nursery."

"Perhaps, it would be for you," Schitz said.

He rested his frame on the Harquebus. Within less than a minute, Scarlet Fever began to quiver. The combined weight of the weapon and the instructor was too much for her.

Harquebus

"Getting tired?" he asked.

She nodded. Schitz took the Harquebus and tossed it to Spanish Influenza.

"Assume the firing position."

Schitz looked at the class. "Extend one leg out in front of you parallel to the ground. Bend the other in a squat."

Spanish Influenza complied. He wobbled a little.

"Maintain the barrel integrity," Schitz said. "Just tilt it upwards in its holder."

Sweat broke out on the younger Demon's face.

"It's not possible."

"Then maybe we should bring out the nursery Demons," Schitz said.

Spanish Influenza blushed. This time, Schitz did nothing to stifle the giggles. Schitz took the Harquebus and handed the younger Demon the steadying rod. He positioned the musket's butt in the crux of his right shoulder with the barrel resting upon his left forearm and completed the squatting exercise.

Schitz handed the Harquebus back to Spanish Influenza.

"When Syphilis carried two fully grown Demons across the battlefield at Teutoburg, she could not have run if she had not first learned to stand. Therefore, despite this young expert's opinion, Lesson One is standing. Do you understand!"

The collective shout of "Yes, sir," rattled the hall.

Schitz introduced the class to the Thirteen Steps. Every day, he brought more and more Harquebuses from the mortal world. By the time he had reached the lessons of humility and surrender, each Demon had been carrying a musket for some time and was gaining comfort with the weapon. Handling the muskets became second nature. The rapport Schitz built with the younger Demons was an additional benefit. He loved and respected them all: Scarlet Fever, the ever-serious over-achiever; Typhoid, positive to a fault; Spanish Influenza, cocky and self-assured; Lung Cancer, flirty and outgoing; Herpes, the prankster; Ulcers the bookworm; Rheumatoid Arthritis, the self-starter.

Schitz learned something about each one and tightened the bonds within the cohorts and across generations as well. He watched with pride as the youngsters developed both skill and confidence.

Hell's halls reverberated with the thunderous report of muskets. The smell of burning gunpowder filled the air. The students progressed rapidly and soon demonstrated target accuracy far beyond anything achieved by mortals. Along the banks of the Styx, squads drilled and prepared Celestial stratagems that incorporated firearms.

"You have completely revitalized our weapons training and all of Hell," Rabies said. She was watching Harquebus training with Schitz from one of the hills along the Styx.

"It has been very rewarding," he said. "A healing process."

She squeezed his arm. "I'm very proud to be your daughter."

"I'm sorry I was not around more," he said.

Rabies waved the comment away. "When I was younger, I wished for the type of family life I sometimes saw amongst others—like the day we had together before you were sent away."

"There was nothing I could do."

"I know that now," Rabies said. "Perhaps now that you are back, and we are instructing together, we can make up for some lost time. I would like you to get to know Pneumonia. He is a good husband."

Schitz draped his arm over his daughter's shoulder. "I would like that very much."

They turned at the sound of shuffling steps.

"Forgive me for interrupting," Smallpox said. "I was wondering if I might have a word with Schitz?"

Rabies walked off toward the drilling Demons.

"How can I help you?" Schitz asked.

I don't trust this one.

"I've come on a personal and political mission," Smallpox said.

Schitz felt a smile approaching. "News of your brother?"

"There is no cure for the Atrophy," Smallpox said. "Those who cling to the belief that Bubonic Plague survives are an affront to reason."

Schitz motioned Smallpox closer. "How can I help you?"

Smallpox's reluctance was evident. "Well... your troubles with my brother are the impetus for my visit, in a way. My daughter Anorexia lost her husband when she was young, and I hate to see her alone. She had always been very fond of you. If you two were to marry, it might put an end to any animosity between our bloodlines."

"I hold no animosity toward you or your children," Schitz said. "The same cannot be said of your brother."

Schitz remembered Anorexia. She was pretty and good-natured.

He enjoyed his friendship with her and her brother Autism, especially since the death of Conjunctivitis.

"Your offer is most generous," Schitz said, "but I cannot accept. I have only admiration for your daughter. Still, I fear the timing is not right. I mean you no offense."

"None taken," Smallpox said. "While I am disappointed in your answer, I am pleased to know that the unpleasantness died with my brother. Perhaps there will be more unity in Hell moving forward."

GOD AND ZINC WALKED along the banks of the Eunoe.

"I am not in agreement with the current regionalism," God said.

"I don't see much of an alternative," Zinc said. "The Houses thought it was a good idea when I stepped away from command. Now they cannot agree on anything. It was naïve to think that each House would operate independently. Sons affiliate with their fathers, even if they have been granted a charter for their own Houses. There will always be a series of cliques, the most natural boundary for which is regional affiliation."

"Indeed," God said, "but I still don't like it. I have always allowed the Angels a great deal of autonomy regarding how they sort their affairs and determine their leadership. However, if I notice things taking a course that runs contrary to my liking, I will intervene."

"What would you prefer, my Lord?" Zinc asked.

"There is too much squabbling and jostling for position within the Angelic ranks," God said. "I would prefer one appointed leader of the Angels. I have never taken such a step because I feared it would be detrimental to morale and because I was concerned that whoever I appointed would eventually fancy themselves my equal. We don't need a repeat of the Gold and Silver fiasco."

Zinc had heard rumors of other ancient rebellions like the one undertaken by Gold and Silver, but he'd always dismissed them as folklore.

"Who would you appoint, my Lord?"

His pulse accelerated.

"Is that of interest to you?" God chuckled. "And don't lie. I can hear your heart from over here."

"It is," Zinc said. "I know self-determination was an idea I sponsored, but I would love to rid myself of the stink I took on when Alexander's Empire collapsed."

"I appreciate your honesty," God said. He pointed to the Golden Halo around Zinc's neck. "But I think you have already cleansed yourself in the waters of considerable success."

"Well," Zinc said, "all modesty aside, defeating the Black Death was a good moment for me."

"Yes, it was," God said, "and that is why I will appoint you as one of two Leaders of Heaven should this regional distribution come to folly."

"One of two?"

"Yes, a little series of checks and balances. No one can rest on his laurels—no one can stretch for too much authority."

"A good solution," Zinc said, though he would have preferred sole control.

"Yes," God said, "but we will implement it only if the Angels prove incapable of handling the sovereignty I have given them."

They walked for a moment in silence, basking in the radiance of Heaven's natural light.

God's next words sounded like someone thinking aloud. "More than anything, though, I would like to know where the Demons have gone and what they are planning since you smashed the Black Death."

Zinc did not care.

I have a chance to achieve a position of leadership beyond my father's wildest dreams. Now all I have to do is make sure the regional system of governance falls completely apart.

Though annoyed by his summons to the Triumvirate Council, Schitz was more comfortable with the group's current makeup. Smallpox,

Autism, and Anorexia were present along with the Wraith contingent of Elise, Mephistopheles, and Anubis, and the representatives of the Infernal Church, Titus, Erin, and Desdemona. For a moment, Schitz found himself distracted by the Priestesses. Erin's fiery hair surrounded a fair complexion; Desdemona, as befitting her Middle Eastern roots, had dark hair and olive features. Schitz wondered if the Priests indulged in carnal pleasures with their appetizing counterparts.

"Thank you for being here today," Titus said, ever the blunt emcee. "Please inform us as to the progress you have made with your training."

Anorexia looked like she'd been crying—bloodshot eyes, puffy cheeks. Schitz snapped back to the present and issued his synopsis.

"I can assure you that all of my pupils have acquired both maximum efficiency with the Harquebus and other matchlock weaponry and a heightened fighting mentality. I am certain our Academy work has elevated our forces in pedigree and stature over those of Heaven."

"We have received your reports and assessments with much joy," Titus said, even though he looked like a man suffering from an attack of hemorrhoids. He gestured toward a leather-bound volume Schitz had previously submitted. "Your proposal for an expedition to the New World is ambitious, to say the least."

Schitz waited.

"You believe your plans are feasible?"

"I do."

"Based on..."

Schitz looked at Mephistopheles, who had asked the question.

"Based on my extensive experience scouting and subsisting in the New World during the... ah... holiday so graciously provided by our Lord."

Nervous laughter trickled across the room.

Titus reinserted himself in the conversation. "The Triumvirate is here to prevent blind ambition from interfering with progress. We want our forces deployed only on the most strategic missions."

"Like you did with Bubonic Plague and the Black Death?" Schitz asked.

He knew better but could not help himself.

Spectators in the back of the hall began to buzz only to be hammered in silence by Titus's spiked gavel.

"We have discussed your proposition, Schitz," he said. "You may have any of the Demons you see fit for your endeavor. However, I warn you. Lord Satan will not tolerate the misuse of his resources."

"Well, there you have it then," Schitz said.

Before he reached the door, he called over his shoulder. "And thank you for all the good wishes."

Outside, Schitz felt a familiar hand tug on his robe. Elise embraced him.

"He has to ask questions, my husband," Elise said.

Schitz rubbed his neck in feigned boredom. "I don't give a fuck what he does or doesn't have to do."

Elise recoiled as though slapped. "I... I... well... uh... I have been investigating this... Spanish Influenza. I believe he is very dangerous. I heard rumors—something about his involvement in Rubella's demise. I think I can set a trap for him."

"Mama, I want to fix things with us. Honestly, I do. However, I need to make it abundantly clear that you cannot meddle in my affairs."

"You didn't mind when I killed those Wraiths in Egypt," she said. Her voice reminded Schitz of a cobra's hiss.

"I was young and foolish back then."

"And you were young when carrying on with the Angel within The Maid of Orléans?"

"Excuse me?"

"I know more than you think," Elise replied smugly. Then, to backtrack the tension that had entered the conversation, Elise grasped Schitz with her sole hand. "But you got yourself out of everything on your own. You're right; you are a big boy."

"It's not that," Schitz said. "I just need to be the architect of my actions and of those taken on my behalf. It's the only way I can achieve greatness."

Elise nodded. "I can live with that. Can I still acquire information for you? I am a Wraith, after all."

"Of course, but I am the only one who will act on it."

"That's reasonable."

Schitz paused to select his next words with great care. "Please never, ever go back on your promise. I must be able to trust you, Mama."

"Of course, you can," Elise said. She hugged him once again. This time Schitz offered no resistance.

"I love you," he said.

And he meant it—at least at the moment.

ANXIETY CREPT THROUGH SPANISH Influenza's stomach. The forces of the Caliphate had recently conceded to the Castile-Aragon Union, and the Moorish mortal inhabitants of Granada mirrored his mood. The Christian mortals had engaged in nearly eight hundred years of conflict to reconquer the Iberian Peninsula. Generations of mortals passed in what seemed a few years to the Demon. However, the recent elevation of the mortal's consciousness (another one of God's bad ideas) had altered the perception of time for all beings—mortal and Celestial. Since the agreement had gone into effect, time slowed; mortal years no longer flew past so rapidly.

During a debate at the Island of Neutrality, Demons and Angels had argued about the possibility of the mortals gaining full mental elevation and knowing about the role their souls played in providing Celestial beings with psychic energy. There was talk of the mortal bloodline that possessed knowledge of past lives and, according to some legends, knowledge of the future. These mortals were seen as the harbingers of the end of Demons and Angels.

Spanish Influenza wondered if he would see the final resolution of the conflict with Heaven.

Probably not, he thought. *Most of my lot falls in Satan's service.*

He thought of his Angelic counterpart, Zinc. Despite having met on the battlefield, the two had maintained a certain level of amicability. He thought of their nights of shared debate and debauchery and wondered if the two kingdoms could ever simply reunite.

Lost in thought, he nearly bumped into Smallpox.

"You asked to speak away from prying eyes. Did you have to choose one of the hottest parts of the map?" Smallpox asked.

"You're a Demon... from Hell," Spanish said. "If anyone heard you say that you could never show your face again."

"It's not like that there and you know it," Smallpox said. "I wouldn't know brimstone if I sat in it."

"Irrelevant," Spanish Influenza said. "We have an image to uphold. To your point, this is a plausible place for us to be since the siege having just ended."

"And why are we feigning to conduct the Lord's business when there is much work to do in preparation for the attack upon the New World?"

I much prefer Zinc's company, Spanish Influenza thought. *At least when we meet, we are civil... and drunk.*

"I conducted certain sensitive transactions with your brother on Satan's behalf," Spanish said. "With Bubonic Plague gone, I require assurances of your favor and of my safety."

Smallpox laughed. "I thought you called me here for something important."

"But I am your—"

"Enough," Smallpox said. "I know all about how we are related. Depending on which side we trace, I am either your great or your great-great-grandfather. There is so much generational bed-hopping, who can keep track. Still, we are of the same line. So what?"

Spanish Influenza had a brief mental image of a long, snort-able line of red dust, then returned to the business at hand.

"I come to you as a member of the same family, and I am asking for help in recognition of your brother and my relationship with Satan."

"Look, sonny," Smallpox said, "I did not survive this long by being naïve or by handing out favors. I surmise that my brother knew some salacious details of your career—why else could you have been forced into his idiotic duel. Rest assured, whatever secrets you have died with my brother. Satan's memory is ephemeral, significantly damaged by his abuses of the flesh. If he needs you again, he knows where to find you."

Spanish Influenza twitched involuntarily.

"Let me give you some advice," Smallpox said. "Your forays into the neutral ground are somewhat legendary, but you did not invent that place. You might be surprised as to the identity of some of the Demons who have found some release amongst the vices of that place. But diving so deeply and indulging so often do not comprise a recommended recipe for longevity."

The younger Demon hung his head. "If your advice were as easy to follow as it is to dispense, the vices would no longer exist."

Smallpox shrugged. "I will not be your handler. It's your funeral. I have my own issues with Satan dating back long before you were born. If you want someone to watch your back, I recommend Titus or Schizophrenia."

If Schitz knew of my part in his wife's butchery... A finger of dread dragged along Spanish Influenza's spine.

"Thanks for the suggestion," he said.

Smallpox jumped into a passing human who was opening a bottle of wine. "Come now, young lad. Join me."

THE CHAMBER SEEMED ODDLY crowded. Schitz looked at Anemia sprawled across his bed, naked. She was thin, fair, and young. She'd been particularly attentive to his Academy instruction.

Not long after he had noticed her interest, she had arrived at his quarters and offered her maidenhood to him. There had been bouts of hungry, ferocious passion followed by lengthy discussions. He wanted to know why Demons had begun giving their children names like Brain Cancer and predetermining the ailment they would develop; she asked him about the ancient world.

Schitz had never engaged in a tryst with such a young partner. He wrestled with the future of the relationship during his preparations for the New World. And he decided to end it.

He began slowly. *Be kind.*

"I cannot tell you how much our time has meant," he said.

"But it can't continue, right?" she replied. She rolled over on her stomach. "That's what you were about to say?"

"It was. I... I'm sorry."

"Don't be," she said. "I had hoped to make you my husband, but I have no regrets. I can use my experience to snare someone else."

"Any would be lucky to be your mate," Schitz said. "I am broken in many ways."

She bit her lower lip. "Not the ones that matter," she said.

"It pains me to let you go," Schitz said, "but I cannot undergo the pain of losing a loved one again—not another mate."

"I understand," she said.

She slithered from the bed and coiled around his body, a seductive python of feminine allure. "If you must go," she said, "I believe you should say a proper goodbye."

He pushed her onto the bed. "As you wish, milady."

THE HEAVING SEA MADE Schitz miss the rhythmic rocking of his bed.

Much more pleasant, he thought. *And I didn't have to listen to Smallpox and his incessant blather.*

Schitz rode the waves from within Hernán Cortés. Smallpox occupied a junior officer.

"Velázquez revoked the charter for the mission. There was nothing I could do; they hate each other."

"But you convinced his mind to proceed as planned?" Smallpox asked.

"Yes, we are still on plan."

The hold of the ship was crowded with Spaniards. Among the possessed, Schitz saw Anorexia and Autism.

"I am honored by the presence of the Triumvirate," Schitz said.

Autism chuckled. "Are you tagging along with Council or the other way around?"

"You're an idiot, Autism," Schitz said, "but I love you. And yes, you are accompanying me. You are not here as members of the

Triumvirate but as the last of the old Demons. We must ensure that these Spaniards are not infiltrated by Angels. That is why we sailed with them from Spain. When we arrive, the mortals' armor and Harquebuses will be a massive advantage over the natives. You will each captain a contingent as we make our way here."

Schitz pointed to a map he had pinned to the hull of the ship. "This is Tenochtitlán, the capital of the Aztecs. You must not allow your squads to become complacent, for although the natives will be primitive, they will be fierce in battle."

Schitz recalled the Jaguar Warriors he had used to defeat Gold. "Any Angels within these mortals will still pose a threat even if they are outclassed in weaponry."

"We are taking a large contingent of Hell," Smallpox said. "How will this be any different from any large-scale, pitched battle we have fought before? Won't the Angels simply bring their superior numbers and slog it out?"

"I don't believe so. There is one thing that separates this campaign from all the others that have been undertaken—"

Autism interrupted. "Location!"

"Correct, Autsy," Schitz said. He timed his shove perfectly with a wave, and Autism tumbled across the subdeck to everyone's great delight. To his credit, Autism scrambled to his feet and laughed along with the rest.

"We have always brought large numbers in the Mediterranean, Europa, the Levant, Persia," Schitz said. "We have never pursued a full-scale campaign in the periphery. I believe that we will mainly encounter Angels that resemble the Natives; Angels gravitate to the regions in which they were raised. Not many European and Near-Eastern Angels will come to the aid of their New World counterparts."

"That is a big gamble," Anorexia said.

"You are correct; everything I said is based on conjecture."

Anorexia blushed when Schitz complimented her input. He wondered if she had been aware of her father's marriage proposal.

"If I am wrong and we find a high level of Heavenly forces committed to the battle, we must disengage. I did not train the new generation for wanton and wasteful slaughter."

As the journey across the ocean wore on, Schitz continued to drive home the objectives of the campaign to his commanders. They, in turn, relayed the mission to their squads. Schitz spent the time reviewing patterns for attack and defense with his commanders and their units. He was accompanied by the three cohorts he had trained along with the Demons who sat on the Triumvirate. Hell's operations were left to Rabies, Pneumonia, Reye's Disease, Encephalitis, Meningitis, Streptococcal, Cancer, and Malaria. Seldom had Hell been so dangerously undermanned.

One afternoon above deck, Schitz found Anemia and Rheumatoid Arthritis looking out across the waves. They smiled and waved from within their mortal Spaniards.

"The mainland is within sight," Anemia said.

"Remember you two, there will be fewer female bodies, so you must be strategic in locating hosts and careful to avoid the melding of minds."

"They drilled that into us in the Academy," Anemia said.

She had looked at Schitz's groin when she said "drilled."

He let the innuendo pass without comment.

"Good," he said. "Alert the others."

Cortés sloshed to shore first, Schitz within him, and assembled the conquistadors and Demons alike. The force was a sight to behold. Polished silver armor glittered in the morning sun. Red and orange banners snapped in the breeze. The horses and weaponry of the force offered a portent of the violence. As the march began, one of the attendants began to strum a lute. The strains of an old Spaniard tune *Non é Gran Cousa* soon wafted through the warm Mexican morning. Voices joined in the chorus.

> *Non é gran cousa se sabe, bon joyzo dar,*
> *a Madre do que o mundo, tod' á de joigar.*[64]

---

[64] We should not wonder that Our Lady gives true judgments, as she is the mother of, He who will judge the world.

The march continued through the jungles and the highlands past Mount Nauhcampantépetl.

Mui gran razon é que sábia dereito,
que Deus troux' en seu corp' e de seu peito mamentou,
e del despeito, nunca foi fillar.
poren de sen me sospeito, que a quis avondar.[65]

They met mortals first, primitives who fell under a hail of musket fire and a wall of pikes like wheat before the farmer's scythe. Soon after, the Angels appeared. Schitz felt uncontainable joy as he watched his students subject the Angels to his strategies. The Demons utilized concentrated fire from the Harquebusiers to target any possessed mortals, while teams of two or three waited within the Celestial along the flanks and dispatched seizing Angels. The Angels who moved into the Celestial to avoid the barrage of lead and pikes faced further hit-and-run attacks from other Demon teams arrayed along the main body of the assault. The formation created three sides of a square around the Angels, within which they were efficiently dispatched.

Non é gran cousa se sabe, bon joyzo dar,
a Madre do que o mundo, tod' á de joigar.[66]

The Demons cut their way to the island city of Tenochtitlán. Schitz recalled sneaking into the city during his years of exile. He appreciated, even more, the pride of entering the city at the head of a conquering army. He had held onto his possession of Cortés to ensure the success of the mission, which required negotiations with the local enemies of the Aztecs. Aside from the practical necessities, he held onto the Spaniard host because he wanted to sit at the head

---

[65] It is not strange that she judges well, she who bore God in her body and nursed him at her breast and never was wronged by him. And so, I am sure that he filled her with wisdom.

[66] We should not wonder that Our Lady gives true judgments, as she is the mother of, He who will judge the world.

of the army of conquistadors and Demons when they entered the Aztec capital.

Perched atop his mighty warhorse, he felt he was fully recovered from his feud with Bubonic Plague and the loss of Rubella.

> Sobr' esto, se m' oissedes, diria, dun joyzo que deu Santa Maria,
> por un que cad' ano ya, com' oý contar,
> a San Jam' en romaria, porque se foi matar.[67]

Autism waved from within one of the commanders. "Congratulations!"

Schitz pumped his fist. "My friend, this is just the beginning."

The strains of the lute and trudge of armored steps echoed across the warm climes of the New World as the flag of España unfurled across its vast expanses. In like manner, the forces of Hell exploited their advantage North to South.

> Non é gran cousa se sabe, bon joyzo dar,
> a Madre do que o mundo, tod' á de joigar.[68]

The Harquebuses cracked and the nose-tickling stench of powder filled the air above the swamps of the Everglades. Schitz shouted for another volley as more of De Léon's Spaniards moved up to fire, while their comrades reloaded. From the flanks, slogging through the watery ground, Anorexia led a crew of Demons on the Angels that had been shot out of the Seminoles and those already in the Celestial trying desperately to defend them. The fight was brief. The Demons deftly dispatched the Angels, running them through and slitting their throats with ease. In desperation, some Angels jumped into mortal natives only to be cut down by the next musket volley.

---

[67] On this theme, if you pay heed to me, I will tell you of the judgement of Our Lady on a man who, as I heard tell would go to Compostela on pilgrimage every year, and who killed himself.

[68] We should not wonder that Our Lady gives true judgments, as she is the mother of, He who will judge the world.

Este romeu con bõa voontade, ya a Santiago de verdade.
pero desto fez maldade que ant' albergar,
foi con moller sen bondade, sen con ela casar.[69]

Smallpox rushed into Coronado's tent with frantic news.

"We are not only spreading our own diseases among the mortals at an unheard-of rate. These Europeans carry the remnants of long-dead Demons: Influenza, Measles, Plague, and others, and they, too, infect the mortals."

"I thought a cure accompanied a Demon's demise?" Schitz responded from within his third conquistador.

"No," Smallpox said. "Our death only enables mortals the *ability* to develop a cure."

Smallpox had possessed a priest.

Ironic, Schitz thought. But he said, "Our comrades are still with us then. Life after death, eh?"

Non é gran cousa se sabe, bon joyzo dar,
a Madre do que o mundo, tod' á de joigar.[70]

Atrocities rained on the inhabitants of the New World, delivered by mortal and Demon alike. Elise, having returned from one of her many scouting missions, felt the urge to relax along the Styx. Schitz's expansion into the lands beyond the sea had stretched the Wraiths to the breaking point. To her amazement, the river jostled and heaved and broke its banks as the deluge of fearful, hateful souls flooded its depths. Elise marveled at the power her little Schitz had garnered.

Pois esto fez, meteu-ss' ao camo,
e non se mãefestou o mesquĩo e o demo mui festo,

---

[69] The Pilgrim indeed would go to Santiago with good intentions, but on this occasion, he did wrong, for first he spent the night with a woman of ill repute, to whom he was not married.

[70] We should not wonder that Our Lady gives true judgments, as she is the mother of, He who will judge the world.

se le foi mostrar,
mais branco que un armo,
polo tost' enganar.[71]

"You have to come to our aid if we ask!" Magnesium stood before the assembled Standard Bearers with his son, Molybdenum.

"According to our agreement," Zinc replied, "we cannot be called into endeavors that lack a clear strategy. And when we decide to send our forces outside of our realm, the magnitude of the force remains at our discretion. Is that not correct?"

Seated in the next seat, Lord Hydrogen leaned in and whispered. "This is not how I intended the agreement."

Zinc's response chaffed like a rasp on flesh. "And yet the slaughter of your House that you fought so hard to avoid will commence if you commit them to this bloodbath," he said. "Refrain from calling me a coward now, and afterwards I will hold your interests close to my mind, despite past circumstances."

Hydrogen was visibly conflicted between his better nature and his love for his House. "A truce then?" he asked. "At long last?"

"Let's not go that far," Zinc said. He could see Rachael's sneering face, he could feel her writhing body. "We will call it an accord."

"And what do you mean by afterward?" Hydrogen asked.

"Well, that you will have to take on good faith," Zinc said.

The two broke from their whispered confab and Hydrogen addressed the assembled. "I am sorry, but that is an accurate interpretation of the agreement."

Magnesium sagged.

"I will offer assistance," Cobalt said, "in exchange for all of the dispensations you hold for opting not to sire new Houses."

"Unacceptable," Magnesium replied.

"Then you may pledge fealty to us and reside within our boundaries once your lands are overrun," Cobalt said.

Fury and embarrassment etched Magnesium's face. "So, we give

---

[71] After this, he set out on his pilgrimage without making confession, and the Devil with great speed appeared to him, whiter than ermine, to deceive him at once.

you either our future or our freedom," he said. "In that case, consider our request for assistance withdrawn."

Molybdenum attempted to dissuade his father from stomping out, but to no avail.

Non é gran cousa se sabe, bon joyzo dar,
a Madre do que o mundo, tod' á de joigar.[72]

Schitz looked at the ruins of the old temple atop the settlement at Machu Picchu. Pizarro's men raped and looted their way through the settlement. At the approach to the temple, Anorexia and Autism stood over the bodies of two massacred Angels within the Celestial. Autism spoke first.

"These two seemed important. The others were protecting them."

He punctuated the sentence by nudging the nearest corpse with his toe. Schitz scrutinized the hacked bodies. Each corpse wore a large, Celestial sword. More ornate than practical, neither of the deceased had drawn their blade. Instead, one had fallen while holding two short swords and the other a mace.

"They were Lords of their Houses," Schitz said.

He reached, drew the ceremonial weapons, and held them over his head. A cheer rose from the Demonic horde.

Semellança fillou de Santiago, e disse:
Macar m' eu de ti despago, a salvaçon eu cha trago,
do que fust' errar, por que non cáias no lago,
d' iferno, sen dultar.[73]

The Spanish Conquest carried across the land. Neither mortal nor Angel could stop it.

---

[72] We should not wonder that Our Lady gives true judgments, as she is the mother of, He who will judge the world.

[73] He took the form of Santiago and said, "Though I am displeased with you, I bring you salvation for the sin you committed, to keep you from being surely case into the fiery lake of hell."

Non é gran cousa se sabe, bon joyzo dar, a Madre do que o mundo,
tod' á de joigar.[74]

LILLY PRESENTED THE RESULTS of the Familiars' latest scouting within the New World to an assembly of Angels, Priests, and Familiars.

"We are now certain that the Houses of Magnesium and Molybdenum have been killed off down to the man," she said, emotionless.

The High Priest spoke. "As the representative of the Lord God, I have come today to announce that our sovereign is most angered by the most recent turn of events and has abolished the regionalism that consigned two of his Angelic Houses to the slaughter."

Schitz's Notebook

Spanish Conquistador

Hernán Cortés

A man of egotism and greed, but a master strategist nevertheless. When technology, tactics, and organization are combined as they were during the Spanish Conquest, the only possible outcome is victory.

---

[74] We should not wonder that Our Lady gives true judgments, as she is the mother of, He who will judge the world.

Zinc looked about the room and felt a palpable sense of shame descend on those assembled. They all knew they had allowed their kin to be butchered to serve their own political interests.

"God hath decreed that a dyad of Supreme Commanders is to be appointed over all of the Angelic Houses. He calls upon Zinc and Uranium to accept the honor and responsibility of these offices."

A commotion of scandalized conversation erupted notably amongst the Asiatic Houses where Uranium was of the younger Standard Bearers. When Zinc looked across the room, it was obvious that Hydrogen now understood the deal he had struck in withholding aid for the mortal and Angelic Natives.

His gaze shifted to Rachael, awash in her trademark composure. Her hand was raised to Hydrogen's ear, blocking anyone from reading her lips. Zinc remembered when he had claim over her hands, and her lips, and all else.

He cursed to himself.

THE PENTAGRAM FIRST CLASS bore the same shape as the Second Class; only it was suspended from a black, white, and red ribbon. Awarded for heroism more meritorious than the Second Class and less than the Knight's Pentagram, the award still alluded many living members of Hell. The new First Class medal rested upon Schitz's robe above his Pentagram Second Class. He could feel the added weight, and it felt... right. The New World had been good to him in terms of decorations. He had a Second Class for killing Gold and a First Class for the Spanish Conquest.

"Congratulations, again," Autism said. He raised his chalice of Brew in Schitz's direction. Schitz swirled his own cup before raising his in reply. Anorexia sat between the two and raised her cup as well.

"Cheers, boys," she said with a smile.

The three imbibed with weary grins.

They looked at the Styx, still engorged with excess souls from the New World.

"I used to come here with our old comrade Conjunctivitis," Schitz said.

Autism patted him on the shoulder.

"It's hard to believe that we're the last three left from our cohort."

"Indeed," Schitz replied. "We die so fast."

"The New World campaign was a walk in the park compared to others," Anorexia said to lighten the mood.

"We still lost HPV, IBS, GERD, and Anemia," Autism said.

Schitz flinched.

"Poor Anemia," Anorexia said with a stolen glance toward Schitz. "And right after she birthed twins to Osteoarthritis."

Schitz broke an awkward silence. "To our heroic fallen," he said, raising his cup.

"Here, here," Autism said.

The chalices clinked, and Schitz reflected on his circumstances.

He had done well to choose loneliness over loss.

Still, he would miss Anemia.

So much for love, he thought.

He drained his cup into the Styx and dropped it on the ground.

L ieutenant Colonel Bradley dismounted his horse with the expertise of a veteran equestrian. A small cloud of dust rose from the
parched ground and smudged his shiny black boots and beige leg-
gings. He made his way to the command tent. Colonel Bradley had
scouts, but still preferred to make his own reconnaissance from time
to time. His officers were accustomed to the routine and abandoned
their own tasks when they saw their field commander striding into
the headquarters.

Schitz removed his riding cap and wiped his sweaty brow. An
attendant handed him a glass. Even watered down, the sherry was
a blessing of a refreshment. He caught his breath and addressed his
assembled officers.

"Major General Wolf plans to capture the city of Quebec," he
said pointing to the map, "a lofty goal complicated by geography,
defenses, and many French."

Someone said, "Yes, Colonel."

Schitz fired a nasty glance at the interruption, then continued,
"As you know, the main army is still on the Southern bank of the St.
Lawrence with the heavy gun batteries. Wolf wants to cross the St.
Lawrence as close as possible to Quebec and the Plains of Abraham,
PDQ. Our battalion has the honor of clearing the area south of the
plains to block reinforcements. I just returned from a scouting run.
The Plains of Abraham are behind us—the army's landing point is
in the opposite direction. But half a day's march away is a French
cohort; they outnumber us two-to-one.

Schitz paused and assessed his officers' response. Wolf had sent
him with one-third of his company but most of the officers, the
backbone of the British military. He had four majors and ten lieuten-
ants, more than enough disciplinarians to ensure that his battalion
would be fierce as lions.

Schitz checked for any sign of fear or doubt. He saw none.

"We will meet them here," he said and jabbed at a field bisected by the only two roads that led to Quebec.

"Lieutenant Barnwell!"

A devilishly handsome officer snapped to attention.

"Sir!"

"You will take twenty of your grenadiers and our contingent of savages to the small copse of trees in the middle of the field." Schitz pointed to the Iroquois allies standing in a cluster just beyond earshot. "Go tonight and conceal yourselves. When the French split their force to pass the trees, as they invariably will, you will open fire on either flank while the rest of us meet them head-on. They will collapse, and the natives will fall upon them in their distress."

Five years of fighting the French and their Indian confederates had taught every man in the tent the value of looking beyond the conventional strategy.

"Gentlemen, ready the men for tomorrow. Glory awaits."

The officers departed, and Schitz closed the tent flap. Pain pricked him behind the eyes, and tension knotted his forehead. There were Angels in the detachment, at least two dozen. Clearly, word had spread of the upcoming engagement in Quebec. For the mortals, it held the opportunity to change the course of the entire war. Schitz rubbed the side of his head and tried to breathe.

He thought, *There will be Angels in Quebec already, but if they need this many reinforcements, the Angelic contingent must be frightfully undermanned. The battalion of mortals numbered six hundred and was a mere smidgeon of the four and a half thousand French troops already entrenched in Quebec.*

It did not take long for Schitz to figure out the Angels' goal. They were not rushing to reinforce Quebec; they were maneuvering to crush the British on the Plains of Abraham. They intended to swoop in from the rear when the French responded and annihilate Wolf's army and the Demons their reconnaissance had told them would be there. Schitz realized his primary problem was his greatest strength.

Even before the epiphany had fully dawned upon him, he knew he would use the copse of trees, but only when he realized his advantage, did he become giddy with anticipation. He had survived long enough to know that if he had seen the Angels, they had seen him. They knew his detachment consisted of three Demons and three hundred mortals. Textbook strategy dictated the three Demons would either attack the Angels' flanks for a hit and run, or simply withdraw in the face of overwhelming odds. The Angels would not expect the Demons to seek out a decisive engagement. The Heavenly forces would press on undeterred by the Demons, confident and focused on the primary encounter with Wolf's main force. To them, Schitz's battalion represented a minor skirmish en route to the main action, a mentality sure to be their undoing. His plan was superb, but he needed more men.

Schitz embedded his strategy into the mind of the lieutenant colonel. Everything would go as expected. The mortal would not deviate. Schitz traced the ancient symbols in the earth at the base of the tent's entrance, sprinkled gun powder from his horn until the symbols were covered. Removing the flint from his pistol, he quickly strode over to a spare musket and removed the black flint piece from the Brown Bess. With efficiency born of practice, he flicked the two flints together. The resulting spark ignited the symbols—earth and fire—and opened the gateway while obliterating the symbol. Schitz stepped out of the lt. colonel and exited.

Earth & Fire

ZINC SAT QUIETLY AMONG the French Battalion encamped below the Plains of Abraham. He could not sleep like the others sprawled out in the various tents. He had seen the Demons standing between them and the main body of Wolf's force. Iron III had assured him they were the rear guard sent to harry and hassle their advance. They would either disperse or conduct a singular attack before being rebuffed or eliminated. However, Zinc had an all too familiar sense of foreboding; no plan is ever perfect, and no foe should ever be discounted. He desperately longed for his new appointment as commander of the Angels to begin with a rousing success. Zinc enjoyed the clearness of thought that sleep gave him when possessing a mortal. However, that night sleep proved to be a more than worthy adversary for him and his host.

SCHITZ STEPPED INTO THE Great Hall and strode to the altar as the chorus of Wraiths began to sing. He kneeled and swiftly formed the sign of the pentagram by moving his right hand from his forehead to the right side of his chest, then to his left shoulder, then his right shoulder, then down to the left side of his chest, and finally back to his forehead. Schitz snatched the chalice of holy wine from the flabbergasted Priest, took the final dreg, and rose to his feet. Before he could hear repudiation, Schitz was already jogging to the doorway that concealed the mysteries beyond the knowledge of a foot soldier.

Schitz banged on the heavy wooden door and was surprised when it was answered by the Devil himself. Amused, Schitz thought, *How does that saying go? 'Knock on the Devil's door enough times and one day he will answer?'* He saluted crisply, then said, "Hail Lord Satan."

"What is it now, Schitz?" the Devil asked. His exasperation was evident.

"I need three men," Schitz said while looking the Lord in the eye.

"Have you gotten your new recruits killed already?" the Devil asked.

"No," Schitz replied. "I have an opportunity to deliver to you two dozen Angels."

The Devil sighed and rolled his eyes. "Exaggeration does not suit you, nor does ambition, but if you must, I can assign another three-Demon squad to work with you."

Schitz felt his blood boil. "No," he replied. "I do not need assistance; I need three more subordinates."

"So, you want a promotion then, is it?" Satan was in a huffy mood. "I'm growing weary of you, which says a lot, considering where we stood at the outset of this conversation. Despite your previous success in the Americas, you are not a member of the Triumvirate and really should be taking up this matter with them."

Schitz composed himself. He heard the clock, its ticking pressing on him like a heavy hand.

"I don't have time to locate the Council members. This opportunity is fleeting and will soon pass. Give me three men and approve our mission. I will give you a victory."

"Fine, fine, fine," the Devil said, waving his hand. "Go collect three that are significantly your junior and be sure you return them to the service of the Triumvirate unharmed, or you will be called upon to answer for your decision making."

Schitz saluted and backed away. By the time he pivoted, the Devil had already closed the door.

Rushing back to the Great Hall, Schitz looked over the available recruits. He was not presented with the luxury of a great selection. He was satisfied to encounter two squads, one led by his academy colleague Cancer with her close friend Meningitis and faculty member Sepsis, the other led by Cancer's great-granddaughter, Brain Cancer, accompanied by the neophytes ALS and Hantavirus. Schitz outranked them all. However, Cancer, Meningitis, and Sepsis were all senior fighters and would likely pose issues with abandoning their own missions.

The explosion of military activity surrounding colonialism had stretched the forces of Hell rather thin. The Triumvirate was conservative about troop allocation and concerned about casualties. Despite his growing reputation, Schitz doubted that he could convince two academy instructors to abandon whatever responsibility they had.

Conversely, ALS and Hantavirus were neophytes, and their leader was barely bloodied herself. Brain Cancer had been in the youngest cohort during Schitz's initial Harquebus instruction had seen limited action in the Conquistador Campaign. Schitz had a gut suspicion that the younger trio had been thrown together for a low-priority mission.

"I have a need of great importance and require three soldiers," Schitz said.

Cancer's reply was clipped. "Who doesn't have an important task?"

"Fair enough," Schitz said, "but this is dire, and I am your superior."

Even as the words left his mouth, Schitz knew he was taking the wrong approach.

Cancer rolled her eyes and huffed. "As I was saying, I haven't seen any Angels in Benin for some time now, but still keep your wits about yourself."

Schitz turned to the younger squad members. "Where are you headed?"

"Africa, sir," Brain Cancer said. "These two are still trainees."

A smile spread across Schitz's face. "You know you make me feel so old. I was a trainee long, long, long before your grandfather was born."

The tension eased a bit. Schitz poured on the charm.

"Okay, here it is. The trainees should be more than happy to take part in this mission; it's guaranteed to produce a handful of dead Angels and should move them right along toward their final vetting."

"Hold on," Cancer said. "Brain Cancer might take your orders because she's young, but I'll not have you taking my kin on some crazy fishing expedition."

Schitz sighed with mock exasperation. "Then how about this: you enjoy Africa with Hantavirus; he's still in the Academy. Let Meningitis, Sepsis, and ALS go with me to the New World."

Cancer laughed. "That's what I like about you, Schitzy, ever the deal maker. We were just on our way back anyway, so I'm sure these two will be more than excited to get right back out there."

Schitz glanced over at Meningitis. "Oh, yes, sir," she said, heavy with sarcasm.

The newly formed sets of three headed to two of the many door-ways that lined the Great Hall.

Schitz turned to Sepsis. "Where have you been?"

"China."

"Do they still eat rats?" Schitz asked.

"You are such a jerk sometimes," Sepsis said.

As the two squads went their separate ways, Cancer called over her shoulder. "Good thing Plague isn't around to hear you joking about eating rats."

MORNING WAS BREAKING OVER the fields of southern Canada on a warm September by the time Schitz had readied his squad of Demons. He was satisfied; he already had loyal veterans in Autism and Pneumonia. Now with the addition of battle-hardened Meningitis and Sepsis, he felt secure in his plans. Even the neophyte ALS was set to be the valedictorian of the current class. Having been briefed, His Majesty's troops, some occupied by His Lordship's Demons, prepared for battle.

Fifes peeped out *The British Grenadiers* and the battalion took to the field, rows of vibrant crimson and shimmering brass moving forward in one concentrated formation. They churned forward to the tattoo of the drums. Schitz had seen the Greek Phalanx, and the Roman Tortoise, and countless other formations, but as he marched at the head of the Redcoats, he was impressed at the discipline and moved by the pageantry of it all.

Schitz heard the words of the march echoing in his head.

> *Some talk of Alexander, and some of Hercules,*
> *of Hector and Lysander, and such great names as these:*
> *But of all the world's great heroes, there's none that can compare,*
> *with a tow, row, row, row, row, row, to the British Grenadiers.*

The blue uniformed French approached in an opposing formation. They were also a marvel of cohesion and discipline—all ranks moved in unison. The enemies drew closer with every precise step.

Schitz was pleased to see the silhouettes of a squad of Angels to the left and right center—six each, as he predicted.

The Conquistador Campaign had been a strategic masterpiece for which he had received only partial credit. This moment would solidify his reputation as a tactical genius.

When the faces of the French were clear—Schitz could see pimples on the faces of the novices—he experienced an orgasmic sense of accomplishment. The French front line reached the edge of the copse where the grenadiers and Iroquois had concealed themselves.

Schitz hummed in his head.

> When e'er we are commanded to storm the palisades,
> Our leaders match with fuses and we with hand grenades,
> We hurl them from the glances about our enemies' ears sing,
> tow row row row for the British Grenadiers.

He signaled the Demons next to him. They began moving in opposite directions across the front line, a tactic devised to prevent the static Angels from zoning in on them. Schitz smirked. "It's like a training exercise."

Each side halted. The officers shouted, "Make ready!" Schitz and his group of five bounded into the Celestial. Bursting forth between the lines with the marching tune in his head, Schitz saw his comrades rushing forward with vigor equal to his own. Their fleet steps closed the divide between the two armies and the doomed, mortal and Angel alike. Both sides heard the command, "Present," when a crashing volley of withering musket fire exploded from the trees.

With ruthless efficiency, Schitz dropped the Brown Bess he'd fired and raised the next readied musket. Each grenadier in the trees had two muskets apiece. The second fusillade from the trees formed a cacophonous duet with the initial first exchanges from the main forces. Once again, Schitz and his comrades (two on either side) rushed forward in the Celestial. Musket balls whizzed past. Schitz reached the front rank. To his delight, he saw six seizing Angels. His hungry sword opened the throat of the first one while Autism and ALS continued past to their own quarry. In short work, each of them had ended two Angels in a brutally efficient fashion.

Schitz howled with bloodlust and took a moment to sink his teeth into the open wound of his fallen enemy. Autism and ALS grinned and followed suit. Brandishing tomahawks, knives, and clubs, the whooping Iroquois fell on the French lines, which were already collapsing. British officers yelled "fire" once more, unconcerned for their Indian allies downrange. Schitz took the momentary reprieve following the volley to jump into the body of an Iroquois brave as he hacked his way through the French. The other Demons followed the pre-determined plan and assumed the bodies of other Indians.

The remaining, isolated Angels stood frozen in terror. The Demonic trio reached the first Angel, still within a French soldier. He parried ALS's tomahawk swipe with his musket, but Schitz and Autism stabbed him simultane-ously in the midsection. The Angel fell to the ground in a fit. Schitz and Autism stepped into the Celestial and hacked him to pieces.

Iroquois Tomahawk

Schitz jumped into a fresh Iroquois and led his men toward the next Angel. The frightened prey jumped from one French to another but could not get far enough away to avoid Schitz's tomahawk. It buried itself in the back of his skull.

ALS threw her hands in the air. "Nice throw!"

Schitz flayed the neck of the seizing Angel. The four remaining Angels clustered together. Schitz had seen the same reaction many a time—Heavenly fighters in an untenable situation who were too scared to step out of their mortals to confront a Demon in the Celestial. Another wilting round of musket fire tore through the French and Iroquois alike. Everything according to plan.

The clustered Angels were all hit. Autism's Iroquois took a musket ball just under his left eye.

"Stay with him," Schitz said. "Do not leave him exposed under any circumstance."

Schitz was a whirlwind of mayhem. He brutalized the four writhing Angels. He tore at their throats and their stomachs, careful not to let his blade lodge in their rib cages. Ecstasy overcame him and he experienced the unusual, a forceful seizure brought on by the delight in the battle. Schitz regained his composure and pulled Autism to his feet.

"You are running up the score today," Autism said.

"Glad you're still with us," Schitz said.

"Glad to be here!"

ALS looked back and forth between the two in awe.

The French broke into a scattered free-for-all of retreat. Schitz saw a solitary Angel flesh-hopping in bewildered terror. Meningitis, Pneumonia, and Sepsis were in hot pursuit.

Drunk with the victory he had so perfectly engineered, Schitz said, "Come, let's cut him off."

Schitz led his trio in a ferocious run. There were no available Iroquois vessels between them and the fleeing Angel, so the Demons opted to pursue at full tilt within their current mortals. Schitz marveled at the pace his nearly naked savage could produce; he was a fine specimen of mortality, sinew, and strength. As Schitz closed the distance to his prey, his eyes cut from left to right. At last, he saw what he was looking for, a loaded, discarded musket dropped by a retreating Frenchman. Schitz scooped it up without breaking stride. Autism and ALS followed his lead and collected their muskets as well.

British Land Pattern Musket
a.k.a Brown Bess

The Angel ran with the terror of self-preservation. Schitz raised his left hand, pointing vigorously in the direction of Meningitis, Pneumonia, and Sepsis and then held up three fingers. Schitz made the motion of snapping a stick with both of his hands.

From within her host, Meningitis unleashed a terrifying scream, "Karònya!"—the Mohawk word for Celestial. Schitz watched as the leading Demons jumped from their human vessels and continued the pursuit in the Celestial. Schitz grinned. If the Angel jumped into the Celestial, he would be overwhelmed there. Meanwhile, it was only a matter of time before his group caught the mortal Frenchman.

A jarring explosion sounded overhead. A transient thunderstorm swept across the open field. Within moments, everything was soaked.

The fleeing Angel's pace was impressive. Schitz's lungs pleaded for air, his legs protested each step. Just as the Angel reached the tree line, Schitz dropped to one knee and aimed. The smooth bore weapon was an inherently inaccurate instrument of war for a mortal. Schitz never missed.

He drew his bead and pulled the trigger. The hammer slapped the pan with a dissatisfying clank. Only ALS's musket discharged, and the younger Demon's skill was insufficient to score a hit. Pine bark exploded a few inches to the right of the Angel, who ducked and disappeared into the trees.

Schitz gave the order to halt, and his five warriors converged upon him.

"Damn, that fucker was fast," Meningitis said.

Schitz gasped for air.

"I almost got him," ALS said.

"You still got a couple of kills, well done," Autism said.

ALS blinked with a startling reality. "My first," she said.

Schitz thought back to his old classmate, Vertigo, then quickly banished the memory. "More importantly," he said, he tapped Autism on the back, "you protected this inept fool when he managed to get himself shot."

Autism's protests were drowned by laughter from the others.

The French had fled the field. The British had reformed and were marching in the direction of the Fields of Abraham and Quebec.

Schitz whooped the Iroquois' war cry, and the others joined in as they ran back. Moments later, Schitz led the others out of the Indians and into the Celestial to join with their colleagues already freed of human form. They reached the copse of trees.

"Take the heads," Schitz said. "No one will believe we killed this many. And let's send the Familiars that come looking for their dead a message."

"What message is that?" Sepsis asked as she began sawing at the neck of a fallen Angel.

"That nobody should fuck with us," Meningitis said.

Schitz grinned. "Precisely."

The receding sea of crimson started up the song, *Lilliburlero*, a jaunty marching tune, perfect for those who had just survived an engagement and were walking off to yet another. The Demons had rewritten the words. The fifes, bugles, and drums accompanied Schitz's booming voice while he sawed away at an Angel's neck.

Brother, did you happen to hear them say,
The news that's come from the front today,
You'll want to hear it,
It'll lift your spirit,
There're no Angels left; our boys cleared the way.

Meningitis joined in, grunting under her exertions.

Sorrow, Sorrow, Sorrow for Angels,
Lucifer's Soldiers, this is our job,
When bugles are calling, and armies are brawling,
Sorrow for Angels, that is our job.

Heaving as he ripped the final stringy bits holding a fallen foe's head to a set of dead shoulders, Pneumonia sang along with the others.

Sorrow, Sorrow, Sorrow for Angels,
Lucifer's Soldiers, this is our job,

> When bugles are calling, and armies are brawling,
> Sorrow for Angels, that is our job.

The sun beat down. The brief storm had left the air heavy and humid. Still, he sang.

> Hopeless and lost, for mercy they pray,
> As we march on taking the field and the day,
> Volleys like showers,
> Fall through the hours,
> As they look on their broken ranks in dismay.

Even the typically reserved Sepsis belted out the refrain with glee and fire burning in her eyes.

> Sorrow, Sorrow, Sorrow for Angels,
> Lucifer's Soldiers, this is our job.
> When cannons are crashing, and muskets are flashing,
> Sorrow for Angels, that is our job.

Schitz patted ALS on the back as she worked at hacking another lifeless head free. The Celestial weapons were better for piercing than outright butchery, but the hatred of Angels and the still unfulfilled bloodlust led the Demons onward as they sang in a grizzly chorus of unity.

> Sorrow, Sorrow, Sorrow for Angels,
> Lucifer's Soldiers, this is our job.
> When cannons are crashing, and muskets are flashing,
> Sorrow for Angels, that is our job.

Schitz walked from headless corpse to headless corpse, his expert eyes darting from one detail to the next. He noticed a Heavenly dagger, an inlaid relic from the now bereft House of Gold, a souvenir. He continued the song with renewed zeal.

Though they send countless numbers our way,
We scatter them all in complete disarray,
Slaying all we see,
To the Lord's decree,
For every step they take, dearly they pay.

Having picked the field bare, each carried two Angelic heads per hand, save ALS, who carried only three in total. They strode toward the trees.

Sorrow, Sorrow, Sorrow for Angels,
Lucifer's Soldiers, this is our job,
When sabers are clattering, and grapeshot is scattering,
Sorrow for Angels, that is our job.

Their faces beamed as they repeated the refrain.

Sorrow, Sorrow, Sorrow for Angels,
Lucifer's Soldiers, this is our job,
When sabers are clattering, and grapeshot is scattering,
Sorrow for Angels, that is our job.

Autism knelt in the dirt and began tracing the symbols for a gateway at the base of two trees.

Forward we march in forceful display,
Of just how at home we are in the fray,
And if the foe doesn't know it,
We're quick to show it,
For our just cause we never betray.

Schitz watched as Meningitis struck two pieces of flint together. The dancing sparks jumped in unison with the tune.

Sorrow, Sorrow, Sorrow for Angels,
Lucifer's Soldiers, this is our job,

> *When shells are exploding, and we're quick reloading,*
> *Sorrow for Angels, that is our job.*

At last, the powder ignited, and the gateway opened. The jubilant squad sang in triumph.

> *Sorrow, Sorrow, Sorrow for Angels,*
> *Lucifer's Soldiers, this is our job,*
> *When shells are exploding, and we're quick reloading,*
> *Sorrow for Angels, that is our job.*

"Ladies and Gentlemen, it has been an honor to fight with you on this day," Schitz said before they stepped through the portal.

> *Swiftly our forces know no delay,*
> *When called upon to the melee,*
> *Ready by day and night,*
> *Itching to fight,*
> *Our courage stands fast, never does it stray.*

"Now, as one, let us return bathed in glory!" They stepped through the portal together—comrades joined in song and connected by blood.

> *Sorrow, Sorrow, Sorrow for Angels,*
> *Lucifer's Soldiers, this is our job,*
> *No matter how much we've battled, we've never been rattled,*
> *Sorrow for Angels, that is our job.*

The Priests, ever attentive at the altar, and many a passerby in the Great Hall, were astounded as Schitz led the jubilant Demons through the portal. They waved the severed heads like pennants and finished their song.

> *Sorrow, Sorrow, Sorrow for Angels,*
> *Lucifer's Soldiers, this is our job,*

No matter how much we've battled, we've never been rattled,
Sorrow for Angels, that is our job.

THOUGH THE DRUMS AND brass bands melody had faded from Schitz's mind, an even louder symphony of gossip had begun stemming from his massive victory and unorthodox return to Hell. The myth was maximally enhanced by the Devil's purported reluctance to provide Schitz with his request for additional troops. Hell was a bustle with news of six Demons slaying twenty-three Angels.

Schitz sat in his chamber awaiting the assembly that had been called for all the forces of Hell. He looked at the dagger from the House of Gold.

"Funny," he said aloud, "we still run into each other."

Thoughts of the past invariably brought back his painful longing for Anna. He could see her in his mind, festooned with golden swords and daggers.

A knock at the door interrupted Schitz's nostalgia.

He composed himself. "Come!"

Elise struggled with the weight. Schitz rushed to assist his Wraith. Each time he saw her, she looked slightly older, a grim reminder that though immortal unless killed, Wraiths aged. She resembled a woman in her early eighties.

"It's time," she said.

Schitz took Elise's one remaining hand and walked with her toward the Great Hall.

"You shouldn't be so rash with the Lord," she said.

Schitz released a bashful grin.

"I know," he replied. "It's just, so often I feel that I have to do what I do for the cause despite him. It seems the Angels are one hindrance and he another."

"You two have had your share of butting heads," she replied, "but no matter how fierce you are, we are all expendable to him. Remember that."

"Relax, Mama," he said. "I think my brasher days are behind me."

"Well, I don't believe you," she sighed, "but it's still nice to hear. Regardless, I believe you will be pleased today."

"Pleased at a funeral?"

"Who said it was a funeral?"

"Well, nobody is getting married, so I had deduced..."

Beyond the main altar in the Great Hall stood a tall black statue of a British Grenadier in full regalia, bayoneting a prone Frenchman. Schitz suppressed a laugh as he gazed upon the outstretched wings breaking from the back of the Grenadier and wilting to the floor.

"Even in our own art, we find the need to add wings," he said.

Elise had faded to the perimeter of the Great Hall with the other Wraiths. He marched to the front of his class and took his place beside Autism.

"Glad you're still with us," Autism said.

"Glad to be here."

Schitz felt immensely proud as he took a second glance at the statue. There were statues all over Hell, but to have one placed in the Great Hall was quite an honor. Schitz wiggled his fingers to keep from fidgeting, but Autism noticed.

"Hold still! This is a solemn occasion!"

The Devil entered, followed by a procession of Priests and Priestesses. Titus swung a thurible. Thick, sweet smoke filled the hall. Six Priests carried ornate silver platters bearing the heads of the fallen Angels.

The solemn file of holy men reached the base of the statue. A section of the stone floor had been removed. In a rather unceremonious fashion, the Priests dumped the heads into the crypt at the base of the statue. With no bacterium in Hell, the heads would remain there forever in the same state.

I wonder if the Angels have already held their funeral mass, Schitz thought.

Every Demon snapped to attention when the Devil stepped to the front. His rasp filled the cavernous room. "Amyotrophic Lateral Sclerosis."

Schitz watched ALS approach the Devil and salute.

"With exemplary conduct far exceeding the expectations of a trainee, Amyotrophic Lateral Sclerosis eliminated two Angels and protected an immobilized superior."

Schitz discretely elbowed Autism.

"That's you, gimp."

"Shut up."

"For her invaluable contribution to this historic mission, Amyotrophic Lateral Sclerosis is hereby presented with the Pentagram Second Class."

He pinned the medal on ALS. She saluted and returned to the ranks. "Sepsis Status Malus!"

Her first medal, too, Schitz thought.

"With exemplary conduct and worthy heroism, Sepsis Status Malus eliminated three Angels on the field of valor. For her invaluable contribution to this historic mission Sepsis Status Malus is hereby presented with the Pentagram Second Class."

Pin... salute... return.

"Meningitis Insidiosa," said the Devil. "For exemplary conduct far exceeding her years of experience, Meningitis Insidiosa successfully led her companions into battle and eliminated three Angels. In her leadership and tenacity, Meningitis is a credit to her family and her cohort and is hereby presented with the Pentagram Second Class and the Campaign Star."

The Devil spoke as he pinned the medal on the dress uniform. "Meningitis Insidiosa is a shining example to all of what is possible through dedication, loyalty, and courage."

"Pneumonia Frigus!"

Schitz was pleased with his son-in-law.

"With exemplary conduct and worthy heroism, Pneumonia Frigus eliminated five Angels on the field of honor. For this astounding display of tenacity and resolve in striking fear into the heart of the foe and contributing an invaluable effort to this historic mission, Pneumonia Frigus is hereby presented with the Pentagram Second Class."

"Autism Retardabitur Motus!"

Schitz grimaced slightly. "Well, I'm one better, or I've been overlooked altogether."

"With skillful acumen and exemplary valor, Autism Retardabitur Motus eliminated three Angels and provided invaluable aid to this historic mission. For this exemplary and admirable display of resolve and courage, Autism Retardabitur Motus is hereby presented with the Pentagram First Class."

Autism was smiling on his way back to the troops.

"Don't get a big head," Schitz said, "you'll always be a second-class kind of guy to me."

Autism choked while trying, unsuccessfully, to stifle a laugh.

Surely, I will not be passed over. I should get a Campaign Star at the very least. "Schizophrenia Incenderos Nervosa!"

Schitz marched forward and saluted the being for whom he had such strong antipathy.

"With heroic skill, innovative thinking, supreme leadership, and courageous initiative, Schizophrenia Incenderos Nervosa led a historic mission that resulted in the annihilation of twenty-three Angels, six of whom were eliminated directly by Schizophrenia Incenderos Nervosa. Not only did Schizophrenia Incenderos Nervosa vanquish the foe from the field of honor, but he did so while ensuring that no losses were incurred on his side. For this exemplary action, Sir Schizophrenia Incenderos Nervosa is hereby awarded the Knight's Pentagram."

Schitz felt as though he had been struck by a hammer. He had only known a handful of the old Demons—Hayfever, Tetanus, Tuberculosis, Diphtheria, Bubonic Plague, Fever and a minority of others—who had this honor. The conference of knighthood was a virtual relic. The honoree received the title "Sir" and was elevated to legendary status.

Schitz drank in the moment. The High Priest handed Satan the award, and the Devil tied the ribbon around Schitz's neck.

When he returned to the line, he whispered to Autism, "Did I salute?"

"You are still alive, aren't you?"

The High Priest chanted. "We give thanks to you, our Lord, for bestowing upon us the courage that we may rightly serve you in our lives and, if need be, in our deaths."

When he finished, everyone saluted. The Devil exited, and the assembled broke into the anthem of Hell, *The Hunter's Song.*

Along with pride, Schitz felt an unquenchable longing for Rubella... or Anna... or Lady Calcium... somebody with whom to share such a special moment. At the conclusion of the anthem, the assembly ended.

Schitz was enveloped by the surviving members of his class and many others.

Autism patted him on the back. "Well done, sir. If I dare say so myself, sir, ah yes sir, indeed sir."

"All right, I get it, peasant," Schitz said.

Cancer shook his hand.

"Bet you wish you'd came with us now," Schitz said.

Cancer shrugged. "It wasn't for me, congratulations nevertheless."

Schitz caught a glance of Spanish Influenza who, though visibly perturbed, executed a brief bow. Schitz knew Spanish Influenza to be motivated by recognition; though the holder of both a First and Second Class, Spanish would not be enjoying himself on a day in which the exploits of others were so heavily lauded.

Schitz fancied himself as a fighter, not hung up on rank or decorations. Most Demons, except for the current crop of trainees, knew him as someone who spoke frankly and was not bothered with protocol or etiquette. However, it was surprisingly pleasant to be recognized. Amidst the hubbub of socializing, Schitz decided to take his leave and strolled back towards his room.

Elise materialized.

"You still always get me," he said.

"I wouldn't be very good at what I do if you saw me coming, now would I," she replied. She locked her arm in his. "Are you pleased?"

"I am," Schitz said. "Satisfied that my fighters and I were recognized for what we accomplished."

"I am very proud of you," she said. "I know that your parents and Rubella would be proud as well."

Schitz bobbed his head but could not speak.

Titus was gasping for breath when he caught up to the pair.

"My boy, my boy," he said.

"How can I help you, Your Holiness," said Schitz.

"This is truly a global war, my boy, from the battlefields of Europa to the New World, North and South America, to India and Africa, the entire world battles."

"The entire world has always battled, High Priest. It is no different. The armies of a handful of nations fight across the continents; we hunt the Angels, and they hunt us, like always."

"It is different," the Priest said. "The weapons, the cohesiveness, the time has come for the final victory, your triumph and the victory on the Plains of Abraham proves that the time has come for us to wipe out the Angels, down to the last man. Then, as the British and their allies march over the Earth in its entirety, we will walk behind them drawing the everlasting shadow over the realm of man, once and for all."

"That has always been the plan," Schitz said. "I certainly hope you are correct and that we live to see it."

"The Triumvirate Council needs you," Titus said.

"I serve the orders of the Counsel," Schitz replied. His disinterest increased with every response. "They tell me to go to Africa, and I kill Angels in Africa; they tell me to go to India, and I kill Angels in India. They send me to Canada… that's how it is. I think the Council benefits from my efforts very much."

"Yes, yes, of course, of course, my dear boy, but when there is an open seat at the table, it calls for your warrior wisdom," Titus said.

Schitz hated the Triumvirate Council mainly because the Priests had the final say on all matters as the Devil's proxy.

"I think my time is better spent fighting. I will leave the broader strategy to the most learned of minds, each to his own role."

"You are very kind with your words, my boy," the Priest said. "Should you ever change your mind, your words of wisdom would be highly weighted."

Schitz declined his head in respect.

Titus addressed Elise. "Madam, a word if you would."

She looked at Schitz. "Duty calls."

"Of course," he said.

Elise touched Schitz on the arm and departed in the company of the High Priest.

Schitz meandered on the way. The alleged new and final global war could wait for a little while. Schitz relished the rare opportunity to be out of a mortal body and to have some time to himself.

Maybe I'll write in my notebook, he thought.

Schitz saw two figures standing by the door of his quarters. He rested his hand on his sword until he recognized the youthful physique of Bornholm Disease, a member of the newest class. Schitz found it hard to remember his own adolescence. He recalled it as he looked upon Bornholm's maturing body. She leaned against his door, her youthful round face half-covered by long blonde hair.

Schitz did not recognize her companion, who wore her red hair in a bobbed cut that Schitz found to be boyish, and yet alluringly attractive. The unknown Demon was sitting on the ground, her arm wrapped around Bornholm's calf, her hand gently resting on her compatriot's thigh just above the apex in the split of her black robe.

"Can I help you, ladies?" Schitz asked.

"Well, finally, you are here," Bornholm said. "We've been waiting forever."

Schitz was not certain how to respond and instead turned his attention to the other Demon.

"Schizophrenia," he said, "and I'm sorry, but I don't think we've met."

"Paratyphoid Fever," the stranger replied in a hushed, smooth voice. "It's a pleasure to make your acquaintance, Sir Schizophrenia."

He smiled, feeling slightly more at ease. "Call me Schitz. The sir thing is just more of a formality."

He fidgeted with the Knight's Pentagram around his neck.

Paratyphoid smiled the way a schoolgirl keeping a secret often does. She stood, dragging her body along Bornholm's and whispering in her ear. Bornholm brushed her long blonde hair away from her face and glanced down at the ground, biting her lower lip. Schitz could not make out the words but felt a growing sense of awkwardness at being left out of the conversation.

"She wants to tell you something," Bornholm said.

Something about that look, Schitz thought.

Perspiration dripped at the nape of his neck. The decoration at his throat got heavier.

"Well?"

He was slightly ashamed of his visceral reaction to the young women.

These women are junior to Anemia. I must control my thoughts. They are here on some foolish errand.

Paratyphoid glanced at Schitz and returned to whispering into Bornholm's ear. This time, Bornholm held Schitz's gaze.

"She doesn't want to tell you here."

Irritation pricked at Schitz's brain. These neophytes were tampering with his solitude. Now he was sure he would open his door to find a drunken group of rabble-rousers who mistakenly thought he would enjoy a surprise party of some sort.

To his relief, his room was empty.

Schitz turned to his guest. "Forgive the clutter. I seldom entertain," he said. "You may sit on the bed if you would like."

"No," Bornholm said. "You've had a big day. You sit; we have to be going once she says what she has to say."

Schitz slumped onto the bed.

"Well?"

More whispering. More floor gazing. More bitten lips.

"She has decided not to tell you," Bornholm said. "She is going... to show you."

Bored of the pseudo-drama, Schitz had been casting his gaze around the room. When he looked again at the redhead, intent on scolding her for wasting his time, he flushed with arousal.

Paratyphoid raised her robe over her head and dropped it to the floor. Schitz's eyes tracked up her thin, muscular legs. He drank in her toned stomach and perky breasts.

Not to be undone, Bornholm slipped out of her robe. Schitz noticed a tattoo—a serpent that started behind her right ear and ran down her neck and over her demure collar bone. The scales of the snake passed under her heavy breasts before disappearing behind her left hip and her immaculately bare womanhood.

Schitz caressed one of Bornholm's generous breasts. She ran one hand across his chest, while grasping at his manhood with the other.

"I've never been touched by a man, Demon or mortal, before today, only her," Bornholm whispered into Schitz's ear.

Schitz glanced at Paratyphoid. She knelt in front of him. Her mouth parted; her tongue slowly moved across her lips. Her hands slid up between his thighs and opened his robe. Bornholm reacquired her grip and began moving her hand with increasing speed.

Paratyphoid paused and looked at Schitz with deep, pleading eyes. She whispered, "Can I show you what I want to do?"

Schitz closed his eyes and thought, *Forgive me, Rubella,* before diving into the carnal festival.

Hours later, Schitz lay entwined among the limbs of the sleeping Bornholm and Paratyphoid. The neophytes had yet to outgrow their need for sleep. He apprised their young, lithe bodies and smiled at the aroma of female pleasure arising from the dampness of the bed.

It was a good day, a good day, indeed.

THE TRIUMVIRATE COUNCIL ISSUED marching orders. The drums thumped, the bugles blared. The push was on to fight the Angels on every corner of the globe. The British and French sought to cut each other to pieces, high and low, near and far. So did the Demons and Angels. Into the instruments' crescendo came Hell's newest knight. Schitz heard the fifes, drums, and pipes, and readied for battle.

A melancholy tune, *Over the Hills and Far Away,* played over and over in his mind. Schitz readied himself for another sortie with Autism and Anorexia. He glanced up to the gallery of the Great Hall, and caught the solemn glance of his Lord, the Devil. Schitz saluted. Satan returned the gesture.

Our 'prentice Tom may now refuse,
to wipe his scoundrel Master's Shoes.

The sun battered the fields of the Gambian countryside of West Africa. Schitz marched in line with his fellow Redcoats as the fifes and drums played.

For now, he's free to sing and play, Over the Hills and far away.

Schitz buried his short sword into the throat of a writhing Angel as the French ranks broke in yet another collapse of their line in Pondicherry. Schitz looked up from the body of his fallen foe and jumped into a charging Redcoat. The tropical heat enveloped him as much in the Celestial as it did when possessing a mortal.

A lieutenant with a heavy Geordie accent encouraged his men as they rushed into the ancient Indian city. "Onward!"

Over the Hills and O'er the Main, To Flanders, Portugal, and Spain.

Cannon shells whooshed past—sea spray hung in the air. Another French ship sank beneath the waves off the coast of Gibraltar. Schitz kept a keen eye out for Angels on any of the beleaguered French vessels.

King George commands, and we'll obey, Over the Hills and far away.

Schitz took cover from musket fire behind a sturdy pine tree. He raised his own musket and shot an on-rushing native nearly point-blank. He hated fighting the Indians and French in the woods. Schitz swore and began reloading his musket. Soldiers of the king fell around him to arrows and musket balls alike.

Courage, boys, 'tis one to ten, but we return all gentlemen.

Schitz walked through the camp. The evening sun's dying rays matched his uniform. He patted the shoulders of war-weary comrades. They wrote home, played cards, or lay on the grass and celebrated another day without dying.

"You did well today, lads," he said.

All gentlemen as well as they.

Schitz swung his bayonet at an Angel who was defending the cannon from onrushing infantry. This was the last living Frenchman. Without warning, he dropped the ramrod he was using to defend himself and raised his arms in the air. He was too panic-stricken to continue fighting, and too anxious to flesh-hop. Schitz heard the old song echo in his head.

All gentlemen as they.

Schitz stopped another redcoat from running the Frenchman through and gestured with a flick of his head for the prisoner to be led off. The Angel met his gaze but remained in the mortal's body and marched away into captivity. Schitz felt a rare twinge of respect.

Over the hills and far away.

He marched to the drum along yet another dusty road, every bit as bedraggled as the humans beside him.

Over the Hills and O'er the Main, To Flanders, Portugal,
and Spain. King George commands, and we'll obey.

The wooden troop boat rocked gently in the waters off the South American coast. Schitz took in his fellow redcoats, soldiers in the service of the East India Company. He looked past them to the mighty decks of the HMS Kingston, renamed the Lord Chive, and then over to the defenses of Montevideo.

Over the Hills and far away.

Schitz stood passively in the Great Hall at the funeral mass commemorating the young redhead who lay still as stone on the altar. He remembered pressing against her in the heat of passion.

When I finally fall to rise, never more.

Schitz fought back tears at Paratyphoid Fever's internment.

As did our comrades who came before.

It felt like he'd met her only days before.

On that day, the fifes and drums will play.

Schitz trudged onward to the endless roll of the damnable drums and perfidious fifes, lock-stepped with his fellow humans and Demons as they stumbled ever forward toward the ranks of the foe.

Over the Hills and Far away.

CHAPTER 16

FIRE AWAY

The Royal Opera at The Covent Garden was an impeccable display of man's architectural and artistic achievements. The structure sported elaborate candelabras for illumination. Luxurious viewing boxes rose from the orchestra floor to the ceiling on the three sides of the stage. The walls and the performing areas were adorned with golden depictions of Angels, clouds, and other Heavenly scenes. It was, in a word, astounding—a jewel among London's many other prized structures.

Zinc did not particularly enjoy the opera. He failed to grasp the point of the frivolity, the excessive amount of time mortals spent perfecting the ability to master a musical instrument, mechanical or vocal. He did not like the ostentatious attire of the social elite or the simplistic stories that retold love and betrayal repeatedly. But he had summoned all of Heaven's Standard Bearers to The Covent Garden on a cool March evening in the year 1742, nevertheless. From his perch within the Celestial, he looked down on those in attendance as they filtered in.

On the surface, Zinc had assembled the Standard Bearers in a place free of human conflict for the purpose of solidifying their unity. *Messiah* by Handel was an inspiring work of great importance to the Angels. In the time since the Nazarene, many in Heaven had clung to the notion that the mortal who had slain so many Demons was, in fact, the son of God and was hidden away somewhere in Heaven waiting with his father for the final victory.

Almost all Angels had carried rosaries and crucifixes in the time since the mortal had been put to death. The symbol of the cross, which had always been important to the host of Heaven due to prophecy, had been enhanced ten-fold following the Crucifixion. Zinc knew the musical performance would lift his peoples' spirit.

As the strains of the violin brought the audience to a hush, Zinc looked out from the royal box. The seating arrangements for the Angels offed him a clear layout of the political map of Heaven. He had assembled the heads of the various Houses under one roof so he could fully plan his next maneuvers.

Zinc first looked at his fellow Supreme Commander; the Angel meant to balance his own power, Uranium II. Zinc's method to install his colleague had shaken Heaven to its core. Yet, none had challenged him over his thinly concealed assassination and installation of a pretender to the Uranium Lordship. The way Zinc prevented a civil war had cast a dark pall over his emergence as the sanctified leader of Heaven.

He closed his eyes and allowed the gentle strains of the pastoral introduction to Handel's oratorio to enter his ears. He reflected on the situation in Asia. The son of Cobalt had assumed the Lordship of the Uranium House, built from Cobalt survivors. At the outset, these Angels were resistant to following Uranium II. To his credit, Uranium II had wasted no time demanding loyalty and obedience from the members of this new House. Although his older brother Platinum had come to heel, there was lingering discontent between the siblings. They mimicked each other in a kind of silent standoff.

When one Angel hoarded dispensations, the others did as well. If one incorporated a House, the other acted in turn. When Platinum awarded one of his sons the House of Silicone, Uranium countered by giving his heir the House of Fluorine. Their offspring had replicated the process. Silicone founded the House of Selenium and Fluorine initiated the House of Bromine. These expansions had set up a massive expansion of the Asiatic contingent. However, the permanent fracture between Uranium (and his client Houses) and Platinum's faction meant that the Asian Houses were irreparably split.

Uranium II had centered his area of control in China, while Platinum controlled Japan.

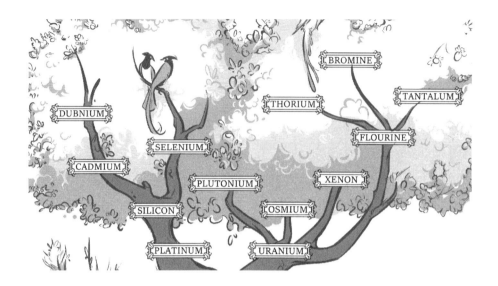

Zinc mused about his own situation regarding the Asians as a tenor filled the auditorium with *Comfort Ye My People.*

I wish my people could comfort themselves, Zinc thought.

He held Uranium II entirely in the palm of his hand. Not only had he installed him as a Standard Bearer, but he had also done so in a brutal manner that inspired fear and loyalty. By controlling his fellow Supreme Commander, Zinc held sway over half of the Asian faction. This enraged Platinum and threatened to turn him into a full-fledged and dangerous enemy.

As a result, Zinc often turned dispensations over to Platinum whenever there was a Grand Gathering. This had severely reduced Zinc's ability to incorporate any Houses of his own, a source of extreme agitation among his nephews, cousins, and their offspring. His sole surviving son, Abraham, had been born late and raised by his older sisters. He took after Cecilia, his mother. Like her, Abraham was mostly suited for reconnaissance missions, a matter of great shame to Zinc, whose other sons had died heroically on the field of battle.

Still, Abraham served a purpose. He was next in line in the Zinc House, and as long as he lived, the others could not raise their voices too loudly. The bass replaced the chorus and began singing, *For behold, darkness shall cover the earth.* Zinc turned his attention away from his own House—he was certain he would always hold it in check—and summarized the Asian situation. He was confident that it was stable; he controlled Uranium II through their conspiracy and Platinum by handing over dispensations. They would jostle with each other, but never seek all-out war for fear Zinc would remove them as he had their father, Cobalt.

Zinc turned his attention among the possessed attendants to Lord Hydrogen. His eyes wandered to Rachael as she sat beside her husband. He saw through the shroud of her possession of a plain mortal to the Angel for whom he still hungered. Zinc forced the lusty thoughts from his mind. Rachael had kissed him in an attempt to manipulate him but had threatened to expose him when she was outmaneuvered by his agreement. She had been icy and distant ever since.

Unlike his wife, Lord Hydrogen was amicable enough. He appeared content with his place, next in succession behind Uranium II for the title of Supreme Commander. In the interim, he continued to consolidate his position by adding to the number of Houses he had founded. Having already sired the House of Bismuth with a son from his first wife, Hydrogen added the House of Beryllium with his and Rachael's first son, Musa.

Zinc considered Lord Beryllium with disdain. The youngster was the spawn of a despicable union. Zinc still wondered how his own offspring brought forth from Rachael would have appeared.

Beryllium displayed a light complexion much like his mother's. Beryllium's offspring looked like him and featured the characteristics of Arabian mortals. Their appearance created consternation among the Houses of Bismuth and Rhodium. Zinc suspected these Houses considered themselves the true shepherds of the Dark Continent and thought of Beryllium's House as an interloper. The attitude mirrored the mortal divide between the inhabitants of the Sahara and the plains of Africa.

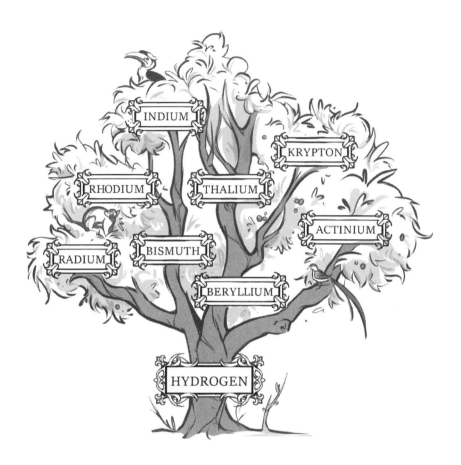

For his part, Hydrogen busied himself to stop the infighting. Though it posed less potential for explosive violence than Asia, Africa was far from unified. The unrest limited Hydrogen's influence and played directly into Zinc's hands. More than anything, however, the agreement that Hydrogen was next in line for the position of dual Supreme Commander provided Zinc with enough leverage to control Hydrogen.

The soprano soloist began to sing *Rejoice greatly, O daughter of Zion*. For a moment, Zinc reined in his incessant scheming and let the beautiful voice wash over him with the melodic announcement of the greatest miracle ever. He wondered where he had been when the Holy Mother had given birth. He suspected he'd been planning the expansion that had ended in the disaster of Teutoburg.

Other than Hydrogen, the only two surviving members of the original Houses were Carbon and Iron. Zinc recalled their mutual ascension after Gold's rebellion in Egypt. Iron III had come a long way from a cowering child forever in the shadow of his father. Now he was stronger and more ruthless in battle than the lord he had replaced.

Behold and see if there be any sorrow bellowed from a tenor's throat. Zinc assessed Lord Iron III. The House of Iron had founded the Houses of Gold and Silver, a tremendous embarrassment considering that the offspring had opted for rebellion—an indelible mark on Iron II's name.

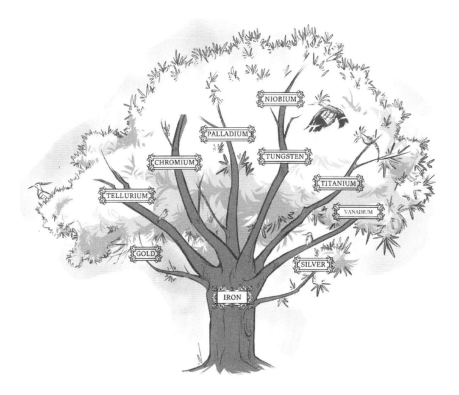

To make up ground after the fiasco, Lord Iron III founded the House of Tellurium, but his son died at Teutoburg. Zinc could still recall Iron III's devastation when Lilly listed Oswald Tellurium among the fallen. Still, Iron III had persevered. He accrued dispensations while he sired more children and soon appointed his heirs to the Houses of Tungsten, Titanium, Vanadium, Chromium, and Palladium. In turn, Tungsten founded the House of Niobium.

These six Houses were established with the sole purpose of feeding back dispensations to Iron III. The venerable House experienced a reinvigoration of power and prestige under Zinc's peer. Iron III was seen by many as the most powerful Angel in Heaven, and the rightful Supreme Commander. His method for running his faction was extremely successful, and he had become a master of war. Had Zinc not initially surpassed him, Iron III would likely be in control of Heaven's Army.

Zinc peered down on Lord Iron III from the royal box. As though perceiving the weight of the gaze, Iron III turned his head to meet Zinc's stare. He nodded politely and turned to the performance.

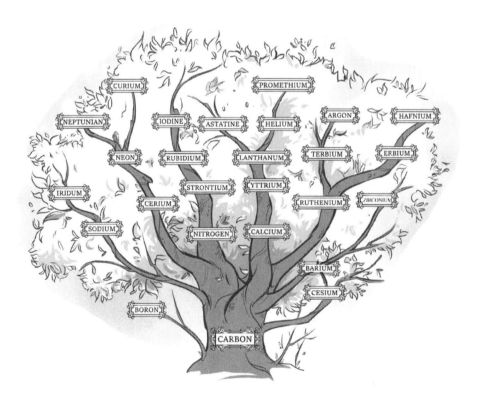

Zinc did not know how he would deal with Iron III's threat. He turned his attention to Carbon VI. Lord Carbon IV, who had also ascended with Zinc, had lost a hand at Teutoburg and stepped aside for the ascendancy of his son, Robert Carbon (Lord Carbon V). Robert had fallen in the duel with Bubonic Plague. However, under the agreement surrounding the duel, the House had remained incorporated and passed on to the next heir, Thomas Carbon (Lord Carbon VI). Consequently, Zinc was significantly older than this Standard Bearer, a young Lord in possession of perhaps the strongest of the Angelic Houses.

Siring Houses like champion race horses, the Carbon Lords (IV, V, and VI) founded the Houses of Calcium, Yttrium, Nitrogen, Strontium, Rubidium, Barium, Zirconium, Sodium, Boron, and Ruthenium. These ten Houses comprised the largest contingent in Heaven. However, for generations, the Carbon Lords had allowed the Houses they founded to hold on to their own dispensations, thus allowing for greater autonomy. Thus, Carbon VI oversaw a federation of Houses that was much looser in affiliation than Iron III's contingent. Nevertheless, the eleven Houses that comprised Carbon VI and his kingdom were a severe threat to Zinc's control as well.

Zinc returned his attention to the performance to alleviate some tension. A bass rattled the audience with an impenetrable question.

Why do the nations so furiously rage together?

A plan unfurled in Zinc's mind. And a tenor warbled.

The kings of the earth rise up, and the rulers take counsel together against the Lord.

First, I will appear to blunder and miscalculate, Zinc thought. *Iron III will see an opportunity for his advancement. He will attempt to assume control of the Heavenly Army. Once Iron III is in charge, I will ensure his zealousness results in a disaster that leads to his death and the deaths of his supportive Standard Bearers.*

Zinc envisioned the resulting feeding frenzy. Everyone would present a case for their own control.

To dispel any chance of civil war, I will use a dispensation to pass a decree that all disbanded Houses are to pledge fealty to one of the Supreme Commanders. Under the guise of maintaining a balance of power in Asia, I will limit how many of Iron III's network go to Uranium II. I can even gift one to Platinum from my allotment if necessary. That will then allow me to press Carbon VI from a stronger position.

The pieces were falling into place for Zinc. He'd crushed the Black Death. Now he would conquer his opponents in Heaven. He was not particularly proud of aiming his talents at his own kind, but he was convinced that the only way to deliver the final victory was if he crushed the incessant politics of Heaven once and for all.

He vowed he would follow through upon the plan he had devised and then never again have a hand in the death of an Angel. Satisfied, Zinc turned his attention to the matter of Heaven's morale. Then... an occurrence Zinc could only label "a miracle." The performers launched into the most glorious chorus the Angel had ever heard.

Hallelujah! Hallelujah! Hallelujah! Hallelujah! Hallelujah!

In a moment of diabolical inspiration, Zinc stepped back from the edge of the royal box and into the body of King George II. He filled the monarch's mind with the singular thought: *Stand.* The chorus continued.

For the Lord God Omnipotent reigneth, Hallelujah! Hallelujah!

Zinc moved into the Celestial and saluted his fellow Angels from the edge of the royal box. The moment the king rose, every patron followed suit. The shuffling of hundreds of bewildered attendees rising to their feet was drowned out by the stirring music.

Hallelujah! Hallelujah! Hallelujah! Hallelujah!
The kingdom of this world is become the kingdom of our Lord,
and of His Christ!
And He shall reign forever and ever.

Within the Celestial, Zinc shouted to his brethren, "Onwards, to the final victory!" He conveniently overlooked that a moment earlier, he had been planning a purge.

> *King of kings, forever and ever Hallelujah! Hallelujah!*
> *and Lord of lords, forever and ever Hallelujah! Hallelujah!*

Swept up in the power of the moment, Zinc flushed with emotions. He thought of his father and his young self before he was a Standard Bearer. He remembered all the things he would never have believed he would do, positive and negative. Tears sprang from his eyes in a veritable deluge as he reflected upon his own life and the scene of devotion he had orchestrated.

I can make it all worth it if we win, he thought as he tried to halt the salty flow.

The crashing of the timpani and the blare of trumpets met with a thunderous storm of strings to construct a magnificent incantation of praise that rose to Heaven itself as the frozen tableau of the once-secular gathering transformed into a pious gathering of devotion.

> *King of kings! And Lord of lords!*
> *King of kings! And Lord of lords!*
> *And He shall reign forever and ever, Hallelujah! Hallelujah!*
> *Hallelujah! Hallelujah!*
> *Ha-lle-lu-jah!*

"YOU COME HERE A lot," Spanish Influenza said from behind Schitz.

Without breaking his stoic vigil of the Styx, Schitz replied, "I suppose I do."

"Trying to remember or forget?" Spanish Influenza stood alongside the sitting Schitz.

"I suppose it is nobody's business but my own, but, if I had to say,

I come here to remember those who have passed on. I particularly remember those with whom I held conversation here along the river's edge."

Schitz ignored Spanish Influenza's superior physical position—an intentional move on the younger man's part—but he refused to be baited into revealing his innermost thoughts.

"And how is it that you have not joined that lot?" Spanish Influenza asked.

"Dumb luck."

"Is that all?"

Schitz shrugged.

Spanish Influenza pressed the conversation. "And the same happenstance led you to a position of power?"

"Am I in a position of power?" Schitz asked.

"I presume so, or at least I did when they let you run riot during the Spanish Conquest. After that, they broke everything down to limited missions."

"Conservatism often follows broad success," Schitz said, "just as large-scale endeavors follow periods of inactivity. It is an ebb and flow. You will learn this to be true."

Schitz hoped Spanish Influenza would take the hint and leave.

He did not.

Schitz continued to stare at the river. "Why are you so eager for power and control?"

Spanish Influenza shifted uneasily. "Isn't it what we all want? Upon the final victory, those in the highest positions will reap the greatest rewards. They will be the satraps, dukes, and marquises of the New Order of Hell and Earth."

"And how do you suppose one rises to such a position?" Schitz asked.

"By killing Angels; by killing the most Angels," Spanish Influenza said.

From the corner of his eye, Schitz noticed the tops of Spanish Influenza's hands. There were tattoos consisting of at least twenty hash marks—a tally of slain Angels.

"And is the reward worth the task required?" Schitz asked.

"Dominion over mortals and lesser Demons? Don't be ridiculous, of course, it is," Spanish Influenza replied.

"Something bad happened to you when you were younger, didn't it? That's why you lust so much after power. There must have been a time when you were not in control. Do you want to talk about it?"

For the first time in the conversation, Schitz looked up at Spanish Influenza. He knew his tone was condescending. And he liked when he saw Spanish Influenza flush.

"I bid you good day, Sir Schizophrenia," Spanish said.

"Quite right," Schitz said as the youngster walked away. "I thought so."

Not five seconds later, Elise emerged as if from thin air.

"I don't know if it was wise of you to antagonize him so," she said.

"Eavesdropping again, Mama?" Schitz asked. He'd long since abandoned being surprised by her arrival. "That young upstart has been trying my patience for as long as I can remember."

"He is power-hungry and dangerous," Elise said. "If you wish, I could—"

Schitz stopped her conversation cold. "No, no, no! We have discussed this, Mama. I must act as my own agent. And do not believe for one second that I inflamed him so without cause. I know he is ambitious, but there is more than that. I believe he has set plans in motion, and I aim to uncover what they are."

"If I can be of any assistance…"

"I will certainly let you know," Schitz said.

FROM HIS BOX AT the Royal Opera, Zinc rolled in his memories while an alto and tenor sang *Oh Death Where is Thy Sting*. He recalled a conversation with Lilly.

"You know I am on the verge of retirement, thrice delayed," she said with heightened irritation in her ancient voice.

"I have never fully asked you how it came to be that you survived the action that killed my late wife," Zinc said. "Do you think an inquest into that series of events and our disaster at Teutoburg thereafter would reflect well on your desire for an honorable retirement?"

Lilly gulped, awash in visible displeasure.

"Ah, there it is," Zinc said. Aware of other Angels in the atrium of the Great Hall, he raised his voice a notch. "Would you like to confess and unburden your soul?"

"All right, all right," she said. "One final mission. What would you have of me?"

Zinc nodded. "This is not the time for a schism within Heaven, not that there ever could be a good time for unrest. However, now is an especially bad time. Cobalt and Uranium seem eager to plunge us into a vile civil war. Cobalt appears unwilling to accept the ascension of his son's House. I know not how God did not foresee this happening."

"He did," Lilly said, "but he thinks Cobalt is too much like Gold, too much enthralled by his own light. Uranium I is a dullard, but never was there a stronger warrior. By pairing him with you, God gets brains and brawn without ego and self-interest."

"A fair assessment," Zinc said.

"As well it should be," Lilly said. "It was constructed for God by the Familiars."

Zinc chuckled. "A fan of your own work, then?"

"Of course, as I am sure you are as well, of yours," she said.

Zinc conceded the point. "Fair enough. This is what I need from you. I need to know when Cobalt will move next onto the field of battle, whether against his son or the Demons. I need all of the particulars of his contingent, objectives, armaments, et cetera."

A grim look passed across Lilly's face. "It's a dreadful business."

"Indeed," Zinc said, "but attend to it well, and you will have your retirement."

WAITING FOR A PARTICULAR entity at the neutral ground was one of the surest ways to ensure a thorough dive into the depths of debauchery available within the abode. Helga had long since retired from her role of matron. She had been replaced by a Familiar named Venus, whom Zinc had enjoyed many times along with all the various intoxicants available.

"You look rough," a familiar voice said with a laugh.

Zinc rose from a listless stupor to see Spanish Influenza standing over him.

Zinc groaned. "I've been waiting for you."

"Why on Earth?" He laughed and pulled Zinc into a sitting position.

When his thoughts cleared, Zinc considered the magnitude of the decision he faced.

Can I ask this Demon to kill Cobalt?

Zinc weighed the severity of the action he was considering. He had already determined that he could not allow Cobalt to fracture the forces of Heaven by refusing to accept Uranium I's elevation. God had decided—the issue was closed.

However, to ask his Demonic associate to kill an Angel was treason regardless of the rationale. In the moment, he lost his nerve and decided he would accomplish his task another way.

"I can't ask it of you," Zinc said. He looked toward the wall.

"So, all that for nothing?"

If the Demon's feelings were hurt, he didn't show it.

"I'm sorry, I have to go," Zinc said.

He scrambled to his feet and bolted from the room.

What an odd fellow, Spanish Influenza thought.

THE UNIFORMS OF THE Qing Emperor's troops formed an endless ocean of blue as they marched south with their matchlock muskets slung over their shoulders. The soldiers of the Green Banner were Asia's most elite contingent. Cobalt's grip on the Qing Empire provided him with the perfect instrument to exert his leverage over Uranium I. In turn, Lord Platinum, Cobalt's second eldest son, had mobilized his House within the forces of Siam. Despite his new elevated position as a Co-Commander of Heaven, Uranium I (positioned within the Konbaung of Burma) found himself beset on either side, north and south.

The rainy season had not yet ended, and the heavens poured on Zinc's head. He watched the procession of Chinese soldiers advancing toward the Irrawaddy.

"Going against God is always dangerous business," Zinc said, turning to one of Cobalt's sons. "There is much for your House to lose."

"I understand your predicament," Xiang Cobalt said from within the frame of a Qing officer. "You are freshly elevated with your promotion and yet hindered by the conflict caused by my father's shameful demotion."

"Shameful?" Zinc asked from within the Celestial.

"For God to pass over the father, he must have seen significant, grievous shortcomings. This is an insult to such an Angel as my father. The Angel who brought the Mongols successfully across the vast swaths of Asia, then properly divided the realm between himself, Platinum, and Uranium—my father should be elevated."

"Well, where is your loyalty to your brothers?" Zinc asked.

"Lord Platinum and Lord Uranium are my eldest brothers, and I venerate them as such," the son of Cobalt said, but his stoicism was showing cracks.

He wiped his mortal's rain-swept face and glanced about awkwardly. Zinc could feel his young counterpart's conflicted nature.

"I am next to receive a House or to inherit my father's," the young Cobalt said. His voice shook. "Now my inheritance will be death defending my father, or whatever wreckage survives this fruitless endeavor."

"You are still a young Angel," Zinc said. "You may yet put an end to this conflict before it spirals beyond repair."

Xiang heaved audibly and looked up through the ceaseless rain. "When you called for an audience, I knew you endeavored to turn me against my father."

"Then why did you agree to meet?"

"Did you not hear me? You are the Joint Supreme Commander of Heaven," the younger Cobalt replied, his voice dripping in sarcasm.

"And because you want to know what I have to offer, I suppose," Zinc said.

Xiang displayed the smile of a hungry crocodile.

"My offer is what they denied your father, the opportunity to rule alongside me as a Supreme Commander of the Angels," Zinc said.

"How is this yours to offer?" Xiang asked, astonished.

"It's not," Zinc said. "However, God appointed Uranium, and after your brother is removed, I will use a dispensation I have saved from not founding a House to install you as the new Lord Uranium the Second."

"That's not how it works," Xiang said. "God appointed my brother. Handing me his House will not grant me his appointment."

"God will allow it, if it affords a swift return to the status quo ante bellum," Zinc said. "All God wants is a warrior lacking in strategy to balance my side of the office. You fit the bill for that."

"As do many of my father's sons."

Cobalt's descendants had earned a reputation as fearsome warriors, a fact that made the impending storm even riper for Heavenly catastrophe.

"I could offer this to one of them if you refuse," Zinc said, "but you will not, so it really doesn't matter."

"I will agree to your terms." Xiang stepped into the Celestial to shake Zinc's hand. "I will be Lord Uranium II."

"Yes, you will," Zinc said.

"You realize that you are compromising my position by calling me away from preparations for battle," Uranium I said.

He walked alongside Zinc through the Heavenly Halls.

"Yes, and I apologize profusely," Zinc said. "And I explained your precarious situation to God, but he was insistent."

Zinc led them through a heavy doorway to a room where Familiars repaired the bindings of ancient texts. The room was filled with tools, material containers, and restoring agents.

"And God said He wanted to meet here?" Uranium I asked.

"Well, yes," Zinc said. "He should be here any moment."

Zinc had left the door ajar. Constance Silver slipped in without a sound. She wore a white scarf across her nose and mouth.

Uranium I continued his conversation with Zinc. "I wonder why—"

Constance's hand slipped over his mouth. Before Uranium I could react, Constance plunged her Celestial dagger into his kidneys and spleen in a series of vicious swift thrusts. He collapsed to the floor. Constance lifted his chin, then drove the dagger into the base of his throat.

Zinc and Constance grabbed the body in sheets and cleaned the floor. Zinc slung Uranium's wrapped body over his shoulder and backtracked through the library. Anna Gold fell in beside him.

Zinc moved through a series of small corridors that led to the Manna bakery. He located the wheelbarrow that Constance had left outside the bakery and, with his accomplices in tow, walked toward the Eunoe. The trio slid Uranium I's cocoon into the water without a sound.

They dispersed. Zinc discarded the wheelbarrow and walked inside. Only then did the weight of his deed hit him.

I have murdered a colleague for no other reason than to prevent discord and to solidify my new position.

Head down, Zinc collided with another Angel. It took him several moments to realize it was Rachael.

"In a hurry?" she asked.

"Not particularly," he said, painfully aware of the transparency of his lie.

"Oh, I can always tell when you are lying," she said.

She rested her palm on his chest and moved her fingers just below the outer folds of his robes. The touch sent electrical impulses through Zinc—directly into his groin.

Having made her point, Rachael withdrew her hand. "Let's get to the point, shall we," Rachael said. "It would appear that you are the sole Supreme Commander of Heaven for the moment though I do not think God will approve of the method by which you have achieved your monopoly."

"I... I... I didn't do it for power," he said. "But how did you know?"

"This place has more eyes and ears than you know, my darling," she answered.

Zinc glanced from side to side.

"Your secret is safe with me," she said, "but that body will remain in the river forever as your damnation."

"What do you want?"

"You know what I want. Hydrogen takes Uranium's place."

Zinc took great care with his response. "When Lord Uranium cannot be found, and his house is disbanded, I will elevate your husband to be Supreme Commander alongside me."

Rachael moved close and kissed him. Her tongue wrestled with his. Zinc's hands wandered along her hips. For a moment, he was sure they would make love in the hallway, but she pulled back.

"I've missed you," he said.

"I know," she replied, "but we can go no further."

Zinc leaned against the wall and allowed the moment to pass. When the throbbing in his nether regions diminished, he resumed the conversation.

"How have you been?"

"Well," she replied, "I still haven't caught Schizophrenia, the Demon with the scar on his face."

Zinc shuddered involuntarily. "I think I encountered him in the New World. We walked into his ambush in Canada. I was the only one who survived, and only because a rainstorm dampened his gunpowder."

"I heard it was a savage slaughter," she said.

"The Demons are uncannily good with muskets," he said, "the way they move and fire; you don't want to be anywhere close."

"And they took the heads as prizes? That is true?"

"Yes."

Zinc could tell that his affirmation of the rumor unnerved his former lover.

"Well," she said, "when I find him, I will kill him."

"Such singular purpose after all these years," Zinc said.

Her eyes glowed with vengeful anger. "I was next to my brother

Benjamin in the womb," she said. "For the entirety of my life, the longest time I was away from him were the moments I spent with you. When the Demon killed Benjamin, he murdered part of my soul. I will have my vengeance."

WELL-DRESSED AND BLINDFOLDED BACHELORS searched the drawing-room of the Pembrook Estate with outstretched arms while shrieking, wide-eyed damsels feigned terror and made little effort to avoid capture. From within the body of Gilbert van Ness, Schitz enjoyed the escapade thoroughly. The effect of the blindfold was lost upon him. His heightened perception had no problem seeing through the cloth that covered his host's eyes. So, when Gilbert succeeded in capturing the young Claudette Sullivan, it was no accident that his hand grazed her breasts before settling around her waist. The young heiress screeched. Her pubescent body's response to the touch both surprised and horrified her. Schitz grinned at the lascivious look etched on the face of Skin Cancer within the mortal woman.

The young Demon was a member of the Hellish Academy's newest class. As had become somewhat of a routine, Schitz had found himself the target of the maiden's affection. Although he did not seek out conquests among his pupils, Schitz saw no need to deny the advances of unmarried maidens. He had taken Skin Cancer to the mortals' gathering as a method of easing her into the dance of seduction. Even though she had sought out his affections, the youth was shy and apprehensive. From within the body of a host, physical contact was less overwhelming. So, as the mortals slyly engaged in passing touches and flirtations, Schitz unwound Skin Cancer.

After they had abandoned their mortal bodies, they snuck off to one of the manor's many boudoirs, just like their human counterparts. They lay unnoticed atop one of the mortals' beds. Schitz breathed in the serenity of the moment; he appreciated taking the opportunity to escape the endless cycle of death and destruction.

In many ways, his entire existence felt unbearably absurd.

To have immortality only to risk it continually until he was destroyed seemed utterly futile. Schitz ruminated on his reality as he took in Skin Cancer's tender body. He had enjoyed taking her innocence. He'd become quite adept at pushing aside any pangs of guilt about Anna, Lady Calcium, and Rubella.

"What are you thinking about," Skin Cancer asked.

Damn, she sounds young.

"Just about the way of things," Schitz replied. "Mostly about this next war here in the Colonies. I wonder who will prevail."

"Our forces have grown substantially," she replied. "I suppose this conflict will be my class's first action."

"Indeed." Schitz decided to lighten the mood. He rolled closer. "You'll be fine; you had an excellent teacher."

"In so many ways," she said. She began kissing his chest and then his stomach.

"I feel the need to be transparent," he said.

Skin Cancer paused in her descent. "You need me to know that we are not mates," she said. "Not to worry." She kissed his lower abdomen. "I know you had Hysteria from the class before me, and before that, Bornholm and Paratyphoid, and before that Anemia, and before that Sepsis."

Schitz cringed as she recited his list of recent indulgences.

"I did not seek them out," he said. His voice more defensive than he'd intended.

"I know," she said. "That's why I say you are a challenge. The girls want to see who has the courage to lay with you, and if any is good enough to win your monogamy."

"Why me?"

"You're sexy," she replied with a coquettish giggle, "and you're esteemed and brave."

"Oh, stop it." Schitz laughed. *I was once considered the class dunce.*

"So, this is what all the girls gossip about?" he said. She was getting closer. He did not have to look. "The young lads must hate me."

"Well, they have their chances with Encephalitis and Meningitis, or they can travel to the Neutral Ground for, ah, relief."

Things have certainly changed, he thought. *Rubella and I were essentially married when—*

She interrupted his thoughts.

"Have you ever been to the Neutral Ground?" she asked.

Schitz shook his head. "I've never seen the purpose for it; it seems like a place for damaged, self-hating entities."

He thought of Spanish Influenza. "Have you?"

"No," she said, "Although I might not tell you given your condemnation—but… no. It can be rough on females. Dyslexia went there and got intoxicated. She ended up sleeping with several Angels, something she continues to regret, especially since she and Macular Degeneration had already agreed to wed."

Schitz's response indicated his sarcastic disdain. "How salacious."

"I'm sorry to bore you," she replied with a devilish grin. "Maybe you'll like this more than Academy gossip."

Schitz groaned as Skin Cancer took him in her mouth. He closed his eyes and thought, *It's a good life, being a challenge.*

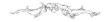

RACHAEL'S FURY BORDERED ON insanity.

"You lied to me! Give me one reason why I shouldn't unveil your assassination?"

"Because I didn't lie." Zinc glanced furtively about the Great Hall. "When Lord Uranium dies, I will submit my dispensation to elevate Lord Hydrogen."

"Lord Uranium is dead," she said, her voice a hiss. "His body is at the bottom of the Eunoe."

"True," Zinc replied, "but the replacement Lord Uranium II was already in place prior to our agreement. Therefore, our accord applies to the *current* Lord Uranium."

Rachael's cheeks inflamed. "You lying sack of worm turds! I cannot believe you manipulated me."

In addition to anger, Zinc heard pain.

She still cares about me, he thought.

"The replacement had already been decided," he said. "Be patient. Your husband will be a Supreme Commander."

Rachael inhaled deeply and regained a modicum of decorum.

"One life is never that great of an obstacle to overcome, whoever it is. You would do well to remember that, my Lord."

She stormed off.

I have to take more precautions for my safety, he thought *If I can eliminate old Uranium, who knows what someone might do to me.*

THE CLOSED-DOOR MEETING OF the Triumvirate Council had been called to order. Titus looked around the room and began to sweat.

This is like being locked in a cage.

Mephistopheles and his insufferable wife Elise, along with their third wheel Anubis sat across from him. Titus hated the way the Wraiths were always skulking about.

Sneaky bastards.

He looked at Smallpox and his children, Autism and Anorexia. They held seats that had once been filled by Plague. *I wonder if he was the Antichrist foretold within our legends, and those of the Angels. Nobody could defeat him in battle. In the end, he proved the only entity capable of destroying himself. The demi-Satan is gone, and I'm stuck with a disinterested ancient, and his dullard children.*

Titus forced his attention to the matter at hand. Inwardly he chastised himself; he was supposed to see the value and good in all Hellish beings. In truth, he was very fond of the Wraiths, particularly the handicapped Elise. He also recognized Smallpox's potency, as well as the prowess of his children.

I am not mad at them. I am jealous. They can survive in the Mortal Realm.

Titus swallowed; his saliva hit the bottom of his stomach like a stone. He addressed the audience through a quivering voice.

"Recent success has prompted Lord Satan to decree the resumption of wide-scale maneuvers. He can only imagine, when looking upon recent engagements during the Seven Years War, the potential devastation…" his voice cracked again, "the potential devastation we could wreak if we combine our forces as we did during the Spanish Conquest. I suggested that Sir Smallpox or Sir Schizophrenia oversee such an operation."

I really do not want to do this.

He pressed on.

"However, Satan has expressed concerns that neither is ideologically devout enough to usher in the Final Victory… which… uh… which he believes is close… at hand."

"Oh, for goodness sakes, man." Smallpox slammed his hand on the table. "Spit it out already."

Shocked by the outburst, Titus snapped out of his uncharacteristic lack of poise.

"It's me," he said to the confused faces. "He has instructed me as the High Priest, his voice in absentia, to lead the army of Hell."

No one spoke. Then a girlish giggle broke the stillness. Titus turned to the seat beside him, where Erin flushed red and desperately struggled to contain her laughter. Her sniggers catalyzed a deluge of chuckles that progressed into outright hysterics.

Titus flushed with embarrassment mixed with rage. "I didn't ask for this."

Even Smallpox was smiling. "I'm sorry I interrupted you earlier, Lord Commander," he said.

Titus rolled his tongue around his cheek and shook his head. "The entire idea is ludicrous." He checked over his shoulder, anxious that the Devil should hear him voice disapproval. "I am not a warrior, but he expects me to lead soldiers on a great endeavor."

Mephistopheles clutched at the few remaining strands of hair on his head. "We are doomed."

Elise patted him upon the shoulder.

"Not necessarily," Smallpox said. "A great commander does not need to be the greatest of all of his warriors, or the smartest of all of his officers; he simply requires understanding."

"Understanding of what?"

"Well," the old Demon said, "even the most limited person

understands where he is— let's call that Alpha. And even the most uneducated strategist recognizes what constitutes victory—Omega. What makes a wise commander is understanding how to get from Beta to Psi when all about him is chaos."

"Oh, is that all?" Titus asked. "I did not know military conquest could be reduced to a linguistics lesson. Why was I worried?"

"Don't be petty." All humor had left Mephistopheles's voice and demeanor. "For once in your life, be quiet and listen. Smallpox has killed countless scores of Angels."

Smallpox raised his hand to quiet the Wraith. "There's a war coming to the British Colonies; we can use it to train you. You will not learn how to fight. But you might learn how to lead."

"So, THEY'RE INFANTRY, BUT for ships?"

Titus was intrigued by the soldiers marching and drilling beside the docks of Chesapeake Bay.

"They're called Royal Marines," Schitz said. "Well, they would be if they were British. I don't know what the Continentals are calling them. The ship is impressive, isn't it?"

"Yeah, she is," Titus replied.

Schitz looked at the hull and masts of the Continental warship.

"But she's a tough bitch, too," Schitz said. "Twenty-six guns, and you're going to learn all about them when you jump into one of those marines."

"I've never possessed a mortal before," Titus said.

"Nothing's easier," Schitz said, "as long as your mind is stronger than theirs. If they bounce you, try another."

Titus nodded his head like an eager pup.

"Come on."

Schitz began jogging alongside the training marines. He slipped into the squad leader and watched as Titus settled into the soldier next to him. Schitz laughed as he watched the High Priest struggle within the mortal.

"Have you ever run before?" Schitz asked.

"Shut up—and no," Titus said.

"It's good for you."

Titus was already gasping. "It's terrible."

"Trust me," Schitz said, "it's not going to get any easier than this."

Schitz began singing an upbeat marching cadence set to a popular sea shanty:

Lift them up and set them down.

The marines running alongside responded.

Fire Providence, fire away!

"See how the raid has unfolded?" Smallpox asked.

He pointed to the Continental marines that were capturing the town of Nassau.

"Had there been Angels here, we would have advanced in a split formation—some within the mortals and others within the Celestial."

The marching cadence echoed in the High Priest's head.

One shot for the Lord and one for the Crown,
Fire Providence, fire away!

Schitz pointed at the American position on Brooklyn Heights and shouted, "Angels in the gap."

Titus watched as various Demons moved into the Celestial in response to the Angelic advance; others remained within the Continental soldiers. The Continentals unleashed a volley of musket fire. The air filled with eye-burning smoke and the smell of burned powder.

There's thunder when the Commanders say,
Fire Providence, fire away!

"Get those guns into position!" Spanish Influenza's bellow carried above the sounds of battle. The British ship of the line moved alongside; the deck heaved and pitched in the choppy Atlantic.

"There are Angels aboard that craft," Spanish said. "We'll shoot them to Hell and then board and engage."

Titus stepped into a member of one of the gun crews and heaved on the ropes. The cannon rattled into place.

> *Pull the tackles, and there she'll stay,*
> *Fire Providence, fire away!*

"We can pick them off from range," Cancer said. She peered down the sights of her Kentucky long rifle, "and then our boys up there in the Celestial will take them out."

Perched in the tree overlooking the advancing redcoats, Titus aimed his rifle from within a Continental sharpshooter. He pulled the trigger. The powder ignited with an explosive crack.

> *Haul the powder from down below,*
> *Fire Providence, fire away!*

Schitz urged a contingent of Demons forward in the Celestial. "Faster—faster!"

He looked over his shoulder to Titus. Titus's head wiggled. Schitz saw him swallow.

It won't be so bad, Titus thought.

When Demons neared the Angels, several of the foe stepped into the advancing British light infantry. However, the possessed redcoats were struck by cannon fire when the Demons arrived. The Angels within the British were instantly sent into departure seizures and dispatched with extreme prejudice.

> *Touch the linstock, and there she'll go,*
> *Fire Providence, fire away!*

"You get it, right?" Smallpox asked.

He and Titus walked past the rows of drilling Continentals. Titus watched the rows of troops advancing in unison under the tattoo of drums and the shrill notes of fifes.

"I have a grasp of the strategies," Titus said. "Just not sure about improvising when things get thick."

When I get back to Boston town,
Fire Providence, fire away!

Titus issued orders from the captain of the USS *Hampden*. "Let out the reefs! Make full sail!"

He stood at the helm, the handles of the ship's wheel in his hands. He guided the ship towards the prize with practiced expertise. Spanish Influenza signaled that the line of approach was good from within the boarding party.

"They have no hope," Titus said. He watched the frantic Angelic movements about the British ship.

I'll drop a line to little Molly Brown,
Fire Providence, fire away!

Titus sent the Continentals toward the redoubt controlled by the British troops along the Mill Creek.

"Forward!"

The crack of musket fire filled the air; smoke plumed. Titus stepped into the Celestial and shouted orders to the Demons under his command.

"Move into the space between the two armies." He pointed. "You, you, and you, take up firing positions within the advancing mortals.

Chain shot's loaded and powder's dry,
Fire Providence, fire away!

"Mon Dieu!!"

Titus ducked. The air transformed into a sea of splinters and shrapnel as the British second rate pounded the deck of the French flagship off the coast of Dominica.

"Allez! Allez!" he shouted to the nearest gun crew. They readied themselves for return fire. His eardrums rang within his host when the mighty gun discharged.

> *Their masts go crack when we let lead fly,*
> *Fire Providence, fire away!*

"We'll maneuver along their supply train," Titus said.

He pointed to positions marked on the parchment map. The canvas tent was illuminated by a flickering oil lamp. There was a moment of heavy silence in the air. Titus looked up at the Continental officers occupied by Smallpox and Schitz, each with a broad grin upon his face.

"What is it?" he asked.

"Nothing," Smallpox said. "We just don't recognize you anymore, Your Holiness."

Titus smirked.

> *Our Providence she's a sturdy little craft,*
> *Fire Providence, fire away!*

Sepsis protested from within one of the gunners. "You'll hit our troops."

"I doubt it," Titus said. "Fire!"

The gun reverberated and sent its deadly payload downrange into the pitched battle.

> *Twenty-six guns from the fore down to the aft,*
> *First Providence, fire away!*

Schitz had just forced two Angels to flee from the Celestial into mortal shields and had himself just stepped into a Continental soldier, when a blur of heat and forcefulness passed over his right shoulder. The ball smashed through the two possessed mortals and left both Angels writhing on the ground. Schitz turned with surprise toward the distant gun crew, shocked that they had attempted the shot. He gave a thumbs-up before he dispatched the two foes.

So hoist the sails and tie 'em down,
Fire Providence, fire away!

Titus walked through the Great Hall with a confident stride. The Priest had been transformed into a commander from head to toe. He hummed the marching cadence of the Continental Marines as he walked past his subordinate Priests performing the Return Ritual.

Let's kick the Red Coats out of Nassau town,
Fire Providence, fire away!
Fire Providence, fire away!

Schitz's Notebook *USS Providence*

9.5/10

-12 4lb. guns -14 swivel guns -6 officers, -22 sailors, -26 marines
A sturdy, reliable vessel. Fond memories of Titus and our time spent training him to lead our army.

"I'M NOT OVERLY CONCERNED about the American Colonies," Zinc said.

He looked across the Chinese highlands and remembered his time with Sun Tzu.

"Is that why you have not asked for help in your new region?" Uranium II asked.

With the destruction of the Natives, the New World had fallen primarily under the auspices of Zinc's European contingent. Even though the old territorial boundaries had been abandoned, many Angels still held to their preferred regions of the globe.

"I have other plans that will require your assistance. But I don't want to weaken you against Platinum," Zinc said. "Your feud with your older brother bores me." He continued, "There will come a time soon when I ask you to hold back in your efforts. I will order you to ensure that your contingent does not sustain casualties. I don't want you to concern yourself with the outcome of the battle, a battle that will surely be an Angelic defeat."

Zinc thought, *Iron III will see Uranium II as a support—a complete ruse.*

"We need victories but not just against the Demons," Zinc said.

I've got those two buffoons exactly where I want them, Zinc thought.

THE TRIUMVIRATE COUNCIL CONVENED a public hearing upon the conclusion of the American War of Independence. Titus was presented to all portions of Hell; Demons, Wraiths, and Priests as the Highest Commander of the Army of Hell, second only to Satan himself. Schitz observed something different about the High Priest, something he admired. The Priest had annoyed him before because he spoke with what Schitz called "the arrogance of ignorance."

The war had changed and humbled Titus. Whereas before, his paternalistic nature had been oafish and rooted only in the notion that his station made him "a father," after leading Demons in combat, the High Priest possessed a genuine sense of concern. He understood the bloody nature of conflict.

Schitz had watched Titus grow pale when Gout was cut down by a trio of Angels at Bunker Hill. The High Priest had also been present when they had lost Reyes Disease and Osteoarthritis during an action on the Atlantic. On a march, Titus had recounted an instance in which he and Spanish Influenza came upon the butchered corpse of Chronic Gastritis, slashed beyond recognition.

There had been countless Wraiths lost in action as well as newborns who did not make it back to Hell safely. The losses had been light compared to those inflicted during the campaign, but they had clearly left their mark on Titus. Schitz could see that the Priest had developed the appropriate level of concern while also refining his courage and his stomach for combat.

Although Schitz missed leading the forces of Hell, he knew that Satan could have picked a far worse leader than the commander Titus had become.

"I will follow you wherever you should lead," Schitz said to the High Priest at the conclusion of the meeting.

Titus clasped Schitz by the shoulders and hugged him.

"You set the bar high during the Spanish Conquest, very high. Maybe that is why the Lord chose ideology over raw battlefield talent. But you and the others have taught me much, and I will not let you down. That I promise."

Titus

Chapter 17

Heroes of Antiquity
Never Saw a Cannonball

"The revolution was a wild and wasteful fever," Jules Fonteneau said. He looked across the harbor of Marseilles. "It sickened the nation; it did not save it."

"How can you say such a thing?"

Marie Beaumont took in the stevedores who heaved and pulled various cables to load and unloaded cargo from around the globe, sailors of the various warships leaving or returning to their stations, clerks and administrators supervising the activities.

"Don't get me wrong," Schitz replied from within the young Frenchman, "I enjoyed the bloodletting with immense enthusiasm."

In his mind, he beheld the divine instrument of execution standing high above the cobblestones and the ragged crowd, her heavy blade adorned in crimson, tireless at her work. The crowd cheered La Guillotine and satisfied its insatiable death thirst with the seemingly endless parade of sacrifices that trudged up the scaffold's steps.

From within Marie Beaumont, Rabies assessed her father's words. "As much as it was a delectable orgy of wanton violence, we focused so much on Robespierre and the revolution that we allowed the Angels to grab Napoleon Bonaparte," she said.

"It is no matter; we will crush him as we did Alexander and the Caesars. The Angels are obsessed with building empires they can never hold together. Besides, that little twerp is locked away on Isola d'Elba," Schitz said.

Schitz took in a deep breath. In his mind's eye, he could see out into the Mediterranean, past the despot's Corsican homeland, to the tiny, uninteresting island where the French emperor was imprisoned.

"I do not think he'll stay there," Rabies said.

"He didn't!"

"Ah, Mama, you made it," Schitz said.

The matronly madame, surprising in her agility, embraced father and daughter, then sat.

"Tell us the news," Schitz said.

"Bonaparte is no longer on Elba and will soon reassume the French crown," the Wraith said. "The Angels will once again lead him into battle."

"There you have it," Schitz said. "But why the concern?"

"Our intelligence indicates a fracture in the Angelic ranks. The commander we have identified as Lord Zinc lost significant sway following our victory at Leipzig. There is belief that the Grande Armée will be led by a new commander when next they join us in battle."

"An unknown factor," Rabies said.

Elise looked at her. "Exactly. An Angel known as Lord Iron III, we are quite familiar with him and his kin, has apparently grown in stature as of late."

Schitz's face lightened. "A change in leadership will present an opportunity for us to strike a decisive blow, especially if we target this new leader head-on."

"I have returned from a closed meeting of the Triumvirate, and that is precisely the thinking," Elise said. "However, there are also indicators that the Angels are calling upon their African and Asian Houses."

"Six coalitions and they've yet to do so," Rabies said.

"Precisely. Mephistopheles raised this concern to the Triumvirate but was largely ignored. Satan is spoiling for Titus to have a wide-scale engagement."

"He performed remarkably in Iberia and Russia," Schitz said.

I should still be leading Hell's forces, but the Priest is quite competent.

"When the Angels take to the field, the Devil will order all of Hell to meet them," Elise said. "That is why I wanted to see you."

"We appreciate the notice," Schitz said. "This is going to be rough."

ZINC WAS GIDDY WITH amusement as he assessed his plan from within the French commander Marshal Michel Ney. Zinc helped facilitate several defeats in the French emperor's fall from grace. Iron III used Zinc's defeats as justification to seize Bonaparte for his own possession. While Zinc still clung to the title of Supreme Commander, there was a broad consensus that should Iron III deliver a stunning victory, he would rise as Zinc's replacement. In a show of support for the impending battle, Zinc exercised his authority and called on the far-flung Houses of Africa and Asia. He knew his move would remove any suspicion that he had acted to sabotage Iron III's efforts. He hoped his efforts would attract Demonic attention and place Iron III and his supporting Houses firmly within Hell's focus.

From within the saddle, Zinc watched the vast columns of blue and white uniformed soldiers march across the rolling, green hills of the Netherlands. The summer air shimmered.

It will get hotter when the lead begins to fly.

Zinc was confident he was in the precise position to inflict his subterfuge upon the ambitious Iron III. The only factor he could not account for was whether the Demons would arrive, but he believed the appearance of so many Angels would draw them to the spot. If he had maneuvered properly, the foe would have Iron III and his supporting Houses squarely in their sights. He spurred his mighty warhorse onward with a sharp kick to the flanks and galloped past the ranks of marching infantry.

Titus had poured over many scrolls which contained academic assessments, field reports, and battle analyses. He had taken great care to pair squads that were balanced in terms of combat skills and seniority. Still, he felt wholly unprepared for the looming battle.

"Anxious?" Mephistopheles asked.

Titus stretched his back. "To say the least," he replied.

"I've watched many battles unfold over the centuries," Mephistopheles said. "Would you like some advice?"

"Gladly."

The Wraith patted the High Priest on the shoulder. "Whether planned or spontaneous, all battles are chaotic calamities. War is unpredictable. No matter how much you agonize over these papers, the outcome will be written in blood and sweat. What matters is that the Demons are prepared and ready to follow your orders."

"Thank you."

The High Priest looked down at the list of assignments and was filled with the weight of his responsibility. His assignments might be the difference between life and death for his Demons. He handed the order of battle to Mephistopheles.

"Please deliver this to Lord Satan."

"Very good."

"Sixty-two names," Titus said.

"Sixty-three," the Wraith replied. "You're going with them."

Titus bowed his head. "I'm not worried about me."

"That's why you will do great, my friend."

SCHITZ SAT ON THE banks of the Styx and focused upon his breathing.

Steady in... hold... steady out... hold.

He appreciated the solitude of the riverbank and wondered if he was looking at it for the last time. He thought of the Viking prayer for the dead, and for a moment, he could see Tuberculosis and Diphtheria and SIDS and Poliomyelitis.

"I will do my duty to honor my ancestors who came before me," he said aloud.

Schitz knew the air would soon be filled with musket balls, cannon shot, swords, and bayonets. He had seen countless skirmishes and pitched battles in his life, but something deep within warned him that the impending contest would be far more severe than anything he had ever witnessed.

SATAN RECLINED WITHIN HIS private abode, and he scanned the order of battle for the upcoming, decisive encounter with Heaven. It had taken thousands of years, but at long last, it would be decided. The Devil felt rewarded for his decision to promote Titus to the role of commander of his army. He knew that Titus would offer no challenge to his own authority following the final victory.

Satan marveled at the Priest's progress and skill. Titus has broken the forces into four corps: I and II containing four squads of four and III and IV containing three squads of five. And he had been quite equitable in terms of skill and age.

Suddenly, the Devil quivered with rage. He noticed an annotation that one Demon per squad in Corps I and II and two demons per squad in Corps III were assigned to a cannon crew.

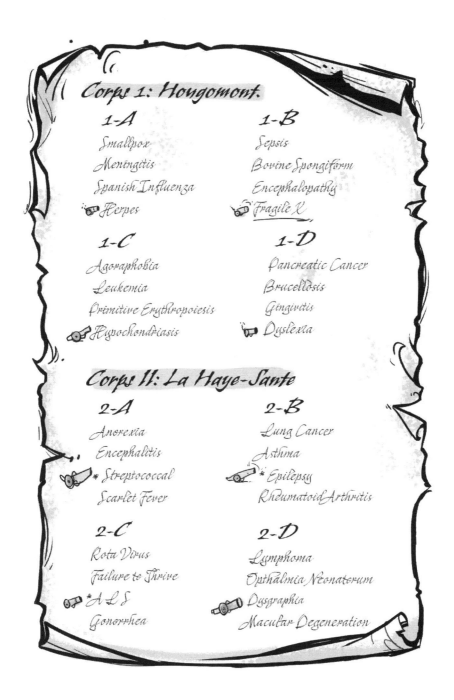

Corps 1: Hougomont.

1-A
Smallpox
Meningitis
Spanish Influenza
Herpes

1-B
Sepsis
Bovine Spongiform
Encephalopathy
Fragile X

1-C
Agoraphobia
Leukemia
Primitive Erythropoiesis
Hypochondriasis

1-D
Pancreatic Cancer
Brucellosis
Gingivitis
Dyslexia

Corps II: La Haye-Sante

2-A
Anorexia
Encephalitis
* Streptococcal
Scarlet Fever

2-B
Lung Cancer
Asthma
* Epilepsy
Rheumatoid Arthritis

2-C
Rota Virus
Failure to Thrive
*ALS
Gonorrhea

2-D
Lymphoma
Opthalmia Neonatorum
Dysgraphia
Macular Degeneration

Corps III: Papelotte

3-A
Autism
Pneumonia
Cancer
Typhoid
Hepatitis

3-B
Gangrene
Ulcers
Naegleriasis
Hemophilia
African Trypanosomiasis

3-C
Guillain-Barre
Osteomyelitis
Skin Cancer
Hysteria
ADHD

Corps IV: With the Prussians

4-A
Schizophrenia
Rabies
Malaria
Trichomoniasis
Liver Cancer

4-B
Visceral Leishmaniosis
Brain Cancer
Lassa Virus
Bornholm Disease
Hantavirus

4-C
Ehrlichiosis
Diarrhea
Dengue Fever
Diabetes
Hemolytic-Uremic Syndrome

"Fourteen!" He shattered a plate against the wall. "Fourteen Demons behind the guns?"

Satan stomped to the Great Hall. A cluster of Priests and Priestesses chatted beside the gate of the Return Portal. They bowed.

"Get me a Wraith," Satan said.

One of the Priests quit cowering long enough to respond. "I'm sure they have all departed for the battle, my Lord."

Satan snarled and lifted the Priest off his feet by the back of his robe. "Deliver a message to the High Priest. Tell him that one, and only one, Demon will be allotted to cannon support. One per corps, not per squad. He will send the rest forward to face the multitude of Angels."

He dropped the Priest, who scurried away like a frightened rat. Satan shouted after him. "My order will be obeyed on penalty of death!"

Satan bared his teeth and muttered on his way to his room. "Fourteen hiding behind the guns! Disgraceful. I remember when I only had fourteen Demons in all of Hell."

ZINC ASSEMBLED THE STANDARD Bearers on a small hill overlooking a series of rolling fields in the Netherlands. They would coordinate this section of the battle. Fully aware that gossip had already pitted him against Iron III, Zinc played the role of the embattled leader and made one final effort to link the outcome to the conflict to Iron III.

Zinc took in the senior figures assembled in the country estate that served as Napoleon's briefing room. Carbon VI, Platinum, Hydrogen, Uranium II, Yttrium, Iron III, and Chromium awaited the briefing.

"I fear we have wagered too many Angels on this roll of the dice," Zinc said. "When I assigned you to Bonaparte, I did not envision such a grand call-up. It smacks of Teutoburg."

Iron III protested from within the French emperor. "You appointed me to this endeavor, so allow me to complete what you failed to accomplish at Austerlitz or Borodino."

Zinc made a conciliatory gesture. "I merely meant that the numbers—"

"The numbers are fine," Iron III said.

Carbon VI tried to sidetrack the impending argument. "I would feel better," he said from within one of Napoleon's aides, "if my various Houses were permitted to fight alongside my own."

"Your Houses are independent," Iron III said through thinly veiled frustration, "and their multitude is needed across various locales. Besides, I am certain Lord Zinc will look after those under his direct command."

Carbon VI executed an intentionally sloppy salute.

"You all know what is expected," Zinc said.

"Carbon VI, your human Jérôme will lead the attack on Hougoumont, supported by the Houses of Barium, Nitrogen Strontium, Platinum, Silicone, and Selenium."

Carbon VI clicked his heels. "Then I bid you adieu and wish you luck."

Platinum followed his compatriot.

Zinc pointed to Uranium II. "Your assignment is to lead the attack on Papelotte. You will be assisted by the Houses of Fluorine, Bromine, Yttrium, Rubidium, Zirconium, and Sodium."

"It is my life's honor to fulfill my duty on this day." Uranium II's salute was textbook perfect.

Not to be outshined, Iron III addressed Zinc. "You will take La Haye-Sainte along with Hydrogen, Bismuth, Beryllium, Rhodium, Calcium, Boron, and Ruthenium. No need to repeat everything."

Zinc barely hid his disdain. "It's always good to plan," he said.

Iron III stood ramrod straight.

He might as well be posing for a statue, Zinc thought.

Iron III's voice was better suited for the lecture hall. "Try as you might, I am Bonaparte, and this is my operation. You will not lay claim to it when we wipe the stinking, grotesque fiends of Hell from the map. The day is mine."

"Then win it," Zinc said.

Once his back was turned, Zinc smiled all the way out.

"Things all right for you?" Hydrogen asked.

They walked past rows of French soldiers readying themselves for the day's battle.

"They could be better," Zinc said, "but they are under control."

"Oftentimes, I wonder why I aspire to rise in stature, if this is the type of thing one has to deal with," Hydrogen said.

Zinc chucked a passing soldier on the shoulder in encouragement. "It's not so bad; you just have to remember who is your friend and who is your enemy."

"And who am I to you on this day?" Hydrogen asked.

"I don't have any friends," Zinc said with a smile indicating he was not kidding, "but I suppose you are the fondest of my enemies."

"Fight somebody long enough, and all that?"

"Exactly."

They continued walking. "I have not forgotten our agreement," Zinc said. You will succeed Uranium II. I have left instructions that you are also my successor should I fall."

Hydrogen stopped. "I am surprised, to say the least," he said.

Zinc put out his hand. "As much as I still envy... everything with Rachael, you have been reliable. I probably owe you my life for the day of the duel. So, if I am dead, what do I care who is ruling Heaven? Right?"

Hydrogen shook the proffered palm. "What an unlikely collaboration," he said. "Still, I hope I will replace Lord Uranium II and not you."

Zinc resumed the pace. "From your mouth to God's ears," he said.

TITUS STOOD IN BAFFLED silence as the words of the junior Priest rang in his ears. Schitz stepped forward and shook him from his stupor.

"He has doomed us," Titus said in a hollow voice.

"Whatever do you mean?" Schitz asked.

"Our Lord has only allotted three Demons to the guns. When I assigned fourteen, I was not sure that was sufficient."

"He sees it as a waste of resources," Schitz said. "He knows nothing of tactics."

"This is not America," Titus said. "There are few trees, if any. We will not have scores of sharpshooters in elevated positions picking off possessed soldiers. We need artillery enhanced by possessed gunners to select specific targets. The Angels will have such."

"Ignore the orders."

"He will kill me."

Schitz breathed heavily. "He threatens that a lot, and I have yet to see him go through with it."

Titus stamped his foot and cursed. "I had a good battle plan. If I thought ignoring his orders would save our effort, I would gladly face execution, but I have already instituted his orders. To change our assignments for a third time would create uncertainty and confusion."

"Well, if that is your assessment as commander, then you must focus on the here and now and not what could have been," Schitz said.

Titus clicked his tongue. "So be it. I wish we had more artillery, though."

"Well, your three remaining gunners will have to do us proud," Schitz said. "Who are they?"

"Dyslexia, Dysgraphia, and Hysteria," Titus said.

"All youngsters—the most recent Academy class." He locked eyes with Titus. "You are our commander. Even if our orders have sent us to the slaughter, you have to find a way to rescue this."

Titus nodded, stoic in the face of potential ruin.

"I must be getting to the Prussians," Schitz said.

Titus thrust his arms into the air. "That's it!"

"I'm sorry?"

"The Prussians," Titus said. He danced in place on his tiptoes for a moment. "Of course, the Prussians. They were meant to arrive through the center at the critical moment after the French attack."

"Yes."

"Well, you can take them wide around the flank," Titus said. "Napoleon will counter the maneuver with his own Imperial Guard and reserve as he did when the Cossacks attacked the flank at Borodino."

"Yes."

"If we coordinate with our push at the main front, the French will disintegrate and create instability among the Angels. They will expect us to have the cover of cannon and will proceed forward with caution. If we can simply hold on until the French break, we will salvage the day and save our forces."

Schitz chewed on the inside of his lip for a moment. "The plan is contingent on one thing."

"Which is?"

"You need the IV Corps and me to break the Angels and mortals within Bonaparte's Imperial Guard and to do so without the cover of cannons."

"And I need the forces of Hell to hold the line until the French army breaks," Titus said, "or Heaven will have won the war."

"This day got very bad, very quickly," Schitz said, "but we will do our duty. If luck is on our side, perhaps we will prevail despite our Lord's horrible strategizing."

He mounted his stallion. "To arms!"

Titus watched as Schitz, within the Prussian officer, galloped toward the forces of Gebhard Leberecht von Blücher.

THE BRITISH HAD POSITIONED four light divisions of guards among the farmhouses of Hougoumont, a tiny, wall-enclosed rural township. As the battle commenced, French artillery fired round after round into the small town. The shells sent fragments of metal flying through the air, tearing at the trees, buildings, and unlucky guards. Within the lines of Redcoats, Smallpox watched a large formation of French troops march across the grassy fields outside the town. Their blue uniforms and brass buckles reflected the morning light. The tattoo of drums and the blare of horns announced their advance.

Smallpox could discern the light aura indicating the possession of many of the French infantry. Additionally, he beheld numerous Angels within the Celestial, advancing in front of the mortal troops.

He issued the order. "Make ready." The first line of British guards knelt and cocked the hammers of their muskets. The second and third ranks readied their muskets as well, barrels toward the blue sky. Smallpox assessed the situation.

He was within the guard officer commanding the forward infantry, as was Meningitis. Spanish Influenza and Herpes were in the Celestial and ready to charge. Sepsis was leading a squad to his right and Agoraphobia to his left. Among the troops farther into town, Pancreatic Cancer and her squad were arrayed among mortals and the Celestial as well. Covering them from within the British artillery was Dyslexia.

Orders were to stand fast. But Smallpox was certain they stood a better chance of holding the town with an aggressive posture.

"Present!" The mortal troops lowered their muskets toward the advancing columns of French troops. He turned toward Spanish Influenza and, with the slightest flick of his head, gave the order to advance.

"Fire!"

Within the Celestial, Spanish Influenza rushed toward the advancing French and Angels. He had closed the distance a few strides ahead of Herpes when the British volley passed harmlessly through them and tore into the first line of French troops. Soldiers in the front of the formation crumbled as the lead tore through their bodies. Spanish Influenza zig-zagged to avoid Angelic throwing stars, one of which sliced his left ear.

He reached to his waist drew a throwing knife in each hand. He hurled the blades simultaneously with a flick and watched with delight as each found its mark within an Angel's neck. When he was closer to the cluster of Celestial Angels, Spanish Influenza stopped and crouched. The Angels were confused for a split moment. Herpes leapt over Spanish Influenza and buried his short sword into the torso of one of the foes. He assaulted another Angel and then another, driving his sword into vulnerable flesh.

On the firing line, Meningitis was rapidly readying her musket for action. A good mortal was expected to fire three rounds in the space of one minute. However, she had spent the morning possessing various maids, while Smallpox had possessed various men of the regiment. They'd filled the mortals' minds with additional expertise. When Meningitis dropped a cartridge down a barrel and pressed it home with the ramrod, the hands of her host were steady.

"First rank, make ready!" Smallpox watched the individual battles unfold. Meningitis returned the ramrod to its holder as the command was issued and pulled back the hammer.

"Present!" With a racing pulse, yet steady breath, Meningitis pointed the musket once more toward the rapidly approaching French infantry.

Spanish Influenza knew the next volley would be accompanied by cannon fire from Dyslexia. This was the time either to fall back or to press the advantage. The action erupted everywhere.

The Celestial was a killing field. Fragile X had arrived screaming and whirling twin katanas. He kicked an Angel in the chest before decapitating her. Hypochondriasis moved like a shadow, cutting, killing, and maiming the enemy.

Things were not one-sided. Primitive Erythropoiesis had just run an Angel through with his sword when he was stabbed in the back. Herpes had been struck in the chest by a throwing knife, then hacked apart by Angels. Spanish Influenza watched as the mortal French infantry, many possessed by Angels, arrived upon the area of their Celestial battle.

He bellowed in rage and frustration. "Fall back! Fall back!"

He looked towards the artillery position. "Come on, you bastards, fire the damn gun!"

Within the battery commander Dyslexia anxiously watched her comrades facing insurmountable odds. She drew a deep breath. "What a day."

Dyslexia had placed a female within the crew of each gun when she had been given word that she would be alone at the battery. She had never tried what she was about to attempt.

She aimed the gun. "Fire!"

As the commander pulled the lanyard, Dyslexia flesh-hopped into the next gun's commander, adjusted the gun slightly, and fired. The cannon roared. She jumped into the next gun crew, and on down the line.

When the last gun fired, she collapsed on the grassy hilltop within the Celestial and gasped for breath.

Spanish Influenza had expected a single well-placed shot. He watched in amazement as projectile after projectile tore into possessed Frenchmen as though they had been individually targeted. Spanish Influenza thanked his lucky stars he had not retreated with the others and began attacking the piles of writhing Angels caught in departure seizures.

He saw a group of Angels butchering Rocky Mountain Spotted Fever. In a rage, Spanish Influenza unleashed a flurry of havoc destined to become legend.

Schitz's Notebook

British Grenadiers

I can honestly say that the discipline and courage of the King's infantry was unparalleled. They are a model for battlefield organization and tactics.

He ran from Angel to Angel, stabbed hearts, sliced throats, stamped skulls, and filleted helpless flesh. He emerged from his run along the line soaked from head to toe in Angelic blood. He fled back toward his lines.

The battle for Hougoumont reached its climax. The French broke down a gate and flooded into the town. Smallpox ordered another volley from the British infantry and stepped into the Celestial. He yelled to Meningitis.

"If they hold the gate, the town will fall to the French, and our flank will collapse. Our orders are to repel the Angels until the French break. Get the reserves into formation, and retake that gate."

"We must converge on the center of the town now," Meningitis said to Pancreatic Cancer. "Ready the reserves and charge the Angels."

"So soon in the day?"

"The day will be decided now," Meningitis said.

Smallpox was wily. He ignored several seizing Angels and attacked the ones who were still standing. All while holding the narrow gate to the town within the Celestial. He fought with his characteristic unorthodoxy. He fought one Angel with a sword, then ripped the carotid out of the next with his teeth. He head-butted another opponent while kicking an attacker in the groin with his heel. He seemed invincible until he was caught in the stomach by a throwing knife.

He pulled the blade out of his innards. Though grimacing in pain, he hurled the knife back and killed its owner. Smallpox finally went down, overwhelmed by sheer numbers, but he took dozens of Angels with him. A violent, heaving scream exited his lungs as a young Angel ran her sword through his valiant heart.

A moment later, more Coldstream Guards arrived and fired a withering volley into the French. Led by Meningitis, the British charged with their Demons and recaptured the gate. A horde of Angels stood at the gate within the Celestial, but there were no available hosts. The Angels lost heart and withdrew.

Sepsis pointed. "They're falling back!"

"They'll regroup," Spanish Influenza said, his voice a stern warning.

The youngsters, Agoraphobia and Gingivitis, looked at the blood-soaked Demon with dread and respect.

Meningitis approached. "You did well, my son," she said. She turned to the others. "This ground was held at a dear price. Dearer yet, it may be before evening's fall. You are all soldiers of Hell and will do your part."

Spanish Influenza stepped forward and raised his bloodstained sword aloft. "For Satan."

The Demons beside him screamed, "Huzzah!"

INCOMING ARTILLERY BATTERED THE British positions along Papelotte. Autism looked down the lines of British troops. He knew the French and the Angels within their ranks would launch their attack in earnest following the bombardment. When he had been informed that he had lost most of his own artillery support, Autism had been forced into a bold plan.

He dismissed Pneumonia, Typhoid, and Cancer from the forward line and sent them to the British cavalry, the King's First Dragoon Guards.

"We need them within mortals," Autism said. "Tell Hysteria to hold off on the gun until the very last."

Hepatitis prepared to leave. Autism grabbed him by the arm. "And hurry back, old boy," he said. "I'm by myself here, you know."

The shelling subsided. Hepatitis returned to Autism's side at full tilt.

"She's up for it," he said, "though she thinks you are mad."

Autism laughed. "Time will tell, but I do not see any other way to hold out."

The lines of French infantry advanced. Autism and Hepatitis stepped into the Celestial. On either side, Autism saw Gangrene and her squad and Guillain-Barré's group.

Please remember the plan, he thought.

His knuckles turned white against the handle of his sword. The British mortals fired their muskets into the oncoming French, and Autism led the charge within the Celestial. Counter to the standard strategy; the Demons were free from a mortal host. They met the Angels in front of the British lines with savage effect. The Angels had split their forces between the Mortal and the Celestial Realm and were caught off-guard. However, they still possessed numerical superiority.

Autism hacked off an Angel's head and turned to see ADHD fending off three Angels at once. She ran one through, used the corpse to block, then struck down a second. The third Angel stepped back in amazement. ADHD drilled him between the eyes with a throwing star.

ADHD waved in triumph at Autism only to be cut down by yet another onrushing Angel. Before he could react, Autism was knocked to the floor and forced to defend against the crashing blows of a furious Angel with Asian features. Hemophilia came from behind, stabbed the Angel, and pulled Autism to his feet.

"Thanks," he said.

"No prob—"

Hemophilia went down with a knife to the throat.

The Demons, though outnumbered, fought ferociously. Gangrene lost her sword in an Angel's skull, drew her dagger, and assessed the scene. The Demons had been pushed back with the retreating British. Gangrene drove her dagger into an Angel's thorax, then collapsed from a blow to the back of her head. She rolled left. A blade whizzed past her ear and stuck in the ground. She jumped to her feet, ready to engage. The Angel rushed—too hard and too fast. Gangrene ducked, flipped the attacker over her shoulder, and drove her dagger through his eye.

One after another, the Angels came; Gangrene dispatched each in turn. Not all of her compatriots were as fortunate. A hammer crushed Ulcers' skull. Naegleriasis, unable to disentangle her sword from a foe, took a blade to the heart. African Trypanosomiasis fell when he was beset by Angels from all sides.

Alone after her squad's decimation, Gangrene stood among a pile of Angelic corpses. She heard Autism sound the call to retreat. Howling like a wounded animal, Gangrene fought her way through the Angels that encircled her. She leapt into one mortal and then another as the gaggle of Angels chased in a bloodthirsty frenzy.

The situation repeated itself among the Demons defending Papelotte. Autism fled through the advancing French and then utilized the retreating British. Skin Cancer lost the rest of her squad, Guillain-Barré and Osteomyelitis. She jumped through the mortals who were in panic-stricken flight. The Demons defending the British flank had been routed.

From the hills farther beyond the lines, the thunderous tread of the king's horses plowed through the tall grass of the rolling hills.

How often has British cavalry swept across the continent over the centuries? Cancer thought from the head of the Dragoons' charge.

Her chinstrap dug into her mortal's neck, and she struggled to draw a full breath. At long last, she cleared the final, grassy slope and came upon the carnage wrought by the French advance. Cancer's keen eyes surveyed the scene. She saw the British infantry falling back in orderly, disciplined formation. With them, she saw the surviving Demons—frantic and flesh-hopping.

So few left? she wondered.

As Autism had suspected, the Angels stepped back into mortal hosts to pursue the fleeing Demons sheltered within the human ranks. For the moment, all the pursuing Angels were within mortals and vulnerable to the cavalry.

From her position at the gun battery, Hysteria watched the cavalry closing in on the French. She had spent the morning pre-sighting the cannons. They were exactly positioned to cover Autism's retreat.

The day had been a challenge. After learning she would be the sole gunner at a battery intended for four, she received a frantic message demanding fire. The young Demon, fresh from the newest Academy class, felt the weight of the moment. She was young, but serious and methodical. She had spent time possessing all of the female members of the different gun crews, filling their minds with her knowledge, making up as best she could for the missing Demons. Despite her nerves, she was certain where the shot would fly.

"Fire!"

Cancer felt the heat of the canister shot; scores of small, metal projectiles, buzz past her like enraged bees. The shrapnel shredded the possessed French infantry in a hailstorm of death and destruction. The possessed mortals that escaped the cannon barrage fell to Cancer's saber.

Behind her, Pneumonia and Typhoid, leapt out of the bodies of their dragoons and fell on the enemy. Pneumonia threw himself towards any Angels that managed to escape their hosts, while Typhoid set about slaughtering the sea of seizing Angels. A handful of Angels managed to step into the Celestial during the shelling and then back into mortals following the arrival of the cavalry. Cancer was more than up to the task of running them down with her dragoons as the French and surviving Angels fell back from Papelotte.

Cancer reached the crest of a hill. Her horse reared on its hind legs. Balanced in the saddle, she raised her bloody saber aloft and shouted a violent, unintelligible battle cry, a shriek echoed by the dragoons under her command.

The Duke of Wellington looked across the field from his post and turned to his aide de camp. "I don't know what effect these men have upon the enemy, but, by God, they frighten the Hell out of me."

Napoleon (Iron III) lowered his field telescope and growled. "Damn Prussians!"

The Angel within the French emperor was clearly conflicted by the emerging threat that endangered the outcome of the mortal and Celestial battles. He turned to Zinc, still within Marshal Michel Ney.

"Shall I deal with the Prussians?" Zinc asked.

"Don't be smug," Iron III said. "I will take the reserves to deal with it. If the Prussians are on our right, they are not in the center. Take your men and capture La Hoyte-Sainte."

Iron III rallied his reserves and his old fighters, the Imperial Guard, the very best of the French troops, and rode to meet the Prussians. Frustration and anger increased with every hoofbeat. His forces had been repelled from Hougoumont. The Angels had been massacred and pushed back from Papelotte. Now the Prussians were threatening to destabilize the entire French Army. If the French collapsed, the

Angels would lose their opportunity to crush the Demons. Worse, they might be annihilated despite their superior numbers. His Percheron carried him toward the Prussians under the command of von Blücher. Iron III had all his descendants with him: Tungsten, Titanium, Vanadium, Chromium, Niobium, and Palladium.

Iron III had only one thought as he thundered towards the conflict. *This will take me to the height of Heavenly power.*

THE HORNS BLARED THE strains of the *Dessauer Marsch* as the Prussian troops marched along the small dirt road through the countryside. Their blue and gray uniforms were immaculate; their buttons polished; their muskets clean. The pride of Germanic society was the military of noble Prussia.

Schitz marched along with the lead contingent, having left von Blücher for a forward officer. Suddenly, he noticed a blur along his flank, the senior Wraith, Anubis.

"I have the intelligence you requested," Anubis said from the tall grass alongside the road.

Schitz abandoned his host and stepped into the Celestial, where the Wraith handed him a plethora of scrolls.

"Will that be all, sir?"

"Dismissed."

Schitz looked through the scrolls that contained remarkably distinctive renderings of various Angelic Lords. Schitz read the names aloud. "Iron III, Tungsten, Titanium, Vanadium Chromium, Niobium, and Palladium."

Schitz waved to Rabies, who departed her host and joined him walking along the columns of soldiers in the Celestial.

"These are the leaders of the Houses coming to face us," Schitz said.

"Are we up to this? We have no artillery support."

Schitz heard the fear.

"We were always going to be without cannon support once Titus decided to send us around the flank," Schitz said. "I would not lead us into hopeless slaughter. I planned this move long before the battle—a little trick, a gift to Titus. The Angels value their Lords; if we decapitate them, there is a chance that the rest will collapse."

"I trust your judgment, Father."

"It will still be rough," Schitz said. "Take Brain Cancer, Bornholm, and Liver Cancer to that grove of trees." He pointed. "Two shooters, two reloading. These are not Kentucky rifles. They're smoothbore. When mortals use them, they are worthless outside of fifty yards or so. You can probably make them effective up to a hundred yards, but that's it. Don't give away your position no matter what you see happening on the field."

"I want to be up front with you," Rabies said, "not hiding in a tree."

"You want no part of what is going to happen."

He cut her protest off with a wave. "I know I have been distant as my father was with me. But like him, let me be good to you now, and protect you during this cataclysm."

"Look after Malaria," she said.

Rabies jumped into a nearby Jäger[75] and summoned her squad. Four soldiers ran toward the cluster of trees between them and the approaching French just emerging over a distant hilltop.

"Schnell und lebhaft,"[76] Schitz said.

He had instructed the Demons to stay within their mortal hosts as long as possible, which might be catastrophic once the musket fire began. However, it would be essential in keeping the Angels within mortals until the decisive moment. They passed under the trees; Schitz looked up and met Rabies' gaze. He had the distinct sensation that it was for the last time but pushed the thought from his head and managed to wink at her.

"Halt!"

---

[75] Skirmisher, Light Infantry, Hunter.

[76] Fast and lively.

The Prussian column stopped. "Rüsten!"[77] The French continued to close the distance. Schitz looked across the front line to his grandson Malaria, who was within an infantryman. If Rabies was a beloved stranger, her son was a full and complete mystery. The horns continued the *Dessauer Marsch*; drumbeats pulsed through the air.

Schitz leaned over to his grandson and whispered. "We are soldiers of Hell. Our family bonds are not the closest, but I want you to know, I am happy to be facing this day with family."

"I am honored to be shoulder to shoulder with Hell's fiercest Demon," Malaria said.

"Whatever happens," Schitz said, the French were close enough to make out individual faces, "stay within your mortal; it is our only hope."

"Präsentieren!"[78]

In unison, the musket barrels lowered toward the enemy. For a moment, the two armies stood facing each other, each filled with mortals who wanted nothing more than to see home again. Schitz beheld the Angels rushing toward him within the Celestial; he saw the ones in the French ranks. The decisive moment had arrived.

Schitz and his French counterpart shouted the same order at the same time.

"Schießen!"

"Tirer!"[79]

The field disappeared, buried by billowing smoke. Soldiers on both sides fell and poured their life's blood into the Earth's thirsty maw. A ball from the second volley punched Schitz's host through the chest cavity. It smashed the young man's ribs, tore through the soft tissue of his right lung, and buried in his back. Schitz flesh-hopped into the mortal to his left and narrowly escaped the onset of a departure seizure. Most of the Demons were still within their hosts. Lassa Virus and Diarrhea had fallen to the ground.

---

[77] Ready.

[78] Present.

[79] Fire!

"Stay within your mortals!"

The command condemned the stricken Demons to their eternal deaths. Schitz watched, helpless, while the closest Angels cut the writhing Demons to pieces. The Angels seemed perplexed by the Demons' decision to remain within the mortals and jumped into the unoccupied Prussians.

Schitz drew a pistol and fired it into one of the possessed Prussians, then drew his bayonet and sliced another. He did not wish to be fighting off Angels within the Prussians.

Everything comes down to the next volley.

Both armies reloaded as fast as they could. Schitz heard ramrods scrape and hammers cock. The Prussians lowered their barrels a moment before the French. Here was the opportunity.

"Schießen!"

The volley ripped through the French ranks. "Vorwärts!"[80]

The Prussians charged. The Angels lurking in the Celestial to dispatch departing Demons could do nothing but wait. Schitz knew there was another volley coming from the Imperial Guard.

He felt the concussion of the simultaneous musket blasts and watched more of his troops—mortals and Demons alike—clutch and fall. There was a momentary thrill when Schitz realized he had not been hit. But his joy was short-lived; ten yards away, Malaria grabbed his chest and collapsed.

A pair of Angels running within the Prussians leapt into the Celestial. Helpless, Schitz watched as one began stabbing the seizing Malaria in his back while the other lifted his chin to slice his throat. Seconds later, Malaria was just another lifeless corpse. Schitz grimaced but pressed on resolutely.

If only I could have kept my promise to Rabies, he thought.

---

[80] Forward!

IRON III WATCHED THE skirmish with disbelief.

"They are not leaving wounded mortals," he said. "The Demons don't even care about their own well-being."

"But they are mowing down our troops. It is obvious. They are trying to alter the outcome of the mortal battle," Lord Tungsten said.

Iron III looked at his son. "Of course," he said. "If they break the French here and gain access to the rear area, the whole Grande Armée will collapse, and we will be unable to coordinate anything."

Tungsten pointed. "Look!"

He raised his arm within a French officer and gestured at the point of impact between the two lines. The Prussians had forced the French backwards. At point-blank range, the Prussians maintained their cohesiveness, reformed their lines, and assumed a firing position.

Potzdam Musket

Iron III's voice was a hoarse croak. "No."

Successive volleys from the first and second line struck the French with unforgiving ferocity. The French howled and scores of the Imperial Guard collapsed to the earth. Those who survived started running. All while a call to "Retraite" sounded from the bugles.

Iron III turned to Tungsten. "Everybody into a Frenchman, now. We will turn the tide of this battle."

THE LONG BARREL OF the Potsdam musket peeked from the leafy branches of the tree. The butt of the weapon rested in the crux of Rabies' shoulder. She rested the long gun on a branch for increased stability. From her vantage point high in the tree, she had watched the battle unfold. Her father had been accurate in his assessment that she "wanted nothing to do with it." She watched as the luckless Demons fell helplessly from their hosts and were butchered by awaiting Angels.

Tears burned her eyes as she watched her last child fall under an Angel's sword. Schitz barely avoided death when his host was struck. Then, one by one, Lassa Virus, Diarrhea, Hantavirus, Visceral Leishmaniosis, Hemolytic-uremic Syndrome, Ehrlichiosis, and Trichomoniasis met the same fate. A dread notion passed through her mind.

I am going to watch everyone die and never fire a shot.

Next to her, Brain Cancer shouted, "This is madness!"

"He knows what he is doing," Bornholm said. The sternness in her eyes steeled the others against the savagery they were witnessing. Then, as Schitz had predicted, the Prussians broke through the French and forced them back. Suddenly, all the auras of Celestial Angels began to rush into French infantry.

Rabies called to her compatriots. "Be certain before you fire. No one misses."

She aligned the sight over a possessed Frenchman close to Schitz and squeezed the trigger. The crack of the musket echoed from the treetop. Before the ball found its mark, Rabies tossed the musket over her shoulder to Liver Cancer, who was perched next to her and caught a loaded one. Rabies set the weapon on a tree branch and steadied her breathing. There was an explosion of powder as Bornholm fired from the tree beside her.

Rabies focused upon her own task. Schitz had already killed the Angel that she had felled and was approaching another. Rabies pulled the trigger.

She heard Liver Cancer from over her shoulder. "Ready!"

"Toss!"

They exchanged weapons. Rabies tracked a possessed Frenchman near to Dengue Fever and fired.

"Ready!"

"Toss!"

Liver Cancer could load in less than twelve seconds, far faster than the best of the King's Regiment. He caught the musket from Rabies, poured powder from a paper cartridge down the barrel, grabbed the ramrod from between his teeth and pushed the musket ball down the barrel.

Returning the ramrod to his mouth, he put a measure of powder on the pan, closed the frizzen, and cocked the hammer. He knew full well that the outcome of the engagement depended on his speed and accuracy.

"Ready!"

"Toss!"

Rabies caught her next musket and drew down on another possessed Frenchman. The process repeated.

And the merciless harvest of Frenchmen continued.

JEAN-FRÉDÉRIQUE HAD BEEN A member of the Imperial Guard for many years. But something about Waterloo was different. He could not place it; he simply did not feel himself. The battle raged... and he imagined he was being moved by an unseen force. He thought back to easier campaigns—Austria and Russia; he remembered his elderly mother, his beautiful wife, his lovely children. He longed for a glass of wine. His thoughts abruptly terminated when a musket ball smashed his larynx and tore through his jugular vein and carotid artery.

Schitz leaped out of the body of the Prussian he was possessing and stabbed his dagger into the throat of the Angel that fell out of the body of Jean-Frédérique. The musket fire from the treetops seemed supernatural. Enemies near to him slumped and fell as though by his will. Their comrades were unable to assist them. By the time the victim fell, Schitz had dispatched them and jumped into another mortal body. He crisscrossed the field. Ever surrounded by Angels, he weaved the deadly dance and avoided his foes. When Angels managed to step into the Celestial, some survived; others died.

Wholesale killing was not his goal. Within his mind's eye, he always saw the images sketched upon the parchment scrolls. He recited their names; he knew that killing the leaders would turn the battle.

At long last, he spied the first of the Angelic Lords, Titanium, a noble-looking Angel with flowing silvery hair, a strong chin, and piercing gray eyes. He appeared through the mortal he possessed as he extolled his fellows to repulse the Prussians. Schitz charged towards the Angel. He hoped the shooters would not fail him.

From the treetops, Bornholm and Rabies had both spotted Schitz's target moments apart. They each fired a fatal shot at nearly the same interval. The mortal Frenchman was stuck in both the chest and the forehead simultaneously. Schitz leapt from the Prussian a moment before a Frenchman bayoneted him through the ribs, hurled a throwing knife into Titanium's throat, and barrel-rolled across the ground to safety. Before the Angels could react, Schitz was already within another mortal host. He turned his attention to the closest Angel, who was summarily felled by the next musket ball.

The slaughter wore on as the Prussians took the field from the French, and Schitz and his comrades chiseled their way through the Angelic ranks. Schitz cut down the Lords he remembered as Chromium and Vanadium in rapid succession. Schitz became aware that he was the sole remaining Demon. Dengue Fever and Diabetes were nowhere to be seen. The young Demons, both graduates of the most recent class, had been given a tough assignment, but they had answered the call of destiny.

Many older Demons had fallen under fire as well. Still, the young-sters had completed their objective. Piles of Angelic corpses littered the grassy field as the French fell back toward the small hamlet of Plancenoit. Schitz was rushed by a contingent of at least a dozen Angels. He recognized the Lords Tungsten and Niobium leading the group. Half the Angels stepped into the Celestial; the other half remained within the mortal Frenchmen. Schitz could already envision the struggle within his mind before it unfolded. He knew that he would likely perish while facing such odds. However, he would not flee. He did not wait for the musket fire from the trees but stepped into the Celestial as well. He drew a throwing knife in each hand and hurled the blades toward the Angelic Lords. Both targets collapsed as searing pain welled from Schitz's abdomen. One throwing knife protruded from his stomach, another from his shoulder. A third blade was embedded in his right thigh.

He felt a shock—a sting on his throat. He ran his hand across his neck. It came away bloody. He was cut but not injured seriously.

Out of weaponry, Schitz yanked at the handles of the knives skewering his body. The barbarism of his move terrified the Angels. He buried the blades in the back of two seizing Angels who'd been brought down by Rabies and Bornholm.

Outnumbered eight-to-one and nearly delirious with pain, Schitz pushed himself into an onrushing Prussian. The Angels, now keenly aware of the snipers aiming at any mortal they might possess, hightailed it within the Celestial back towards Plancenoit.

Schitz slowed the mortal's run, then fell to his knees. He raised his musket over his head. Though the images blurred through the haze of his injuries, he was sure he could see the Jägers in the treetops waving back to him.

WITHIN MARSHAL NEY, ZINC had spent a significant portion of the day coordinating the French assault on La Haye-Sainte. Once Iron III (and Bonaparte) left to take on the Prussians, Zinc had enjoyed considerable freedom. All reports indicated that the battle was progressing better than he could have hoped. The Imperial Guard had been routed for the first time in its history; Iron III and the Houses of his descendants had been smashed by the flanking Prussians. Additionally, the Angels had sustained severe casualties at Hougoumont and Papelotte.

Zinc had taken a measured approach in probing the British and Demonic forces. He utilized updated assessments from the Familiars when they informed him that the Demons occupied a solitary gun battery and would be vulnerable within the mortals.

He led the main contingent forward across the field.

"Avance!"[81]

Once they approached the small town, the British opened a barrage with cannons and muskets. Grapeshot and bullets ripped through the mortal infantry. Zinc and his comrades slipped into the Celestial and continued their progress. They saw the Demons arrayed among the British lines—half in the Celestial, half within mortals. Fully aware of the presence of death, Zinc held onto every sound, sight, taste, and smell.

Hydrogen called from his left. "Faisons-les payer!"[82]

Zinc saw Rachael next to her husband, her fierce eyes burning within a Frenchwoman. On closer consideration, what he first thought was her leather cape was, in reality, the tanned skin of a flayed Demon.

He shook his head. *And still, I want her*, he thought.

He raised his arm.

"Se préparer!"

With a flick of his hand, he sent the advance elements of the Angelic warriors forward into the Celestial. They rushed headlong to meet the Celestial Demons. Half were under orders to engage the Demons; the rest would continue past toward the rear of the Demonic position.

"Présenter!"

Both Zinc and the French officer he possessed looked down at the grapefruit-sized hole in their torso. Zinc had experienced a departure seizure before, but his understanding of the process made it no less agonizing.

The world shook. His body convulsed as if being stabbed while

---

[81] Advance

[82] "Let's make them pay!"

underwater. Rachael stood over him in the Celestial for a moment, then rose to defend herself, and him, against a quartet of Demons.

Confusion reigned.

We outnumber them. We maneuvered perfectly. We surrounded them. How are they attacking? How are so many of them here at the front lines? What is happening with the assault?

He wanted to help Rachael, but nothing moved. He watched her as if from a long distance. She was a whirl of blades and spins, slashes and death.

A Demon flung himself at Zinc and buried a blade in the stricken Angel's left arm. Rachael stabbed the attacker, spilling his innards on the ground. Rachael leaned over Zinc.

"Are you al—"

Zinc winced at the sound of bones crunching. A Demon wrenched the spiked iron ball of his Morningstar from the remains of Rachael's skull and raised it to end Zinc's life. Zinc grabbed for Rachael's sword and, summoning the little strength he had left, thrust it at the Demon. The blade slid neatly between the Demon's ribs; he stared wide-eyed at the protruding handle as he slumped to the ground.

Zinc crawled to Rachael. The back of her head looked like a fractured eggshell.

"Don't try to speak," he said. "Manna heals all kinds of damage."

Zinc recognized one of his former students from the Academy, then realized it was one of Rachael's many sons.

"Jacob!"

The boy abandoned his host.

"Justin," he said, but his focus was on his mother.

Ever the commander, Zinc issued orders. He gripped the boy's arm.

"She is alive, but barely. Get her out of here. Make a portal. Get Manna immediately."

The boy looked from his mother to Zinc, then towards the raging battle.

"Go—now!"

Justin picked up the limp body. He looked at Zinc, tears in his eyes.

"They sprung a trap. They have killed Calcium, Bismuth, and Rhodium."

"Your father?"

"My father rallies our forces even now," Justin said, "my brother Beryllium as well."

"Good," Zinc said. "Now, make haste!"

Justin Hydrogen departed. Zinc used a sword as a crutch and pushed to his feet. His left arm hung by his side, useless. He limped across the field, then stepped into one of the multitudes of onrushing Frenchmen crossing the field toward the burning town of La Haye-Sainte.

SCARLET FEVER FINISHED WRAPPING a bandage around her wounded hand. "We are defeated," she said. "We must return to Hell."

They had fallen back to Dysgraphia's position. Anorexia looked at the haggard survivors of the encounter: Scarlet Fever, Lung Cancer, and Lymphoma.

"I did the best I could," Dysgraphia said. "I picked off four of the Lords from those sketches the Wraith gave me. There were supposed to be three others."

Anorexia patted him on the shoulder. "You did great. They defended their Lords with unexpected ferocity and skill."

"We have felled many Angels," Lung Cancer said. She ran her hand across her face and wiped blood away from a superficial facial wound. "We should not retreat now. The French have not taken the field. Our entire strategy is based upon holding until Schitz and the Prussians shatter the French. We can kill scores more Angels when their hosts fall into disarray."

"They have taken La Hay-Sainte," Scarlet Fever said. "The British center is about to collapse, and if it does, we will be the ones fleeing for a portal in terror. We must retreat."

Anorexia sighed. "There are still seventy to eighty Angels down there. The odds have gotten worse."

"Must be sixteen-to-one by now," Dysgraphia said.

Anorexia weighed their chances. "Fine," she said. "Fuck the orders. We were supposed to have four gunners; let's have three now. Scarlet Fever, Lymphoma, you stay with Dysgraphia and man these guns."

Anorexia walked over to Lung Cancer and punched her on the shoulder. "We will go forth to meet them."

Lung Cancer clasped Anorexia's arm and head-butted her.

"You two against seventy to eighty?" Scarlet Fever asked. "No matter what we do with the guns, you will die."

"It will not be a bad death," Anorexia said. "I just wish there were more Angels to take with me."

Lung Cancer unleashed an unholy laugh. The two charged down the hill away from the gun crews and back toward the British lines.

Meningitis groaned and readjusted her head in Spanish Influenza's lap.

"Night will come soon, my son," she said, "and then you can slip away back to Hell. No one will call you a coward."

"Victory must come first," he replied.

Or death, he thought.

Spanish Influenza winced from a variety of wounds and stroked his mother's hair.

She will die soon.

They sat in the Celestial. The British guards had held the town of Hougoumont despite the hordes of attacking French and Angels. But the cost had been dear. The Angels outnumbered them and had surrounded the town within the Celestial, but cowardice prohibited them from attacking. They had suffered grievous losses over the course of the day.

With the death of Smallpox and the impending demise of Meningitis, Spanish Influenza assumed he was in command. Gone too were his daughter Sepsis, Fragile X, Hypochondriasis, Agoraphobia, Brucellosis, and Gingivitis. He looked down again at his mother and realized she was gone. He laid her head gently on the ground, stood, and possessed an officer of the Coldstream Guards.

Addressing his fellow Demons, who were within the surrounding mortals, he said, "They have surrounded us in the Celestial thinking that we will be on the losing end of the mortal battle. However, if the British still hold this position, their center has not been broken. So, we will wait here safe within these mortals for now. Should there be a general retreat of the French and the Angels, we will pick off the edges of their formation one at a time as they fall back. Should night arrive without a British victory, we have done all we could, and we will exit."

He heard a mumble of consensus.

"You've all fought well," he said to both the mortals and the Demons. "I'm proud of each and every one of you."

THE REGIMENTAL STANDARD OF the French 45th Regiment De Infanterie had flown over the army of the emperor for many years. But, as the day concluded, it lay in the hands of a soldier of the Royal North British Dragoons, a fate shared by many of Napoleon's flags, standards, and soldiers.

As the Grande Armée disintegrated and retreated, the army of Heaven lost its footing on the battlefield. The edges of the Angelic forces stood vulnerable to the nimble Demons. It was a deadly progression. Panicked French mortals left the field... the Angels had no hosts; the surviving Demons picked off numerous Heavenly soldiers without suffering further losses.

Zinc completed the Return Ritual with Lord Uranium II and walked into the Great Hall of Heaven. Iron III and Palladium stood in one corner.

"How many of your contingent return from the field?" Zinc asked.

Iron III's voice trembled. "Fifteen."

"Not from your House, from your contingent?" Zinc kept his voice loud. He wanted all the attention he could get.

Iron III clenched his teeth. "I said fifteen."

"Fifteen of one hundred and twenty?" Zinc pivoted. He pushed Iron III, goading him to begin walking.

Uranium II gave Palladium a shove and he trudged behind Zinc and Iron III. A crowd had gathered by the time they reached the small island used to resolve disputes. Zinc gestured for Uranium II to stand beside him. He addressed Iron III.

"Turn and kneel."

Iron III's face went ashen. "You can't do this."

Zinc's response was without emotion. "Your Houses are scattered to the wind; who will intervene for you?"

Iron III sank to the ground. Uranium II forced Palladium to his knees. Zinc addressed the spectators.

"We are the Supreme Commanders of Heaven's army. The Houses of Iron challenged us and demanded the opportunity to demonstrate their leadership. You all know this to be so. You all heard the whispers that Iron III should be Supreme Commander. Look at what his leadership has wrought. He did not capture La Haye-Saint. He did not kill any impressive number of Demons. His failure and his hubris will now be punished."

Zinc drew his dagger and plunged it into Iron III's neck. Before Iron III's face hit the dirt, Zinc shoved the body into the Eunoe.

Uranium II dispatched Palladium.

Zinc watched the bodies sink below the surface.

Now they are with Uranium I—more challengers removed.

He wiped his blade and went to find Rachael.

SATAN'S VOICE SOUNDED LIKE iron nails scraping on slate. "I should have you boiled alive."

Titus knelt in front of the other members of the Triumvirate Council. The High Priest was exhausted.

"If that is your desire, I remain your humble servant," Titus said. "I only wish to see the Demons I commanded one last time."

He looked up, neither defiant nor fearful.

The door opened.

Satan roared his displeasure. "Closed meeting!"

Heavy footsteps echoed on the flagstone. Titus turned. Schizophrenia was standing next to him.

Schitz saluted crisply, removed his Knight's Pentagram, and hung it around Titus's neck. Schitz stepped back and saluted again.

"You should have had your guns, sir," Schitz said.

Schitz saluted Satan, executed a precise about-face, and limped from the room.

The Devil opened his mouth but was interrupted again when Autism entered. He repeated Schitz's moves exactly, though this time, he placed his Pentagram Second Class upon Titus's robe.

"It was an honor to serve under you today, sir," he said.

Footsteps sounded again but stopped when Satan rose.

"How many more are out there?" he asked.

Anorexia saluted. "Spanish Influenza, he has his decoration and his mother's. Cancer—"

"Get out!"

His last word hung in the air like a roar of thunder. Cancer bowed and backed out of the room. Defiant, she never took her eyes from Satan.

Satan chucked. "Well, that was easy, your last wish came to you. Now—"

The door opened again.

Elise glided across the floor and saluted with her good arm. She pulled a scroll from her belt. "The battle report," she said, then winked at Titus as she withdrew.

Satan perused the parchment. He then tossed the scroll to Titus; the High Priest's hands quivered.

"Read it aloud," Satan said.

"An... An..." Titus coughed. "The Angels fielded approximately five hundred and ten Angels (about eighty percent of their total forces). Three hundred and seventy-seven were killed in action. So, there are still at least two hundred Angels left in Heaven. We fielded everyone we had, sixty-two in all. Thirty-nine went down. We have twenty-three Demons left."

Satan's sneer could have curdled milk. "You're thinking that if I had allowed more on the guns, we would have achieved the final victory," he said.

"Not my opinion, my Lord," Titus said. "It is the grim reality of the after-action report."

"Of course, you are correct."

Titus had never heard such candor from the Dark Lord.

"But you are also fired," Satan said. "You are no longer my army's commander. Go back to being the High Priest and my voice on the Triumvirate Council. Now, go."

Titus scrambled to his feet.

On his way out, he heard a malevolent whisper from the throne. "And if you know what's good for you, never speak of this again."

"How is she?" Zinc asked.

"She lives, thank God," Hydrogen said.

"She saved my life," Zinc said.

"Would you like to see her?"

Zinc stepped into the room of his longtime nemesis. Every other Standard Bearer that he knew decorated his abode with captured Demonic weapons or prizes from mortal warriors. Hydrogen's dwelling place was adorned exclusively with the skins of African animals: lions, leopards, giraffes, elephants, and a few that Zinc did not recognize.

Zinc's attention moved to the bed, the site where Rachael had unleashed her considerable passion and skill on another. She was obviously damaged, but serene.

"The Familiars have told me the Manna will heal her," Hydrogen said. "She should awaken as she was."

"I pray for that," Zinc said.

He turned for the door, then reconsidered and extended his hand. "Thank you."

Hydrogen shook it. "Thank you," he said, "for being worth her sacrifice."

"Pardon?"

"You lead when others falter. You make decisions others do not face. We are all eternally grateful."

Zinc walked down the hall toward the oppressive loneliness of his own empty room.

"THEY TOLD ME YOU'D be here," Titus said.

He tossed Schitz's Knight's Pentagram through the air. It hit Schitz in the lap.

Schitz looked up from his meditative state along the banks of the Styx.

"I appreciate everything you did on the field and afterward," Titus said.

"I did my duty," Schitz replied. "I have been reflecting a lot about what that means of late."

Titus chuckled. "You are not alone."

"You see that we serve an imperfect Lord?" Schitz asked.

"I do now."

"Well, there you have it," Schitz said. "And yet, there is nothing to do but march along to the beating of the drum."

"Indeed."

After a moment's silence, Titus said, "He's demoted me."

"At least he didn't kill you," Schitz said. He sat for another moment, then hopped to his feet. "Wait here."

"Where are you going?"

"Brew," replied Schitz. "We need Brew. Then we can converse about battles won and lost."

Titus reclined in the grass and waited.

"I can't think of a better way to end the day," he said.

ORIGINAL LYRICS
BY J.L. FEUERSTACK
FROM OVER THE BROAD EARTH VOL. I

ENGELLIED
(THE ANTHEM OF THE ANGELS)

We stand on guard with not a single hint of trepidation,
We stand on guard, to the foe's ever-present consternation,
Yes, we stand on guard, battle-scarred, weathered, and hard,
Ready for any possible situation.

We fight for God, the primogenitor of all creation,
We fight for His honor, and it brings us the greatest elation,
Yes, we fight with might, for all that is good, noble, and right,
That his temple may never know any desecration.

We wait for the Holy Spirit that Its guidance may always command us,
We wait for Its blessing, which will render us invincible and glorious,
Yes, we wait for that day, patiently, hopeful, we pray,
For when we will be left standing victorious.

We clear the way for Christ, the bringer of all Holy Redemption,
We clear the way with demonic purging, for Earth's reclamation,
Yes, we clear the way, one step further with each serpent we slay,
So that all are free to partake in the Lord's adoration.

If we should fall amidst the battle's havoc, turmoil, and confusion,
We will not beg, nor offer our foes collaboration, parley, or collusion,
Yes, if we should fall, we will fall having given our all,
Let that be our final rest and consolation.

THE HUNTER'S SONG
(THE ANTHEM OF THE DEMONS)

We stand firm, though the foes volleys fall upon us like showers,
We stand firm through the passing of many countless hours,
Firmly we stand, awaiting the Lord's command,
Ready to unleash our company's many powers.

Forward we bound, when unleashed upon the dastardly foe,
Forward we leap, like hunting hounds upon the beleaguered doe,
Eagerly we spring, letting the battle cry ring,
Swifter than any arrow loosed from a bow.

Proudly we take our place amongst the Lord's trusted appointed,
Bathed in the blood of the foe and in the oil of victory anointed,
Proudly we feast on the flesh of the vanquished deceased,
Our enemies dismembered and disjointed.

We bring forth the peace of the everlasting and the tranquil night,
We bring forth all that is needed and what's more all that is right,
Justly we come, to undo all that must be undone,
We will never tarry or weary in our fight.

If victory calls for us to offer ourselves a sacrifice on the altar,
We will not hesitate, nor will we cower or will we falter,
Preparedly, we go forward, no loss is too untoward,
Merrily we go forth to the slaughter.

THE ASCENSION
(HYMN OF THE ANGELIC ARRIVAL CEREMONY)

Let glad tidings reverberate and resound,
Telling all of redemption's greatest story
That which was lost has now been found.

Renewed in the light of Heavenly glory,
Delivered from the suffering of Hellish plight,
And all that which is sickly and gory.

Now walk onwards towards the light,
You have paid your fare with contrition,
Suffer no longer in the darkness of the night.

Your destination is not solely for saints' admission,
Though you will walk on Holy ground,
But for all who will engage in sin's abolition.

Bathed in the grace in which all evil is drowned,
Go towards that place where love and light abound.

Redi In Gloria
(Hymn of the Demonic Arrival Ceremony)

Let all passersby hear this our hymn and declaration.
We emerge clad in the trappings of victory.
Purged of all weakness through the test of conflagration.

Rewarded for our devotion and our loyalty.
Let all join in the triumphant battle cry.
In honor of the true and only Royalty.

Our Lord that reigns over all on high
He imbues his subjects the might of lions,
And gives us strength to pull Angels from the sky.

Armed with his wings our environs,
We proudly are free to take our flight,
Over the world that we claim as his proud scions

Victorious in our just and noble fight
To cover all in the peace of darkest night.

Buona Notte
(Angelic Funeral Hymn)

Hear how, the bells tolled,
When Requiem, was told,
With darkness, descending,
And sadness, unending,

See how, widows cry,
Nary an eye is now dry,
Of all those assembled,
Fraught and quaking; how they trembled

Feel now, the dead corpse,
Cut down, without remorse,
Note how, the veins chilled,
For all blood has been spilled,

Taste now, the acridness,
There is no cure for this sickness,
Of eternal silence,
Brought upon by unholy violence.

Smell now, the foulness,
As death now, surrounds us,
Wrapped in the putrid wings,
That envelop all mortal things.

Weep now, with full remorse,
There is no other recourse,
The living; for the dead cry,
Knowing that one day they too will die,

Honor now, the sacrifice,
No other price, will suffice,
For it is the lot of those who serve,
To give all, and never lose nerve.

Offer yourself, to God,
Who all on Earth and Heaven laud,
And your own death will have meaning,
Long after you are no longer breathing.

Tearful
(Demonic Funeral Hymn)

Weep no more, dear,
Feel no fear here,
All that is dust, must return to dust.
All that is Ash, once again becomes Ash,

Weep no more, dear.
Feel no fear here,
All that has been awoken, must be unspoken,
All that has been born, must one day be torn.

Glory fades like the ebbing light,
As we are all overtaken by the creeping night

Rest in the Lord's arms,
Safe from all harms,
Peaceful in the deliverance from all of life's pains
Nothing but the Lord and his attendants remains.

Amen.

DEMONIC LILLIBULLERO

Brother did you happen to hear them say,
The news that's come from the front today,
You'll want to hear it,
It'll lift your spirit,
There're no Angels left; our boys cleared the way.

Sorrow, Sorrow, Sorrow for Angels,
Lucifer's Soldiers, this is our job,
When bugles are calling, and armies are brawling,
Sorrow for Angels, that is our job.
Hopeless and lost, for mercy they pray,
As we march on taking the field and the day,
Volleys like showers,
Fall through the hours,
As they look on their broken ranks in dismay.
Sorrow, Sorrow, Sorrow for Angels,
Lucifer's Soldiers, this is our job.
When cannons are crashing, and muskets are flashing,
Sorrow for Angels, that is our job.
Though they send countless numbers our way,
We scatter them all in complete disarray,
Slaying all we see,

To the Lord's decree,
For every step they take, dearly they pay.
Sorrow, Sorrow, Sorrow for Angels,
Lucifer's Soldiers, this is our job,
When sabers are clattering, and grapeshot is scattering,
Sorrow for Angels, that is our job.
Forward we march in forceful display,
Of just how at home we are in the fray,
And if the foe doesn't know it,
We're quick to show it,
For our just cause we never betray.
Sorrow, Sorrow, Sorrow for Angels,
Lucifer's Soldiers, this is our job,
When shells are exploding, and we're quick reloading,
Sorrow for Angels, that is our job.
Swiftly our forces know no delay,
When called upon to the melee,
Ready by day and night,
Itching to fight,
Our courage stands fast, never does it stray.
Sorrow, Sorrow, Sorrow for Angels,
Lucifer's Soldiers, this is our job,
No matter how much we've battled, we've never been rattled,
Sorrow for Angels, that is our job.

FIRE AWAY

Lift them up and set them down.
Fire Providence, fire away!
One shot for the Lord and one for the Crown,
Fire Providence, fire away!

There's thunder when the Commanders say,
Fire Providence, fire away!
Pull the tackles, and there she'll stay,
Fire Providence, fire away!

Haul the powder from down below,
Fire Providence, fire away!
Touch the linstock, and there she'll go,
Fire Providence, fire away!

When I get back to Boston town,
Fire Providence, fire away!
I'll drop a line to little Molly Brown,
Fire Providence, fire away!

Chain shot's loaded and powder's dry,
Fire Providence, fire away!
Their masts go crack when we let lead fly,
Fire Providence, fire away!

Our Providence she's a sturdy little craft,
Fire Providence, fire away!
Twenty-six guns from the fore down to the aft,
First Providence, fire away!

So hoist the sails and tie 'em down,
Fire Providence, fire away

Let's kick the Red Coats out of Nassau town,
Fire Providence, fire away!
Fire Providence, fire away!

Coming In Volume II

The village of Lushno was not sizeable on any map but it was the only place in the world that mattered to the Demon AIDS. His entire existence currently consisted of the small pit of sandbags surrounding Fritz Christen's 108mm anti-tank gun. Christen's detachment of the Waffen SS Division Totenkampf, the infamous Death's Head Division, had been wiped out to the man from a withering barrage of rifle fire.

Christen managed to repel the Soviet skirmishers with several well-placed rounds from his Kar98 rifle, all while incoming rounds whizzed by him like angry bees. The young soldier was certain that he would be killed any moment, but he held firm to his training. When he had manned the anti-tank gun and fired a well-placed shell amongst the Russian infantry, the attackers had temporarily withdrawn. The Angels in the Celestial Realm had not.

Now they stood around the possessed Christen and awaited the trapped Demon. AIDS was baffled to find himself in such a position—a treed opossum. He could not run; he could not attempt to fight six Angels simultaneously; he was stuck. The Angels tried to shake his focus by taunting him.

AIDS fired the anti-tank cannon once more. The recoil set off a paralyzing whine in his ears. He saw the turret of yet another Russian tank jolt upward, flames engulfing the armored vehicle.

One of the Angels hissed at him. "We're going to kill you slowly for making us wait."

AIDS ignored the catcall and raised his Kar98. He fired another round and struck the closest Russian in the chest. He chambered another round before the soldier hit the ground.

The heckling continued.

"Are you too scared just to pop out and face us?"

"He's a frightened bitch!"

"Come out and fight like a warrior, you sissy!"

AIDS pulled the trigger three more times in succession, sending three more letters to grieving mothers and wives; he was not in the habit of missing. More incoming fire sent Christen ducking behind the small pile of sandbags. He reloaded his rifle and began firing again. The sun beat down without mercy; the wind was a dry cough. AIDS was in a heightened sense of awareness. He felt everything—the slightest movement of infantry even hundreds of meters away, the mechanical groaning of enemy tanks, the breeze raking his face, every bit of dirt on his boots, the spent shell casings somersaulting through the air each time he yanked back the bolt of his rifle, the hiss and pop of incoming rounds—everything came to him with magnified clarity.

He saw the Angels' lips moving but blocked out their jeers. Instead, he focused on a muzzle flash emanating from a first-story window, squared his weapon, and spewed death from the barrel of his weapon.

A MILE FARTHER AFIELD from the entrance to Lushno, the Wehrmacht sniper, Maximillian Hessler, scanned the landscape from his perch high atop a massive oak. His mountaineering shoes dug into the bark. The scout had applied leaves and sticks to the mesh covering his helmet. His rifle was swaddled in dull canvas; every reflective surface had been coated in grease. Not even the most discerning eye could differentiate between Schitz and the upper reaches of the mighty tree. Cradling his Kar98 in his left arm, he surveyed his surroundings through his binoculars. Schitz saw AIDS and marveled at the young Demon's composure. It was an interesting balance. As long as the lone survivor killed Russians at range, the Angels could not move in to slay him. The Angels needed a single round from a member of the infantry or a tank shell to take out the pugnacious Demon.

A *perfect encapsulation of the Demonic cause,* Schitz thought. *Outnumbered, outgunned, but denying Heaven the ultimate victory because of our innate savagery.*

Karabiner 98 Kurz a.k.a Kar98

He smiled and began to whistle Chopin's *Nocturne in E-flat major, Op. 9, No. 2.* Panning away from the town to the east, Schitz picked up a massive formation of troops moving across the open country-side towards the town. He let the binoculars dangle from their neck strap and peered through his telescopic sight.

"Sixteen and a half," he said aloud, calculating that the foe was just under the length of seventeen football fields or one thousand seven hundred meters away. The man's execution was delayed only by his lowly rank. Schitz navigated through the mass of infantry until he found the commanding officer. The Demon ran the calculations— the east wind, his elevation, the enemy's distance, the bullet's path. When he reached a pause in the *Nocturne*, he pulled the trigger.

Coming in January 2022

ABOUT THE AUTHOR

J.L Feuerstack holds a BA from Washington & Lee University and a MA from Queens College, both in the study of Psychology. He has worked in various investigative and supervisory capacities for the City of New York. He is a diehard supporter of Liverpool Football Club and the German National Football Team.

ABOUT THE ILLUSTRATOR

Alana Tedmon has worked as an illustrator since 2012. She graduated with her BFA from the Art Institute of Dallas and also studied illustration under award-winning artists, including Edward Kinsella and Sterling Hundley. She enjoys skiing and cycling around her hometown Philadelphia, as well as spending time with her three pet rats.

ACKNOWLEDGMENTS

The author would like to thank:

My wife Eileen Feuerstack for her unwavering support and encouragement as well as her companionship in traveling to many of the locales featured in the story. She also puts up with the copious amount of time I spend writing.

Editor, Arthur Fogartie, for his unparalleled skill and patience. His insight and wit were paramount in ensuring that this story was told.

Illustrator, Alana Tedmon, for her talent and dedication. Her creativity was vital for the creation of the characters of *The Saga of Fallen Leaves*.

Printed in Great Britain
by Amazon

15987099R00334